Praise for
The White Mare

"With nods to Marion Zimmer Bradley's *Mists of Avalon* and Diana Gabaldon's Outlander series, newcomer Watson presents an ancient Scotland tightly laced with romantic tension, treachery, and cliff-hangers aplenty....Mightily appealing."
—*Kirkus Reviews* (starred review)

"Watson deftly blends fact and fancy, action and romance in her splendid historical fantasy debut....An appealing love story, well-researched settings, and an interesting take on goddess worship."
—*Publishers Weekly* (starred review)

"It requires a special sort of imagination to create a plausible vision of Britain at the time of the Roman conquest. Jules Watson rises effortlessly to the challenge." —*Daily Express*

"In the grand tradition of the historical epic, this is a tale of heroic deeds, kinship and kingship. Truly sumptuous reading."
—*Lancashire Evening Post*

"A sweeping tale of the struggle for love, honor, freedom, and power." —*Home and Country*

"Strong characters, a compelling story, and sound historical research make this a winner. A stunning debut novel." —Juliet Marillier

"Lovers of all things Celtic will find much to satisfy in this incredible tome." —*Good Book Guide*

"She breaks new ground targe... the border, a road few historical n...

Praise for

The Dawn Stag

"Richly imagined...Watson brings first-century A.D. Britain to vivid life with just the right details at the right times, and successfully keeps the tension high, balancing violence and tragedy with romance and religious transcendence." —*Publishers Weekly*

"Epic and spellbinding...The exploration of period gender roles and the intriguing diversions into pagan mythology enhance this enchanting tale. And while the tale is dense and leisurely paced, its emotional impact is significant....If the components of a novel are a volley of arrows, then Watson hits her targets every time."
—*Kirkus Reviews* (starred review)

"A scorching read that will keep readers breathless."
—*Good Book Guide*

"The writing is smooth and pleasing. If you like your Celtic historical romance well written and constantly interesting, this book is for you." —*Historical Novels Review*

The
Swan Maiden

JULES WATSON

BANTAM BOOKS

THE SWAN MAIDEN
A Bantam Book / March 2009

Published by Bantam Dell
A Division of Random House, Inc.
New York, New York

Book design by Virginia Norey

Library of Congress Cataloging-in-Publication Data
Watson, Jules.
The swan maiden / Jules Watson.
        p.   cm.
ISBN 978-0-553-38464-2 (trade pbk.: alk. paper)
ISBN 978-0-553-90630-1 (e-book)   1. Deirdre (Legendary
character)—Fiction.   2. Queens—Ireland—Fiction.   3. Ulster
(Northern Ireland and Ireland)—Fiction.
    4. Mythology, Celtic—Fiction.   I. Title.

PR9619.4.W376S83 2009
823'.92—dc22   2008041339

Printed in the United States of America
Published simultaneously in Canada

www.bantamdell.com

BVG 10 9 8 7 6 5 4 3 2 1

To my dear friend Graham Swinney,
who taught me about courage and love during the writing of this book

ACKNOWLEDGMENTS

I would like to thank Patricia Crook for help with the Gaelic yet again, especially when I conjure up such problematic nicknames.

My deep and endless gratitude goes to Claire Swinney, who even in the midst of the darkest of times still somehow gave to me of the great light in her heart.

And as always, I am awed and overcome by Alistair's willingness to be plot-shaper, reader, writer, cook, dishwasher, and margarita-maker while holding down a job as an international man of mystery. *A stór mo chroí*, always.

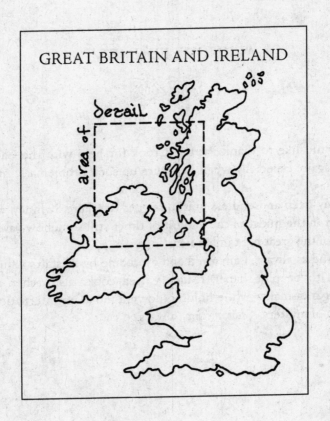

GREAT BRITAIN AND IRELAND

area of detail

CHARACTER, PLACE, AND PRONUNCIATION GUIDE

THE FOUR ANCIENT PROVINCES OF ERIN

Ulaid   *The tribe who lived in and gave their name to Ulster*
Connacht   *An old name for Connaught*
Mumu   *An old name for Munster*
Laigin   *An old name for Leinster*

CHARACTERS

THE FOREST

Deirdre
Fintan, *her foster-father*
Aiveen, *her foster-mother*
Levarcham, *druid teacher, King Conor's talking-woman*

EMAIN MACHA

Conor, *the king of the Ulaid*
Nessa, *his mother*
Cormac, *his eldest son*
Fiacra, *his youngest son*

Fergus mac Roy, *the former king and Conor's stepfather*

Buinne, *his elder son*
Illan, *his younger son*

Cathbad, *the chief druid*

Red Branch warriors:
Cúchulainn, *the king's champion and nephew*
Ferdia mac Daman
Naisi, *eldest son of Usnech*
Ardan, *second son of Usnech*
Ainnle, *youngest son of Usnech*
Conall Cearnach
Leary
Dubthach

ALBA

Cinet, *king of the Epidii*
Bridei, *his nephew and heir*
Fidech, *his huntsman*
Talan, *his cousin and chief of a northern dun*
Carnach, *Talan's nephew*

PRONUNCIATION OF NAMES

Naisi	NEE-sha
Deirdre	DEER-dra or DAIR-dra
Ainnle	AN-la
Aiveen	A-veen
Cúchulainn	Koo-KULL-lin or Koo-HOO-lin
Cinet	KIN-et
Ferdia	Fair-dee-ah
Cathbad	KA-fa or KA-had
Dubthach	DUFF-ach
Fedlimid	FAY-lim-i
Badb	Bive
Emain Macha	OW-en MAK-uh or Avvin MAK-uh
Muirthemne	MUR-hev-na

SPOKEN AS WRITTEN:

Ardan
Fintan
Conor   anglicized form of *Conchobhar*
Levarcham
Conall
Leary   anglicized form of *Laoghaire*

OTHER WORDS

Sídhe (shee) The fairy folk, Otherworld beings

Fiáin (FEE-aw-in) "Wild," used as an endearment: "wild one"

A stór (ah stoar) Common Irish endearment: "Beloved"

A chuisle mo chroí (ah KOOSH-la muh cree) Common Irish endearment: "O pulse of my heart"

Curragh (KUR-rack) Light boats made of wicker and hides

Banshee (as written) "Ban" means woman and *"sídhe"* means fairy

Fladorca (as written) An anglicized nickname, derived from *flaith*, said "flah," which means "prince"; and *dorchas*, said "dorkas," which means "dark, secretive"

Samhain (SAH-win) The festival held around November 1, giving rise to All Hallow's Eve. It is the start of the ancient Irish and Scottish New Year, a feast of the dead, and was a time when the veils to the Otherworld grew thinner, allowing the *sídhe* to pass forth into mortal worlds.

Imbolc (IM-bulk) The festival held around February 1 to mark the coming of spring and the lactation of the ewes. It is sacred to the fertility goddess Brid or Bridget.

Beltaine (Bee-YAWL-tinnuh) The May Day fertility festival, celebrated around May 1 to herald summer. Sacred bonfires were lit on hilltops and cattle driven between them for blessing.

Lughnasa (LOO-nah-sah) The festival celebrated around August 1 that marks the harvest; sacred to the sun god Lugh

The
Swan Maiden

CHAPTER 1

Leaf-fall

She was silver, an iridescence that arced along its trajectory like a falling star. The eagle hovered against the sky, wing-tips spread, and Deirdre imagined her spirit as a net that would capture it in a glittering sling of light.

Her body still lay in trance by the fire and she had to summon immense focus to keep sending soul-breath along the thread that joined spirit and body. *Now let the light sink in.* It was Levarcham's sibilant whisper, chanted into her ear. Her teacher's will flowed beneath her, a current pushing her forward ... *upward.*

The druid had fasted and sung with her for days, striking the drum until the sonorous pulse rang through both their bodies. Levarcham had endured the spasms and nausea of the herbs, all to fuse her energy with Deirdre and give her this fleeting chance of sacred flight.

The determination to stay focused on the soul-cord and the eagle at the same time was a keen pain, honed over moons of torturous practice. Deirdre was exhausted. It would be easier to fall back into her body. But she would not fail or waver.

Her own frustration had provided the force that initially flung her free, Levarcham's will then lifting her, helping her break through the boundaries for one, long breath. *There ...* She caught a flash of sensation: arms spread, a strange lightness of bones. The shock blanked her mind. *Breathe, breathe!* Levarcham urged.

Deirdre was gazing from *other* eyes. The rush of air peeled back wing-feathers and there was a blur of mountains, sunlight and shadow flitting across bare rock. At once, the eagle plunged into a dive and the land spun toward her. The bird opened its beak and screeched in ecstasy: *freedom!*

The one thing denied her. *The one thing…*

A resounding crash tore her from her trance.

She found herself sprawled in the rushes by an overturned stool with a jug glugging water into the rushes. A moment later, pain lanced her brow. "Deirdre!" Levarcham rasped, but she could not answer, clutching at the floor as it bucked beneath her, the walls of her little hut spinning.

The whirl of the room gradually slowed, and eventually lurched and stopped. A sense of her surroundings began to seep back in. Not air, not sun… but flickering light on curved mud walls and low thatch roof. Crackling flames drove the chill from the door-hide, and there was a lingering tang of herb smoke. Then Levarcham tossed something different on the fire—*cleansing betony*—and it flared, the light flashing off jewelry scattered on the dresser.

Deirdre's belly did not stop moving with the room, however. She sat bolt upright, and Levarcham, now settled on the hearth-bench, shoved an empty pot at her with her foot. Deirdre's mouth quirked and, grabbing it, she vomited up the dregs of the potion. The clenching of her stomach felt good, the violent retching emptying her of anything that was not the sensation of soaring. At last, she groped for a cloth and wiped her mouth, draining the last drops of water from the jug before slumping against a chair.

Her druid teacher was used to such travails and had swiftly regained her composure, only her slight pallor and labored breathing betraying her. She was frowning at Deirdre's brow and, with a shaking finger, Deirdre touched her forehead, smearing the tip with blood.

Levarcham's staff struck the floor. "What did I tell you, foolish girl?"

Deirdre dabbed at the blood with her sleeve. "Not to move my body."

"It is only your spirit that you merge with the bird's—*you must keep your body still*. And so? I feel you lose focus, and when I open my eyes there you are, waving your arms and launching yourself into the air!"

Deirdre bit her lip to stop that mental picture showing on her face. "Hmm."

The staff cracked the floor again and Levarcham leaned over her crooked leg, all traces of the trance gone from her piercing gray eyes. "What if you fell hard and hurt yourself? Or rolled in the fire?"

Deirdre drew a steadying breath. "You have good reason to reprove me." As Levarcham's brows nearly disappeared into her hair, Deirdre smiled. "But, with respect, we could assume you already have and I've apologized profusely, so we can move on." She clambered to her knees and hooked a finger around Levarcham's, linking them as they had been in flight. "*I felt the eagle this time.*"

The expression on Levarcham's long, stern face warred between pride and severity. She thinned her mouth toward the latter, squeezing Deirdre's finger firmly before returning it to her. "There are three things I told you to do, one of which you obviously forgot. What are they?"

Deirdre gave in with a grin and sat cross-legged, palms up. "Strengthen the thread between body and spirit. Retain my own awareness. And keep my body still."

"Exactly." Levarcham gripped her staff with both hands, mollified. "It is the most demanding of druid skills and takes years of practice to achieve alone. We don't fully understand how we do it at all, except that great discipline and a strong will are essential." She snorted, her gaze sweeping Deirdre. "The will you have by the cartload. The other I'm still waiting on."

Deirdre ignored that, the thrill of flight still lingering in her aching limbs. "I'm sure I felt the feathers move, and saw the mountains." She arched an innocent brow. "You're always telling me to notice details."

Levarcham was silent for a long moment, and when she spoke again her voice was ominously quiet. "This is no idle trick. It is a sacred act to touch the spirit of another creature, let alone share its body. It should only be attempted after the proper prayers and fasting to lighten flesh and soul; the songs of honor and exhortations to the gods." The druid's stony face and crooked limp had always been daunting, her long, dark hair frosted over despite her only living for forty years. Her power was not in her lean body, however, but in her eyes, luminous as twilight on water. "You know I should not be teaching you any of this at all." Those eyes darted away, hiding her thoughts. "I could be banished from my order and exiled from the king's service altogether."

Deirdre's thrill faded. "I haven't forgotten." The idea of any harm coming to Levarcham or her foster parents, Fintan and Aiveen, was enough to sober her at once.

Levarcham stood, cupping Deirdre's jaw. "But this is not about me. If the thread breaks, your soul will be lost and your body will perish." Despite the fire, a shiver nipped all the way up Deirdre's back. "You could die."

"Then why show me?" All the ecstasy had flown from Deirdre and she hauled herself upright, still unsteady. At nearly eighteen, she had reached the same height as her teacher and they gazed at each other, breathing hard.

"I don't entirely know. I felt I must—and the fact you have gained even a glimpse hints at some gift for it. Nevertheless, it's serious—*death* is serious. The crossing into the Otherworld is no time for jests."

"Perhaps it's the best time for jests." Deirdre couldn't keep the fierceness from her voice. "I'd rather go boldly, anyway. At least the gods would know I'd *lived.*"

A shadow passed across Levarcham's angular features. "Fledgling." She reached out a finger again. Deirdre did the same. The tips touched, the younger woman smiling wryly. The druid limped to the door, her head brushing the sprays of rowan-berries over the lintel, the tiny, red fruits shriveled on the bough. "Bathe that wound and put a compress on it." She braced herself visibly. "The king is coming from Emain Macha any day now. There is knitbone in my saddle pack that will help the bruise; I will have Aiveen pulp it in her mortar."

Deirdre merely nodded, keeping her face still—something she had perfected with practice. It was a mask that stopped Levarcham, Fintan and Aiveen from hurting for her more than they already did.

After the druid left, she turned to the loom against the wall, threaded with an unfinished strip of cloth. Her hands gripped the oak beam, knuckles white, her head tilted so the long, golden strands of her hair mingled with the colored wool. The loose threads bled out at the bottom, unraveling as she was...

Lately the pressure inside had grown more potent, a force welling up that seemed too large for her body. Her skin felt stretched and thin, muscles straining to contain it. Levarcham said she was merely filling out since her moon-bleeding had at long last begun, but Deirdre knew it was something deeper.

What she felt herself to be wasn't what they all saw: fair-haired, green-eyed, soft-skinned. She had never been that, even as a child. Then, her tiny world seemed like a vast adventure, and she gleefully embarked on all the journeys her imagination could conjure from three little huts, an encircling wall and a narrow valley. Oceans! Endless plains! Glittering caverns!

As she grew, she took to wandering the woods alone, for only in that silence could she hear the whisper of her emerging spirit, that glimmering promise of hidden depths *beyond*. She expanded and grew, but the valley did not, and wonder turned to frustration.

The whispers inside her turned into a murmuring sea, its secrets surging and ebbing before she could catch them. In desperation, she paced between the ash trees, walking in spirals that drew ever tighter. She stood with dew trickling down her brows and prayed that the bark would flow over her like a silvery skin so she could disappear. She crept into the boles of oaks, sank into leaf-mold, but she could not quiet that restless tide. All that happened in the expectant hush was that she heard her pulse, counting down the moments.

The king is coming.

She rested her forehead in her hands and let the room fall away, conjuring the image of an unfettered eagle against an endless sky.

⬡

The stag launched itself across the stream and landed with a stumble, before recovering and tearing up the bracken slope. Naisi saw the flash of its pale belly as it scrabbled through the brown ferns, dappled sun glinting on its antlers.

"Around this way!" Ardan hissed, thudding along behind his elder brother.

Naisi barely heard him, his pounding heart filled with the roar of the stream in the undergrowth before him. His thoughts raced along with the tumbling rapids. *Could go around...shallow to the south...that will lose time...on the hill he'll escape...*

The ground dropped away into a ravine of churning water. Teetering on his heels, Naisi whipped the cocked arrow off his string and looped the bow over his back. "Naisi!" Ardan growled. "Don't you dare..."

Naisi sized up the distance, gripped the arrow between his teeth and flung himself over the edge, hands outstretched. The gorge yawned below him, the foam only thinly veiling the teeth of the rocks.

His fingers caught a fallen oak leaning across the gap, its bark slippery with moss. Every muscle screamed as he wriggled his hands along, feet dangling over the drop. He swung a leg into a crevice of wet rocks, then levered himself on top of the trunk, standing up to balance precariously. Arms out, he danced a few wobbly steps between yellow-leaved branches, then threw himself up the steep bank.

"Ainnle," Ardan bellowed, "we'll circle around to the ford. Come on!"

His youngest brother's voice floated to Naisi above the roaring of the stream. "I go where *he* goes."

"You'll snap every bone in your body if you fall."

"See you on the other side!" Ainnle sang out.

Naisi wiped spray from his eyes and stuck the arrow in its quiver. He forced his straining legs up the slope, the dying bracken clinging to his calves in wet fronds. The hide of the deer had become lost amid the turning leaves of brown and gold, but he still felt confident they'd catch it. This one already trailed scarlet down its side from his first arrow, and it had landed badly, laming itself. Somewhere up there it must be slowing.

He reached a ragged escarpment and saw the ravine up which the stag must have leaped. The breakaway was filled with tumbled rock and tree roots and he stormed up it, scrabbling with bleeding palms and barked shins. The slope gave way to flatter ground scattered with boulders and scree, and he immediately spied the stag. It boasted only a few antler tines, and in its youth and inexperience had blundered into the rocks, snapping its leg.

Trotting forward, Naisi spat on his hand and wiped the blood down his hide trews, drawing out his throwing spear. He and his two brothers had devised the short hunting lance and the carrier that went across the back, so a man could run after game for days. The sons of Usnech did not stick to the safe, lowland trails, pursuing boar on horseback, only for hounds to bring them down.

Unlike some.

Naisi frowned and leaned on the spear, still panting, the cold breeze lifting his sweaty braids from his neck. The branches of an overhanging rowan scratched at the rocks, making the deer's dark eyes roll at him in terror. He should finish it off. He lifted the spear, his arm fatigued from the chase.

All at once, the stag stopped struggling and merely lay there, its breath turning to mist on the crisp air. The spear remained hovering, and Naisi found himself rooted to the spot, unable to look away.

The deer's red flanks were foamed with sweat, and the nostrils in its soft muzzle flexed and closed, pulsing in time with Naisi's blood. His breath quickened as he watched its chest rising and falling, emitting puffs of vapor. *It breathed in time with his heartbeat.* The stag's eye swiveled to fix on him, as if staring straight into his spirit. Its pupil was a pool drawing him in, the waters dissolving them so *he* was the stag and the stag was him...

Ainnle and Ardan came pounding up. "I don't want to know how you got up that ravine so fast," Ardan panted to Naisi.

"I nearly made it after him." Ainnle flicked sweat from his thick, black hair. "Nearly."

Naisi ignored them, locked in the communion with the stag. All the while he'd been running, the thrill of the chase had been swelling in his chest, but now it was collapsing, sinking in on itself. The stag strained against the rock and Naisi's own leg cramped, shooting pain up his thigh. *It was trapped.* It had no way to run free now. Naisi mac Usnech, famed as a hunter, could not make the killing blow.

His middle brother, Ardan, hefted his spear. "It's suffering." He glanced at the youngest, Ainnle. "We normally have to rein *you* in. What are you waiting for?"

Ainnle's green eyes were as always fixed on Naisi. "It's his kill."

The stag slumped against the boulder, and despair pooled in Naisi's belly.

"If you won't release it, I will," Ardan declared, and then his spear was soaring through the air, embedding itself in the stag's chest with a solid *thunk*. It was a thing of beauty, that throw: a perfect arc, a clean kill. Naisi tried to summon an old stab of pleasure, a heated thrill, but all he felt was coldness.

The beast stiffened when the point entered its body, its spine arching back before sagging. Naisi imagined its spirit being released, soft and light as smoke, while its ribs slackened and it spilled blood over the mossy rock. Only when its neck finally bowed could he breathe out. He clasped the hunt amulet strung at his neck, the tiny deer carved of antler browned by his touch. *We honor your death,* he said to the deer. They would feast on meat tonight, and tomorrow their own limbs would fill with strength.

It was right and good, he told himself—and then told himself again.

"Gods," Ardan exclaimed, bending over the downed beast. "What is that?"

He was peering at something Naisi hadn't noticed because he thought it was blood: an arrowhead that had broken off in the stag's rump and lodged under the skin. Faint shreds of scarlet-dyed threads trailed from it.

Ardan's dark head dipped as he poked at the barb. Then his shoulders stiffened and when he looked up at his elder brother, his skin was blanched beneath the flush of exertion.

A pang hit Naisi's heart. "What?"

Ardan swallowed. "It is the king's mark."

CHAPTER 2

The young warriors circled each other, sweat-soaked and grimy, bare chests gleaming in the sun. "Come on!" Conall snarled. "Or are you pups still on the teat?"

One youth attacked, sweeping his wooden sword across his opponent's thighs; the other blocked it and the oak shafts cracked and locked at the hilt. The fighters struggled, pushing on each other until Conall swiped his own blade between them. "Stop farting back and forth. On the battlefield you'd be dead already!"

Beside the sparring green, Ferdia, Leary and Dubthach chuckled. "He's testy today," Ferdia observed.

"Too much ale last night." Leary leaned back on the bench, picking shreds of meat from his teeth. "He's puked twice this morning, and he's not happy it's his turn to play teacher."

And indeed, the tall, rangy Conall was stooped, his bleary eyes almost as red as his shock of wild hair and beard. The practice yard was ringed by stable blocks and the high timber rampart of Emain Macha, and despite the cool wind the weak sun bounced off the daub walls, casting a sickly hue over Conall's face and coating the pack of young warriors with sweat.

Ferdia glanced at Cúchulainn, who was observing the action with folded arms. He was the king's nephew and champion, and war-leader of the Red Branch—the elite squad of three hundred Ulaid fighters that protected Emain Macha and led the rest of the army. It was Cúchulainn's responsibility to ensure there was good blood coming through the Red Branch ranks. As usual, little could be read on Cúchulainn's deceptively mild face, his cool, blue eyes assessing.

Conall urged the youths to pace through their sword-moves again and they began hacking at each other, the grunts, thwack of swords and thud of feet rebounding around the yard. They puffed out chests and tensed their arms, all conscious they fought before the great Red Branch heroes—Conall, Leary and Cúchulainn. *And me*, Ferdia thought wryly. He remembered the pride of being picked to train for the Red Branch, sparring on sacred ground below the thatched hall of King Conor on the hill.

Simmering bloodlust was also never far under the surface, and soon furious insults began flying, along with dirt kicked up by bare feet. The thrusts and lunges quickened, sword-slashes went awry and hilts began to smack into skulls and bellies. Conall's eyes narrowed. "Get that foot back! And you, by Manannán's breath, stop pummeling him and let him up!"

A pair of fighters danced before Cúchulainn and, when Conall's back was turned, one spun in a showy lunge, whipping his sword around. He jumped too fast, the tip merely grazing his opponent's ribs, but the second youth screamed and brought his hilt down on his attacker's arm. All the fighting stopped when the first warrior let out a loud howl, leaping about in agony, his face turning red. Squinting, Ferdia decided three of his fingers were definitely broken.

Conall waded in as the injured man jiggled about. "Idiot!" Conall snapped. "Get off to the temple and find a healer, then. Hurry up." He turned on the one who'd inflicted the blow. "And if that's the best you can do, you'd be dead by now, too." The youth's triumphant grin faded. "If your enemy fights two-handed, he might have lost his fingers, but right now he'd have his sword stuck up your arse from underneath!"

The others snickered and the young fighter flushed. But jutting his chin, he retorted, "Then perhaps Cúchulainn can show us the right way."

A hush fell over the yard, and Ferdia glanced at Cúchulainn. The Hound of the Ulaid rarely sparred if he could help it. Renowned for the battle-fire that smoldered constantly beneath his mild exterior, he could not fight by halves, and that was why he never raised his voice or brawled.

Conall's scowl said what he thought of the pup's insolence, but before he could reprove him, the others began clamoring. "Let Cúchulainn show us!"

The Hound let their voices wash over him, and so they grew bolder, the yells turning into a chant…*Cúchulainn, Cúchulainn!* Ferdia rose, wondering how to quiet them, but to his surprise Cúchulainn stepped forward, and the crowd fell silent.

The champion was blond and beardless and of modest size, with a compact, lithe build which surprised those who knew his reputation. All the youths drew back, their eyes bulging, while he stripped off his tunic and refastened a bronze ring over his bare arm. He wore no other regalia besides this Red Branch badge—a circle of braided bronze whose join was a spear-point. The braid showed the mystical Red Branch bond, all the warriors woven together; the spear, that they were protectors of the Ulaid.

"Cheeky sods," Leary muttered.

Ferdia sat down. "Sometimes he makes his points better this way."

Leary's expression turned sour, though it was hard to tell with his blunt, broken nose and protruding jaw. He was jealous of

Ferdia's close friendship with Cúchulainn; they all were. He and Cúchulainn had fought in Gaul and the British lands and all over Erin, and for some reason Ferdia could calm the Hound after battle when no one else could. He was an obscure blacksmith's son who had shed flesh and blood to be Red Branch, and yet this brotherhood with Cúchulainn was more valuable than any bronze badge.

Conall came off the field holding his belly, leaving the Hound demonstrating one of the battle-feats. "If they made me yell any more, I was going to puke on their feet." Conall sank down and rested his head on the wall.

They were silent, soaking up the sun, until Leary suddenly lifted his chin. "Look at that." They all turned to the stables, while Conall groaned and opened his eyes.

A magnificent chariot had been wheeled outside by servants, its fittings of bronze, coral and amber glittering in the sunshine. King Conor stood by while his driver polished the gilded hubs and oiled the yoke, and another servant fixed shields to the wicker platform. The king's lean body had been encased waist to neck in a burnished leather breastplate, a green cloak pinned over it with a gold brooch. An ornate helmet was set on his fair hair, the iron and bronze cheek-pieces framing his proud, bony face.

Conall squinted blearily. "It's that time of year again." He snorted, sinking back. "He should wield that sword and shield for real, show these boys how to face Connacht's armies instead of slavering after some simpering green-maid in the woods."

Young Dubthach frowned in puzzlement. "What maid?"

At Ferdia's warning glance, Leary merely shrugged. "Dubthach is Red Branch now. Why shouldn't he know about Conor's little obsession?"

Dubthach remained perplexed, and Ferdia grunted in exasperation. "He's going to visit his betrothed. Now forget about it."

"Betrothed!" Leary sneered. "And here's his marriage to Princess Maeve of Connacht barely over, and her running back to her royal kin in the night. He should be after *her*, wrestling her down and getting a Connacht heir, instead of sniffing around some useless chit."

Dubthach was still looking confused, and Conall snorted. "Gods, lad, surely you've heard of Deirdre, Fedlimid's daughter?"

Their attention was interrupted by movement on the field, where Cúchulainn had apparently decided to fight the boy who had called him out.

Demonstrating the thunder-feat to his challenger had limbered Cúchulainn up. His muscles sensed the gradual flood of battle-light, the energy pushing up from within and quickening his pulse, speech and thoughts. The others looked on while he ad-justed his young opponent's stance. "Sink into your hips." He tapped the boy's foot with his sword. "Focus on each toe and feel the ground. You have to draw that in, *and* the resistance of the hilt against your palm, *and* the force of the wind, *and* the correct ten-sion of your legs—*all at once.*"

The youth's face creased in concentration, and he crouched lower.

Cúchulainn stood with his blade held upright. "Then, pause to summon the Source-of-All from the air around you, the earth, and let it fill your body. It's a heat, a light inside your flesh." His body vibrated, the crowd of faces beginning to blur. "And you focus it *inward,*" Cúchulainn heard himself saying as if from far away, "and use it to drive your legs and arms *outward.*"

The flame of the Source was licking around Cúchulainn now, and he held it at bay, remembering that he was here in peace. He turned, holding the sword over his head, left arm out. Years of training and repetition so that his muscles knew the precise weight and swing of sword, the heft of spear, and all of it came down to…*surrender.* The Source was the One flame of divine light that surged through everything, and all the tiny sparks that made him—flesh, bone, spirit—were drawn in a flood to that bril-liance behind the world. And when he sank into it, losing the edges of self, his awareness became expanded and minutely focused all at once, color and shape so bright and sharp they looked surreal. It was this willing loss of boundaries that took courage, not the simple wielding of a blade.

Just as he surrendered into flame when he lay with his wife, his treasured Emer, and the sun seemed to rise between them…

The blade. The pressure of the hilt in his palm brought him back, anchoring him. In battle, the incandescence of the Source lit up every detail of every moment so vividly that time itself seemed to slow for Cúchulainn. Men thought he read minds, yet all he did was melt into the substance that made them all. He could see the halo of flame around his opponents, the glowing corona flaring with his challenger's intent a moment before he moved, allowing Cúchulainn to block a sword-slash, stabbing under a guard.

His Red Branch brothers felt this between themselves, to lesser degrees, and this was the Ulaid's secret. When they surrendered into the Source, they fought as one, constantly sensing the presence of their sword-mates around them. With one stroke, they could dispatch an opponent and, on the return arc, down their comrade's attacker behind them. But it took years to grasp *that*—a lesson for another day.

"Put up your sword," Cúchulainn said to the bold youth, who was now looking both boastful and terrified. They ran the first four feats together, their sweeps and blocks gradually growing faster. The youth was soon struggling, dripping with sweat, while Cúchulainn barely felt the ground, reflecting back every strike as if he was the boy's mirror. He savored dancing on the blade-edge: one side the beckoning lake of fire, the other solid ground, for this was only a game.

They leaped around so swiftly now the crowd shuffled back, the boy's face contorting into a fierce snarl. All at once, Cúchulainn saw the burst of light at the end of his arm…just before the boy's desperate thrust came toward his groin. But Cúchulainn was already ducking, sword clattering to the ground. He slid *inside* the lunge, one hand on the boy's chest and the other on his belly, and with a shout that bounced off the walls of the fort, he pushed out the energy with a ripple of his arms. The slight movement sent the youth flying backward to land with a thud several paces away.

There was a shocked hush. The boy lay winded, his face white, his companions looking from him to the Hound. Cúchulainn was burning, the urge to catch up a glinting blade flaring. Sucking in air, he tried to dampen the flame, relieved when it began to fade and the stable walls took shape around him again. "Cúchulainn." It was Ferdia's voice, calling him back.

He drew in the Source from each limb, holding it together in a fiery ball in his chest. Then, with a long sigh, he let it flow down his body and back into the ground. He was left with every hair on his neck standing up.

The young warriors were helping up their friend, muttering over his impudence. Cúchulainn fixed his eyes on him, blinking to clear them. "In rage, you flung your limbs out with no power behind them. If you had been in the light, you would have sensed what I might do next." The winded youth nodded, all bluster gone.

Cúchulainn turned for the benches, shaking his arms and rolling his neck from side to side. Ferdia, Conall, Leary and Dubthach all avoided looking at him as he sat against the wall, giving him time to come back to himself.

"You lot!" Conall bellowed. "Get back to practicing what the Hound showed you—now!"

Ferdia watched his friend for a moment and, seeing how softly his breath came, his own shoulders lowered.

Looking uncomfortable, Dubthach cast about for something to say, turning back to Leary and Conall to break the silence. "You didn't tell me where the king was actually going."

Cúchulainn's eyes opened as Leary leaned forward. "There was a feast while this Deirdre was still in her mother's belly— nearly a score of years ago now," Leary said. "When the chief druid, Cathbad, put his hand on the woman, he foretold that the maid would be fair beyond all measure, but she'd cause strife among the Ulaid fighting men and bring ruin to Conor's kingdom." All the men were uneasy, a whisper of superstition chilling the air. Leary folded his arms, scowling. "She should have had a spear put through her then and there, I reckon."

Cúchulainn spoke up. "And what warrior of the Red Branch would kill a child still smeared with its own birthblood? Conor was right to ignore the calls for her death, and let her be reared alone."

Except that he should have sent her into obscurity, Ferdia thought darkly. No one knew precisely where she was, for Conor always drove the last leagues himself, only that she was still within the Ulaid's borders. Some thought she must live on a sea-rock, others on an island in Lough Neagh. It was forbidden to find out, and the druids had joined with Conor in that prohibition. The warriors were happy to comply because they'd prefer never to hear of her again. Only, Conor would never let them forget.

Cúchulainn gazed out through the tall, wooden gatetowers, where the sun outlined the yellowing trees along the river, the falling leaves speckled with red and brown. "Only the gods direct men to their fates," he said softly. "I don't fear some girl-child to bring mine to me."

"We already know your prophecy," Leary retorted. "The greatest glory and renown of any warrior…"

At the general intake of breath he stopped, but Ferdia was already finishing the sentence. *And in payment for this…a short life.* Thirteen years ago, when Cúchulainn was twelve, Cathbad announced that this dark, glorious fate would belong to any boy who took his first weapons from the Red Branch hall that Samhain Eve. Everyone stayed away—except Cúchulainn.

Ferdia wiped his sweaty palms down his trews, while Leary looked as if he regretted his outburst. Cúchulainn, however, only nodded. "Aye, and my end will have naught to do with some little maiden. She deserves a chance at life, same as we do."

Conall was glancing between them in disbelief. "Sometimes I want to knock your heads together. Conor didn't hide her away to protect *us*, he took the girl to gloat over. That's why he gallops off so proudly with his prick in the air!"

Cúchulainn eyed him. "We are Red Branch. We should protect the king's honor, not attack it."

"It's not just us saying it, Hound," Leary broke in. "Some of the border chiefs think Conor should be leading us against Connacht while they're still reeling from their king's illness and Maeve's flight. My wife says the women whisper that the king needs to *find* his balls, not empty them."

"Fergus would have held on to Maeve," Conall grumbled.

"If he kept his throne long enough," Leary quipped. "*He* was led by his balls a bit too much."

"He still is." Conall and Leary guffawed. Dubthach joined in uneasily.

"Don't let him hear you say that." Ferdia was irritated by such unguarded words about the former king, Conor's stepfather, Fergus mac Roy. "He might be sixty, but he can still match most of us on the battlefield—and in the bed-furs."

Conall sobered, shrugging.

"I honor Fergus," Cúchulainn said, "but he would not have forged peace with Laigin and Mumu as Conor has done. The king is not a warrior, but he *is* clever."

They all exchanged disgruntled looks, and just then Ferdia lifted his chin with relief. "Ah, look! The sons of Usnech."

A trio of young men spilled through the gate, leading horses and laughing. Ferdia rose to greet the new arrivals, glad that the distraction would shut up both the young and old warriors. "Naisi! Just in time to quiet these cubs for us." The sparring youngsters had already begun arguing again, voices rising.

The three brothers looped their reins over a post. They were alike and striking with it—tall and black-haired. Ferdia put a hand on Naisi's shoulder. "The Salmon Leap," he said. "That will strike them dumb for the rest of the day."

Naisi's smile was, as ever, guarded, his intense blue eyes flicking over Conall, and Leary behind him. "We've been hunting for days and I strained my leg."

"On an ill-advised jump over a gorge," Ardan put in.

Naisi's glance was full of discomfort. "It got us the stag, and your belly is fat enough to vouch for that."

"I went over, too," Ainnle put in, until Naisi sent him a warning look.

Cúchulainn spoke up from the bench. "Take a leap with Ferdia, Naisi. The cubs have had enough of me for the moment."

Though Naisi was five years younger than Ferdia and Cúchulainn, his command of the Salmon Leap was second only to theirs because he'd already spent years perfecting it. Ferdia still remembered his slight, solitary figure on the green as dusk fell, when the rest of the boy's troop had gone to eat. Naisi's face beneath its crop of dark hair was always set with absolute focus, those vivid eyes alight with a hunger to conquer himself.

Naisi's attention darted to the pack of younger warriors. Though they were close to him in years, they had yet to pass their initiation feats, and there were scowls at the favor shown him by Ferdia and Cúchulainn. In response, Ferdia was pleased to see Naisi's chin go up as he immediately began peeling off his tunic and unbuckling his sword. Ardan slung an arm about Ainnle's neck. "We'll watch."

While Ferdia and Naisi went to the barrel of blunted spear-hafts, Cúchulainn addressed the adolescent warriors in training. "To appreciate this feat properly, we need an enemy." His eyes swiveled toward his comrades. "Dubthach, Conall and Leary make good Connacht warriors."

Leary and Conall groaned. "I've got spears to make," Leary said, jumping up.

"And I've got sleep to get," Conall protested.

Cúchulainn merely grinned, raising his voice. "And they are going to form a defensive group for Naisi and Ferdia to attack." Grumbling, Leary and Conall gave up, making their way onto the practice field with Dubthach following. All three turned and lined up in a half-moon.

Ferdia and Naisi faced them on the other side of the yard, their spears over their shoulders. Ferdia glanced at Naisi's bright eyes.

"Go," he muttered. They both took off, running at the crescent of three warriors, the spears held in front.

Ferdia's sight narrowed to the gleam of the band on Dubthach's arm, and he let go into the light and dug the blunted spear into the ground, clenching every muscle to propel himself using the shaft. His body arced up, bending the spear, and at the top of the thrust he flipped into a somersault that took him over the line of defense. His lance clattered onto Dubthach's head as Ferdia landed lightly behind him, Naisi coming down a heartbeat later. Dubthach pretended to be surprised, and in a moment Ferdia's dagger was at his throat, Naisi's pressed against Leary's side.

Leary shrugged Naisi off in irritation, flexing his shoulders, and the younger man stood back and sheathed his dagger. The warriors in training were still exclaiming when Cúchulainn joined Ferdia and Naisi. "*That* was a Salmon Leap to be proud of," he said, slinging an arm about Naisi's shoulders. He turned to the youths. "The positions of the body are honed by discipline, and Naisi has expended more of that than most." He smiled briefly at him. "But the thrust and flight need passion and surrender. If you are stiff you'll unbalance yourself, and if you're not swift enough you'll miss the spin and hit them with your body."

Ferdia grinned at Naisi. His own blood was still singing from the leap, and he saw the answering spark in those brilliant blue eyes as Naisi buckled his sword back on. Then the younger man's face changed, and Ferdia turned.

The king had come up quietly behind them. He held his power about him as he did his mantle, his hawk face giving little away, his eyes shrewd beneath lowered brows. He was Cúchulainn's uncle—the brother of the Hound's dead mother—but there was little family resemblance beyond their fair hair, though Conor's was now threaded with gray. His beard was braided into two spear-points, which served to sharpen his features more.

"An impressive display," the king said, his voice resonant and measured. He inclined his head at the warriors in training. "And there are some fine fighters proving their blood here this day, Hound." Cúchulainn nodded a little warily, before the king swung to fix his gaze on Naisi. "But the sons of Usnech have not graced my hall for weeks. Where have you been?"

Naisi's eyes hardened. "Hunting."

Ardan and Ainnle had joined their brother now, their cheeks flushed. They stood shoulder to shoulder by habit, never noticing how uncomfortable it made some men when faced with that wall of dark heads and tall bodies.

Conor studied them coolly. "Your sword-brothers have already brought us boar. I would be most honored, therefore, if you would engage yourselves in something more useful to me."

Nothing he said was inflammatory, but Ferdia did not miss the subtle tension between Naisi and the king. He did not understand it. Naisi was a strong warrior, yes, but young—and entirely loyal to the Red Branch and the Ulaid. And the king was…the king.

Naisi's hand had balled on his hilt. "We are at your service, as always," he replied stiffly. "I hear there is a wolf ravaging Forgall's herds. Ainnle is an expert wolf-tracker. Or do you need us to ride the Connacht border?"

Conor smiled thinly. "Neither, though I acknowledge the honor you do me for pledging such bravery." The ritual words did not do much to lessen the tension. "Clever men are required to supervise the carpenters at the Emain Pass."

The pass was a gap in the southern hills, a gateway to the plains beyond. Conor was closing off a ring of them with palisades to control entry to the sacred heart of the Ulaid territory. The Gates of Macha, they were called, after the goddess who built Emain Macha eons ago.

Naisi didn't seem to hear the compliment, for a muscle twitched in his jaw. "You want us to build walls?"

"They are an important defense," Conor said. "Why would I trust such a vital job to anyone other than three of my best Red Branch warriors?"

Naisi bowed his head, though Ferdia felt sure it was only to

hide his face. "Any skills we have are yours. We will leave for the
Gates tonight."

"Tomorrow is adequate. Though I myself will be absent
tonight, it would please all the warriors if you would grace my
hall with your singing." With that, Conor returned to his chariot.

No one would meet Naisi's gaze. "Why will he be absent?" he
muttered.

"He's off a-courting," Leary replied dryly.

A scornful snort was the only answer to that. Naisi stalked
back to the horses and his brothers closed in behind him, all the
laughter bleached from their faces.

Naked and shivering, Deirdre trickled the mead between her fingers into the pool. "We honor you, Flidhais of the woods, and beg
leave to enter your sacred waters." She pressed the last honeyed
drops to her lips, closing her eyes in the pale sunshine.

Standing beside her, Levarcham let out a small murmur of approval. To their right, the stream gushed from a bank of amber
and gold-leaved trees down a terrace of rocks and into a pounding waterfall. One arm of the swirling water calmed into a pool at
their feet, while the rest tumbled farther away down the valley.
The stream-bed glittered in the cold sun, ripples of shadow passing across it from overhanging ash trees.

Deirdre dug her heels into the gravel. Why there was every
other comfort in the steading but a large bath was a mystery.
Levarcham made her splash herself standing in a little tub—
something about instilling discipline, no doubt. "You might wash
your hair for the king," Levarcham suggested. "It's got things in it
I can't even identify. Have you been poking about fox dens again
or just lying on dead logs?"

Deirdre's eyes flickered open. Today...it was today. Levarcham
was holding out a flask of soapwort wash, and Deirdre glanced
between it and the river. "Hold it for me," she said, turning away.

"Deirdre." Levarcham's voice was sharp. "Don't..."

She didn't hear the rest for she was already bounding barefoot up the path through the coppery ferns. Racing headlong, she took a deep breath…*Flidhais, please understand*…and holding it, flung herself off the rocks into the pool beneath the waterfall.

Levarcham's shout was cut off—her words about the king, Deirdre's despair, all of it snatched away by the agony of the freezing water. She kicked herself under the falls until they pounded on her head, pummeling her with their boiling fury. Again she went back under, letting the force and cold crush every last feeling from her.

Panting, she swam out of the turbulence into calmer water. Levarcham had given up speaking, planting herself on an oak stump, and when Deirdre guiltily glanced at her she was surprised by the pain that flitted over her teacher's features. Deirdre wondered if she was the only one dreading the return of the king.

She let her body float, forcing a smile. "The king is called Conor mac Nessa after his mother because his father was a druid, isn't that so?"

Levarcham peered at her, tossing over the flask. "The king was conceived at a Beltaine rite. Nessa was part of that rite and so was Cathbad, the chief druid. But no one is sure who his father is."

"Then he is a god-sired child." It was the last thing she wanted to think about, but this repetition of Levarcham's teachings was restoring the druid's composure. Deirdre rubbed soapwort into her hair, stoppering the flask. "So that's why he became king, even though he was no warrior."

Levarcham had only recently shared the details of Conor's youth, and Deirdre read from that there was something unusual about his kingship. "With no noble sire to give Conor arms or train him, he was drawn to the druids, to matters of the mind," Levarcham clarified. "This made him shrewd, and won him the kingship in the end."

"Because King Fergus—who *was* a great warrior—wanted to seek his own adventures. And Nessa, by then Fergus's wife, convinced him to let her son Conor guard the kingship for a year though he was barely twenty." The hollow words tripped off her tongue; she wanted to show she had memorized this. "Conor proved so clever the warriors decided to keep him on as king when Fergus got back." She tipped her head to wash out the soap. "But doesn't Fergus mind?"

Levarcham's mouth pursed. "He found kingship a burden— and he is still a mighty warrior, with men loyal to him."

Deirdre threw the flask to the bank and sank back in the water. "Conor then tricked Laigin into exchanging some of their best cattle and pasture for an Ulaid marsh. And then he gave the pasture to the Ulaid chiefs and the cattle to the warriors, and they all got wealthier."

"Yes." Levarcham was watching Deirdre closely. "And this is why Conor has held power for thirty years. He used his cunning to forge peace with Laigin and Mumu, and was trying with Connacht when—" She cut that off. "*Ach!* I forgot to bring a robe for you." She beckoned impatiently. "I will go back. Come out and comb your hair."

Deirdre numbly crawled out and sat with knees up. *Conor.* A powerful king who took her in when her mother died at her birth and her father, the king's harper, followed her through the veils. As Conor's ward she knew she should be grateful for her comfortable home and good food. Political marriages were often made from such ties, Levarcham had always said; it was a natural extension of the king's care. And after all, she didn't know any other way to live. Only it had begun to *feel* unnatural, and Levarcham also seemed more disturbed lately…

Deirdre squeezed water from her hair. Her teacher was the king's talking-woman, his satirist, who stood high in his favor; Deirdre must be imagining she was unhappy about the king's visits. *Enough!* Deirdre snorted and promptly closed her eyes.

She shivered for a time until a tingling began to spread over her, the sun sinking into her wet body. She felt every tiny, tightening sensation. She moved her head to feel her hair trailing over her shoulder-blade. A cool wind skirled over the stream, stroking her arms and caressing the plump, white tops of her breasts like a trailing finger.

Deirdre's eyes sprang open.

The breeze lifted her hair and left a kiss on her nape. Then it licked lower, brushing her bent knees and buttocks, sliding between her thighs. Her hips loosened and she stared at the light dancing over the gold hairs on her forearm. Her hand moved of its own accord, smoothing over waist and flank. The lines of her body flowed in and out now, and there were hollows and sheened curves where before there had just been bone. She glanced at the blue veins under the milky skin. Fintan, Aiveen and Levarcham were brown-skinned, with creased eyes and graying hair. She wanted to be like them, not this entirely different creature. *Then she could fade into the bark and never be found.* Her hands traced her nose and lips, and still she could not transform this pattern into an image of her face. She had tried peering in the pool, but the trees cloaked her in shadow and the wind puckered the surface.

She did not know herself.

Her fingers closed into an empty fist. Conor kept her isolated to protect her from his enemies—from Connacht, Levarcham said. It was so she could have the quiet and space to learn, away from the rivalries of Emain Macha and those who would jostle for position against her as his bride. Levarcham said these things in a rational way that was supposed to make sense. And they used to, when she was an unformed child, but they grated against all her instincts now.

Staring across the water to the woods, she slowly uncurled to her feet, holding out a trembling hand. She felt it again: that invisible pressure, that thickening. The air quivered with minute vibrations, a density through which she could almost push. She slitted her eyes.

The trees across the water, the clouds, the rocks...they shimmered for a moment in the broken sunshine, as if everything she saw was partly veiled, its truth only glimpsed. It was like firelight catching one edge of something, as the shadows hid its entirety. The world was there, and behind it was another.

And she was barred from both. She looked up at the mysterious, towering forest, and all that was numb kindled into searing, furious life. She was a flame against the wall of trees, burning alone where no one could see.

Now the king was coming with more gifts, a landslide of gifts, when she only wanted the one he would never give: the right to leave the valley alone and climb a hill to smell the sea.

CHAPTER 3

That night, Levarcham sat on the bed behind Deirdre and bound her hair from her face, ready for the mask she would wear in her dance for the king. The silence between them was heavy.

The druid wove feathers through those long hanks of spun gold—a color all the maidens at Emain Macha would weep for, but for which Deirdre cared nothing. Levarcham sucked her lip between her teeth to keep her feelings similarly bound. For years she had told Conor Deirdre wasn't ready—but her moon-bleeding had come at last, and now it was a lie.

The girl had learned all the noblewomen's arts long ago—spinning, dyeing, weaving, embroidering—as well as how to walk with a graceful sway, carve beef, pour ale and make light conversation. She had mastered these with impatience, eager to turn to tasks more suited to her questing mind.

She'd been too disarming a child for Fintan and Aiveen to curb. Conor had picked them as guardians because they were simple, good-hearted people who had lost their own babe and could never bear more. Ignorant of the subtleties of parental bonds, Conor didn't realize they therefore loved Deirdre blindly and could deny her nothing.

Levarcham had never enlightened him on this.

Aiveen let Deirdre rush out with the spinning unfinished to play in the stream like an otter, watching her with indulgent eyes. Fintan, a massive, rough-hewn man, was soft as butter underneath and allowed Deirdre to trot along at his heels when he checked his snares for hare and marten, and caught and butchered the occasional hind. She seemed oblivious to dirt and cold, and fascinated by the workings of life as any druid, her small hand hovering over each limp animal to give the death-blessing, the honor for meat and fur.

Levarcham's cynicism squawked like a crow on her shoulder. *And all you've done is polish that fine mind into a king's jewel.*

She chewed her lip. *I've done all I can,* she protested. *I've bent the rules and can go no further.* The crow was ominously silent on that.

She thanked the gods that at least Deirdre's bleeding had come so late. The moon-tides of the maids closeted in the women's hall ebbed and flowed together, so perhaps Deirdre's isolation accounted for this late bloom; neither Aiveen nor Levarcham's blood still hearkened to that call. And Conor had been too embroiled with the Princess Maeve of Connacht to demand her earlier. Considering Levarcham's sole task had been to mold a fit consort for Erin's greatest king, this reluctance to discharge her final duty was vexing. It was just…the girl's restlessness had become so unbearable lately.

"The moon stirs woman-flesh as it does the seas," Aiveen had sighed one day, watching Deirdre pace the walls.

The simplest thing, the crow pointed out now, *is to tell Conor she's ready and let him bed her.*

Levarcham's thumb tugged a knot and Deirdre let out a hiss of pain.

Ach. Levarcham shouldn't resent a king who had bestowed such an honor upon her, or question the chief druid Cathbad's prophesy that the girl's blood was tainted with ruin. After Conor decided to have her still but raise her in secret, Cathbad told Levarcham the best she could do was make the child biddable. But what was pliant about Deirdre?

In the end, she'd settled on a perfect druid paradox: to faithfully prepare the child to be queen while delaying the day as long as possible.

Tying the braid, Levarcham limped to the dresser to fold the crushed robes of finely-embroidered linen—anything to occupy her hands. *The king's gifts.* Deirdre had pushed them aside in favor of hide trews and wool tunics, her preferred clothes when Conor was absent. Levarcham laid a gentle hand on the worn leather, and her smile was sad.

Feet padded up behind and she sensed Deirdre hovering, before the girl pressed her cheek for a moment against Levarcham's shoulder. Levarcham held still, enjoying that rare closeness, as if a deer had come to her from the forest. She sighed and Deirdre immediately straightened, and when the druid turned Deirdre's green eyes dropped to veil her thoughts, her lashes fringing wide-set cheekbones above a determined, narrow chin. The druid nudged aside her fair hair to check the cut from the fall. There was only a shadow of a bruise now.

Deirdre braced her shoulders. "So, do I look presentable?" Her gaze had become opaque. *She was no girl now, but a woman with secrets.*

Levarcham could barely nod. She had ordered long ago that there would be no mirrors or polished metal in this homestead, and no large baths. Deirdre had never seen her features clearly. This was Levarcham's last, hidden rebellion. If Conor made beauty a trap, then it would be banished from this place while Deirdre grew. She had been taught to nurture her mind, and for this, Levarcham felt no guilt at all.

Conor wiped his beard and belched a waft of buttered trout into his hand. Half-eaten dishes were spread across the low table: honey-roast turnips, venison steeped with cherries, fresh hazelnut cakes. It was a change from all that interminable boar-meat at Emain Macha.

The belch produced no change in Levarcham's grave expression, and he gave up any attempt to goad her for his own amusement, stretching his boots to Fintan's fire and letting his muscles sag into the cushion. It was so peaceful after his raucous hall, stuffed with youngsters all locking horns.

Youngsters. By Lugh, he was only fifty. He irritably hitched his trews, trying not to notice the slight paunch that now padded his lean body. "My compliments to you on that fine meal," he said to Fintan's plump little wife, who shyly bobbed her head. He glanced at Levarcham. "So, the last time you tried to convince me the girl was not yet proficient in all the womanly arts." He had been so absorbed in taming Maeve of Connacht, his erstwhile bride, that a full year had passed since his last visit. Still, the memory of that time was vivid. When he took Deirdre's fingers by his chariot, she had pulled her hair from her eyes in the wind, and though they once glinted with a child's curiosity now they were mysterious and shadowed, like the deep reaches of the woods.

"She has...come along," Levarcham said stiffly. "Though we don't have to tell you the details if you don't want them."

No, nothing happened here except by his will. This valley was a little haven where he ruled unchallenged and didn't have to constantly prove his strength to squabbling warriors who thought you could hold a kingdom by force alone—if they thought at all. They had no conception of the shrewdness required to balance the complex webs of alliances and grievances. They didn't have to. They could eat and drink until they fell, and hump a dozen women a night. Well, for such denial, he would reward himself with the greatest prize of all: Deirdre.

Keeping her isolated meant that he would avoid the darkness of the prophecy and only savor the light. A thrilling whisper threaded his mind. Could Conor mac Nessa be the man to outwit the gods? After all, they admired courage and cunning. Smiling, he held out his cup. "More ale is what I want."

While Aiveen poured, he watched his hand waver and realized he'd drunk more than he intended. *Ach*. He deserved it, after what that vixen Maeve had done to him, spurning their marriage and running back to Connacht to squabble with her brothers over her dying father's spoils. A glimpse of auburn hair and flashing eyes entered his mind like a blade and he thrust it aside, replacing it with a soft mist of golden tresses. Deirdre wouldn't shame him.

At the thought of what changes a year had wrought, his prick stirred satisfyingly beneath his robes. See, she made him virile as a stallion already. "Enough. I want to see her." He did not miss the glance between Levarcham and the granite-hewn Fintan. The druid was perfectly straight as usual, but Fintan's massive frame was hunched, his cup crushed between callused paws. "What?" Conor demanded. "Is there something wrong with her?"

Fintan's mouth turned down in his short, graying beard. "No, my lord."

"Come out with her, then. I've waited long enough."

Levarcham nodded at Fintan's dormouse of a wife, brown-haired and timid, and the woman scurried to summon Deirdre. The druid snuffed out all the lamps so Fintan's hut was lit only by firelight, the curved walls in shadow. She picked up a bone pipe and, seating herself, began to play.

Wreathed in that keening melody Conor's muscles relaxed, his swift mind slowing. Maeve's image faded into the trilling notes, and just as he was sinking into his seat the door-hide was pulled back and cold air swirled in. Conor sat up.

A slim, bare foot appeared, twirling slowly to the time of the music. Little bells were tied around the ankles and, above that, pale wool hugged a lithe thigh, the cloth so fine it was nearly translucent. Then, for a pause…nothing else. The king leaned forward, breathing hard. Wrists appeared next around the doorway, and arms that gracefully turned in time to the music, the rest of the girl in shadow. He ignored the waft of white feathers sewn on the sleeves, or how the spirals her arms traced suggested spreading wings, focusing only on that hint of thigh.

And then *she* stepped out into the dappled firelight. The shock rocked him back, and for a moment he thought it a spirit of the marshes and not a girl at all. Her hair was bound back, the lengths woven with white feathers and her face covered by a crudely painted wooden mask. An orange-and-black beak jutted from white cheeks below long, tilted eyes. Deirdre's eyes were also wide-set and slightly slanted, cheeks broad above a narrow chin, so this bird mask had taken her essence and twisted it into something more primitive, even savage. Conor's shoulders tightened with a delicious chill.

The bird-spirit spread her arms and the sleeves fluttered, her feathered braids swirling around her waist. Now Conor recognized the haunting tune. It was an old tale of the swan maiden, a girl turned into a swan by the *sídhe*, the denizens of the Otherworld, and doomed to wander the land until she was released by love and so died. Transfixed, Conor forgot to breathe as Deirdre began to dance.

He had never seen anyone move like that, losing all trace of the maiden, becoming the bird. She twirled around the fire, her slim arms capturing the beat of flight, the fold of wings as she alighted, the glide over water. Arching her graceful neck, she preened and shook her feathers. The tale unfolded. She played out the maiden's shock at her capture, the realization she was trapped as a swan and the years she floated on mirrored lakes, staring down at her reflection. Her loneliness and longing were so palpable that Conor was momentarily diverted from his lust. When she beseeched the water gods for release, Levarcham's playing faltered before righting.

The moment came when the swan maiden sees her love. She follows him, beating her wings, mutely begging for help. But the boy, a hunter, does not hear the song of her heart and shoots her in flight. As she falls to earth, she resumes her human form of great beauty, and in that moment the youth takes her in his arms as she is dying, and she is released from pain.

Conor knew the story and only vaguely followed it with his mind. It was his body that ruled him. He could see the flesh at her ankles, arms and neck, the skin glowing like the inside of a shell. Every line of her body was a harmony, from firm thighs to tiny waist to flared hips. His mouth went completely dry.

When she bent at the waist, her breasts fell into the neck of her gown, and when she stretched up, the thin wool outlined the nipples and shadowy cleft between her legs. *By the Dagda.*

The heat grew in his loins as Deirdre's limbs became a blur, the tune rising to a climax. The pipes let forth an endless, keening note…and Deirdre mimed falling from a great height and sank gracefully to the floor, wings outstretched. The music stopped and the hut fell silent.

Conor gulped to suppress the galloping in his chest. He glanced at Fintan, who was looking upon Deirdre with utter bewilderment, his heavy brow rumpled, then at Levarcham. The druid was staring at the girl with the only shock he had ever seen branded upon that grave face.

Conor remembered who he was then, and forced himself to clap. "Wonderful!" he cried hoarsely. "Magnificent, my dear!"

After a moment Deirdre rose and she was a young woman again, brushing off her clothes. "Come!" Conor demanded. "Sit by me and let me look at you properly." *Let me look at you until my bones crumble to dust; let me look at your flesh, white and soft, forever.*

Hesitantly, she stood before him. The beak on the mask was sharp, the slanted holes giving her own eyes a fierce cast. A breath of superstitious fear brushed the king's mind but he batted it away, gesturing her to the bench beside him.

Deirdre perched as far away as she could, hands between her knees. Conor frowned, frustration wiping out everything else, and without thinking he reached across and tore away the mask.

CHAPTER 4

Deirdre disentangled the thongs of the mask, looking at the wall over the king's shoulder. The fringes of her body felt blurred, shimmering in time with the urgent beat of wings she still sensed at the ends of her arms. Dazed, she could hardly remember who she was, her heart still consumed by the swan's fear and longing to be free.

Her attention was caught by Levarcham, surprising a look of panic on her face. Deirdre's eyes darted to Fintan, who was scratching furiously at his beard, and Aiveen, whose hazel eyes were limpid with an odd resignation.

Conor cleared his throat. "You dance exquisitely," he murmured. "You honor the gods—and me."

They were familiar words, but the expression on Conor's face was new. His eyes roamed over her, studying every feature, even the dip below her mouth. Deirdre rubbed her chin as if she could hide it from him. "Thank you. I did practice a lot this sunseason. There wasn't much else to do, after all." She rubbed her chin again. She hadn't meant for that parry to slip out.

But Conor didn't seem to hear, his gaze roving from her cheeks to the neck of her gown. It didn't feel like the wind's wild caress now, but a smear of grease. She itched to wipe each place his eyes lingered, wishing she was in her muddy trews and worn tunic, hair bundled off her face.

"You have certainly grown." Conor's voice was low.

Her reply stuck in her throat. "Indeed, I am as tall as Levarcham."

Conor smiled, the firelight glancing off his faded golden beard.

His face was long and bony like his body, carved with deep crinkles around eyes and hawkish nose. "That is not exactly what I meant." He reached a hand toward Deirdre's cheek.

Once, he had dandled her on his knee. Now, as the king's long, elegant fingers extended toward her, Deirdre saw how they trembled, and her belly churned when he grasped her chin and she felt his clammy palm. His thumb brushed her lip and she tried not to be sick. She did not understand her own reactions. Levarcham's stories were full of men touching women and it sounded pleasurable. She would be Conor's wife and that meant he owned her. *Surely a king can touch whatever he likes*, she thought faintly.

Her body didn't listen, though. Her legs forced her up, sending the mask thudding to the floor with its eyes now empty. "But do you not want a tale, my lord?" Pressing her tongue against the roof of her mouth, she tried to look as if she had risen naturally. "I've practiced those for you, too."

Conor blinked with irritation. Levarcham started from her stool, then stood with the pipe clasped between her fingers. Fintan and Aiveen stared at the king, clearly afraid. Deirdre's chest drummed with her own daring, but this only drew Conor's gaze to her breasts.

He slowly sat back. "Why, yes," he replied evenly. "I do like to hear you recite."

Levarcham's instructions had been for something *calm*. Another wilder Deirdre was asserting itself, though, as it had taken over her dance. "I will tell you of the heroes at Emain Macha." At Conor's evident dismay, Deirdre added forcefully, "For the renown of a kingdom's heroes is only a reflection of the greatness of its king."

Conor regarded her warily, then nodded. "The poets of Erin do speak of the wonders of my hall."

With a frown, Levarcham sat back on the bench and everyone turned to face Deirdre.

She collected herself like a bard, closing her eyes and stretching her throat to loosen the anger from it. Then she began to recite the list of Ulaid heroes and their attributes: the un-matched Cúchulainn, champion of the Ulaid; Ferdia mac Daman, dark with mystery but bright-skilled; Leary, winner of battles; Conall Cearnach, of the five spears; Illan, son of Fergus mac Roy; and Conor's own son, flaxen Fiacra. More came after, many more.

Defiance fired her, as if the warrior names she tasted made her braver, too, and she was not afraid to meet the king's eyes. Spots of color had appeared on his lined cheeks as she outlined the virtues of his young men, describing their muscled legs and strong shield-arms. Levarcham had taught her these names so she would know those close to Conor's throne—and she was only repeating bard-song, wasn't she?

She came to the warriors that intrigued her most because they were three brothers and she had no siblings. They were famed for fighting, hunting and singing.

> *Deep their delight in trebled song*
> *That twists brightly its wing-feathers*
> *And circles over Ulaid's plains*
> *Blithe their sweet voices together*
> *Beasts hearken, sleek cattle*
> *Yield milk with great increase;*
> *Men, bound in spell, hearken*
> *And halt for music mid-pace*

Deirdre progressed through the poem, eyes glazed. She vaguely noticed Conor's mouth begin to twist.

> *Swift their joy in the noisy chase*
> *They race eager hounds for quarry*
> *And fell in flight the gasping stag*
> *That flaps the red tongue of panic*
> *With happy shout, tired champions*
> *Loose the shrill hounds at the prey*

Quick also to sweep with courage
Iron swords brandished together

Lost inside herself, Deirdre's voice was rising, and she closed her eyes for the last lines.

Into battle the joyful brothers
Naisi, Ardan and Ainnle

She flung each name out like blows of her fist, like war cries, hardly knowing what she was doing. At last her voice faded and she came back to herself, and those fine names died on her tongue. Conor's eyes had ignited, the contours of his face set into hard lines.

Deirdre gulped down the remnants of the song, and Levarcham took her by the shoulders. "That's enough," she said sharply. "You have had a long day. Go to bed now. The king would want you to rest."

Conor made no move to stop her, and as Deirdre grabbed her mask and fled she saw only that he had gone stiff-backed, like the old dog when it heard a distant wolf.

With one look at Levarcham's face, Aiveen and Fintan hastily excused themselves to take refuge in the salthouse.

The druid turned, bracing herself on the roof-post. Sweet Brid! Where had Deirdre learned to move with such sensuality? With no sign of the moon-tide, Levarcham had postponed her sexual education. And with no exposure to men other than a father, she assumed Deirdre's desires would slumber until the king woke them. *You were avoiding it all*, the crow squawked, and she cursed her blindness. The swan dance was chosen to show off her grace, but the girl had unknowingly turned it into seduction, her carnal nature instinctively unfurling, unrestrained. And that was more powerful than any artifice.

Levarcham glanced at the pacing Conor. She had hoped to beg another year this night, to say the girl was still unformed. With one turn of her ankle, Deirdre had demolished that lie.

Conor spun on his heel, his gray eyes fiery. "And just why did you teach her this ridiculous drivel about young cubs barely out of their breech-clouts?"

Levarcham stared. She had not been thinking of Deirdre's poem, but her dance. "I had to teach her about the warriors at your hall. She will be queen. She must know about alliances and old grudges, who to trust and who not to—"

"Ballocks." Conor rarely cursed, too cunning to give way to emotion. "You fill her head with nonsense about callow youths. You will cease this *immediately!*"

It was the roar of a man used to being obeyed. Levarcham, however, was his satirist. She was meant to spear a king's folly with words, reminding him of the proper boundaries of royal power. "They are the same tales your own bards tell," she retorted. "And do you want a milkmaid for a wife, or an accomplished queen? She is young, and will look at younger men. I warned you of that when you sent her here."

"She will not." Conor raked his hands through his hair, tearing the carefully-combed curls apart. "She must obey me—and she would if you hadn't let her grow up so wild and uncurbed, like a sprouting weed."

Wild, yes, Levarcham agreed in despair, but not like a weed. Like a storm. "The more you push her, the more she will rebel."

Conor glared at her. High, bony cheeks and heavy eyebrow ridges framed an unflinching gaze, giving it a force that was increased by his constantly drawn brows. Few could face down Conor of the Ulaid. "I can rule her, and I will. I want her by my side as soon as possible."

Levarcham's jaw clenched. "She's not ready yet."

"You're telling me *that* wasn't ready?"

Levarcham reached desperately for excuses. "When you gave me this task, I accepted on condition that you would respect my judgment. The teaching is not yet complete." *When you gave me this task,* she lamented, *I knew in my heart it was wrong.*

The tempest in Conor's eyes was now leashed tight. "You don't understand. She is a triumph. I *have* to have her now. I will not go a moment longer without her."

The frustration in his face made Levarcham's pity waver, and some of her anger ebbed. Was he just misunderstood? She thought of Maeve's betrayal, the stress he must be under, the shame. "With her by my side," Conor said, his gaze roving over the walls, "my hall will be even more admired. With her by my side, no one would challenge me, or question my strength."

No one would think I was aging if I had won her.

The thought arrowed from nowhere, piercing Levarcham's druid senses. "My lord," she whispered, unseeing eyes fixed on the fire. "Let pride and greed rule you and you will plunge down a dark road. The gods ask for surrender to the natural laws, for grace and wisdom." She drew a shaking breath. "Perhaps you should let the girl go, after all. You've given her too much of a hold on you—"

"When I have waited all these years?" He took a threatening step toward her. "I took her as mine on the day she was born, and I will have her and no other."

Her eyes narrowed, her voice steadied. "You own no one. You are king solely by the will of the people. Your nobles voted you into the kingship for only so long as you rule justly, bringing wealth and honor to the Ulaid. If you cease to do so, they can depose you, too." His nostrils flared at that, for he hated being reminded of how Fergus had been tricked out of his rule by Conor's own mother, Nessa. Before he could react, she disarmed him. "Nevertheless...you are right. I have not been as strict as I could be with the girl." The belligerence began to leach from the king's expression. "Give me another year, and I can mold her into a woman who understands her place, who will honor you as husband and king." Every word hurt. *Why put off the inevitable?* the crow taunted. She would see Deirdre more at Emain Macha.

There would be no change in a year, as she well knew. So why did she feel compelled to delay?

Her gaze locked with the king's, both unwavering.

Conor exhaled through his nose, tapping his fingers together. Levarcham prayed for the gods to change his mind. At last he stroked his beard, and she knew she had him. "Six months," he countered. "But not a month more, woman."

Relief swamped Levarcham. "It will be for the best."

Conor tilted his head away. "The anticipation of her alone is power." He smiled to himself, gazing into the shadows. "And there are always other ways to curb her later."

CHAPTER 5

Wild geese began arrowing over the forest, seeking shelter for the long dark. Their poignant cries arrested Deirdre as she trudged to the storehouse with baskets of berries and hazelnuts, her chin stretching to follow the flocks across the pale clouds.

The morning after the dance, Levarcham had left with the king, and for once Deirdre had been glad not to have to look into her teacher's deep, all-seeing eyes. She did not want to be questioned about why she picked that poem—for she had no answer—or hear how angry the king was, or why. She didn't want any reminder of that night, for it brought back to her the sensation of his touch on her skin.

Then Levarcham reappeared at the steading one day with a face like a storm, her dark cloak falling from rigid shoulders. Her gray hair was bound so tightly her face seemed all bone. "Come with me. We are going out."

Deirdre did not pause to puzzle out that terrible expression, for she had not left the steading for days. She, Aiveen and Fintan had been butchering a pig Conor sent them, brining and curing the meat and turning the rest into blood puddings. Now she eagerly wiped salt from her hands and grinned at Aiveen, who flapped her apron to herd her out the door. They all knew Deirdre had to be among the trees to breathe.

She ran back to her hut for warmer clothes and boots and rejoined Levarcham at the gate of the timber rampart surrounding the little homestead. The druid did not speak as they made their way through the leaf-fall woods, leaning on her staff in a rolling lope that favored her crooked leg and gave her surprising speed. Hastening to keep up, Deirdre looked at her teacher, but the grim set of her mouth forbade any conversation.

Levarcham swept past the bushes holding the last, shriveled brambles and the scarlet hips clinging to the leafless rose stems. The forest canopy was a mingling of speckled russet and gold, and bracken coated the clearings in rusted fronds, glowing in the shafts of weak sun. "When is Samhain?" Levarcham snapped, making Deirdre skip a hurried step.

She thought fast—she had a druid sun-disk that helped her track the stars and moon. "Twenty-one days."

"What's that plant?" The druid pointed at a withered patch of leaves barely attached to a trailing stalk. Deirdre frowned at Levarcham's back. It was hard to tell the herbs at this time of year. "Candle-flower."

"Used for…?"

"Fever, blood-cleansing, increasing the flow of urine, rashes." There were many more uses for candle-flower, but baffled at Levarcham's mood, she asked boldly, "Is that enough or do you want more?" Levarcham only grunted, shaking her head.

It took time for Deirdre to notice they were passing far beyond her usual haunts, and eventually they reached a place where the path began to climb, leading them out of the valley. Her step began to quicken when she saw the forest thin up ahead, and at the end of the trail the trees gave way to a wide meadow of frost-browned grass, bounded by a ridge of hills. Deirdre broke into a trot, eager to climb that beckoning slope.

"*Wait!*" Levarcham cautioned, holding her back. "Don't go tearing out there. It's dangerous."

"Why?" A stream sprang from the peak, foaming toward them through a cleft of ferns, and Deirdre was distracted by an urge to plunge through that bracken, soaking her trews to smell the spray on her skin.

Levarcham was listening for something, and Deirdre's questions were driven from her head by a hoarse bellow that boomed off the valley sides. A second cry answered. "Stags!" Deirdre exclaimed breathlessly. She'd heard them from afar before in leaf-fall, and Fintan had brought back their discarded antlers to carve into combs and toggles. She'd only ever seen one with her own eyes, though—an old stag that blundered into the woods near her home.

The two bellows clashed like groans of thunder, the echo thrown to the clouds. "Stags in rut," Levarcham corrected. "Which means they are fighting—and if girls get in their way, they could get trampled."

Deirdre's head swung around. "I'm not a girl," she said quietly.

A ripple ran over Levarcham's face, as if something moved beneath that hard mask. "No." She drew a labored breath, pointing up the hill. "They fight in the open this time of year. We are going to watch."

Torn between curiosity and concern for her teacher, Deirdre followed. As they crept up a narrow ravine, Deirdre was sure she was about to see the world outside, the leagues of the Ulaid. When they crested the peak, however, she sagged with disappointment. Below, birch trees dotted a high plain of brown grass and on the other side rose more hills. She still could not see far. She contained that ache and followed Levarcham to a line of boulders halfway down.

In the middle of the dying grass, two stags were squaring off. Their sweaty flanks were russet as the bracken, their hides fringed with pale bronze. Their antlers spread above them like tree-crowns, and drool streamed from their nostrils and chins. Beside them, a cluster of hinds watched the proceedings impassively, lowering their necks to crunch at the withered plants.

One stag pawed the ground, snorting clouds of breath. The other bellowed a challenge with chin stretched out, the sound emanating from its barrel chest. That moaning roar vibrated through Deirdre and she clutched the rock in front of her.

The stags ran, tilting their heads, then threw themselves at each other with a resounding *crack*. The antlers tangled together as they scrabbled back and forth. First one would gain ground and push the other, then the second charged, forcing the first to dig in its hooves, tussling and snorting.

A prickling had come alive inside Deirdre's belly—no, lower—and with every roar and crack her breaths shortened. Their lust to fight invaded her. She sucked it in from the air and it thundered up from the ground, and the thrill and aggression filled her. All her muscles contracted in one ripple. She wanted to fight, growl and bellow, run and strike out, free all that restless energy. "They are magnificent," she breathed.

"They are male." The odd tone in Levarcham's voice drew Deirdre's head around, and that is when she saw the tremble in her teacher's chin. Levarcham coughed to cover it, fingering the jet beads at her neck. "They can hurt each other, kill each other."

"Then why bring me here?"

"It's not the fighting I brought you to see. Wait until one triumphs."

The pattern was repeated: the circling, the run and crack, the struggle. One beast was slightly bigger than the other, its antlers many-branched, and after the third fight the smaller stag broke the antler-lock and galloped away. The larger ran after him, bellowing, until he finally halted and stood puffing out his cheeks, flanks streaked with sweat. "Watch," Levarcham instructed in a faint voice.

The triumphant stag was huffing around the hinds' back legs, nosing them. Coming to one, he reared up on his hindquarters, and for a fleeting moment Deirdre's unsettled mind thought he would fight her, too. The female stood still, though, while he rested his forelegs across her back. Whuffling, the stag curved over and something extended between their rear flanks that Deirdre could not make out, before the male thrust close to the hind and began undulating. Deirdre stared, and for some reason her pulse skipped. She had seen doves flap about like this, and foxes mating in the woods. The stag was groping the hind with his forelegs, and with a cool part of her mind she thought, *It's a beast rutting, that is all.*

When she knelt back, though, her palms fell on the turf and her body was swept with heat, the vibration in the ground traveling through her wrists into her blood. She struggled to breathe, and the warmth and heaviness centered between her legs now and throbbed every time the stag thrust. Her cheeks burned and she glanced uncomfortably at Levarcham.

The druid's expression shocked her out of all sensation.

Her face was white and still, her eyes glittering with what could be...not tears? The stag levered himself off the female, shook his head and trotted away, and Levarcham extended a shaking hand. "That is mating. The stag puts his male parts inside the hidden hole between the hind's legs—her female parts—and in leaf-bud the fawns are born." The words were perfunctory, but the corners of the druid's mouth had folded in, and it took Deirdre a moment to recognize her anguish.

Understanding roared through her, for the power of earth had entered her and she was exquisitely raw, with no numbness to protect her now. She was instantly on her feet.

The druid started and went even paler, lifting her hands. "My child..."

"*No.*" Deirdre turned and scrabbled back up the hill then down the slope on the other side, sliding on the wet ferns and rocks. Stumbling back to the path, she wove blindly along it through the forest.

At last she stopped, swaying there, and soon Levarcham caught her up. At her approach, Deirdre turned on her. "Do you think I am a simpleton? That when I see the beasts do this—

when you tell me of desire between men and women, and when Aiveen speaks of babies—that I would not *understand*?"

Levarcham was struggling to speak, but Deirdre drew away from her outstretched fingers. "I know that Conor will lie on me and thrust his man-parts in me, and I can't stop him." She struck her temple with her palm. "And now you *make* me see, so that I can no longer escape the pictures that crowd my mind?" The blow of her hand brought back a startling memory of bursting into Fintan's house as a child and glimpsing a soft thing hanging between his naked legs. Conor's belly would be as wrinkled as his face, and below it *that* would dangle… Her chin jerked up and her throat burned, but she would *not* weep because of him.

"I…did not know how to tell you." Levarcham's voice cracked. "I held it inside for so long. But now it comes…"

Deirdre stared at Levarcham's hollow eyes, the pupils so wide they were black. Never in all these years had she seen her teacher undone, and her body went cold, the power of earth and hot blood and raging stags snuffed out. She knew then that Levarcham hadn't done this mating herself. *There was something Levarcham didn't know.* The druid held a veined hand before her face as if she could not bear to see herself reflected in Deirdre's eyes, her head bowed as the wind kicked up dead leaves around them.

Deirdre watched her teacher's bent head, and then she was taking her by the shoulders, tall enough to rest her chin on the older woman's gray hair for a moment. The trembling that came through them both made her feel as if the ground itself quaked.

Levarcham raised her face and gazed at her, before unexpectedly drawing her into a fierce embrace. Now Deirdre knew something had changed forever. The druid was not distracting or debating; she could offer nothing beyond sorrow. Deirdre's arms rose until she was clutching Levarcham to her, and for the first time they shared an embrace of commiseration, between women.

There was no one with the power to protect her here anymore.

Through a fug of ale, Conor savored the swelling in his groin as he lolled with his women on furs and cushions around his great chair, close to one of the roaring fire-pits. It was a foul day and rain beat upon the thatch roof of his hall, arching far above.

One of his youngest bed-mates giggled at his interest, and an older slut nudged her away to pour ale from a bronze pitcher into his horn cup. He stared at the glimpse of breast in the neck of her gown, gilded by the soft light of sheep-fat lamps scattered on low tables of shale and polished oak. Servants and warriors filled the cavernous room and he wasn't one to rut before others. He would savor this later.

Since he returned from Deirdre, his manhood would not lie down, rising each night and often in the day. The women's eyes turned toward him again as news went about of his vigor, renewed after Maeve's shaming. His warriors showed more respect. Even Levarcham had noticed, her eyes unreadable when she bid him farewell to take provisions to Deirdre for the long dark. Good. She knew now he would not be placated much longer.

Warriors sat drinking, mending leather and polishing weapons around the wall-benches beneath rows of shields and spears. The lethargy engendered by rain and ale stifled conversation, and no one bothered him with demands. Even his mother, Nessa, was absent, saving him the lash of her tongue. Servants threw armloads of wood on the fires, flinging up showers of sparks, while hounds lazed nearby on scattered deer-hides, eyes glowing in the flickering light.

The great oak doors creaked open and freezing air rushed through the entrance porch along with cold, gray daylight. Conor glanced over when one of his stewards hurried toward him, bowing. "The sons of Usnech, my lord."

Three shrouded figures came in, hanging their swords on pegs struck into the ring of massive carved and painted oak posts that held up the soaring roof. Two paused with their friends to shrug off dripping cloaks while the third made his way through the benches and cushions to Conor. Naisi dragged back his soaking hood, his eyes stony in his chilled face as he looked down upon the king. Conor realized he was at a disadvantage, and unhurriedly wrapped his cloak around his robe and sat with exaggerated ease on his carved oak chair.

Disrespectfully, Naisi spoke first. "The fortifications are finished, my lord." The bitter edge to his voice traveled around the hall, and the warriors on their benches looked over.

The king stared down his nose at him. Naisi's black hair was plastered to his forehead and mud crusted his boots. The rain ran off his cloak in a steady drip. *He is no more than a drowned pup,* Conor thought contemptuously, pressing himself into the chair for strength. The boy's dead father, Usnech, had also challenged Conor for the sake of it; he would have put him in his place but for the many Red Branch allegiances Usnech had formed over the years. And these sons of his were still milk-wet, in no way as dangerous as the proud tilt of Naisi's head endeavored to suggest. "We are grateful that you discharged your service," Conor said, rising to dismiss him.

"There is someone else to see you, my lord." Naisi's deep, still eyes always managed to radiate a knowing contempt, and that, matched with his scrupulous politeness, made Conor's hand itch to strike him. "We spoke as we came in. A man from Cullen's dun."

The steward hastily bobbed again. "It is true, my lord."

Irritably, Conor beckoned in the sodden messenger lurking at the door. Naisi retreated to the crowd around his brothers, watching. The messenger's cloak was soaked and he was also coated in mud from swift riding. "What?" Conor demanded. All the desire in his loins had vanished.

"One of the Connacht border-chiefs has raided Cullen's lands from the south," the man informed him. "A stud bull was taken, its handlers killed."

Conor's sight clouded over as all the warriors crowded the hearthfire. "We must get it back," Dubthach declared.

"Cullen's dun isn't far," Conor's elder son, Cormac, leaped in.

"We must catch up with them. They will be slowed by the bull."
All their lethargy had melted away, and they were like hounds
straining at a leash.

Conor glared. "*Must* we?" Cormac was a little bold for comfort. Conor did not like this slight challenge, this faint testing of
his authority. He wasn't gone yet.

Fergus's eldest son, Buinne, broke in, tossing a pigbone in the
fire. "Cullen has a special bond to Cúchulainn. Perhaps he should
go, and me with him." Buinne was growing as massive as his father—red-haired and permanently glowering, so that everything
he said sounded belligerent.

Conor's mind raced. It did make sense. When Cúchulainn was
a boy called Sétanta, he had been attacked by the huge guard-
hound of the cattle-lord Cullen. He killed the beast in self-
defense, but to recompense the chief he guarded the gates of
Cullen's dun himself for a year. That was how he earned his adult
name: Cúchulainn, the Hound of Cullen. Conor was sick of the
story, but Cullen *was* powerful and he needed to satisfy his
honor. There were always rumbles from the chiefs bordering
Connacht's lands, and that discontent was growing greater now
that Maeve had slipped his net. Any chance of keeping Connacht
at bay had gone with her.

Naisi's voice slid into Conor's heated thoughts. "Cúchulainn is
at Dun Dalgan, too far away. If someone doesn't go after the
raiders now, we'll lose them."

"Then I shall go!" someone shouted.

"No, it should be me," Buinne growled.

Conor ploughed through his squabbling warriors. "Silence!"

He was glaring around, summoning his answer, when Naisi
stepped forward. "Send us, my lord. We have just come from the
road, we've readied fresh horses and we know Cullen well."

Conor didn't even look at him. "No," he snapped. The last
thing he needed was the upstart son of a rebellious chief going to
Cullen's rescue and earning himself renown. His eyes raked over
the throng of warriors, searching for someone of the stature required. "Where is Conall?" he barked. "Leary?"

"They are at their own duns," someone said.

"We can go." Naisi's voice was a buzzing gnat, undercutting the eager shouts. "We know the westlands." One of his brothers put a restraining hand on his arm, while Conor looked fixedly over their heads.

"We'll go, Father!"

Conor almost slumped with relief when his youngest son, Fiacra, strode in. Close to his side, as always, was Illan, the younger son of Fergus mac Roy by a different wife than Buinne's mother. Fiacra had long, flaxen hair and Illan boasted a shade darker, so they looked like twin stalks of barley in the sun.

He relaxed. Cullen would be suitably impressed and indebted when he sent his own son to track the raiders. He stifled a pang of fear that warred with pride. Fiacra was young and brave— some said foolhardy—but at least he had no ambition to grab Conor's throne when his back was turned. He was uncompli- cated, loving the hunt and dice games with his friend Illan. His loyalty to his father was unassailable.

"What are you doing?" Ardan hissed, watching Naisi grope for his saddle in the darkened stable. The pools of light thrown by their lanterns were hazy with dust and hay, the air warm with horse-breath.

The taut lines of his brother's face gave little away as he side- stepped a pile of dung. "Leaving."

"The king has not released us." Ainnle cast worried glances at the half-open door, the sky outside darkened by a squall. Rain blasted in at an angle, wetting the straw, and he shut the door and leaned on it.

Naisi was trying to get the saddle on his stallion but it kept shifting, stamping one hoof. Ardan wasn't surprised, for his elder brother's shoulders were too tense and his hands moved fever- ishly. They all felt the frustration—gods, no one knew how deep Ardan's ran—but Naisi had always held his at bay. He'd always kept control.

"If we stay," Naisi muttered, "he'll have us guarding his sodding women at their looms all day."

Ainnle wiped rain from his face with a forced smile. "That will be warm, at least. I've had enough of rain and mud." Ainnle was always first to leap for scabbard, bow or saddle and last to the hearth, Ardan thought. But Naisi's discomfort had finally penetrated even his youngest brother's high-blooded eagerness for fighting and game.

Ardan itched to place a comforting hand on Naisi's arm and stretched out his fingers, but the wildness in his elder brother's eyes stopped him. "I know where you want to go, Naisi, but it was the king's arrow we saw. No one is supposed to venture into his royal hunting grounds. We were told not to go past the lake and we did, even if it was by accident."

"And why does he keep that herd to himself?" Naisi rounded on him, his mouth a drawn line. Ardan scanned his face. This was not about hunting, but about the way Conor had treated them in the hall. Even when Naisi was a boy, he and the king had scented something about the other; some instinctive dislike. Conor was always quick to judge Naisi's mistakes, slow to acknowledge his triumphs. And Ardan had felt every blow through his own body, and knew the way it festered. "He guards those stags so tightly because he's too poor a hunter to track any others," Naisi went on. "He should be proud of us, celebrate us—and instead he can't stand to see another succeed where he does not!" This thread of jealousy in the king was most unseemly and unsettled them all, but for some reason it enraged Naisi.

Wide-eyed, Ainnle was watching his eldest brother as if the earth had just shifted beneath his feet, for he was used to Naisi's cool head.

Ardan breathed out, lowering his voice to a whisper. "We are too young to defy him now, but Conor is growing old, brother. He may not rule much longer."

Naisi slapped the girth-strap about his stallion's belly, the leather slippery from the burnishing of his palms. The horse's ears twitched and he lifted a hoof and pawed the straw. "And every year we grow older, too. I did not exhaust myself learning the sword only for it to rust in its scabbard, or my bow to rot and snap. I did not train in the cold and rain so that he would bind my hands with his own weakness." Before Ardan could speak, Naisi swung toward Ainnle, making him jump. "I saw the tracks of bigger stags in that valley—a fourteen-point rack at least. We'll leave the horses with Finbar so we can get to the steeper parts on foot."

Ainnle's eagerness died when his eyes met Ardan's frown. He glanced uncertainly between his brothers. "Perhaps we shouldn't go there again. The lake grounds are forbidden…"

Naisi's gaze was on the lamp-flame, his black pupils reflecting points of fire. "No one can own the beasts that roam. To do so is an affront to the gods. It is him they would be angry at, not us." Those terrible eyes rose to Ardan. "I am going. I have to. He can't take the forest from me."

Helplessly, Ardan could only nod, comforting himself that no one would discover them in those uninhabited valleys. Turning to his own horse, he vowed to stay by Naisi's side until he had exhausted this rage and defied Conor in his own small way. That would assuage it, and then Ardan could get him home.

And no one would be the wiser.

CHAPTER 6

At the sacred end of the year, as the last leaves fell, Levarcham was summoned again to Emain Macha.

Deirdre kindled the Samhain need-fire all by herself, relighting Fintan and Aiveen's hearth and her own with a taper of rowan-wood. She set out the honey-cakes for the spirits of the dead and poured libations of mead for the *sídhe*, the spirits of the land who slipped more easily through the veils at the turning of the year.

The longest night arrived and she shivered in a gale, sheltering a wildwood flame to plead for the sun god Lugh to ride north once more.

After that she prowled the rampart of the steading, ignoring her streaming nose and cold-pinched ears, memorizing every angle of the overhanging black branches. She made up names for all the shades of gray that filled her world, from the swirling fogs and sheets of rain to the shadows thrown by the low, slanting sun over the frosts. She and Aiveen poured milk into the stream for the rite of Imbolc, begging the goddess Brid to bless the land with fruitfulness.

It was after this that the dreams began.

Huddled away from the endless storms, she would wake in the night with a flail of her arms, the curve between her breasts slick with sweat. Though she had no memory of the dream itself, her hand was always clenched between her thighs, all the urgency in her body now focused there with unbearable pressure.

And then, at the end of the first moon of leaf-bud, the gods sent a last fall of snow on a howling wind. The heavy clouds made day as dark as twilight, and Aiveen and Fintan coaxed Deirdre from her bed to roast hazelnuts by the fire. "The cold will pass soon, lass," Fintan said with a worried smile. His great hands, able to tie a delicate snare and nudge the fur from a stoat in one piece, were clumsy around her when she was sorrowed, his fumbling fingers dropping hazelnuts into the rushes. She crouched to pick them up and pile them in his palms, squeezing his hands and wiping from her face the knowledge that each waning moon only brought her closer to Conor. After forcing down a few crumbs of nut-cake she pleaded a headache, embracing Aiveen and Fintan so fiercely they at last smiled and let her return to her own hut.

She burrowed under the furs and slept fitfully until another dream came—and this time, she *saw*. It was a stark image of a hand gently cupping a white breast. The woman's skin was dove-soft, the man's faintly tanned. *Young and unlined.* The hand reverently hefted the pale globe, the thumb brushing its dark center. A scattering of gooseflesh rose in its wake and the nipple stood up, swollen…

Deirdre startled awake, clutching the bed. The shapes of the hand and the breast were still branded behind her eyes. Feverishly, she tossed back the sheets. Her skin was damp, her linen shift stuck to her and she pulled it from her belly and legs and paced the hearth. After a moment, she cocked her head, listening.

In her sleep the wind had died and there was the muffled sense outside of snow on the ground. Spreading her quivering fingers, she gazed down at them. *I can't order my dreams. I can't.* That tanned hand had nothing to do with Conor or being his wife, or submitting to him. She bit her lip, shamed. She had been druid-taught; she should be in control of this.

Coming to a decision, she twisted her damp hair into a knot. She would creep in and sleep by Aiveen's fire. Her old child's pallet was still there under the eaves, and no invading dreams could reach her there, she was sure.

Outside, the starlight glowed on a silver world. She skidded over the rimed cobbles by her door and crunched over grass blanketed with snow. Fintan's house was a snug, dark shape against the white, the layered door-hides bound to their frame with buckhide thongs. Deirdre was about to untie them when a groan from inside halted her. Was someone ill? Apprehensive now, she pressed her ear against the hide.

The second moan was guttural and another voice throatily answered it: Aiveen. Fast breaths came, and a whimper that knocked Deirdre back a step.

"*A stór,*" Fintan gasped. *Beloved.* "Always open to me, lass…"

Deirdre's legs buckled and she slid to her knees, sheltered from the snow by the eaves. Some of the hide was frayed and she glimpsed firelight from the corner of her eye. She turned her head a little, knowing as she did that it was wrong. But her face was drawn to the gap as if someone forced it there. Her foster-parents sounded pained even as they laughed. The mystery of it swept all her scruples away, because she *had* to know. She trembled on the fringes of knowing, could barely function from lack of sleep and the gnawing of her mind.

She pressed an eye against the hide. She could vaguely see two heads at one end of the bed, the shape of their bodies beneath the furs rising and falling, the groans in time with the movement. *This is wrong.* She went to turn away, but just then the breathing became faster and Aiveen's pale hand rose from the hides and clutched at her husband's shoulder, her whimpers turning to gasps. Deirdre's breath unconsciously merged with theirs, rasping in her throat while her heart galloped painfully.

She tried to think of deer, of Conor…but how could she when her parents were caught up in such oblivious pleasure? There was no fear there, no force, just…surrender, abandon. A hiss escaped from her lips as she saw that dream-hand again, stroking the curve of that white breast.

The groans rose and ebbed more swiftly, and now she could do nothing but sink with her back to the damp wall. The memory of her dream merged with the sounds, and she found she was clenching her thighs together, wiping beads of sweat from her lips. At the moment she could bear it no more, the noises erupted into twin yells of pleasure. The cries seemed to be endless—Fintan's a bellow and Aiveen's faint and high—until at last they faded.

Deirdre slumped, gazing out blindly into the dim whiteness of the falling snow. This was nothing like the stags, or what she had pictured with the king. This was uncontrollable. As their cries peaked, her own body had also strained toward something—an indefinable sense of being about to burst, to shatter into fragments. And after…she didn't know. They had sounded their release, but she had gained nothing, and now she was left huddled here, swollen, shivering and confused.

She dragged herself back out into the snow with no sense of where she was, staggering through the pale cloud of flakes against the dark sky. She would have kept going, dissolving into white, but came up against the wall of her own hut instead, and at last groped for the door.

The next day Deirdre sat hunched in her cloak on the rampart, watching snowflakes land on her shoulder through bleary eyes. She huddled here, hoping the cold would numb the misery, for she had woken that morning knowing those whimpers of pleasure were not for her.

She had seen Fintan's eyes lingering on Aiveen's rump whenever she bent over, glimpsed the warm gaze that brought such a blush to Aiveen's plump face. She had heard love in their voices when they spoke to each other—an intimacy she could not breach. With Conor, there would be none of that. She would be no more than a hind, waiting stoically for the stag to mount her. She clenched her eyes shut, chin tucked into her knees.

A croak broke into her thoughts.

She opened one eye. Along the palisade a raven was perched, regarding her with head cocked. Its hooked beak gleamed like polished jet and as it shook its head the loose feathers under its throat rippled. Behind it, two more preened themselves. The nearest raven cawed again and she flicked a finger at it. "Let me be," she muttered, her nose running from the cold.

The bird squawked and opened its wings, hopping out of her way. Once safe, it strutted back and forth along the walkway, its talons clacking on the wood.

Deirdre eyed it balefully, but the raven merely cocked its head again, dark eye glinting. She detected both admonition and pity in its gaze. It hopped to an overhanging oak branch, and as she watched, it tipped itself over and hung upside down from its claws. Its brothers stared, impressed.

She couldn't help a snort of amusement. The raven jumped effortlessly back to the palisade and Deirdre sat up, cursing herself. Her pain had addled her. She knew what such birds augured. Most were just carrion-seekers, but some were messengers of the gods, wild spirits of the *sídhe* who had taken on raven form. Omens of battle. Signs of destiny. Companions of the war-goddess Morrigan. This one seemed persistent. "Forgive me," she whispered, reaching out a finger.

The bird huffed, ruffling its glossy feathers and turning its shoulder, pecking at something in the wood as if it didn't care for her, after all. She sat still, wondering if she was mistaken, until it decided all was forgiven and with another flap hopped to one of the posts. It glanced at her and, stretching out its throat, it cawed. The cry rebounded off the low clouds, pinning her there while its brothers raised their heads and screeched. In the tension of their bodies she read that they would fly again soon—and that the raven was including her in its summons.

A more intense pain split her chest, as if breaking her ribs apart so her heart could at last fly free. *The raven was calling her.* She knew she should not attempt the bird-flight alone. She couldn't do it; she had not prepared. It was sacred, Levarcham had said. But when the raven cawed once more, it was as if it had hooked its talon deep in her bowels and was yanking her out of herself, turning her inside out.

Deirdre gasped and closed her eyes, and the sharp pull of the claw became desperation, a yearning that consumed her utterly. She breathed out and, as the birds spread wing, they sent a gust of wind that blew back the hair at her brow. The cries soared up into the air, and she flung everything she had after them in one hopeless howl of despair.

A light…shrinking.

A spinning vortex.

Infinite speed and rush…a shock of collision.

Darkness.

CHAPTER 7

There was a slight density beside her, an awareness in the surrounding ether. It was the raven's spirit, tiny fast heart beating. She clung on with her will, her thoughts shattered into babbling chaos. *It could not be…could not be…*

Other ideas began to dart around her, fluttering impulses that were not hers. *Deer…many deer…wolves…* She caught an image that was memory, and in it she was floating above a landscape of snow-clad ridges that circled a winding stream that emptied into a shining lake. *Wolves. Dead deer. Go there.*

Reeling, Deirdre thought, *It is a dream. I am dying. I froze in the snow.*

Something jerked in a rhythmic movement—wing-beats—and, startled, she thought about opening her eyes and then somehow she did. Only she was gazing out through *its* eyes.

A heartbeat later, she was sucked into a sensory storm.

The forest below rushed by in a dizzying swirl of shadows and snow-glare speckled by black trees. The raven's nostrils tasted cold as a message, not a pain, the shifts in temperature making it tilt its feathers to graze above the icier ridges, then swoop low along warmer updrafts. Now she saw the multitudes of tiny movements on the ground—animals digging into snow, running up trees, chasing prey. In the raven's eyes, they glowed with myriad hues of red, violet and orange, so the sweep of forest sparkled with life. *Food.* The awareness of the darting creatures was a pulse joining the bird's eyes and belly, for it scented the heat of life as well as the carrion rot of death.

All at once the raven soared, and Deirdre was lost in the

sensation of flight. The air was a living thing, dense in places, thin in others, and the bird climbed those invisible slopes with its wings. The wind-rush pierced Deirdre with an ecstatic pain. She felt the tug of the cord to her body, the light threading away behind her, and she wanted to let go of it. *She needed to let go…*

A cry snapped her back, and the other two ravens swooped alongside her. One swerved close—the one who had called her—forcing Deirdre to glance at it. *Its eye was a star.* The raven-sense had gone and something infinitely knowing looked back. She stared at the glow, mesmerized, and the star spun, dragging her from the tiny shell of her own awareness into a glimpse of raven-mind that lasted one rapturous breath.

An intense rush of life…visceral…a simple knowing that Thisworld was an island surrounded by the oceans of the Otherworld. Time was a great and ancient wheel that spun beneath Thisworld, weaving the rhythms of life and safety. Dark and light. *Sun soars and sinks…moon grows and fades…rain sweeps in and away… wind roars and dies…night, day, night again.* Day.

She was still reeling from that when her raven plummeted, swooping her back into the here and now.

A taint had crossed its tongue, a metallic scent filtered from the wind. *Blood.* Eagerness surged through the Deirdre-raven and she was flung around as it spiraled down. She had the presence of mind to absorb where they were—a white path leading through the woods to a shining lake—before the land blurred, rushing up to her. She glimpsed a vivid splash of scarlet and pale figures moving around it, and then her raven spread its wings and alighted on a dead oak furred with frosted lichen.

The other birds were already lined up beside her. A stag was stretched out dead in the clearing, a stream of blood flowing from its throat over the thin snow. A ring of footsteps had broken through to the mud beneath, speckling the white crust. Arrows and spears stuck out of the stag's body. Deirdre's eagerness to see eclipsed the raven's will, and it turned its head from the bloody stag. The figures were men clad in thick trousers and overtunics made of sheepskin. They didn't have beards like Fintan, though their chests were also wide, their hides obscuring a suggestion of bulky shoulders and corded necks. Their waists were narrow and straight, and their shoulder-length black hair was knotted into tufted braids stuck with feathers. The raven jumped with her shock, flapping its wings. Their skin was like an unmarked fall of snow, unlined and smooth. *It was like hers.*

"Phew!" one puffed. "I thought it would never weaken."

Another one elbowed him. "Getting old, Ardan? You could always stay with Conor next time."

"We shouldn't speak his name, even out here." The third youth's voice cut through the laughter. He was leaning over the carcass with his knife, his face hidden.

The second youth shrugged. "Who will hear us, big brother? And anyway, *you're* the one who dragged us here. It's a bit late to be careful."

The elder brother dug his knife into the hide. "I'm angry, Ainnle, but not witless. Unlike some of us…"

The one called Ainnle pulled a face, and Deirdre's raven nearly fell off the trunk, its claws scrabbling to right itself. Ardan… Ainnle. These were the sons of Usnech—and that one must be Naisi. Her raven squawked at her leaping thoughts and she desperately held to the cord…remembered to breathe into it as it snaked back to her body. It was a disconcerting feeling, like she was tiny and hovering in space, and yet there was this shell about her of feathers and bone infused with a light, an awareness that was flavored with a wildness and savagery.

The cry had caught the brothers' attention and they looked up. One of the other birds immediately hopped to the stag behind them and began pecking at its eye, but the Deirdre-raven didn't move as she gazed into the upturned face of the eldest brother. The world-wheel seemed to slip askew, and time paused and locked, for all Deirdre's thoughts had been arrested by the youth's coloring, which was an uncanny echo of the scene around him. His curling hair was as glossy black as raven feathers, and beneath a pelt of stubble his skin was pale like the snow. The flush of lips and cheeks reflected the hue of the spilled blood.

Raven, snow, blood. *Black, white, red.* Druid colors.

The world-wheel creaked and groaned before the spokes clicked into place and it lurched back into motion. By now, the raven's tiny heart was fluttering erratically and Deirdre had to grip the cord again, clinging on. *All is well,* she told herself. *All is well,* she said to the bird.

She dared another glance at the eldest brother. His features were determined, his nose much longer than her short, up-turned one—a keen ridge thrusting from his face, with flared nostrils. His lower lip was fleshy and full, his long upper lip tilted with a sardonic expression. His cheekbones had dips underneath that formed two lines down his face, and the weak sunshine could not leach away the startling blue of his eyes.

"Oi!" Ainnle ran at the pecking raven, shooing it. "Get away!" In contrast to the brilliant sky-hue of Naisi's eyes, Ainnle's were greenish and Ardan's more gray, though they were all similarly black-haired and clear-skinned.

The youths turned back to their kill. "Don't worry," Naisi said. "It's only at the eyes, and we haven't split the hide open yet." They paused to strip their fleeces down to shirts of green-and-brown-check wool, and bent to butchering the stag. She could see now that their forearms bulged with lean muscles as they wielded their knives. Three leather packs bound to hazel carrying frames were strewn on the ground. Something long stuck up from each one, wrapped in hides. Her senses flickered with excitement. Swords. *Warriors.*

At first the brothers were silent in concentration, except for Ardan, who hummed under his breath. They sliced membranes and peeled back the hide, opening the stomach and pulling out the guts. Their breath was a pale cloud over the dead beast. "I don't know about going after the king stag, Naisi," Ardan said, breaking his singing. "We might have pushed our luck now. We should go home."

Naisi's face set and he dug at the flesh with his blade. "It had nearly a score of points on its antlers."

"Nevertheless, we saw smoke over the lake."

"Other people live here, then, so it can't be entirely forbidden, despite what Conor says." Naisi spoke quietly, though his steely tone cut the chill air. "I want that stag." He ripped the knife through sinew.

Ainnle cleaned his bloody hands with snow, exchanging glances with Ardan. "You just want Anya and all her friends to coo at you." Ainnle put on a high, squeaking voice. "Oh, Naisi, you must have been *so* brave to bring down *such* a big stag!"

Naisi's face didn't change, he merely leaned over and in the same movement flung a handful of snow at his brother's face. It smacked Ainnle in his open mouth, and as he spluttered, Ardan laughed. Ainnle gathered snow with two hands and flung it at Naisi. Naisi ducked away, but the disintegrating ball caught Ardan's arm and, in a moment, the three of them were dashing about as snowballs flew in all directions.

Deirdre's raven took advantage of the chaos to flutter down, perching on the curved belly of the stag. She was too entranced by the snowball fight to notice.

Powdery flakes drifted over her as fierce cries echoed around the silent forest. She had never seen siblings play, but she recognized the joy in their sparkling eyes and yearned to run after them on two legs, screeching and laughing. She wanted to drink the crisp air and feel splatters of ice on her cheeks.

While the youths were distracted, the other ravens had turned from the entrails to strips of flesh, and spotting them the brothers raced back, breathlessly trying to wave them away. Naisi's face was on a level with Deirdre's raven, who had not retreated, and as he resumed skinning she studied him intently. The cynical lift of his mouth and tension around his eyes had gone now, replaced by a savage glee. Flakes of snow melted in his dark hair. "I'd lay bets that Conor rarely comes here—it's too far from his fires, and the trails are hard-going—and the carcass will be just bones soon. Anyway, when I present him with the rack for his hall, he'll be spluttering too much to ask where it's from!"

Deirdre wished she could tell this opinionated young man that the king did indeed come all this way from Emain Macha. By now, however, her raven had been waiting too long. It spread its wings and hopped to the bloody entrails on the snow. Before she could gather her wits it pecked at a scrap of meat. Her senses were overwhelmed by a sour, copper taste as the slippery flesh slid down the raven's gullet.

The part of her that had been focusing on breathing silver into the cord shuddered—and the connection to the bird snapped. She was wrenched out of its awareness, the pinprick arcing back along a trail of confusing dark and light and whirling shapes. There was a sense of falling and a disconcerting thump and she came back to herself sprawled in the snow, her hands and face icy.

Deirdre's eyes sprang open to snowflakes drifting down from the clouds. They melted on her lips with a metallic tang, reminding her of blood in a raven's beak.

That night she gulped her mutton stew, answering Fintan and Aiveen's questions as well as she could. Fintan had seen her lying on the wall in the cold. "Are you sick, lass?" he asked.

She smiled sadly at him. "No."

"Is it...you know?" He arched his brows toward Aiveen, who was parching barley grains in a pan over the fire.

Aiveen shot him a look. "Fintan! Don't you dare mention 'women's troubles' now."

"No." Deirdre shook her head. "I am just tired, that's all. The long dark is hard." They all looked intently into the fire, leaving unspoken what might come with the greening of the trees.

In the flames, she saw again the enticing starlight in the raven's eye. A tremor of excitement ran through her. Did she call the ravens somehow? Were the *sídhe* speaking to her? That wild hope hurt too much, and she shifted her thoughts instead to those three young faces flushed with fierce delight. She had once felt jealous observing a litter of fox cubs: their rough and tumble, the way they leaned together when threatened. She had seen that bond today and never wanted anything so much in all her life—

more than the slaking of her body's strange desires, more than Levarcham's approval. *Belonging*.

At length she excused herself, and on the way back to her hut was halted by an enormous bronze moon soaring over the black hills. The sky was clear, the air crisp with a hint of ice. She stretched her head back as if drinking the cold light, and as always her eager imagination burst into life.

The moon rose in the east, where the lake was. The path that Fintan had made down the valley would lead through the bare woods in a shining ribbon, like a spirit-cord she could follow. She would be able to see everything, as if the moon-goddess held a lantern up just for her, the flame spun of silver.

Her thoughts snagged. *No, she couldn't*. There was a pause where the world held its breath.

She could. She could go a little way and be back by dawn, and no one would know. She knew the woods most of the way down the valley, and in her raven-flight she'd seen the path fork over the hills. All she had to do was take that eastern trail to the lake. It was easy in snow.

She stood at her door, her heart straining. She had flown that path in another form. Now she needed to breathe the lake air with her own body, run toward that abandoned laughter on her own strong legs, her lungs burning.

CHAPTER 8

She dressed in wool shift and tunic, and sheepskin trews and cloak with the fleece turned inside. Her boots were of oiled hide, and she looped a rope about her wrist and stuck her meat-knife in her belt.

At the door, she surveyed her house. A glimmer of white caught her eye and she gazed at the swan costume hanging from the bed-screen, its feathers fluttering in the updrafts from the fire. Something impelled her fingers to close on the wooden mask and then she was settling it over her cheeks and looking out through the eyeholes.

A savage impulse descended over her, to take flight with nothing chaining her, nothing touching her but air.

She clambered down the rampart on the rope and crept across the snow-filled ditch, and then she was racing along the trail, intoxicated. She had walked in the valley in sunseason, when the trees were pillars of pale bark against dark earth and leaves. Now the world was turned upside down and inside out: the trunks black with damp and the ground white. Vapors of mist rose from the hollows and surrounded her, until she wondered if she was attached to the ground at all.

She reached the edge of the clearing where she first saw the sons of Usnech. The trees shone with frost, the lake glinting beyond. She carefully approached the stag. Something had stripped away the remaining flesh and pulled off its legs, leaving its ribs a gaping arch. She slowly withdrew her knife and held it before her. Her nostrils were stifled by the mask's beak, but then ... there it was, a hint of woodsmoke. A trail of tumbled snow, dark with dirt and blood, showed the way the brothers had gone and, warily, she followed it.

She had just stopped again to sniff the air when an unearthly howl rose before her, squeezing her heart up into her throat. It swelled into fullness before fading away. Deirdre's legs were paralyzed; she knew wolf-song when she heard it. The stripped ribs of the stag loomed behind her eyes. An answering howl sounded from farther west: a fainter lamentation, richer and more haunting, with notes weaving around the main arc of song. .

The first call burst out again and Deirdre backed into a tree, panic charging her body, before the hush was shattered by a roar of laughter. The second pack answered and she heard the difference then—the first sweet and high, the second many-layered and deep. "Arrooo!" someone called, interspersed with snuffles of amusement. "Come and get us, wolves. We'll make warm cloaks of you all!"

"Ainnle, shut up. If you sound too convincing, they'll come back."

"No, they won't, Ardan was far too croaky." There was a scuffle, punctuated by growls and more laughter.

Irritated, Deirdre pushed the mask back and wiped trickles of sweat from her face, gazing into the darkness as she waited for her heart to slow. After a moment, she narrowed her eyes. The ghostly glow on the frosted ground seemed to be growing brighter, then fading. Brighter again. Softer. Was it in time with her pulse? Everything looked more vivid, the trees appearing to glimmer now, the lake to glow with its own rising luminescence.

Pulling the mask down, she was overcome by a yearning to savor the sensation of the earth falling away beneath her again, her body becoming lighter. As she surrendered into that memory, into the spirit of the mask, all awareness of her heavy bones and dense flesh dissolved. Now she was gliding through the hushed forest, though she must be lost in a desperate dream, for surely the shadow below her was winged.

As Deirdre flew along, the argent tide of light that poured from the trees scattered into pearly flecks on the fringes of sight, and her passing stirred them into whorls until she had the dazed impression of flying through a sparkling cloud. A dream, yes. *A dream.*

Gradually, softly, Deirdre at last woke from that strange trance. She had arms and legs, and two feet planted on the snow. Her heart filled her again, pounding forcefully.

A campfire glowed on the other side of a tangled thorn-brake. She dragged in shuddering breaths and clutched the trunk of an overhanging oak, vaguely recognizing a familiar sound. She struggled to focus until the noise resolved itself into something she understood. Voices.

The brothers were sitting on their packs around the fire. Sticks propped up between stones skewered meat that dripped juice into the flames. Ardan poked at the deer-flesh with a dagger. "I'm beginning to think this king stag of yours a ghost, Naisi. We've looked all day."

"He's close," Naisi snapped. "I saw his antlers on the ridge." He checked himself, a rueful smile softening his expression. "A few more days, Ardan, that's all. We can get him, I know we can."

"Even if we run ourselves into the ground?"

Naisi looked away into the woods, his jaw outlined by the flames. "So much the better. Conor hasn't sent us to battle for some time; he prefers his treaties and tricks. We've won a name already, but we should take any chance we can to make it greater."

Ainnle pulled meat off a stick, blowing on it and testing it with his tongue. "Illan and Fiacra are solid fighters," he proffered, smiling to cheer up his eldest brother. "It's no shame they went to help Cullen."

"They are brave," Naisi agreed. He leaned a hand on his sword, which was propped against a log in its scabbard. In the firelight the hilt glinted with some kind of gilded decoration, and Deirdre's heart quickened. A sword from the bard tales. Naisi ran his fingers over the raised design as if it were alive. "But we are brave, too. And for that, the king keeps us leashed like dogs, so we do not shine too brightly."

Deirdre was instantly alert. Conor? The bitterness in Naisi's voice went right through her, stirring the coals of her own long-nursed pain. Across that gap between snowy tree and flickering campfire, she felt a leap of kinship. Surely such men were not like *her*, trapped by the king of the Ulaid?

"At least," Naisi added with a shrug and a tight smile, "we're all tied up together. Woof." He darted a glance at Ardan, who rolled his eyes as if unimpressed, before passing a skewer to Naisi and another to Ainnle. They all fell to eating, their white teeth tearing at the meat.

They had been chewing for some time when Ardan's soft voice lifted into the icy air in a wordless humming, wandering up and down as he unfastened a plug from a leather flask and handed it to Ainnle. While the youngest brother drank, Ardan opened his throat into song, his eyes on the flames. His voice was sweet and powerful, soaring as Deirdre had flown, and her body felt lifted again by it. Levarcham encouraged her to sing but despite being a bard's daughter, her voice could only produce a throaty croak.

Ardan let go into a soft tune about a ghost stag that appeared to men as a white beast in the moonlight, enticing fair hunters into the Otherworld. Recognizing the gentle chiding, Naisi smiled ruefully and rested his chin on his hand. Ainnle joined in, holding the flask to Naisi, and both younger brothers sang to the eldest, their pure voices flowing out with no trace of shyness.

At last Naisi gave in, and together their voices wove about one another in mingled harmonies that entranced Deirdre, their melodies like sunlight, like splashing water. When Naisi sang, that troubled shadow over his face cleared and it shone.

Ardan then slipped into a faster tune about a man wooing a maid, the descriptions of her teeth, eyes and hair outrageously exaggerated. He began listing attributes Deirdre had never heard in song before: a woman with breasts and buttocks like hillocks and—her mouth dropped open—a cleft as wide as the River Bann, fringed with ferns of gold. The brothers began laughing, until at last Ardan couldn't continue, his song dissolving into snorts. Her cheeks flaming, Deirdre held still as their gales of amusement faded into hiccups.

Ainnle fell to tearing more meat off his skewer with his teeth. "For some reason that song brings our dear, departed Queen Maeve to mind."

Ardan snorted again. "That she-wolf? She'd bite your hands off before you could get near her hills!"

Ainnle shook his head, chewing. "I enjoyed watching Maeve fling herself about Emain and so did you, Ardan, if I remember rightly." He swallowed and grinned. "I heard she needed humping ten times a night, and her screeches nearly took the roof off!"

"No wonder Conor looked so tired," Ardan returned. "Bet he didn't expect *that* when he took her to wife."

Deirdre's ears pricked up and she forgot about the song. *Wife?*

"Still." Naisi's voice was so quiet the others fell silent. "She's the only one who has ever defied him."

Ardan sent him a pointed look. "It was easy for her to run away back to her kin in Connacht. She's a princess—she had a king to protect her from Conor's wrath."

"Her father is gravely ill, by all reports."

Deirdre barely heard the rest, for each word was falling into her mind like precious offerings scattered in a pool. *Queen. Wife. Defied. Run away.* Her fingers sunk into the frosted moss that covered the oak trunk. A wife, not just a betrothed. *She* was just a betrothed. A tingling rushed up her spine.

"On second thoughts…" Ainnle hastened to change the subject. "It sounds much more like that ale-maid at Fergus's dun, Eithne." He handed Naisi another stick of browned meat, waggling his brows. "After all, you have to climb *mountains* to reach her river, even if it is worth drowning in."

With a swift glance at Naisi, Ardan also grinned. "Except her ferns are black, not gold."

"And the fact you both know that scares me," Naisi said dryly, allowing himself to be coaxed away from the dark thoughts written on his face.

"Just because Anya practically rips the throat from any girl you dive into, big brother."

"Better than having to be dragged by the neck from so many rapids."

Deirdre blinked, forcing the whirl of thoughts about Maeve into her belly, where they sat churning. These boys were talking about women as if they were nothing but bits of bodies to entertain them—prodding them as they did the meat! It made her skin crawl when she remembered Conor's eyes upon her. She rocked on her heels. The thrill of the wild bird-flight was still clinging to her like mist, daring her on. Perhaps she could gift these boys a song of her own.

Levarcham had taught her a tale about the goddess Clíodna, whose three magical birds trilled songs to heal warriors. At one point, the storyteller whistled a little bird-tune, repeating it until all the listeners joined in. Now she crept between the over-hanging branches of the oak and, pushing back her hood, waited until the youths fell silent. She cupped fingers around her beak and let loose a whistle.

The men all sprang up, instantly on guard. "What was that?" Ardan demanded.

Naisi peered around, frowning. "An owl?"

"It didn't sound like an owl."

"Perhaps it's just the wind."

While they bickered, Deirdre crawled to another spot, the snow muffling her progress. There she crouched and warbled again, breaking into the tune from Clíodna's story. "What now?" Ainnle exclaimed. Naisi stood with head alert, scanning the woods.

Ardan alone seemed unafraid, striding to the boundaries of the firelight and gazing out. Deirdre held her breath. The moon-glow caught his face and it was transfigured, his eyes lit by won-der. "I know that tune," he muttered. He paced to the other end of the clearing and Deirdre ducked under the bushes before singing the melody again: five notes up, four down and the fifth repeated three times.

Ainnle looked around warily. "I recognize it, too," he whis-pered.

"It's that song from Senan's tale." Ardan stared into the dark-ness, his body leaning toward the woods. "The goddess Clíodna."

"Goddess?" Ainnle echoed. "I wonder if she heard us?"

That would serve them right, Deirdre thought, abuzz with her own daring. It would make them think about their treatment of females, for all women were sacred to the goddesses. Ainnle surprised her then by lunging for his pack, straightening with his sword braced. *Great Brid*... At the same time Naisi ducked and then spun back with an armful of dead leaves and branches. Before she could react, he threw them on the fire, making the flames roar up.

She staggered back, and one of the brothers cried out, "What's that white thing?"

"It had a beak…gods…"

"Grab your swords and stop babbling."

Deirdre blundered sideways, but when she faced the dark she was almost blinded by the afterglare of the fire. She glimpsed a strip of open path and flung herself at it, driving straight into a thicket of hazels instead. The thongs of her mask caught on the branches, and she wriggled back in panic, stepping on a dry twig.

It broke with a resounding *crack*.

"That's no goddess!" Naisi shouted. "I *knew* it."

Biting back a yelp, Deirdre could think of nothing but fleeing. She pushed blindly into the dark, stumbling and then pulling herself up while one of the brothers crashed through the woods behind her. She bolted along the moonlit path, her pursuer's feet thudding far more swiftly. Though she tried to run faster, she couldn't get enough breath. The mask was stifling her, her lungs burning. Finally he caught at her cloak, spinning her into a drift of snow. "Stop right there!" Naisi cried.

Ignoring him, she dragged herself up and tumbled over a bush, releasing a grunt that was unmistakably human. He exclaimed, leaping over the bush and yanking at her sleeve, rolling her over. In her desperation, all the simmering fire of months—of years—went rushing along her leg in a wild kick toward his groin. Her heel hit his thigh instead and he growled in pain. When she swung again he cursed and threw himself over her, pinning her legs. With a gasp of rage she punched and bucked, and he was half thrown off as he struggled to grab at her flailing arms. Finally, he simply sat on top of her, squashing her arms with his shins. Wiping snow from his mouth, he gazed down. "So," he panted, "it seems we've caught a wildcat rather than a goddess!"

"You don't know what I am," she wheezed furiously behind the mask, crushed by his weight.

At her voice he tensed, drawing himself off her, and Deirdre crawled to her feet and backed up, winded.

"Gods' balls," Naisi swore softly, and before she could react he deftly flicked her braid out. It tumbled down her back to her buttocks. "You're just a girl!"

Her enraged retort died on her tongue, for when his wrist brushed her neck she was shaken by its unfamiliar softness. The sensation was so unexpected it remained on her skin as if his hand still rested there. The scents of dried sweat and tanned leather wafted from his shirt, and she smelled birch glue on his hands along with the pungent taint of dried blood. Hunter smells. His sheer otherness took her breath and anger with it.

"Well," he demanded, "why did you try to scare us with that trick?"

Dark brows shielded his eyes, the shadows cutting his face into sharp angles and planes. The dip above his full lips drew her. Absurdly she wanted to trace it, to see what was different to her own mouth when she touched it. A man. A young man.

The silence drew out, and now Naisi became gruff rather than angry. "What's the matter? Here, come to the fire where we can see you."

Taking hold of her cloak, he led an unresisting Deirdre back to his camp.

CHAPTER 9

When they appeared from the shadows, Ainnle lowered his sword. "Look," Naisi said with grim humor, "here's your bird goddess." He gave her a little shove and she stumbled in front of the flames. Ardan and Ainnle both regarded her open-mouthed.

"Oh." Ainnle frowned, embarrassed. "I see."

Ardan, however, laughed. The sound was shocking, so warm and real that Deirdre found herself smiling back. In the aftermath of that wildness, she felt oddly giddy.

"She won't talk." Naisi rotated his shoulder and flexed his arm, his tunic spotted with melting snow and mud. "I think she might be simple."

"I doubt that," Ardan said, watching her eyes.

Naisi's insult gave Deirdre her voice back. "Simple? I'm just getting my breath after you chased me and hit me and nearly squeezed my lungs flat."

"Me? You're the one who tricked us, sneaking about like a thief, eavesdropping when you shouldn't." She blinked, a cold memory rushing back of creeping to Fintan and Aiveen's hut. Twice now her judgment had been overruled by her feelings. Naisi rubbed his jaw. "And you thumped me back pretty well, I can tell you. You've got a good fist for so slight a girl." His gaze raked her up and down. "Although most sane girls wouldn't dress like a boy and go running about at night taunting grown warriors and mocking the gods!"

Her heart sank. "I heard you singing to the wolves." She turned to Ardan, the one with the kinder face. "I didn't mean to spy, I just enjoyed your singing." Ardan looked surprised at her frankness.

Ainnle scowled. "And the mask?"

She touched the wooden beak. "It was made for a dance. I meant you no harm."

"You were trying to make fools of us," Naisi muttered, folding his arms.

"And you were talking rudely of women," she returned hotly, "and I thought…" Her words trailed away.

"You thought you'd teach us a lesson." There might have been a glint in Naisi's eyes then.

Ardan interrupted with a crow of amusement. "She's got us there, brothers. If Mother had heard that, she'd give us a tongue-lashing we wouldn't forget."

Naisi tilted his head, looking less angry. "Where have you

come from, then? And why won't you take that off?" He indicated the mask.

Her hand still held its carved wooden edge. She could not help but think of Conor's mouth growing slack as he looked in her face. "My steading is over there," she said, waving vaguely behind her and ignoring his other question.

The brothers looked at one another, no longer relaxed. "But we only saw smoke on the other side of the lake," Ardan ventured.

She glanced from one to the other. "Yes."

Naisi frowned. "You've come all the way from there on your own at night, with wolves around?"

She didn't know how she'd flown so far—it still felt trancelike and hazy—but she was unable to resist a slight, unconcerned shrug. "I knew the wolves weren't *that* close."

Ainnle's curiosity outweighed his hurt pride. "Gods! We didn't think anyone lived here. Everyone else is forbidden—"

"Ainnle," Naisi growled, cutting him off.

Forbidden. For the first time, the gravity of what she had done hit Deirdre. If these men were not meant to be here, it was also forbidden for her to seek them out. *I was just going to watch them from afar.* The power of the night had made this all seem so thrilling and unreal, but these were flesh-and-blood men, not the products of her fevered imagination. Since that's all she'd had for company for years, it was hard to adjust.

Ardan glanced at his brothers. "That walk alone is worth a rest before our fire. We have forgotten ourselves." He offered Deirdre his pack to sit on and thumped Naisi's sore shoulder. "You go on about Conor's lack of generosity, but it's us who have no manners."

Naisi shrugged, abashed.

Warily, Deirdre sat by the fire, beginning to shiver from the snow that had gone down her neck in the fight with Naisi. Ainnle and Naisi returned to their seats, and Ardan squatted nearby.

Now she had the time to study them, their faces bore such a

marked likeness beyond their dark hair and light eyes it was un-canny. There were differences she did not notice when she was the raven, though. Ardan was heavier-set around the head and shoulders, his features broad and blunt compared to Naisi's. His gray eyes were frank, too, and less guarded. Ainnle was still lean and boyish, his chin jutting proudly, his glance challenging.

"Well." Naisi broke the silence. "We'd offer you mead and meat, but you can't eat unless you take that off." He flicked a finger at the mask. "You seem very attached to it. Are you deformed or something?" He said it with a faint smile.

"What, deformed as I am simple?"

The others snorted with amusement, and he had the grace to look uncomfortable. "You might at least tell us who you are, then," he added. "You seem to know a lot about us."

"Only because you talk about yourselves so much," Deirdre returned, emboldened by their own teasing.

Naisi's eyes grew sharp. "Just how long have you been follow-ing us?"

Appalled, she backtracked. "I mean, listening to you tonight. And don't worry; I didn't hear much beyond you complaining about—"

"You heard something about the king." Naisi's face changed completely.

Deirdre gulped and glanced into the fire to avoid his eyes, re-alizing she had set herself careering down a slope that might prove too steep after all.

A knot of wood exploded and a cascade of sparks spiraled up, soaring around the flakes of ash with a will no real fire possessed. She watched them, confounded, until their gleeful whirl spun so madly it drew the blood up her body, and she was engulfed by a hot flood of daring and boldness. A stream of words were pulled out of her belly by that savage rush of sparks. "It doesn't matter what I know," she heard herself saying, "for I am also held pris-oner by the king of the Ulaid. He forbids me to go as far as the lake or leave my steading at night and I've done both, so I'm in as much trouble as you." With that unraveling came a surge of intense relief, as of immense pressure being released.

There was a baffled pause. "Why would Conor care what you do?" Ardan said.

Any moment now they would be sure to reason this out, for Levarcham said her betrothal was known at Emain Macha. But she would do anything to keep them talking, to hold to this contact with the outside world. "There is a forbidden place near here," she improvised, the lie choking her. "A river where the king finds his gold, and a cave where he stores it. He tells people to stay away so no one knows of it. My father is the guardian of the valley, and our family has to stay here and not talk to anyone." Three sets of eyebrows rose. "So you … won't tell anyone?"

Naisi grimaced. "We don't care for Conor's *gold*. Courage, honor, sword-skill—these are all that matter in the world. That and the Red Branch."

His eyes showed far more than his words, though—a wild flare of pain that tore the last of Deirdre's own hurt from her. "How can they be the only things? At least you can roam about and swing a sword, shoot a bow and sleep under the stars. He stops me doing *anything*." Her voice cracked and she jumped up. "I must go," she mumbled. "I have stayed too long as it is."

"What's wrong?" Ardan said, but she shook her head and turned so she did not have to see their dawning understanding. She was plunging through the woods when Ardan called from behind, "We will stay here one more night."

She threw a glance over her shoulder at his shape outlined against the flames. She wanted to say, *I'll come back*, but clamped down on the words.

I can't, she mouthed as she fled back along the paths to take her home. *I won't.*

The rope burned her palms when she hauled herself back up from the ditch, and she rolled it into a knot and clasped it to her chest. The unbridled flow of life she'd glimpsed in the sparks urged her to turn her back on rules, shackles and sense. She threw herself under her door-hide and collapsed on all fours by the coals, shivering. "I can't go back," she said forcefully aloud.

I have to.

She undertook her tasks feverishly that day, her gaze so glassy that Aiveen stopped and placed a hand against her cheek. "I think you *are* sick," she declared, her soft, hazel eyes searching Deirdre's own.

Hauled back from her thoughts, Deirdre watched her foster-mother rummage among the dried herbs on the shelves, muttering about making her a draught of mint tea. Deirdre understood then that Aiveen needed to do something, however small, since she could not hold back the greater change coming.

As Aiveen hovered there, Deirdre walked toward her, her feet barely touching the rug. Hardly breathing—hardly here at all any more, her spirit already flying—she circled her arms around Aiveen's plump waist and rested her head on her shoulder as she once had as a child in her lap. And all the while her thoughts were a tumbling stream, words glittering like leaping water catching the sun. *Maeve was a queen, and she ran away from him. She took her own fate in her hands, and she left.*

Aiveen's brown hair always smelled of warm bread. "Thank you," Deirdre said past the lump in her throat, constraining herself from looking down the path that would not fade from her mind. The silver trail stretched before her, luminescent and tantalizing. "Thank you." She meant gratitude for all the years, not just today.

And when Aiveen patted her hand and wiped her own cheeks, she thought perhaps her foster-mother understood that, too.

The brothers were singing when Deirdre came to them that night. They appeared to have won their king stag, for an enormous deer skull was propped in the fire, its antlers scattering eerie shadows over the snow.

Its base was set in a hide bag of water over the flames to boil off the flesh, and she wrinkled her nose at the smell of singed hair, though the mask shielded the worst of it. Some perverse impulse had called her to wear it again, perhaps because, behind it, she felt distanced from her actions. It made this all seem unreal, nothing more terrifying than a dance or play. She was not the king's betrothed—she was a swan gliding over a dark forest. Her rational mind said this night of freedom existed out of time, and in the morning they would be gone and real life must dawn again for her.

By the oak she paused, listening from the shadows. This song was not as rude as the other, but was again about a woman. Was that all the bards could compose? The three intertwined voices eventually fell from soaring beauty into silence.

Ainnle hauled the dripping antlers out and, resting them on the ground, began to scrape the boiled flesh from the bone with a knife. As if resuming an earlier conversation, he said, "Aye, that bird-girl was an odd one, all right. And gods, but she's easily riled."

Ardan hissed at him to hold his tongue, head cocked to listen for Deirdre in the woods.

Just as unwilling to hear anything about herself, Deirdre forced her legs to move, striding through the undergrowth so they would know she was coming. With hearty greetings, they set her down before the fire and Ardan picked up his flask and wooden cup. "We are failing in our hospitality if this night we do not offer you drink and food." He gestured toward the mask. "But you'll have to disarm."

When Deirdre hesitated, Naisi's glance was challenging. "What could be so bad you don't want us to see you?"

She made her dry lips move. "No. It's not that."

"Then what?" Ardan sat down with the flask between his knees.

Her need to hide her soul from Conor had given her an instinctive fear of revealing herself to anyone, but now this wrestled with an unbearable yearning to meet the gazes of these three youths unafraid, as herself.

Naisi was watching her. "We're not brutes," he murmured in exasperation. "Give us more credit than that."

She nodded, feeling dizzy. Now she was back at this fire, the kernel of the wild idea sown by Queen Maeve was suddenly growing into a painful, overwhelming rush. Possibilities hovered, if only she had courage.

"Come," Ainnle prodded. "We don't bite."

At last she released her breath and lowered her chin, tugging the mask up. She kept it down as she pulled away the buck-hide thongs, grasping those last moments of protection.

Then Deirdre braced herself and lifted her head to face the sons of Usnech.

CHAPTER 10

There was a long pause.

Ardan struggled to tear his gaze from the girl before abruptly squatting by the fire, reaching his knife to the skinned hare over the flames. "See? The sky hasn't fallen in." He began to carve the cooked flesh, catching it on a scrap of bark.

Naisi had no such scruples about staring. She'd tracked them and tricked them, and his shoulder still ached from her fist, not to mention his bruised thigh. She sat rigidly, gripping the mask as if the mere revealing of her face would be alarming. Irritated, Naisi scrutinized her.

Judging by her clothes, he was expecting a solid, plain girl, as boyish as her dress. He tried not to show surprise. Her features were unsettling and exotic in the firelight, as if they kept shifting into something else. Large eyes were set far apart, and broad, flat cheeks tapered to a narrow, pointed chin. Her pale forehead was wide, too much for her delicate lower face, her cheekbones so high that when Ardan gave her the meat her smile slanted her eyes.

For some unknown reason, he thought of the ale-maid Anya at Emain Macha, dark-haired and lean. He'd been intrigued by her snapping black eyes and clever tongue, but like all his conquests she soon resorted to sulking when he took off to hunt, and desire slaked with so little effort soon palled. He cleared his throat. "Now we've seen your face, we need your name. You know ours, after all." He glanced at the sky as he said it, all the tension flowing out of him. He'd seen her and she was undoubtedly striking, but in the aftermath of that he felt oddly restless. Time was moving on. They'd come out here to *hunt*, and now that they had the king stag, they must leave.

"Yes," he heard her say.

"So…?" Ardan prompted, handing her a cup of mead.

Naisi narrowed his eyes at the stars, wondering how late it was. They must get up early to be back at Emain before nightfall.

Deirdre desperately chewed the mouthful of meat and took a sip of mead. She had to savor every taste of this freedom before they found out who she was. The mead was fiery, and the hare meat was lifted by a musty tang of the thyme on which it fed. She would melt the scents of the wild places on her tongue and remember this glimpse of escape.

She closed her eyes as the wind creaked the branches, bringing the scent of snow and rock, mud and wet leaves. The desperation hammered. *Lie.* But she could not. She had eaten and drunk at this fire, and that was a sacred act.

The mead trailed down her throat and she opened her eyes and looked straight at Ardan. "Deirdre," she said, quiet but clear. "Daughter of the harper Fedlimid."

The second silence seemed endless.

Ardan froze and Ainnle, who'd been wolfing down the meat

and only half listening, now blinked as if waking. The gods alone knew what Naisi looked like—but he was sure they were laughing. The fire flickered in his eyes.

Manannán's breath. He was on his feet, the whisper falling from his lips, but for once it was not a lighthearted curse. This was a prayer, fervent in this moment of terrible dawning. Conor's face formed before him, amid the wavering shadows and bloody licks of flame. Ainnle threw the bone away and belatedly leaped up. "Gods' balls," he muttered as Ardan joined them. Shoulder to shoulder, they gazed down at Deirdre. She shrunk before them, her eyes huge.

"What have we done?" Ardan murmured.

Visceral panic flooded Naisi. "We must get away, right now." He cast about wildly for his sword, and even as he said it he hated himself, feeling for a moment like the child he once was, quailing before Conor's throne.

"Gods," Ainnle could not stop saying, shoving random belongings into his pack.

Naisi paused with his sword, fingers roving over the raised design cast into the hilt of bronze and polished horn—a wolf's head, brave and strong.

Ardan was arguing with Ainnle. "I knew we should never have come here in the first place."

"But how were we to know this was why Conor forbade us these hunting runs?"

"He will not forgive this. A stag, perhaps…but not this."

"We should have guessed who she was last night."

Yes, Naisi thought, *how could I have been so blind?* Except if he had ever imagined the king's betrothed in passing, he had pictured a noble lady, all fluttering skirts and expensive scents, walled up in a lavish fort. Everyone thought she was on an island in the sea, far away: a myth barely believed by the young men, barely remembered by the old. Conor's arrogance at keeping her closer to Emain, albeit among the barren uplands, took his breath away. That the king thought his word alone was enough to keep his warriors at heel, like slavering pups!

Deirdre halted them by springing up. "Stop talking about me as if I am not here!" They all stared at her, speechless, and she spread her palms. "Did you not listen to me? He keeps me against my *will*. All I've ever had to look forward to is one day being dragged to Emain Macha like a cow mated to an old bull."

The torture in her eyes pricked Naisi's pity. He remembered the trapped stag with the broken leg—and in the same breath thought of himself.

"I'm sorry for that," Ardan muttered. "We understand something of what you feel." He glanced at his brothers. "We do."

"Do you?" she retorted. "So you'll be pinned down while he mounts *you*, will you?"

They were all shocked, but Deirdre didn't care. The crude words were a sharp blade in her hands stabbing into her own flesh, making the rest hurt less.

Ainnle sat down with his hands over his eyes. "Conor's anger at our hunt will be nothing to this."

"Ainnle, grow up," Naisi snapped, to Deirdre's surprise. "You're not a boy anymore, to crumble before that man." His face was stark with anger and she thought: *That's not fury at me.*

"And how could you put us in such danger, anyway?" Ainnle turned on her instead, narrow face flushed a dark red. "You said you were forbidden to see anyone."

"You said you were forbidden to come here. I don't recall making you."

Ardan stepped between them. "There's no real harm done." He faced Deirdre, lowering his tone. "If you don't tell anyone, then we won't. It was all a mistake—we'll leave and you just pretend you never saw us."

His tone was calming the others, but Deirdre was consumed by a flame of anguish and desperation. A vision had opened before her of what she must do, swimming in and out of focus. It all came together—the unexpected freedom of raven-flight, the sparks soaring unfettered in the fire. "No," she heard herself say.

"What he's done isn't right. I must find a way to break the betrothal and leave him, just as Maeve did."

Naisi's eyes blazed from his pale face. "What are you talking about?"

She ignored her suddenly unsteady legs. "I'll find a safe place and send Conor a message that I will not marry him."

"You are betrothed!" Ainnle exclaimed.

Naisi was staring blankly at her. "*You* are going to defy Conor? You?"

Defy was a word that had never crossed her mind in the dark nights of despair. Her voice wavered. "Just to find out if there's another way."

Ardan raked fingers through his hair. "He'll punish you. You're a fool to unleash that on yourself."

She whirled on him, fists balled. "*He already has punished me.* He imprisoned me, took away my right to choose for myself. If he beats me now, that is nothing."

"Easy to say if you've never been beaten!"

She plunged on with determination. "If he discards me, then at least I will be free." She met their bank of firelit eyes with braced shoulders.

"Gods' breath." Ardan's glance was reluctantly admiring. "I never thought any girl would…"

"You want us to take you." Naisi's harsh voice cut the chill air. "You want us to take you to this safe place. How else can you escape? You have no food, no weapons, no idea where to go." He strode to her and gripped her elbow, eyes glittering savagely. "Did you intend this all along?"

"No! Until you spoke of Maeve, I never knew I could choose at all!" He released her and turned to the darkness, and she chafed the imprint of his fingers from her arm.

Ainnle regarded his brother's back with horror. "Naisi, you're not seriously thinking about helping her? She might be running away, but it's *our* lives that will be forfeit."

Naisi spoke over his shoulder, strangely brooding. "The king lied to all of us about the hunting grounds. Every step of his is dishonorable, and it sticks in my throat…"

"I can feel you thinking, brother, and you can stop it right now." Ardan threw a frantic look at Deirdre. "We are sorry for your pain, really we are. But you are a woman and you won't be punished more than you have been. As for us…" He stared at the back of Naisi's black head. "He hates us. He hates Naisi. It's too dangerous to help you."

Deirdre barely listened, her eyes fixed on Naisi. He hadn't refused. The desperation erupted once more, the silent howl struggling to break free. She had to make him help her. She walked toward Naisi, and his brothers drew back. She stopped so close her breath stirred his hair.

No! Her conscience wavered and she looked into that dark heart inside her: the hunger for survival that had possessed her, her craving for vibrant life. This was the only way. "Just take me to the nearest dun," she murmured. "It would only be a few days." The dancing glow of the fire entered her flesh again, urging her on.

A quiver ran over Naisi's skin, and she had the irrational thought that she might as well be pressing her lips along that firelit curve of neck, the strength underlying the tendons so utterly unlike her own. It was a new power that flowed through her as naturally as breath. Her voice dropped. "I have heard many tales of the sons of Usnech, and one thing is said above all: here are three brothers who never refuse aid to those in need, lest they forfeit their dearly-held honor and pride. Everyone knows it."

Naisi raised his head to the canopy of bare, frosted branches, his shoulders lowering.

"Naisi," Ardan began.

"I need to think," Naisi croaked.

"But—"

"I need to think!" Without looking back, Naisi forced his way through a drift of snow, banked up by wind, and was gone.

Naisi broke out on a path behind the trees and paced a little way before sinking on his haunches. He bent his head into one arm, dragging his fingers over his scalp to help him think. Deirdre's words wove through his mind like smoke, binding arguments and contradictions together. *Honor. Pride.*

At last he raised his face with a bitter smile. Two women would defy Conor and yet he, Usnech's eldest son, would not? There were many reasons to refuse, but as he wavered there the old impulse stirred again, the black river flowing through the buried caverns of his spirit. Was this secret hunger the source of the hatred for Conor...or did it stem from the hatred itself? He did not know. His early memories were tainted with a sense of hostility as he watched Conor subtly scorn his father, Usnech, and since then it had grown in the darkness like a mold, into something far more deformed—for Naisi was a warrior of the Red Branch, and that was a byword for loyalty. It was a drive he didn't dare voice, even to himself, for the reek of shame that rose from it. *And this girl could be key.* She came from the woods like a gift, a message after so much struggle. Is that what she was? Or did she just want to use him? If so, then perhaps he could use her, too.

When he stood, he felt as if he'd left his belly on the ground, but he had to do it now before he changed his mind. He was so tired of sense, of forbearance.

At the fire, Ardan and Ainnle looked up. "I will take her to Aed's dun," he announced. Ainnle began to protest, but he held up his hand. "It's only three days on foot. I will deliver her, and that's the end of it. Conor can only be so angry at that. His rage will be eclipsed by what she says to him." He did not miss the flinch that crossed Deirdre's unsettling face.

"No," Ardan said. "You cannot be serious."

"She's only going to attempt it, anyway—look in her eyes. And if she dies of cold or injury, we could be in even worse trouble. Once we hand her over to Aed, she can have it out with the druids themselves over the *brithem* laws that govern betrothals.

It's not for us to stop her going just so Conor can get what he wants." His rapid speech was confusing Ardan. Good; his brother always saw too much.

Deirdre spoke up, her voice unsteady. "I'll say I'd left already and came across you in the woods when I was lost. I'll say I didn't tell you my name."

Ainnle glared at her. "You could have done that to start with, and then we wouldn't have known the difference."

She stared back. "I could not do that in honor while I supped at your fire."

Ardan's brows rose and he sat heavily on the nearest log. Naisi also glanced at her in surprise, then dragged his attention back to his brothers. "I don't want either of you coming, nor can you dissuade me. She's right." He drew a deep breath. "We do have a name to protect. Father's name. I think it's best for us—in the long run—if we are seen to help her."

Ainnle was silent, struggling to come up with more arguments. Ardan was staring at the hare, which had turned black over the flames. Face furrowed, he tipped the burned carcass into the snow. In the pause, Naisi turned to Deirdre before his own resolve weakened. "We have to go by dawn."

She blanched. "Tonight?"

"Yes." He spoke as if they were the only two there, so for a moment he didn't have to deal with the anguish in his brothers. "Do you have sleeping hides?"

She nodded. "I've got beaver-fur blankets Conor gave me, and sealskins…"

He shook his head. "They are too fine. You need a cowhide and blankets, something thick and old." She nodded again, her teeth beginning to chatter. See how she liked being faced with the realities of the outside world now. "Bring whatever you need of warm clothes, but otherwise pack light." He studied her critically. "We have to move fast. This could be hard on you."

She shivered. "I often ran up and down the valley path. Just to run."

"Very well, then." Their gazes locked. She needed his help; he wanted something of her. That seemed simple enough, except there was a shadow of vulnerability behind her eyes and he had to quell a pang of unease.

As soon as she left, his brothers' protests began again, and he parried them. It was only a few days, and they'd say they didn't know who she was. "We might even be able to turn this so the king has to thank us for rescuing his beloved. In public."

Ainnle was eventually resigned, too used to following Naisi to resist. Relieved, Naisi went to the stream to drink. He was scooping water in his palm when Ardan came up behind him, boots crunching on the frosted leaves. "What's this really about? I feel sorry for the girl, too, but...there's more here than you're telling me."

And you will not know it. Ardan was too pure, too steeped in warrior honor, to understand. To forgive. Naisi brushed spilled drops from his hide tunic before it froze. The moonlight glowed on the churning foam at his feet, and he thought of one shining truth he could tell his brother. "Remember my fasting trial for the Red Branch?" At fourteen, Red Branch initiates had to withstand cold and hunger for five days. On the third day of Naisi's trial, he fell into a trance by an icy pool, pleading to the gods to be the best, for Conor's eye to fall on him with favor. That had been a vain plea, but the gods *did* answer part of his prayer—or rather, a goddess did. He remembered the glimmer of the swan gliding over the dark water toward him, the Otherworld glint in its eyes. Its stern demand for his oath had shot through his heart without words. "Brother, I didn't just swear to that goddess— Macha, Brid, whoever She was—that if She would raise me high in the Red Branch I would protect the *Ulaid* with my life. She wanted more: that I would protect the weak who had no one else. Children." He paused. "Women."

"Oh." Ardan's brows shadowed his eyes.

"Our success with the sword and bow has surely been god-blessed since I made that vow, just as Mama says. But it brings obligations, too."

Ardan was quiet, their misty breath mingling. "Then that goes for all of us." When Naisi protested, he bestowed on him a troubled smile. "The gods spoke to Cathbad at the girl's birth and told Conor not to bring her into the heart of the Ulaid. He didn't listen. The goddess asked you to protect the weak ones who beg your help, and then the girl stumbles across us. Perhaps nothing good will come if we, like Conor, defy such signs. I don't like it, but there it is."

Ardan had always been drawn to the druids and their misty realms of prophecy and dreams. *My brother*, Naisi thought fiercely, nodding in relief.

When Ardan told Ainnle he would go with Naisi, Ainnle frowned and kicked at the buried hare. "Of course I'm with you, too—though I'm more concerned about men and their swords than gods."

Naisi was throwing more wood on the fire while waiting for Deirdre to return. "There is no chance any Red Branch warriors will set themselves against us. Conor would bring down upon himself the wrath of every chieftain of the Ulaid if he did that. He is many things, but not foolish."

Deirdre held the ache of loss at bay while she rolled up old bed-hides and tied them to a leather pack she used for walking in the woods. She braced the inside of the soft leather bottom with the swan mask. Levarcham had helped her make it; it must come. She held the sun-disk in her hand, gleaming in its frame of polished yew. Levarcham had been showing her how to mark the passing of seasons around the rim. It was her only druid gift; she carefully wrapped it. She took an extra fleece cloak, tunics and trews and meat-knife, and when her eyes swept over Conor's jewels she nearly turned away but changed her mind and tossed in a few bronze arm-rings and pins, and necklaces of amber, glass and jet. They would be returned to him as a mark of the severed betrothal.

She was surprised how familiar this felt, as if she'd made this decision long ago and had only been waiting for her wings to grow. For her chance to come. Pain hovered, too, but she told herself it would all be over soon. She, Aiveen and Fintan could live together wherever they chose then. Free. The faint trembling that ran beneath her skin told her she would not be barred from anything again.

One task remained.

She had always drawn pictures of animals, absorbed by the tiny details of their character and movements. Now she found old shreds of bleached kidskin in her dresser and dug charcoal from the hearth. *First Levarcham*. She drew a crude outline of three blackbirds and a fourth behind them with wings spread. Blackbirds were singers, dark-plumaged. She dared not say more, but surely Levarcham would know that she went of her own free will. And now something for her parents. Two small animals took shape beneath her fingers, flowing and sinuous. Aiveen watched her swim when she was small, laughing at her little otter splashing about. Fintan said she was his fox-cub, quick and clever. The charcoal otter was diving gleefully, the ripples trailing off the kidskin, and the fox trotted along a trail that led far away, ears pricked. There was no message in that but love.

She fled before she could change her mind.

This time when she rejoined the track, she was running, and took no note of the moonlight or the frosted trees. A force pushed her feet on in long, urgent strides, kicking up the snow behind her.

CHAPTER 11

Leaf-bud

The next day, the wind turned westerly, bearing a stream of warm, salt-laden air. The frosts and thin snowcover swiftly began to melt, as if the land intended to rush headlong into the second moon of leaf-bud.

The ground became muddy and all the streams were swollen, which slowed the progress of Deirdre and the sons of Usnech. For the first two days the skies were clear, though, the catkins feathering the hazel branches, and thorn blossom scattering the bare undergrowth with banks of creamy white. Deirdre felt the forest coming alive around her.

She thought she would stumble along exhausted, but the exhilaration of being free bore up her limbs with a sweet fire, and she flew along with a light tread. Naisi loped in front and never turned his head—all three brothers could trot in silence like that for hours at a hunter's pace. He had strapped the enormous rack of antlers to his pack across the shoulders, and he appeared in Deirdre's half trance as a stag-spirit leading her through the forest, each step taking her farther into the unknown.

At night, they huddled around a tiny fire and gnawed their trail-food: cakes of fat, dried berries, barley grains. There were no songs or jests now, for Naisi's somber mood and the weariness of travel leached all conversation away. The only exception was when they were striding in the rhythm all three shared, and then she heard as a murmur the song they chanted to fire their steps.

Soft the tread of hunters
Cleave the silent forest
Triumph over wild ones
Hearts as fierce as they

Strong the tread of fighters
Cleave the roaring armies
Triumph over brave ones
Hearts as bold as they

Red Branch
Red Branch
Red Branch

Soon the song wove through Deirdre's own heart, and she was pierced with the longing to claim it for her own, to feel such pride flowing through her veins. Red Branch…the greatest warriors in Erin.

The three youths were careful of her honor at night, bending branches of yew and juniper to make her own little shelter, their evergreen needles forming a thick, scented tent. As soon as she finished eating, she crawled in and slept.

She had never been so cold, yet though she shivered in her hides and blankets, her nose pinched by the freezing air, the wilderness did not feel threatening. When the rain began, she did not huddle away from it. Instead, she pushed back her hood. The sluice of drops was like being bathed by the sky, and when it ran into her mouth it was like the world slaking her thirst.

The more she opened herself, surrendering to the cold and damp, the less discomfort she felt. Her body grew tired, her feet sore, but it was a satisfying ache of exertion. She watched to see if fear would fell her; then she would know she'd done the wrong thing. But it did not come.

Naisi watched Deirdre with suspicion. In daylight, her skin was disconcerting in its fine-grained whiteness, her eyes as green as moss on pale birch-bark. Her golden hair threw glints across the irises, which fired them into something almost hungry, searching. She paid little attention to him or his brothers, and there were no sly glances or giggles. If he addressed her, her unguarded thoughts passed across her expressive face before she spoke aloud. She did not complain as expected, but peered at her blisters around the fire at night with curiosity.

He soon forgot to wonder about her, however, because his dread at what he'd done was peaking. *So rash...* He had leaped on impulse and now was free-falling through air that was far too thin. He sucked it in as he ran, unable to draw from it the relief he needed, the knowing he had done right. Every time they stopped, he heard the whisper inside. *Was it too late to go back?* No one at Emain Macha knew what they had done.

On the third night, he had to keep fighting the urge to wipe their footprints from the forest floor, retracing their steps back to the lake. Gods. He growled at himself for that moment of weakness, and turned his attention to Deirdre, who was chewing a strip of dried deer-meat by the fire. Her slight jaw ground away with determination. His guilt prodded him. "Having second thoughts?"

She swallowed. "No." She glanced frankly at his brothers. "This is what I longed for, to walk free under the sky. Nothing of this could be hardship."

Ardan's face softened at her words. Naisi only hoped he didn't look like that. "It is a hardship, but you make it easier by not saying so," he replied gruffly, forced to be fair by his own conscience. This was his choice. His. He had to remember that, but it was difficult when he seemed to have a gag lodged down his throat. He dug his knife into the soil, tracing shapes to distract his mind while Ardan asked Deirdre about what she learned from her druid teacher. He drew a circle, a long nose, a pointed beard; it was crude, but it helped him to summon Conor's face.

As Deirdre and Ardan's voices hummed around him, Naisi

took a breath and stabbed the dagger into the ground once, then twice. Panting, he gazed into the vacant eyeholes of Conor the king and saw contempt gazing back.

Fintan brought the news to Emain Macha, so overcome with fear for Deirdre and an urge to protect Aiveen from the king's wrath that he rushed to Conor and burst out with it before the entire hall. Aiveen, however, crept to Levarcham's side all unnoticed by the men and folded shreds of kidskin in the druid's palm.

While Conor was distracted by his own fury, Levarcham slipped from the hall, hobbled to her hut, and unrolled the messages. Slowly, her thumb smeared the charcoal, savoring the last thing Deirdre had touched.

She did not understand fully, only that the child wanted her to know she had chosen this. Her eyes stung, blurring the dark lines on the pale skin. She was shocked that she was not struck with horror at Deirdre's flight, only cursing that she herself had not discovered it. For she understood in an instant that she would have hidden it. She would have left Deirdre free as long as she could. *You should have freed her yourself*, the crow squawked. Yes. A maternal pang pierced Levarcham, and she knew it would have given her the unassailable power to face down the king.

At the moment she finally understood that force, it was already too late to wield it. Deirdre's fate was gone from her own hands, which had proven so useless after all.

"We will reach Aed's dun today," Naisi looked at his brothers. Wafts of sour sweat rose from their clothes and they were spattered in mud. "Aed is a powerful chief. It is important we come to him as the nobles we are, not as fugitives."

"I thought we weren't fugitives," Ainnle said sharply.

Naisi sent him an exasperated look while Ardan ruffled his younger brother's hair. "This stinks—I swear it has badger scat in it. Stop whining; start swimming."

Ardan and Ainnle went to bathe in a nearby stream and Naisi settled on a log with his sword unsheathed over his legs. "Go upstream, Deirdre." He pointed with his chin. "I will stay on watch until my brothers get back."

Later, hair scrubbed, chin shaved, Naisi himself climbed up the bank from the stream. Icy water ran from his naked skin, and snorting with cold he wiped his limbs to flick it off. He heard a noise, and thinking it was his brothers he turned with his tunic hanging from his fingers.

Deirdre was standing on the other bank. Paralyzed, he waited for her shriek of embarrassment, but it never came. Her wet hair was the hue of dark barley, eyes vivid splashes in the paleness of cold skin. Unafraid, that brilliant gaze slid in astonishment from his shoulders to belly to ... *Ach*. Naisi reacted, dropping the tunic and throwing himself back into the stream. The cold made him gasp and he turned on her, safely covered in water to the waist. She still hadn't run away. "What are you doing? I told you to bathe up there."

"I know, but ... I came back the wrong way." She was frowning in confusion, a little wrinkle marring that smooth brow.

Naisi pushed his tongue against his teeth, his legs going numb. "Well, can you leave now so I can dry myself?"

She wasn't listening. Instead, her gaze was roaming over his body, her eyes widening a little as they reached his shoulders, neck, chest and belly, then narrowing intently to follow the line of hair from his navel into his groin, now hidden underwater. He had to resist the urge to cover himself, and with an effort kept his hands on his hips. "Why are you doing that?" Now it was his turn to be confused. She had been brought up to be the king's betrothed. Surely she wasn't learned in seduction already? Then with a jolt, he recognized curiosity in her face, not slyness.

"Because you are ..." she searched for a word, "... fair."

He blinked. "What?"

She gingerly stepped forward, and his nostrils flared. He leaned back, even though they were separated by the water. "I admit I did wonder," she murmured, "whether I was different from others, and not in a good way. If I was kept separate because, in fact, there was something wrong with me, and Levarcham couldn't tell me." Her smile was wry, and then it flickered out, her gaze returning to his body with the same intensity. Now she spoke softly, as if to herself. "The skin *is* the same—it must feel the same—but I didn't think a man would look so...smooth and hard at the same time. The shape is so different—not like me at all, in the end."

Now Naisi didn't feel the cold. She spoke as if he couldn't hear her, as if she was used to thinking aloud and dissecting things. Baffling thoughts thundered through him and he realized he had no idea what to say, and so ended up at the truth. "That is the strangest thing anyone has ever said to me."

Her eyes darted up. "Is it?" Knowing dawned over her and she backed away. "Gods, everyone is going to think me such a fool. I'm sure Levarcham never had anything to do with young men and what women should say to them. All I know is how to ask chieftains about their *fat cattle* while pouring ale that doesn't spill."

Naisi was trying not to laugh, even though he was in agony from the cold. The strangeness of her provided a welcome relief for his dark thoughts. He wondered if he should comfort her, but had no intention of revealing the cold-shrunken organs between his legs. "It is obvious you are not a fool." His teeth chattered. "And you will soon work out how to be with other people."

That idea, to his surprise, didn't thrill him. For he realized that if Anya was standing there, he could predict their entire conversation: the flirtatious quip, the knowing smile, the flash of dark eyes followed by her opening her legs with barely an effort made. But he had no idea what this girl might say next.

Which was why she should be swiftly passed on to someone better able to deal with her. He shifted his feet on the pebbles. "One thing you do need to know," he said loudly, "is that men feel the cold just as women do."

"Oh." *Now* she blushed. "I am thinking too much of myself. I'm sorry. I'll go." She dashed off through the trees with that odd way she had of running: small bursts interspersed with long leaps, as if something in her strained to fly.

The huntsman bent to the stag carcass, its ribs arching from the boggy ground. Up here on the fells, the skeleton had been gnawed by wolves, but something had obviously caught his eye among the splinters of brittle bone and trampled mud. He dug his fingers into the icy soil and Cúchulainn found he was instinctively bracing himself.

"What is it?" Conor snapped from horseback.

"I think…it is a shred of fletching, my lord. It looks like the beast was killed at the same time as the other by the lake. This one's lost its antlers, though."

There was a silence. "Someone was hunting where they should not."

The second tracker appeared in the distance, loping up a long ravine that disappeared west. He had been gone all morning. Eventually, as Cúchulainn stood beside the king in the bleak wind, the man hurried up and went down on one knee before Conor in a mud puddle. "It was very hard, but I finally found some new tracks that went down into gravel," he puffed. "They were nearly washed away, and—"

"What did they show?" The king's voice cut him off.

"They are hard to separate. Some men, indeed, though I am not sure how many. And smaller prints—a woman."

The silence returned, broken only by the creaking of the bare branches of a lonely thorn tree, its roots gripping the crevices of an outcropping of rocks. "So," the king murmured at last. "There, it appears, goes Deirdre." He was swathed in ruddy furs of beaver and fox, the only warm thing about his pinched, gray face.

Cúchulainn moved up beside Conor's horse, fingering the end of his bow. "Nothing can be known for sure in such conditions. The ground is a mire."

"We know she's gone, Hound. Who else would it be out here?" Though Conor's dead sister, Dechtire, was Cúchulainn's mother, the king only called him nephew when he was in an expansive mood. Now his eyes were as cold as the leaden sky. "So whose tracks were they? *Who stole her?*"

The second tracker began babbling. "It appears she went of her own will, my lord. There are no signs of a struggle."

The king's look silenced him. The first huntsman turned with the fletching. "I can tell you." He walked to Conor's horse, glancing nervously at the silent Cúchulainn, who stared straight through him. "Your warriors that play at hunting fletch their barbs with patterns, to boast."

We do it to mark our kills. Anger kindled in Cúchulainn's belly. He knew whose arrow it was, and at that moment fought an urge to sink his fist into the tracker's face to close his mouth. What did he know of the discipline, the danger, the courage required to hurl yourself against a blade in what could be your last breath? A man who did that must be celebrated, not scorned.

Conor leaned forward in his saddle as if he also might strike the man. "Whose?"

The tracker smiled smugly and handed over the tuft of black and white feathers, raven and swan. "That," he announced, "is the mark of the sons of Usnech." He spat on the ground. "They all three have the same mark, as if one."

Cúchulainn closed his eyes, setting his face to the icy wind. The land fell away from rolling hills into a blanket of brown forest, where skeletons of bare trunks littered slopes threaded by foaming streams. *Naisi.* The dismay almost choked him.

The Hound had not known that this was where Conor had secreted the girl, and Naisi couldn't have known, either. What the warriors *did* know was that, yes, it was a foolish vanity of Conor's to declare his own hunting run, but it was a minor thing to concede. *There are countless leagues to satisfy your bow, Naisi*, he silently berated him. What drove him to pit himself against this particular folly of the king's, and so by accident reveal a far greater danger?

Cúchulainn gnawed on that, wondering if he'd missed some deeper disturbance in Naisi that had led inexorably to this. The cold air hurt his chest as he gathered it in, but he smoothed all emotion from his face when he turned back to the king. "Do not leap to conclusions," he warned. "They are good lads, and loyal to you and the Red Branch. It is likely they were trying to help the maid."

"By taking her away from me?" The king's voice cracked. The light in his eyes was savage now, the only animated thing about his cold, white face.

A darkness entered Cúchulainn's heart. "We do not know the truth of this. They will no doubt be back at Emain Macha by the time we get there, and we can laugh about it over an ale."

Conor ignored him and addressed the second tracker. "You said they were traveling west?"

The man nodded, pointing over his shoulder. "They go west and a little south, toward the borders with Connacht."

"Past a point they could turn north." The king spoke as if to himself. "Their steps, then, do not take them to Emain Macha." Cúchulainn fixed his eyes on his horse's neck so he did not have to see Conor's proud face contorted with helpless rage. "Or back to me."

CHAPTER 12

Aed, son of Cumall, fingered one tip of the magnificent antler-rack Naisi had just placed at his feet.

"So you can see why we had no choice, my lord." Naisi felt his words tumbling out too fast. "We had to help her."

Aed's white hair still flowed over his shoulders in a thick mane, hiding the slight wasting of that once-powerful body. His craggy face had remained still throughout Naisi's explanation, his eyes on the antlers, not meeting his gaze once. Naisi tried to quash the fear triggered by this unnatural reserve.

At last the old chieftain sighed, glancing at the only other person in the empty, echoing hall—his druid Lassar. "I see how you thought that, my boy." Naisi warmed a little at the tone of affection, for his father, Usnech, had hunted and fought his way across Erin at Aed's side. "This situation, however, is not as clear as it would at first seem."

Naisi's hope plunged. "Any warrior worth a Red Branch shield would have done the same. She's a noble-born lady of the Ulaid. She pleaded for our help." Even now, Deirdre's whisper still breathed across his skin. The moment of clarity replayed itself, when her need to run met his own rage and flashed together, spark and tinder.

Aed waved a hand, the veins stringy beneath the papery skin. "We must confer, Lassar and I. Leave me now, my friend. We will speak again soon." At Naisi's stricken expression he forced a smile, his crinkled blue eyes under shaggy white brows looking much more like the Aed he knew. "Do not despair! Conor is ruled by his head, not his heart. We will work this misunderstanding out, I am sure. In the meantime, enjoy the hospitality of my dun."

Naisi was swamped with relief. "Thank you, my lord."

As soon as Naisi left, Aed looked at Lassar—a thin, clever young druid standing quietly behind his carved chair. Lassar stepped forward, his hands tucked into the sleeves of his robe of undyed wool. His long, brown hair was shaved over the forehead, making the pale dome arch higher. The lengths were braided with gold beads, denoting his earthly bonds to his chieftain, Aed, and raven feathers which marked his Otherworldly travels.

"What do you think?" Aed tapped the arms of his chair. He felt as if a dark shadow had flown into his hall and was now perched somewhere near the rafters, quiet and still. "Does she have a claim for clemency? Or has my bold Naisi gotten himself embroiled in something dire?"

"The *brithem* laws cover most eventualities, my lord, marriage being one of the most detailed areas. Betrothals less so, since they are often broken, at least before gifts are exchanged."

"Broken? Then there is precedent for this?"

Lassar looked troubled. "This is a most unusual situation. There are provisions made for nine classes of marriage, the first four to protect the property of those entering the marriage, and the latter to protect any children born from the union when there is no property at stake." His voice took on the singsong cadence of a druid summoning words from memory. "Since no lawful marriage contract or exchange of goods has actually been entered into, she is not restricted by the tenets of the first four. I suppose we would also have to rule out the last, the union taking place between insane people, since we are dealing with our king."

Aed grunted. "He was mad to pursue her to begin with."

As lord of the rich cattle plains bordering Connacht, Aed avoided being drawn too deeply into Conor's fortunes. Kings changed, allegiances shifted. He did not want the king demanding the services of his own warriors in order to discharge some imagined debt, or risk the next king's wrath for supporting this one too wholeheartedly. As a buffer between the Ulaid and Connacht, he was too exposed to real enemies to risk the king's intrigues. He could only focus on his own borders.

Conor's treaties with the kingdoms of Laigin and Mumu had subdued Connacht's king Eochaid for years. The brief marriage of Eochaid's daughter Maeve to Conor had kept Connacht further at bay. The borderlords' wealth of cattle and crops meant strength of numbers, and that had ensured that Connacht and the Ulaid exchanged cattle raids but never descended into all-out war. All in all, a balance of sorts. But now Eochaid had fallen ill, and Maeve had run. It made his head ache.

Lassar had raised one brow at the muttered insult. Now he continued. "A fifth degree union is cohabitation through the mutual consent of the man and woman to share their bodies, or the man to visit the woman with her family's consent." He paused. "I can safely rule out that the maiden has consented to this union?" His only answer was Aed's snort. "Nor have they eloped together, since she was a child, nor can consent be proffered by her family since her mother died in bearing and her father a moon later, leaving no kin."

Aed was glowering. Put so baldly, this betrothal was a terrible idea. No one had been sufficiently driven at the time to stand against their powerful king on behalf of a newborn, kinless child. They had been embroiled in a war with the province of Laigin and had greater worries. But after looking into Naisi's troubled face today, suddenly he cared very much about that babe's fate because of how it reflected on the boy.

"In fact, the king justified this by taking her under his protection as a ward, which puts him close to foster-father status. But if he claims her as family, this raises another issue entirely—incest."

"Spare me!" Aed exclaimed. He peered back through the years to the night at Fedlimid the harper's house, where he had sat drinking with his young king. He had seen the light in Conor's eye when Cathbad told him to leave the girl's beauty alone. *A bloom that should never be plucked from the wild places,* Cathbad said.

"Indeed." Lassar took a breath. "Then that only leaves as guidance a union formed by abduction, but this has legal validity only as long as the man can keep the woman with him. Clearly, Conor has not been able to keep her with him. Perhaps he relied on her passivity and acquiescence too much."

Aed sat up. "That is the legal flaw."

"It comes closest," Lassar agreed. "And taking into account that the union has not been consummated and there are no children to protect under law, the issue of the woman's consent or that of her family becomes the only paramount consideration. In this case, where she has no family, her consent becomes paramount." His smile was expansive. "It seems fairly clear."

"It does, doesn't it?" Aed agreed, feeling pity for this girl-child he had never seen. "Conor has temporarily lost his wits to greed, that's all. Now that the girl has removed herself from the situation, we can all deal with this on a more reasonable and rational level." And perhaps it was not such a bad thing for Aed to remind Conor of his own independence and power.

Lassar bowed. "I take it, then, that you intend to offer this girl and the sons of Usnech shelter in your name?"

"Naisi and Ardan saved my lands from a Connacht raid when they were barely initiated," Aed growled. "As for the girl…" He tapped his teeth, ground to pegs from years of gritty barley-meal. "I will see her first. Then we will decide what to do."

Lassar bowed. "It would be wise to deal carefully with the king, my lord, of course—but your reputation among the other chiefs, and indeed the druids, will be enhanced by such an act of compassion and wisdom. And we do not know how many years Conor has left as king. It may be a wise idea to gain the loyalty of the three sons of Usnech, young and growing in power, which may stand us in good stead in the years to come."

Aed was feeling much better. "Then summon the lads and tell them to bring the girl, too."

Deirdre stood behind Naisi in the largest building she had ever seen. The great hall was a vast cavern made of wood with soaring posts like the trees of a forest, holding up a sky of pale thatch that met at a peak far above. Two fire-pits each as long as her own hut roared with burning wood, sparks lighting expanses of decorated hangings and piles of cushions and furs. The firelight sparkled on the array of swords and spears that bristled the walls.

Though she was upright, her body reeled as if it might fall into a stupor and she wanted to clap her hands over her ears. Her head rang with all the noise of the din outside—things she had never been exposed to before: the shouts and chatter of many people, horses neighing, the ringing of smith hammers. There was a constant rumble of cart-wheels and the frequent blare of bronze horns from the high walls. And her eyes…There had been too much to see, to grasp. Children running, dogs squabbling, and the flanks of high-stepping horses gleaming in the sun.

Banners that flew from carved timber gates. Marching ramparts of oak stakes. Layers of thatch roofs all clustered together over little roundhouses, their walls painted with curving shapes. And a chaos of color, of people. Their clothes—yellow, orange, brown, green; their hair—black, brown, gold, white—and all of them with their curious attention upon her. She had been jostled by crowds when she was rarely touched; dizzied by voices when she knew only silence; stared at when she had so often been hidden.

The cacophony had entered her head and she was quaking, daunted and elated by the glorious chaos into which she had plunged. Then she heard her name and she had to draw her wits together, to see and hear clearly again.

Aed was expecting a soft maiden with hushed voice and downcast eyes. He barely heard Naisi's introduction as an urchin in dirty hides stepped forward instead, ash smeared across one cheek. Her hair was not piled in curls like that of other noblewomen, but scraped back and tied in a careless knot at her neck.

"You are Deirdre," he heard himself saying.

"Yes." Her chin was high, arms folded behind her waist. It was almost a defiant stance, and he wondered at it until he picked up a slight tremble of her mouth and remembered she was fighting for her life.

He was a compassionate man with many grandchildren, and so pity overcame him. That skin of unusual clarity and the startling green eyes created a different kind of beauty, but the odd composition of narrow chin and broad brow was unsettling. It was not something he would be drawn to, not plump and pretty like his wives. Instead, she reminded him of a fox cub, alert and fierce. "Come closer, Deirdre." He made his voice deliberately mild. "I may look like a bear, but I do not bite." Warily, she stepped forward, wiping her palms down her trews. "Naisi told me of your difficulty. This is unprecedented; nothing I have ever dealt with before."

There was only the briefest pause. "Me neither, my lord."

Aed's gaze darted toward Naisi. The boy was embarrassed and trying not to show it, grasping his sword-hilt, eyes proud. *Has he put his hand to the cub and found she nips?* Aed glanced back at Deirdre and understood then she was not being provocative; she only stated truth. "Then we have something in common." He hid his amusement in his hand, arm braced on his chair. "We are both perplexed by this unusual situation, and—"

"Oh, I am not perplexed," Deirdre broke in. "I accepted my fate only because I thought I had no choice. But now I know differently." She seemed oblivious to Naisi's mortified glance.

Aed was enjoying himself. The little wild thing was now pinning him there with those intense, slanted eyes. He straightened his face, trying to focus on her words.

"Maeve, Conor's wife, divorced him by choice. If she can do that, then I can break a betrothal. Indeed, I hereby *withdraw my consent* from such a union. Not that I ever gave my consent to start with." She frowned, before her eyes lit up savagely. "So I am sure such a thing was never therefore legal at all."

Amazed, Aed could not help meeting Lassar's eyes. The druid leaned in with perfect composure. "She was tutored, I believe, by Conor's talking-woman, Levarcham," he murmured.

Aed sat back. *Manannán's breath and balls!* "Well, Deirdre," he said, for once in a long life lost for words. "My druid and I were wondering the same thing. I think the most appropriate action would be—"

"I know what I must do," she interrupted once more. Her lapse in manners was forgiven when Aed recognized the haunting desperation in her face. "Send a message to Conor telling him I am of an age now to make up my own mind, and though I thank him deeply for his care of me, I look upon him as a foster-father and must dissolve this betrothal made without my consent."

Aed imagined Conor receiving that message, especially the *foster-father* part, and winced inside. "Lassar and I have also concluded that would be the best course. We must discover the king's position as soon as possible. But perhaps I can lend you Lassar's services to help you to…couch your message in a language Conor is used to? If that is to your liking," he added, amused by the flash of her eyes.

She glanced at the druid, then turned to Naisi. The young warrior was glaring openly at her now, and to Aed's surprise it was only that which at last made her falter. "I...that would be most kind, my lord."

Aed's smile included them all. "Then until we hear back from Conor, you are all under my protection. If you have any needs, let us fulfill them."

"Thank you," Naisi answered formally. "But we would not dream of imposing on you. My brothers and I would be pleased, with your permission, to bring some good meat to your fire."

Aed nodded, and, relieved, the two younger brothers filed out of the hall, Deirdre and Naisi following more slowly. Aed turned to Lassar. "Help the girl compose what she needs to," he muttered. "And by the gods, do not let her inadvertently insult Conor's manhood, or mention the words *old, aged* or *fatherly*!"

Lassar bowed. "Indeed, my lord. The gods willing, this will all be over within a week."

"Deirdre." Naisi cornered her on a path between a row of houses, their thatch roofs nearly sweeping to the ground. Ainnle and Ardan had gone ahead. "You speak your mind without thinking, and though that may be acceptable with us it is not so when you address a chieftain like Aed."

Lost in dazed, hopeful dreams, it took a moment for Deirdre to hear what he was saying and come back to herself. As the words sank in she grew hot with shame. "His eyes were kind, and I—"

"What he is, is very powerful." His dark head reared above her, his eyes narrowed with anger. "You're not in the woods anymore, with your birds and trees. You have to curb that runaway tongue. This is *real*."

She bit down on a retort. The thread of freedom for which she had grasped was now tenuously leading her on, first to the sons of Usnech, then to Aed, who said he would help her. Perhaps she could even stay with him and have her own little pallet on the floor and have no one look at her that way again—least of all some snooty youth who thought himself so important he could scold her. Then it came to her. "You are worried about your own standing," she said slowly. "You don't care about me, you just want to make sure *you* don't look foolish."

His fingers clamped her elbow and the force pushed her back against a slope of thatch. A woman edged past them down the laneway with a basket covered by a scrap of hide, glancing at them curiously. Naisi lowered his voice. "This is no game. You may see us as sweet singers, as laughing hunters—but we are warriors. It's all I've trained for, to be Red Branch at Emain Macha, the greatest honor in the world. And now you come along and you—"

"Stop right there!" Deirdre tugged her arm free. The soaring fear and crash of relief in Aed's hall had unraveled her, and before she knew it her finger was pressed under his rib, like a spear. She barely refrained from jabbing it in. "*You* at least are free. You can stride out of here and do whatever you want—hunt, run, fight. Women can choose nothing. We have to marry old men and be stuck inside *forever*. So don't try telling me this is all about your honor!" *Conor*. It was his features she saw wavering over Naisi's face, and she was taken by the impulse to strike at his chest, that great shield of bone and muscle that would always be stronger than her.

Naisi took a step away from her finger, his head knocking drips from the thatch into his black hair. "I aided you in the defiance of my king. Of course it's about me!" The trickles beaded his brow and he swiped them away, making his forelock stick up.

"You agreed so Conor would think you brave, so the warriors would admire you. You did it for yourself!" She hardly recognized the words that leaped out, her fingers forming a cage over her mouth, belatedly trying to trap them. *And after all he had done for her …*

Naisi's vivid blue eyes flared even brighter, as if she had indeed struck him, and she was swept by the bleak memory that she had forced him to help her with a lie, exaggerating tales of his honor to pluck at his pride. But, sweet Brid, she *had* to, or she would not be here…

She glanced to the side. Aed was standing there, shrewd eyes studying them. "Don't get too worked up on my account," was all he said, and chuckling, shook his white head and walked away.

They were rooted there in mutual shame until Naisi made a strangled noise, turning on his heel. She tried to stop him, desperate to apologize, but he brutally shrugged her off and strode away. Deirdre sank on her haunches against the damp wall, huddling under the dripping thatch as if she could hide from the awful thing she'd just said. Words could be weapons; she *knew* that. She gulped a breath, faintly hiccuping. Poor Levarcham. The druid had tried so hard to instill dignity and discipline in her, and look what she did with them at the first showing.

A distant cry interrupted her thoughts. Wiping the drops from her face, she got up and put her head around the curved wall of the house, peering down the path and through the gates. The sun had come out from the clouds again and now she heard a high-pitched shout and a muddy ball of reeds went bouncing over the ground outside the rampart, a flurry of children in pursuit.

The innocent joy of the screams and laughter drew her down the rutted track and through the crowds until she stood on the green meadow that spread to the river. The youngsters raced back and forth, and she marveled at their high voices and smooth skin, and how small and fast they were. She felt a presence over her shoulder: Aed again. "My grandchildren—and great-grandchildren." A tender smile softened his gruff face. "A few wives, a few concubines; it doesn't take long to add up." As Deirdre tried to form a reply, he said softly, "I assume you had no one to play ball with you?"

Her throat closed over. "Only the wall," she answered, with a rueful smile.

"Then by all means join in. The little cubs scream like banshees, but they're quite safe."

"I . . . surely I am too old for games!"

"Nonsense! They crawl all over me, pulling my beard and making me pretend I'm a bear until I catch one—and me with my creaking knees."

Deirdre was smiling now, picturing that scene. Just then the ball came flying out of the pack of dashing bodies and rolled across the uneven grass at her feet, toward the edge of the meadow.

The running and laughing scoured Deirdre's soul clean, but there was no chance to speak to Naisi until nighttime.

In the great hall, people clustered around the fires as sides of beef sizzled over the flames beside simmering cauldrons of mutton stew. Baskets were piled with bread hot off the hearthstones, spread with the first pats of early sheep's butter.

Daunted by the noise and curious gazes, Deirdre lingered outside the doors on the frosted grass. Mist curled up the paths and over the roofs, and her breath joined it, her nose prickled by the icy air. Here, she was half in the wild dark and still close to people. She could smell the damp forest and the smoke of human fires, see the moon even as her face was warmed by the pitch torches that flamed on posts around the entrance.

People came and went and at last one of them was Naisi. She moved from the shadows. He stopped, his face instantly guarded. She tangled her fingers together. "I'm sorry. I absolutely didn't mean it."

He chewed his lip, regarding her. "You do everything rather absolutely, I've noticed." Encouraged by the wry glint in his eye she shrugged one shoulder, acknowledging that truth. The silence drew out and he tilted his dark head the other way, studying her in the flickering light. "Actually, you were right about the pride."

Her brows rose. "But you've put yourself in great danger for me, and I should have only thought of that."

"And I that this might be hard for you." He straightened and sighed, as if he had been holding tension in his chest. "I made the decision to aid you and I must stand by that. Anyway, if you are a free noblewoman—free enough to leave Conor—then I'm afraid you can say what you like, to whomever you like. Though I expect I'll come to rue pointing that out."

She smiled tentatively. "Then I'll stop being guilty if you will."

"Agreed."

She fidgeted for a moment, then realized now was the time to make her escape. She had been given a bed in the lodge of one of Aed's sisters and it would be quiet there; her head ached from the unaccustomed noise. As she ducked to move past him, Naisi abruptly spoke. "What will you do when he releases you?"

She couldn't see his expression in the shadows, the darkness as blank as her mind. She had not thought further ahead than the moment she was in, glimpsing nothing but vague ideas of freedom and peace. "I suppose I'll return to Fintan and Aiveen." She couldn't keep the tremor from her voice, and even she didn't know if it was because she missed them, or quailed at the thought of going back to that lonely steading.

The door opened and he glanced at it, the torches lighting up his lean face and the blade of his nose. His cheeks hollowed as he pursed his lips, his eyes far away. "I'd stay among the laughter and music if I were you and had been for so long alone. Once Conor gets over it, you might even go to Emain Macha and live with your druid friend there."

"Perhaps. You'll be back hunting for its cookfires by then."

She did not think she imagined the fell shadow that flitted over his face. "Perhaps. Either way, we'll be leaving here soon."

The chill brushed her neck and she crossed her arms, stamping her feet. "Of course."

He became brisk, brushing the mist from his hair. "As soon as we've heard from the king."

CHAPTER 13

Levarcham was praying in the temple when the summons came from the king.

The great fort of Emain Macha was ranged on a low mound in a landscape of rolling green hills. Huts, storehouses and stock pens spread up the slight slopes until, near the crest, the buildings grew grander: the Red Branch Hall with its russet banners, and at the very crown the king's hall with its conical thatch roof that caught the sun. Across a gentle valley rose its Otherworld twin: the sacred mound, crowned not by a king's hall but by an enormous round temple of wood and thatch, dedicated to the founding goddess of the Ulaid, Macha. Around it were placed smaller shrines to other gods and goddesses—simple huts with idols and altars.

The roof of the great temple was held up by four concentric rings of massive posts, growing taller as they neared the center, the circle cut through by three long aisles for druid processions. At its heart was an enormous oak tree shorn of branches, black now with age and the blood from old sacrifices. Its face had been crudely smoothed by the axe into a faint suggestion of a woman's features, grave and enigmatic. There were slight rises for breasts and an axe mark for her cleft, showing She nurtured them all. She was daubed in ocher, and fresh boughs of flowering hawthorn were wound about her feet, marking the season of fertility. Levarcham's heart had not joined with the women's chants, though, and it sat as a cold knot in her breast, as if the frosts could not melt from it.

Around the walls were ranged the talismans of the kings:

battered shields, swords, ceremonial armor kept lovingly burnished; many-colored cloaks, faded with age; cups, bowls, platters and mead-horns—everything that spoke of a king's sacred
communion with Macha to protect the land and give it life.

Levarcham had been praying for Deirdre, of course, and also
for Cathbad, the chief druid, who had taken a cough and fever
this long dark that would not shift. At her knee was a net bag of
bitter-root she had been collecting, to brew a draught for his
chest.

As Conor's servant delivered his message and left, she slowly
dragged herself up and kneaded the crooked joint of her hip.
This summons could mean only one thing.

She did not go straight to the king but to her own tiny hut
within the walls of the fort, washing her hands and rubbing at
the juice stains, combing out her gray hair and securing it behind the ears with the owl feathers of prophecy. She pinned her
gold-and-amber brooch on her cloak with shaking fingers. She
must draw her power around her as she did her woolen mantle.

The fort was subdued, for everyone had been affected by
Conor's simmering rage when he came back with his trackers,
even though Levarcham had not been able to find out anything
of Deirdre because he wouldn't see her. Until today.

The king was alone in his chamber, an alcove in the second-
floor gallery of his royal hall. The gallery floor was open at the
center, admitting the light and heat from the roaring fires below.
The alcove was hidden from passing servants by screens of
carved oak, and today was lit by only one sputtering lamp, which
cast shadows across the king's face.

Levarcham peered at him, hiding her shock. He was haggard,
his brows drawn low over glinting eyes, his jowls sagging from the
weight of his downturned mouth. His fingers hooked his knees
like he was clinging to something—or crushing something. For a
terrifying moment, she thought Deirdre must be dead.

"The girl is at Aed's dun."

A rush went up her legs. "Thank the goddess! I will make
ready to ride—"

A croak of laughter silenced her. "Before you do that, druid, you will listen to what she said."

Warily, Levarcham lowered herself to one of the oak benches.

"She sent a courteous greeting to the king of the Ulaid: dainty words that must have tripped so sweetly off her tongue." Levarcham was desperately trying to read his voice. "And, under the protection of Lord Aed, she wishes to exercise her right to sever a betrothal that was not of her own consent. She wishes to be released from the betrothal to *me*." His breath rasped, like nails scraping the mud wall. "And what do you think, oh learned one, of such a claim? You know the *brithem* laws." Conor swung to her with feral eyes. "Did you put her up to this?"

Levarcham tried moistening her dry lips but her tongue was stuck to the roof of her mouth. "You doubt the word of a druid?" she replied hoarsely. "You know that I had no forewarning. I have been here all through the long dark and you will find no messenger that bore my orders to her."

Conor's face twisted. "I don't care. Is what she says true?"

Levarcham was struggling to keep her wits beneath a tide of emotion. *My precious one! Not lost to the woods, but alive.* Then a darker rush came: *Foolish maid! You strike such a king and think no blows will be returned?* Terror for Deirdre spun her thoughts about, but in the wake came something she did not expect. Pride. The pupil had at last outshone the teacher. Deirdre, not Levarcham, had seen straight to the heart of the matter after all.

Levarcham had sought ways to cushion the blow, to buy more time, but she had never questioned the *very right* of the betrothal. When she came to Conor's service, it was already spoken of as an unassailable right. Because Conor believed it so forcefully, he made everyone around him believe it, too. Her trembling hand shielded her eyes from him. She had been blind.

"Woman!" Conor's hiss struck at her. "Answer me!" Fury rose from him like a heat haze.

Breathlessly, she lowered her hand, and if her heart pounded with triumph, she did not show it. "Given the unique circumstances of her birth, it's possible she has a claim in legal terms."

"It is not possible." He struck the arm of his chair. *"It's not possible!"* he bellowed and, dragging himself up, swept the ale jug to the rug, splattering the fine wool with dark liquid, like blood.

Levarcham clasped her hands in her lap. "Of course, it is Cathbad you must consult. The *brithem* laws are exceedingly complicated, and sometimes open to interpretation."

Her voice was admirably calm but, taking her by surprise, Conor crossed the room, his bony fingers fastening around her jaw, forcing back her head. His eyes were wild, his long gray hair uncombed. "And did you know," he whispered, "that she was stolen away by none other than Naisi of the black heart and his brothers? Did you?"

Levarcham kept still. She had never seen him lose his wits enough to lay hands on the sacred person of a druid. It was an outrage, but the sense in his eyes had been shattered by something she now recognized as humiliation—a force greater than anger. "You forget yourself," she gasped. He released her and staggered back, and she rubbed her windpipe. "No, I did not know." *I did not know for sure,* she amended. Blackbirds: the singing sons of Usnech. Deirdre would be drawn by their life-force, their laughter.

Conor spun about and gripped the back of his chair. "You told me she would be pliant. Even if you were not there when the theft occurred, still you have responsibility for this travesty. Still you bear blame!"

Hiding her wrath, Levarcham decided to divert him. She had never faced a greater challenge as satirist, but she would not fail now. "You use words such as *theft* and *steal* in relation to this...incident. Yet may I remind you that every piece of evidence points to Deirdre leaving of her own free will. And the proof is that she sought shelter from a powerful chieftain," she lingered over the word *powerful*, "and now seeks to dissolve your betrothal in a way that leaves no room for misunderstanding."

Her words merely bounced off the king's brittle rage, his eyes fixed on the wall. "It would have to be Aed, would it not?" he murmured to himself. He took a shuddering breath, his shoulders lowering. "Then he will be the first to learn that I will have no one stand in my way to her."

"This is not about the sons of Usnech, or of Aed," Levarcham snapped, "or about a girl defying you. It is about the law—laws that were designed to protect your own subjects."

The king would not listen. "Get me Cathbad," was all he said, his voice icy.

Outside, the chill wind hit her, pushing Levarcham so hard she had to wade through it, limping along with head down, her legs trembling to expunge her anguish. She ran straight into Cathbad on a path between the houses and told him what happened. He listened in silence, his tall, thin frame stooping to hear her, his breath laboring through his cough. At last he shook his head, the golden beads woven through his white braids clinking. His breastplate of shining jet was smooth against his thin, wrinkled neck, and bony fingers held a staff of polished oak. "So it comes," he said softly.

"What do you mean?" Against all propriety, her hand closed about the chief druid's forearm and only then did she feel the wasting of the muscle, the brittle bones. His bald crown was spotted with age, the veins on his brows blue and knotted. "She has as bright a heart-fire as the dawn itself." Her voice was uncharacteristically ragged. "Do not condemn her, I beg you."

Cathbad's fathomless eyes bore the milky cast of age, though his gaze still radiated power. "I will not lie to the king; I must ponder the legal weight of this. It is a strange situation. Clouded…"

"Yes!" Levarcham hissed. "Strange because there is no precedent, and if there is not, then perhaps the betrothal was not legal in the first place."

Cathbad coughed, his frail hand over his chest. "Perhaps."

Anger loosed Levarcham's tongue and she forgot he was ill. "You were there at the beginning. *Your* words condemned the babe before she'd even taken a breath. The least you can do is reverse the evil set in motion by those words."

Cathbad peeled off Levarcham's fingers and held them, his long, hollowed face grave. "Do not let love cloud your mind, daughter of the oak. Or your training," he added pointedly.

Levarcham could have cried out in frustration. Did the rigidity of druid minds sometimes veil a truth that more open hearts could feel? Levarcham had never learned so much about humans until she watched one grow from when it couldn't speak to when it lived such blinding truth. *She ran because it was the only way to hear the song.*

Levarcham had taught her that each spirit was a light shimmering with a different hue, vibrating to a different note. She had taught Deirdre to recognize the song of her own soul, know its color and melody well enough to leave the body for the birdforms and still come back. She had revealed that sacred path to her—*know thyself*—and all Deirdre had done was to follow that, wanting to be herself alone, not a shadow of someone else.

"My words did not curse the babe," Cathbad corrected. "I spoke only what I saw, what had already been set down. I argued with Conor at the time, and I bade him send her far away. That was all I could do."

Levarcham pulled back, her words choked. "Then in this, you can do more. You can set her free."

Cathbad shook his head. "You aren't listening. Druid power is that of the sacred, reaching through the veils from Thisworld to the Otherworld. A king's power is of Thisworld only: land, crops and beasts, the force of the iron blade. Both should wheel in balance, and indeed when one is out of balance the gods restore order. But Conor did not listen to me on this matter, which he sees as relating only to fleshly lusts and the marriage bed, not the sacred, and there was no divine prohibition or punishment I could reasonably bring to bear on him. Conor's will has often been contrary: he believes in his own cleverness too much."

"Then if he is not doing the will of the gods, he should be condemned as a fool and unseated from the king's hall," Levarcham whispered harshly.

Cathbad held her eyes. "There is no one who knows without

doubt the will of the gods except the gods. We can guess—we can feel and think—but we don't know. Don't fall into Conor's trap of deciding only you know the truth."

Levarcham remembered her training and returned tartly, "No one should be denied the natural freedom of their own hearts. That seems like a divine truth to me, Father, and not open to debate."

Cathbad nodded. "So it seems from the view of one heart. But these matters are part of a larger flow, pulling in not only the will of the warrior-nobles but matters of the Ulaid's safety itself. Eochaid of Connacht is sick and his daughter, Maeve, has run back to her brothers, and we do not know what will emerge from our great enemy now. Do you think anyone will upset the balance of power—the iron hold of Conor, who has been a strong king—for the sake of a kinless girl no one has ever seen?"

The cold wind scoured Levarcham's skin. "Yet one overturning of *her* right and wrong could change the fate of a kingdom. You taught me that."

"And that is what we tell kings," Cathbad agreed, "for our eyes are always on the stars, searching within their patterns for the fates of all. But a king's eyes are on his warriors, weighing up loyalty and bloodlust and how much hold he has over them, and how to *increase* that hold. And for some reason, in Conor's heart, your little Deirdre has become swept up in that. As chief druid, I have to think of all the people as a whole, not one."

"Nothing that blocks the powers of the wild spirits, the desire and fire, can be the best for the people!" She wondered where that came from, for she did not live that way; she stayed wrapped in the cool comfort of her mind.

"Ah, there you are wrong, indeed, child. For if everyone went about letting out their free-flowing desires, we would be in bloody chaos. " Suddenly he smiled, his spare, wrinkled face kind, if troubled. "I will do my best for the girl," he said. "That is all I can leave you with."

Skimming bark off a shaft of arrow-wood, Naisi paused at the
sound of voices. He was glad the budding hazel branches hid him
from sight so he could ignore them and be alone with his
thoughts.

His eye was caught by the gleam of Deirdre's golden hair in
the cold sunshine, and before he could stop it his gaze was seeking her through the trees. A crowd of young people came up the
slope from the marshes, the youths balancing bundles of willow
on their shoulders, the maidens swinging bags and sacks. Their
faces were flushed and they were chattering brightly.

"Say it again," one young man urged, walking at Deirdre's side.
He was dressed in rough-spun clothes and bore no weapons.
Deirdre did not spend much time with the nobles, preferring
the company of the craftspeople who turned wood into bowls
and wove baskets and cloth, for they were often outside gathering timber and rushes. Naisi had noticed she did not feel comfortable within walls.

She was shaking her head. "They were druid chants to bless
the willow and alder. They shouldn't be used lightly, I told you."

"But our druids certainly don't look like you!" The others
chuckled, and one of the girls dug the boy in the ribs with her
elbow. He ignored her, turning his shoulder to keep Deirdre to
himself. "Please?" he wheedled, the admiration clear in his smile
and eyes.

It was Deirdre's look that arrested Naisi: a sideways glint of
secret amusement at the clumsy flirtation. "No," she answered.
She glanced over into the bushes to hide her smile, and so only
Naisi saw it. "I sang it over the willow-beds, but you're not a willow so I won't sing it over you."

The youth's face flushed, and, compressing his lips, Naisi tried
to ignore them, holding the new arrow-shaft to his eye to check
for straightness. He could not while away his time in idleness.
Anxiety had been sitting like cold gruel in his gut now for a
week, and he kept making arrows and spears, as if ringing himself with blades would help. Unfortunately, he was too jaded to
fool himself like that.

The young man would not give up. "Look." He pulled a muddy tuber from the pile in the basket on his shoulder. "What do you sing over that?"

Deirdre took it and gravely examined it, rubbing the skin clean with her thumb. "Nothing," she said at last, and without further ado bit off a piece of the starchy flesh. "Though it's better roasted," she added around her mouthful. The others all burst out laughing and the bold youth scowled.

Naisi swallowed the obstruction in his throat. Didn't she know what danger they were all in? Then he stopped himself, fingering the adze in his hand. The lack of a response from the king was an expectant silence that was spreading through Naisi day by day—and Deirdre must feel it, for what he recognized in her was not flirtation but a desperation to savor every taste, smell and sound. He'd watched her eat with her eyes closed, halt in her tracks just to feel the wind. Didn't she drink it in because she knew any moment it could be torn from her?

He threw the shaft down and rose, suddenly restless. Deirdre saw the movement and shaded her eyes, before peeling away from the group and striding toward him. The young people carried on, the boy trudging along with a downcast face.

"Don't let me disturb your fun." Naisi gathered the arrow-wood shafts, confusion making his speech stilted. "I have something else to do."

Her smile faded. Her bones looked starker in the daylight, the hollows in her cheeks more pronounced. Guilt made him pause. She was more strained than he thought.

"If you are so busy," she replied, "I could help you instead." In contrast to her cool tone, her eyes flashed from under her brows, bright with irritation. Challenging.

The transformation was so swift Naisi had the breath knocked from him. "It's not something you could help me with."

"Try me." She held up her fingers, one by one. "With my foster-father I laid traps for hares and skinned them, gutted pigs with him, mixed brains to tan leather. I polished his daggers with wool-fat, set tallow candles and boiled birch-tar for his spears."

Naisi stepped back from this onslaught. "That might be so, but I doubt you'd want to scrub the dirt off my back in the river." What he knew was how to use a sword thrust when cornered.

Her neck mottled from collarbone to chin. "Well, I certainly wouldn't do that for *you*." Her words were weighted to suggest she might for someone else, and he regarded her with astonishment as she set off after her departing friends.

She was the cause of all this, his pain muttered. *Ach.* Would he give up the little honor he had to blame a girl for the momentum of his own limbs? *You agreed so Conor would think you brave,* she said. *So the warriors would admire you. You did it for yourself.* How Deirdre's words had needled him when he lay in his bed in the guestlodge watching the fire-shadows on the walls. It wasn't that simple and he wasn't so vain, but the sentiment had lodged in him like a shard of broken bone, pricking him whenever he drew deep breaths down to the dark cavern inside. He did do it for himself…and he had no idea where it might lead.

He realized he was staring at the outline of her thighs as she walked away. She had peeled off her hides down to a wool tunic and trews, and she wasn't as graceless as he'd first assumed on glimpsing her bundled up by the fire. She was formed of compact curves, with a small waist and strong buttocks. And her stride was not girlish. He'd already seen how she sensed the earth through her boots, feeling for the ground. Both warriors and hunters had to be alert to the tilt and density of the soil lest it give way, know the direction and force of wind, taste and sort scents. But how had she, a girl, learned a warrior's rhythm, a hunter's walk? Out of nowhere, Naisi was struck by a vivid image of her endlessly circling through the forest. Pacing. *Yearning.*

He turned on his heel and strode away, fixing his eyes on the rampart. They must leave as soon as possible. He had done what he said he would. She was here now. He drew an arrow to his nose, drinking in the familiar smell of raw wood, comforting and simple.

"The king has still sent no word," Ardan commented on Naisi's return to the guestlodge. He was sitting by the fire stirring a pot of sticky black birch tar. Beside him were an array of spear-hafts, iron points and rolls of dried sinew. Ainnle was fitting the points into the shafts, pausing to swig from a cup of mead.

Naisi leaned the bundle of arrow-wood against the wall and squatted by the fire. "It's not our concern." He spoke with a harsh edge. "We delivered her to safety, as we said we would."

"And now it's time to get out of here." Ainnle spoke around the strand of sinew he was softening between his teeth.

Ardan frowned. "And go where? The king will know we did this."

Naisi shrugged uncomfortably. "So? We haven't compromised her virtue after all." He lunged for Ainnle's cup and gulped mead, wiping his mouth with a rigid hand. "It might mean a barren few moons in some far-flung outpost, but by sunseason he'll have re-lented."

Ardan looked baffled by this contradiction of his earlier, bolder words, but Naisi's mind was churning. So he had used Deirdre to defy the king. What next? He ground thumbs into his eyeballs, thinking. Aed was a powerful chief who had always kept his distance from Conor. To make anything of this daring risk, he must ensure he was drawn into the old chief's confidence, and as a man now, not a boy. As a powerful warrior in his own right.

His thoughts simmered, dark as the tar. *Did* he still want to make something of this? That would bring what was long-hidden into the light, make it real. But he could still get out. They could go back and beg Conor's forgiveness...Naisi nearly retched at that thought. He didn't know what to do—a blankness now lay where days ago frustration had fired him.

Ardan smeared more tar around the hafts and handed them to Ainnle. "Perhaps we should just stay put for a few more days. Then we can see what happens to Deirdre."

"Why?" Ainnle said. "It was her choice. She made us take her."

"As I recall, we agreed of our own will," Ardan replied. "And now our names and hers are linked. The least we can do is make sure the king releases her."

Naisi got up, trying to shake off that numb indecision. "If there's a problem, she can stay with Aed."

"And if Conor does not agree?"

"Then her gamble failed, and she'll be carted off to Emain Macha as she would have been." Naisi's own dismay at the hole into which he'd flung them sharpened his voice.

"Into slavery!"

"She's going to be a queen; it's hardly slavery."

Ardan vigorously stirred the birch tar. "She can't stay if Conor refuses to release her from the betrothal. Aed has too many people under his protection to set himself against the king; too much to lose." He held Naisi's eyes. "Let us stay until we hear word, and then we will know what to do."

CHAPTER 14

Aed called his sons and nephews to attend him at the open-air temple of oak trees, where he sacrificed a new lamb to bless the sowing of the barley. Afterward, he wiped his hands as they all gathered near the entrance to the grove. "Conor's man came three nights ago." Aed could not meet their eyes, pushing up his sleeves to rub away the last traces of blood.

"In the night?" his son Niall repeated.

Aed's voice was grim. "It was a simple message: yield up the girl and the sons of Usnech immediately."

"*Yield up?*" one of his nephews repeated. "That is provocative language indeed!"

"Yes." Troubled, Aed gazed through the greening oaks down the hill, toward his fort, nestled on a low mound in the weak sunshine. The houses were wrapped in a comforting smoke that spoke of safety and warmth.

"Or what?" Niall demanded. Behind them, Lassar and the

other druids finished the rite, bending to peer at the entrails of the lamb with their divination sticks.

"There didn't have to be an 'or.' *Yield* is something you say to an enemy. *Immediately* is a bold demand that should only be wielded on lesser vassals than I." A nephew handed around a beaten gold cup filled with mead that had been blessed on the altar. Aed drank silently. In all these years, Conor had been wise enough not to try to force him to heel. He guarded the most dangerous length of the Ulaid borders—those butting up against Connacht—and in return was left alone to rule his own dominions. It was his choice to whom he offered shelter.

"What did you do, Father?"

"I sent him back a message of my own: the girl has a claim that needs to be legally debated. I asked him to send his druids and it could all be sorted out civilly. I made no mention of our other guests. This has naught to do with them, and Conor needs to keep his focus where it belongs."

The younger men all grunted in agreement, but Aed did not feel as confident as he sounded. No return answer had come from Conor, though enough time had passed. "I made no mention of this to you because I hoped it would be swiftly resolved. And I do not want the sons of Usnech knowing any of this yet; this is a *fidchell* game between Conor and I as we move our pieces on the board. They are not to go hunting alone anymore, but join them in companionship, not as guards. One whiff to Naisi that I am concerned, and he will leave, taking his brothers and the girl with him." He paused, Deirdre's sad face drifting through his mind, pushing her golden hair out of the way as she ran with his grandchildren. "If they leave, they are in danger. I want them here, so Conor knows that my power protects them."

One nephew darted glances at his cousins, then spoke with a frown. "But uncle, is this wise? You would only be worried if you think Conor is a threat, and if so we should be wary about sheltering these fugitives."

Aed sent him a severe look. "I was friends with Usnech, and in memory of his departed spirit I must help his sons. And if Conor thinks me weak on such a small matter, he will assume that age has wearied my body and addled my mind. He must be made to back down."

"And if you are too stubborn," another kinsman muttered, "you may give him an excuse to flex his authority. It is a dangerous game."

The sun broke out from beneath the clouds, flooding up the hillside and investing the grove with a warmth that entered Aed's aching bones. "I must follow my own conscience, or I have lost my power already."

As he edged himself back down the slope to the fort, trying not to hobble on the uneven path, his favorite nephew, Dallan, was behind his shoulder, with Aed's two younger sons, Sencha and Lugaid. "We will accompany the sons of Usnech this day, uncle," Dallan offered. "It might be prudent to stock up on our stores of meat."

Just in case, Aed finished for him, his heart darkening. The fumes of the mead burned all the way down his throat.

Naisi had his head down as he came back across the marshes, sling and bow over his back. It was a somber, gray day that matched his mood, the moor stretching out flat and featureless but for the wind soughing through the brown reeds, blowing fitful showers of rain into his face. The honks of geese came from all around, as if mocking him.

With every day drawing out with no word from Conor, he felt the dread rising in him. He and his brothers should be gone, but they were still here and he wasn't sure why. It would be better to know what Conor had said before they disappeared into the forest and lost contact with their allies, he reasoned. That was practical.

He was weaving along a narrow path through the high grass when a cloaked figure straightened from a crouch and blundered backward into him. She yelped and spun around, dropping the muddy fistful of plants at her feet. Unbalanced, Naisi's hands came out to steady themselves on Deirdre's shoulders.

She recovered, breaking into a relieved smile and pushing her hood back. "Sorry. I'm collecting bulrush roots and I have to keep my eyes on the ground."

He was too surprised by the warmth under his fingers to let go. "You should take care." His eyes were on her mouth, and confronted by that mysterious, self-contained smile, he was appalled to feel a rush of anger. He wanted to delve his nails into those shoulders to bring her back from her secret thoughts. How could she shrug off all this weight by picking reeds in a marsh? "Warriors are not geldings. You might find yourself in trouble if you come across one like this." That was all that came to him.

Not surprisingly, her smile faded. She swiped tendrils of wet hair from her cheeks and pulled back, ducking to pick up the discarded roots and shoving them in her net bag. "So far, I've seen they have better manners than that." The implicit lack of his own hovered in the ensuing silence.

He knew he was wrong, which only made his discomfort worse. "Manners don't come into it." He walked past her and turned, rolling the stone inside his sling. "You are in a different world now. You must grow wise in its ways." *It will fail you, disappoint you.*

She paused, her eyes bright and hard. "Thank you," she said steadily. "I'll remember that next time I get accosted on the marsh by a flock of geese."

He watched her stride off then break into a run, the soles of her boots showing brown against the bleached rushes. His irrational anger turned on himself. Why did she make him spout such things? It seemed he never knew what to expect of her, and that threw him, and all his darkness got twisted around.

"Naisi!" He looked up with relief at the sound of a male voice, seeing Dallan, Sencha and Lugaid loping jauntily toward him. "We've been looking everywhere for you. At dawn we leave on a deer-hunt, and we want you and your brothers to lead it. There's a valley we've left alone for a few years. It should be stocked with some beauties now."

Naisi instantly forgot about Deirdre and let himself be drawn along with the young warriors, their arms slung around his shoulders. Talk swiftly turned to which weapons to take, what weight of arrow-points—all manner of things he found more agreeable because they were straightforward, like his best hunting spear.

Two days passed, and the next morning the deer-hunters climbed over a pass in the hills to a cold plateau.

Naisi wriggled on his belly over patches of frosted mud, the crisp air prickling his throat. The group of young stags huddled together in the valley below, pawing up the sedge and chewing the thin buds on hazel branches. From behind a dead oak, Naisi peered down through the tangle of brambles and counted them. Ten.

He had taken refuge in a familiar world now, senses attuned to each faint noise in that hushed wood, his nose to the minute changes of wind. To either side, he was aware of the other hunters creeping through the bare woods, as if their bodies were joined on some primal level. After stalking the prey all day, they had stripped their hides down to dun-colored tunics, barely visible against the mottled background of bare earth, green buds and patches of frost.

Naisi leaned his cheek against the rough bark, sizing up which stag was weakest, with drooping head and thin girth. He wanted to leave the strongest, for they would be next year's challengers of the king stag. His brow still itched. Before the hunt they smeared themselves with the blood of a previous kill to invoke the kinship with their quarry, and purged their bodies with druid herbs, sending an unconscious part of their spirits to call the deer. His belly ached from the vomiting and his mind felt clear, a light shimmering at the fringes of his sight.

There were two good contenders for the kill. He signaled to

the line of hunters and Ardan and Ainnle nodded back. Aed's kin were watching his gestures; they looked to him to lead the chase. *It is honor for the Red Branch*, he told himself, though he could not help the bound of pride inside him. He paused to press the amulet around his neck to his lips, whispering to it. *We will honor you, and your gift will strengthen the herd.*

They all became still, the valley enveloped in a hush broken only by the crack of sticks as the stags pawed the ground. As one, the hunters smoothly came to their knees, each behind a tree. Naisi held his breath as he bent his yew bow, pulling the string back with its notched arrow. It was half his height and required great strength to draw the sinew, the grip shiny with the oil from his palms. His arms trembled with the effort and he breathed again, steadying his body, one knee up.

His would be the first barb to find its mark, he vowed to the Goddess. *And if you give this to me today, I will know I have done the right thing by aiding the girl.*

A flash of vivid color darted through his mind, blotting out the brown woods—moss-hued eyes and yellow-gold hair. A small wrinkle appeared between those imagined eyes and she rubbed it as she did whenever she was thinking hard. Naisi bit his lip. *Go away.*

The string stretched back. He savored the spring of the bow in his palm, the arch pushing on his wrist, the tensed strength of the wood stirring him with excitement. His eyes sighted down the shaft to the iron point, his mouth already watering at the thought of the rich deer liver roasted over a fire to return strength to them after the long trek.

He heard no noise but as one the stags' heads came up, dark eyes turning toward the slope above Naisi. A curse was already rising up his throat when he heard the whine of an arrow. *Who has taken my kill?*

No arrows flew toward the stags, though. Instead, swinging around, Naisi watched in shock as a white-fletched barb thudded into the ground by his thigh. He could not take it in and so for a breath did not move. *It came from behind.*

Suddenly more were falling all around. The stags snorted and spun around, thundering away across the valley. From somewhere to his left, Naisi heard Ainnle's curse, and from his right came a scream. Shouts erupted and Naisi staggered up, his own arrow escaping his fingers in a wild, skewed shot, the string flicking against his cheek with a harsh sting. Another scream came— *Aed's men, Aed's sons*—and he tried to wrench himself about, feeling for the sword that he'd left back at the dun.

His legs slid in the mud just as another whine came, then something struck Naisi in the left shoulder, and it was as if a flame had been kindled in his flesh. He gasped, the pain felling him, and dropped on all fours. Ainnle barreled past him, firing off arrows as Aed's men tore after their assailants through the woods. Ardan was looming over him, sinking on one knee while Naisi tried to speak, the shock twisting up his tongue.

Ardan shouted in wordless anguish, gathering him to his chest. But the force moved the arrow in Naisi's flesh and he cried out again as the dark took him.

CHAPTER 15

Deirdre was helping one of Aed's wives to roll thread from her spindle into a ball by guiding it around her spread hands. Suddenly the spindle stopped turning, the older woman's head lifting at the sound of shouting at the main gates.

Then a scream rose, high and shrill—a woman. Rushing outside with the others, Deirdre almost dropped the ball of thread when she recognized the ragged group of men limping between the gatetowers.

Instinctively, her eyes strained among them for dark heads,

black and sleek. She couldn't see them. Her senses were suspended, sound and sight faltering. Most of the men were grouped around a bier made of looped branches, heads low as they lifted its burden. Deirdre at last pushed her feet forward, the wool trailing from her cold hands into the mud…and she saw Ardan and Ainnle behind the bier, holding up a staggering Naisi. His body was almost hanging in their arms, head lolling. A little cry escaped Deirdre but it was drowned by an anguished wail from the women clustering about the bier.

Deirdre's fright stopped her tongue when she got close to the brothers.

Ardan's eyes were eerily blank. "We were attacked," was all he could get out. Ainnle's glance seared her, full of accusation and pain.

Then Deirdre saw an arrow haft, broken near the point, protruding from the muddy hides across Naisi's shoulder. All sensible thoughts were driven from her head. Naisi groaned and staggered, and only then did she hear Levarcham's voice taking over her mind, dry and cool. "This…this should have been drawn out."

"No," Naisi gasped, flinching away from her.

"It's only in the muscle, but he wouldn't let us cut him," Ardan panted. Deirdre hovered beside him, with no right to touch or offer comfort. "We must get him to Aed."

Deirdre followed, eyes on the shard of wood protruding from Naisi's back, his tunic stained with blood. The stain blurred in her eyes, the hue growing more lurid. *Your fault.* She knew it in her bowels.

They sat him by Aed's hearth, Ainnle bringing ale, Ardan and Deirdre wrapping a discarded cloak around Naisi. He shuddered, eyes glazed as if he couldn't see them, teeth bared in a snarl. His white face was streaked with mud and blood, like warpaint.

The hall was in chaos. Wounded men were being attended by their women while crowds surged around the bier, crying out in grief. Ainnle forced ale down Naisi, and Ardan chafed his hands, and there was a flurry at the door then as Aed rushed in. He went on one knee by the bier. "Dallan," he moaned. "Nephew...no..."

A woman sank at Aed's feet, sobbing incoherently. "My son... my son." Aed held his sister in his lap, his hands on her shaking shoulders. She became angry then, lifting a tearstained face and screaming, *"Who took him from me?"*

The cry was taken up by the other women as Aed's sons gave a stumbling explanation. An attack from behind, by stealth, on the chieftain's kin. Who would do such a thing? Deirdre gazed into Naisi's stark face with its deathly pallor. Her hand fell naturally on his, squeezing his limp fingers. "Let someone remove the point," she murmured. "It may fester—"

"It will stay," he hissed, his pupils dilated into emptiness. Before she could stop him, he staggered upright. Ardan scrambled up to support him, but Naisi shook him off. People stopped keening and stared up at that tall, bloodstained figure. "Who would do such a thing?" His voice faltered, he stared at Aed. "We know who would."

Aed moved his sobbing sister into the other women's arms and grabbed a bench to haul himself up. His wrinkled mouth was contorted with pain. "It is not possible."

"No?" Naisi's smile was terrible and he reached back and before anyone could stop him tried to wrench out the arrow.

"Naisi!" Ardan cried, as the point, its bindings loosened by the impact, broke off in his flesh.

Naisi staggered before feebly tossing the shaft at Aed's feet. There was no fletching on it, nothing but blood and splintered wood. "I give you your answer from Conor of the Ulaid."

A hush fell on the hall, broken only by the desperate sobbing of the dead man's kin. Aed's face was ashen, his shoulders slumped. "It's not possible," he repeated through bloodless lips. "No king—no lord, no *man*—would attack from behind, unprovoked. You are strained beyond reason to think Conor would commit such a cowardly, base, dishonorable act—"

Naisi's wild laugh cut him off. "And yet he is all those things." Holding his left arm, he wove drunkenly for the open doors, his brothers and Deirdre hastening after him. The stillness of the man on the bier was branded on her mind like the afterglow of fire. She gritted her teeth as a wave of sickness passed over her. This is what that urge for flight had wrought, what she had been driven to.

In their empty guestlodge, they managed to sit Naisi on a bed. "You must get that out," Deirdre said, eyes on the glint of metal amid the shredded flesh. At least it had not gone in far or hit a vein, for he had not fainted, and was no longer bleeding.

Naisi's mouth spasmed. "No."

She turned on Ardan. "You deal with such things all the time. You're warriors, aren't you?"

Ardan's face was unrecognizable. "We've never had to," he faltered. "People only shoot barbs in the hunt. We've taken sword cuts but not…this."

"Then get Lassar," she cried. "A healer—anyone!"

Ardan shook his head. "He won't let us," he kept repeating, and Deirdre recognized that horror had taken him. He was still caught in the moment when he thought he'd lost his brother. He would be no good, and nor would Ainnle, who just stood there panting and looking like he might kill someone with his bare hands.

A shudder went through Naisi and he turned savage eyes on her. "I will keep this in my flesh as a reminder of Conor's mark. For this has taken the Red Branch from me."

Ardan's legs gave and he sank on his knees. "Don't say such a thing," he gasped.

Beads of sweat were breaking over Naisi's brow, his words slurring, eyes glazed with delirium. "I will bear it to remind me of what he has done—he who betrays me now to the utter end— and if any of you take it from me I will count you an enemy, too!"

"Gods, Naisi!" Ainnle threw the cloak on the bed. "Calm down or you'll bleed again."

Ardan barely turned his head. "The shock has addled him. He doesn't mean it."

"I do, damn you," Naisi croaked, and he swayed on the bed, his hands digging into the furs. Ardan shook himself awake, ignoring his brother's protests and levering Naisi's legs under the covers in one movement, turning him on his side to avoid the wound. Naisi grasped his hand. "If anyone takes it out, I will kill them," he whispered.

"We heard you," Ardan replied faintly.

"I will not sleep."

"As you wish."

Deirdre tried to find Lassar and beg him to help Naisi, but he was closeted with the dead man's family. When she came back, Naisi was clutching his dagger to his chest as if Ardan was about to attack him. His eyes were closed and every breath was labored.

Ainnle had gone to find out what he would of Aed. After a time he returned. "They are deep in mourning," he said to Ardan. "He was Aed's favorite nephew."

Ardan collapsed by the fire and rested his forehead on his knees. Without thinking Deirdre placed a hand on his shoulder. When he raised his face, she saw branded there the moment when the arrow struck his brother.

Naisi's rasping breath calmed as dusk approached. His eyelids lowered and Deirdre thought he slept, but when she checked him they were still open a slit, the dark pupils fixed on the fire. She had no idea what thoughts made his gaze so intent, and he did not speak them. At last, she made up her mind to get the brothers to hold him down and take the point out by force, and went for water to bathe the wound. When she came back, the bed was empty, the lodge deserted.

Cursing, she hastened to the hall, to see Naisi standing before Aed once more, though this time the chieftain was alone but for the servants that crept around the hearth on hushed feet. Ardan and Ainnle hovered behind their brother, stricken.

The old chief was sitting by his nephew's bier. Outside on the meadow, a pile of branches was already being assembled for a pyre. The hall doors were open to let the spirit pass forth, and

Aed sat in the freezing draft of evening staring down into his kinsman's gray face. The body had been covered with an embroidered blanket, and the man's bow and sword placed by his side.

Naisi stood with loose hands, his eyes no longer delirious. He swayed a little. "You have to see the king for what he is: a betrayer of oaths. Of hearts." His voice broke.

Aed's breath rattled his chest. "It must have been Connacht—"

"The other kingdoms raid our cattle in horsebands, or openly challenge us to combat. No Erin warrior creeps up from behind, or kills by stealth." He paused, adding hoarsely, "But the king is no warrior—he has never taken our oaths."

"That is unimaginable. It must have been someone else—a blood feud, perhaps, for you have killed many men. Or someone taking revenge on me..." Aed trailed away, lifting reddened eyes to Naisi's face. "You can fire such accusations at the king because you are young, and have no one to guard but yourself."

"Then we will leave you," Naisi answered. "We are putting you in danger."

Deirdre's gaze was on his bloody tunic, and she barely heard the words that would tear her away from this one chance of safety at Aed's dun.

Aed winced as he stood, then placed a gentle hand on Naisi's good shoulder. "No. Here I can protect you from whoever seeks to harm you. But for the sake of the gods, let that wound be cleaned." Naisi wavered, and Aed cupped his black head with a veined hand. "Would you inflict the added grief and shame of *your* death on my hearth?"

That was the right thing to say. Naisi nodded. "As you will. For you."

Back at the lodge, he asked his brothers to take his condolences to the dead man's family. When they had gone, he let his weakness show, sinking on the bed into the hollow of the deerskin covers. To Deirdre's dismay, he thrust his dagger at her, hilt first. "There is no one else. You take it out."

She gaped at him. "Me?"

"The druids are engaged in funeral rites, and I cannot..." His lashes lowered. "I cannot face the women of this dun who tend to such wounds, not when they mourn so...when in my heart I know I was the target. I cannot see Aed's kin." When she remained silent, he barked, "You said your Levarcham taught you everything."

She chewed her lip, keeping her distance. "Not this. I picked herbs with Aiveen, but they were the same hearth-herbs any woman knows."

"Well, you're a woman, plainly, and I am not."

Deirdre thought of Fintan showing her how to skin a hare, shaving between the tiny membranes with nudges of the blade. She *had* found it fascinating, appreciating the elegance and beauty of the animals, seeing the sacred mark of the gods in their intricate designs. The thought of touching him wasn't fascinating, though, only daunting—for he was large, angry and undeniably alive. "But...your brothers..."

"They care too much about me to do it."

She was surprised by the bleakness his blunt words triggered. He was right. She stood outside all kin bonds, all sense of belonging to anyone here. She was just a useful pair of hands to him.

Silent now, she left water boiling and went to procure yarrow, knitbone and sponge-moss from women in the nearby huts, and a set of dye tongs. When she came back, she tore up one of Naisi's tunics into bandages and poured boiling water over the herbs to steep, except for the knitbone, which she ground against the hearth using a meat-knife. She took up a cup of willow-bark syrup she'd begged from one of Aed's wives and moistened her lips. "I have to cut the skin, and this will help the pain."

The smoldering flame in his eyes had now turned inward. "Will it blur my mind?"

"No."

He turned his chin away. "I would rather feel the pain Conor caused."

"Gods, you're stubborn!"

"It's the way I'm made. If you don't like it..."

"It's not a good idea to insult the person tending you."

"Or harangue the patient."

She sucked in her lower lip, biting it to steady her temper. "Take off your tunic, then." She turned the dagger in her hands. In the firelight, the blade glinted with engravings of curled designs, like vines, and the hilt was antler, carved into a deer's leaping body. He wore another figurine like this on a dark leather thong around his neck—a smaller amulet of gleaming deer horn, brown and cream, that nestled in the hollow of his throat beside the stained tusk of a boar.

Her patient lay facedown, his skin pale against the ruddy hides. His shoulders were formed of great slabs of ridged muscle, his upper arms molded by unfamiliar furrows and rises. She did not possess those ridges, that bulk, and their strangeness only made the situation feel more surreal. His black hair fanned across the pillow and, despite her pity, the set of his jaw triggered a jolt of frustration. He should have got someone else to do this. He should have ripped it out in the forest. Instead, he seemed to want to hold on to something that pained him, just so it would pain him more. *Conor.* He held on to rage at Conor.

She had not questioned Naisi's assertion that the king was responsible, for though she knew little about warrior honor, her rage could suspect *him* of anything. She still heard the grief in that woman's voice. She still saw the pain in Aed's kind eyes.

The dagger-hilt felt hot to her touch and she was taken by a primitive impulse to stab it into flesh and wrench Naisi open, to join with that fury that men could let out in war-cries and sword-strokes, and blood-scented air. *Gods. She was going mad.* She had to use all her will to focus on the shredded edges of the wound, closing her eyes and summoning the memory of Fintan assessing her knife skills. It had been a challenge, something to conquer. Just like this. "Hold on," she croaked, and made two firm swipes at right angles to the wound, where the arrow was caught. The skin gave just like that of dead hares, but her stomach turned when Naisi stiffened, a whistle of breath escaping him.

Fresh blood oozed over the dried crust and, gnawing on her

cheek, Deirdre clasped the iron tang of the arrow with the tongs and slowly teased the tip free. Naisi grunted as it slid out and blood spilled down his shoulder blade. She staunched the wound with the sponge-moss and peered at it; it didn't seem deep after all. In silence, she bathed the cuts and smeared on pulped knitbone before bandaging.

She'd been holding her breath to put some distance between them, but heat radiated from his downy skin and raised the hairs on her arms until at last she was forced to gulp air. She inhaled a waft of Naisi's sweat, and salt, and something that lurked beneath all that—a subtle musky scent. Hurriedly, she finished and stepped back to a safer distance.

"At least it was not my sword arm," he murmured, edging onto his good side and staring at the wall behind her. "I will need to wield my blade again soon."

Though his voice was hoarse, the tone was silky and danger-ous. It reminded her of the way he traced his sword with a finger-pad when he polished it at the fire. She shook off her unease, fetching the draught of yarrow. He peered at the cup with suspi-cion. "Another potion to take my wits?"

"It will leave any wits you *do* possess—though the quantity is up for debate." His brows lowered. "Gods!" she exclaimed. "It's only to cleanse the blood, so no fever takes hold." She busied her-self washing the tongs and knife as he gave in and drank.

Soon he lapsed into silence. And then, after a time, though his jaw was gritted, it at last slackened. Even he could not resist sleep. Ardan and Ainnle came back in, checked on their brother and, comforted by Deirdre's assurances and thoroughly ex-hausted, crawled into their beds and were soon flat-out snoring.

Deirdre didn't want to leave the stool by Naisi's bed, even though she kept dozing then waking with a flail of her arms as she thought she was hitting the ground. After a time, she couldn't fight her heavy eyes and so slid to the cushions on the floor and rested her head on the bed-furs.

In the quiet hut, Naisi woke. For a time he was occupied with fighting the agony of the wound, with its ceaseless burning. He wiped sweat from his brow, looking at the others to take his mind off it. Deirdre's face was lost amid a tangle of fair hair, her breath wheezing. He tentatively reached out for the presence of his brothers, but the cut cramped again and all other feelings were eclipsed by the *one*. Betrayal. The pain inside his soul was greater than in his flesh, exquisitely sharp. And wound through it was a terrible, burning shame. In allowing that sliver of secret desire to escape, had he drawn that arrow to him? *To Dallan*. Dallan had died.

He went back to the hunt in his mind, floating above the scene now as the arrow spun again through the chilled air. He saw it enter his body. He watched the barb part the layers of his skin and muscle, cutting the tiny threads that wove flesh together and all that had bound him to the Ulaid, to the Red Branch. He imagined it all with excruciating clarity, and that was better than hearing the howl in his heart.

It was a sundering—of veins, of bonds—and now only pain joined him to Conor. For just as if the unmarked arrow trailed a thread back to Emain Macha, the tug on his instincts, the sense of his body, knew without doubt that the shaft had been loosed at the king's orders. Aed did not allow himself to believe. Naisi's brothers were suspicious, but ultimately not ready to conceive of such an act. Naisi, though, had felt it cleave his flesh, and so he knew.

He could not digest the speed with which his choices had been torn from him. For years he had mentally played with his ties to the king, drawing them out, testing them. Now that which bound him to the Red Branch had been brutally cut—their shared oaths to protect the kingship and Emain Macha; the freedom to spar with them on the green and drink beside them in the hall. For they gathered about the throne of the Ulaid, at the feet of one who had betrayed him.

Wincing, he reached up to touch the Red Branch band that was always about his upper arm. One arrow-head had severed all other paths. There was no going back. There was no making amends. There was no pride in guarding that king or his dun, only humiliation and shame if he returned. There was no way to retreat, only to stumble forward now like a hunted beast, pushed along one trail.

Outcast.

"Deirdre." His voice swam through her dreams, calling her back. She found it imperative to struggle out of slumber. "Deirdre."

When she forced her eyelids open, her face was next to his. The firelight over her shoulder set a tiny reflected flame in his black pupils. She sprang upright, rubbing the creases from her cheeks. "Are you in pain?"

"No." His features were more vulnerable than she had ever seen them. "I didn't mean to bully you to cut me, I just didn't think you'd actually do it." Pain softened his mouth.

She leaned her elbows on the bed. They were cocooned in a circle of ruddy light. "There are many things you don't know about me."

"And you me. Though you've found out that I'm stubborn."

She smiled warily, relieved he was no longer delirious. "You are not alone in that. I used to think it drove Levarcham mad, but now I wonder if she secretly loved it."

He grunted. "I don't think anyone loves it in me." He eased onto his back, wincing, one hand under the blanket on his chest. He glanced over at Ainnle, who smacked his lips, muttering to himself in sleep. "It's because I had to look after them when they were little, after Fa died..." He trailed away.

There must only be two or three years between all the brothers, Deirdre thought. He would have been small as well. *And now I've forced him to protect me.* Since the attack, she had been thinking of immediate things: the horror of his injury, digging out the blade and stopping the blood. Like a shadow that had been waiting with wings spread over her, now she at last looked up into darkness. She knew in her flesh that it was Conor who had attacked—and if so, he had refused her. "If the king did this, it's because of my presence here." A shiver unraveled her voice.

There was a pause. "Our presence."

No, the danger had flown after *her*, and struck with deadly swiftness. Now she had looked into a dead man's face. She had seen an arrow lodged in that smooth expanse of Naisi's skin. She may as well have sliced through those two bodies herself. "I cannot bring pain like this to Aed. I have to leave." She summoned the memory of playing with the children, all those sweet rushes of freedom. Then, holding them for a moment to her heart, she let them fall away. This was no game.

"I agree. We must go."

"What 'we'? I have to release you, I should never have risked this." As Naisi's face hardened, she hissed, "And don't say you have no choice." She would go back and agree to wed Conor. That was a fair price to pay to save people like Aed, Ardan, Naisi and even the glowering Ainnle. She would send another message to Conor tomorrow, at dawn . . .

"Deirdre." He was looking at her hand clutching the blankets, and she wondered if she imagined the faint stirring of his fingers toward hers. "It is plain that though he wants to wed you, he wants to kill *me*." His breath was forcefully expelled, the words tumbling out as if he had nursed them for hours. "I can never go back to Emain Macha now. With you or without you, I am outcast, and so there is no sense in us abandoning you."

"It is too dangerous," she stammered, frantically switching her gaze from his eyes to the wall so he could not see how she longed to grasp for that safety.

"You are quite the master of a skinning knife, but you'll last no time on your own, and you know it."

"I can't ask that of you."

"You are not asking. I am telling."

She steeled herself, meeting his determined eyes. "I don't care what you say. You *are* in more danger with me—and *you* know it."

He smiled bleakly, and faced with that naked despair, she distantly felt something shift in her, like burnt embers in a fire. "The deed is done. Conor lost his chance to end this when he sent such traitors after me. I could never abandon anyone to him: man, woman nor child."

Deirdre sat back on her knees. "Then there is ... no way out for you?"

"Not even if you went to him right now—and that would be a pointless bravery. Dallan's life is worth more than that." He glanced at the roof, his fist curling up under the deerskins. "*Live,* or that death will have been in vain." He said this so fiercely she felt he spoke it to himself.

"But there must be a way to resolve this! Perhaps we can seek aid from someone else, someone more powerful than Aed."

Naisi shook his head. "The same would happen."

"What about going to Maeve of Connacht? She left Conor, so she will understand..."

Naisi's obvious revulsion stopped her tongue. "I would rather die than join the Ulaid's enemy. That would be like renouncing my gods. Do not ask that of me."

"Then I will go alone, so you are in no more danger."

"You're not listening!" His voice broke and his clenched fist came out from the blanket. He opened it. The cleaned arrowhead lay there, the light moving along the point as if it breathed. "The danger is already among us."

She folded her arms and leaned her forehead on them, afraid for him to see her. She had to find a way to stop this. He grasped her wrist. "Only one thing has come to me in my dreams: find a place to live namelessly, as common folk. Buy time for Conor's anger and pride to cool, time even for him to be overthrown." Her head came up and she caught the spasm of his jaw that he turned into a cold smile. "See it as an adventure; I'm sure you dreamed of them as a child."

She took her hand away, because the sense of his pulse beating against her wrist was unbearable. "I never dreamed of blood and death."

"That's what makes up the other half of bard tales."

The fire hissed with jets of blue-green flame, filling the room with a sibilant noise as Deirdre tried to form words to beat him back. But there were none, for despite her pain, something had sprung to life.

Hope came in a fierce leap, and it would not let her lay down her head and wait for the wolf, her throat stretched back.

CHAPTER 16

There was a port on the great expanse of Lough Neagh, a gathering place for the tribute that flowed to Conor down the River Bann from his northern chiefs. Flanked by banks of rippling oars, hide curraghs and log-boats flew south across the wind-whipped waves of the lake, avoiding a difficult trip by cart through the marshes. In the storehouses at the southern shore, the tribute was counted and then carted to Emain Macha on Conor's royal road—a trackway of oak planks cut from an ancient forest.

On a fine day, Conor rode to the port in his chariot, and ahead of the horses went lines of bards blowing long, curved bronze trumpets shaped like ram-horns. The wailing song spread far over the water, sounding like a flock of the *sídhe* riding the skies to battle, or a march of gods. Ranks of Red Branch warriors rode behind the king. Their bridle trappings were set with coral and amber, shields fixed on their saddles so the hammered bronze fittings caught the strengthening sun. Their hair was lime-washed into peaks, like long manes. People lined the road to see them, and crowded the shore to watch the bobbing boats and the king with piles of bronze, hides and sacks of barley at his feet.

By midday, the wind had swung around, cutting across the cold waves with the sharpness of knives, and Ferdia blew into his hands—a habit to keep his fingers supple for the sword. He stood beside Cúchulainn in the Hound's chariot so they had a good view of the proceedings. Cúchulainn was wrapped in his champion's cloak, the wool dyed with costly imported Greek scarlet. The ridged disk brooch holding the cloth was so large it glowed like a sun on his breast. He did not shiver in the wind as it tugged on his fair hair, his face watchful. His chariot-driver, Laeg, leaned with folded arms on the yoke between Cúchulainn's horses, the Gray of Macha and the Black of Saingliu.

Ferdia cast an eye over the warriors on the rocky shore as chieftains landed and presented their tribute to Conor, and his druids tallied the marks on rolled leather. He sensed restlessness among the younger men, and shaded his eyes. A man had come ashore from a large curragh, directing servants to heave sacks at the king's feet.

A rumble of voices rose and Cúchulainn's head went up. *Ah*, Ferdia realized. It was an uncle of Naisi's, gifting his clan's tribute. Ferdia tried to sort the whispers breaking out among Conor's retinue. *Where were the sons of Usnech? Where was the girl?*

"He knows something," Ferdia murmured into Cúchulainn's ear. For days the king had been closeted in his chamber, leaving the hall to seethe with rumors. Whenever Ferdia glimpsed his face, he was shocked at its pallor, the hollow pupils devoid of feeling. "But he won't face us. He's humiliated."

"A man is only humiliated by choice," Cúchulainn answered. "If his own pride is strong enough, no one can shame him."

Ferdia glanced wryly at his friend. It was easy to say when you were the Hound of Cullen and your pride was utterly unassailable because of your prowess. The Source flowed through Cúchulainn like a wide river. For all others, Ferdia thought bleakly, it's a patchy trickle of water. The sun was making him sweat beneath his ceremonial armor—a set of breast and belly plates made of scales of polished horn, thin and gleaming. "I think the nuances of that might have escaped the king, Cú. But if it's merely a rut he's after, he should empty himself into a dozen maids and be done with it."

Cúchulainn snorted, and the Hound's wife, Emer, glanced over from her place among the noblewomen, her smile tinged with concern. She somehow sensed her husband's mood across the breadth of that crowd. Ferdia did not see the Hound glance back, but Emer's eyes warmed as if the sun had touched them. Ferdia quashed another surprising pang, then smiled grimly at himself. Such joinings of the heart were rare and, after all, he had Cú, his sword and the Red Branch. *Such desires can also kindle darkness*, he thought then, watching the shadows in Conor's eyes.

A hooded druid was making his way through the crowd, approaching the king with a forceful stride. Conor's personal guards stepped forward, hands on sword-hilts. A hushed silence fell when the druid revealed his head, though Ferdia could only see brown hair wound with feathers. At the sight of him, the hollowness in Conor's expression was eclipsed by something else.

"I have terrible tidings," the druid declared, the words carrying over the water. It was rare for one to speak so boldly without the king's leave.

"You will address me in the proper manner in my hall," Conor said, mustering a cold authority, "and perhaps Cathbad will approach you about your lack of respect."

The young druid flung up his head, and Ferdia got the impression he had chosen this public confrontation. "I am Lassar, servant of Aed, son of Cumall, and I bear news of a traitorous attack on a Red Branch warrior!" All the men exclaimed. Ferdia's lungs deflated at the same time a hiss escaped Cúchulainn.

"Of whom do you speak?" Conor cut in.

"Naisi mac Usnech, who is under the protection of my lord's oaths."

A mass breath was released by the surrounding warriors. "Aed," Cúchulainn was muttering. "Why didn't I think…"

Conor seemed just as shocked, and in the silence Lassar kept going. "The traitor loosed an arrow at him from the woods—*at his back*. In the same attack, Aed's nephew—a man most dear to him—was slaughtered."

The grumblings were punctuated by a horrified shout, and Illan, mac Roy's son, demanded, "Who would do such a thing?"

Cúchulainn turned to meet Ferdia's eyes and his gaze burned. Such an attack violated all warrior codes.

"And what of Naisi?" The king's pallor was now distinctly gray. Ferdia saw shock in his face, yes, not calculation, and the knot in him loosened. The sons of Usnech had enemies. They were too fair, too successful at battle and hunt. Men had died on their blades: men with sons and brothers and cousins. Someone had taken advantage of Naisi's predicament—a coward who was not Red Branch.

"Naisi lives," Lassar announced. Another rumble of noise ran over the crowd.

Conor did not move for a moment, then turned toward the water. He passed a hand over his eyes as if in pain. The wind lifted his graying mane from the thin gold circlet that crowned his brow. "That is welcome news, though it comes with the grief of a death." When he swung to face them again his face was furious. "I condemn this act and Naisi's attacker. Being so close to the borders, it must have been Connacht—curse them to mortal agonies!"

Connacht-men raided openly, Ferdia found himself thinking, and were unlikely to attack a few deer-hunters. It must be a blood feud of some kind, instead. Meanwhile, the other warriors had joined in with Conor's righteous dismay, all shouting and speaking over one another.

Lassar's mouth thinned as Conor strode toward him, the king's heavy embroidered robes filling out in the wind. "Tell my loyal chieftain I am sorry for his senseless loss, and this is another reason for him to draw closer to my protection." The druid's eyes smoldered, though he nodded as Conor continued. "Tell him I will make amends, that it was obviously the presence of *my* warriors who drew this attack."

Cúchulainn leaped off the chariot, striding so fast that the men around him drew back, wary as always. "Let me go to him, my lord. This crime only makes it clearer that Naisi and his brothers should return to the bosom of the Red Branch, where they belong."

"Why are they with Aed, anyway?" some of the young men wondered aloud. The king's youngest son, Fiacra, shifted uncomfortably while his friend Illan, Fergus's son, openly glowered.

"They made a mistake," Cúchulainn said, his steady voice cutting through the noise. "They fell in with company they did not anticipate."

"They dishonored me," Conor returned softly, though when he met Cúchulainn's eyes there was the slightest hardening of his face. "If they bring the girl back and beg me for a pardon, I will relent and they can come home. *That's* when they will be safe."

"Send them a pardon first, make it clear you forgive, and it will all be over." Color crept back into Conor's thin cheeks, and Cúchulainn persisted doggedly. "Your quarrel is with the maid alone, for she went willingly. The brothers must have thought they were helping you by aiding her."

The king had been cornered by the Hound before all the warriors and most of the population of Emain Macha. He straightened with one arm behind his back, the other hand stroking his beard. It was his familiar stance, carefully chosen to appear composed in contrast to his boisterous warriors. He addressed Lassar, who had been watching this exchange with sharp eyes. "Was he chastened at least by this...incident?"

Lassar chose his words. "He is understandably angry."

"See?" Cúchulainn broke in. "He will not be thinking straight. Let me go to him—"

"No. Not unless he asks first for my forgiveness." Conor met the eyes of his warriors one by one. Many dropped away. "Would you have it known a young stripling got the better of your king? How do you think the Connacht-men would react if they heard that? They would assume my power is slipping, and might seek to take advantage once more in our perceived moment of weakness. This is what Naisi has wrought with his willful disobedience."

Ferdia's mind was buzzing so much he wanted to shake his

head. Again Conor was invoking a danger to the Ulaid. *He links the threat of Connacht to one willful maid and a rash young warrior?*

Blunt Leary spoke up. "The king is right," he said gruffly, avoiding Cúchulainn's hard gaze when it swung toward him. "We all love him, but the boy has been an abject fool. He is endangering us with his pride. He must learn his place." Leary, too, had always been jealous of Naisi.

The other men were unsure, darting dark looks about. "Take this message to them," Conor said to Lassar. "Send the girl back, ask for a pardon and have them come here with swords over palms and knees bent. I am a forgiving man."

Lassar spoke through gritted teeth. "My king is aware that Aed has offered the maiden Deirdre protection. *That* is a druid matter. The young men are his guests, which is a separate issue."

"Whether a druid matter or one of marriage," Conor snapped, "the fact is, they must all come to Emain Macha so it can be laid to rest. Tell them that, and tell your lord that, too. My man will travel with you bearing the mourning gifts I promised."

Lassar's eyes spoke volumes but he bowed again, stiff-backed, while the king dismissed him with a wave.

The crowd parted again as Cúchulainn clambered back into his chariot, Laeg leaping forward to hand him his ivory spear for the ride. Cúchulainn turned away to mutter in Ferdia's ear, "We must be in the saddle to Aed's as soon as we return to Emain Macha."

In Lassar's absence, there had been a mysterious raid on one of Aed's homesteads near the Connacht border, with many killed. Aed told Lassar this on his return, though the chieftain was finding it hard to speak, for age had suddenly crept into every cavity in his body.

Visibly alarmed at Aed's haggard appearance, Lassar whispered Conor's words into his ear. Before Aed could react to them, the king's man who had accompanied Lassar from Lough Neagh hastened forward to say he had a message of his own to present. He said the king's order was for him to speak to Aed absolutely alone. Despite Lassar's protests, Aed was too heartsick and weary to argue. He waved his druid and the servants away, until he and the king's messenger were left in the dim, echoing hall.

The man did indeed bring mourning presents from Conor, including bronze rings and bolts of cloth. The true gift, however, was hidden in the bottom of his pack, and he laid it at Aed's feet as if in homage.

It was an arrow, a hank of scarlet-dyed threads trailing from the tang like a trickle of blood. The sign of the king of the Ulaid. The kneeling messenger kept his face averted while Aed stared down at the gleaming point, as all the warmth drained from him.

The man's voice dropped to a hiss. "If you had returned the girl and her lover, there would have been no barbs flying from the silent forest, no kinsmen dead or steadings burned. But worse will come if you do not yield them up now—or if you breathe a word of this to another. This is his last warning to you."

Ainnle stared at Naisi stuffing belongings into his pack in the guestlodge. "I don't understand. You should be resting."

Naisi worked one-handed, his fist on his wounded side clasped to his chest. "I am rested enough. The cut looked worse than it was." Ainnle glanced at Deirdre, crouched on a bench with arms tight about her knees.

Ardan came from their beds with sleeping hides and dropped them by the fire. "There was a raid on Aed's lands."

Naisi grunted as he added his shaping piece to his pack, his sharpening stone, his flints and tinder rolled in buckhide. He turned to wrap his bow-string. "They say it is Connacht, but I know." He paused, his wounded shoulder twitching, and the stab went through Ainnle as if the same point had pierced him.

"I still don't…you can't really believe the king did this…" Ainnle's voice sounded frustratingly young to his own ears, asking a question for Naisi, as always, to answer.

"Even if you don't believe me, it's too much of a coincidence after so many quiet moons." Naisi looked at Ainnle. "And if there's any chance at all—will you risk the safety of Aed's people by staying?"

Ainnle shook his head. He knew he should be pained at the news of the raid, and he was, for Aed. But he was instantly consumed with the desperation to get Naisi away from here.

His eldest brother reached for his scabbard and, still favoring his sore side, awkwardly belted it over his back. "Aed will try to hold us here out of love and pride, of course, but we cannot have it. That is why we must go now, in secret."

Ainnle could not help the relief that broke over him. There would just be the three of them again, and these torturous days of waiting, of inaction and dread, would be over. Three and only three: the core of his heart. He only felt like Ainnle mac Usnech when they were alone in the forest together. Other people fractured them and he lost the sense of himself. Other people thought him nothing, the youngest, the last-born. When three ran as one, they *were* one.

"We will leave Aed gifts for Dallan's family." Ardan took a bronze-and-enamel ring from his finger, placing it on the hearth as Naisi did the same with a buckle off his belt. One of Ainnle's brooches clanked on the pile. Then he saw Deirdre untie something from her neck, raw amber chunks strung on sinew. The necklet clattered on the stone and Ainnle realized what it meant. "She's not coming." He turned on his eldest brother. "If what you say is true then she's bait for he who follows, Naisi!"

Naisi's glance pierced him. "So you would spare Aed and his family but not a maid? You shame me."

The words hit Ainnle and burrowed in painfully. Anger at *her*, and humiliation that Naisi would say such a thing. "She *did* heal him," Ardan reminded Ainnle. He glanced warily at Naisi, doubt warring in his eyes. "And it's not her fault, and we cannot take the chance of leaving her if Conor's wits really have deserted him. He could kill her, if he's as mad as Naisi says."

It is her fault, Ainnle thought fiercely. Now was not the time, though, for he cared only for getting his brothers away.

"Ainnle is right," the girl spoke up, and he glanced at her in surprise. He expected petulance, and the lack of it inexplicably made him more ashamed and therefore angrier.

"We've had that out, Deirdre," Naisi growled. "That's enough, from all of us. We have to leave before anyone realizes. Hurry up."

Ainnle applied his frustration to assembling his own belongings, pulling the thongs so tight about his pack that they escaped and burned his fingers.

CHAPTER 17

Cúchulainn and Ferdia arrived at Aed's dun two days later to find the brothers and Deirdre had already fled. They went back to tell Conor they had lost the tracks. The king was conscious of all his Red Branch warriors eyeing him as he strode about the stable yard trying to contain his wrath, summoning messengers, trackers and huntsmen.

Cúchulainn and Ferdia changed horses and demanded to be given leave to continue the search. Conor could find no way to refuse, though the Hound's blind love for the brothers made him suspicious of his intentions. Conall and Dubthach set out in another direction and Illan and Fiacra stayed together, their flaxen heads bobbing down the river trail as they cantered their horses northward.

Conor watched them go, then called to him Leary and a group of other warriors who were not Red Branch. Standing on the rampart of Emain Macha, he twirled a gold arm-ring that would buy fifty fat cows for the man who won it. The warriors eyed the shining ring. "This goes to he who returns Deirdre to me," Conor murmured. "The betrothal was legal, and so it will be proven. Now the brothers are alone and no longer hiding behind Aed's shields, they will be more easily…convinced."

"Do you want them captured?"one man asked eagerly.

"They will be hard to subdue." Leary's eyes were on that gold. He had never been the richest of warriors, for though he captured booty, he had to give much of it away to make women lie beneath his ill-formed body. No black hair, blue eyes and full lips here.

"I do not care about Naisi." The king forced the name between his teeth. "I just want her back."

Another warrior spoke. "I have heard Naisi guards his honor jealously. He'll soon see that its loss is not worth a mere poke of a—" He cut himself off, gulping.

Conor's mouth moistened with bitterness. The jealousy was a sickness. "Then you'd better find him first, if you are so sure you will be successful."

"Indeed, my lord."

"One last thing." Conor lifted the ring so that sunlight reflected over their faces. "Go to Usnech's dun in the territory of Dalriada and apply to see Naisi's mother. Tell her you seek them to deliver my pardon, if only you could find them."

"A pardon?" Leary frowned. "I thought…"

"Ask where her boys played as children, the secret places they loved." Conor saw only the glints of the sun on the stream below. His mouth moved, but he hardly felt his mind make the thoughts or his lips the words. Some other ruthless part of him could take over to keep his kingship, to hold up his world from crumbling as the great oak pillars did his hall. "Tell her they are in great danger if Connacht's warriors find them first. It is always prudent to listen to a mother's heart."

Leary grunted. "That is clever."

"There is as much worth in minds as in sword-arms," Conor retorted. When they had gone, he leaned on the timber palisade to stare out over the river meadow, fastening the arm-ring over his wrist. Farther along, the guards covertly watched him from the shadows of the gatetower. He shifted the other way, toward the sun, and slitted his eyes until his vision blended into one mist of gold, and the world became light again for him.

Deirdre came dancing toward him through that gilded cloud, until at last she saw him and spun about, the feathers fluttering into stillness at her wrists. She smiled at him, eyes glowing like a wild animal beckoning from the darkness. She wanted him to tame her; she needed it. His heart banged so hard against his palm he thought it was the faltering of age, that he might die spread-eagled on the damp oak. *Wait for me*, he said to her. *I will seek you through this dark dream. I will.*

The brothers stuck to deer- and sheep-paths over ridges, avoiding open tracks and fields. In the two weeks they had been at Aed's, the birch, oak and hazel trees had misted with a haze of leaves, and patches of primroses and violets splashed the forest floor. Only the ash trees still lifted bare limbs to the sky.

Deirdre drew in lungfuls of air, forcing herself on with the knowledge that she was still free. Unable to spare time for hunting, they lived off trail-cakes and dried meat, sometimes picking the new tansy and dandelion tops to boil in a water-bag over the fire. Despite the sparse food, her limbs grew strong and wiry. Her fingers traced new hollows in her face and her ribs formed a ladder under her breasts, but she didn't care. That was Conor's plumpness she burned off, bred into her as if he fattened a calf.

Her stride parted the woods, feet landing unerringly as she let her soul sink into the earth through her boots. The rhythm sent her into a place where she didn't think of *before*, aching for loved ones and sorrowing for Aed, nor *after*, where fear stalked her. There was only the *now*, running through a greening world that trembled on the threshold of full life. In turn, she who had walked so long as a wraith became aware she was gradually solidifying into vital, breathing flesh, and the rush of sap beneath the bark of the trees seemed to flood her own limbs.

The emptiness between the four of them was charged, however.

Naisi's rage smoldered and he loped along with neck thrust forward as if to outrun what filled his heart.

He did not melt into the forest as she did, only cleaved it like a dark blade.

They made their way north and west to Finbar, an old friend of Naisi's who had already inherited his father's hall. However, when they came to his gates he did not invite the fugitives inside, taking them downriver where a line of fish-traps netted a rushing stream.

Finbar led Naisi into a salting hut furnished with a long oak table, and only then eased down his hood. Naisi searched his friend's rough-hewn, freckled face, fringed by ruddy hair. They had trained for the Red Branch together. "Am I to understand from this lack of hospitality that you will offer us no help?"

Finbar glanced out the doorway. Ainnle, Deirdre and Ardan were crouched on rocks by the fish-traps. Ardan filled Deirdre's flask for her and handed it over with an encouraging smile that lifted her taut face. "The king has made known the consequences of harboring you."

"And you would cower before him?" Hurt bloomed in Naisi, eclipsing the rage that had given him strength as he pounded the forest paths.

Finbar's hazel eyes were anguished. "I have not had my dun long. I am still gathering my power."

The well of darkness glinted inside Naisi, and a few words leaked out. "But *now* is the time to defy him. If we gather enough chiefs, if we all work together..."

Finbar fell back a step. "Why would I want to defy him?" Naisi's skin crawled and he longed to grab his thoughtless words back. "I've heard that Connacht might have started raiding again, Naisi. People are confused and afraid. Men want to bar their duns at times like this, not launch some pointless challenge of the king, who might be the only thing holding Connacht at bay!"

"The Red Branch holds Connacht at bay."

"And the king wields loyalty among us."

"You are betraying our friendship."

Finbar shook his head. "I have your horses here still, and I will give you food and clothing—anything you need. But I cannot keep you. Never have I heard the king so set against any Red Branch warrior." He smiled grimly. "You have won notoriety, my friend."

Naisi spread his hand over the bloodstains and silvery rime of scales on the table. He imagined the women here filleting the trout and salmon, cheeks apple-red, hands chapped. He almost heard the banter they would exchange with the men hauling in the traps. Home scents, hearth-chants, the working songs that beat out the rhythms of life from which he was now barred. He saw his mother's soft face wreathed in steam from the cauldron of porridge she stirred, her voice rising and falling as she sang blessings into the grains. His healing shoulder cramped, shooting a twitch of pain through his heart. "I have done nothing wrong." His voice cracked. "The girl came of her own will."

Finbar peered outside again and Naisi glimpsed Deirdre sitting on a rock, face lifted to the sky. Ardan was speaking, peeling open a bulb he had dug from the mud, and she nodded, her eyes closed. Naisi had been glad of their emerging friendship, for it kept Ardan's worry occupied. Now he noticed the small smile shadowing the corner of Deirdre's mouth and knew it for what it was, a simple reveling in the strengthening sunshine. Something stirred in him, making him feel sick. He was under too much strain. "She is untouched," he said, sounding hollow. "No finger has been set upon her by any of us. "

Finbar was still looking. "Then you are a stronger man than me," he murmured. He turned to Naisi and hesitated, scratching his stubbled chin. "It wasn't the wisest thing you've done. You should have sent her away."

Naisi walked to the door, trying to soak sunshine into his chilled skin. "Because of the king, this small thing has grown into a monster."

"And we are young men with friends, but little power." Finbar came to his shoulder. "You should know he's sent out trackers."

So Conor hunted them like prey. "We will take the food," Naisi said hoarsely, "but I ask that you send our mounts home to Dalriada. We have to stick to the high trails where no horse can go."

The guilt in Finbar's eyes did not make Naisi's friend relent, though they stared at each other in silence. It was clear Finbar would rather suffer that than suffer Conor.

⌘

They saw the first trackers from a ridge in the rain. Crouched behind rocks, Ainnle could not recognize horses or men. "They're Ulaid, though."

The two riders squatted by a marsh the fugitives had been forced to cross that morning. "They're good if they've found any tracks at all," Ardan murmured grimly. He looked at Deirdre. "That's why we made you walk on the crushed reed-beds, away from the mud." He always included her, because he said she must know what to do if they had to keep running.

"I did assume that," Deirdre replied, with the ghost of a smile.

"The king sent them." Naisi's voice sliced between them. Deirdre glanced at him. Raindrops ran down his face like it was a cliff, his features unmoving as he stared out into the drizzle. "A king who on the day he was crowned vowed three things: to serve the gods, to ensure the earth is fruitful and to protect the people with his might. He should be just and generous, and rise above petty jealousies. He is supposed to be a father for all. Isn't that what the druids tell us?" His fingers gripped the arrow-tip now strung around his neck with his deer talisman and boar-tusk. Deirdre fought the urge to prise his fingers from that stained shard of iron and fling it to the ground.

When they crept away over the sodden moors, she found herself walking behind Ardan. "I'm sorry," she blurted.

Drops spangled his eyelashes and ran down his blunt face. He smiled, sympathetic when the others only glared, in Ainnle's case, or ignored her, in Naisi's. "The king's rage has roots that go back further than you know. Conor was suspicious of our father, too; it must run in the blood." His ability to be kind even now warmed her chill skin.

That night in the dripping dark, Ardan said, "We should stay away from the noble duns now, from people like Finbar. They are too afraid of Conor. The herders and farmers will not have heard of this, so the more remote areas will be safer."

Naisi held on to Ardan's reasonable tone. "We could head to the sea."

Deirdre's shadow shifted. "The sea? I've always wondered if it's as beautiful as I imagined it."

Ardan's head dipped to look at her. "When we get mired in the dark, you think only of light."

The note of intimacy between them echoed inside Naisi's empty heart. However, he could spare nothing for any of them. He still felt choked, as if the wound had sent creepers of scar tissue to his lungs, which would not let him breathe. He rubbed his chest, summoning instead the places they went as boys, for the coast was not far from their own dun. "There are good reasons to make for the sea. We can eat shellfish, there are caves along the cliffs, and most of all, few people."

"Why are there few people?"

Ardan patiently answered Deirdre. "Because raids come from Alba over the sea. The rich cattle plains and great duns are inland, behind the defenses of the cliffs and marshes."

"We can't go home, though."

Ainnle sounded so lost that Naisi shook off his own desolation and sat by his youngest brother, slinging an arm about his narrow shoulders. "No, we can't go home." They had to stay away from Mama, and her soft eyes and calm hands. "We'll go east and north, where only the fisherfolk scratch a living from the rocks."

They received unexpected help from a cattle chief who had fallen from Conor's favor. He gave them hot bowls of beef broth, and promised to send a message to their mother. Naisi wanted her to leave some of their other weapons and clothes hidden in rocks near a sacred thorn of the *sídhe* on a lonely marsh above Lough Neagh.

Soon after that, they saw the second trackers. Ardan, posted lookout, scrambled over a crumbling wall to where the others sheltered from the rain in the ruins of a collapsed stone hut, hissing at them to grab their packs and run. When they at last collapsed in a tiny ravine on the other side of the moor, Ardan squatted next to Naisi. "I knew them." His eyes were as bleak as the weeping sky. "It was Dubthach and Conall." He and Naisi locked gazes. "If the king has set the Red Branch itself against us, then...by the gods." His voice was hoarse with pain; his teeth were clenched. "You were right all along. He will not stop until we are dead. There is no going back now."

The cold from Naisi's sodden clothes seeped far inside him, icy fingers that for a wild moment he thought might stop his heart. The Red Branch had joined the hunt.

They heard from a shepherd a few days later that the cattle-lord who helped them had been taken away by warriors in polished mail. His hall was fired in a conflagration that bruised the sky with smoke.

No one else was hurt, the whispers said, for Conor was a merciful king.

CHAPTER 18

A week later, Naisi stood at the mouth of a sea-cave in a ravine that ran down to the eastern shore of Erin. The dawn wind buffeted his chest like an invisible barrier, but there before him lay the real obstacle: the gray ocean heaving with stormy swells. On the horizon, a sliver of rose heralded the sunrise.

His frustration fought back against the battering wind. He had been *driven* to the sea. The sons of Usnech…*driven*…leaving behind smoldering huts and people weeping. His father's face was there before him, sorrow in his eyes.

Usnech's imagined pride had over the years taken on the status of a myth, Naisi told himself for comfort whenever the king lashed out at him. He had died of a battle-fever when Naisi was only seven, a stern father who said little but whose eyes glowed when he watched his three sons sparring with wooden swords. At least his *father* would be proud, Naisi would tell himself to soothe his bitterness after another of Conor's snubs. Look how admired the brothers were for their fighting prowess, their hunting and singing! Hear what the bards chanted! If Usnech still resided in the Otherworld and had not yet been reborn, he would have been rejoicing at every feast.

Now when Naisi thought of that cattle-lord being led away in bonds, he knew his father would be ashamed. They had picked up the extra packs their mother left for them at the thorn of the *sídhe*, and his father's torc was again around his neck. Every time he touched the cold bronze of the neck-ring, though, the shame bit deeper. How could this have happened? Such a short time ago they were racing after the stag, and laughing and drinking mead

in the Red Branch hall. And it was his fault. If he had never listened to the dark whispers inside…His face crumpled and in
horror he put a hand over his eyes, grinding his fingers into the
sockets.

"Naisi." Deirdre had climbed the path up the cliff, a net bag of
seaweed and shells dripping down her hide trews. "You didn't answer me."

He turned his chin toward the cave wall, scraping his fingers
over the rough surface as if inspecting it. "I couldn't hear you in
the wind."

She squeezed past him and dropped the bag, tossed more
driftwood on the fire and came to string up seaweed to dry at the
cave-mouth. He wished his brothers were here, but they were
scaling the cliffs, after gull-eggs.

To his discomfort, Deirdre stood next to him and looked out
at the sunrise. He saw her fill her lungs, closing her eyes, nostrils
flaring. Her gold hair was bound in one long braid that reached
her waist, roughened by dried salt-water. The sleeves of her
green tunic were rolled up and her forearms had gained new
muscles digging shellfish from rocks and sand. The loss of flesh
from her face had left her jaw starkly outlined, her pointed chin
and broad cheeks even more prominent. She was rosy with
health, though, not bowed with pain like him. She lifted her face
to the dawn, lips slightly parted as if she tasted it.

Naisi watched and could not move.

All at once she turned, catching him unawares with her frank,
green eyes. "You are suffering badly, Naisi. Before anger helped,
but not anymore." Her hand drifted toward his belly, and he instinctively sucked it away from her touch. "You grip your tunic…
here. You don't even know you do it." While he scrambled for
something to say, she firmed her mouth, pinning him with a
fierce look. "You must go back and make peace. End this now. It's
not too late."

His blood leaped with…was it hope? "But what of you?"

She sighed. "Sunseason is coming and the woods will soon
grow warmer."

"You can't live alone! You are lost in a dream. How will you find food?"

"I can make do with plants, and I know how to set snares."

"In the next long dark you will freeze without shelter."

She paused. "By then, I will find someone to take me in. I will work for my keep: grind grain, cook, skin, dye, anything."

He had to brutally expel the next thing. "Any man seeing you will take your body by force. You are different, set apart..." He hardly realized what he was saying.

Admirably, her hands showed no tremor as she lifted them, palms spread. "I will stay away from warriors, find herders, farmers. I'll go into Mumu or Laigin, or west to Connacht, to Maeve." When his face fell, she glanced at him. "I know that is betrayal to you. You are Red Branch, and thus you cannot leave the Ulaid or you'll be killed as an enemy. I made no oaths to break."

This bravery was a knife through his heart. Why had he not shown such courage years ago—defied Conor openly like she did? But then, Usnech's torc had always been at Naisi's neck: the badge of leadership, family protection and kin ties, trapping him between duty and the longing for something more. "There is a lookout that watches the north coast," he found himself saying. "The lord there fields only a few old warriors, and he hates Conor. If we risk one foray, we might get aid from him to send you to Connacht."

At least she will be safe there, his fervent thoughts ran, and he did not pause to question them.

Another secret meeting ensued, a horn lantern swinging in the dankness of a cave. This chief was a scrawny, weasel-faced man whose beady eyes darted over them. "Everyone knows the king hunts for you. He uses not only threats but the promise of reward to any man who betrays you." His narrow face was scarred by sword-cuts. "I owe much to your father, but though you have many allies, you also have enemies."

"You are saying your people would *sell* us to the king?" Ainnle demanded. He snorted. "Still, I suppose we can expect no less from warriors who are not Red Branch."

The chieftain scowled. "It is the Red Branch that is after you, Ainnle, if you remember."

Deirdre held the edge of her hood across her chin and mouth to shield herself, eyes lowered. Naisi knew she was afraid, for somehow he could sense her emotions now as he did those of his brothers, like tasting a change in the wind. The chief peered at her, small eyes glinting, and Naisi decided he and his brothers would see her safe ashore in Connacht.

The brothers could move faster then, hiding among the islands in the western sea. Without her, perhaps this dark dream would fade, and sense would return to Conor. Naisi found it hard to clear his throat. "We thank you for your help."

Gruffly, the chief said he needed time to arrange this in secret, and a few days later they returned at dawn. Their ally was waiting in a hidden bay, cloak whipping around his shoulders in the sea-wind. The sun brushed the choppy waves, blinding them as it came over the sea—and there was no boat tied to the rocks. "Come," the man said, picking his way up the cliff. Naisi asked him where the boat was, but he would not answer. Naisi had his hand on his sword, demanding explanations when the chief disappeared over the top, and he had no choice but to follow, for with no transport they were stranded.

The chief led them along hollows still shrouded in sea-mist, the damp turf bitten down by sheep. Farther along the headland, a stone tower reared from the rocks, its thatch roof leaking smoke, and huts sprouted around it, roofed with dried seaweed. "Our spring," the chief spoke at last, turning into a copse of bent rowan trees where a stream burbled into a crude well. The sight of dead sheep heaped about the clearing drew Naisi up short. Slowly, he nudged the nearest carcass. The sheep's back was arched in a rictus of pain, its tongue slumping from its jaw.

His eyes rose. A woman sat nearby, so still he'd not seen her against the rocks. Two small bodies lay at her feet, covered in blankets. Shreds of mist still clung to the shadows, wreathing her

silent form. "The children kept the well clear of leaves and dirt."
The chief's voice was toneless.

Naisi walked toward the woman and squatted by the bodies.
"I…" Sense deserted him. "Please let me see them." Behind her
matted hair, grief-glazed eyes glanced at his ornate scabbard before she turned away. He peeled back the nearest blanket. A
small girl lay there, skin creamy at the neck then spreading in
shades of mottled purple over her face. Her half-open eyes
showed only whites. Her lips were slack, the black tongue too
swollen to stay in her mouth. Though his belly protested he stared
at her, absorbing her, because he had to. "I am sorry," he said,
though the mother did not move again.

He approached the bubbling pool, sheened by the dawn.
Curls of vapor rose in spirals from its surface. Conor must have
sent spies out across the Ulaid territory when he first discovered
they were at Aed's; he knew they would run. He must have left
instructions, even then, of the warnings to give if people har-
bored them. Naisi imagined him passing gold to petty lords to
watch their neighbors. Only kings had access to the sorts of poi-
sons that could do this. He kicked at the stones of the pool, conscious that here they were, and no armed party had come for
them. The local traitors were too cowardly to take them alive,
then. They waited for the Red Branch.

Gods. His eyes slanted toward those tiny bodies. An arrow in
the back was nothing to this, even if it had hit his heart. He had
lived more than twenty years already, and done more than most.
These children had not. He saw for a terrible moment the swan's
eye on him by the frozen pool, heard his own vow to the
Goddess, in his heart. *Protect the weak.*

His pulse ran slow and thick as he stared down into his own
reflection, seeing the bruises beneath his haunted eyes. The
water rippled and when it cleared another face hovered over his
shoulder.

She had sensed his hurt before.

Deirdre and Naisi's faces were framed in the pool, as they should be, she thought grimly. They had wrought this together in the moment she whispered a lie in his ear, and he accepted because of that strange darkness that always lurked behind his eyes.

In the poisoned water, they looked at each other and understanding passed between them, as if they were alone. Her hand moved in an instinctive gesture, reaching toward his fingers before she stopped it. His nostrils were flexing and he broke the reflection to turn his gaze on her real face. Pain strained his mouth and her eyes went to his lips, unable to drag themselves away. She wanted to put her fingers on them to still that slight tremor, to disarm the silent curses he must be inflicting on himself even now.

Naisi spoke to his brothers. "I will dig a grave for them."

"This ground is too rocky." The chieftain's voice held a faint contempt. "We will burn them."

Naisi stared intently at him. "I don't care if it's hard. The mother must have somewhere to come and be with them. To sing to them."

"With the three of us, it will not take long to dig," Ainnle murmured.

"I will do it on my own."

Ardan hesitated. "Red Branch warriors will be on their way already. We have to leave."

"I will make a bed for them with my own hands," Naisi repeated in a low voice, "or I wander as a ghost, no longer able to call myself Usnech's son."

The chieftain shrugged. "Then, as we have no water, perhaps your strong brothers could help us dig out another well at a spring on the ridge there, which we rarely use."

Naisi nodded, his eyes pleading with Ardan. "Go and give what aid you can." Ardan sighed grimly and prodded Ainnle along.

Naisi asked Deirdre to get a shovel and mattock from one of the herder's huts by the tower, and before she went she paused by the children's mother. "We will make a place for them to sleep

near you." The woman did not acknowledge her. "Is there anywhere special you would like the…like us to dig?"

The woman's throat bobbed as she moistened her tongue.
"Under that hawthorn. They loved the blossoms…made gar-
lands for me…" Her dark head bent over words she could not
voice. Deirdre tentatively rested her hand on her shoulder until
the woman grew still again.

She procured the necessary tools from some hard-faced farmers and handed the mattock to Naisi, who was marking an area
under the hawthorn among the pale, fallen petals. He glanced at
the second set of tools she had brought. "Leave me," he said.

She dropped the other shovel and pick by the hole. "I think
someone should stay with you." When he glared, she added,
"These people do not feel kindly toward us; we must keep together. But I'll sit over there on the rocks if you want."

He applied himself to the hole, toiling as the sun rose, stripping off his tunic when it was dark with sweat. As always, he bent
the Red Branch armband off his sleeve and, dropping his tunic,
swiftly clasped it back on his bare arm. He did it instinctively, as
if it was still part of him. It shone against his clenched muscles
and Deirdre watched him covertly, her own body straining in
sympathy. The ground was harder going than the chieftain had
said. Suddenly she was hopping into the trench alongside Naisi,
the smaller shovel in her hands.

He looked up, sweat flicking from his black hair. "What are
you doing?"

"Helping." She stuck the shovel into the rocky soil.

He flung a heap of earth out of the hole. "This is my responsibility."

Deirdre hacked with determination. "It's my fault, too."

"I said I would do it."

"And you are!" she cried. "But so am I."

He watched her push the blade down with her foot, dragging
up earth and rock and heaving it out. When it was clear she
wouldn't stop, Naisi bent back to his task and soon they were

puffing in unison. Unfortunately, Deirdre's righteous anger couldn't carry her far, and when the sun was high the blisters on her palms and fingers began bursting, and she had to swallow each grunt of pain. She could hardly straighten her back and sweat stung her eyes.

All at once, Naisi stopped with an exasperated snort, leaning on his shovel handle. "When you said you were stubborn, you meant it."

She kept digging and heaving. "I always say what I mean."

Even as they emerged, the words were tainted. *No.* She drew a breath, raising her head. "That's not true. I lied about one thing."

Naisi's short braids had unraveled and waves of dirty hair were plastered to his cheeks, a few fallen thorn-blossoms speckling the black. His shoulders were dappled by the budding branches and she fixed her eyes on his face rather than the amulets in the dip of his throat, stirred by his breath. The heaviness she'd been carrying came rushing out. "I said what I did about your pride to force you to help me. But I never heard that. You are known for many things... I heard many things... but not that."

He squinted into the sun, licking sweat from his lip. "I said you were right, anyway."

"But I didn't know it then."

"That doesn't make it a lie."

"It was at the time." She was starting to feel foolish, for she'd thought this a sin he would not forgive. "By Brid, do you always fend off well-meant apologies?" She suspected she was getting off far too lightly and did not know why.

Amusement glinted in his eyes. He looked down and, after a moment, tilted his head, changing tack. "Why are you always dirty?"

"What?" She rubbed her chin with her knuckles. *Make sense,* she thought furiously. "I suppose... I have never cared how I look—perhaps because *he* cared so much." The ghost of the un-named hovered between them.

Naisi nodded, studying her face. She wondered if he noticed how it flamed. "I can see why you could not marry him," he said at last. "The Red Branch won't understand; they will think you a banshee who has ensnared us. But I see it—you would wither away. You might as well be dead."

The shovel lowered in Deirdre's hands. Though brutal, that was the most perceptive thing anyone had ever said about her.

With a frown, he flicked a clod of dirt from her cheek and she froze, then realized he had done it unconsciously. The sun reflected on tiny flecks of silver around his pupils she had not noticed before. The desperate sorrow all around them and the presence of the tiny bodies fueled a shocking craving in her belly: the need to feel a man's touch before she died. And death might even now be thundering toward her on the fleet hooves of Red Branch horses.

The halo of warmth around his fingers grazed her and she had to resist the urge to turn her head into his palm. *He doesn't mean to touch me.* He was too strained, too distracted with keeping his brothers safe. His hand dropped away. "You did what I would have done," he finished, leaving her speechless.

Her chest moved again as he clambered out of the hole and stood looking down at her. He hesitated, and words came to her for both of them. "There is no one else to help us," she murmured. "There can be no more of this." She gestured despairingly at the bodies in their shrouds.

"No," he said, and the kinship that was reflected in the pool glimmered between them again. "Nothing like this can be done in our names again. We are alone."

She watched him walk to the bereaved mother, telling her she could now lay them to rest with their own druid, in their own way. The woman would not even look at him.

He went to seek his brothers and Deirdre followed him. The mattocks rested across his wide shoulders, his wrists looped over the handles. She clutched the shovels across her chest. *We are alone*, he had said. She was now one of the *we*.

She withdrew her fingers from the handle of his shovel and pressed them to her nose, inhaling the musk of Naisi mac Usnech imprinted there by his palms.

CHAPTER 19

Naisi chipped at the limpet shells on the wet rocks with his dagger.

Deirdre often crouched like this around the fire, breasts pressed against her thighs. He hacked furiously, but more unbidden images crept into his mind. When she placed shells in the coals, her tunic gaped and he saw the globes of pale flesh pushed up on her knees. He would almost *feel* her nipples rubbing against the cloth as his own chest prickled.

Now he expelled a low growl, frustrated at his weakness. After being cooped up in a sea-cave for many days, was it any wonder he could find nowhere to look? The hiss of waves sometimes sounded like voices coming closer, and they all tensed whenever the rustling trees on the cliffs above cast shadows over the cave entrance.

I am a man of honor. He flipped a limpet off, dunked it in a rock-pool and placed it in his sling. *I will keep my honor over this.* One day he'd have to face his Red Branch comrades, and as Conor had not released her, in their minds she was somehow still his.

Dusk was creeping over the beach. He stared at the last finger of sun reaching down their tiny wooded ravine from the west. The light warmed the gray, restless sea—and he thought of the previous night, of Deirdre washing her hair in the stream and drying it before the fire. Her fingers had been a weaving comb through that gold thread, lulling him into a daze where none of this was real.

A cry came, so faint it could be a gull. He squinted down the rocks to the pale crescent of twilit sand. Two weeks they had kept hidden. The cliffs were too rugged to support steadings and the trees that spilled down the ravines were in their full growth, hiding them from the sea. Their cooksmoke leaked away into the fissures in the cave roof.

Over the wind the cry came again, more urgent. He straightened, the knife dripping. *That was human.*

Naisi sprang across the rocks, sheathing his dagger as he went. His feet slid in the kelp and he leaped between the bare knobs of stone until he could drop to the sand, hardly noticing the growl of denial that was rising in his throat until it burst out in a shout. "Ainnle! Ardan!" His brothers were around the point behind him.

Another whaleback of stone protruded from the beach ahead, and when he leaped up it, he saw four figures outlined against the gloom of evening: Deirdre clutching her bag, her cloak streaming in the wind—and advancing on her, three men. The last lick of sun picked out the shine of metal in their hands.

Naisi roared as he ran, feeling his sword-hilt in his fingers though he could not remember drawing it. He knew the build and hair color of one man there—Leary, winner of battles. The warriors saw Naisi coming and began to run, with Deirdre caught between them. Naisi bellowed something incoherent and at last she turned, stumbling toward him before getting her legs under her and streaking across the sand. Panic twisted her face and it was that which broke Naisi's long-dammed temper and set it free in a flood. She was defenseless.

He caught her before the others reached them, flinging her brutally behind him and squaring off, shielding her. "Run! Down the beach, now!" She scrambled up and over the rocks and disappeared.

The three warriors halted, swords up and shields braced against their chins, panting. "So you show your faces at last," Naisi gasped. "But you, Leary, I didn't expect. So is this better than releasing a traitor's arrow at someone's back?"

Leary's eyes widened. "I would never!"

"And yet you stalk us now like beasts."

Leary lowered his shield, his blunt face even grimmer. "We

have been scouring the land for you, aye, but only to put a stop to this foolishness before someone else gets hurt! Give the girl up and we can all go home. We don't want to fight."

"Then why attack?" Naisi's blade wove in front of him.

"You stole what belongs to the king."

"I stole nothing. She asked for my help as a noble warrior of the Red Branch. Would you turn away a maiden who pleaded with you, Leary? No, you'd have her on her back as payment!" His rage hammered him.

"Enough!" One of the other warriors spat on the sand. "She isn't just any maiden, and the king wants her back. It's simple enough: give the girl up."

There was red behind Naisi's eyes. *Give her up*... He might have done before that point pierced his shoulder, leaving a scar that still ached—before she tried to soothe his pain, reaching un-flinchingly to share his burden of guilt.

"You can still come back from this." Leary gritted his jaw to ignore the insult. "Put down your weapon and hand her over. With her at his side, we all think the king's madness will pass and we can get him to forgive your infernal pride." When Naisi only raised his sword, the tip wavering, Leary burst out, "Come on, man! If you've lifted her dress we'll not tell him, just for some sweet peace around here."

Struck, Naisi wanted to say, *But she doesn't wear dresses*, and in that moment knew this was not about his pride. "Swear you've heard no word of us, and I will not harm you."

Their eyes fixed on the grim gleam of his blade in the fading light. "We can't do that," the third said, another Naisi knew only by sight. "We've been ordered to take her, no matter what."

"What, trussed like a fowl? Conor will sink to that?"

The man merely shrugged contemptuously. It was too much. Naisi again saw Deirdre's face lifted to the scents of dawn. Conor would not let her walk through the woods alone, the night hushed and silky-dark around her. "Put up your blades," he said quietly, and Leary's face fell.

Behind him, Deirdre and his brothers appeared on the crest of the rocks. Ainnle cried his name. "Stay back," Naisi barked. "This is on my head only."

"Balls to that," Ainnle growled in answer, and spitting something at Ardan he barreled down onto the sand, unsheathing his sword.

Deirdre's nails bit into Ardan's arm. Ainnle had told his brother to stay, but she could feel the strain in the muscle beneath her fingers. "Go to them," she choked.

Ardan shook his head. "They will have to come through me at the last."

She could barely make sense of the fight that broke out below as the men began spinning and lunging, stabbing out and leaping back. Sand was kicked up and the dusky light and shadows confused her further. Slash was blocked by thrust, blades reaching in then darting back.

Naisi's sword rose, its scything plunge met by Leary's blade in a terrible grate of iron. Deirdre stared as those familiar flowing muscles of Naisi's formed new shapes—hacking, jabbing, stabbing, the whites of his eyes showing in the dimness. She was amazed at his speed and grace; she'd seen the brothers run and climb but this was more like a dance, blades spinning so fast they were a blur, legs leaping, arms whirling.

The two brothers stood back to back, using each other as shields, and as they were taller they could get in under the strokes of their stockier opponents. The clang of blades traveled through Deirdre's shaking body.

Her gaze was tied to the curve of Naisi's head. She had once held it to peer at his healing wound, and it came to her now in exquisite detail how the bones fit her palms, his black hair caught between her white fingers. Heat swept over her with no warning—an urge to stroke his waist and back, his underarms, his muscled flanks, to see if they also molded to her touch. Absurd at such a time—so late, so blind!—but the need roared through her at the very moment she might never feel his skin again.

"It's a duel," Ardan was muttering. "First cut only and it's over. No Red Branch has ever killed another."

She dragged her mind back, shuddering. There *was* something controlled in Naisi's movements as he tried to target not the flanks of his opponents but their swords, and at last succeeded in twisting one blade away. When the man stumbled, Naisi struck his head with his hilt and he collapsed on the sand, unconscious.

"We are matched in number now," Naisi croaked. All the warriors were soaked with sweat, their hair stuck to their foreheads. "Let us go freely."

"We can't," Leary panted, flinging his shield to the sand. "Before I left, the king demanded my clan oath to return her, even at the cost of you."

A chill drenched Naisi. "He asked for one Red Branch oath against another?"

Leary nodded wearily. He spread his fingers, and they trembled from strain. "I won't have you destroy so much for your pig-headed pride. It was always too ripe in you—in all of you."

Naisi rocked on his heels. "So now it comes out. You would ignore your conscience for the king's gold."

Leary sucked in a breath, launching his unshielded blade at Naisi with a yell. Naisi's sword swept up to block it. Gulls exploded from the cliffs in alarm, whirling around their heads and shrieking against the darkening sky. Back and forth the two men twisted and cut, Naisi forced from Ainnle's shoulder by Leary's attack, both men reckless with anger. Leary was thicker-set, stronger, better controlled; Naisi, lithe, his reflexes quicker. The fight was so furious that Ainnle and his opponent stopped sparring, their swords lowering.

Naisi took a cut on the forearm and grunted at the sting but did not falter, nor did Leary halt his attack. All pretense of a duel had died.

Blood trickled down Naisi's hilt now, making it slippery, so he flipped his sword into his left hand. He had not only practiced the Salmon Leap into the night as a boy, but also taught himself to fight from either side, like Cúchulainn. The blades met again and slid along each other until they locked at the hilts. The two warriors' faces were so close that Naisi's spittle flecked Leary's cheek. "He's wrong, and you know it," he gasped.

Leary's eyes were clenched with effort. "Bend just a little and you'll live! But you never can."

With a growl, Naisi pushed his sword sideways like a staff and Leary's foot sank in a patch of softer sand behind him. It was only a slight imbalance, hard to detect. But Naisi saw and didn't hesitate, kicking out with his heel to knock Leary's legs from under him. As the older man wobbled, Naisi sprang forward in a last act of desperation, thinking only to cut his sword hand and disable him.

Leary dropped his weapon, however, and leaped for Naisi to wrestle him over. Naisi didn't see the dropped sword, only the movement. Years of practice had honed his instincts, melding blade with body, and as he brought up his arms to defend himself, his sword came with him.

From a dazed distance, he watched the blade disappear as Leary drove himself onto it.

Deirdre heard a scream like a dying animal and ran toward it, only she realized when she reached them that it didn't come from the stabbed man sliding to the ground but the one who held him. Naisi. Ardan shoved her aside as he stumbled to his brother's shoulder. Ainnle was standing with his mouth open, sword dangling. The third warrior had by now dragged his friend up, still dazed, and without a word they both fled across the sand.

Naisi was rocking the dead man, his dark braids falling over those staring eyes and white cheeks. Deirdre's stomach heaved and she shoved her fist in her mouth, sinking on her knees. The pool of blood soaked into the sand while the wind rippled the dune-grasses.

Naisi shrank back, pulling his bloody sword with him and flinging it away as he let Leary's body slump to the ground. He crawled toward the sea, head down, and when he had gone a little way opened his throat and retched up bile. Deirdre heard the keening between the splashes of vomit on the sand, a raw sound wrenched up from his bowels. His brothers did not take their eyes off the dead man's face, utterly confounded.

At last Naisi staggered up, swaying. His hands were bloody— one from the cut trickling down his forearm, the other from the sword grip. He shook them as if to rid himself of that gore, then wove toward the water. When he reached the curling waves, he plunged in, his head going under. Deirdre looked at Ardan, her cheeks stiff with dried tears. "He won't...hurt himself?"

"No." Ardan's face was bleached of feeling. "He must make Leary's death worth something. He will take the victory."

Darkness fell and the wind rose, and Ardan, Deirdre and Ainnle crouched around the driftwood fire in the cave. Naisi had dragged himself out of the water and disappeared over the rocks, and he hadn't come back yet.

Dazed, Deirdre stared at the strips of deer-meat drying on their frame. A few days ago the brothers had crept into the hinterland and hunted a hind, roasting it in a pit on the beach. They laughed openly for the first time around that fire, Naisi's face softening in the glow of the flames. The guilt was strangling her. "I must go to him." She brushed past Ainnle and his accusing eyes, averting her gaze from Leary's bundled body.

Outside the wind was raging as if joining them in grief, the surf foaming under the thin sliver of moon. She searched one end of the beach to the other before glimpsing Naisi on the whaleback rock. Heart in her mouth, she climbed up to him. He didn't turn, watching the waves sweep up on the sand in front of him, his fingers curled over the slash on his forearm.

"You didn't mean to hurt him," she blurted. "It was just the way he leaped—"

His shoulders moved convulsively, halting her words. "Our swords should never have met in anger, not one Red Branch against another. It cannot happen. Surely it did not happen…" He trailed away.

"Naisi, I'm so sorry," she murmured. When he did not reply, she drew the salt wind in through her nose to clear her mind. "Tomorrow I leave for Emain Macha." His head whipped around, the moonlight turning his face to bone and hollows. "I never want to see your body wracked like that, Naisi. Not you…never you…" She gulped down the rest of those sweet, anguished words. "It will be your death next."

His eyes were pits in the dim light. "I will not allow Conor to triumph."

"This isn't about victory! It's about *saving people*." She grasped his shoulder. "Once, I wanted what you had more than anything— to sing and chase deer, taste the grease on my lips from game I had hunted. But in wanting this, I have taken it from you." She shook her head. "I must end this."

The bitterness of his smile took her breath. "You betray your innocence, Deirdre. I will always be a wanted man now for killing a warrior of the Red Branch."

No. He was wrong. There must be a way out. She had wrought this; she would mend these broken threads, if she had to submit to Conor's desires until the day she died. She got her quivering legs under her. One more moment of the moon on his face, shaping it into those bleak planes, and she would have no strength to leave him. "I will remember how you fought for me." Her voice broke and she clambered down the rocks, wind-blown spray coating her face.

He caught her by the shoulders halfway across the beach. Beneath his flying hair, his lips curled in a snarl, and she smelled blood on him. *"He will not have you."*

So she was just a *thing* to him, too, a possession to snap and squabble over. She flung up her chin. "As Conor's bride, I will tell him this death was an accident and gain a pardon for you. It will be a wedding boon, the last thing I ask of him—"

"I don't need you to ask it. I'll sink a sword into him before he looks even once upon your face."

"You're not listening!"

"Because you're insane!" His eyes were wild, his fingers biting into her arms.

The wind buffeted her body and her temper was torn free by its force. "So now you seek to bridle me as he did? To deny the choice of my own heart, to end this, to save you?" She struck at his belly with her palm as if vainly beating a rock to release that rage, knowing it was for Conor.

Naisi braced himself, easily absorbing the blow, and the implacable hardness of his body shattered her control. She went to kick out but he pulled her against him, his fingers burying themselves in the unraveling braids at her ears. "Don't do this to me, Deirdre. Not this night…" She barely heard his mumble, the wind pushing their tangled hair into her mouth. She was dragging it free when he crushed his palms to her temples, and looming in, ground his lips to hers with brutal force.

She went rigid with a moment's shock before the storm broke over her. *The mingling of heated lips…blood-scented breath…spatters of cold spray on flaming cheeks…* His body pressed against hers in hard lines down her belly and thighs. "N-N…" The sound of his name tried to form behind her bruised lips, but all rational thought was driven away when he opened his mouth and she *fell* into him, in wetness and warmth and the slickness of silky tongues. Her legs gave out against him, leaning on his thighs for strength.

He devoured her, and she drank of him. It was a melting, consuming heat, and with it came the desperate realization that this thirst had been building in her for weeks. And when Naisi's hands pulled her rump in closer, grinding her against him, she dimly knew he had thirsted the same.

The kiss was furious with need, almost wrathful. His mouth roved over hers and his teeth were behind, trapping little folds of her lips and drawing them in. He went deeper, sucking on her tongue, licking at the tender skin inside her cheeks. Her hands helplessly grasped him around the waist as the sand tilted beneath her.

It was then she felt the change in him.

Naisi had grasped for Deirdre mindlessly, overwhelmed by grief. He kissed her to expend his fury, to stop the terrible words she kept speaking. For if she went back to Conor, she would shame him unbearably. If she went back, he had failed.

As the first storm passed, though, he became aware that Deirdre's body had grown pliant against him, felt her hands creeping up to bury themselves in the thick curls at the dip of his skull. Her fingers smoothed his head, growing more frantic as she used her grip to push his tongue deeper into her mouth. She came up on her toes in her need to consume him, elbows crossed behind his neck, and pushed her groin into him so hard one thigh parted his own so they were entwined.

The anger rushed from Naisi like water through sand, and his hands were sliding over the wondrous curves he had watched all these weeks—that small waist and fleshy bottom, high and hard with muscle. He cupped it and pulled her in so now his knee parted her legs, and as he ground into the soft, giving flesh between her thighs, she whimpered. It was that tiny noise of surrender that made him at last understand it wasn't any woman-flesh he hungered for. It was *this* body, imbued with all that naked will and emotion, that disconcerting fierceness that wrestled with his own.

He broke the kiss and held her face with one hand, struggling to be still. A star hung low over the crashing sea behind her. With one finger, he traced the fine line of her jaw and sockets of her brows, shadowed by hurt, and the dip in her temple, which pulsed. There was a dark stain on her cheekbone, and it took him a moment to realize it was his own blood from the cut, smeared on her skin.

Overcome, he trailed lips into the hollow of her throat, pausing to lap at the indent as she arched away in his arms, his tongue sliding to the plump tops of her breasts where they disappeared into her tunic. Her skin was so fine-grained, it was as white as the sea-foam. "Deirdre," he murmured helplessly, and at last drew her to his chest to tuck her under his chin, squeezing his eyes shut to hold in the rush.

The path ahead was no longer twisted, as it had been all the years he prowled the walls of Emain Macha. It reached across the waves in a straight trail painted by the moon. *Escape. Life.*

He would never let this flesh be pawed by Conor. Her fiery gaze, the life in her movements, the scent of her—the loss of these would rip something visceral from his flesh. His body must have known it before he drew his fateful blade.

Deirdre was gripping his tunic, nuzzling his throat. "Naisi," she croaked, "you have turned me from my path."

He ground his chin into her hair to feel the tender curve of the bone beneath, his eyes blurring the moon on the water. "Then we have to find a new path," he said. He wanted to kiss her in the salty darkness, enveloped by the sound of rushing waves, until he could feel nothing more. But it was late, and more warriors would soon arrive. "Come," he murmured, forcing himself to pull away, letting the cold air rush between them.

Only the tips of her fingers burned in his as he led her back to his brothers.

Naisi and Deirdre came into the cave with the same blood streaked on their cheeks. Ardan saw it and a coldness crept over his features, though Deirdre could make no sense of it with her skin still smelling of Naisi.

Naisi looked at his brothers, touching the edge of his naked blade. "I will not be forced to hold another dead friend in my arms."

"Conor upholds the betrothal." Ainnle avoided looking at Deirdre. "If she goes back, this will be over."

"She's not going back."

Ardan said nothing, his elbows resting on his knees and his chin dropping. Ainnle's head, however, reared up. "Why can't you see sense?"

Naisi pinned Ainnle with a look. "Deirdre's not going back to Conor."

Ainnle glanced from one to the other. "Oh, I see. It's like that, is it?" The lost expression that flitted over his face surprised Deirdre, as he got up and turned on his eldest brother. "We can't go on like this, Naisi, waiting for the arrows, the blades…"

Naisi's brow creased. "I know." One fist grasped his sword-hilt, holding it to his heart. "If I thought single combat would decide it—"

"And face Cúchulainn?" Ardan huddled into crossed arms. "He is Conor's champion after all."

"Not Cúchulainn!" Ainnle gasped.

Naisi leaned his sword against the wall and drew Ainnle into his arms, their foreheads leaning together. "I won't be hurling myself on any blades soon, Ainnle-lad. I only seek some way out."

Ainnle clutched Naisi's shoulders. "Let us return to Emain Macha, then. We can all ask to be forgiven, even Deirdre."

Naisi sighed and straightened, keeping a hand about Ainnle's neck. "Over the years, we have all had our own way in turn—seeking mischief most often in your case, and ale in Ardan's." Ainnle smiled faintly with shadowed eyes. Naisi held his gaze. "Now I will have my way on this one thing, if I never do again. For I must have…" His chin went down and he drew a breath, and Deirdre was pierced by wonder to hear him struggling to speak. At last, he just bleakly shook his head. "You cannot tilt the world back to where it was before."

In that moment, Deirdre's thoughts broke through the confusion that had flooded her body. She had drunk from Naisi's lips, felt the beating pulse in his neck. Now she could never touch another—not Conor, not anyone. If she had to let him go—if he did not feel as much as she—her skin would still burn with the memory of this fever.

"Leary is gone," Ainnle whispered.

"And I will pay for that one day," Naisi answered. He glanced at Deirdre. "But this cost would be too great."

All three brothers regarded one another, and the tension rose in Deirdre as the silence lengthened. At last Ardan spoke. "I can almost hear your thoughts turning. If you're about to announce that this is all on your head and you'll flee with Deirdre, save yourself the trouble." He kept his eyes on the dagger in his hands, twirling it with small, savage movements. "We won't leave your side, and you say you will not leave Deirdre's. So we stay together."

Naisi's shoulders lowered. "Then there is nothing for it but to flee. And Alba is the closest coast."

"We can't leave Erin," Ainnle stammered. "We can't leave the Red Branch!"

"Conor will hunt us from the northern cliffs to the southern beaches. There will be no peace, no rest, and all who shelter us will be slaughtered." Naisi raised his eyes to Ainnle. "You know this."

Ainnle rubbed both hands over his face and dropped them. "Not the Red Branch..."

"The Red Branch act for Conor, and it is he who expels us." Naisi spoke harshly, but grief was etched across his face. "Erin shelters us no more."

CHAPTER 20

They moved fast, conscious that news of Leary's death was even now reaching Emain Macha.

By starlight, they took a curragh from a fishing settlement—a long, narrow hull of tarred hides over hazel ribs with four oar benches in a row. They did not know the ocean, but drowning was a better end than Conor's spears. Naisi left a gilded dagger in exchange for the boat, stabbing it through the frayed rope.

They rowed north along Alba's coast for days, fighting the seasickness and currents, hauling up on islets to replenish fresh water. The gods did smile on them, though, for the seas were calm enough, a brisk wind pushing them from the southwest.

At the steering oar, Naisi spent so much time gazing into the water Deirdre wondered if he saw Leary's face traced there in foam and weed, and his fingers cradled his bandaged cut as if trying to force the blood back into it. When she sat by him, the face he turned to her was taut with grief and a more elusive darkness that only faded when his eyes focused on her, kindling with hunger once again.

"How far north will we go?" she asked one day, to break the spell of their wordless staring. Her voice was husky with the nerves she felt around him now. She had seen those muscles swing a sword with lethal power and deadly grace, kissed that dangerous, unknown flesh and found it salty and sweet. When she stared at his forearms straining on the ropes, it kept coming to her that although his hands brought death to others, every part of her was alive with the anticipation of his next touch.

Naisi glanced down at his scarred palms as if he read her mind. "Cúchulainn trained at the warrior-queen Skatha's battle school in the isles of Alba. He said a great valley, or glen, slants from this west coast to the northeast coast, and it's filled by a chain of lochs that run as far as the northern sea. If we enter the sea-loch here, we can travel inland without leaving the safety of the water."

Ardan and Ainnle were rowing, faces twisted toward the bow, and Naisi reached to cradle the nape of Deirdre's neck, rubbing it so slowly and gently it was even more intense than passion. The sunlight reflecting off the water merged the sea into his eyes, casting a glowing net about her. A startling image came of his fingers tracing the path his lips had taken that night on the beach, grazing the soft skin across her collarbones…then drifting lower. It was easier to surrender into that sensation than remember the hurt and fear that lurked behind them.

The sea-wind was icy, but Deirdre burned.

Alba's coasts were circled by thriving trade routes that reached to the northern amber lands and south past the tin mines to the Middle Sea, and Rome. Although they saw many sleek timber traders and curraghs, no one challenged such a tiny boat and they kept their swords and spears hidden.

The land they passed was craggy. Russet mountains soared from scattered islands and looming inland ridges, the rocky shores clothed with forests of spreading oaks and the slender, pale spears of birches. Spires of smoke marked out countless forts and steadings on the sea, which shaded from dark and glassy to an iridescent blue in the sandy bays.

Deirdre was worn out by the ceaseless wind and the sickness in her belly, and by the time they entered the inlet that cut deep into Alba, she was huddled in the bow, cheek on the railing of the hull.

They crept along the southern shore of the great loch. Each headland was crowned with rings of timber ramparts or clusters of thatched huts, and jetties reached out into the water on stilts, anchoring bobbing flocks of boats.

Spreading south from the great glen were the lands of the Epidii, Naisi said.

"The greatest enemy of the Ulaid bar Connacht," Ardan added softly, staring at the shores. "And we have come straight to its heart."

"Yet where better to hide from Conor?" Naisi's voice was roughened by the wind and salt. "Few Ulaid traders gain entrance to the harbor at their fort of Dunadd, and even fewer warriors walk its mountains."

"Except us." Ainnle's face was grim.

"We agreed this is the best course," Naisi said a little sharply.

"The greater risks offer the greater prizes. No one will search for us here."

All at once the curragh juddered, making Deirdre sit up. They had been caught in a slight current rushing out from the shore. She stared at that dip in the land, mind and body suddenly awake.

Alba's hues were painted in dusky layers, the ridges near the water greening with new bracken, and farther away a faint suggestion of mountains that disappeared into a purple haze. "A river must come out here," Ardan ventured.

Deirdre found herself answering, "Then that is where we must go."

"Go where?" Ainnle shaded his eyes, peering at the shore.

She gripped the side of the boat. It was hard to see against the backdrop of the hills, but the land narrowed either side of the river mouth, and she felt drawn toward it by a curious pulling sensation. "If we can go inland up a river or lake, then the mountains become higher there, see? *That* will hide us." She met Naisi's eyes.

He paused, kneading the back of his neck, looking from her to shore. "Cúchulainn said many lochs cut into the mountains. This waterway is too busy for my liking, anyway; perhaps it's time we sought somewhere quieter." Ardan grunted in agreement, and so they turned and began to row against the ripples, realizing it was not a river they approached but another lake, emptying into the sea-loch.

As they got closer, Ainnle softly swore. A plume of disturbed water poured from the narrow entrance, and behind that rapids roiled across the center of the loch mouth like the maw of a vast sea-creature. They stared at it in horror. The maelstrom was sucking in the lake behind it and then spewing out foaming waves toward the sea. To either side, whirlpools were stirred as if by the lashing of a great tail.

"What is this devilry?" Naisi cried, wiping salt from his eyes.

Ainnle shouted, "The loch is against us! If a god guards it, he is wild with anger. Look, he calls up the waters to push us back!" The little boat had been skewed out of the current into an eddy near shore, where the water lapped in disjointed slaps against the rocks.

Deirdre's freezing hands gripped the boat and she stared down at the water, breathless. Her wet lashes broke the reflected sunlight into fragments and she began to lose all sense of the shore, the boat, of the men in it. Whirlpools drew her head down, the spray coating her cheeks until she tasted the salt and grit of churned foam. The whorls spun in tantalizing patterns she could not grasp. Spirals beckoned her like swirling arms...in and up toward those far hills. *Goddesses lived in lakes,* Levarcham once said, *floating with their palms on the glassy surface, watching us.*

Naisi began to turn the boat with his oar, and she gasped and twisted around. "The goddess of the loch roars not to keep us out but to protect us from those who come after us!"

"Protect us?" Ainnle pointed at the waves pummeling the boat. "Kill us, more like."

Deirdre staggered up, making the boat tilt. "She demands courage, that is all! The brave can pass; the cowardly cannot."

Naisi's sunburned face showed his exhaustion, his hands blistered from the damp chafing of the oars. He seemed torn, and on impulse Deirdre clambered over the benches. Grasping the fourth set of oars, she shoved them in the water. The brothers stared at her uncomprehendingly as the curragh was caught by the current.

Naisi cursed and leaped for his oar-bench. "Come on!" he bellowed to his brothers, and they stabbed their paddles back in, bracing their feet against the ribs of the hull. They hauled the boat through the dark band of water near the shore, edging around the maelstrom of whitewater in the center of the straits. *Are you the brave? Are you?* Deirdre could almost hear the murmur underneath the thunder of the rapids. Naisi must have understood it, too, expending his last reserves of strength in a low, furious growl. "I am!"

With those conquering words, they grazed the far edge of the foaming flurry, desperately pulling as the curragh was buffeted. Deirdre was thrown hard against Naisi, bruising a rib on the oar.

If you want us, she thought crazily, *let us pass*. They pulled again, crying out with the strain, with defiance.

Their muscles cramped in agony, lungs choked by spray, until at last peace unexpectedly descended. They raised their heads.

They were gliding over a sheet of smooth black water, the rapids falling away behind. The men sprawled in the hull, Ardan spitting out spume while Ainnle wiped his own cheeks. Naisi had his eyes shut, his arms braced on the oar as he regained his breath.

After a time they began to row again, nudging the boat inland up the now-calm loch, all of them spent. Only when the shores began to narrow again did Deirdre crawl back to the bow. Ahead the loch was a sheet of dark glass dotted with islands. To the right, she glimpsed a settlement on the southern shore, the sky smudged with smoke above it, but to the left the loch turned north and east. There it speared up into ramparts of immense, rearing peaks, shrouded in rainclouds—a veil that would close behind them, taking them from Thisworld into mist.

Deirdre's gaze ranged over those mountains. They rose almost directly from the water in great sweeps, hunching their shoulders to shelter their valleys from the world, hinting at hidden places, trackless wastes. "In there," she croaked, "we shall find a home."

She leaned forward, hands spread in supplication, and four swans floated out from behind a rocky island, their white wings glowing against the dark water. Their wake drew a shimmering arrow eastward into the secret hills.

Ardan turned from the swans to Deirdre, eyes dazed. "The goddess *did* call us," he murmured. "And now the *sídhe* show us the way."

The funeral of Leary, winner of battles, took place on a blustery day that spattered the mourners with rain. His dun was by the sea, so his pyre was of driftwood, the smoke blown over the gray sands on a salt-laden wind.

Conor watched the flames eating the pitch-soaked wood. Leary's body was wrapped in a fur robe, his spears by his hand, a jar of mead and a joint of boar-meat at his feet. The king felt the anger of those about him thickening the air, and so he studied the boar-fat instead as it melted and caught alight in runnels of flame.

"May Lugh's light guide you across Manannán's plain to the Isle of the Ever-Young," Cathbad chanted, his voice cracked by the remnants of his fever, as he weakly sprinkled sacred water from a rowan branch over Leary's head. The dead man's widow rocked and keened.

Conor was acutely aware of his Red Branch warriors crowded together at the end of the pyre—away from him. He turned his cheek from Leary's eyelids, translucent and blue-veined, and his gaze fell on Levarcham, who was staring right at him. The unearthly, luminous gray of her eyes was now the cold glint of iron.

That contemptuous look increased the pressure in his head, like a weight pushing it down. As if he would bow his head before her! With an irritated snort he straightened his aching shoulders. The wind was biting, and he tucked his red hands into his fur sleeves. Conall, Dubthach, Illan and sly Ferdia glanced sideways at the movement, and though they immediately turned away, he saw the accusations behind those blank expressions. *You killed him.*

Conor shifted on his feet, loosening his knee which had been wrenched by the uneven ground. *I did not,* he snapped inside. This disaster had been wrought by Red Branch pride—and anyway, a warrior knows he risks death when he takes his oaths.

Cúchulainn's attention was on the body, but his very stillness, his obvious sorrow, needled Conor, even though the Hound did not glance at him or even look angry. Conor's rage flared along with the hungry flames. Cúchulainn was breathtaking with a sword, but he was a fighter, not a ruler. How dare he judge a king, and the difficult demands and challenges he had to navigate? The Hound's damned purity was enough to make any man feel soiled.

As soon as the ceremony ended, Conor turned his back on the pall of dark, sickly-sweet smoke and stalked down the slope to where turf gave way to beach. The waves were gray and fitful, their white-tops marching far out into the whipped ocean. The wind buffeted him, tugging against the gold brooches that held his sealskin cloak.

Unbidden, Conor was taken by a distracting memory of Deirdre's leg stretched out in her dance, muscles taut beneath fine wool. He unclenched his palms on his thighs as his long robe was molded to him by the wind. One more glimpse of that would be enough, he thought fervently, just the chance to kneel at her feet and hold that unlined flesh to his wrinkled face and breathe in her perfume, let her purity cleanse him.

The bitter brew inside him curdled. *Naisi.* He hissed the name, as if it might drift out in a poisonous mist and strike the boy down unto death.

The peaks in the hidden glen towered over water that was now puckered by droplets of rain. Deirdre tipped back her head, letting them fall on her tongue. The drops held the essence of the smoky, peat scent of Alba—her first taste of its earth, its rocks.

"Grim, isn't it?" Ainnle ventured, with a doubtful frown.

Never. Deirdre swung around, marveling at how the mountains on either side formed a great cup of stone that held the loch. The russet slopes reared above the water's dark surface, their sweeps of brown bracken and pale gold sedges beginning to green with new growth. White streams poured from bare, gray peaks, washing down fans of scree. The valley sides were dotted with birch and pine trees, the hollows and streambanks clothed in thicker woods of budding hazel, ash and oak.

Something was watching her, and she turned to see a sleek domed head floating just above the water, dark eyes fixed on her. Then the seal lifted its snout, taking a breath, and sank beneath the surface with barely a ripple.

At the head of the loch, a saddle of green valley carried a river from the east, which spread out into marshes of pebbled banks cut by winding channels. "Look," Ardan breathed. The boat's ripples had disturbed scores of ducks, which lifted in flurries against the gray sky, squawking. "That's some fowling," he exclaimed, his grim face brightening despite the rain.

"And on that peak—isn't that deer? Oh …" Ainnle looked crestfallen. "And there's smoke up the valley."

Naisi scrubbed his salty face on his sleeve. "There's bound to be some, little brother." He scanned the sky and Deirdre watched the rain beading on his cheeks, resisting the urge to break the drops with her finger-tip so they trickled down his chin.

The rain had awoken something as she stood there in the hull, ankle-deep in water, her soaked clothes stuck to her skin. She felt naked, unformed, as if it poured through her insides as well, dissolving her down to the core. It left nothing of what she had been before; the only memory her body would take to this new shore, the imprint of Naisi's lips.

"Cúchulainn said the king's seat at Dunadd is days away," Naisi continued. "It looks empty, just as we need it to be." He turned and saw Deirdre's lips parted to the rain and he started, his burnished cheeks darkening.

"I can't see any forts or large steadings," Ardan agreed, cheering up.

"They are more likely to be sheepherders." Naisi held Deirdre's gaze, his voice remaining even though the heat in his eyes brought an answering tide of blood to the surface of her skin.

"Nevertheless, we should lay low at first," Ainnle said.

They landed and crouched beneath an oak tree, chewing smoked fish to recover their energy, and when they had rested they followed the cooksmoke up the valley to the nearest steading. There they squatted behind a thorn-brake in the rain, watching.

The stone walls of the little hut were topped by a heather roof weighted with nets. A crude pen protected a few ewes and their lambs, which slid about in the mud, splay-legged. These people were herders, isolated and poor.

Muffled voices floated from behind a sheep-fleece hanging across the doorway. "Get the lambs in, man," a woman urged. "If this gets any heavier they'll drown in muck." To Deirdre's surprise, she could understand the words. It was a strange, thick accent, but not unintelligible—Alba and Erin were close to each other across the sea after all.

Before the herdsman came out, they quickly crawled away. "We'll camp higher up," Naisi decided, "and only approach these people once we've recovered some strength."

Deirdre's braids had been dragged into tangles, and the brothers' black hair was encrusted with salt. After weeks on the run, their clothes were filthy, the fine blues and reds of their tunics faded by rain and muddied into dull russets and browns. "No one would know we were warriors, anyway," Ainnle observed, ruefully rubbing his sprouting beard. Ardan smiled wearily, though Naisi did not.

They went back to the shore to seek a sheep-path up the slopes, and as Ardan and Ainnle turned along the trail, Deirdre paused and bent down. A single swan's feather lay across her path like a little bow. She picked it up and tucked it behind her ear, glancing back at Naisi. He was still looking over his shoulder at the loch that led west to the sea, and to Erin. This time his hand hovered over his heart and he did not seem conscious of it, his eyes hollow.

They made camp as they had done many times beneath the overhang of a cliff in a little ravine, staking out hides for a lean-to and covering the ground in pine and juniper branches. Naisi and Ainnle gathered wood while Ardan and Deirdre kindled a fire just beneath the lip of the cliff, spreading out their sleeping hides and cloaks to dry.

"Will we survive here?" Deirdre asked Ardan in a low voice, piling bracken for the beds.

Ardan paused and looked right at her, catching her wrist. "Don't feel guilty, Deirdre." So often he read her thoughts before she had fully felt them. "It will eat at you, and we are all weakened enough." He had grabbed her hand naturally like he did mere weeks ago, only now when he realized it he dropped her fingers as if they stung him. He smiled bleakly, then turned to kick the bracken up for his own bed. "We will live," he muttered, "as long as we are together."

By the time Naisi and Ainnle came back, the rain had thickened into a dark soup.

They all collapsed, pulling off wet boots to uncurl shriveled feet. Despite the flames, the wind made Deirdre shiver, and Naisi glanced at her. "You should get out of those clothes and wrap up." Nodding, she retreated to the rear of the shelter and as usual the men turned their backs to give her privacy.

Ardan and Ainnle spoke in listless voices, tired from lack of good meat. That was the first thing that must be solved, Naisi told himself, trying to focus on the rumbling in his belly. Yet he could not ignore the soft sounds of Deirdre's movements at the back, and he found himself straining toward her.

No one would come hunting them tonight.

His relief was needled by bitter pain. *Leary.* His mind kept whispering that name as if it would bring their sword-brother to life again. And what good was Naisi's own safety when others he loved were vulnerable? He thought of his mother and uncles who ruled the dun when Usnech's sons were absent. *Absent far too much.* He bore that pain with straight shoulders, because he would not bow to it; because he had to retain something of himself when the shame crept over him, or fracture utterly.

Deirdre came back with a deerskin wrapped around herself and tucked into her armpits. Her bare shoulders were rosy in the firelight as she spread her clothes out to dry. Ardan and Ainnle tilted away, their eyes avoiding her. Naisi went rigid, his will fleeing the anguish that lay behind him and focusing solely on her. *Conor wasn't here.* He was free of the pressure to defy him. He *had* defied him.

Immediately, Naisi was taken by the urge to press his lips to Deirdre's polished flesh, slowly teasing the hide off and letting it fall free. He needed to lose himself in white heat so he could feel no pain—so he could feel nothing. He jammed his tongue against his teeth as if he could taste her already.

Deirdre shot him an intense glance, before turning her back to draw the hide around her shoulders and curling up by the fire. For the first time in his life, Naisi wished his brothers gone from his side. When he looked in their faces he saw himself, and right now he wanted to be someone else, give in to this desire as if it had no tendrils of guilt running through it. "Your turn," he muttered to his brothers, and while they got changed he flung more sticks on the fire.

"Come on," Ainnle mocked, coming back with a hide about his waist. "You've got us all at a disadvantage."

Naisi unbuckled the tools from his belt, carefully placing the axe and dagger to the side along with his sword and bow. They formed a crescent of blades, a vain effort to protect him from the blows of his pulse. He undressed and sat down with a cloak folded about his hips, and when Deirdre's eyes slanted toward his naked torso, her secret smile was for him alone. Naisi watched the slow uplift of her mouth and made himself breathe out.

The sunseason nights in Alba would be unguarded, the twilights long. He could lose himself in her so there was nothing left to remember, make a bed for her, and walls around it...He trapped that idea with a frown, remembering Anya's fingers tangling in his limbs and hair, seeking to hold him by her hearth when he wanted to hunt and spar with his brothers. There had been no time and no desire for a wife, a mate.

Naisi reined in his wandering mind, focusing all his will on the reflection of fire on Deirdre's pearly shoulder. Simple, feverish desire was all that mattered, because it was consuming, a burning dream that would hold him through the dark.

Deirdre barely slept that night, too aware of Naisi on the bracken beside her—and his brothers squashed in next to him. Though she was utterly exhausted, her body was still tense, her nerves

tightened by an ache she couldn't name. She tugged irritably at
the tunic she'd dried by the fire, now stiff with salt.

The wind moaned through the crevices in the rock, and a
rowan tree creaked outside. The land felt lonely and vast beyond
their tiny shelter, and far away she thought she heard the plaintive howl of a wolf. Something rustled beside her, and Naisi's
hand covered her own. Deirdre's eyes sprang open, the warmth
traveling up her arm.

She spent the rest of the night staring at the cave roof, her
heart racing too fast for slumber. His thumb stroked her palm
and then her wrist, and only when her breathing quickened did
he stop and link fingers again.

In the darkness, she strained across the distance between
them, for the air of Alba was clear and icy, and in it she could
truly breathe him in.

CHAPTER 21

By dawn the rain had lifted. Bleary-eyed, Deirdre looked over
at the brothers in the gray light. Naisi was curled on his side,
his hand under his chin. He muttered in sleep, rubbing his
mouth, and only when his skin grew rosy did she realize the sun
was rising. She eased herself from the sleeping hides and, quietly
donning boots and her fleece cloak, crept outside.

The morning was hushed. Dew dripped from the birches that
clustered in the shadowed ravine, their pale limbs ghostly
against the sprouting bracken and dark rocks. The stream between them was a winding ribbon hung with veils of mist.
Above, the east-facing hillslopes were splashed with orange sun.
A thrush sang from the top of an ash tree.

She squatted among tiny bluebells on the streambank, wetting her hands and face in the icy water. When she opened her eyes she grew still, before slowly uncurling. The sun must be distorted by the mist, for the leaves and branches, the stream and rocks were rimed for a moment with a silver glimmer. Deirdre wiped her eyes on her sleeve then stopped, spreading her hands. The coating of moisture shimmered a little, forming a thin band of light around each finger.

Once at Beltaine, Levarcham had allowed her a sip of the herbs of seeing. Now the same dizziness seemed to have entered her, that faint ringing through her flesh. The shapes around her lost their definition and she thought the ghostly trees quivered, though it must just be the swirl of mist. Dazed, her legs led her along a deer-path that slanted skyward, moving without conscious will through curtains of vapor shot through by sunlight. She felt she was not walking but floating, gradually dissolving into iridescence.

At last she broke out into a high meadow bathed in the cold dawn. A hand-hewn stone leaned at an angle at its center, its shoulders mottled with lichen, and another stone had fallen beside it. Deirdre paused. A yew tree had grown up beside the stones, its heartwood dying and leaving saplings that sprang from the ring of the ancient trunk. The Otherworld tree of transformation, the doorway to the spirits. It was the bough of the death goddess Badb: a bringer of dreams.

Deirdre crunched across the frosted grass and when she got into the pool of sun at the fallen stone, her legs gave out and she folded back on it almost without volition. She clung to the cold rock with spread hands while the pale sky spun around her, sweeping all her mind-sense away with it. Her breath swung back and forth, like a feather floating to earth, the rhythm making her sink lower...

Her eyes closed, her breath halted.

A pulse came up through the stone into her palms, almost below hearing—a vibration that was so low and long that it could have merely been a gust of wind funneling over the peaks.

Yet it was centered here. One of her feet slipped off the stone to the ground, and she knew it rose through the earth then, a thrumming pressure that was gathered here in the clearing. It flowed up her in waves until her body sang in tune with it, in tiny ripples of blood and muscle. The vibration lapped into her mind, thoughts quivering...images stirring into life.

Impressions bloomed across that dark void like lightning-bursts, bright before fading.

A circle of the fresh-hewn stones stood upright with people weaving through them in a dance. The rough surface under Deirdre's fingers throbbed in memory.

Further back...the meadow was once a forest, and at its heart was a clearing that held an oak stump. Someone in ragged hides knelt there with bowed head, placing an offering at its base: a haunch of meat. The air shimmered, and the song came through the ground into the hunter's knees, summoned by his reverence, anchored here by the touches of many hands that had darkened the wood. *Join me to my spirit brothers,* he chanted, *all held in the womb of the Mother.* It flooded Deirdre's body now, a drumming inside her, and she felt him.

Her flesh shivered along with his into the fluid light around him and...

...now the hunter sensed the eagle flying above, and knew its thoughts. The bird heard the same faint song he did, but in the mountain realms of cold updrafts that resonance was behind the sky. It passed through skin and feathers, lifting the bird's wings along with the rush of air. To eagle-eyes, the clouds were stream-ing currents of radiance, and below, the heartbeats of animals wove a vivid tapestry. *Life, swift and urgent.* There is what the man sought. *Deer.*

Deirdre tumbled with him down into blackness, spiraling to a shocking halt. The light grew again. Four legs trembled in the undergrowth, antlers brushing the branches. Muscles flooded with alertness, nostrils twitched, sorting scents. Rotting wood. Bitter sap. The meaty whiff of larvae chewing leaf-mold. Then a waft of something that turned the deer to stone. Wet fur, pungent urine. *Wolf.* The stag slowed the tremor of its lungs until it slipped into being one with the trees, disappearing into the web of light.

Another plunge, a pause.

A long snout stretched to the wind, ears pricked. High on a ridge the wolf halted, tilting its muzzle, testing the smells. Warm hide, and the sharp overlay of fear. *Deer.* Its head was lifted by the growing pressure in its throat and chest as the howl took shape, powerful and urgent. The cry wrenched free of its jaws and bounced off the valley walls, reflected back until its ears rang with the sound of its own soul. *This I am*, it sang, *I am here, I am life.*

Hunter, deer, eagle, wolf, the heartbeat of the earth itself—as one it crackled through Deirdre like a bolt of lightning, and her soul erupted in a great flash. She saw her body as a pinprick and her spirit-self billowing outward from it at immense speed, exploding into a vaster form. Surging back through memory to what she had been; soaring onward to what she might become.

A jolt of terror went through her, and the flash imploded into darkness.

Suddenly, Deirdre was awake, sucking in a labored breath as if surfacing from a dive, her galloping heart trampling her thoughts. She must have fallen asleep, and mad dreams had entered her from the land beneath. Her fingers pressed into the rock to stop the yawing of the ground, the scent of yew needles filling her nostrils.

Mortals were taken by the *sídhe*, the untamed spirits of the wild that could appear as beautiful men and women or animals. As a child, she had longed to glimpse them; as a woman, she had strained to hear them, to know what lived in the mysterious woods. A raven had beckoned her once, but this was different. The visceral force of animal sense had utterly consumed her. She hadn't called it; it happened *to* her. Her eyes widened. What could the *sídhe* want of her?

To leave herself, lose herself, entangled with the wildwood?

No one could control the *sídhe*. She sprang upright, panting a white cloud on the morning air. She could see nothing now but

the dew on the sunlit bracken and the pale trunks of the birch
trees surrounding the meadow. An aching cold seeped into her
hands from the fallen stone. She rose and crossed the meadow,
and with trembling fingers broke a sprig of rowan blossom off a
small tree at the fringe of the woods, tucking it in her tunic next
to her breast along with the swan-feather. Rowan protected people from enchantment, Levarcham had said.

Deirdre carefully crept down the path, her eyes on the stony
trail at her feet and away from the spreading rays of the sun that
had blurred her mind.

Shivering, she nestled into Naisi's broad back. It moved gently,
like the shores of a quiet sea. In the growing light, she touched a
thread of hair where it had escaped his braid, curling in the soft
dip at the base of his skull. This was where she belonged, what
she was. She turned her cheek against the blade of his shoulder,
and now she could only hear his heart beating in her ear.

As the morning passed, the sun burned off the lingering mist
and a cold, brisk wind chivied the clouds away. Naisi and Ainnle
decided to go back to the herder's hut they had passed the day
before.

At their appearance, the old woman stirring porridge in her
doorway let out a hoarse shriek. Her bowl went flying, spilling
congealed barley over the step while Naisi closed in, hastily trying to explain. Still screeching, she backed into the dark, low-
beamed hut, flapping her skirt.

Her wizened husband came hobbling from the sheep pens,
lunging at them with a knobbed staff, eyes fiery beneath bushy
white brows. "Away, yeh blasted sods! Away!"

Ainnle's astonished chuckle became a grunt when the staff
got past his raised arms and connected with his head. Naisi managed to shout, "We mean no harm, we come as friends!"

"Friends? Creeping up on my Arda—I'll give yeh a knock to remember!"

It took some time to calm them down, but at last Naisi was

able to get through to the couple that he and Ainnle had not come to attack them. He studied them as he rubbed his aching shoulder. The old man was still on guard, his staff held before him. He was as bleached as broken driftwood, with salt-white hair and gray eyes that were sharp in a nest of wrinkles. His wife, Arda, was stout, with wind-bitten cheeks and gray braids. Their cloaks were of raw sheep's wool, mottled brown, their boots pieces of fleece wrapped with flax rope.

The brothers had decided to change their names to hide themselves from Conor. Ardan was now Bran and Ainnle was Conn. "I am Finn," Naisi introduced himself, summoning a smile that felt stiff, for it had been so long since one came naturally.

The old woman wavered, lowering her spoon and scanning him from head to toe. After a few courtly words about the weather and the difficulties of lambing in rain, they were convincing enough that the old man at last relented, and warily invited them inside.

Swinging from terror to fervent hospitality, Arda bustled about seating Naisi and Ainnle on benches by the smoky fire and urging bannocks upon them, the moist bread still hot from the hearth-stone. The hut was tiny, with a loom set by the door surrounded by baskets of creamy, pungent wool, and a bed-box covered in fleeces. Little linen bags of cheese curd hung in pale globes from the rafters, dripping whey into wooden bowls, and the air was tangy with the scent of soured milk.

The man's name was Urp, and Naisi swiftly discovered from him the most important thing about their new home: there were no forts or homesteads close by, beyond a few herders' huts like this one. Urp pointed with his chin. "East up yon glen is Mairi and her father, Necht, and her daughter, and a few others, then beyond that it's barren moor and mountain until the Venicones lands on the other side. South and west over the loch is the king's seat at Dunadd, four days away." He shrugged one bony shoulder. "We're left to do as we please." Naisi nodded gravely, hiding his relief.

"And how many are yeh?" Arda asked, pouring ewe's milk for them.

"Three brothers," Naisi answered, taking the tiny cup of alder-wood off her. He held Ainnle's eye, willing him not to mention Deirdre. "We were forced to leave our home, an island in the Erin sea."

Urp's beady eyes moved from the gilded terminals of their bows to their dagger-sheaths, the embroidery dirty and frayed though still fine. Naisi silently cursed himself. Their riches—arm-bands, torcs, brooches, furs—were buried in their packs, but he'd become so used to his filthy clothes he'd forgotten their weapons. He met Urp's thoughtful gaze. "We had a disagreement with our lord, and thought it better to make our own way." At the old man's alarm, he hastily added, "We came here to live quietly. We mean no trouble to anyone."

Urp sat back, his fingers tapping his staff. "It's the king's leave to stay yeh must seek. Though as we name this place the roaring glen on account of the winds, yeh may want to reconsider."

Naisi returned his smile. "If we are not crowded by others, we mind little else. We will apply for the king's leave when we can. In the meantime, though, it might be better if the news of our arrival did not travel far."

"There'll likely be no trouble if yeh leave the sheep alone."

"Husband," Arda scolded, pouring more barley into a battered pot on the fire. "Finer young men I never saw!"

Ainnle looked down, stifling a smile. "What about the hunting?" he asked Urp.

Urp's white brows twitched. "We're a mite too old to be leaping about rocks like goats."

"Then what we kill we'll share with you," Naisi offered.

Arda's smile revealed the gaps in her teeth, her red cheeks bunching. "I've not had fresh deer for years," she murmured, sucking her lip appreciatively.

Urp asked where they had camped and they gave him vague directions. "Be careful up there." He leaned in, voice dropping. "*They* live in the wild places, the *sídhe*." He tapped his veined nose, the nostrils sprouting pale hair. "The *calleach* herself is heard up there on stormy nights, screaming to the rain. Best yeh ask *her* for the game."

Naisi drained the single mouthful in the cup and placed it on the bench. "We'll dedicate the first kill to her."

Arda was studying their shoulders with a glint in her eye. "And remember she can be a maiden, too, beautiful as dawn. She makes young men lie with her, but she's dangerous." She poked her spoon at Naisi. "Be careful not to be ensnared, for yeh surely have the face to stop a maid's heart, goddess though she be."

Naisi's blood was inexplicably pounding. "I'll be careful."

When they left, Arda pressed a trug of butter into Ainnle's hands while Urp hauled a skinned shoulder of lamb out of his lean-to. "To get yeh started," he said. Naisi took it from him, the generosity robbing him of his fine words, so he could only mutter a gruff reply.

When they got back to camp, Ardan was gutting a hare. He told them he didn't have to set a snare, for it just sat there while he cocked his bow. "Not much of a challenge," he grumbled. He flicked shreds of intestine from bloody fingers. "We'll have fresh stew tonight, anyway."

"No, we won't." Naisi laid the lamb on stones by the fire. He indicated the hare. "Go and introduce yourself to Urp and Arda, and give that to them as a gift."

"But I just caught it!"

Naisi cuffed him over the back of the head, making Ardan duck away. "We'll have roast lamb instead, and the sooner we repay the debt and gain their trust, the better."

Naisi found Deirdre in a lochside clearing among hazel trees, picking violet leaves and nettle tops and rolling them in a hide bag. Her gaze was glassy as she listened to his report of Urp and Arda, all the while combing her fingers through the hair she'd rinsed in a nearby stream. His words faded as he was overcome with the sensation that her mind had turned inward, away from him.

Her eyes were opaque in the shadows of the leaves, and an instinctive fear drove him to kneel beside her. Strange thoughts tumbled through him. She wasn't his to lose himself in after all. Curled up in her deerskins, she was a doe glimpsed for a moment in a forest clearing...a *sídhe* in deer form. And now that she was free of Conor's snare, she would leap away into the hills and he would be left with this crushing weight, alone.

It was the exhaustion, the fight with Leary; it had addled him. Unnerved, he reached and cupped her cheek. Her sight wavered back into focus and her chin tilted to him, her hair a glowing corona around the heart of her face. The heat was there in her eyes again, naked and earthy, and his mind cleared as the lingering heat of sun-warmed skin brought her musky scent to his nostrils. When he saw her lips part slightly he buried a hand in her hair and dragged her to him, his tongue capturing hers. *Come back*, he wanted to say...and then she was back, her mouth opening hungrily, melting into him. His desire lashed him. *I must take her at last...here...*Anywhere.

If she were Anya he would pause only to pull up her dress. But not Deirdre. She was still unbroken—they had shared no more than kisses and burning touches—and he would not rush and cause her pain. And Ardan or Ainnle could come upon them at any moment, and somehow he knew if he could not keep her unsettling beauty from his brothers, he must at least hide how naturally she opened to his touch.

He broke off, his hands falling away as the truth roared over him. Even that was not it. It was that when he thought of them rutting in the woods, he clearly saw Conor's smirk hovering over them. For this is what everyone would expect—that they were nothing but animals, that he broke his Red Branch vows because he could not control himself. He could not banish that strangling vision of the knowing contempt in Conor's eyes. He could not allow him to be right. Naisi turned on his belly, hiding the swelling between his legs and trying to get his breath back.

Deirdre placed her hand on his shoulder. Her eyes were penetrating, her cheeks flushed. "Don't treat me like a child." She struggled to push the words out. "I know what you want."

Startled, he raised himself on one arm and her eyes traveled down his body. With a wondering look, she brushed the sliver of belly exposed by his rumpled tunic, until he grabbed her hand. "I don't know how safe these woods are—"

"You just told me they were very safe." A tinge of mischief hovered around her mouth.

Before he could summon anything sensible, unexpected words leaped from him. "Wait until I make us our own home." Her body subtly tensed and he also froze, astonished at himself. Sharing a hearth built with their own hands—food and fire— this bound people together beyond the pleasures of the body. When he had gripped her shoulders on the beach, he'd had no thought of anything but keeping her from Conor. *Mated. Handfast.* He wasn't even sure he wanted that. He didn't know what he wanted...

She cut through his churning thoughts by bending her lips to his palm. "Only if you promise to show me everything then." Her eyes swept up, fixing on him. "I want to know it all, and all of it with you, Naisi." He stared, speechless, until she suddenly disarmed him with the flood of her smile. "Until then we can kiss, though, can't we?"

The air rushed out of him. *Yes, though it might kill me.* He leaned over her among the violets and she put her arms over her head with a sigh and stretched her hands as if grasping for the sun.

CHAPTER 22

"I never want to see another fish, let alone eat it," Ainnle grumbled, hauling the curragh up on the riverbank among the marshes.

Ardan slung a brace of trout over the oar bench, their scales gleaming and gills still pulsing. "And all that hare leaves me hollow."

The leaf-bud days had turned gray and wind-bitten, with flurries of raindrops slanting over the loch. A curlew called mournfully and nearby a pair of swans drifted close to shore, sheltering from the wind. Naisi was spreading their new fishing net over a bush to dry and Deirdre came to help. All her time had been taken by picking stinging nettles, shredding out the fibers and weaving the net together, as the welts on her fingers could attest. Naisi's hands were cold from the water, and now he turned her palms up and pressed one of the nettle blisters to his lips, his lashes spangled with rain.

With her other hand she brushed the chafed corners of his mouth, roughened by the wind and their kisses. His smile faded as his eyes bore into her with strained desire, and she cleared her throat, drawing away. "You could always pick bulrush roots," she said to Ainnle.

Ainnle glanced at her, and she felt his accusations land in pinpricks all over her skin. *This is all your fault—being stuck here, being hungry.* She wrapped her hide cloak more tightly against the cold wind, unwilling to meet his eyes and give him the satisfaction of her guilt, for their thoughts were more alike than he could know.

"The deer should be easy to hunt." Ardan stuck the oars upright in the pebbles. "But they seem to disappear into the rocks themselves."

Naisi faced the water, his hands resting loosely on his hips. He shifted the rocks with his toe. "Perhaps we have not appeased the gods of this place. After all, the king of the Epidii has not given us leave to stay." The darkness in his voice drew Deirdre back and she placed her hand against his side, disturbed to feel his ribs with her knuckles. Even with Arda's butter the brothers were growing thinner, for they spent their days scouring the hills for game. They were young, and they needed red meat.

The rumble of Ainnle's stomach interrupted them, and he grimaced as he unloaded his bow. "We should take service with another lord, brother."

Naisi's head came up. "No. The Ulaid are a sworn enemy of the Epidii. We cannot be discovered yet."

"Then we must go somewhere else," Ainnle argued. He scowled, his eyes straying to Deirdre. "It's what we are made for. Grubbing for plants is for women. We are warrior-born."

Deirdre kept a blank expression. *Then you'll starve as a warrior, too.*

Naisi exhaled and spun about, making them all startle. "Lugh's breath, why can't we hunt? Are we god-*cursed* now?" It was a rare outburst, and for a moment none of them could speak. Naisi scraped wet hair off his temples, struggling to compose his face, but Deirdre had already glimpsed the fleeting fear behind that frustration.

They did not only lack meat. At the village at the mouth of the River Awe, they could barter for grain and iron pots, arrow-points and cloth. But so far, they had no hides to trade.

"We do have *something* to exchange for food." Ainnle's voice was low, his eyes lighting on Deirdre's wrist.

She had pulled on Conor's armbands to make the weight of her pack easier, and had grown so used to them that in the flight and these early days of exile she had forgotten to take them off. The bronze was starting to tarnish in the salt air, but the graceful swirling designs marked their quality. Impulsively, she dragged one off and tossed it on the ground. "So you think I hold to these out of greed or vanity?" She met Ainnle's challenging eyes. "Sell them, then."

Naisi sighed, his shoulders lowering. "They are yours."

"They are not mine." Her back drew straight. "They are the king's. Ainnle is right. I don't care anything for them." Ainnle looked almost disappointed at her swift acquiescence.

"No." Naisi's face was tired and grim. "I won't have us giving up everything of what we were." A thread of fierceness ran through his voice. "You, Ainnle, your torc would buy a storehouse of barley, yet I don't see you volunteering it." Ainnle's fingers went to his warrior neck-ring, his scowl deepening. All three of them still wore their Red Branch armbands under their clothes, too—but at least they were sacred; they had been earned. Hers had not.

Deirdre stared at Naisi. "You don't understand me. Am I any less when you take the king's gilding away?" She twisted the other armband off, and it was Conor's eyes she felt upon her as she flung it to the sand with a noise of defiance. How could she, even in weariness, forget his shackles had still been on her arms? The ring bounced over a patch of sprouting chickweed and settled, glinting up at her. Another band followed it, and as they left her she felt lighter. "I don't need the marks of a man's regard to make me myself."

Naisi was regarding her with concern. Behind him, Ardan's smile was admiring and rueful, while Ainnle rubbed his stubbled chin, at last looking shamefaced. Had he ever given thought to a woman's heart, she wondered, or were maidens just playthings to him, gilded and embroidered to make his life more pleasurable? An irrational dart of fury made her want to fling one of the rings at him, to make him truly *see* her, but a cooler impulse quashed that. For despite it all, Ainnle's bow had downed meat to feed her and he had raised his blade to defend her.

The hurt went from her in a rush. "I care for nothing but you who shelter me," she said in a low voice, looking right at Ainnle, "and for the woods and water, and to be free whether alive or dead." Her gaze went to Naisi. "So never make my hunger the reason to take service with another lord. I need nothing of that world. It is not mine."

Naisi broke the silence by stepping up and holding her tense body to his chest, her face in his neck. "Gods," he muttered in her ear, "don't turn that flame on *me* any time soon. You'll singe my brows off."

She flung back her head to look up at him, and then she saw the deeper glow in his eyes that did not match his wry smile. "It depends if you annoy me enough," she murmured breathlessly.

His smile widened. To his brothers, over his shoulder, he said, "One of us will take the bronze over the loch and buy grain and beef, and when that is gone we'll find another way."

Ardan sat on the rail of the beached curragh, looking over the water, his arms folded across himself. "The deer have to come to our spears sometime."

A few mornings later, Deirdre woke to a hushed dawn, the trees seeming to float in a sunlit mist. Ardan's words echoed from the remnants of her dreams. *They have to come to our spears sometime.*

Over Naisi's shoulder, Ainnle was a snoring lump, while at the end of the row Ardan had begun stirring, yawning and slapping at the hordes of tiny biting insects that descended on them each dawn and dusk from Alba's damp woods.

Naisi was watching as she blinked herself awake. "Today," she whispered to him, still walking in her forest dreams. "Today you shall hunt, and I will come."

He touched his thumb to her cheek. The rising sun sent a ray across his face, setting a glow in his eyes and making his hair gleam like raven feathers. "I heard it was bad luck to take women hunting."

"Men say that just to be free of their wives for a day." He acknowledged that with a snort and she rested her hand over his, the calluses on his palm grazing her cheek. His otherness still caught her off guard, both his smell and his way of moving. His long muscles were honed by the repetition of skilled sword feats and the bearing of heavy weapons: an utterly physical life. It gave all the brothers a startling presence, as if they claimed the earth beneath their feet with every step, shaped the air to let them pass. "We must ask for what we need in reverence, together," she murmured. "The four of us are alone, and subject to the land itself now."

He searched her eyes. "The druids taught us our hunt chants. Is this something Levarcham said?"

She hesitated. "It's something I feel to be true. There is a knowing here, a presence unlike anything I have felt before. Perhaps it's because there are so few people—the wild seems vast, powerful."

He absorbed the determination in her face. "Well, there's only us to please now after all. We can make any rules we want." She saw how crooked his smile was, though, and shadowed.

When he told his brothers that Deirdre was coming, Ainnle said nothing, stabbing a stick into the fire-coals and stirring them up. One arm-ring had bought them meat, barley grains and two iron pots, though the beef was gone now, the bone sticking out of the congealed porridge.

Ardan cocked his head at her. "Why is it important you come?" He wasn't being challenging, she realized, meeting his deep gray eyes. He sensed something about the expectant still-ness of this morning, too, with the mist curling from the damp bracken. He always asked her about her strange intuitions and never scorned them.

"The spirits of the mountains are strong here. Their slopes shelter all the animals and plants and we have to honor them, promise we will bring more life in exchange for what we take." She spread a hand. "I am druid taught and, as there are only the four of us, we need as many prayers as we can muster."

Ardan nodded to himself, and Naisi, who was checking his spears, glanced over with a somber look. Flustered, her gaze slid to Naisi's hands smoothing his spear-shafts, testing the bindings of the points and feeling for straightness. He was unconsciously enlivening the weapons with his touch, waking the barbs and binding them to his will. Desire quivered in her. What surge of life would they kindle between them, in return for the deer?

Naisi slid the spear-butts to the ground and leaned on the shafts. "We all understand when honor is demanded by the *sídhe*." He looked pointedly at Ainnle. "We have been rushing off to hunt with only the briefest of blessings, as if we are still at home. Let us sing the full chant now from the sacred hunts at Emain Macha. After all, we have an almost-druid to help us." His glanc-ing smile was warm on Deirdre's cheek.

There was no blood from a previous carcass with which to mark their faces and so invoke their kinship to the deer. Instead, the brothers unbound their hair and removed all belts and bind-ings to allow the flow of spirit through them. They piled their deer amulets on the ground and sat in a circle around them in a pool of sunlight.

Resting cross-legged, Deirdre's eyes sank closed as one by one the brothers began their sacred chant, a low murmur of barely recognizable words, asking the *sídhe* of the deer-forests to bless their endeavors. The gods ruled men's fates and warded the distant realms; the *sídhe* were the nature-sprites, wild guardians of beasts and plants, streams and springs.

Now they struck the rhythm of the song out on their knees in a primitive beat, pleading for sustenance. The thumps of their palms formed a racing pulse, weaving a spell that went deeper than mere words and into the flesh itself. The blows of their hands thudded through Deirdre, stirring up her blood as her head grew light, resonating with sound. Words came alive on her lips before she could stop them, a song pulled up from some ancient memory glimmering in the recesses of her mind. Her fear flowed strong and then ebbed, drowned in the vision that opened up behind her eyes.

It was a cave, and her own hand painting an ocher outline on rock. A crude stag came alive under her fingers, the tracing and the husky song summoning the ghost-deer, pleading with them to draw their flesh-and-blood brothers to the grasslands in sight of the hunters' spears. She knew then that in other lives she had crossed these liminal boundaries between spirit-place and Thisworld...walking the soul-trail for the people, the clan. Shaman. She did not know the name that breathed through her soul.

She had been unconsciously threading that ancient tune through the hunt chant, and together the four voices sank down into earth and soil and rock, becoming breathy and sonorous. The galloping song beckoned the deer to run with them now through these mountains of Alba, guttural and urgent. Primal. *Come...come...*

Deirdre's body swayed as it loosened with song, and she had the frightening sense of its outline shivering into light, her eyelids flickering uncontrollably...

The deer thundered through the forest, the thudding of its

hooves in time with the ragged chanting and pounding fists of the men. It snorted hot breath through soft nostrils, drawing in the dank, rich scents of the woodlands that had now burgeoned into fecund life, the thick cover of leaves filtering the sun into a green haze. The dawn had wakened its blood, and now it must expend its nervous energy. It lifted its antlers to gaze up at two peaks with a ridge running between them. There...high ground ...safe ground.

Two peaks that speared the sky above the roaring glen.

Deirdre was on her feet, staggering. Her fingers spread before glassy eyes. "We must go," she croaked. "I see him." Her hand was a white arrow pointing the way up the ridge.

The brothers grabbed their weapons and hastened away from camp and she fell into step behind them. The sons of Usnech did not speak, moving up the ravine with the flowing bounds of wolves. She hardly felt herself running, her feet sensing the echo of the song through the earth.

The sun was past its peak when they broke out onto slopes of stately pines, their spreading boughs swaying in the mountain winds. The needles dappled the light, turning the brothers' clothes into spotted pelts, black hair streaming out behind them. The thread pulling Deirdre on grew stronger the higher they went. She felt the heartbeat of the deer as a swifter current within the ocean inside her.

At the top of the slope, the brothers hesitated, but Deirdre wheeled along the ridge past them and began climbing a narrow crevice in the rocks between two sharp peaks. The hunters scrabbled up behind her and at last they were all standing at the crown of the world, the slopes falling away from their feet like gray sea-waves frozen into rock, their bodies buffeted by the icy wind. In the shelter of the hill-crest, a stand of pines spread a raft of branches, and something gleamed there between them. Russet fur caught in sunshine.

In a daze of sweat, the hunters sank behind the rocks, drawing in shuddering breaths as one. Oblivious, the stag dipped its neck to chew at a crop of rowan seedlings, its hide rippling. Deirdre looked at Naisi's transfigured face and beyond him to Ardan, whose cheeks were flushed, his eyes glassy. Ainnle had lost his scowl, the power of the chant casting a glow of purity and power over his young face.

Silently, Naisi drew a spear from his carrier and all Deirdre's rational thoughts disintegrated. An instinct came in their wake, a gradual knowing rising through her like a wind, enveloping her with wordless meaning.

"We must get closer," Naisi murmured.

Deirdre hardly heard him, for at that moment the deer's antlers swept through the overhanging needles. It turned to look at her, and the power of its gaze reached out and bound them both together. The irresistible force dragged her to her feet.

"Deirdre," Naisi hissed, catching at the hem of her tunic.

"Wait," she heard Ardan say.

She almost floated over the ground toward the stag, and it did not startle but remained still, apart from one twitching ear. Its dark eyes fixed on hers, and in the shelter of the peak the slopes became hushed, the wind dropping, the bird-song fading. She walked with her fingers out in supplication, and let her heart fill with gratitude. The deer trembled in answer, shivers spreading under its hide.

Its eye followed her every step until she was there before it. At last, she reached out and touched a wild beast as she had longed to do in all the years she paced the ramparts of Conor's prison. Its antlers branched above her, its flank moving under her fingers with potent, powerful life. It felt kin to her. She could put her arms around it and cling to its back as it ran, its hide merging with her skin.

She savored the rough texture of its coat and it shuddered when she stroked its neck and softer muzzle. *You will be held in our hearts always, the imprint of your life in our spirits, your blood in our blood.* Her reverence was like a druid blessing, and it flowed from her into the stag, and she held its head so that its leaf-scented breath mingled with her own. Its pulse thudded under her fingers as her gaze drowned in deer-thought, and she wondered what she must give in return for this gift. Her body showed her, summoning an image of two pale figures entwined under moonlight, a white fire burning between them. A rush went through her of stag-sense, of simple lust for life and rutting, the feel of wind and sun. *Naisi.* Naisi must come to the deer. Was he connected to her enough to hear that call?

The combined life-force of deer and girl reached for the young hunter, and at length she heard his feet, each step slow and careful. Naisi held his dagger poised in one hand and the deer's head turned toward him, their gazes locking. The stag's eyes were knowing, the man's glistening with emotion.

Naisi gripped the hilt, steadying himself, and his other hand spread over the deer's trembling flank. They stayed in that communion, the trust naked in the beast's eyes while Naisi murmured to it under his breath. At length, his fingers felt tenderly along its muscular neck for the artery, and he bent his head so his loose hair fell in a dark curtain, shielding Deirdre from those last moments of hunter and stag together. She felt rather than saw the dagger slide in. Pain mingled with light and the stag's body slowly crumpled. Deirdre had to draw back as it sagged to its knees and then toppled to one side. Naisi, though, followed it all the way down, pressing his cheek to its flank, holding its neck while its blood ran through his fingers.

Deirdre turned, still lost in her dream-state. Wisps of dank mist were creeping down from the clouded peak now, and outlined there she saw the deer-spirit, its substance finer than smoke. Her mind adrift, she did not question how it came to be there. The spirit deer paused, unsure, and an old instinct made Deirdre raise her hands. The senses that had overcome her on the fallen stone rushed through her: the eagle's awareness of the light behind the sky, the wolf's urge to howl its existence, the dissolving of the deer into the forest. The song of the stone was in her flesh, and it flowed from her outstretched hands, stirring the air into a stream of light that was cradled and focused by her reverence. Her blessing. *You are safe...go well.*

The deer pricked its ears toward the light, which unwound

before it in a bright thread, and step by faltering step it was drawn toward that shining path that led it onward. Gradually, the outline of the ghost stag wavered and the memory of its form melted back into radiance, until there was only the lowering sun in Deirdre's eyes.

They silently burned the liver on a small fire as an offering to the spirits, and while dusk fell packed the meat into bundles. Deirdre was washing her hands in a stream when Ardan squatted beside her. "Can you teach me to call deer like that?" he murmured. His expression was awestruck.

She wiped her hands on her trews, shivering. The stars were glowing in a pale, hushed sky. "I don't know. It wasn't a calling, it was...joining." She could barely speak now, as if her body was a stranger to her; her lips clumsy, tongue thick. "The druids say that to reach through the veils you must be still, and listen, and sink into them, like water." She didn't even know how she'd done it, for the experience was already fading from her mind.

Ardan sighed. "I try all that, to no avail." He glanced strangely at her. "Perhaps now I will try harder."

She turned to him. "You are drawn to druid lore. Why did you not enter the training?"

His smile was faintly bitter. "With a father like ours and brothers like mine?" His gaze went to Naisi, rolling up the bloody hide, and the glimmer of light in the sky illuminated something in Ardan's eyes that was not resentment. "We are a pack," he said softly. "How could I be anything but a warrior, born to a den of these cubs?"

She watched him with sympathy. "Then I will tell you what I know," she said, wondering if that betrayed Levarcham. She thought her teacher might see it as payment to one who had saved her, in the most fundamental way, from imprisonment.

Ardan's gaze came back to her and the grim shadow in his face lifted, and his smile was gentle again. "I would like that."

As they walked back down the mountain, the brothers sang a

softer, twilight song, and Deirdre picked sprigs of thyme and crushed them to her nose to smell the wild mountain and draw it deep inside her.

The three hunters stripped and bathed before entering camp again, washing all traces of the animal-trance away, dressing in their human form to return to the fire. Deirdre stuck the thyme sprigs in the deer-flesh before they rolled it in leaves and nestled it in the coals, and they ate the tangy baked meat as dark fell. When they crawled exhausted into their sleeping hides, Naisi turned his back on his brothers, placing his face beside Deirdre's on the bracken. It smelled of the myrtle leaves she'd sprinkled there to ward away the gnats.

"So you are a *calleach,*" Naisi whispered.

The untamed, woman-spirit of the mountains. A sudden heaviness descended over her. What was reaching to her from the wilds? Ardan was already breathing slowly and Ainnle twitching. No one could see them. She leaned over Naisi and brushed his lips with her fingers. "I am me—don't make me into something else." She paused. "That's what Conor did."

With a muffled curse, Naisi pulled her down until their faces were level. The faint glow that remained all through the sun-season nights in these northern skies caught his cheek, and shadowed by his brows, his eyes were deer-dark. "What you are is my *fiáin*—my wild one. I do know you; I was there." He smoothed the hair from her temple. "I was there with you."

She kissed him, her elbows crushed together on his chest. It was tender this time, almost tentative. She had never revealed herself so much to anyone. As a child she had been groomed to be a royal bride, and that had changed how Aiveen, Fintan and Levarcham had seen her. Now she wasn't anything but herself, yearning for the freedom of the forest, challenging her courage, testing her limits as she had always wanted to test them. Did he understand that without words?

Unlike the storm of lust, this surrender into tenderness was silent and gradual, the kiss a slow dive into a great, hushed space.

He felt the change, too, pulling away to touch his mouth to the corner of her lips, softly caressing her eyelids.

A different chill crept in then, slinking up on Deirdre like the shadowy twin of tenderness. She found herself glad her arms were wrapped over her chest, shielding her suddenly exposed heart. He could turn her inside out with one glance, see all the hidden things in her she did not yet know herself. She felt raw, and fought the urge to curl her body up, making her heart safe and contained again.

In the dim light, she glimpsed an answering vulnerability in Naisi's face, and then she could not look anymore, resting her head on his chest.

Cúchulainn rode into the tiny cluster of huts by the sea. People peered from their doorways, while rain poured down around him in the gloom. A few boys freed themselves from their mother's grip, darting between the puddles and disappearing into a house at the end of the track. It was so gray that they would not recognize his features, but his Red Branch shield was tied to his saddle. Everyone knew that sign: the gilded tree painted on the polished leather, one trunk spreading into many branches, each tipped with a gold spear-head.

He stopped his pony amid the dripping circle of thatch roofs. The horse flicked rain from its eyes with a shake of its head, and Cúchulainn followed suit, slewing it from his face with a cold hand. Thunder cracked over the sea beyond the hill.

A man hurried out of the far house, holding a sheep-hide over his head. "My lord," he stammered, blinking up at Cúchulainn through the rain.

His pale eyes were tight with fear, taking in Cúchulainn's sword and the spears sticking out of his saddle-pouch, tipped with wolf-fur. Cúchulainn dismounted. "Don't be afraid. I need a bite of something warm if you have it."

The headman bowed and clumsily led the way into his hut.

The walls inside were webbed with drying nets and fish-spears, baskets and oiled cloaks. Cúchulainn stretched his sodden boots to the crackling fire and accepted a bowl of thin shellfish broth from a terrified woman.

After slurping down the broth in silence, watched by a circle of eyes, Cúchulainn sat forward. He held the headman's gaze. "I seek news of fugitives—three men and a woman."

The man's eyes slid away. "We know nothing."

Conor's threats had traveled far. He dropped his voice, spreading his hands. "No one knows I am here; I swear as the Hound of the Ulaid. You have my honor on it."

The villager's scrawny throat bobbed, though he still looked too scared to speak.

"I lost the trail of these people some time ago," Cúchulainn continued gently, "and they mean much to me. Now I have heard rumors…" The man's glazed eyes flickered, and Cúchulainn's voice grew firmer. "Has there been any trace of strangers in your lands these past moons?"

The headman's mouth pursed beneath its rough beard.

"Did you see anyone?"

A vigorous headshake.

"Fires?"

A nod.

"And where they had camped?"

The man's tongue came back to life. "We saw shells and hearths. And we heard…" he hesitated, "…*singing*. Once, in the middle of the night."

Relief washed over Cúchulainn. "Do you know where they went?" The man hesitated again and Cúchulainn reluctantly rested his hand on his hilt. He summoned a faint throb of the battle-light, that focused force that with a ripple of his hands could send a young warrior flying. "I need to know."

The villager sucked in his lip, then spilled out words. "We never saw them, never! But…a curragh disappeared. We thought a storm had got it."

A boat…so they'd left the shore. But for where? Naisi would

never abandon his homeland, so they must have headed for an island, and there were hundreds of those. Cúchulainn's thoughts raced. Naisi had not handed the girl over after Leary's death, even though Cúchulainn knew it must have been a terrible accident. Something else had happened to make Naisi give up the Red Branch. For some reason, an image of his own wife's face arose in Cúchulainn's mind. *Emer.*

Naisi had always burned to be the best; he was single-minded, focused. He slaked his body with the ale-maids, but he had not taken a wife for convenience, as many did. Could it be...? Not Naisi—he had always been wedded to his brothers and his sword. Then the Emer in Cúchulainn's mind gave her slow, secret smile, dark eyes shining, and the Hound remembered indeed what was possible between man and woman.

"That's all I know," the villager was babbling, teeth chattering, "we never helped them. No one helped them..."

"Peace." Cúchulainn was already on his feet, his cold muscles filling with a new determination. "You've told me what I needed to know. Now someone must show me from where the boat was taken."

The headman grasped the collar of a lurking boy and shoved him at Cúchulainn. The boy darted out, and at the door-hide the Hound paused, twisting one of Conor's gold rings from his finger. The headman's eyes widened as it soared in a glittering arc in the fire-light and landed on the bracken floor.

"For the boat," he said. *From the king,* he added silently, as he ducked back out into the rain.

CHAPTER 23

Sunseason

The game did not avoid their bows now.

Deirdre's instinct was that the bond with the deer had been summoned only by desperation, and the impulse that came the day of the hunt was that it was a single gift, to give them strength. In honor of that, she never tried to reach out that same way again.

They built a fire-pit outside the cave for fine days, dotting the clearing with tents of hazel branches under which they dried the deer-meat over smoke. Deirdre gathered the rich harvest of uncurling leaves and stalks that covered the riverbanks and forest floor, and Arda gave the brothers cheese curd and barley bread.

When she was not gathering, Deirdre tended the tanning pits the brothers dug on the loch shore, along a rocky path where the old people did not venture. She often spent all day there, poking hides into a soup of oak bark and water, and scraping hair from staked skins with a blade. When she rinsed the hides she paused, struck by the sweep of gray peaks and green turf, and streams carving gullies down the mountainsides to empty waterfalls of foam into the dark water. The immense silence was pierced only by the cries of circling eagles, and the etching of wind across the mirrored loch.

Wandering the rocks, she picked up the swan feathers that drifted endlessly ashore, thinking she'd make a mattress with them one day. Naisi never hunted the swans, telling her about his vision of the goddess in the forest. To Deirdre, they were a guarding presence, their pale shapes gliding past her through morning mists and in the gloaming of dusk.

She was afraid to stumble across the high meadow and the stone, her heart shying away from the memory of her loss of control. She kept reliving the lurch as her body fell away from her, though, and for days every time she closed her eyes she felt that rush toward the vast moment of knowing, that calling. She would startle and open her eyes then, and busy her hands. Forcing away that fine trembling of fear beneath her skin, she tried immersing herself in the rhythms of gathering food and sewing hides—something simple and peaceful.

And still the quickening came for her.

It somehow soaked into her from the land, saturating her like the trickle of rain through soil. If she fell into the mindless rhythm of scraping hides or weaving twine, her sight glazed over before she could help it and…a spark would fly past the corner of her eye. The moment she focused, there would only be wind stirring the leaves. Her gaze would be caught by the gleaming hide of a deer bounding up a hill, or the wet glint of otter fur on the shore, and when she folded leaves in her pouch in the dappled woods, she kept glimpsing the same little darts of light on the boundaries of sight. It was like the glitter of sun on water, but when she dared to focus and stare hard, it was gone.

At night, the darkness around the tiny shelter felt vast and knowing. Just as she drifted into sleep in her nest of hides, she sometimes detected a ripple of sound on the boundary of her senses…a sibilant whisper that emanated from the air itself. Or perhaps she dreamed.

One night, Ardan and Ainnle sat pounding dried sinew on rocks by the fire, separating the fibers for bow-strings and bindings. Naisi sharpened his knives while Deirdre crouched on a log, finishing off a bowl of lamb stew flavored with ramsons, savoring the pungent, herby broth of barley grains and meat.

The evening was still, the sky alight over the horizon. A few stars hung like lanterns over the black spears of the pine trees on the ridge, and the air was so clear they could hear the rushing of a thousand streams all around them. Deirdre couldn't tell Naisi about her fears because she didn't know for sure that she was sensing anything real. And he would think her strange experiences stemmed from some druid training, and they did not.

The glimpse of bird-lore was one thing, but Levarcham had not taught the king's betrothed to tap into the savage, sensory song of the beasts. It consumed her whenever Naisi was near, and when he came to her at the loch she crushed his mouth to hers, her arms binding his head so she could drink from his lips, thirsting for his taste.

Naisi's voice interrupted her thoughts. He told his brothers about his visit to Urp and Arda that day. The old man was suffering pain when he passed water, and had taken a fever. Deirdre cleared her throat. "Has Arda given him a tonic?"

"How would I know?"

"She probably cannot climb high enough for bear-berry." She eyed him. "I have a little. I have been collecting everything I can."

Naisi picked up his dagger, closing one eye to sight along it. "No."

There was a pause. "I never agreed to obey you," she said, struggling to keep her voice even. When he restricted her, even in small ways, she had to fight an instinctive sense of panic, even though she knew it was foolish.

Naisi tugged the toe of her boot. "I don't expect you to obey me except in matters of safety. Everything else is up for debate. I don't want any word getting out of you here with us, that is all." When she moved her foot away he grinned, his teeth white in his tanned face, and edged up her trews with a finger. Turning his back on his brothers, he flashed her a look like a hot dart before kissing her bare shin. She kicked out and he gripped her foot, his face vivid with unguarded amusement, and rubbed his stubbled chin over her skin to send little sparks up her thigh.

At the sound of her stifled chuckle Ardan glanced over and swiftly turned away. Deirdre stopped struggling. "All right. I won't let people see me."

Satisfied, he turned to pick up his axe, and watching the back of his head Deirdre's smile faded into thoughtfulness. He had obviously never lived with a druid, where every word spoken was well chosen. She hadn't said she would not go, only that she would not be seen.

It did not feel good to resist his intent, but being trapped was worse. Urp and Arda had fed the brothers meat, and every time Naisi returned from their hut, a little more of the haunted tension had leached from his face. It disturbed her she could not express gratitude for that. Levarcham told her such a balance in the Source must always be maintained.

The four of them still slept beneath the overhang, for it was one of the few rock shelters protected from the prevailing wind. Naisi had shuffled their hides over to the other side of the narrow cleft, at least, and later that night he waited until his brothers' breathing deepened and, turning his back, slowly and inexorably drew Deirdre into his body, exploring her mouth as if for the first time, his hand cupping her chin. The slide of his tongue over hers filled her with a hunger she could barely restrain. But when her fingers crept to the warm sliver of skin beneath his tunic, he immediately crushed her knuckles.

"They're asleep," she whispered.

"No, not here with them." The back of his hand brushed her breast. His skin was burning, and his voice constricted. "I want to take the time to show you properly, so it doesn't hurt."

She began to protest and he pulled down her shift and softly bit her neck. "*That* is cruel," she gasped with a laugh. Then after a pause, "Go lower."

"Lower is dangerous," he murmured, but he did move down her body a little so he could rest his head on her ribs and tilt up his chin. She felt the watchfulness of his eyes, shadowed by his dark hair and the glimmering sky behind him, until eventually they closed and he slept.

Deirdre remained alert and instead of getting sleepier, an agitation began to creep over her. She tried to rein in her mind, but she kept imagining the valleys stretching away into the wild, the life awakening under cover of the dark. The air outside held a sense of expectation, and her limbs became unbearably restless.

At last she slipped from under Naisi's sleeping body and crept past the wind-break of heather and pine branches. After lacing her boots and tying her cloak, she stood in the blackness of the little valley with arms spread, feeling the night. The coals of the campfire had been banked with turf to protect them from rain, and the stars glittered in an inky arch of sky.

The herbs she'd gathered were drying on a willow frame, and with one hand out she felt her way there and picked some leaves by smell. There was meadowsweet for fever, and in her pack by the shelter she had the bear-berry and some willow-bark for pain. The path to Arda's hut was well worn by the brothers now, and she thought she could navigate by the sliver of moon. She dug coals from the hearth and rolled them into a little bronze fire-pot Naisi had brought back from the village, taking a bundle of pine tapers with her in case she needed to light her way.

The trail followed the ravine and she crept along, nursing the glowing bowl in her hands. The mist of the foaming stream soon drowned out the lingering scent of woodsmoke and coated her skin, washing away the vestiges of warmth that still clung to her from Naisi's body. At the ford she paused, the shallow water sheened by moonlight and a faint glow from the pot. On the other side, the path disappeared into a dark bank of ash trees.

Her nostrils flared. The darkness between the trees stirred with almost-movement and those hints of a murmur below hearing. Then something brushed her cheek.

Deirdre recoiled and stumbled into the water. She strained into the dark for an endless time, her blood pounding, but the air had become still again, the murmurs just the babbling stream. Bracing herself, she leaped across the river-stones and plunged through the trees. When she reached the pastures above Arda's house, she flew along the moonlit trail, frustrated at not know-ing…afraid to know.

Panting, she placed the herbs at Arda's doorway with a blessing and turned to go. The alertness faded as quickly as it came, and she rapidly slid into a haze of exhaustion, as if a hand was pressing her down into sleep. She crossed the ford and sensed nothing now but damp mist on her skin, and with relief nestled back in beside Naisi.

She yawned, thinking of Arda brewing Urp the herbs, filled with the satisfaction that she had done something for others at last. Holding that thought, the dark lake of sleep drew her down into its depths.

And she dreamed.

…she was an immense cloud of radiance, shimmering, rippling.

She paused in the void, before scattering her vast self into a multitude of tiny stars. Now she could sink down through all the filmy layers of spirit to Thisworld again.

She dreamed…

…she was sídhe.

As a cloud of star-dust, she floated among the vapors of Thisworld for a moment, pausing to exult—she was back! She could play! But first she had to shrink once more, condensing that scatter of sparkling consciousness down, down to one brilliant, fiery speck that held All of her.

Now she soared through air, immediately drawn to a spire of flame standing by the stream…the human. Ah! See how the girl resonated with such a fierce melody…a fiery will, endlessly seeking. The maid savored her senses so intensely she held time suspended and did not even know it…tasting the mist, scenting the earth, absorbing the warmth of the fire-coals. See how she quivered, filtering those senses through every particle of her being, and at the same time straining *out*, wanting more.

She did not mean to reach out so—look, she throbbed with fear! But the constant ebb and flow, surrender and searching, nevertheless made her burn with Source, and that called more toward her.

Laughing, the *sídhe* dived down and brushed the girl's cheek, and the light in her faltered. Poor thing…look how her flame guttered, the thread of seeking snuffed out. And a moment later, the girl leaped over the water and ran away.

The *sídhe* soared out into mist and paused again, bobbing. Joy! Thisworld spread all around, formed of the scattered dust of existence—tiny specks of star-motes, vibrating sparks of pure Source. They might be birthed in the otherworlds, but here they could be shaped by thought into matter. What fun! So the air was a radiant mist, the water luminescent, the moonlight silver fire.

And the souls here were like stars, too, and they did not know it, either.

For they were all shining fragments of the One, which long ago splintered apart, and scattered its shards through all the realms of Source. And each shard—people and *sídhe*, and what humans thought of as gods, and all the other souls—had to grow and learn, seek and remember, and so gradually wend their way back to One again.

And what a place of play Thisworld was! So many forms for the *sídhe* to love, as they summoned the flow of Source for plant and animal, water and earth.

Many others of its kind were diving past now, plunging through the whirl of dancing dust. Rock, hill and soil were glimmer-webs whose songs reverberated in long thrumming beats…their matter dense and slow-moving. But the sparks of plant and beast beat faster, their substance singing of life. This *sídhe* enjoyed them above all.

An alder tree spread out in a raft of glittering motes, held in patterns of bark and leaf, root and trunk. The *sídhe* shrunk again and plunged through that sparkling cloud with glee, zipping along a spiral path as it watched each tiny tree-spark vibrating with the god-song. It soared through a leaf…and there, one group of the minute, resonating motes were faltering, their lights dimming. If they forgot their dance and scattered apart, the specks would become air and soil, but the leaf itself would die, its form broken.

The *sídhe* began to croon the alder song, and as it did, it gathered to it reams of Thisworld light that flowed all around it, through the earth and water. It also summoned a glowing thread from the veils of the otherworlds, a beam of spirit-light. Focusing the light, it streamed it through the leaf. The beam stirred the little motes and the *sídhe* laughed and spun, coaxing them back into harmonic patterns again. All the sparks quivered faster with a pure note, and glowed more brightly, and the Source in the leaf became fluid silver again and the tree pulsed. Life!

The rush took the *sídhe* and it soared on high. There was the girl again! It hovered over her once more, as she lay in slumber with others of her kind. The *sídhe* was irresistibly drawn to the emotions that flickered like lightning across her dreams. *Wonder, love, anger, desire.* Dark threads of her fear kept halting the flow of Source, but a fierce drive nevertheless forced them aside—a hunger to shape the sparks into patterns of her own making. *Creation.*

With a pulse of delight, the *sídhe* grazed the edge of those dreams with human meaning. *Closed eyes cannot see the light falling from darkness.*

CHAPTER 24

Lying beneath an ancient oak tree, Deirdre stared at her hand, spread against the sun. She kept reliving a vague sensation of falling beneath the surface of something that should be solid, sinking down through stars. It was elusive and hazy, like a distant memory of a dream.

Behind her fingers, the leaves stirred in the wind, their delicate veins outlined by sunlight. Her eyes drifted to the glowing vessels in the webbing between her fingers, and then to the faint lines of blue that ran down her wrists.

The veins that knitted her body were echoed in the spreading webs across the leaves...or perhaps they merged. Did the fragile vessels of blood branch from her beating heart, flowing into sweet sap and gray bark, then on through the limbs of the tree? Her thoughts took wing and she imagined floating above the mountains and looking down...and there, the rivers also spread in gleaming branches and veins throughout the land, coursing with water and silt...*water like her own blood.*

She brought her eyes back to the spots of afterglare dancing across the leaves, and found herself straining to see specks streaming in filaments along the veins. As if she remembered something—

An eerie wail of grief interrupted her.

It took her a moment to realize it was a real sound, and not part of her daze. Fox, wildcat—eagle? She sat up too fast and her head spun, the spots racing around before her eyes. The moan rose and fell again. Human. She sprang to her feet. *Naisi...Gods, Naisi.* Then her thoughts intervened. It was a high, thin scream and it came from up the glen to the east. A woman.

By the time she raced back up to camp, the brothers were dragging weapons from the cave and throwing bundles of arrows down by the fire. Naisi looked at her, a glimmer of excitement suppressed by the grimness in his face. "Urp came to us. That widow Mairi's homestead—the one near the moors—was raided by strange warriors this morning. She barely managed to escape and make it to Arda's."

"Raid?" The word made no sense in her mind.

"Men came from the high ground in the east." Naisi squatted and rested the arrows beside his bow on a hide. "She said they had tattoos of wolves on their faces—Venicones. Her father was killed, and the raiders have her daughter." He paused, then added harshly, "Those are Mairi's cries of grief you hear."

Deirdre's hand covered her mouth. For a moment she thought only of Mairi and her daughter, and didn't take in what the brothers were doing. When the sun glinted along the iron blade Ardan had unsheathed, however, the warmth of the day was extinguished. She whirled on Naisi. *"No."*

He kept stabbing arrows into his quiver. "Mairi said they've never used this valley before. If we let them escape, more will come, because they'll know it's unguarded."

Deirdre gripped his arm. "They won't come back. There is no plunder here..."

"They slaughtered an old man with only a sheep-staff to defend him."

She had not seen the implacable warrior in him since the fight with Leary. His eyes were dark, his lips pressed together as if he had summoned something savage and now held it leashed. He wore a helmet she had not seen before, either, a cap of leather bound with bronze rivets. The metal reflected a harsh shaft of sun into his eyes, drawing a vertical slash between his dark brows.

His lean torso was crisscrossed by the buckles and straps that held his weapons, and he reeked of the wool-fat that greased the leather. He had retreated to a place she could not follow. Feeling sick, Deirdre watched Ardan bind his sword-belt over his back. *Fighting...they were going to fight.*

The grate of the blades from their sheaths had brutally shattered her reverie. "H-how many men?"

"Six, Mairi thinks." Naisi pursed his mouth. "She didn't get a chance to count them before they skewered her father and dragged her girl away."

Deirdre's teeth trapped a soft noise of dismay. Naisi took up his naked sword which had been resting against a log and hefted its weight, limbering his shoulders. His fingers curled around the hilt with familiarity, intimacy, and her belly contracted. Those fingers had touched her skin. The air vibrated with a tension she had never felt before, alert and focused.

When Ardan and Ainnle went back to the cave, Deirdre fiercely grasped the neck of Naisi's tunic, the only piece of cloth she could find. "This is no task for only three men. You must go to the nearest chieftain and ask for aid."

He blinked, pursing his lips. "That will take many days, by which time these wolves will have scoured this glen and killed everyone in it."

She realized she was trembling as he took her shoulders. The shadows thrown by the helmet made the planes of sunlit bone in his face more pronounced, and he looked like a stranger. Then he drew her in and kissed her behind the ear. "Do not fear." The words caressed her even as the metal buckles grazed her neck. "These raiders are expecting no resistance. We'll take them easily."

She squirmed back in his arms. "Get help first," she forced between her teeth.

He crushed her to him, looking up at the mountain peaks. "My heart will know the day of my death, *fiáin*." His eyes came back into focus. "And it is not today." He grinned savagely and kissed her again, his lips lingering long enough for her to taste the sharpness of excitement, and in that moment she felt his soul brush hers. Closing her eyes, she swayed toward him, clutching his arms.

The sound of Ardan and Ainnle's footsteps broke them apart, and Naisi smiled and let go of her trailing hand, the cold air rushing between them. "Go back down the shore and stay in the woods," he said. "Don't come out until it is safe." With a jingling of weaponry and thud of boots they finished arming themselves and Ardan and Ainnle turned to go. Before Deirdre could absorb Naisi's last, fierce kiss he, too, had followed.

She ran back down to the tanning pits at the loch shore, standing on the rocks and ceaselessly watching the trail of smoke against the sky above Mairi's farmstead as afternoon wore into evening. Her mind was filled with an image: a flash of light that was a blade descending toward Naisi's chest. She gasped under her breath, pushing her knuckles into her own throat as she paced.

The shriek of a buzzard circling above grated her raw nerves into agony. *Naisi.* She sent his name out like a fervent prayer, a yearning to reach him. The mewing cry came again, piercing and urgent, and she clapped her hands over her ears. Before she could look up, an enormous winged shadow soared across the rock at her feet, and a heartbeat later the bird itself swooped in low over her head. The rush of air from its mottled feathers blew her hair back, and she flung her hand out, clutching at the empty air.

Her mouth went dry as the great hawk soared over the water, keening again and again, the shrillness of its cry lifting her heart into her throat. Only in such desperation had she been able to follow the sons of Usnech once before, to see...She had to see, and she didn't care about being lost, because if he was dead she was cut adrift, anyway.

Rooted to the spot, she watched the buzzard spin on its wings and, against all its natural wariness, swoop back toward her as though it would plunge through her heart.

Naisi and his brothers crouched in the bracken behind the smoking homestead. Following the dark plume, they had tracked over the marsh and reed-beds to come up the valley on the south side, where the rock peaks were steeper.

The raiders had thrown a skinned sheep on the embers of the burned hut and were now sprawled around it, picking off shreds of charred meat. Mairi's daughter huddled against a ruined wall, clutching her torn dress over her breasts. In the slanting afternoon light, Naisi could see the smears of blood on her legs.

He shifted his cold gaze to the warriors. They were clad in leather and furs, their dark hair wound with fat and lime into long tails of striped black and white. Naisi stared at the tattoos that covered their cheeks and brows. Ferdia and Cúchulainn bore small animal designs on their temples from their time training with Skatha in Alba—Cúchulainn's the war-raven, and Ferdia's a fox. However, the curling lines of these tattoos broke the men's features into inhuman shapes, invoking snarling animal faces. They were well armed, but shields were casually thrown aside and blades were splayed over slack legs. Despite the savage decorations, these men were far from alert.

The brothers watched them until the shadows of the sinking sun crept across the bracken. The raiders belched, got up to piss, swigged ale from leather bags and jested in harsh voices. "They're not moving tonight," Naisi whispered.

Ainnle rubbed sand into his palm to roughen his grip. "We should spread out and come at them from different directions. If we fly from the gloom, they will think us more than three."

"They're too sodden with ale to be much sport." The scorn was thick in Ardan's voice.

Naisi shrugged. "They don't deserve a fair fight."

Keeping their heads down they crept closer, hidden by the purple shadows and the flicker of flames from the bonfire.

Deirdre's buzzard twirled on its tail-feathers, shaking itself in agitation. She tried to summon something to soothe its spirit, but it was hard when her pinprick of awareness was yawing and spinning around.

She didn't know how she'd projected herself without Levarcham's energy. Just like the last time, it was a dim throb of knowing that sank back into some hidden depths of her soul. The druid training must have imprinted something in her. Frustration had fueled her before, but now she was consumed by fury that Naisi might be harmed, and her terrible fierceness to protect him forced the bird on.

She glanced back and the chord of dream recognition chimed again. The connection to her body was a stream of quivering resonance in the air that was somehow alive, not the silver thread Levarcham had told her to see.

The buzzard's mewing call brought her back. Ahead, flames glowed against the dusky slopes of heather, and smoke billowed above a ruined hut. Summoning all her will, Deirdre nudged the bird down through the clouds of ash to a dead elm tree, overriding its turmoil. One sharp hawk-glance took in the raiders by the fire and, in their midst, the weeping girl. Deirdre's awareness plunged with sorrow and the bird, not knowing what to do with this unfamiliar sensation, stretched out its throat and flapped its wings.

It was then she spied the stealthy movement in the bracken—three dark shapes approaching from different directions. The buzzard nearly called again, but with a desperate will she held it silent.

One man got up on all fours to crawl toward the girl, and she shrank back against the wall. He reached her, pushing up her dress and fumbling with his trews while she desperately struggled to hold down her skirt, weeping.

Squatting behind a ruined wall, Naisi was taken by surprise at the breathless growl that forced its way out of his throat. He was keeping his desire for Deirdre so fervently crushed he was sick with it, and all because he found he could not claim her with this fugitive taint hanging over him, his pride too strong to allow Conor to be right. And now this scum would release lust mindlessly, taking what was not his. The fury flushed Naisi's loins with eager blood. Now there might be some release, at last.

After a moment, he cupped his hands and let out an owl's hoot—the agreed signal to his brothers, who were approaching the hut from the other side. The raiders did not react, and Naisi slowly reached over his back and withdrew his sword from its scabbard. The metal let out a faint hiss as if it, too, thirsted for blood. He shoved his naked dagger more firmly down the side of his boot and tensed, giving the second call as he straightened.

Ainnle burst out of the undergrowth with a yell and danced past the nearest raider in a graceful spin, biting his sword into the man's neck while Naisi was still vaulting over the rubble. Ardan had also joined the fray with a bellow that rebounded from the peaks all around, as if scores of men were converging on the farmstead.

Naisi slashed across the unprotected neck of one of the raiders just as another warrior grabbed for a spear. Still in the flow of the first lunge, Naisi flipped his dagger from his boot

with his left hand and stabbed up into the belly of his second attacker. Ardan meanwhile ducked under the wild stroke of another, leaving the man and Ainnle behind him while slicing at a
fifth warrior, who stumbled up from the bracken. They worked
together as Red Branch, one fighting beast with many limbs.
Ainnle's sword struck his opponent's blade in a clash of iron that
mingled with dying men's screams.

Naisi was conscious of an uncontrollable force flowing up his
body—the old, dark river of secret shame about Conor now shot
through with red gouts of rage. He turned for the man attacking
the girl. The ravager was still tangled up in his trousers, scrabbling for his weapons while the terrified maiden dragged herself
into the undergrowth. She reached a fence and cowered there
with her arms over her head.

Naisi stalked across the clearing with his sword trailing at his
side, the point slicing through the bracken. The black and red inside him mingled together, searing him. It was as if the touch of
his hilt again and the marks of rape on the girl's thighs had un-
leashed it from its chains. *A fight that is righteous and noble, at last.*
The bitter force burst from him and he was hacking at the man,
striking aside his sword. Wildly, Naisi stabbed into thick, giving
flesh, and each blow of his arm relieved more of the banked pressure, letting it bleed from his own body and run away into gore.
A cry was wrenched free by that release, savage and high, a howl
to the deepening sky.

As he stuck his sword upright in the dead man's ribs, Naisi's
eyes cleared and he saw what he had done, the blood wet on the
pale stones, spattered across the white arms of the whimpering
girl in the ferns. *Red Branch,* his mind screamed. *Remember the Red
Branch.* His wail of fury became a war ululation, and as Ainnle
and Ardan joined him, heads back like a pack of wolves, he
hardly realized he cried into it: *This is what I am! I am still Naisi!
Naisi!*

Now it was light that he saw, not blackness—the light of
Cúchulainn's spirit leading him into battle as it always had, the

thread of silver running through the dark. He let himself go into the glorious flow of it, holding to the lifeline.

The war cries and yells of the wounded men rose in a din that forced the buzzard up into the air. The bird thrust its wings away from that terrible noise and Deirdre struggled to gain control, at last wrenching its head around and looking down.

Her shock made the buzzard squawk.

Four other warriors were hurrying down the slopes above the burning hut. As they got closer they withdrew swords from scabbards, heads cocked to the sounds of fighting. There were ten raiders, not six.

The sons of Usnech were beginning to lower their guard, breathless with exertion. *Naisi!* Deirdre cried, but she had no human voice, no body to scream and run to give him warning. Her fear jabbed at the bird and it shrieked for her, mad with pain.

Naisi looked up at that cry, his jaw outlined by the flames, and so he and Ainnle were both facing the ruined wall with swords raised when the other raiders burst upon them. These men were not drunk or taken by surprise, and the fighting resumed far more fiercely, Deirdre's terror keeping the buzzard circling above.

Fear and panic had snapped the last shreds of human thought and she fragmented into bird-sense, clinging to its light as the only forceful presence nearby. The sons of Usnech were obscured by a burst of silver fire, which reached out in long plumes as they lunged, whipping back when they spun and leaped. *Source.* The bird saw the Source. It was vibrant and searing, and it reached into the bird and to Deirdre as pure emotion. Instantly, she was filled with the brothers' savage need to protect one another, the fierce bonds that linked their hearts and forged those three separate flames into one fiery blade.

Ardan overbalanced one man with a blow of his hilt, leaving Ainnle to finish him off while Naisi leaped upon another. The force of his attack bore them both toward the fire that was now eating up the collapsed roof-timbers. Their feet kicked up flurries of sparks as they grazed the fringe of the flames, lunging in and scrabbling back.

Naisi became blinded by billowing smoke and his foot caught on a burned stump, making him stumble. Deirdre saw the hazy shimmer in the air around the raider's blade a moment before he moved his arm, and her spirit had already flung itself down through the flames, dragging the bird with the force of her fury. She swooped at the raider's face, flapping her wings in his eyes and slashing out with her talons.

The man cried out, flinging an arm across his eyes. Naisi righted himself and ducked beneath his flailing sword as Deirdre swooped up again, the buzzard shrieking its terror. She watched Naisi grasp his hilt in both hands and drive it up into his attacker's belly with a yell of triumph.

The tide of relief that hit Deirdre took her power with it, releasing the buzzard from her will. It soared madly into the air, screeching and tearing itself away from the smell of burning and the reek of blood. The twilit loch rushed away beneath her in a stream of light and shadow, until she fell down through the world into senselessness.

And then she knew her body was lying on the wet sand, shivering.

The lowering sun was gilding the sweep of feathered clouds over the mountains when the brothers returned. They appeared on the edge of the clearing and stopped, Naisi throwing down a large hide-wrapped bundle that clanked.

Deirdre put aside her cup of nettle tea with trembling hands and launched herself at him, ignoring the gore that covered his clothes and splashed his face. He clasped her close, laughing. "*Fiáin*, don't touch me!" Smoke had roughened his voice. "We need to bathe before we can come to the fire."

She burrowed into his shoulder, heedless of the dried blood and sour sweat, and as she clung to him she was confused by her senses, that she still had feathers on her fingers, that her arms seemed thin and awkward. When she gazed into Naisi's blood-smeared face, it was hard to make her lips move, for she felt a beak opening to the wind.

Ardan spoke hoarsely behind them. "And then we need a victory feast, our first in Alba. Look!" He held up two leather flasks in each hand. "Urp gave us mead." Ainnle pushed past him, a haunch of mutton balanced over his shoulder. His grin was a gleam of white in his bloodied face.

While Deirdre speared slivers of meat and propped them over the fire, the brothers went to the deepest reach of the stream with their swords, stripping off and wading in. Their bellows of laughter at last began to loosen the knot in Deirdre's chest. They cleaned and blessed their blades, and weighted their clothes in the current before going to the cave for fresh ones.

Naisi squatted to warm his hands at the fire, his pale blue tunic stuck to his damp skin. Deirdre took the linen towel from him and stood behind to dry his hair. *He lived.* She closed her eyes for a moment, drinking in his weight against her thighs.

He tilted his head up. "We gave Mairi and the other herders all the armbands and torcs to trade, though we kept the swords. Mairi is taking her daughter to live with kin in the great glen, so she'll need something to start over." Though she heard the deep note of satisfaction in his voice, it still bore a tense edge, and looking closer Deirdre glimpsed a hint of distracted hunger in his eyes. She must be imagining it, or perhaps all men looked this way after battle, their blood still on fire. She gently brushed the damp hair from his brow and kissed it, and in answer he pressed her fingers to his mouth, his breath rushing out between them.

That night, Deirdre tasted an echo of what Emain Macha must be like when warriors returned from battle: the eating and drinking, the singing and jesting. The brothers reminisced of past fights and then turned to the expedition of the night, excitedly describing a blow here, a leap there. Deirdre sat next to Naisi on a log, the mead singing in her veins. She had shared this, she had defended him.

Naisi was explaining how he was hard-pressed until he thought he saw a bird swoop at his opponent's face. That was impossible, though; he must have imagined it. Deirdre broke in without thinking. "You misjudged your footing and went too far into the smoke, that's all."

The brothers all turned to stare at her. "Deirdre," Naisi said quietly, "how do you know that?"

A shred of mutton lodged in her throat, robbing her of words. Naisi's hand shot out to grasp her fingers, spilling mead over her lap. "Did you disobey me and *follow* us there? I cannot believe this of you!"

"No," she stammered. *I did not follow in body.*

Ardan and Ainnle glanced between them while Naisi let go and slowly rose. The hurt in his face stabbed her to her core. "I didn't follow you that way, I swear. I went as…" She sucked in a breath. "I flew as a bird—inside a bird. Levarcham taught me how. I know it sounds impossible, but the druids do it." A hush fell over the campfire. Naisi's wide eyes had now filled with confusion.

"What are you talking about?" Ardan asked. "You turned into a bird?"

She desperately held Naisi's stunned gaze. "No. You let a piece of your spirit slip out of your body and somehow…catch hold of an animal, like in a net. I picked birds because they are free." Wordlessly, she begged Naisi to understand, but he only rubbed his temples, backing away from the fire.

Ardan leaned forward, his face alight. "Our father's druid hinted of such arcane skills, but I thought he was just mocking me to make me leave him alone! So you can make a bird do what you want?"

Biting her lip, Deirdre watched Naisi staring into the flames. "Only turn its movements a little, and only for a short while."

Ainnle let out a loud whistle. "That's incredible!" His face was flushed with mead, his eyes glazed. "So you were a bird in the woods that first night in Erin?"

Ainnle had been quiet enough about her since the day of the stag hunt, his contempt sliding into a prickly wariness. "That *was* just me playing tricks. This was real." She looked at Naisi. "I followed you, and when you stumbled, I flew into the man's eyes."

His expression was still blank and her fingers went slowly to her mouth. She could still smell his touch on her, the scent of the river. Did he think her fey now, or mad? Levarcham said that druids were set apart from others, but she wanted to belong here now, and share this. "Please," she said softly. *Please, it's still me.* As if he heard, his gaze came back into focus upon her like a lamp-flame, and she saw then his eyes were full of wonder, not fear. A tremor went through her and her arm dropped weakly to her lap.

Ardan straightened. "I don't know why this is a shock. We saw her call the stag." He paused, trying to read his elder brother's thoughts. "She is druid-taught after all."

Deirdre caught her breath when Naisi sat back down and took her hand, looking intently at her fingers. "What she is, is surprising." His eyes tilted up, his gaze going right through her now with its heat.

Ainnle's laugh shattered the tension. "By the gods! I thought only druids could do such things."

"Well, it takes a *lot* of torturous practice." For once, she thought of those firelit nights with Levarcham without any pang of pain. "As long as it is undertaken with the proper reverence, I can show you."

Ainnle snorted. "I can just see that. We'd probably overshoot and get lost somewhere up there." He waved drunkenly toward the stars.

"*You'd* get so carried away, little brother, you'd spur some poor bird headlong into a rock-face," Ardan put in.

Naisi squeezed Deirdre's fingers, regarding Ardan. "And you'd never come back. You'd catch an albatross and go dreaming across the seas, forgetting all about us."

She tugged Naisi's hand. "And what about you?"

"I'd be an eagle and fly so high no one could tether me again."

Ainnle rolled his eyes. "I'd be happy with a kestrel but *you'd* have to be an eagle."

Naisi's smile was mysterious. "An eagle can do what he wants."

"Well, I for one want to know what it's like to be a druid," Ardan said softly. He glanced at Deirdre, his awe clearly struggling with bemusement. Then he just shook his head and got up for more mead, staggering slightly.

When Ardan turned to pour for Ainnle, Naisi and Deirdre looked down at their linked fingers. The warmth of his thigh melted into hers. "You fought for me," Naisi murmured.

She picked at the peeling bark, oddly shy. "You are not angry?"

"Only my brothers have ventured into danger for me." There were still tiny flecks of blood around his nails. He had come so close to death.

Swallowing, she nestled the back of her curled hand against his face and brushed it down his neck, savoring the thud of his pulse. "You did the same for me once."

His mouth quirked. "When you said you would never obey me, you meant it."

She went still, and her face was grave. "I will never wait helplessly and watch you die." The words slipped out of nowhere and, as a chill went over her, Ardan appeared with the flask, and Naisi held out his cup, smiling.

The rest of the night was carried away on a river of mead until the empty flasks were scattered about their feet and the fire was a pile of burning embers, though it was the height of sunseason and the entire sky was still faintly glowing with that lambent northern light. At last Ardan wrapped himself in his cloak and slid down to curl up in a mead-sodden sleep. Ainnle sprawled by the fire on the drying clothes and, after croaking a last joke or two, promptly began to snore.

Deirdre managed to drag a hide over him before Naisi grabbed her hand. His eyes were glassy as he backed up, unsteadily dragging her along the path into the cave. There he tore off her cloak and flung it away before falling on his knees before her, swaying like a tree in the wind. Lifting Deirdre's arms above her head, he stripped off her tunic and she gasped with the cold, her skin puckering into goose-flesh. The gasp became a stifled yelp when his warm lips fastened around one nipple, before he lost his balance so thoroughly he tipped over, and it slipped from his mouth. He sank down with her, wriggling into their hides and claiming her lips with clumsy kisses instead. Enveloped by the potent fumes on his breath, Deirdre reached out to fumble with his laces, her eager hands nudging down his trews as she had been longing to do for weeks. It had to happen sometime…

It took her a moment to realize her burrowing fingers had skated over wiry hair and a soft dip of skin in his groin, and then closed around nothing but limp flesh between his legs. Naisi hiccuped, his head falling to her bare chest. "Too much …" he mumbled, his weight pinning her down. "Ah, *fiáin*…" he murmured into the curve of one breast, and astonished, she lay there while he hiccuped again and then fell silent.

After a moment, she sank back and stared at the rock above her. He was falling asleep *now*? When he let out a snore, she could not help but snort with amusement. Then she smiled to herself.

At least he could not push her hands away anymore. She swept a palm over his tunic, along his shoulder-blade and waist, wriggling her fingers down inside his trews to possessively cup the side of his buttock. The muscle there was hard and an image winged through her of the russet flank of the stag bunching over the hind. It did not bring fear now, and there was no thought of Conor, or Fintan, or anyone. Her senses were consumed by this man alone…his smoky scent, the soft wheeze of his breath, the sprawling length of his body on hers. She felt a tiny, prickling sensation inside her, low between her legs, and savored the unfamiliar weight of him parting her thighs. Breathing through her nose she tried to shift a little, to increase the friction of his belly against hers, but he was too heavy.

Instead she reached under his tunic and drew the line of his spine up from his rump, pressing every warm ridge of muscle and wondering how they would feel tensing under her fingers. Her face was burning now, and he was still snoring and oblivious. She bit her lip to trap a laugh, placing her hands flat on the smooth planes of his back.

Now she held his heart beating in her palm, and that was all she cared about. He was alive.

The next day, the brothers went with thumping heads to pay their respects to Mairi and dig the grave for her father, up the hill under an ash tree. Deirdre gave Naisi some rowan-leaves on a stalk to place in the grave for her. The weeping woman clung to Ainnle and Ardan, blessing them for rescuing her daughter, though the girl sat huddled by Arda's fire and only sent a few terrified glances their way, no matter how gently Naisi spoke to her.

Urp eyed their swords as he farewelled them, leaning on his sheep-pen. "Arda says the gods brought yeh here to protect us."

Naisi glanced at his brothers. Beneath the seediness of his churning belly and the ache of his head, his limbs were still faintly resonating with the power that had filled them in the fight. "It's what we are," he said, his voice roughened by mead. "We would never stand by and allow such slaughter."

Urp nodded, squinting up the slope before suddenly meeting Naisi's eyes. "Not wandering hunters after all, then."

Trapped by that shrewd glance, Naisi realized he didn't want to lie to this man, a spirit as steady as the seams of rock threading the hills. "We are wanderers," he said, wiping the grave-soil from one palm down his trews. "Though it's true we were not born in a herder's hut."

"It's also true we want no trouble," Ainnle broke in, with a worried glance at Naisi.

Urp barked a laugh that set off a coughing fit. He thumped his chest. "Trouble! Yeh saved *us* from trouble, lad, so don't look like yeh might stick me with that knife o' yers."

"I'd never do that!"

"Aye." Spluttering, Urp could not hide the curious twinkle in his eye. "Which is why none will hear aught of yeh from me. Every family here has feasted on good meat and Mairi has her daughter's life to lay at yer feet as well. Arda said the *calleach* herself must have given yer presence Her blessing—for the *sídhe* have already left us some wee gifts of herbs in the night."

Naisi frowned, his bleary mind struggling to make sense of that. But Urp was resting his staff over the pen now, staring hard at him, and Naisi's chest began to drum. He felt the tug—that in exchange for silence, Urp wanted something from him. In a flash, he understood. *Trust.* The ties that bind people as they were being bound to this place. "We are in hiding," he admitted, making Ainnle and Ardan look sharply at him. "If I told you from whom, you would be in great danger, so leave it at that. Our presence must be kept secret for as long as possible."

Ardan blew out his breath, turning to Urp. "Otherwise we will have to leave."

Urp nodded gravely. "Ye've given us more than ye've taken. What price a steady tongue for that?"

"There could be a price." Naisi had to make him understand. "If those who pursue us come, it could go badly for you." He was struck by inspiration. "And for that reason, never seek our camp, but let us come to you. That will be safer for you, for if they find us you can keep your distance and tell them in truth you don't know where we are."

Urp absorbed all that, then shrugged. "I'm more afraid of Venicones than yer mysterious pursuer. But I know enough to soothe my suspicions. Keep yer secrets."

Trailing back up the slope, Naisi rested his wrists on his bow over his shoulders, stretching his back. He could draw in greater lungfuls of air now the cloak of secrecy had been eased a little, clearing his pounding head. The people of the valley were bound to them, and they to the valley now they had defended it. A little house...yes, they could build it now—just a circle of stones—for they had surely staked their claim with their own blood, at last. Somewhere he could be with Deirdre inside stout walls.

He could have found a place for them to lie on the mountain these past days. But he was still wrestling with the superstition that once he joined with her, some path back to Erin would be

barred forever. Everything the king and Naisi's Red Branch brothers believed about him would be true—that he was a betrayer of
oaths.

Naisi, it already is true, he reminded himself bleakly. In the hidden darkness of his heart, it had been for years, long before he
met Deirdre. And it came to him like a hammer-blow. Was he
willfully blind? *There was no going back.* That chance had already
passed, and so there was no sense in struggling with it now. And
with this drawing of swords, of blood, they were not fugitives
here anymore but protectors, weaving themselves into the fabric
of the land.

So it all surrendered from him in a rush. If there was a hearth,
and a bed, and fishing nets and a hunting bow over the door, and
his meat in the pot, then, yes…he and Deirdre would be mated.
And no one could say then that they were rutting animals, or
lovesick children, or anything but Naisi and Deirdre.

Deirdre noticed a change in the brothers in the days that followed. She realized that the fire of battle had only been smoldering in them after all, and now a furtive flame had leaped back
into life. They began to speak of old fights, their voices becoming
unguarded once more, their songs echoing off the rock peaks.

She had seen their fire through a buzzard's eyes, and so she
knew.

They had surrendered into the deadly dance again, their limbs
lifted and flowing with power. They had felt the ecstasy of skill
and speed no longer suppressed, and renewed the connection of
sword-brothers. Now they simmered with that excitement, and
Deirdre endeavored to understand it and welcome back their
smiles.

Her heart was shadowed, though, as if brushed by a dark wing
in passing.

CHAPTER 25

When Conor's mother, Nessa, came to Emain Macha from her dun in the north, she occupied a lavishly decorated house near the crest of the hill.

On this grim day, Conor sat by her hearth, the scattering of Roman lamps glowing with small, refined flames that did not cheer him as much as the crackling fire-pits of his hall. He sourly watched his mother crook an imperious finger at her girl to pour ale for him, though his eyes already watered from his own breath.

Nessa's back was still perfectly straight, her unbound hair falling over her bony shoulders in a curtain of gray. Her wrinkled face was powdered with flour and her lips reddened with the *ruam* herb in a vain attempt at maidenly allure, even though sixty-five wheels of the sun had withered her wrists to bird-bones and spotted her skin.

As a fifteen-year-old widow with a baby, and devoid of illustrious kin, she had clawed her way to influence with intelligence and the arts of her body, moving through a succession of older husbands and amassing great wealth. Widowed again at thirty-three she had set her sights on the new king, Fergus mac Roy, five years younger than her.

Conor accepted the ale, thirsting for the cool tang so much he barely looked at the pretty maid who gave it over. If only he could forge bonds with his warriors by drinking more and being the last man standing, like Fergus. For him it was a secret thing, taking the edge off the constant gnawing in his belly. It restored some blurred calm, allowing him to order his messengers and warriors off on the hunt for the sons of Usnech, scouring the barren hills, the islands and marshes of the Ulaid. The more Red Branch he sent away, the less he had to listen to their jests, or the battle tunes that reminded him of how *they* sang in his hall...

He narrowed his gaze on the knobs of red enamel embedded in his bronze cup. He had to remember that Fergus's fighting, drinking and rutting had proved his undoing in the end. Nessa had tricked Fergus into leaving Erin, but Conor told himself fiercely that the rest had been his: the treaties; the appeasement of the chiefs, disgruntled at Fergus for abandoning them for his own pleasures; the devious ploys to make them choose Conor as king. He gulped, his hand shaking. It was all his, and would not be taken from him now by some mewling black pup.

Nessa dismissed all her women and, as soon as they were alone, she pinned her son with small, shrewd eyes. "I hear you've sent the warriors off on some ridiculous quest while you moon about here over that ungrateful, impudent chit."

He should have known this was coming. His tongue was clumsy in his parched mouth. "She's not—"

"There's been no more attacks from Connacht." Nessa was on her feet pouring Greek wine from an expensive glass flask she let no servant touch. She splashed blood-red liquid in a bronze goblet, her jangling bracelets betraying agitation. "Is Eochaid ill, or dead? They might be licking their wounds, fighting over the kingship—who knows? But *now* is the time to raid!" She spun on her heel, gazing at him with contempt. "Instead you have your warriors chasing around after some loose-thighed slut. How shamed I am!"

Conor peered up balefully. "And of course this is about *you*."

She was across the hearth in a stride and he had to crush the old instinct to flinch away from her. "It is when I worked so hard to put you in this hall," she hissed.

Worked hard on your back. A hoarse laugh tickled his throat. "You craved being a king's wife and mother, and that's all you have ever cared about." The lurid hues of the wall hangings and gleam of furs and polished bronze all beat on his aching head, as stifling as the wafts of her Egyptian perfume.

He closed his eyes to her furious gaze, trying to erase her words from his head. Raid? He could not share the mead-cup of battle with his men when Naisi and Deirdre could be slipping his net! His thin shell of control would not bear that. "If the Connacht-men are squabbling among themselves, let them waste their own blood. They cannot see me shamed by this milk-pup of Usnech's…" He blotted out that name with a ragged swallow of ale.

Nessa let out a frustrated sigh of wine-scented breath and he opened his eyes. When she reached out a bony finger, he grew warily still, but she only tapped his forehead. "I won the throne for you with *this*—Fergus lost it despite his sword strength. Brute force cannot stand up to cunning for long."

Conor's lip curled with revulsion. She could never understand what he felt when he saw those glints of contempt in the eyes of his warriors—or how his mind could not wipe them away, no matter how it mocked his weakness and smirked at his pain.

"So to catch him, you must know your enemy's *mind*." That drew his attention back. "Naisi." Her tongue touched her lips. "Do you think that delicious boy would be happy to cower in exile?" Her eyes glazed and her fingers caressed the beads of amber at her throat. "I saw the fire in him, a dark fire, always burning."

"Control yourself." Conor got up, towering over her though his back was bowed by the tightness in his belly. "Your old paps would smother him."

She looked at him with distaste. "I mean that fire must flare into life again somewhere. He will not survive with power quenched. He will still want more." She gripped the back of his neck before he could step away and he pulled against that stringy strength. "Look for him at the courts of great kings, not in the wilderness." Conor merely stared at her and she spun away. "You fool!" she muttered, tapping her foot under her long gown.

"Not Connacht?"

"The pup is too proud for that."

"The kings of Laigin would not hide him from me."

"Look for other bases of power." She studied him critically. "Goddess. If I were a man, I could have done away with you and Fergus long ago."

In answer, Conor drained the cup and tossed it on her fine cushions, and her eyelids slitted when dark drops spattered the bleached hide. The satisfaction gave him enough strength to walk to the door with some control in his legs, though he felt her gaze on his back all the way.

As soon as Nessa was alone, her body sagged against the roof-post, the intricate carving digging into her shoulder-blade. Every year it grew harder to ferret out the rare scraps of sense men possessed.

She was combing her hair by the fire to soothe her wrath when her serving girl held back the door-hide to admit Fergus mac Roy. Once-husband, once-king. He had moved on to other wives but still wanted her—something she had made great efforts to ensure.

Nessa carefully set aside the gilded bone comb and got up, summoning the mysterious smile that heated his flesh. "Welcome back," she said huskily. Fergus had been visiting kin for some moons now on the borders with Laigin.

Fergus shrugged off his cloak and shook the rain from it, then stretched his back. "Long ride," he grunted, though he only did it to show off his massive shoulders. At nearly sixty, he remained a magnificent specimen, incessantly training at war so that even though his chest hairs were white, they furred muscles that remained hard beneath slackening skin. His thighs were still as thick as young trees, and he kept his hair limed in a halo of luxuriant gray, matched by a drooping moustache and shaven chin in the old fashion. He flung himself to the bench and, when the girl poured him ale, drank it in one gulp. "Some welcome home," he grumbled, wiping the fringe of raindrops from his moustache.

"I gather you don't mean the weather." Nessa clicked her fingers for the servant to feed the braziers with more wood, as she sat down in her rush-woven chair, crossing her ankles and arranging her skirts.

"All this fool business of Conor and Fedlimid's daughter! My son Illan says the youngest Red Branch warriors can speak about nothing else."

Unease pressed on Nessa's temples, and she gestured for the girl to leave them. "I assume they don't upbraid Naisi for being the fool," she said when she'd gone. Fergus's shoulders twitched in a gruff shrug. "In fact," she went on, "I suppose they're speaking of this whole escapade as some sort of great, romantic adventure."

"Hardly, considering Leary is dead." His voice had grown sharp.

"By Naisi's blade," she snapped back, quick as a fox.

Fergus's face became troubled, his eyes glinting with pain. He frowned and applied his attention to the liquid in his cup. "You might want to tell Conor that the best way to protect himself is to wash his hands of the whole thing." His mouth thinned in bitter mirth. "Imagine risking so much just to sheath his prick in some green-maid!"

Nessa made herself smile at his crudity. "I can't think of anyone who's risked anything like *that* before."

Fergus's dark eyes glinted ruefully beneath his bushy brows. "*You* were the fiercest, most elusive, most exciting minx in the whole of Erin—and I was bored." He toyed with his cup. "I like fighting and feasting, not babbling about treaties and struggling to keep all the chiefs happy at once. It nearly split my head in two."

She stood behind him, kneading the knots in his shoulders, and he sighed and rested his head against her. Fergus inspired great loyalty among the men even now; she was wise to keep her options open. "It's a heavy burden, the kingship," she murmured. "I always knew it would sit on Conor's shoulders more easily. He was a sly child who preferred strengthening his mind to his sword-arm. I wanted to spare you, and you've been much happier since."

His head lifted. "Your son is wily, but he is not Red Branch."

She dug harder, interspersing the kneading with caresses behind the ear. "The Red Branch fight, but they need their king to be cunning."

"They need a king to lead," he grumbled. "And for thirty years, Conor has done an admirable job, or he wouldn't be king. So why risk it all now? He's starting to look as if he's weakening, his mind addled."

Hearing her own fears flung back at her was highly unpleasant. Crushing her wrath, Nessa purred in his ear. "I'm sure we could be speaking of more soothing things." She peered over his shoulder. His manhood was already standing up for her, even after all this time. As always when their blood was stirred, the years fell away—the wrinkles and slack skin—and they were young again and hot for each other. She knelt between his thighs, drawing her gray hair around her neck and across her breasts as if she was naked and smooth-skinned. She rubbed her belly against his hardness. "The sooner Naisi is found, the better," she murmured. "So Conor can mend this."

His eyes were glazing over. "The men are all looking," he breathed, watching her moisten her lips with a small tongue.

"And if you or your sons find him, you must get him back to the king as soon as possible. You must trust Conor in such matters. He knows what's best."

"He always has done," Fergus admitted, but it was grudging and she saw the lingering doubt. She unlaced his trews, creeping her fingers down his belly to the curling hairs, and now he smiled lazily. She knew the tender places no other had ever taken the trouble to find in him. Lesser women might like him banging away on top of them like a charging bull, but it took something else to find the erotic heart of a man and draw it out, make him discard his control.

She had worked for years on that, and there was nothing that could stand in the way of Nessa once her mind was trained on it.

Naisi dumped the armful of hazel saplings at Deirdre's feet where she sat on a fallen log, narrowly missing her toes. A little circle of rocks had taken shape in a clearing by a stream, the walls already head high. Around them lay piles of heather she had been collecting for the roof, and bracken and the creamy, scented fronds of meadowsweet for the bed.

Deirdre was looking at her druid-disk with its sun- and star-marks, and the staves she had nicked to trace the days. "I hate that we missed Beltaine after we left Aed's dun. I always marked the druid festivals with Levarcham."

"I am sure the gods forgive us." Naisi wiped his brow, his bare torso running with sweat, for the days since the raid had grown much warmer. "We were somewhat distracted at the time."

"Well, now it's nearly the longest day." She bit her lip, looking up at him. "Naisi, the house must be finished by then."

Naisi ruffled his damp hair, deliberately spattering her with sweat. "How long do we have?" The sky was hazed by banks of low cloud, and the air was heavy with sultry heat.

She pursed her lips and shuffled away from him down the log. "Three days."

"Are you trying to kill me?" He sat beside her, flexing his arms.

The house site they'd picked was halfway up a low hill near the mouth of the river, hidden by a tangle of hazel and oak trees. Ardan and Ainnle were building their hut farther up the slope. Through a gap before Deirdre, the wooded slopes fell away to the expanse of loch, the water glassy in the hushed air.

The hairs on Naisi's naked arms tickled her wrists and she was conscious of the heat coming off his skin. She couldn't look at him, though she felt the weight of his stare. This would be a home with a man. A firelit place where they would have a bed, and be alone. "Why the longest day?" He breathed it into her ear.

Levarcham's voice replied in her head, speaking in a brisk tone that did nothing to cool her heart. "A hearth-fire cannot first be lit after the turning of sunseason," Deirdre repeated faintly. "The retreating sun will take the life of the house with it. We have to build the fire now to hold a piece of its soul in the flames when it's at its strongest."

"Then I will kill myself to finish it," he murmured, and she was mesmerized by the tendons moving in his hand as he reached out his little finger to stroke her thigh.

The next day Deirdre stood back while the brothers levered an oak lintel into place to hold the weight of the stones above it. *I have a real home. I am mistress of it,* she thought, and wondered why she had to keep telling herself, and why she was so heavy inside. One mysterious realm hovered, murmuring at the fringes of her senses—and now it had been eclipsed by an even more urgent fear. She didn't know how to *be* a mate, a wife, to have walls around her again…

"What you put into the house is returned to you," Naisi said, "so smile." Ardan and Ainnle had already left to go to their own house, and tentatively, she rested her hands on Naisi's waist. It felt so possessive now, standing before their own doorway. She trailed her fingers up his bare arms, tracing the details she was already coming to know: the bulkier right side he favored for the sword, the bundle of tendons where shoulders met neck, the angling of waist and thighs into a leanness bred of a hunter's lope. She had explored it all with her eyes, and now she would sink into him with her body. Her throat constricted, but somehow she made herself smile, and satisfied, he turned to follow his brothers up the hill to cut more heather.

It was the eve of the longest day when they finished Deirdre's roof. Naisi went to complete his brothers' house and she was left alone at her own doorway.

It was dark inside, smelling of dried mud, damp rock and crushed heather. The hazy daylight behind her distorted her shadow on the floor, and she found herself wondering what shape she would take when Naisi at last lay between her thighs. Her muscles tightened and even she did not understand the confusion in them—desire, apprehension...

A storm had been building in the west all morning, yellowing the swollen bellies of the clouds. She walked back to the cave, her thoughts disintegrating. There were druid rites to bless a new house and she followed them, her mind hanging in a void, unable to move past this day into what night would bring.

She spread their hides on the bed-platform delved of earth and piled with heather and bracken, and making several trips arranged all the new belongings they had bought in the village, setting the sack of flour by the door along with the bronze water-pot, and iron cauldrons and the spit in the fire-pit. She stripped down to her linen shift, her legs bare, and loosened her hair so it fell around her shoulders. Finally, she took a branch of rowan and drew a spiral around the hearth, singing a druid blessing under her breath.

> *On the path*
> *from womb to death*
> *And hearth to pyre*
> *She guides us.*
> *Brid, curve our steps*
> *Macha, light our hearts*
> *Dana, draw us to you*
> *And let us find the heart of all*
> *Goddess bless us.*

She shivered, remembering Levarcham's words. The spiral was a symbol of eternal seeking and transformation, the sacred journey to God and Goddess. It curved both outward, expanding with new growth, and inward, toward the ancient heart of creation, and the One. It was carved on tombs by the ancestors. Traced by the pearly walls in seashells. Echoed in the patterns of the seed-heads of plants and petals in flowers, by the spin of winds and water.

In this house she would become a woman, as she must have walked that spiral path many times before...and as she would again. So the cycles turned. *And what else would she be, besides woman, lover...mate?* That strange pang kept echoing around her conscious thoughts, like eagle cries rebounding off the peaks.

Searching through Naisi's clothes, she found a black hair left on a shirt. And after plucking one of her own, she moved back a hearth-stone and placed both hairs in the hole. They nestled there, gold and black entwined. Her blood throbbed, and as she sprinkled the ewe's milk over them for Brid's blessing, she felt the ripples of the more primal energy that was held in the very soil reaching for her again. She dropped the stone back, breathing hard.

She circled the room, placing a palm on the oak lintel set into the stone-and-mud wall. Her thoughts tried to comfort her. Though the house had been hewn from rock and trees, it was not a barrier against the wildness, but a part of it still. The dreams of the oak wandered through the wood beneath her hand, a memory of branches lifted to wheeling stars. She moved to clasp the cold stones. Something entered her from that un-yielding surface, a warmth—*the Source*—and it, too, felt alive under her fingers.

The first spatters of rain came and Deirdre became aware she had been sitting by the fire-pit for some time, half in a trance. The sky was darkening with cloud and she lifted her sweaty hair off her neck, her pulse thudding too fast. The somberness of the rites suddenly felt stifling, as if she was rooting herself so inex-orably into the earth she would dissolve into it, losing herself. As if the magic of gold and black hairs kept her entwined, tethering her to...

She looked up into Naisi's face. It was indistinct as he passed from daylight into the shadow of the house, smelling of streamwater, his hair damp. He hooked his cloak over a protrud-ing rock, placed his dagger and bow on the earth floor and solemnly unbuckled his sword. In the open doorway, the scab-bard of polished wood and gilded leather caught the bruised light of the stormy sky; it would always be there to protect her now. She had a mate. The curled shape of the tangled hairs burned behind Deirdre's eyes.

"Let us light the fire." Naisi's hoarse voice was strangely stilted. Perhaps he felt the charge in the air, too.

They piled sacred woods in the little fire-pit, starting whenever their hands brushed. With flint and striker, Naisi got a spark and the tinder smoked before a tiny flame spurted into life. "The blessings of Brid and Macha be on this house," Deirdre murmured, and Naisi groped for her hand to watch their newborn fire struggle into life.

She dared a glance at him. His eyes were glazed, the surface of his pupils shimmering as the fire danced. She knew that line of jaw and cheek, the long nose, the flared lips. *I know it*, she reminded herself. A shower of raindrops pattered on the thick mat of heather above their heads, followed by a peal of thunder that rolled across the sky. The trees around the house creaked in a strong gust.

The groove of Deirdre's back ran with sweat. All at once she felt trapped, just as on the night of Conor's dance. *I am not those girls Naisi once knew. Nor am I a hearth-mate like Aiveen.* She wasn't sure what she was. But to belong to someone, answer to them, *need* them . . .

Her hand tore itself from his. "I have to go outside," she gasped. The damp wind brought the scents of rotting wood, rock and pine. She took a gulp and the power of the storm rushed through her, as the rain began to pour over the roof. *Be reborn in storm and lightning*, it sang. *In chaos*.

Naisi's brow was creased with a dawning hurt, but the moment she drank of the sultry air, desire began to sweep through her body again, immediately clearing her confused heart. She cupped his cheeks and sucked the swelling of his lower lip. When he groaned she stepped away, extending her hand. "Come with me and be my husband, then."

He shook his head, blinking. "What?" He went to catch her but she danced away, and flashing an impish look over her shoulder darted out the open doorway.

Indignant, Naisi paused to grab her cloak before following Deirdre out into the rain. The clouds had obscured most of the evening glimmer, spilling sallow light over the wet turf. The wind whipped the trees back and forth, and he could hardly see for the water being driven into his eyes. He squinted, his fist warding away the drops, and made out a white shape weaving down the hill. He ran after her, the rain hammering his exposed head until he got into the sheltered undergrowth. "Deirdre?" he yelled again, and then spied her in a clearing beneath an oak tree whose branches creaked and swayed.

The first burst of lightning flashed and showed her laughing, her head tilted back, her mouth open to the rain. "Deirdre," he repeated brokenly, and took a step. And then was helpless to continue.

She blinked her lashes with a delighted grin. "Isn't it wonderful?" She opened her mouth to drink again, exposing the shiny pink inside, her tongue licking the rain from her cheeks.

The cloak fell from his fingers to the ground. Her shift was stuck to her by the force of the downpour, turning the blush hue of her skin beneath. The soaked cloth outlined her curves and caught in the secret folds of her body that he so urgently needed to explore. How could he have waited? This could never be tainted by Conor's claim or his own shame.

She laughed at his gaping. "Come on, stand where the rain can really hammer you." He gave in and came closer, his hands on her shoulders. Her nipples were darker buds pushing out the wet linen, her breasts running with water. She shivered and laughed at her own weakness. "It pounds your soul and washes you clean." She grabbed his hands and spread his arms out. "Doesn't it stir you up so you can't think?"

Naisi blinked raindrops away, his eyes upon her. "Yes." At the intensity in his voice her expression turned somber, her gaze fixing on his dripping lips, her eyes deepening. "Manannán's breath," he muttered, and pulled her in, the rain running into their mouths. He swallowed it from her as if drinking her essence, the run-off perfumed by her skin. Her tongue was startlingly warm amid the cold water. And when she clung to him, throwing back her head, her shift slid off her shoulder and he lapped the runnels from her bare skin.

The clouds were underlit by a great flash of lightning and they leaped apart. The flare contracted her pupils into points of fire before they widened again, fathomless and beckoning. "Will it hurt?" Her voice was the groan of the wind.

He dragged his mind back, his tongue thick with heat. "There are ways for it not to." His fingers brushed the dip between her lips. "You touch for a long time, making your body open, and then it doesn't." He held her dripping hair with both hands, looking around. "But to do that we must be somewhere warm and dry, where I can take the time to soften you…"

"No." She tore herself from his arms and danced away before whirling to face him. "The earth is my bed, and it always has been!"

"Come back here."

"No!"

That wild mingling of defiance and elusiveness released his frustrated anger and dammed desire in one roar. "So you'll force me to take you on the ground? Gods, but you try me, *fidín!*"

She wiped water from her face. "Surely rain doesn't wilt your manhood?" Her grin was savage, firing his loins so they strained painfully toward her.

He growled and went to catch her, but she ducked behind the tree. He charged around the other side and his feet slipped and he slid into the trunk with a thud. "Deirdre!" he shouted, losing his temper and smacking his hand on the bark.

There was a silence and then she stepped into view. With a tilt of her chin, she held his eyes and, wriggling her shift over her head, flung it away in a sodden heap. "It's making me cold."

Naisi leaned on the tree, panting. Her skin was gleaming and fine-grained, and the aureoles of her breasts were puckered in the chill air. Below the indent of her waist and swelling of her hips, the mysterious cleft between her legs was fringed by dark-gold hair. He got his legs under him and propelled himself forward, catching her before she could run, pushing her back against a birch tree and trapping her between the bark and his own body.

Plunging his tongue into her mouth, Naisi lifted her buttocks and pulled her bare thighs about his own, and at last she clamped on with desperate force. He ground his hips into her, and with his soaked trews he may as well have been naked himself, his swelling flesh pushing into a deceptively yielding openness. Only a slip of wool stopped him from sheathing himself.

He staggered back, breaking from her lips to peer around him. Up the slope, above the house, there was a drier nook beneath a copse of yew and pine trees, the canopy thick and sheltering. He bent down for Deirdre's cloak and shift and she tried to twist away until he growled again, straightening and boosting her over his shoulder. She pummeled his back, chuckling, and only stopped struggling when he slung her down beneath the yews. He pinned her with one arm at a time while he shrugged off his tunic, throwing that and her shift on the ground to lie upon. Finally, he pulled the cloak over them like a dark tent. The branches let through only a few patters of rain, and though their clothes were soaked, the ground was soft with needles.

While Naisi breathlessly tackled his trews, Deirdre's palms were already sweeping over his shoulders and down his thighs. "From the day we met, I wanted to feel all this," she choked out.

Twisted up, Naisi untangled one ankle. "Even when I scolded you?"

"Even then." Her lips came down on his wet shoulder. "Because when you are annoyed, your eyes burn right through me."

Naisi pushed his trews out into the rain, and then they were naked together, sleek as two otter cubs. "And when you speak like *that*," he pushed her down to nuzzle her ear, "I wonder if I need bother teaching you anything at all." His hand drifted across her belly. "You might be ready to take me inside you."

She slapped him on the chest. "You won't get out of it that

easily. I want to know everything." She wriggled her fingertips down to brush the hair at his groin. "*Everything*, and don't you be lazy."

He had been strained now beyond all reason. "Then know this," he murmured and, moving down, took a nipple in his mouth.

She yelped and then choked on her laughter, and he pulled back to tease around the nub with feather-light lips. Her breath came in little puffs now and her fingers clawed his shoulder, trying to push her breast up into his mouth until at last he gave in and suckled her with his tongue. The cry she let loose tore the nipple from his mouth. "If you keep screaming like that you'll make me deaf," he murmured.

In answer she grabbed his head and dragged it to her other breast, squirming under him until one thigh lay between his legs, pushing deliciously against his groin.

Deirdre had slipped into a dream of Naisi's tongue and fingers, and warm expanses of skin brushing her in so many places at once she felt drugged by touch.

She couldn't see what he was doing and so every movement was a delightful shock. His fingers went to the tender arch of her foot, stroking up her calves and inner thighs and then falling away, and when they moved back to her breasts, she realized the flesh in her secret place had become engorged with heat, and she was exquisitely aware of the woman-parts Levarcham had named so dispassionately. *If you had ever felt this, you would not have done so,* her dazed thoughts ran. But then no one had ever felt this. She and Naisi were lost in their own world of musty darkness, and breath across shivering skin. This ecstasy had surely never been brought into the world.

Naisi suckled her nipples again and she smeared beads of sweat across his shoulders, glossing them with the moisture of her lips and tongue. Immersed in that, she tensed when his hand unexpectedly brushed the hair at her groin. Now those searching fingers went lower and did not lift away, and she groaned when they gently parted her hidden lips, stroking the unfolding petals of soft, swollen skin. "See?" His voice was husky. "It makes you silky, to take the length of me and feel only pleasure, not pain."

"Then I need…that…" All her senses were focused on the pleasure radiating out from his fingers, until he again surprised her, rubbing the heel of his palm in a slower rhythm where the petals met. Little burning darts reached up inside with every slide of his hand, and she arched her back. "Now, Naisi, now…"

"Not now." His voice held a smile and he slipped down her body. With no warning, he nudged her thighs apart with his hands…and she was utterly lost, for he parted those swollen lips with his tongue and began lapping at her, reaching the hidden places where his fingers could not go.

Her heels dug into the pine needles and she knotted her hands in his hair to drag him closer, all sensation focused there. She was lifting from her body, barely tethered by the sparking knot of pleasure under his tongue, and just as she began tearing at his hair, Naisi slid up her body. "It is I who cannot wait," he breathed, and bracing himself over her, slowly pushed the hard tip of him inside that opening of damp flesh.

Deirdre's instincts ruled her and she tilted her hips, raising herself on her elbows to force him deeper. "Wait…" he gasped, and she felt the resistance, her body pushing back against his. He thrust once, sharply, and though she bit back a cry, the burn of pain was just as swiftly lost when her body opened to draw him in.

She collapsed on the ground and Naisi sheathed himself and they were joined. She clung to him, tears in her eyes. She did not want to move in case that moment was broken. *He was inside her body*. She thought nothing could be better than that, but then Naisi began to rock, pulling out before burying himself again. Every time he sank up to his hilt, he ground his bone and flesh into hers. It brought her a deeper, wilder pleasure that moved through her body in a rolling wave.

She wrapped her legs about him, their hips moving together in a long undulation. He lifted her to him, rubbing the base of his shaft into the bud between her lips and she caught alight with an intense burn of pleasure. It centered there at the core of her, and swiftly became a rush that flared up her body and out, flinging her spirit to the dazzling sky. She remembered a dream of being splintered into infinite shards...and the shards that made her shimmered outward in a wave, into ecstasy. She was Source and she was One, and she was everything for an endless, exquisite moment, the stardust of Naisi fusing with her own. They clung together and he shouted his release in a wordless voice, and she heard in it his surrender.

The light penetrated Deirdre's closed eyelids as if the woods all around them were flooded with their white fire...blinding-bright...consuming them...

At last even that faded, and they fell together into a darkness of no time or sense, the night holding them.

Her flesh and bones slowly re-formed around her.

She remembered that she was Deirdre, and it was Alba. The pattern of the stars placed her here, now, joined to Naisi and Levarcham and the druids and the tribes. It was this time she lived. *Remember.*

Naisi's weight was making it hard to fill her lungs. He felt her stir and rolled to one side, and she sighed when he slipped from her. She grasped his rump and held him close and they lay side by side, their breath mingling while their hearts slowed.

"I can't breathe," Deirdre whispered, and clawed the cloak away from her face, exposing her shoulder to the damp air. So much time had passed that in Thisworld the rain had stopped and the storm had spun away over the hills, taking the wind with it. The trees dripped, the only sound in the hushed forest, and down the hill a bronze moon struggled from behind the clouds.

"Stay there, *a stór*," Naisi murmured, and rearranged the cloak so they could huddle with it around them, knees drawn up.

When he sat back down he stifled a grunt and she glanced sideways. "Cramp," he muttered. "My leg's gone to sleep."

"Mine, too." She nestled into the hides, teeth chattering. "And something's dripping from me."

He slid an arm about her and pulled her into his warmth. "It's just a little blood, and the seed from me…" His tone changed. "How do you make us speak of such things, like a druid poking at entrails?"

Amusement burbled up in her, the remnants of shock sliding into giddiness. "*And* I'm sore, and it's wet."

"You didn't notice all that before, did you?"

The trees brushed shadows across the angles of his face. She nudged a sliver of hair from his brow, the faint light picking out glints of wonder in his eyes that must mirror her own. "No," she whispered.

He shifted, plucking at something under him. "And now the needles are finding their way into crevices they shouldn't." They both began to snuffle with laughter, like children, and all traces of embarrassment were gone.

She nuzzled his neck, then pulled away to look at the arrowhead that had just scratched her cheek. Wordlessly, she untied the leather, holding his eyes. When he realized what she was doing, his shoulders relaxed, and as the arrow dropped into her palm he sighed. She tied the deer amulet and boar tusk back in place and they moved up the slope and dug a hole beneath a hawthorn bush with their fingers, burying Conor's blade together.

They sat back beneath the pines. Deirdre bent her head on Naisi's shoulder and he tucked it under his chin and in the stillness kissed her hair. It was only then she remembered he had just called her *a stór*.

Beloved.

CHAPTER 26

The long sunseason afternoons were spent lying on the warm rocks that scattered the hillsides, Deirdre trying to impart some of the bird-spirit lore to the brothers. Ainnle was too impatient to even begin to slow his breathing, and he usually gave up, wandering away to stalk hares with his bow. Naisi possessed the focus, but he told Deirdre ruefully that he could only make himself shrink down and down, and then he disappeared altogether and found he'd fallen asleep. Deirdre allowed him this, considering they spent much of the night exploring each other instead of slumbering.

So it became her and Ardan cross-legged in the sun, sharing druid lore, or crouched around their hearth when it rained. Then Deirdre would draw pictures in the earth floor that Naisi and Ainnle would glance at upside down, grinning and shaking their heads. Glowing threads…spirits shrinking into dots of light…how could she explain something she felt only with her body?

At least it was apparent that Ardan had a gift, though he only managed to glean a faint sensation every now and then of lifting from his body. Once he did seem to sink into a trance, and when he opened his gray eyes their depths reflected a hint of misty clouds in a distant sky.

Deirdre crouched on the rock, smiling down at him. His awareness only returned gradually, and he flushed when he saw her watching. "It feels so odd to wake," he murmured, blinking, "so heavy. The lightness is what I always…" He stopped himself, though Deirdre heard the meaning run on in her head. *It's what I always longed for.*

She had yearned for freedom, but what did Ardan need? He had his freedom.

Naisi rolled over and braced his chin on his hands, yawning. "As long as you don't go wandering across the skies and we lose you altogether, brother. You might not come back."

Ardan turned his face away so his loose black hair hid his eyes, flexing one spread hand. "Perhaps not." There was an uncomfortable silence, before he returned his gaze to Deirdre. "Let me try once more."

Naisi sat up, stretching his arms. "Then I'll find Ainnle and see if he's got dinner." He leaped off the rock, his glance at Deirdre full of heat.

She looked down at Ardan's closed eyes, and moved by the whisper of hurt around him squeezed his hand. He immediately tensed, and flustered she let go, crouching back on the rocks with arms around her knees. After a moment he took a great breath, relaxing his shoulders.

She softened her voice. "Nine breaths, then, and with each one imagine you are growing lighter and smaller…"

A hush fell over the hillside, broken only by bees humming around the fluted pink trumpets of woodbine that wound over a nearby thorn-brake. "Smaller and smaller…" Deirdre's voice slowed. "Breathe into your chest and feel your body on the rock. Feel the stone's hardness, its sun-warmth, its damp smell. Feel the sun on your eyelids… hold that… breathe." She paused, watching Ardan's chest swelling and falling like waves on a beach. These were Levarcham's words, but for the first time she found her mind circling the idea of what they really meant, what truth lay beneath this practiced skill. "You are Ardan, brother of Naisi and Ainnle; sword-wielder; singer. And you are the spirit that flies." Her voice dropped to a whisper and her eyes went out of focus, the sunlight on the dewy bracken blinding her. "You are that light, no matter what people call you. Nothing can hold you."

Those words arose from a deeper place, and she wasn't sure if she spoke to Ardan or herself.

The four of them threaded their way down the path in the warm dusk, Ainnle with a hare dangling from his sword-belt. The slanting light turned the loch into a pool of molten bronze and set all the purple-blooming heather aflame. As the air cooled, a wind rose, making the birch leaves quiver on their feathered branches. Naisi was bringing up the rear and Deirdre was clambering between a scatter of boulders when he tugged her braid, nearly pulling her over. His hand clamped over her mouth and he pressed her against his belly, his lips tickling her ear. "It's too fine a night to be going inside just yet, *fiáin*."

Ahead, Ardan paused. Ainnle turned and flung an arm about him, making some joke, and they disappeared among the rocks.

Deirdre stuck her tongue into Naisi's palm and he dropped his hand. "That feels like an eel!"

She turned in his arms. "You didn't say *that* last time I used it on you."

"You didn't make me think of eels then." He linked his arms about her waist, kissing her neck. "I said it's too beautiful to go inside."

Deirdre closed her eyes, rubbing her belly into him. "Every time we come back from the mountain, you leap upon me in the woods."

He raised his head, eyes glinting warningly. "I won't leap upon you at all if you don't like it."

She wriggled free and scrambled up the nearest rock. "Oh, I don't *like* it," she declared, balancing there to drink him in. The drawn look was gone from his face now, the muted dusk gilding his skin and lighting his eyes with a feral glow. *I melt with it*, she finished inside. Breaking into a slow smile, she leaped off the boulder into the bracken behind, racing toward the trees, his feet thudding after her.

In this haze of abandoned pleasure, the real world and dream-world had been exchanged. This pool of heated desire was true life, saturated in sensation; the times they had to rise and pretend to be human were stark dreams. Deirdre's existence was formed now of Naisi's essence in her nostrils, under her tongue, palms and fingers, inside her flesh. Her world was all about melting tastes and musky scents, stroking hands and the sensual weight of him between her thighs.

He laid her in the ferns beneath the hazel trees now and lifted her to him, rocking her bones against his as she knotted his thick, black hair and drew it through her fingers like the dark mane of a wild creature. Deirdre's senses joined with the roar of the wind in the branches and the smell of rushing water, and she could not tell where her body ended and the earth began.

Sunseason slid into leaf-fall and the world flamed into red and gold.

The bracken rusted to copper and the wide swathes of grasses and sedges on the hillslopes bleached to a pale, gleaming bronze. The leaves of the trees curled into flutes of yellow and brown. Brambles dotted the bushes with gleaming drops of purple, and Deirdre collected baskets of them, her clothes splattered with dark juice if Naisi came, too. Ainnle had found a bees' nest and Deirdre soaked rowan-berries and rose-hips in the clay pots of honey, sealing them with wax, and roasted hazelnuts and ground them into meal.

Naisi tended the tanning pits with her and she went with him to hunt; there was no question now of her bringing bad luck. Their hunger for touch was all-consuming, and they could not be apart. Naisi's years of hunting always outweighed her natural abilities, though, and when her endurance gave out she'd wait for him on the rocks and they would bring the meat and hides down the mountain together. They set sinew snares and pit-traps, and the houses were dressed with furs of hare, marten, stoat and fox to make them warm against the coming cold.

The langorous desire that soaked through Deirdre drowned all other awareness and she only felt the glimmer of the *other* like a hidden spring running faintly beneath her feet. She was absorbed by Naisi, reaching inward only to their hidden world, sinking only into the waters of sensation that held him.

One day he offered to make her a little log-boat because she could not take the fishing curragh out on her own. They spent a day searching for a suitable oak and, after lopping off the branches, put down the axes and took their pleasure beneath a rowan tree, its feathered leaves a crown of gold.

Now Deirdre was rocked by something deeper than frantic desire. He knew she loved to glide over water, the seals turning their sleek flanks alongside, the swans watching her with dark eyes. He knew her.

Tenderly, she straddled him, cradling him with the shelter of her body, tangling her hair around his shoulders as this time she made the slow rhythm her own.

They were on the shore smoothing the boat with adzes when Naisi became alert, turning toward something Deirdre couldn't even hear. He stared into the trees, then said, "Stay here."

Ainnle and Ardan had been on a hunting foray in the wilder glens to the east, but when Naisi strapped on his sword Deirdre knew it was not their footsteps he had heard. He disappeared into the trees with a flick of the bracken fronds and she took a rest from grinding wood, leaning her cheek on the little boat, murmuring blessings under her breath.

Naisi came back and told her it was Urp calling for him. The old man had been herding his sheep down from the pastures when he saw three warriors walking along a ridge toward the moor.

To Naisi and Deirdre's relief, Ardan and Ainnle returned unharmed that night, though empty-handed. "We were tracking two stags." Ardan slurped slivers of trout from his fingers. "Until we ran into three strangers coming the other way. They didn't hear us in the wind."

Stripping flesh off the fish propped in the smoke, Naisi ventured, "Venicones?"

Ainnle was scooping Arda's curd cheese onto a wedge of Deirdre's honey-baked bread and wolfing it down. He appreciated her for her food, at least. "We never got a chance to find out. We were going up a ravine and they were coming down, and before we could say anything they began shooting arrows at us and we had to take cover. When we drew our blades they fled over the crest of the mountain. They looked like scouts to us, with bows but no swords."

Naisi turned on his haunches. "And they got away?"

Ardan stopped chewing and raised a brow. "Sorry we didn't manage all three for you, brother."

Naisi's smile flickered, though his frown remained. The next day he announced that he and Ainnle would take the curragh across to the village.

They returned at dusk lugging sacks of grain. "We heard rumors," Naisi said to Ardan, throwing one down inside the doorway of his house. Naisi stepped back when Deirdre went to untie it, rubbing his shoulders. "People say there is a new Venicones king, and now trouble is brewing between him and the Epidii king, Cinet. Perhaps that's why the Venicones have sent more men down the glen. They must be testing the defenses."

The barley seeds slipped through Deirdre's fingers.

"Then they are testing us," Ainnle said in a low voice, and all three brothers looked at one another. "Though they don't know it yet." As one, their eyes lingered with speculation on Naisi's sword, propped against the wall of the hut.

CHAPTER 27

Leaf-fall

At the festival of Samhain, the turning of the year, great bon-fires roared on the frosted plain of Emain Macha.

Under an arch of stars, the druids exhorted the gods to ward the land for the long dark. With raised arms and soaring voices, they drew divine power into the soil to nurture the sleeping seeds, and into the byre and sheep-fold to nourish the young in the womb. On this night, the boundaries between Otherworld and Thisworld blurred. The *sídhe* arose and the dead passed between the vapors.

It was a night of mystery, and outside the fort people clustered close to the fires, driving away the fear of the spirits with singing, spits of sizzling meat and barrels of ale. Music threaded through slurred laughter, and hide drums beat out the rhythm of thudding feet, as lines of dancers wove between the piles of embers.

Cúchulainn and Ferdia were quiet at their fire, heads bent over cups. The herdsmen, servants and guards from the Hound's own dun were milling about a pit of stone-baked beef from which rose tantalizing curls of steam. Cúchulainn raised his cup to his wife, Emer, bouncing another woman's babe on her hip. She smiled back, the shine of her eyes full of promise. He sighed. It wasn't safe this night to try for a babe of their own amid the furs on the frosty meadow.

Sunseason had been a fertile time for crops other than barley; the duns were all seething with dissent. At least Connacht it-self was quiet. The yearly rhythm of cattle raids by the young

warriors testing themselves, and the counter-raids of the Ulaid
Red Branch, had been interrupted on both sides. Cúchulainn
still simmered with frustration that the king would not command a more serious attack while Connacht was recovering
from Eochaid's death, but he had ensured that despite so much
effort being bent on Naisi's capture, warriors still guarded the
Gates of Macha and the other defenses. He himself spent what
time he could away from Emer and the rule of his clan riding
Connacht's borders, but Ferdia had no wife or family ties, and
being far more unobtrusive, had been busy gathering news.

"Aed has been stirring up the southern chieftains," Ferdia muttered, swilling the liquid in his cup. In all the years Cúchulainn
had known Ferdia, his friend would only ever drink honeyed
water, for he said ale made him belligerent and morose—though
Cúchulainn found that hard to believe. "Leary's wife and kin are
also directing their wrath at the king since there is no Naisi to
blame." Ferdia's voice dropped. "They question Conor's fitness to
rule, and are complaining about the Red Branch."

Cúchulainn grunted. "Leary was Red Branch."

"I know. But they say he should have died in honorable battle
against an enemy; that we are unsafe—too proud and quarrel-
some." Cúchulainn took a grim sip of ale, and Ferdia glanced over
his shoulder. "Cú, everything Conor fears *is* being said: that he's
lost his manhood, that he's an old fool with a withered prick."

"Gods." Cúchulainn didn't know how to stop this fracturing. If
they could only fight together … That's why he'd urged Conor to
send them raiding, but the king countered that they must find
Naisi first, so no one would question his authority. Without the
tightening of Red Branch bonds in war, however, idle voices
gained power. Cúchulainn kicked a shard of charred wood back
in the fire. "When men take sides, we are all endangered."

Ferdia shrugged, his mouth a thin line. "The young ones admired the sons of Usnech and think this is about the jealousy of
an old king for a young buck. As for the older warriors, the way
Conor won his hall has never sat well, even after all this time.
Men think he should be grateful; they see this as indulgence."

One of the novice bards had been tuning his harp at the next fire, surrounded by a band of youthful warriors who shouted and staggered into one another. When the bard's voice at last grew loud enough to hear, Cúchulainn turned his head.

His heart sank. The song had been written by the king's bard two years before, to celebrate the battle prowess of the sons of Usnech. Ferdia glanced at Cúchulainn in dismay; but how was he supposed to halt every utterance among the Ulaid? He took a slug of ale to ease his throat. He would not prevent their names being honored on their own soil.

Then the song changed, slowing into a poignant lilt. The raucous young men crowding around quieted and the bard's voice soared unfettered. It was a new composition—a lament for an unnamed youth, a fair warrior cruelly cast aside by a spiteful king.

Cúchulainn and Ferdia were immediately on their feet, striding toward the bard and the gathered warriors. But before Cúchulainn could reach them, he heard raised voices. The king's son Fiacra was swaying before Illan, fists balled. "You dare say that about my sire?"

Illan and Fiacra had been raised as brothers, and indeed looked like twins with their fair hair. But Illan's lip jutted now and he yelled back, "No one can tear the great warriors from our hearts! *You* are Red Branch—that's your first loyalty!"

The bard's song faded into silence. Fiacra's eyes were glassy, his locks tinted red by the flames. "Naisi and his brothers betrayed us from the start by stealing the king's bride. Why can't you see it?"

"They didn't do any such thing," Illan slurred. "And I won't see them shamed. Tonight's for honoring the dead, isn't it? Well, they may as well be dead!"

Other youths weighed in on both sides, bellowing over one another, and it was about to descend into a fistfight when Conall appeared, dragging himself from his own fire, his wife and kin. Conall began trying to calm Fiacra just as Cúchulainn reached Illan. Fergus's youngest son had begun exhorting the bard to play again, his voice whipping up the baying mob as he punched the air, singing, "*Into battle the joyful brothers—Naisi, Ardan and Ainnle!*"

Conall's eyes blazed at Cúchulainn. "Shut him up, Hound!"

"Illan," Ferdia growled, slinging an arm about the boy's neck to cut off his drunken shouts.

Illan cried out and ducked free, and before anyone could move he took a wild swing at Ferdia that missed him, Illan's fist then soaring toward Cúchulainn. The Hound stepped aside and the young man went sprawling. As soon as Cúchulainn bent to haul him up, Illan began stammering, "Gods…I am sorry… sorry…" The bard, meanwhile, was watching all this with a satisfied smile. Stirring up such emotion was a great triumph.

Conall shoved Fiacra toward his friends and loomed before Illan, now swaying in Cúchulainn's arms. "Don't touch him," Cúchulainn warned Conall. "He's just full of drink."

"He's a fool," Conall hissed.

Cúchulainn was getting tired of stifling his feelings. "He is grieved—as I thought you'd be."

By the unsteady way Conall raked his hand through his red mane, Cúchulainn knew he was not in control of himself, either, and a warning struck at the back of his mind. "I'm not going to see the Red Branch brought low by a pup as proud as Naisi," Conall muttered. He paused, his eyes pained. "He killed Leary."

Cúchulainn's own head was spinning from the ale. "He must have been trapped, you know that." When Conall's face remained hard, Cúchulainn's patience snapped. "It's bloody madness," he ground under his breath, "but then, you were jealous of the brothers, too."

Conall's eyes flared with anger, and at that moment all the sound of voices around them was cut off, like a harp-string breaking. Conor was there. A hush settled over the crowd, punctured by the spitting of sparks from the nearby bonfire and the wail of a babe. The king gazed around at every man's face, marking them, before his eyes fixed on the young bard. "I gave no permission to sing that song."

The harper had courage, bracing his shoulders, his head flung up. "With all respect, my lord, the words of a bard are druid-blessed and no man can silence them."

There was a general muttering and men and women began to slink away toward the other fires. But Conor's hooded eyes did not waver from the bard, and though he only betrayed a slight tremor in his face, his voice grated with palpable fury. "No one will name those exiles who have brought so much pain to us—*I will not hear it.* And you..." He swung toward Illan. "It is treason to take the side of a traitor."

Cúchulainn's lips thinned. The air almost crackled with tension, and he was about to speak when a deep voice boomed, "Treason, Conor?" Fergus shouldered men aside to stand by his son. "Illan did nothing but repeat a song your own bard wrote. It was *yours,* for the sons of Usnech."

Conor's mouth pursed into a hard knot. "Then I forbid it now."

Fergus's hair had been stiffened with lime into a spiked mane for the festival, his massive neck banded by a torc of bronze and gold. "*Treason* is a dangerous word for anyone to utter," he growled.

Cúchulainn struggled to guard his emotions, for mac Roy's words churned the ale in his gut. Treason was turning on the Red Branch, endangering the kingship. Was Conor not treasonous, too?

The king was momentarily silent with astonishment. "Words and thoughts are free," Fergus said softly, "and if my son honors the comrades with whom he shed blood, then he is fulfilling his Red Branch oaths." In his dark eyes was the message that Conor wouldn't know about those vows, because he had not taken them.

Conor tilted his long nose back and, instead of answering, snapped at the young bard. "You are impudent, and I am sick of the trouble made by rash young men. A bard needs a king's favor, and chieftains to give you shelter because of that favor." He paused, his white fingers stroking the fork of his graying beard with suppressed agitation. "Sing of the Red Branch, but pick a tune that names no man above another, for see the anger you have caused."

The bard's face was beaded with nervous sweat now. He snapped his heels together and bowed before making for the temple mound. The king avoided all their eyes, striding unsteadily toward the gates of the fort while Fergus led Illan in the opposite direction. Conall flung his cloak around his shoulders and stalked away into the dark.

"This is a pit of smoldering coals," Cúchulainn said bleakly. "Soon we won't be able to quench it."

"Then let me finish what I was about to tell you before that damned harper began squawking." Ferdia gripped Cúchulainn's shoulder and turned him. "I've been spending time with the slut who serves Conor his ale."

Cúchulainn's brows rose. "She's a dangerous one to bed, my friend. He tups her, too."

"All in the name of gathering information."

Cúchulainn snorted dryly while they sat on stumps away from their fire. "It's torture, I'm sure."

"It's pleasant enough. But what she tells me is better."

Cúchulainn rolled an abandoned cup close with his foot and shook the grass from it, pouring mead from a nearby jug. He swallowed it in one mouthful. "It can't be worse than this."

"The king has sent secret messengers to the British lands and Gaul."

The cup lowered to Cúchulainn's lap. He and Ferdia had fishermen scouring every dot of island and wind-blasted rock in the Erin sea. "So Conor does not believe they are anywhere near Erin anymore." He looked at Ferdia. "How many messengers?"

"Who would know? He has spies he keeps to himself."

"Then we have to find them first."

Their eyes met. "Skatha," Ferdia agreed. The warrior-queen's battle school was situated on a windswept island off the coast of Alba. Warriors from different peoples went there to learn arcane skills that melded the female mind with male strength and skill. Britons came, and shaggy men from the northlands, and even hardy Roman and Greek adventurers from the Middle Sea.

Skatha still held Cúchulainn and Ferdia, her prize pupils, in great affection.

"If she hasn't heard anything herself, some of her pupils might have," Cúchulainn said. "Not even Conor can call on men who travel over so much territory. Go as soon as you can."

"Leaf-fall is an odd time to sail—and a dangerous one. I'll need an excuse to get away from the king."

"We'll find one. We have to do this for Naisi."

Emer came to Cúchulainn's side, playing with the fair curls at his neck. "This is a night for laughter," she scolded in her husky voice. "And here I see you two with faces as long as spears." Cúchulainn rose and pulled her close to smell the comforting scent on her of soap and bread, women's herbs and wool. She batted his kiss away. "Not before Ferdia!"

Ferdia forced a strained smile and poured out the dregs of his cup on the grass. "I think I should find my own company," he said. "A certain maid who pours a better head of ale."

Baffled, Emer watched him leave. "But he doesn't drink ale!"

Cúchulainn nuzzled her neck. "He's so dazzled by your beauty he forgot himself."

"Hmm, I see you drank enough for both of you." She went on tiptoe to kiss his nose. "I can think of something better to bring your smile back, though, husband."

Cúchulainn gazed down into that beloved face and blessed it for its quirky flaws: the frizz of untameable black curls; her snub nose; the wry, lopsided smile. Emer was no pampered maid, nor did she possess the beauty to set warriors at odds.

She pouted at him mockingly. "You are far away."

He smiled and buried his face in her neck, lifting her off the ground. "I'm right here," he said, breathing her in.

In Alba, Deirdre built the Samhain need-fire far down the loch, watched by the sons of Usnech. The air was icy and the stars blazed over their heads. They had extinguished their hearths and found their way by starlight on the water—they would relight their torches and then their own fires with the sacred flame, marking the new year.

The fire crackled into life and Ardan's voice rose in a lament for Erin, for Samhain was a night to remember what had passed into memory. Deirdre beseeched the Mother Goddess to protect the seeds while they awaited the returning sun, her breath lit by star-light into an ethereal cloud, like the spell of the Goddess herself. They set out honey-cakes for the dead, and it was when they stepped back that, to Naisi, a face seemed to take shape in the lurid glow of the flames.

It hovered in the nether realms between the light of the living and the ghostly flickers of the spirits under the trees. Usnech. *Father, his eyes full of disappointment.*

A stray crumb stuck in Naisi's throat. With that one look, the flood of heat that had soaked through him all these moons in Deirdre's arms drained away into the cold ground. Her hand slipped from his—or did he clench his fist, pushing away her touch? She bent to break another of the honey-cakes, and he turned his face to the shadows of the cliffs.

So the defense of Mairi and her poor daughter was not enough to lay this gnawing shame to rest, to make amends for his soul betrayal. The betrayal of the Red Branch, long ago; his brothers; the Ulaid itself. And look what it had led to—far worse consequences than the hidden anguish inside him. Dallan and Leary dead, his brothers exiled. One brief skirmish could not assuage all that, let alone be a balm for his heart.

He did not know what would be enough.

CHAPTER 28

Leaf-bud

By frost and moonlight, she was a carving of marble, smooth and silvered.

Though the endless moons of the long dark were at last over, ice crystals still glittered on the banks of the spring behind the houses, and the full moon lit the running water into streamers of glass.

She stood bare-legged on the grass, one hand hitching up her long shift, her other clothes left discarded on the ground. She was the moon-maiden, argent light formed into rounded curves and lithe muscles he could glimpse through the damp linen. Then she breathed and her exhalation was an all-too-human warmth that released a cloud around her head.

Ardan's stomach clenched. She was Deirdre, and not his dream at all.

Even though the trees had at last grown their tight-closed buds, the air was still freezing. Did Naisi know she braved this cold, drawn to the spring when the moon bathed it with luminous light? Ardan knew. Against all sense and his love for Naisi, he followed her, pulled from his slumber as if she called his name. She was a dream-maiden who passed his door in deepest night, her soft footfalls beckoning him from his bed.

She reached down for a flask and poured a splash of milk into the pool, her hands moving reverently, her chin outlined as she raised her face and said something under her breath to the moon. Ardan gasped, his pain too sharp to suppress. She colored this gray world of frustration and anguish with tantalizing threads of mysterious Otherness. The branches of the alder trees appeared to reach across the pool to her, rimed by frost. The fallen leaves and twigs glinted as if alive, and the dark peaks leaned in over her head to hide her from mortal view, sheltering this bower of enchantment.

It was just like his bird flights. When he practiced alone, his gains were fleeting. Only when Deirdre's husky voice guided him was he filled with a lightness, an almost-glimpse of sky. On waking from his trance, she was always waiting beside him, legs drawn up, face lifted to the dusk sky. She gave him the freedom to *fly*.

Now Deirdre cocked her head as if listening, and after a moment pulled her shift over her head and tossed it down with her other clothes. Beads of sweat broke over Ardan's face and he bitterly cursed himself, all the while devouring that expanse of naked back and smooth, curving rump. Naisi had her in daylight, by firelight. There was no realm where Ardan could look upon her except this mantle of night where she was another creature. This girl wasn't Naisi's. Splinters of ice seemed to enter him with every breath, while she paused there on the banks of the pool.

The long dark had been unbearable. Unable to hunt, driven inside by storms and rain, he either had to huddle around a fire with Naisi and Deirdre, watching the play of light over her fine bones, or even worse, know that when they disappeared Naisi would be buried between those slim thighs. They spent so much time in the furs that when they did emerge, they floated about in a mist of desire Ardan could smell. Deirdre's skin bore a perpetual flush, the surface gleaming as if burnished by Naisi's hands.

Ardan looked down at his dagger. He held it in his hands when he watched her, pressing the blade into his fingers to make himself feel pain so he would walk no farther down this dark trail. Instead, he managed to fool himself for a few moments that this night-maiden was his, made of sea-foam and moonlit water. He closed his eyes to suppress a hiss of anguish. *Beloved brother.*

A soft splash brought him back. She had stepped into the pool, and just as she always did, ignoring the cold, she lifted water in a scallop shell and quickly streamed it over her head. She shuddered and paused with dripping hair, staring into the dark woods. That absorption, that tilt of yearning toward the frosted trees, set Ardan alight. What did she hearken to? When she flung water from her hair and smoothed it down her legs, he instinctively understood that to her it was *light*. She bathed in this moonlit luminescence, savoring it as a living thing, and for days afterward it glowed from her eyes. But what did she glimpse beneath the surface of the world?

In a moment she would come out with her breasts facing him, the soft curl of hair between her legs...But he'd only imagined that, for he would never let himself see. Ducking his head, Ardan crept away. The farther he got from her body, the more he could let go of that sick desire and invoke the silvery reverence instead, allowing it to fill his heart. Only a plea for Naisi's forgiveness at last let him descend back into sleep.

In his dreams, he was caught in a flurry of waves. Slim arms twined about his neck in the turbulent water, and a sinuous body pressed against him. There he had release, the heat from his body mingling with the water, as the long tendrils of the selkie's hair wrapped around his eyes so he couldn't see.

Deirdre stepped out onto the crackling grass and turned in a shaft of moonlight.

The only time she could drag herself from Naisi's embrace were these nights when the pool was bathed in radiance. She braved the cold because the water and moon-glow mingled into one and, as if it cast a spell, she could not resist that call to at least touch the beauty of the night. She reached out a hand, her breath a cloud around her. An idea darted through her before she could stop it: a musing that the Otherworld veils might be as taut as the surface of water...for didn't her finger-tips feel the boundary?

Her hand pulled back. *Naisi.* She thought she heard his step.

As she turned, her eyes were caught by a glint across the water, like a diving fish. An impulse seized her to plunge back in after that elusive gleam, before a shiver enveloped her instead, and she saw herself crawling in beside Naisi and letting his heat soak into her. She relaxed her shoulders into the sensual caress of water trickling down her flanks. And all the mysterious stirrings in the moonlit air were completely swept away by a physical memory that was so potent she still sensed it with her body: Naisi's limbs encircling her, their legs tangled up, his breath on her neck.

She could almost smell him. She raised her fingers to her nose and then touched her belly. This night was Imbolc, the festival of the goddess Brid, who set a protection over the young of the beasts and nurtured the seeds as they waited for Lugh, the sun god, to return. It was a woman's night that invoked the power of the goddess, the womb of creation. Could a child be seeding itself in her, even now? Perhaps soon, then, she would know what she would become. *Mother.*

She dressed and left her palm over her navel as she walked back, her chattering teeth making her smile. She moved the hazel and heather door aside and the thick hide hanging inside it, and crossing the hearth knelt on the bracken bed, watching Naisi.

He lay with arms flung in abandon, chin tucked into his shoulder. The glow of the coals gave his skin the sheen and hue of oiled wood, and her hands hovered above his chest, drawing his warmth into her palms. One finger accidentally drifted onto his belly and he flinched, his eyes springing open. They were glassy for a moment. "You're cold," he croaked.

"Sorry," she whispered.

He mumbled something and pulled her down among the furs on the springy mattress, curving her into his body. "What were you doing out there?" he muttered, sounding more awake. "Your hair's wet."

She shivered again, pressing her cold nose into his arm. "You shouldn't ask a maid why she goes outside at night."

He lifted her chin with a thumb. "I can warm you up," he murmured, and bracing himself over her he pushed her mouth open with his tongue, tasting her. She relaxed with a sigh and let herself be consumed.

Afterward, they lay sprawled among the tangled bedcovers, Naisi instantly falling back into sleep. Deirdre had unconsciously rolled away from him, though, her naked body exposed to the air while the sweat cooled on her skin.

She drifted into slumber, barely aware that one leg was hanging over the bed with toes brushing the floor, as if poised for flight.

Though the wind still blew in icy gusts and snow dusted the highest rock-peaks, blossoms began to halo the thorn-bushes with white among the bare, brown trees. A raft of cold, sunny days lit the dead bracken into a glowing swathe of copper, and the slopes were reddened by the russet crowns of the birches. Even at the bleakest time of year, Alba blazed with color, its heart too fierce to be dulled by the gray and cold.

Ainnle was on the marsh stringing nets for salmon in the channels one day when a long, narrow curragh came sweeping up the loch from the west. The wind was whipping the water and Ainnle had been toiling with head bent into the stiff breeze, so he did not see the low-slung hide boat until its occupants were close enough to observe him. He heard a faint hail and straightened to see a hull with so many oars along its sides it churned a white wake as it slowed to a halt. In that moment, Ainnle decided he had no choice but to brave this out.

The curragh glided to a stop just short of the gravel bank. Boatmen jumped over the sides into the shallows, and pulled it to shore by its ropes. Before it was even beached, though, a tall warrior joined them, wading through the clear water. His hand was on a sword at his waist, and a helmet of beaten iron sat on his long, fair hair.

Ainnle stood blowing into his chapped hands, his mind racing. They had come from the west, in a boat, so they could not be Venicones. And this man was a person of some standing, his

checked wool mantle held on the shoulder by two enamel
brooches, his wrists circled by thick bronze rings. His wool tunic
and trews were embroidered in swirling designs worked in
many-colored thread.

"Well met," the warrior said, with all the confidence of command.

Ainnle nodded, chafing his palms together. Like the Venicones,
dark tattoos wound over the man's cheeks and brow, the whorls
now suggesting not wolf-teeth and muzzles but horse-heads with
pricked ears and flying manes. The other warriors who stepped
ashore bore variations of the same designs, giving their faces a
fierce cast that chimed with Ainnle's warrior blood, instinctively
quickening it.

Fascinated, Ainnle's investigation of the leader came to a halt
when it collided with a pair of sharp, gray eyes. "I seek a man
called Finn, and his brothers, Conn and Bran," the tall warrior
said. His face was long and spare with thin nose and lips, and his
slanted eyes were narrowed in the glitter off the water.

"I have heard of no Finn."

"Really?" The man stepped closer, shaking the water from his
boots. He was shadowed by three other warriors, all of them
looking up at the surrounding hillslopes. "At my dun in the great
glen, we have heard tales passed on from a widow about this
man and his two brothers. She said her own valley stretched
back from Cruachan, the horned one." He spoke of the great
mountain to the west that guarded the loch, raising twin peaks
to the sky. His glance was shrewd. "I am sure her mind was not
addled."

Ainnle's limbs had flooded with a familiar alertness that was
almost pleasurable. "They might live farther up toward the
moor," he offered with a shrug.

The warrior glanced the way Ainnle was pointing and back.
"Then if you see this Finn, tell him I come in peace from Cinet,
the king of the Epidii and lord of Dunadd and the isles. I wish to
speak with him." He smirked, looking Ainnle up and down. "I'm

sure there were no strange young men about last time I hunted here."

"I am a simple wanderer, and the old ones welcomed me in return for fresh meat." Ainnle looked the fair-haired man in the eye, disarming him with a grin. "I apologize if I have offended you."

He said this so boldly the warrior smiled despite himself. "No matter. I hear the herders here have suffered trouble that has twice been put right by this Finn and his kin. I look forward to meeting him."

"Well, it's an easy walk," Ainnle said cheerily, lifting a last rock to hold the net.

"If you lead us, yes."

"But I have hare-traps to check. You wouldn't want me to starve, now."

The warrior pursed his lips. A jet ring on his finger sparked in the sun as he tapped his hilt. "Next time I see you, perhaps you'll be more amenable."

"As much as my belly lets me," Ainnle returned. He saluted with one finger. "So if you'll excuse me, I have dinner to catch." He loaded his bow and quiver on his back and stuck his dagger through his belt. From the safety of the woods, he hid behind an oak tree and watched. The curragh was left with a small guard while the remaining five warriors set off up the glen with their blond-haired leader. Ainnle turned and scrambled up the hill the other way.

Naisi was alone outside his house. Ainnle expected his eldest brother to order them into hiding, but after listening he only paced for a time before ducking under his door-hide. Baffled, Ainnle was about to go after him when Naisi came out with a bundle in his arms. He shook out a wolfskin cloak, one of his most treasured possessions. It had lain in the bottom of the pack their mother had left at the thorn tree in Erin, for he only wore it at feasts and on festival days. Now Naisi drew it on for the first time in Alba, the shaggy gray-and-black fur gleaming in the sun.

The wolf's head formed the hood, bound beneath Naisi's chin with gold-tipped leather ties, and the tufted ears and long snout carved his familiar features into something much more fierce and threatening.

Ainnle let out a faint whoop of delight. "You mean to face them!"

Naisi settled their father's torc over his collarbones. "If this man is a warrior, he will have sniffed out the same in you already. I'd lay bets you spoke boldly and looked him in the eye." Ainnle thought about arguing and then swallowed it. Naisi's grim smile was softened by the understanding in his eyes. "It's too late for pretense now, little brother. If we run, they'll know we have something to hide."

Thank the gods Deirdre and Ardan were not here to stop them, Ainnle thought fervently, already anticipating the fit of his hilt into his palm as he paraded his blade before this nobleman.

His brother was frowning now. "The old woman Mairi must have blurted it out when she went to her kin over the mountains." He stabbed a bronze brooch into his cloak. "I should have asked for her silence again, but she became hysterical every time she spoke to me."

Ainnle shrugged, hiding his bright eyes, and began to arm himself.

Urp was speaking to the strangers from the safety of his sheeppen, though at Ainnle and Naisi's approach he hobbled to the gate. There he halted. The two brothers were aglitter with armbands, torcs and brooches, harsh in the leaf-bud sun, and Naisi's head was framed by the wolf-hood with its ruff and snout. Naisi saw in Urp's wrinkled face the question of just whom he'd been entertaining at his fire these past moons.

The king's men also turned and Naisi snatched the advantage of surprise. He pressed his hood back. "I am Finn."

The pale slashes of the leader's brows rose, creasing up his tattoos, and his sharp glance went to Ainnle. Naisi had given no father's name and no place to which he belonged. Ignoring that lapse, the man nodded. "I am Talan, son of Nectan, of the Dun of the North Loch, near the falls. Cinet, king of the Epidii sends his greetings to the esteemed warriors who defended his territory from attack by an enemy force."

Naisi's bow was faint, his smile stiff. "I thank you, but I don't know about a *force*. Nine men, I think." He turned to Ainnle. "Or was it ten?"

"Ten," Ainnle replied swiftly, drawing himself up. "Three each, and the fourth to me."

Naisi spread his hands to show his father's armbands—heavy twists of bronze studded with red enamel. "Ten isn't an army. Your king had no need for such gratitude, though we are, of course, glad to receive it." He had to walk a fine line between insolence and respect—too little arrogance and he appeared weak, too much and he risked a fight. It was a warrior's game, and his blood was singing with that familiar challenge.

Talan's wry gaze was sweeping over Ainnle's finery. "And which one are you?"

Ainnle grinned. "Conn."

"Not a hunter after all, then."

Naisi swiftly answered. "We do not belong to any place, and we *are* hunters. We reacted because we were forced to." His thrill was rapidly fading. He had not appreciated that by fighting those raiders they had exposed themselves so thoroughly, and to the king of all people, a sworn enemy of the Ulaid. *And if we did not,* he reminded himself, *we would all be dead.*

Talan's keen gaze took in Naisi's scabbard of gilded wood and leather, and then he turned to scan the hillsides above. "So where is the other, the third brother?"

"Nearby." Naisi's lips had gone cold.

Talan's tattoos lent his smile a sardonic twist. "Do not look so grave! The woman said that three young men arrived like the gods themselves, and everything has been bountiful since, with abundant meat and a safe bed. My king cannot leave such brave warriors unrewarded for protecting his people and the paths into his lands. This glen was never used by the Venicones before due to the difficulty of access at the loch, though it seems their new young king may be bolder. And so Cinet desires to meet you. You are invited to Dunadd."

Naisi ignored Ainnle's intake of breath, keeping his own face still. "I am exceedingly grateful for the honor of this offer. However, if we are to hunt enough to survive this season, I cannot come soon. In the next long dark, I could be spared."

Talan's smile hardened. "I am the king's cousin, and he ordered that you would travel in my own ship, which leaves today to sail down the coast to Dunadd. I came for you in passing; I can tarry no longer."

Naisi was trapped, and torn. Cinet didn't want to thank them; he wanted to discover if they were a threat. He made himself shrug one shoulder. "Then I will meet you at your boat when the sun is one handspan lower."

Ardan and Deirdre were returning from the tanning pits a different way when they stumbled across a bare oak tree wound about with the shiny leaves and berries of mistletoe—a rare find. Excited, Deirdre begged Ardan to climb the oak, for this sacred plant must never be cut by blade. The druids pulled it away with their hands and, if the tendrils released from the oak bark beneath, it was a gift of the gods. Nor should it touch the ground, so she stood under the tree with her cloak spread out, and caught the boughs as Ardan carefully dropped them.

Later they sat with the cloak spread on the ground outside her door, both cross-legged in the sun. "It is called all-heal because of its many healing uses," she explained. "Though I know you are not so interested in *that*."

"Because it's also sacred," Ardan swiftly replied, his elbows on his knees. His blunt face, which had been so heavy and brooding throughout the long dark, was animated again, his gray eyes bright. "That's what I want to know about."

"How could I guess?" She handed him a little sprig and he gently twirled it, peering at the white, waxy berries. "These berries are yellow throughout the long dark, scattering the leafless trees with gold—a sign of Lugh, to remind us he will bring the sun back with him at leaf-bud." Ardan nodded, and Deirdre raised a finger, enjoying herself. She always felt close to Levarcham when she explained such things to Ardan. "*And* it grows far up on the branches of other trees and never touches the ground, and its leaves are green all year so ..."

"It is an Otherworld plant," Ardan broke in. "It is clearly a mark of the gods, for it is immortal and it lives above the earth between ground and sky as they do."

"Exactly." She beamed at him.

"As a boy, I thought the druids cut all-heal at longest night just for decoration." His color deepened at her smile.

"Every part of druid lore boasts more than one layer of meaning." Deirdre's voice gentled as she touched the glossy green leaves. "In this case, we also hang this plant in our houses for protection and abundance." She did not speak the rest aloud. *And the sacred boughs gather and hold love within the walls of a house.*

She felt the force of Ardan's glance from the side, an intense look he never bestowed on her directly, and her face also grew warm. She did not know what lay beneath the unfathomable depths of his eyes. How could she? He was Ardan, straight and true, and his love for Naisi was greater than anything. He must feel the kinship of minds between them, as she did. She looked right at him, and he started, and applied his attention back to the berries. "And finally," she finished softly, "it brings beautiful dreams."

"Does it?" He held the sprig before his face so she could not see his eyes. "A sacred plant indeed, then."

The wistful note in his voice was eclipsed by Naisi and Ainnle's return.

As they appeared on the path, Deirdre and Ardan hastily rose, and Deirdre's greeting died on her lips at Naisi's savage appearance in the unfamiliar cloak. Then he broke the spell by shrugging it off and ruffling his sweaty hair into peaks. As he told them what had happened, Deirdre sank on the bench outside the door and regarded the sprig of mistletoe she still clutched in her fingers. *Protection.*

"We can't let you go alone," Ardan protested. "What if this king harms you?"

Naisi was already pulling his pack out of the door. He paused to smile grimly at Ardan. "There are two other brothers braver than me on the loose. No king would induce a blood feud without knowing the identity of our kin or our lord." He went inside for fresh clothes, Ainnle trailing after him.

"*I'm* coming with you," Deirdre heard Ainnle declare.

"No." Naisi came out pulling a wool tunic over his bare chest, another piece of clothing she had not seen before. It had been colored a deep red with imported dyes, the sleeves and hem worked in silver thread. The rich color set off Naisi's black hair and flushed his cheeks and lips with the same hue, and a little shock went through Deirdre. The gold torc and armbands, the rich clothes and cloak, all boasted his noble bearing; he looked like a prince. And she realized he was going to stand once more before a king. "I'm not risking all of us at once," he was saying. "You two must ward the valley." His eyes rose to Deirdre's stricken face. "There is something to guard here more precious than my life."

Ainnle's glance grazed her. "To you, perhaps, but I—"

"If you love me, then to you as well." Naisi donned his cloak again and hefted his pack. His expression was determined now, his shoulders braced, and there was a faint glint of excitement in his eyes. "And think: I could gain an advantage by meeting this Cinet, for what he has heard of us is good." He forced a reassuring smile, holding it on Deirdre. "It is just how I would want to be introduced to a king."

Deirdre rose and, unable to speak, tucked the mistletoe inside his tunic. For a moment, he rested his hand there, over hers.

Later, she lingered at the fringe of the woods and watched Naisi grow smaller in the stern of the curragh as it plowed back down the loch. Ardan and Ainnle stood close together until the boat was lost in the glare of the sun on the water.

Ainnle turned and Deirdre was struck by the sick anxiety on his face. Without thinking, she lifted a hand toward his arm. He drew away from her. "If it weren't for you," he said unsteadily, "we would all remain shoulder to shoulder, as we always were."

Her hand fell to her side. "I always wanted you to stay hidden together, instead of fighting."

"Ainnle," Ardan said sharply.

Ainnle's eyes flashed at his brother. "But it's not fair."

Deirdre's smile was pained. "Nothing about this is fair, for any of us."

"And it's Conor's doing," Ardan said wearily. "You know that."

Ainnle glared at Ardan before looking back at Deirdre, and she saw the warring of his conscience in his lean face, the sharpness of blame ebbing from his slanted green eyes until at last there was only frustration. He let out an expulsion of disgust at the world—it wasn't thrown at her—and stalked across the riverbank, sloshed doggedly through a shallow channel of water and disappeared among the alder trees.

"He's always been hard to handle," Ardan muttered, "especially when he is barred from Naisi's side." His mouth quirked bleakly. "You have no idea the nightmare he was when Naisi was initiated first and Ainnle still had two years to wait." He watched his brother's stiff back and defiant head before turning and catching Deirdre's eye. "Now we must all wait."

Deirdre realized her hands were trembling and she tucked her loose hair behind her ears, forcing a smile. "Let's row the log-boat down to the island and pick some mussels," she said, "and paddle as fast as we can there and back."

He pondered her a little warily, then sighed and looked out over the water. "Aye," he murmured. "Or we'll go mad, too."

Dunadd was the stronghold of the Epidii, the People of the Horse.

The fort was set on a solitary crag that rose from a marsh, its base skirted by the River Add, which snaked over moorland to the western sea. It boasted a small, bustling harbor downriver on a sheltered bay, from where the Epidii taxed all the ships that ran between the northern amber lands, Erin, the west British coast with its tin mines and on to Gaul and the Roman Empire.

Their kingdom did not possess a wealth of gold and cattle, Talan drawled to Naisi, but was rich instead in the hides and furs borne by the beasts that inhabited these wilder mountain realms; the hardy horses they traded and the fine hounds they bred to fight bears and wolves, which were fashionable among wealthy Romans.

Looking suitably impressed, Naisi passed through a massive timber rampart on the river meadow that circled a village of thatched huts, then under a carved wooden arch to climb the rock crag at the center. Here the decorated houses of the nobles clung to the green shoulders of the hill, perched high above the plain with an unimpeded view of mountains and glinting sea—a majestic eyrie indeed.

A second arched gate led to the king's hall on the very crest of the crag. The royal hall was a vast roundhouse whose horse banners streamed out in the sea-wind above a sweeping mountain of a thatch roof, the golden reeds gleaming from a recent rain-shower.

Inside the cavernous interior, the round walls were covered with stallion hides, their fringing of black manes stirred by the updrafts from the fires and the great oak doors. Stakes hung with horse-tail pennants marked out a ring of cushioned benches and low oaken tables around two roaring fire-pits. Horse skulls lined the walls, and Naisi had the uncomfortable sensation that the ghostly bones were peering down at him from their empty eye-sockets.

Cinet sat chewing a goosebone on a chair carved from an inverted oak trunk, the roots forming the arms. He was squat and powerful, with immense bearlike shoulders and a barrel torso. His boots were hemmed in fox-fur, a short tunic showed his muscular thighs and a leather breastplate strained over his paunch. A thick cloak of brown wool and beaver-fur rippled in lavish folds from his shoulders, and there were glints of gold brooches and armbands.

A bard harped to one side, his strumming drowned out by the roars of laughter from warriors at the fire, pulling flesh from a haunch of spitted pig and ignoring the bustling servants and all the people hovering in the hope of speaking to the king. An enormous gray hound lay at Cinet's feet, paws stretched out and yellow eyes unblinking.

Naisi had been so absorbed in these new sights that the fact he had walked into the den of one of the Ulaid's greatest enemies did not fully descend on him until he heard that boisterous sound of warriors, those aggressive shouts and rousing laughter. As it did, all his nerve fibers tightened on instinct, his feet shifting their balance to his toes, his hands gripping his belt, his shoulders rising. Gods. Let Manannán be with him now. The metal clasp of the Red Branch badge burned into his arm beneath his tunic.

A steward announced their arrival and, after speaking with Talan, the king waved everyone back and beckoned Naisi forward with his gnawed bone. Glittering eyes watched Naisi's approach. The king's brows were tattooed with horse ears and his cheeks with tilted eyes, his ruddy mane and beard threaded with narrow braids tipped in gold. On the wall behind him, an enormous rack of antlers appeared to crown his head.

As Talan moved back, a warrior perhaps ten years older than Naisi detached himself from the throng at the fire and stood next to the king's chair, swallowing a glistening shred of pig-meat and wiping his hands down his trews. He also sprouted a mane of red hair.

Cinet cleared his throat with a phlegmy rumble. "Where do you hail from, then, wolf-killer?" He flicked an indolent finger at Naisi's shaggy cloak.

Naisi stood absolutely straight. At every step, his honor had been compromised, and it would be again if he lied. He had Deirdre to think of, though, and Ardan and Ainnle. And since he'd failed his brothers so utterly already, he would do whatever he must to secure their safety now. "On an island, my lord, out toward Erin—an isolated place, bypassed by everyone except fishermen." He scrambled to think of the tribes that did not bear tattoos, and remembered the traders that came to Emain Macha. The west British were dark-haired, and that would explain a strange accent, too. "We are Silures by allegiance, but in truth we are of no land now."

"Fishermen, eh?" Cinet glanced at Naisi's finery and smirked at the young red-haired warrior. "So why come so far to settle here, without my leave?"

The question was meant to unbalance him, but Naisi's lord had been Conor and he was used to thinking fast. "Forgive us, but we intended only to scratch a meager living that takes nothing from your own people. We want to cause no trouble, nor attract any."

Cinet tossed the bone to the dog and watched the slavering jaws snap, and so it was the other man who spoke. "You've attracted trouble, though, we hear." His pale blue eyes were curious, rather than cold.

When Naisi stayed silent, wondering how to answer that, Cinet waved a hand at the man. "This is my nephew Bridei, the heir to my hall and kingship."

Naisi moistened his lips. "It was not of our own making. Talan said they were Venicones, testing the defenses of your borders." He paused, unable to hide the lift of his chin. "We merely gave them some pause for thought."

Bridei's mouth twitched. "And they have not returned?"

"The raiders? No. Three scouts came, but we ran them off and there's been nothing more from them, either."

Bridei nodded while Cinet absently picked at his teeth. That must be a front—what king would not be concerned about his borders? Cinet extracted a shred of meat, flicking it away. "So tell me why you left your home, then, Finn-of-no-sire."

"My...wife's...kin did not approve of the match. I had to have her and so decided we could not stay." That was near enough to truth to come out naturally.

Cinet snorted. "Brave—and rash. We've all wanted the cow and had to run from the bull, though, eh?" As Naisi absorbed that keen shot—keener than Cinet would ever know—the Epidii king grinned and slapped his meaty paw on his chair. "Enough! I understand you have done us all a service. Now you must tell me what lavish reward you ask for this protection." The king's dark-blue eyes were half-lidded, like a jaded cat batting a mouse, his smile sly.

The steward had demanded that Naisi surrender his sword at the door, though he still had a hunt dagger tucked down his boot—some small comfort, at least. He breathed out, forcing his voice above the noise. "Nothing but the leave to dwell in our own steading in peace."

Bridei broke in again. "You are nobly born, whatever you say of fishermen." His eyes glinted with dry humor. "You wish no tracts of land, then? No great duns, no arm-rings?"

In time. Naisi's heart gave a queer thump at that unguarded thought, for since getting here the promise of what he could gain was dawning on him. He'd been thrust from secrecy into the full glare of torchlight, and though at first he'd cursed it, now he wondered… was this the hand of the gods? He crushed that ruthlessly, for such hope of divine salvation, for forgiveness and honor, weakened him. "Riches are no guarantee of contentment. We want nothing but your blessing."

"Ha!" Cinet exclaimed, resting his chin in forked fingers. "Men want gold and bronze, willing girls in their bed, ale and food. You jest with me!"

Naisi left a fitting pause. "Then one small favor only. In exchange for leave to stay, my brothers and I will guard this pass for you. We also need a few simple things we cannot hunt for: grain, pots, iron tools and points, wool for clothes. That is all."

The king wiped his greasy hands down his tunic. "Any men who can triumph when so outnumbered must be handy with their swords." He belched. "You shall have what you need and, in return, give me your allegiance to guard my pass." He grinned at Bridei. "No one else wants to live in that wind-blasted place, anyway!"

Talan and Bridei duly chuckled, though Naisi was barely listening, his heart soaring. He would get out of this so lightly, for something he would already do to protect Deirdre and his brothers. He had to be honest about one thing, however. He cleared his throat. "I regret to say I have already given allegiance to my old lord, so cannot be forsworn." He didn't care about any oath to Conor—that was broken by the point that parted his flesh—but neither was he in any mood to be bound to a man he did not know.

Cinet's cold eyes probed Naisi. "You appear to be utterly honorable," the king said. The irony of that stuck in Naisi's throat. "Such a trait is as rare as a faithful wench, and valuable to any lord you serve, even without an oath." Cinet heaved himself to his feet. "I accept this, but in return for my tolerance, you and your brothers will join my war-bands whenever I request it. If this conflict blows up with the Venicones, we will need every good sword we can muster."

Naisi bowed as Cinet passed him on his way out. "As you will, my lord."

By the time he returned to the glen carrying gifts from the king, his mind was galloping with a host of new possibilities, like a yoked horse at last set free. He reported it all to Deirdre, the excitement quickening his voice, but when he saw how her face grew still, her eyes shielded, he found he could not tell her of the promise he had made to the king. He let it sink back into his memory as an impulse that would be faced only when necessary.

I do what I must, he thought, watching her slowly unroll a length of fine, checked cloth, a hint of pleasure softening her features. His thumb brushed the single, tiny freckle at the corner of her mouth and he brought her close to kiss it, concentrating on the sensation of here and now.

CHAPTER 29

The supplies of meat were low after the long dark, and the brothers took it in turns to hunt and fish, heading out in the morning and staying away all day.

One morning, Deirdre paddled her little boat west along the loch to a scatter of rocky islets and, pulling the hull up onto the shore, picked mussels from the seaweed. Seals sunned themselves, bodies curved up like bows, and when she sang to them they didn't hump their way to the water and sink under, but stayed where they were and watched her with their dark, liquid eyes. As the day faded, she followed a pair of swans home along the shoreline, their white feathers glowing against the greening banks, hazed by the unfurling buds on the branches.

She walked back from the loch sunburned and with sore arms and back, though wearily content. Passing Ardan's house she stopped, and the little tune she'd been humming trailed away.

Ardan was kneeling outside his door, securing spears into his back-carrier.

A messenger had come over the hills, he told her, avoiding her eyes. The Venicones had sacked an Epidii dun in the southeast—a valley where they sifted gold from the streams. The men were slain and women and children had been captured for slaves. The Venicones were making their way home east over the mountains, slowed by the stolen carts of ore and captives. Talan was gathering a war-band of young, swift-running warriors to overtake them, and they were using this glen to reach the moors. Ardan's chin lowered, and he fingered one of his spear-tips. Talan was calling in Naisi's promise of aid to the Epidii king.

"Promise?" Deirdre repeated, the sack of mussels dripping down her trews.

Ardan looked at her and chewed his lip. "Ask Naisi."

She hastened home and came to another halt when her shadow fell across Naisi rolling up his sleeping hides just inside the open door. Her black shape mingled with the sun on him, darkness piercing light. "What is this promise?" she demanded hoarsely. "You are *leaving*?"

Naisi dusted earth off his sleeping roll and got up, bracing himself to meet her eyes. "I am sorry I kept it from you. But I vowed to King Cinet I would help him against the Venicones in return for letting us stay."

The wet sack slipped from Deirdre's hands to the grass. "You didn't tell me." *Gods*, she'd thought it was over; surely Cinet had now satisfied himself they were no threat. Then she remembered the set of Naisi's proud head that day, his determined bearing in his fine tunic and wolf-cloak. How could Cinet turn from that? She clasped her cold, wet fingers in her other fist, shivering from the touch of the water.

Naisi's expression was a strange mingling of resignation, sorrow and also a shadow of guilt; he knew what he inflicted even as he did it. "I did not know it would ever come to anything, *fiáin*, and certainly not so soon. I didn't want to upset you with no cause." His voice constricted and he stepped out of the doorway to take her arms.

She'd gone completely cold, though, and knew she could not bear his touch, moving back into a pool of sunlight as if it would protect her. It was a visceral, sickening reaction. They had been joined, his essence soaking right through her until the very pieces of body and spirit had melded. Now he was leaving; he risked death. It was like a brutal slash of a sword through their ecstatic dream, ruthlessly cutting it in two. *Cutting her in two.* "I would rather live under the trees if this was the price of these walls around us." Her voice sounded far away, her instinctive panic making it hard to think clearly.

"There's more to it than that," he said quietly, and ran a hand

through his black forelock, his eyes dropping. "We can't hide forever—"

"Why not?" She braced her unsteady legs. "You should have
avoided those raiders in the first place. In Erin, you hid when you
had to, ran when you had to!"

He flinched. The sun drew lines of tension and weariness between his eyes, and she suddenly realized that no rash impulse
had made him agree to go. He had been sunk in dark thoughts
for hours, for they were carved on his brow. "And will you always
have us running?" he murmured. "Let everyone in this glen be
murdered? You can't make the world go away, Deirdre. There
will always be kings struggling for power, and warriors battling."
Before she could move again, he caught up her cold hand, folding his palm around her fingers to cradle them. "We have been
discovered, and we can't risk Cinet guessing we are of Erin. The
best thing is to leap into the heart of the fire and prove ourselves
to him as soon as we can. *That* is what will make us safer."

Her hand remained limp in his, for she felt the scrape of his
roughened calluses—the marks of his weapons. The scar left by
Leary's sword was a stark slash across his sunburnt forearm. "Do
not speak to me of safety," she said, uncontrollable tremors running through her. "How safe am I when you leave me here alone?"

He dropped her fingers, stepping back from her rigid body. "I
will ensure the glen is guarded, but the best way to deal with the
Venicones is by beating them back so they will never venture
here again."

She did not answer, watching his mouth form those empty
words. Struggling to breathe, she flexed her fingers, endeavoring
to imprint his touch on her memory. He must have thought she
was trying to rid herself of it.

"You don't know all we are," he said, and now his voice was
harsh with pain. "What we were before..."

"Perhaps I won't get a chance to know." Something was surfacing from her racing heart. Ever since the raid, Ainnle had been
growing more frustrated, Ardan distant, and Naisi restless. It was
there as a faint vibration running through him whenever he was

not buried between her thighs; something she'd been happy to ignore, pretending it was the remnants of desire. Now it had grown into an excitement she could scent. She raised her gaze to his, the realization dawning. "You are leaving because you long to fight," she said slowly.

He swallowed and stretched his chin to look up, as if reaching for breath. "*Fiáin.*" Then he looked straight at her with those intense blue eyes, that gaze that always jolted her with surprise at its blazing force—only now his dark brows framed a plea for understanding.

And she could not understand.

All at once, she was walking blindly away from him. She scrambled up the slope behind the house, grabbing for the jagged stones and not caring that they grazed her palms. Higher up, the spine of the hill broke through the turf in a ledge of smoothed rock and she flung herself across it, pushing her knuckles into her mouth. After a time he came for her, parting the ferns to climb the rock. She didn't move, her heart unable to find its rhythm, and he looked at her intently before pulling her against his belly. She rested her head on his knee, gazing at the loch through the unfolding leaves of the birch trees, though she could not absorb their beauty.

"You know me as a hunter, a singer, but above all that I am a warrior." At the sound of his husky voice, she buried her cheek in his leg. "You asked me to see you, *fiáin*, and you must do that for me." His breath released. "Because, yes, I miss the Red Branch."

Deirdre rolled over to look up at him. He'd shaved with his dagger and the stubble speckled his neck, the skin streaked red. They had fused so completely together, and still he was unavoidably different from her. His thicker bones framed a jaw that was wide where hers was narrow. His nose was a determined ridge where hers was small and upturned. His upper lip was long and fleshy; hers formed a bow. That habitual expression of stubbornness and self-containment might be the only thing they did share.

Disturbed by the pain in her face, he looked over her head.

"Ach, *fiáin*. We were bound to yell at each other sometime. My father and mother often did."

Her hand curled up under her chin. "Isn't this life good? To be free, with no one to rule us?" She whispered the horror that rose through her. "Because fighting brings you closer to *him*." She did not mean Cinet. "I fear that he'll be able to scent you somehow, when you draw your blade."

He watched her, stroking her cheek. "When I fought those raiders, a kind of fire went through me…" He trailed off, his eyes glazing in memory. "I felt truly myself again…as if the pieces of me are pulled to that dance." His mouth twisted for a moment and he swallowed some hard pain, before his gaze sharpened on her. "I saw it in you after you touched the deer. You know it."

Now it was Deirdre's turn to flinch. She did not want to know what she was drawn to; she did not want to be torn away from him. The pulse in her neck beat out the bleak truth against her fingers. From the start she'd sensed a slumbering flame in him, a passion that could ignite at any time, and then saw it made real through a bird's eyes.

That flame in him caught alight in the bed-furs—and when he held his sword.

"In the end," Naisi said quietly, "I was standing before Cinet when he demanded this oath of me, and I had no choice but to agree. I had no choice."

She drew into a tight ball with her head on his lap, and he stroked her hair and they spoke no more.

The next morning, they took leave of each other, hidden in the forest away from Talan's boat beached on the sandbank. The Epidii warriors were arming themselves to continue up the glen on foot to the moors.

A stiffness lingered between them, and when Naisi kissed her and turned to go, Deirdre held him back. "Why won't you look at me?" Though he had loved her fiercely in the night, there was no meeting of eyes and souls in firelight, no dark pupils drawing her in.

He sighed. "Being torn in two like this…makes it hard to

fight." He brushed her lower lip slowly with his thumb, staring at it intently. "I am sorry."

She rested her forehead on his chin. She was struggling with a baffled anger she could not soothe no matter how she tried, unable to quench it in the night when she nestled into his side, breathing him in. *Perhaps for the last time.*

But she would never knowingly weaken him. She could not feel the warmth of his skin because of the leather breastplate, and his hilt dug into her side. "Go with my blessing," she murmured, pain roughening her voice, "and promise you'll only think of me when you turn for home."

He tilted up her chin and searched her face, before nodding, his shoulders lowering. His last touch was a nudge of her hair out of her eyes, light as air.

Days slid by, and all human rhythms were lost.

There were no rousing voices, bustle of cooking and eating, or sound of steps at dusk to mark the return of the hunters. There was no touch of Naisi's to bring Deirdre into the here and now, anchoring her with nerve-pleasure and white heat.

Her simmering pain did not fade but grew into an unbearable restlessness. She felt too sick to eat. The barley porridge congealed in the pot and the leftover bread was too dry to get down her sore throat. Nor could she sleep. All she could do was numbly feed the fire with branches and crouch there before it, mesmerized by the sinuous leap of the flames, her chin on her knees.

She tried to immerse herself in mundane tasks, softening the stiff deerskins with the smoothing stone, watching glaze-eyed as her sewing needle plunged in and out of the wool, barely feeling her hands. The lack of food made her light-headed, and she began to feel hollow and insubstantial. She wore a path in the bracken from the loch to the house, a circle within which she was bound by the ache of Naisi's absence.

Huddled on the shore rocks, she peered through the morning mists as if she might see him in the vapor…until it broke into shreds, burned off by the rising sun. She would suddenly come back to herself to find the tide had been pushed up by a swinging wind, lapping in icy splashes about her feet.

The silence of the land came for her, slowly, inexorably; an absence of sound so immense it became presence.

In that expectant hush, the vibrations beneath the earth rose to an endless murmuring as of voices all about her—or did they whisper her pain? Her eyes became so gritty and swollen that when she labored at her tasks, tiny silver flames seemed to lick around the fringes of her sight, running up the trees and rocks as if riming them with frost. The flickering did not fade now when she blinked.

On rising from the shore, a brace of swan feathers clutched in her fist, she found herself staggering as the certainty of solid ground fragmented beneath her.

Naisi's steps on that path across Alba became more charged with battle-fire the closer the Epidii drew to the fleeing Venicones.

Like a rising sun, it blotted out the gnawing of guilt— Deirdre's face, the anguish in her eyes—and replaced it with determination. He touched her in his mind, a hand buried in her hair as he cradled the curve of her head to the shield of his body.

This—fighting, winning—is how he would claw back all he had lost for his brothers through his own weakness of soul. And this is how he would keep Deirdre safe. She was not a warrior; she could not know this. She was an elusive, unknown creature, and her mind had been shaped by different forces than his. Now he would wrestle a still, safe place from this turbulent world, one forever removed from Conor's reach, and once he had it he would have the time to discover all the impulses that formed her as a child, the patterns that made her.

These thoughts ran feverishly through him, quickened by the urgent rhythm of his legs and the great draw of cold air into his lungs. *If I fight I will win...and only then can she know all of me—when what she sees will make her proud.*

He glimpsed the same exhilaration in Ainnle's face. His youngest brother's need for excitement drew his neck out and brightened his eyes, and he bounded along like an eager hound. Naisi glanced from the corner of his eye at Ardan. He'd been so subdued these past moons, and now he pounded the path like he was stamping on something, a frown etched between his brows. He seemed to be suffering the isolation, even though of all the brothers he was most inclined to time spent alone. The guilt was a hot stab through Naisi. *Ardan*. It was the blackness in Naisi, the lack of nobility, that had sentenced this most noble of men to a bleak life.

When they stopped to fill their water flasks, Naisi swallowed his guilt and made a joke, ruffling Ardan's sweat-soaked hair. Though Ardan muttered a familiar retort, his smile was slow in coming.

They ran with a column of forty Epidii warriors led by Talan and his gray-eyed nephew, Carnach. Young and muscular, their tattoos broke up the fair expanses of skin on face and arms, so that with their tails of russet and black hair and horse-hide capes they blended into the landscape of dark rock and red moorland. The thuds of their feet all around him had induced Naisi's warrior-trance, as if they were battle-drums rousing his blood. This was familiar. Track the enemy, unsheath his sword, bring it down.

They had left guards at the entrance to their valley, then turned south and crossed an immense moor. It was pocked with pools—scoops of reflected sky and jagged peaks that were fringed by lone rowans—and where they ran their footprints seeped brown water. On the other side of that bleak plain, the scouts reported that the Venicones were struggling over the eastern mountains, moving slowly because of the carts.

The brothers had been sharing their thoughts, and around the campfires at night Naisi began to speak those ideas, encouraged by the friendship they struck up with Carnach. Words came to Naisi's tongue, hot and urgent, as if they arose from somewhere deeper than his own body. They must avoid the valleys, he said, and spear across the high passes, using the precipitous deer-paths to cut off the Venicones. They should pick a narrow ravine to attack, falling upon the raiders like eagles diving from the sky.

Talan watched Naisi with his sardonic smile and measuring eyes. Carnach, however, argued for the bold plan with all the fervor of youth trying to establish its place.

Youth won, and the Epidii took their chances across the peaks, still crusted with snow on slopes that never saw the sun.

By the loch, Deirdre sought Naisi's fate among the sun-shadows at the edges of the water. She grew warm and then cold as the light ebbed, and stars came out in the darkness above her.

A pain brought her back, centered low in her belly. As the sun rose again it resolved into a familiar ache that was nothing like hunger. She stumbled home, her fingers groping for the dried bundles of moss she collected on the moors.

Blood. She stared at it on her thighs before slowly washing it away. The air muttered around her and the cramps reached up into her heart. Her moon-tide...no child had been made between her and Naisi. She bound the moss to her and, dressing again, walked outside, shielding her eyes from the sun. Her mind had fragmented with the delirium of sleeplessness and the endless searching of the mists. Now it summoned strange fears that spun around in cold flurries, like flakes of snow.

No child. Nothing to bind them together, to anchor her and say she had loved here. A dream formed of lust could be blown out by one gust of wind, severed by one fall of a blade. Was that all it was? And what would be left for her if he was gone?

All at once, she was staggering up the hill, toward the peaks with ever greater urgency, until her meager strength gave out and she had to push on her knees to force herself higher. She had crushed those glimmers of knowing, that rush, to sink into desire with him. She had been too afraid to look down the paths that beckoned her. But if he died and did not come back...then there was no desire, no child, no woman-rhythms of hearth and home to fill her. And she was supposed to sit here helpless in this dream and know *nothing*?

She broke out into the meadow, swaying on the spot before plowing through the high bracken. She reached the ancient stone, sank on it cross-legged, closing her eyes and gasping. The drumming of her heart was a savage chant of her own. Warriors, kings…Naisi binding himself with weapons so she could not touch him. To be left behind—blind, deaf, dumb—while men decided fates…decided *her* fate. This was not Deirdre; never again.

The sun pooling on the stone released the resinous vapors of the yew leaves and, panting, Deirdre drew in the tang and it seeped through every part of her. Death. Change. Rebirth. The doorway to the spirits.

Naisi!

She let the pain burn through her and out, and in the immense, echoing pause after that silent cry, the expectant stillness that had been hovering for days was sucked into her. And suddenly it was not silence at all, but *life*.

The sonorous vibration thrummed up from the stone again, focused through this slab that had been rooted here by human hands. It grew more powerful with every inhalation of yew-scent, which dizzied her mind like sacred smoke, and took over her blood until her heart was swept into its rhythm, and she resonated with its song.

She must always forge her own fate…and in the delight of Naisi's arms she'd forgotten. She wanted to be *joined;* not left alone. And here was another world, which had been waiting for her.

The ringing of stone and the sunlight and the surge of her anger all poured through her in a powerful charge, centering at the base of her spine. Its force pushed her to her feet and she stood on unsteady legs, like a newborn fawn.

Her eyes sprang open, and at last Deirdre *saw*.

The substance of the air was silver light, finer than mist, brighter than the moon. It was not on the liminal edges of her senses anymore, but a tide of luminescence that engulfed her.

She moved her head and saw a glowing aura around each tree. Close to the bark the halo was brightest, then came fainter echoes of the same outline of leaf, branch and trunk spreading farther out, ghostly impressions that overlapped until they shimmered away and disappeared altogether.

And she remembered the glimpse in Erin. *Behind this world is another.* There was a constant glimmering among the leaves and undergrowth, animals coursing with life. If she focused on a shred of grass, she saw each dewdrop beading its surface; if she stretched her head back, the sky swirled in filmy layers of shifting hue.

A thought winged into her. *The Otherworld is not* there. *It is here.* The resonance from the rock was still echoing through her, making her vibrate in time with that powerful wave. And gradually she noticed that streamers of the light were contracting now into blinding sparks that whirled around like moths. This time they would not flicker and fade; she would *know them.*

She staggered after the sparks over the silver grass and came to the bank of the stream that spilled from the spring. Scores of the luminous ones hung over the water like clouds of glowing insects at dawn. Delirious, Deirdre swayed there, gazing down at her feet. The stream carved the hardest of rocks; something so light could shape the unyielding. And so *she* would decide her fate among men, not with a sword but with herself alone.

A stone came to hand and she flung it in the water to cause a ripple that would carry down the loch and far out into the ocean—through the sea-lanes with their great ships carrying spear-men and warriors—all the way to Erin. To Conor, in defiance.

A glimmering plume of silver glass splashed up before her eyes and shattered into droplets. The plume fell—but some of the drops remained hanging in the air. Deirdre's breathless yell cut off as they also broke away to spiral around her. She clapped a hand to her mouth, a laugh escaping her fingers. They were shards of something that was alive.

The glowing specks streamed about her as if agitated, gleeful;

and their will was a physical force that pulled at her. She was being drawn downward, the surface of the stream alive with the glitters of sunlight.

The next moment Deirdre was sprawled flat on her belly, plunging her arms into the water.

Naisi streaked down the steep slope that fell from the knife-ridge of rock. Below, the line of Venicones warriors and their lumbering ox-carts were squeezed onto a narrow path, the mountain on one side and a drop to a foaming river on the other. Their tattooed faces all turned up in horror at the sudden descent of screaming warriors, appearing as if from the sky.

Shouting a war-cry, Naisi was about to throw his spear when Ardan came barreling past him, leaping with a roar and flinging his lance a moment before Naisi and Ainnle did. All three spears arced into the Venicones ranks, and the brothers slid down the fan of scree, reaching the path in a cascade of pebbles, the clatter and hiss reverberating off the hillside.

Many of the Venicones were clad in wolf-pelts, the shadow of the peaks dulling the sheen of their leather helmets and iron weapons. They were hardened warriors and swiftly began to recover from the hail of spears, yelling to one another and backing up over skewered bodies to the stalled carts, whipping swords from scabbards.

The Epidii collided with the Venicones line, and both sides were immediately mired in chaos, the men fighting in desperate hand-to-hand combat.

Icy water trails through her spread fingers.

She sees that it is not a fluid at all but a cloud of tiny sparks that break apart when her hands stir them. She lifts her palms. The sun pours through the webbing of her fingers and ... *she* is not solid, either. Her flesh is also made of these glitters of light, floating together in a pattern more closely woven than the air and water.

So if everything is fragmented light ... can she merge with the other streams of radiance? Rock? Air? *Water?* Even as the idea forms she feels herself *dissolving*, melting out into that cloud of luminescence.

Yes! Her own sparks scatter among the motes of water, and each one holds a glint of her vaster self, so her conscious still retains some awareness.

And then she is flying through a world of tiny, dancing stars.

They vibrate more slowly to shape the forms of bone, bark and rock; they are diaphanous showers as air and clouds. There is no awareness in those shards but there is a charge of Source, the force of existence that flashes across the motes like branched lightning. And it imprints each spark with the pattern it must follow to spin matter from star-dust.

One of the *sídhe* zips past. She knows it from water and air by its fiery brightness and purpose of movement. It arcs close to the stream and the water motes are drawn toward it, pulled into long strands that shimmer with resonance.

Glancing through the droplets, her mind sees an image of rain falling on a gray ocean. And she knows. All the sparks of air, water, rock and even flesh are joined to one another by the charges of lightning, the Source. And the *sídhe* can shape them with will.

She could do that. What does she want to join to? *Naisi. Naisi's life-force.*

Her longing is intense and she summons the sparks without thought. Water sings to water, that is easy. Her will leaps out through the clouds of water sparks, and travels as the lightning flash through the vapors, rain and mists. Down along the cracks in rock, the underground rivers and veins of moisture trapped in stone, it runs. Up through the droplets seeping through soil and evaporated into drifting clouds, and there ... to the rain falling on mountain-peaks. Water ... thundering along a ravine as a roaring stream and flung up in a fine spray to the air. Now the charge flashes the shape of *that place, that time* back to her, drawing those patterns in the liquid that soaks her flesh.

She is aware of her body again, her palms hovering above the glistening stream. The water rises between her fingers now, writhing like a water-spout, summoned by her fierce need. *I must know that he still breathes!*

The man forms out of droplets that shimmer between her hands. She sees a suggestion of his features, transparent and glistening. His nose, his jaw...just as she touched them with her body. And there...the tilt of a mouth she once kissed.

Ripples begin spreading beneath the surface of the water, called into being by the crackling light running from her hands. She stares, not breathing. *Let me see. Let me know.* Now it is many men, their heads and shoulders emerging from the stream for a heartbeat and sinking back. The shapes of their running bodies roll like swells along the surface. Long plumes rise up and sway between her fingers. They are a racing mass of pounding feet and whirling arms. The plumes are crested then by sharp, gleaming peaks, like wind-blown waves.

Spears. Swords.

Naisi skidded to a halt before the second cart, the heaving mass of men in mottled hides and armor all blending into one around him. The ox pulling the cart wrenched its leadrope free and in a panic lost its footing, sliding over the edge of the path. Its yoke dragged the cart over and it plunged out of sight to the stream below. Naisi braced himself for screams, but there were none. He had no time to wonder at that, for a streak of movement behind him caught his eye—someone racing up with a raised sword. Before Naisi could spin to defend himself, Ardan was there, twisting around with a grimace of effort, his blade slicing two-handed. It bit into the attacker's arm and the man screamed and fell to his knees, his shattered bone gleaming white in the spurt of blood.

Ardan was still unbalanced by his swing, and as a second

Venicones warrior sized up his teetering body, Naisi leaped in to hack him down. His blade slashed the artery in the warrior's throat and hot blood flecked Naisi's lips as the man dropped. Using the same momentum, Naisi ducked under Ainnle's horizontal swipe toward someone at his side, and stabbed a fourth warrior, bearing down on his little brother from behind.

The flame beckoned Naisi, the glorious fire of the Red Branch, and he dived into it with fierce abandon. There he was joined to his sword-brothers by the invisible threads of that mystical joining, attuned to the movements of those they loved. Immersed in that bond, Red Branch could protect one another in the same flow of attack; defensive blocks and twists woven through aggressive lunges and stabs. Each fighter tapped into a mysterious aura of sensory alertness that gave them an exquisite awareness of wind and scent, ground and weight, stance and thrust.

Red Branch! Red Branch! He shouted it inside where it would not betray him, the power surging as he had not felt it since... gods, so long. Better than a brawl with drunken raiders; better than memories. He looked up from his bloody blade and saw the answering light in his own brothers' faces, and was shot through with the ecstasy of knowing them all one again—Ardan's brooding, Ainnle's frustration, his own pain all burned away by that roaring flame.

The three brothers scythed across the ranks of desperate fighters. All around them, the Epidii attackers and Venicones guards had broken into knots, hacking at one another in disarray. Some of the enemy ran up the slope to flee and were cut down by whizzing Epidii spears; others crawled to shield themselves beneath the carts.

Naisi's expanded instincts picked up the ripple of an enemy's muscles a heartbeat before the man leaped, and his own legs thrust him under the wild sword-swipe, a flick of his wrist parting tunic and flesh. The man screamed and clapped his hand to his side, blood weeping between his fingers, and Ainnle danced up with a spear and sunk it into his back.

Someone spat a curse in Naisi's ear and he whirled, to be presented with a blur of tattooed fangs that stretched his attacker's grimace into a snarl. The warrior's sword was already soaring toward Naisi's belly, and Naisi curved back just as Ardan swept up a spear and flung it. The shaft cracked across the Venicones's neck, and Ardan stabbed him with an upward sweep of his dagger. Over the fallen bodies the brothers' eyes met, a faint challenge in Ardan's blood-streaked face that Naisi had never seen before.

A great cheer went up from the rear of the baggage train and the brothers paused, alone for a moment in the space they had created.

A huge, dark-bearded Venicones warrior had clambered up on one of the carts, a string of spiked wolf-teeth clattering on a thong around his neck. He hauled a wounded Epidii warrior up over the broken yoke with him—Talan. The Epidii commander's helmet had been knocked off and his fair hair spilled over his shoulders, dark and sticky with blood from a deep cut on his brow. His arm ended in a bloody stump at the wrist and he was dazed, unable to stand.

As the screams around them intensified the big warrior spat in Talan's face and, putting a foot on him to hold him down, swung with his sword two-handed, almost severing the wounded man's neck. A wail went up from the Epidii fighters and Naisi saw how they faltered, the momentum of their attack splintering.

They were not Red Branch. The Epidii did not feel the light drawing them together. They stumbled, losing the passionate edge to their fighting the moment their chieftain was cut down. *One trunk, many branches.* A Red Branch chant: break one limb off and the trunk stays strong, like an oak in a storm. The realization of what he had lost speared him, agonizing.

The Venicones fought with renewed vigor as the huge warrior on the cart held up Talan's dripping head. Everything seemed to slow down, and Naisi tried to breathe in the radiance flickering between him and his brothers, until it lifted his body so it was

light on its feet. "We must keep them strong. They are weakening!" The idea crackled between the three of them like lightning.

Naisi was already digging a fallen spear out of the bodies and
wiping the blood from its shaft, sheathing his blade and looping
its belt over his back. "Sing with me," he cried, and began to run
with the spear.

His brothers caught him up, parting the remnants of the scattered Venicones guard with sweeping blows. Naisi tested the balance of the spear in his hands, keeping his eye on the fallen cart
with the capering warrior brandishing Talan's head. The ox had
been cut from its traces and the abandoned yoke formed a platform up to the seat.

> *Strong the tread of fighters*
> *Cleave the roaring armies*
> *Triumph over brave ones*
> *Hearts as bold as they!*

They didn't care now if anyone heard, for the rhythm of Ardan
and Ainnle's shouts counted down Naisi's steps. His awareness
narrowed to a channel of time and space, a bright pathway
formed of his body's will, and his mind's focus…*and his heart,
Cúchulainn said, the blaze of his heart*. The stream of brilliance made
everything stand out in minute detail. The gleam of the yoke,
worn smooth with use. The slippery streaks of blood. The rise in
the ground where he could dig in the spear-butt. He traced the
soaring path of the salmon leap in his mind…and as he ran he
saw Cúchulainn's measuring eyes again, felt the Hound's hands
making small adjustments in his stance. *Let go. Your instincts and
training mean your body will know what your mind cannot grasp*. Naisi
flicked sweat from his eyes, his heart thundering as much for the
memory of Cúchulainn as the effort of his legs.

The warriors near the cart spun about as Naisi stabbed the
spear down and flung himself into an enormous bound. The
lance bent under his weight and he heard only wind roaring. His

fingers released the spear and he tumbled, flying, his hand reaching to grab his sword-hilt as he plunged.

Time resumed with a shock.

Naisi landed near the lip of the cart, his back facing the enemy warrior, his blade in his hand. He absorbed the impact with a dip of his legs and in the same movement whipped his blade around in a spinning slice. The edge caught the throat of the Venicones fighter, who was standing motionless, still gaping, Talan's head clutched by its trailing hair. The blow snapped tendons, carving flesh, and the warrior gurgled and crumpled, tumbling over the side of the cart. Ardan and Ainnle leaped on him to finish him off.

Gasping for air, Naisi raised his sword, the blood running down his trembling arm. "The Mare! The Mare!" he shouted, the Epidii war-chant ringing out over the throng. "To me! To me!" All the Epidii warriors were cheering raggedly, and once Naisi had their attention he jumped to the ground, Ardan and Ainnle lining up beside him so their bodies formed one shield. Carnach came running, backing up against them to strengthen the line. "To me!" Carnach bellowed.

Screeching, the Epidii rallied to him, and with the combined power of their tight wedge of bodies they thrust against the fragmented Venicones warriors, rolling over the fighting men until many broke and scrambled in a hopeless retreat up the hillslopes.

Ardan and Ainnle climbed the abandoned carts, chanting exultantly and stabbing their swords into the air, while the Epidii ran down the fleeing enemy with renewed energy.

Naisi stood alone while the fighting turned from battle to rout, his body shaking with the force that had consumed him. The elation was already running from his muscles back into the ground, and all at once he became conscious of the wind cooling his sweat, his nostrils steeped in the reek of blood.

Deirdre fed the hearth-fire with glazed eyes, barely conscious of the iciness of her hands. The warmth of the flames crept into her and she grew still, staring into the fire's burning heart. A finer trembling than cold ran beneath her skin, the song of the water still ruling her even though she had come back to her mantle of body and blood.

And there was wonder—a wonder so profound it had shattered her mind.

She slowly collapsed on the pile of furs beside the hearth and curled up, shaking fingers drawing Naisi's wolf-cloak over her, her nose buried in the ruff. She knew that he walked alone after battle, sweat and blood drying in his hair.

Naisi stood at the bottom of the ravine beside the broken cart, poking the splintered sacks with his boot. The stream roared in his ears, and he could barely hear the shouts of the Epidii on the path above as they cleaned up after the battle. The body of the fallen ox lay in a tangle of birch trees, buried amid a mass of crushed ferns.

The elation still throbbed through him and he watched it leaping beneath the skin of his wrist. Everything since the skirmish with the raiders had been leading him to this—a grasp for glory, a bound into the light. And yet as the battle frenzy left him, he'd suddenly felt exposed before all those Epidii eyes regarding him with awe and admiration.

Admiration. He wanted it, and he didn't trust that need for glory, for surely that was what had led him to the betraying darkness in the first place. He raised his face to the sky and then clamped his lips together. *This will carve a place for us again,* he reminded himself. He remembered how Ainnle and Ardan looked in the battle, that light blazing from them as they fought together. They needed to taste again what he had taken from them— he would focus only on that, and bind anything for himself up tight.

He squatted and tore open the rent in the sacks with his dagger. Inside one bag of shredded wool there were only chunks of dark rock, and in another, tiny pebbles of gold. They weighted his hand, heavy and cold, and as he hefted them the tingling charge of battle drained away.

A step sounded behind him: Carnach. The young Epidii warrior took off his helmet—an iron dome crested with a battered horse-mane of bronze—and tucked it under his arm. His weary face was sorrowed and smeared with blood. "Gods, man, I've never seen anyone fly through the air like that," he said. "The warriors are still speechless." When Naisi didn't smile, Carnach placed a hand on his shoulder. "By my uncle's honor, I will ensure the king hears how you saved this fight. What a leap! You'd have men lining up to learn that at Dunadd."

"It takes years of practice," Naisi replied, looking around at the remnants of the splintered cart.

Carnach tilted his head, staring at him curiously, and Naisi remembered that the Red Branch were known for their unusual skills. He threw the nuggets back in the sack, brushing gold dust from his fingers. "I thought we were rescuing captives."

Carnach frowned. "No one was sure there were any; it appears it was just rock after all." He clapped his helmet back on. "And what does it matter? This hoard is the gold with which to pay armies. The king will sing your praises at Dunadd for it." He grinned bleakly. "So, let us go now as fast as our feet will carry us, and I will take the first sip of ale with you."

Naisi endeavored to shrug off his unease as they clambered back up the rocks. And when they appeared again on the path, the Epidii all started cheering, and then he found he didn't think at all.

CHAPTER 30

The ancient stone called to her endlessly now with a song of ecstasy…joining…belonging. Power.

She sank on her back, using the sun's heat to melt into rock, wind and soil. For days she was empty of thought, filled with the heartbeat that throbbed through earth and sky as if the light behind the world was the blood in her veins. She watched in a daze as the Otherworld echoes around tree and hill, stream and rock also pulsed in time with that beat.

Little spear-jabs of fear kept jerking her out of the trance. She might sink away into stone and never wake…dissolve into the motes of light and never remember her own form again. What drew her made her afraid, for it could consume her.

Only when she sank into moments of mindless flow did she glimpse the *sídhe*. Some soared around her still, but if she reached for them too desperately, a different fear gripped her— *being left behind in Thisworld, being trapped here*—and that drenched her veins in a cold flood. Then the sparks slipped away from her.

When the animals darted through the forest or the birds flew overhead, she tried to project herself into them, but they were too swift of body and spirit for her slow-turning mind. And she realized she was not fueled by the power of Levarcham or her own desperation to see Naisi; that fire had exhausted her for now.

Instead, she could not stop herself from fragmenting, sinking deeper into the silence around her that was unbroken by any human voice calling her back.

It was a day of low, scudding clouds and wild winds, and Fidech, the king's huntsman, eyed the glowering peaks above him with a scowl. His horse limped along the narrow path behind him, its head drooping. When spatters of rain began hitting his face, Fidech hunched his shoulders and growled to himself.

King Cinet had an insatiable desire for luxury, risking the lives of fishermen, traders and hunters who pushed themselves to procure only the best for his favor: delicacies from the deep sea, bird eggs from far-flung cliffs, rare furs and hides. A huntsman could gain a substantial reward for bringing in the many-pointed tines of a king stag for Cinet's collection.

Fidech cast a glance back at his hobbling stallion. Its leg had been caught by a snare, unexpected in this remote glen. He had some salves in his pack, but if the leg was damaged...He screwed up his face and spat on the ground. It would take a year of constant hunting to afford another mount.

He skidded down an incline, so intent on encouraging his horse along that when he rounded a boulder and saw a flurry of movement, he leaped back with a curse. A mass of hair streamed from a dark hood into the wind, and below that he saw mottled hides. His fingers thrust out in an instinctive warding sign. *Calleach!*

The terrifying spirit also exclaimed, however, and threw herself against the rock. Fidech was startled to be looking into a pair of angry but nevertheless human eyes, and then he saw the glint of a knife braced in her hands. "Are you trying to kill me?" he demanded.

"I couldn't hear you in this wind!"

Fidech could see little beyond that flying hair. "You should take care skulking about these hills clad like a deer," he growled, indicating the bow slung over his back.

"What hunter would loose an arrow before discovering the nature of his prey?" she snapped in exasperation.

Fidech gaped, until his stallion whinnied and pawed its good leg, releasing his tongue. "I am Fidech, the king's huntsman, and these are his lands, so I suppose I might do as I will." He gestured at his horse. "Donnan got caught in some infernal trap. His leg is cut, which means I can't get back to Talan's dun." He cocked his head. "Your snares, I presume?"

The girl let her breath out, her features obscured by hood and hair. "Gods." Throwing a fold of her cloak across her chin she bent and, despite her fierce voice, ran a gentle hand down the stallion's leg. To Fidech's surprise, Donnan stood still, his shoulders quivering. Eventually she straightened, averting her face so he could only see a glimpse of brow and nose. "I feel…the muscle is torn."

"That's obvious."

"And the cut will not be clean if it was on a snare." She glanced back the way she had come, burying her chin in her shoulder. "I do not see any way, without you coming down for me to see to the horse…"

"Well?" He was hungry, cold and tired, and right now cared for nothing but that. "Have you never heard of hospitality, lass?"

The young woman's gaze dropped to the horse's leg. At last she spun about, looping her net bag full of muddy roots over her back. "I suppose you must come, then," she murmured, though to Fidech's ears she sounded most reluctant.

Deirdre gestured the gruff huntsman to a seat, ducking under the bunches of drying herbs hanging on the rafters. His skin was worn, his hair grizzled black and silver, his clothes smelled of dried blood. She turned her back to kindle a lamp, a soapstone bowl filled with sheep-fat and a rush wick. It burned with a low, fitful flame which would help to obscure her features.

Her hands made the pine taper waver. She had sunk so far into this strange floating trance, absorbed by the shifting layers of the world about her, that the sight of another person and the harsh sound of a voice tore at her filmy tendrils of awareness, causing a physical pain. No one—not even Urp and Arda—had come this far down the valley, let alone an outsider. An animal had been hurt by her hand, though, and she could not ignore that.

She served Fidech sorrel and hare stew, her chin lowered, her cloak wrapped around her though she sweltered beneath it. While he gulped down the food she went to the shelf of salves and crushed herbs that she stored in hollowed deerbones and folds of hide. "I must see to your mount."

She felt the man's eyes on her back. "I will do it—"

"No." She turned away, reaching for another lamp. "It is my fault. Stay and dry your clothes."

She went outside to where Naisi had built an overhang to stack their firewood. There the hunter had tied his stallion, sheltering under the turves of heather.

The horse was standing with its head low, the injured leg bent. She soothed him with an old druid song about Flidhais, goddess of beasts. It was something she had sung as a child over Fintan's old hound, smoothing its coat while it slept. Donnan snorted and shook his neck, dropping his head onto her shoulder, and setting the lamp aside she sank until she was cross-legged at his feet. The gash from the snare was a dark crust against his moonlit hide, and as her fingers reached for his skin, the horse twitched but did not pull away.

The moment she put her hands on the swollen muscle, she remembered that her own flesh was formed of the sparks she'd molded in the water. Their dances enlivened bone, skin and blood, and they were lit by those charges of lightning that flashed along the filaments of nerve and muscle. She just had to think of it like the water, dissolving into the tiny sparks of Source.

She breathed down into herself, felt herself slipping…and her eyes leaped open, her heart pounding. It was difficult to surrender into that dreamy sense of melting and dissolution while also directing it with will. It was even harder to let her boundaries shimmer away into the ether when there was an intruder in her house. But she must help the horse, for it would be killed if she did not. She thought of Levarcham. *Bring a blessing to everything you do.*

Someone, something was with her.

The *sídhe* brushed her and it felt like an invisible cloud drifting by even though all she saw was a tiny, bobbing glow. Its touch brought a memory, though, of aligning the sparks of life to create a clear flow of Source.

The scattered motes of her own self grazed the horse's aura. She sensed the rending of the flesh, the tiny sparks of matter weaving broken dances, the resonance disrupted. Blood leaked, muscles swelled, nerves were shredded.

Blessing. That was an act of will, her heart opening to reverence, to love of this wild creature, to sorrow she had harmed. She had blessed things thousands of times...but this time, she felt the actual vibrations of Source that she was summoning from the world about her, concentrating and streaming it with that intent into one river of light. There was something more, too: a deeper radiance that filtered through the glittering pinpricks of air. Perhaps it came from the rippling veils *beyond.* Otherworld light.

The blessing poured from her palms and, instinctively, a speck of her consciousness soared among the star-dust of the stallion's flesh, and she saw it being enlivened by the flood. Then a spark of the *sídhe* sailed past her, and in its trail of light she caught a glimpse of an ethereal horse as she had once seen the ghost-deer.

Understanding flashed through her.

Every creature in Thisworld was just an echo of a spirit-self that lived among the planes of the Otherworld. The stallion unconsciously yearned for that touch of its spirit, whose memory was imprinted in every mote of its body.

These rents in flesh could not be healed by her touch. Instead, she must call to the wounded parts, drawing a thread to that glimpse of the horse's spirit in that other place. *Here,* she soothed. *Feel the vigor of its life, see how the threads join.*

The stream of Source she was directing through its body attracted the disrupted motes in the torn tissues and they hearkened, drawn to the memory of the pattern. Like a plucked harp-string, they began to resonate in harmony with that song, which beckoned them to be as one again.

Dimly, she was aware of the stallion's hide quivering under her fingers.

Deirdre slowly came back to herself. Her head felt heavy and, when she moved it, her body seemed to lag behind her senses for a moment, as if her spirit was not quite contained in this shell of flesh.

She blinked her eyes open to see a glimmering halo still hovering around the horse and her own hands, and when she blinked again it was only moonlight.

"By Taranis…what are you doing?"

Her hands jerked away from the horse's coat. "I am dressing the injury," she said over her shoulder, willing him to remain behind her. Her tongue felt clumsy and she found it hard to summon human words. She reached to the bowl of warm water floating with yarrow and the bundle of knitbone beside her. The stallion was standing with its head up now, its ears pricked as if watching something in the darkness.

"That's not what it looked like."

Gods, she wished he'd leave her alone. "I was druid-taught. There are certain things we must do before we bathe a wound— prayers to the gods." She paused. "It's best done alone."

There was a silence behind her, before his footsteps slowly retreated. She bound the stallion's leg and, after drawing deep breaths of the cold air to clear her mind, returned to the fireside. Her body was prickling with heat now and she could not keep covered up anymore. So be it. She set the lamp on the hearthstone, took off the cloak and bathed her burning face in the water-pot by the door.

Fidech was watching her back. "I have never seen such a thing." The belligerence in his voice had been replaced by awe. "He is cured?"

She wiped her hair back with wet hands. "No one has that magic. But with luck, it will start to heal itself now."

The huntsman chewed his lip. "I must leave in the morning,

and if he is lame he is no use to me. I will leave him with you, see if he recovers." He was looking at her intently, but her damp hair still shielded her cheeks. "I'll come back to get him."

The heat rose in her scrubbed face and at last she turned to him. His eyes widened in their deep creases, and conscious that her tunic was damp with sweat she crossed her arms, clearing her throat. "I hope you will be able to speak with my husband then."

His face fell. "Husband?"

"Of course."

"I thought you lived here as a wild maid all by yourself." She tried not to flinch beneath his scrutiny. "You stalk the hills, you hunt, and you cure a horse by laying hands on it. What else do you do?"

Every muscle in her shoulders had gone taut. "My husband and his brothers enjoy a quiet life here, and I with them." She hadn't meant to say *brothers*, but the three of them had immediately lined up in her mind like a row of shields.

The hunter's eyes alighted on the pegs set in the mud mortar over the door. Soot had darkened the stone walls and outlined in the lamp-light was the faint shape of Naisi's absent scabbard. Deirdre followed his gaze as Fidech thoughtfully scratched his wiry beard, his attention shifting to the fish-traps and crow-berry nets, and the long boots by the door. "He is fortunate to have a wife with such unique talents."

"It is I who am fortunate," she said forcefully. "He's the best mate a woman could have."

"Even though he leaves you alone and unprotected."

She kept her gaze steady. "He has responsibilities to others. And I am not so weak I must tie him to my side." She smiled, proud and cold. "We are strong because we are bound even when apart."

His eyes traveled between her and the sword-shape on the wall. "Indeed."

Late in the night, Fidech tossed in his sleeping hides by the fire. The girl had retired to the other house, but every time he closed his eyes he saw the line of her neck as she raised her face to the moonlight with that bewitching smile. He had never seen such luminous skin matched with such blazing eyes, or features that seemed to shimmer in the firelight. She was astonishing and disturbing—hardly a woman at all.

He pounded the lumpy bracken pillow and resettled his head. She had offered him food at her hearth and that was sacred. He could no more lay hands on her than chop them off, for fear of being forsaken by his hunt gods and chased by the *calleach* until he stumbled off a cliff.

He rose early the next morning and gave his thanks to her in the dawn mists. She had drawn her hood up and he was not able to feast his gaze on her face in daylight. As he walked away, she was gradually swallowed by that ethereal vapor, until he wondered if he dreamed it after all.

A strange impulse dogged him all the way along the loch, where he took a boat to the Awe village. It turned his mind, propelling his feet south toward Dunadd.

The brothers hurried back from Dunadd with the ale barely dry on their lips. Accolades had been sung, the boar eaten, Cinet's thanks given with a cynical smile and sharp gaze. The pride Naisi felt when he saw how his brothers were lauded and the answering glow in their eyes settled deep into his aching soul.

Clarity returned with dawn, bright and cold as the morning star, and he realized that nearly two weeks had passed since he had left Deirdre alone. He drove his brothers homeward then, as eager to return as he had been to venture forth.

The fire of battle and the pleasures of the raucous victory feast animated their speech and they sang as they walked the trails north from Dunadd to Loch Awe, and along its banks to the narrow pass that led to their own loch. In the bustling village, people stared at them and their bright faces, and this time they did not hide their swords but wore them proudly.

With a payment of a bronze finger-ring they persuaded a fisherman to take them across the water to the head of their loch. Dark was falling by then, and Ardan and Ainnle gave the boatman a bed for the night, while Naisi hastened the last few steps home to Deirdre.

She'd fallen asleep with the sheep-fat lamp lit, curled up among the furs, and his sight was still adjusting to the guttering flame when she sprang awake, her eyes wide and glazed. A moment later she threw herself at him with faint, animal whimpers. She peeled back his tunic, her nose drinking in his scent, her legs wrapping around him. With a grunt he dropped his pack so he could hold her hips with both hands. Only then did he realize that she was bare under her shift, as he discovered when he cupped her buttocks and encountered only warm, smooth skin.

He let her feet slide to the ground, unbuckling sword-belt and spear-carrier while she nuzzled his neck. His roving hands felt her ribs pressing through her skin and the prominent ridge of her spine, but his concern for her was eclipsed when she bit down on the tendons under his ear, her hands pulling at his lacings. "Deirdre." He tried to laugh, surprised at her vehemence.

A moment later her fingers were clasping his shaft and it immediately leaped to life at her touch, engorged with a flood of heat. He shook his trews to knees and ankles in his urgency to reach the bed, nudging her backward. There he managed to extract her arms and tossed her once more to the furs, and she lay with tangled hair, eyes glazed, teeth slightly bared.

Naisi stared down, panting. She had lost weight and her face was hollowed, her chin pointed like a fox, her cheekbones carved into high, slanted ridges. That savage look on her face, those glassy eyes looking right through him, made him wonder in what dreams she'd been walking. Superstitious fear prickled up his neck, that a *calleach* had taken her over after all, as Arda said...that she would devour him with passion then disappear with a ghostly laugh, leaving him alone, bereft. His conscience hammered at him. *And if she had wandered far, then whom could he blame but himself?* He had wandered, too, drawn onward by the taunting of his own dark secrets.

She cut off his thoughts by dragging his tunic over his head, nipping the skin of his belly. Guilt drove through him like a spear, pinning them together as he sank on top of her. She gripped his neck and her tongue claimed his mouth, sucking on him.

Bring me back. Her voice.

He did not know if she breathed it into him or it was her thoughts he heard, their minds crossing the borders between them. *Gods, yes, bring me back,* he echoed, crushing his mouth to hers. She fought against his arms even as she devoured his tongue. It was like holding a wildcat caught in some rush of anger... yes, in a terrible fury, her nails scraping his back, her legs kicking out. He trapped them with his own, and her futile writhing only inflamed him more.

The bed was against the wall. Naisi flung her against the stone and, bracing himself with both hands, rammed into her. She did not need softness; she needed taming. When she gasped and raised her hips to him, he yanked her hair to grind her face into his shoulder, letting him thrust deeper. She cried out, a challenge flung into the dark, and its savagery shattered the remnants of his control. He bellowed as he crashed over the peak, and though he had not roused her, she threw her head back and snarled with guttural pleasure. Her throat fluttered beneath his fingers, echoing the clenching of the muscles inside her.

They collapsed back on the bed, panting, still locked together. For a dazed moment he was afraid of the wildness he had called up in himself, wondering if he had hurt her. But as their breath began to slow, she curled into a ball, dragging his arms around to her front. "I am sorry..." he heard her whisper. "I needed to re-member...to remember you..."

He leaned up on his elbow, touching her face. "Deirdre," he said gently.

She drew a shuddering breath, then turned over to look up at him. Her face was her own again, her eyes slowly coming back to recognition. "It's your fault," she said hoarsely, sounding herself once more. "If you didn't do that so well, I wouldn't want it so much."

He smoothed her hair, watching it gleam through his fingers like streamwater. "A woman showing her fire is like a draft of mead to a man." He paused. "I am not afraid." And he wasn't now, for passion had melted all his gnawing pain into unbridled release, robbing it of its power. Behind his eyes he saw himself poised on the cart again, and he let himself glory in that elation now, with no guilt and shame tainting it...

Deirdre's hands alighted on him, tracing then pausing over a scar on his arm. Her face was now hidden in his shoulder. "You have so many of these." She was silent for a moment. "How did you get that one?"

His mind was blurred by the glow of surrender, and he ignored the strange note in her voice. "A Connacht-man got under my guard, two sunseasons ago. Luckily he caught my arm, not my side. And that there was my first sword-cut." For a breath, the space inside his ribs felt hollow again. "I was fourteen, it was my first battle and I was more scared than I would ever show. My body didn't listen to my heart, though, and I emptied my belly over my opponent's boots. It halted his killing blow long enough for Cúchulainn to take him down." He touched it, as the ache inside peaked and ebbed. *Red Branch.*

"And this?" Her hand moved unerringly to a raised welt behind his knee, as if she had already mapped every scar, and gnawed on what they meant.

He pulled her hand back. "I...ah...was absorbed in something and fell on a stick. Don't worry about it; it's not from a blade."

Deirdre went still, then slowly peeled her hair from her mouth, her chin still turned into his chest. "You were doing this with another girl. And there have no doubt been many of those."

Her fierceness unnerved him, so he tried to be light. "Have you seen Urp's sheep scratching their backs on a tree?" he murmured, tilting his chin down to her. "Poking those maids was just like that: itchy before, bliss in the middle and soon forgotten."

He felt her throat move as she swallowed, and then she rolled on her back, looking up at him. "So I'll be scratched and forgotten, will I?"

There was a challenging note to that, despite the merest hint of a smile. He stared down at her. Passion had left her cheeks dewy with a fine sweat, her damp, golden hair framing suddenly uncertain eyes. Her mouth was slightly parted, reaching to taste him even now. *Never forgotten.* He closed his eyes to avoid that intense gaze, kissing her brow. "No. With you it's like drowning in an ocean."

She left that hanging there, and every moment the silence drew out between them, he felt more vulnerable and exposed. He put his face beside hers on the pillow and the guttering lamp sent strange shadows over her eyes. Where had she gone while he was away? *Who was she?* No, that was fear; he would not listen to that.

"Naisi," she said after a moment, her eyes drawn away from him to the shadows reaching up the stone wall. And she took a deep breath and told him about the visit from the king's huntsman and the horse tied up on the other side of the house.

Naisi was dismayed that she'd been seen, but she defended herself, saying she could not leave an animal in pain, that it would disturb the Source.

He didn't want to lose the heat between them, uncertain of her now, and so he closed a hand over her breast to cut off her arguments. His brown fingers spread possessively over that pale globe and Deirdre started and stared at their mingled skin with a look of profound realization. "You'll never see the man again, I am sure," Naisi murmured forcefully. "Leave it now."

She placed her fingers over his own, still staring at her white breast in his brown hand, a flush rising in her cheek. "I will gladly."

He wanted only to feel her now, his mind too tired for words. He reached out to pinch the rush wick of the lamp, extinguishing the flame, and held her as they drifted off to sleep. Only then did he remember to say, "Our swords triumphed, you know."

There was a pause. "I know."

A man emerged from the clamoring crowd around the doors of Cinet's hall. After the steward waved him over, he came to bend a knee before the great oak chair, his bow clasped over his chest in salute.

Cinet blearily peered down at him, head pounding from the ale he'd consumed over the course of the night. "What have you brought me from the hills, then, woodsman?"

Fidech bowed again, gripping his bow for all he was worth. "I met with an accident, my lord, and lamed my horse. I was unable to win either antlers or furs for you this time."

Cinet's brows drew together. He was welcoming a trading party from a far northern tribe and had hoped to present their king with a fine rack in exchange for the fabled white bear fur from the icelands. He had already imagined it glimmering on his shoulders like he was some kind of god. "I am surprised to see you at all, then," he growled.

The hunter's dirty hides gave off a whiff of sweat and old blood, mixed with a hint of damp and salt from his hair. Cinet didn't mind too much, for it reminded him of the wildlands beyond this crowded hall, with all these gabbling people seeking his favor. The cloying perfumes of his women and the greasy steam wafting from the spits suddenly stirred in his belly. He tugged at his belt, disgusted at the flab that bulged over it.

"I did discover something that will please you, though, my lord," Fidech said in his grating voice, glancing up uneasily.

Cinet grunted, his eyes on the dancers who leaped about the fire with hard faces. He'd bartered gold for those foreign slaves, dark-eyed and dusky-skinned. All the warriors were watching them, but Cinet had savored that bought flesh until he was sick of it. He regretted the gold they had cost now.

"My king has refined tastes in women." Fidech glanced at the sinuous dancers.

"And what of it?" Cinet snapped. All that writhing and he was *still* as soft as uncooked dough between his legs. Blasted sluts all tried to please him the same way. His mind slipped on ale and the room tilted disconcertingly. "Spit it out, man."

A sly look flitted across Fidech's weathered face. "On a stormy day in the mountains of your borderlands, I met a maiden as wild as the wind."

Cinet eyed him. He'd been listening to too many bards. "Tupped her, did you?"

Fidech shook his shaggy head. "She is too fey and fair for the likes of me—an uncommon beauty, golden-haired, with pale, glowing skin and a fierce look, like a wildcat." Fidech's eyes had lost focus and he seemed to be reliving something, forgetting to whom he spoke. It was that which at last drew Cinet's attention.

"She lives alone on a mountain, untouched by the shallow concerns of women," Fidech continued, warming to his theme. Cinet glanced aside as two of his bed-mates bickered, fighting to get close to him on the cushions at his feet. "She is a huntress, lithe and skilled, and lives in the heather like a *calleach*—and so I thought her at first glance, until I felt the heat rise from her skin as I brushed by her." Fidech licked his lips and Cinet could not take his eyes from that hungry face, stirred by the fact this dour hunter's awareness of his surroundings could be banished by a mere memory. "And she has the healing hands; she cured my horse in one night. She is unlike any woman of Alba, an untamed spirit of the glens. The other kings will marvel as she feeds you meat downed by her own bow and cures your ills with her hands."

"You sound as if you have devoured her already." Cinet's eyes bored into him, though for some reason his breath had short-ened most pleasurably. "Why not keep this loveliness to your-self?"

Fidech came back to himself, dipping his head. "Because she is mated, and only a king could command such a woman to his side."

Cinet smirked. "I do not grub in the mud of sheep-pens."

"She is mated to a great warrior." That pricked up Cinet's ears. "Though I could not discover his name or those of his brothers." Fidech rested the end of his bow on the ground, his shoulders slumping as the fervency drained from him.

Cinet frowned. "Where did you say you found this maid?"

"In the roaring glen."

Cinet turned to stare at the dancers as they whirled, their movements making the ale slosh around in his gut. He rubbed it, belching loudly. Perhaps he should get outside, dig under this growing fat for the hunter in him, the warrior who once could run for days and climb mountains.

The clear air would surely make him feel less stodgy ... less *old* ... and ready him to face down this aggressive young Venicones king. He needed a fresh entertainment to make his prick spring up as it once had, flooding him with the vigor he needed to triumph in the battles that were no doubt coming.

"Brothers," he muttered.

CHAPTER 31

The Beltaine festival at Emain Macha was subdued. There should have been shouts of drunken revelry heralding the season of warmth and growth, stamping feet whirling in a dance to the fertility gods. Instead, only the lowing of the cattle rose through the smoky dusk as they were driven between two great bonfires and blessed by the druids. Afterward, the nobles and leading warriors returned to their duns to feast, preferring to nurse their grievances by their own fires.

At Dun Dalgan, the merrymaking of Cúchulainn's people was interrupted by a muddy messenger who came racing along cart-tracks turned to mires by leaf-bud rains. Beneath a clouded sunset sky, the man knelt to give Cúchulainn his news. The trilling of bone pipes and thump of drums faded into silence.

Connacht had at last sprung back to life; a hundred raiders had attacked an outlying steading in the southwest. It breached the peace of the sacred festival and was timed to catch the Ulaid off guard. All the Red Branch warriors with their own duns had scattered to them.

The Hound immediately broke up the feast, putting his own messengers into the saddle. Emer's kiss this time was hard and worried, and he paused for a moment to bestow on her his slow, spreading smile, the one that said *I am safe; I will see you.*

The following afternoon he was pacing the earthbanks of the Gates of Macha, grinding his teeth with tension. He hadn't even slept, racing to get his men here, and where were the others? Conall at last arrived with a handful of his warriors. "What took you so long?" Cúchulainn had by now raked his hair into peaks with restless hands.

Conall dismounted, his eyes red-rimmed. "I thought this was more trouble about the sons of Usnech. Your man had to drag me from my ale sleep, and it was a profound one."

Fergus arrived with both sons—Buinne the Red and the younger, Illan. They had retreated from the king's unpredictable moods to their dun in the northwest. "Conor says little and prowls a lot, dulling his pain with ale," Fergus complained to Cúchulainn while they took a turn on the ramparts alone. "Since Samhain, he can barely look me in the eye and I am struggling to rein in Illan's temper, so I vouched to keep my sons away from him for now."

Another fracture, Cúchulainn thought. An ache in his belly reminded him also of Ferdia's absence. After nearly coming to grief in a leaf-fall storm on the way to Alba, Ferdia had barely made it to Skatha's island and then been forced by the weather to stay there for the long dark. A hardy trader had brought the news from him that there was, as yet, no news.

Another sword-mate forced from Cúchulainn's side by Conor.

Fergus planted his spear in the earth along the furrowed bank, gray hair blowing in the wind. He had brought twenty warriors who were now milling with their horses inside the rampart. Cúchulainn counted the growing war-band. "Not all I called have come. Can this be? That they would risk the Ulaid because of their squabbles?"

Fergus hawked, and spat in the mud, squinting blearily at the low sun breaking through the drizzle. He rubbed a paw over his red face to clear his head. "Men are trying to avoid Emain Macha and the Red Branch, Hound. They don't want to be seen to absolutely set themselves against the sons of Usnech and so anger you, or support the three lads and so anger the king. They wonder what will happen if Naisi and his brothers come back to favor." He scowled. "And some are so bitter they will ignore any summons on the king's behalf, no matter what the reasons."

"What, and put the Ulaid at risk?" Cúchulainn strode back and forth, forcing his frustration out through the heavy steps. "Men should be stripped of their halls or Red Branch shields if they give in to such lowly cowardice or spite!"

Fergus stood back uneasily, disturbed by Cúchulainn's rare show of anger. "The gods alone know what Conor thinks to gain with this obsession. No man, as I know, can assume he holds the kingship by right, or even by his men's love."

Cúchulainn got his anger under control with effort and looked at the former king, taking heart from Fergus's towering strength. "I heard you did the best by the Ulaid when you ruled."

"Until I gave up its protection to another," Fergus muttered, staring out over hills veiled by the last slanting rain.

Cúchulainn swung around. Cormac, the king's eldest son, was riding in at the head of a column of warriors sent by Conor, accompanied by his youngest brother, Fiacra, and a host of other Red Branch, including Dubthach, Maine, Curoi, Lugaid, Aengus,

Fachtna and Brecc. This made thirty Red Branch warriors, their
retinues lifting the numbers of all fighters to close to a hundred.
So few Red Branch, Cúchulainn thought with a sinking heart.

Scouts reported that the raiding party had looped around the
hills and begun to swing back to Connacht. From their movements, their path was clear, for a cattle chief near the border had
a particularly fine herd and a renowned bull. Their apparent
carelessness beat a deep note of unease in Cúchulainn's breast.
They know we are weakened; they smell it. What had they heard of the
sickness among the Ulaid?

Illan and Fiacra had wandered far across Erin together, like
Cúchulainn and Ferdia when they were younger. Although they
were still awkward with each other after Samhain, they did manage to confer and agree, pointing the warband toward certain remote paths over hills and treacherous marshes. These trails
would cut off the loop of the Connacht-men who were slowed
by the stolen cattle.

The next morning, the Ulaid warband found that the cattle
chief in question, alerted by his neighbors, had already confined
his herd on a hilltop protected by earthbanks. Cúchulainn ordered him to bring the kine back down to use as bait, cheerfully
promising a large part of Conor's gold in compensation if they
came to harm.

The rain was beating down again, puckering the puddles on
the rutted paths and obscuring the squat thatch roofs and mud
walls of the steading in curtains of gray. The warriors used the
cover of the drizzle to hide themselves in sheep-pens and storehouses, crouching behind the palisade and up on the gatetowers,
and squatting in the mires of the cattle-pens among the stock as
the chief's people fled to the hills.

The Red Branch settled down to wait.

The attack comes like a dream.

The war-crow of the *sídhe* croons to Cúchulainn as he leaps down from the gatetower like another raven in flight, his dark cloak streaming out behind him, his fair hair feathered by rain.

Come, my love, my Hound, the *sídhe*-crow sings. *Be Battle and Courage incarnate, a blade honed by gods...*

The shouts surround Cúchulainn...Ulaid war-cries split the air as the men erupt from their hiding places. *One trunk, many blades. Red Branch...Red Branch!* Connacht bellows of fear and fury ...thuds of sword on shield...whine of spear and thunk of iron-tip into soil...into flesh...

He surrenders to the flame now and is consumed by the One. He becomes a clear channel, a pure column of air that draws the Otherworld fire like a gust of life to flame, and so it roars through him unimpeded by thoughts, fear, doubt.

He is empty of darkness and filled with brightness, and it forges him into a towering blade of power and fury and he dances in glee through a rampart of iron swords. Connacht-men screech: "It's Cúchulainn, Cúchulainn!"

He reaches out with the aura of Source, a cloud of brilliance that penetrates all things. And he feels all the moments of existence at once and together...and so time slows for him.

He is absorbed into utter silence and white-flame-light.

An exhaled breath, a faint moan of the wind through his soul, and he is suspended in stillness. Minute details come into focus. The glint of water in the soil, the earth softened by the rain under that warrior's foot...and lo, the man slips and Cúchulainn's blade is there. There, the sun is about to break through that cloud...and it flashes off the polished iron of that blade and forms a moment of blindness in an enemy's eyes. A heartbeat later, he is downed by Cúchulainn's spear. A gust of wind grazes the Hound's cheek and he looks up to see a lance arcing down upon that breeze. He knocks it away with his sword.

Joined with Source, he sees the corona around each enemy warrior shimmering and flickering with their fear, hate, thoughts. He focuses on the man before him. The movements of the warrior's limbs are a slow-dance, and in the great hush and molten mist Cúchulainn sees the halo around each arm and leg shift. They flow with the warrior's intent, extending out in a plume of light that streams along the ground just before the man leaps. Cúchulainn is already there before the warrior lands the swing, and the plumes shatter into glittering drops, rippling outward when the body falls.

Red Branch! Red Branch! Alone for a moment with blood around his feet, Cúchulainn tilts back his head in exultation, aflame with ecstasy. And he reaches to feel his brothers all joined in one river of white fire that floods the land around them with the throb of life...forming the heart-flame of the Ulaid, of Erin...

Something is wrong.

Dark stains of discord are scattered through the streamers of Red Branch light. A single tear, a momentary rent and there will be no One...and now there are many breaks, many rents, as if a black wind has shredded the glowing veils. Bloody voids of fear and doubt savage the fabric of connection between them. And where is Ferdia, heart-brother? He should be here, their flames gusting together.

Part of Cúchulainn's awareness soars on high, and he can see it all.

The Red Branch had broken into knots, their movements clumsy and increasingly desperate. The backup of brother and comrade was not there when they turned, their strokes no longer mirrors of each other. The flowing dance of stab and thrust, whip and duck, had dissipated into chaos.

Illan and Fergus fought together, but Buinne was dueling alone, his father roaring an order to fall back in with them that Buinne either could not hear or ignored. Conall and his own men struggled in the mire of the cattle-pens, forgetting the plan to drive the raiders into the ditch of the steading. The other Red Branch were scattered among the lower-ranked warriors, who were all sound fighters but distanced from one another.

Their suspicions and frustrations were like shards of iron

driven deep into their bonded flesh, shredding it before Cúchulainn's eyes. Now there was no graceful flow, no power of One; it was down to every man's own strength and desperation alone. The war-crow squawked at Cúchulainn's shoulder, invisible wings beating his face. *They have let you down; they have faltered.*

The screams were no longer war-cries of power but shouts of pain that became the names of men he knew, and each was a thunder-strike through his heart.

Cúchulainn did not wash the blood from his face when he stormed into Emain Macha to face Conor. He wanted the dead men's blood on him, peeling off in flakes. The guards at the hall jumped out of the way as he flung back the doors and passed through the cavernous building like a flaming brand.

He finally discovered the king in one of the storehouses—a long shed set on stilts to keep it dry. Cúchulainn took the stairs in a bound. Conor was inside with his steward, tallying the Beltaine gifts. The two men stood in a pool of light from a horn-shielded lamp, which outlined the dim shapes of barrels and baskets piled against the timber walls. Chinks of daylight fell through the cracks in the boards.

The king jerked around when Cúchulainn appeared, the Hound trailing his unsheathed sword from a bloodied hand. "Tell me this was no defeat," Conor croaked, the veined whites of his eyes glowing in the dimness.

"Connacht's warriors fled and the cattle were retrieved, if that's what you mean." Cúchulainn's lips felt strangely numb, his voice hoarse from shouting.

Conor's eyes darted to the steward, whose ink pen was still poised expectantly over the sheet of bleached leather. "Go," the king said. "We will continue this later."

A storehouse would not have been Cúchulainn's chosen ground, but the sides of drying beef, the sacks of musty grain and vats of cheese hidden in the darkness whispered to him that if the Ulaid warriors faltered, the fortunes of the people would be next—their safety, their survival. As soon as the steward was gone, Cúchulainn's head snapped back. "Maine, Brecc and Curoi are dead, and many others with them."

Conor did not blink, though one cheek spasmed, drawing his mouth down. "When warriors fight, they die."

"If you had not been sunk in your own madness, Connacht would not have raided at Beltaine. They know of our weakness."

The king squeezed out a grunt of protest but Cúchulainn strode toward him, still crackling with the aftermath of the battle-fire. Conor took an involuntary step back, his eyes striped by the sunlight that fell through a gap in the walls. There Cúchulainn saw a gleam of real fear surface from those glazed depths.

The king's long, graying hair was uncombed, and there was an ale stain down his robes beneath the heavy fur cloak. His face was hollowed at cheeks, temples and eyes, as if his flesh were being consumed from within. Still, it invoked no pity in Cúchulainn. "We surprised the raiders, and we should have had them easily. Instead, men died because of this rift that has come between us!"

Conor worried a loose tooth with his tongue, his eyes receding now beneath their hooded lids. "There would be no rift if the Red Branch turned their backs on those traitorous boy-cubs once and for all. The men should be obeying their king—"

"Are you so blind you cannot see how you have shattered not just our peace but our strength?" Cúchulainn roared. He thrust out his jaw and Conor barely suppressed a flinch. "This sickness is rotting the very roots of the Red Branch. Connacht will see we have lost strength now, and they will come back again—and soon with an army. Then you'll have no chance to mourn Deirdre, for we'll all be dead."

Conor's hand curled into a white claw over his chest. "They will rally. The Red Branch are the strongest, the bravest. I spent my boyhood steeped in that myth." Bitterness tainted his words.

Before he could stop himself, Cúchulainn flipped his sword into both hands, retaining the presence of mind to tilt it along his own cheek. The king's gaze ran along the blade. "You still do not understand the mind of the Red Branch."

A pause. "You are not the first to venture that."

"Then listen. In battle, we share in the Source. Our love for our land and one another weaves a net, and in that *we are One. That's* what makes us strong. But it depends on unity—the very thing you risk destroying with your lust and pride." Conor's throat bobbed in angry denial until the sword tip wavered closer. "Unless you do something to right this, the Red Branch trunk will fall and the way will be open for the other kingdoms and even Alba to fall upon us. People will be slaughtered in their beds or enslaved, and *there will be no more Ulaid.* No one will remember us, or sing of us, or light fires for us." He paused, the torrent burning his throat. "And if they sing of you, great king, it will be with scorn."

Conor's face slowly bleached of all color, making his eyes burn with a fury he would not release. His collarbone strained through his wrinkled skin as he swallowed. "You threaten me, nephew?"

"Not with treason, uncle." Cúchulainn dropped the sword. "But my oath is to guard the Ulaid and whichever king sits the throne. I pledged my sword to you only because *you* in turn took oath as the land's protector." He sheathed his blade and at the door he stopped, reaching out to touch the sacking that contained a wealth of grain. "There is still time," he said quietly, "before you have forsworn that oath forever."

When Cúchulainn walked blindly from the storehouse, he saw Levarcham hovering beneath the eaves of the hall and, changing direction, strode toward her. "We need them back," he said hoarsely. He chewed his lip, wary of her unkempt appearance, her glazed eyes. "Have you gleaned nothing from the fires, Sister?" He remembered in his wrath to use the proper form of address.

A tremor went through her at his words, and her gray eyes

struggled to come back into focus. She put up a trembling hand to brush away wisps of what looked like uncombed hair from her brow. "I have looked," she whispered. "I have done nothing but look, and seek, and rend myself to catch a glimpse of them—in fire, in water, in smoke!" Her hands fell to her sides, empty. "I do not know why, but I give all and I see nothing."

That is why he had not seen her for so long. She had not been able to stomach being by Conor's side, but had been searching in her own way nevertheless—inward, as he and Ferdia searched without.

"Perhaps I did not love her enough to catch a thread of her essence through the mists," Levarcham said brokenly. The pain weighed down her face, her shoulders.

Cúchulainn caught himself, straightening and thrusting aside his own emotions. "Perhaps they do not want to be found," he said. "But the Ulaid need them, or we will die."

CHAPTER 32

Sunseason

Carnach sent a message asking the brothers to join his warband in guarding a shipment of furs to the Caledonii in the north. Deirdre convinced herself it was the companionship of warriors Naisi longed for, and though she did not yearn for such company, he had known a different life. *Take me as I am.* He had asked that of her.

The brothers left on a sunny day, and she was unnerved by the strange relief that came over her when their curragh slid away down the loch. She stood on the shore and held the sigh of released tension to her chest with a fist, afraid to face what it was.

The fight had not quenched the subtle hum of frustration that still ran through them. Perhaps it had stoked it. Naisi loved her savagely and then went to hunt alone, driving himself over the highest peaks after deer. Ainnle's moody eagerness to be away made him even more short-tempered. Ardan still debated druid lore with her, but rarely met her eyes, and in between often disappeared for days. When they were home, their nervous energy sent disturbed ripples over the shining surface of the pool around her.

The pool that beckoned her.

She threw back her head and gazed at the green sweep of hillside, its slopes of heather glowing in the afternoon sun. A haze hovered over the trees, its shimmer carved into swirls by the wings of a circling eagle. The boat-wake had sunk back into the loch, leaving no trace of men, and the glassy surface now only reflected the hidden realm in an otherworldly mirror of light.

She bent to the rocks lapped by its waters, and as she walked from the shore she loosened her braids and threaded more swan feathers through her hair, until they drifted about her cheeks. She barely felt her cloak shed itself from her shoulders, or her shoes drop from her feet as she reached the high meadow, her toes buried in lush grass.

By the standing stone, her clothes slid from her skin, their last touch a sigh as they left her. Now her flesh could bind with earth and rock, and the dews could coat her, letting her dissolve into light.

More messages came from Carnach, and each time, the brothers hearkened to his pleas for aid. Deirdre gleaned from Ainnle that they were not peaceful trade missions now, for some of Talan's chiefs were rebelling against Carnach's accession to his hall. Then she discovered that Naisi had drawn his sword to threaten a recalcitrant lord into submission.

For a time, she did not confront him, for whenever he returned, that tension in his body and eyes was a tiny, cold shard lodged between them, a rent in the oneness of their joining. One day, they were stretched out naked on rocks after a swim in the loch. "Surely you've done this Carnach enough favors now." She glanced at him warily over her shoulder, her skin contracting as it dried.

Even here with him, a dreamy part of her was already reaching to the seductive gleam of the rainwashed peaks above them. That world sung to her in a low, beckoning voice, and her body resonated with it. She bit her lip. She should want to sink into *him* instead. But almost unconsciously, unwillingly, a part of her was recoiling from the pain of his absences, and the fear of the danger that slunk along at his heels whenever he left the valley, like a wolf at dusk.

"It isn't enough," Naisi said quietly, his brows knitted against the glare of the sun, his slitted eyes far away.

Abruptly, he came back to himself, pulling her rump close to his groin and tangling their legs together. He kissed her neck and she closed her eyes as he drank the water from the groove of her back, moving his wet body over her, sliding the moisture between them. With relief she melted into sensation, her belly pressed into the warm rock, until Naisi paused, turning her jaw with a finger.

His fierce gaze reached for her, and as she met his glance it expanded into something deeper than desire, turning her inside out. His eyes softened, his pupils dilated. That gaze sought a connection, a belonging, the whisper of *I know you*. And then his mouth clamped and his brow creased, as he tried to force more along that joining, something he could not say but wanted her to *know*—and she didn't know.

A thread of confusion wound through her, as chill as the wind on her wet skin.

Deirdre strayed far up the mountains in her wanderings. One day she surfaced from a strange trance where she had been reaching down through the rock veins beneath her, catching a memory of stone flowing like glowing water. She blinked her eyes open to see someone watching her from the bushes. Those beady eyes widened in fear and then disappeared, but moments later, Deirdre caught up with Urp as he hobbled down the slope with a bleating lamb in his arms.

It took Deirdre until they were on the lower pastures before he would answer her entreaties that she was no *calleach*, only Finn's mate. She followed him to his door, and then it was Arda's turn to cry in fear. That turned to a rant at Naisi—Finn—for keeping her from them, and then a cosseting of motherly pity at Deirdre's thin arms and hollow face.

Urp was wrathful that Naisi had lied to him, until Deirdre returned the next day with bundles of herbs for Arda, which made his lips at last twitch in a gruff smile.

After that, her circles took her along the ridge above their steading, weaving the Source in a blessing over their house and flocks. When they saw her wandering the hills in deerskins, singing under her breath, she knew they secretly thought her *sídhe* after all, and no amount of teasing Urp or wolfing down Arda's cheese and bannocks seemed to entirely convince them. Their smiles were always tinged with respect.

She warded the valley with the light she summoned, which felt like something familiar she had done once, long ago.

The brothers were gone, and Deirdre had walked the horse along the shore, leaving it tied up to pick dandelion, chickweed and sorrel from the damp woods. A movement caught her attention through the trees and she looked up, blinking to clear her eyes, her song of blessing dying on her lips.

A small curragh was hugging the shadows of the loch, gliding silently toward the river mouth. She dropped the leaves, her legs tensing to flee, but it was too late. The horse was hobbled near a little stream where it emptied in the loch, in the open.

She watched the boat from behind alder scrub, and recognized the king's huntsman splashing ashore, having seen his horse. She had no choice but to come out.

"Hail, horse-healer." Fidech nodded, patting his stallion's neck. "I told you I'd come back."

Another man had come ashore with him, clad in the same kind of plain hide clothes. He boasted a broad chest and belly, and the ruddiness of florid cheeks and veined nose bled into his mane of red hair. Unlike Fidech, the fading outlines of tattoos extended up his heavy cheeks, curling around his brows. He swept Deirdre with small, dark-blue eyes, and a shock went through her body when his glance touched her—an instinctive coiling of her flesh.

It was so warm she'd wound her hair up and stuck it with bone pins, and she wore only an old deerskin dress and buck-hide shoes, her legs bare. "Donnan has been well for some time," she said warily, moving around the other side of the stallion's flank.

Fidech glanced at his companion, but before he could answer the other man spoke, his voice grating yet powerful. "What did you do for him?"

She bridled at his insolent scrutiny, though she endeavored to hide it. "Merely herbs and rest." As the man leaned to pick up the stallion's leg she glanced at Fidech, puzzled, but he only stood back with a blank face. "Are you a healer, or just a horse expert?" she asked the other huntsman boldly, stepping away from the odor of stale sweat that wafted from his tunic. He rested the hoof down and there was a glint of amusement in his eyes. Up close, she thought there might be elongated animal ears among the tattoos on his cheeks.

Fidech scratched his graying head. "We are not just here to get Donnan, lass. We brought gifts as payment for your care."

Deirdre rubbed her bare arms, crossing them over her breasts where the hide was worn and thin. "I needed no payment."

The other man waved the boatmen to begin unloading bundles onto the sand. "It's not just for the horse. Our king has sent gifts to Finn and his brothers, in gratitude for their service to Talan's people."

Deirdre's shoulders lowered slightly. If these men knew Naisi enjoyed the king's protection, and that she was Naisi's, then she must be safe enough.

They gave her another cooking pot, and needles, cloth and barley meal, and she realized she could not avoid inviting them for food. The other man was called Galan, he told her as he and Fidech lugged the sacks up to her house. Deirdre felt his presence behind her all the way like a shadow amid the murmuring pool of lightness.

There followed an uncomfortable meal. Sitting on piles of deerskins, they gulped down her fish stew and Galan asked questions about how she spent her days, lingering over her stilted explanations of how she fed herself when Naisi—Finn—was away. He wanted to know about her herb knowledge; her healing of the horse; how she fished from her log-boat and gathered plants. She was trapped. Word could not get back to King Cinet that Naisi's mate had treated his hunters badly. Did she sing and dance? Galan wanted to know. At mention of that, Conor's slack mouth was there before her again, and she splashed the ale as she poured. No, she did not dance, she replied.

The sun dropped lower, slanting through the open door, and at last Galan belched and lumbered to his feet. "Fidech has far to travel over the hills with his mount, and we must not overstay our welcome. Maidens should be treated with respect, so they are well disposed toward us men, eh?" He jabbed Fidech in the ribs, smiling.

As they sat by her hearth, Deirdre had been conscious of the growing tremor in the air, the thrum of instinctive danger. Now she faced Galan, her pulse thudding against the delicate bones of her wrists, making her conscious of the slightness of her body. "Respect should be given unasked. A man doesn't do a woman a favor by treating her as he expects to be treated."

Galan's eyes flashed with delight. "Ha! Hear that, Fidech? Not only fair and skilled, but a wit, too."

Deirdre's lips thinned. She was exhausted now. "I do not display 'wit' as if it's something to please a man. It's just good sense."

Galan's smile widened and he wiped his red face, for the air was close, reeking of their sweat and smoke-tanned hides. "Not many women have the sense, as you call it, to think like that, mistress. You have had some education." She pushed her tongue against the roof of her mouth, silencing herself while Galan peered insolently around the room. "It seems a waste, you moldering away here. Don't you long for richly-hung halls, music and feasts?"

Deirdre met his eyes. "I am happiest here—I don't need anything else."

Galan grunted, looking her up and down until her skin crawled. "Aye, I can see you flourish here as a flower among stones, as willful and wild as the winds themselves."

"Such romantic terms do not apply to me. I prefer plain speaking."

"And that is an even greater beauty." Galan sketched her an odd bow and, mystified, from her doorway Deirdre watched them leave. She kept her palm pressed against the door-post that had been smoothed by Naisi's axe, drawing strength from his absent touch.

⚬

Cinet stood on the wicker platform of his chariot, as the barley pits dotted through Dunadd were filled with the harvested grain and ritually sealed. Bridei sat a pony by his side, his shield of hammered bronze on his arm.

At each pit, the priestesses, led by his sister—Bridei's mother, Eithne—laid offerings of earthen pots filled with mead in the base of the empty holes, along with bone spindles and bronze combs. Sprinkling blessings of sacred water, Eithne beseeched the Mother Goddess Rhiannon to ensure the grain was kept safe and unspoiled in her womb, the earth. The women of the dun then came forward with baskets on their heads, and bending at the waist poured a pale bronze stream of seed into each pit.

Cinet's mind was not on the grain, however, nor on whether his people were watching him with the requisite amount of awe.

He ignored the droning priestesses and shaven-haired druids, captivated by the women's plump buttocks as they emptied the baskets, their breasts swinging in the open necks of their dresses. Their outlines wavered into an entirely different vision, a vivid and sensual memory.

Tanned limbs in a short deerskin dress, the soft hide hugging lush curves. A fall of hair gleaming with the mingled hues of queen's gold and warrior bronze. Flushed lips against creamy skin. He conjured her eyes then, glowing fiercely with a mixture of bold intelligence and an untameable will. His prick began to swell thinking about that look alone. She was a wild vixen and a priestess—and not one of these horse-faced, muttering ones, either. She moved with the grace of his dancing girls, and yet her face was stamped with the defiance of one who could never be enslaved. Her memory alone brought the clear wind of the mountains into his constricted throat.

Like any wild thing, though, she required careful handling. Too brutal a move and he would crush the spirit that so intrigued his jaded appetites. He could throw down any woman and ravage her, but he'd done that enough and fear was no longer exciting. No, he would *tame* her, and in the chase through her mountain realm the fat on him would melt away and his limbs would regain their vigor. That would silence the whispers he was sliding past his prime.

"What of this Finn and his brothers?" he murmured to Bridei, as the priestesses sealed the pit with clay and sang over it, palms outstretched. "How are they conducting themselves?"

The scent of the slow-flowing river was pungent on this hot day, and Bridei shifted his circlet, wiping his brow. "Carnach and his men can speak of little else. The brothers have his entire warband hanging from their every utterance. During the feasting here after the Venicones raid, they exhibited some skills with the sword no one has ever seen. Many of our best warriors are eager to fight beside them."

"Indeed?" Cinet knew all this. He merely wanted to gauge Bridei's tone.

"The warriors have named Finn *fladorca*, dark prince, for they think he is of royal blood, exiled by some jealous kinsman. Whatever the truth, the brothers will be an asset to any king who can secure their loyalty."

Cinet gnawed his cheek, gesturing his driver to lead the horses around for his progress back through the village. He'd let the British interlopers join his warband because they guarded a barren place too far from the trade paths to tempt his own warriors. The game had changed now, though. After all, what was the loss of three swords, no matter how great the skill of their wielders? It was the *how* that mattered.

They had already gained the support of Carnach's men, Bridei was impressed by them and his nephew's insolent young swordmates—all waiting for Cinet to die—desired to fight beside them. They were being noticed, followed, watched...so the chance of doing away with them quietly had already passed. There was nothing so unyielding as the honor bonds between those who'd shed blood together, or the harsh view men took of kings who violated those codes. Cinet's throne was already under scrutiny. It was too delicate to risk cries of betrayal now.

He looked over his shoulder at Bridei. "They seem intensely eager to fight."

"They are first to unsheath their swords, and always to the fore."

Cinet smiled. "Then we must make more use of their need to outshine everyone else."

"How so?"

"They are young and brilliant, and it is better to expend foreign blood than that of our own bucks."

His nephew frowned, unsure how to reply. Cinet merely smiled as the chariot rumbled up the muddy track, the horses led by his driver. He nodded as people paused outside their houses and bowed. He was bored enough to draw out this challenge for a little time yet; it made his blood run pleasurably hot and swift.

Battle was danger: drawn swords, flying spears. Add in an ea-

gerness to prove yourself and, in one slip, it was over. Such deaths
were expected among the brave.

CHAPTER 33

If Carnach's calls for aid were distant bird-cries, something
Deirdre's heart could just keep at bay, a vaster span of wings
soon swooped over them from the west. A message came from
the king of the Epidii himself: Cinet wanted the brothers to join
his scouts on their patrols across the moors.

It was not long before they were called to guard trade ship-
ments along the coasts, and there were more secret missions that
Naisi kept from Deirdre, for he knew how she would fear. Their
lack of tattoos, Cinet said, meant they could penetrate Venicones
territory to gather news, pretending to be travelers from Gaul.
Or Erin, he added, with a glint in his narrowed eyes.

Naisi dared not refuse.

The king rewarded them with royal gifts: gold-rimmed drinking horns and soft wool, sealskins and bronze platters and jugs.
He also sent a glass bottle for Deirdre that contained not perfume, as would be expected for a nobleman's wife, but red-
flower syrup, a rare herbal remedy. It was an unusual but fitting
gift, for Deirdre was more interested in her plants than female
fripperies. Drying herbs hung in boughs over the fire now, and
the shelves held earthen pots of salves and powders, the air
sharpened by the tang of curled leaves and flower-heads.

Cinet had also sent an array of fine kidskins, bleached white
and sewn into a long bolt, like transparent cloth. That was an im-
practical and expensive offering, and Deirdre sat looking at it for
a long time across her lap, her face still.

In piling the gifts against their walls, Naisi did not see the gleam of bronze or fur, however. He only remembered the glowing eyes of the Epidii warriors in Dunadd's hall every time Cinet hailed them for their bravery, describing their expeditions to his noblemen in the most rousing terms.

All those fiercely tattooed faces were turning to the sons of Usnech, and Naisi knew they were winning their place, at last.

Ardan and Naisi huddled around their fire in a hollow away from the scouring moorland wind. The other Epidii scouts nursed their own fires, scraping together bits of dead-wood where they could find them.

Naisi lifted his cold knuckles to the flames and picked up his knife again. The clouded sun was still above the horizon, for they were close to the longest day, and it cast a sickly light over their exhausted faces. They had been on the move for hours, and the wind had swung to the north, cold and biting despite the season.

He glanced over his shoulder. He and his brothers once prepared food without need for words, Ardan piling stones to heat, Ainnle digging the baking pit, Naisi skinning the deer. Now Ainnle had disappeared to one of the other fires, and Ardan would not meet his eyes, their movements out of rhythm.

Ardan had once been the least eager for battle; now he strained to be away from home. *He gnaws at the bonds I put around him. The exile.* Naisi's throat ached as he watched his brother stare over the dusky grassland toward the far peaks. Ardan's eyes were like the skies now, always clouded and distant, for there was no Red Branch to fire them in battle, only these tantalizing glimpses among the Epidii of what they had lost. But it was close now... the belonging. Naisi closed his eyes. *Fla dor ca! Fla dor ca!* Dark prince.

Ardan squatted, jabbing the rocks to turn them. They had sporadically clashed with the Venicones scouts, and Ardan had always fought savagely, though his relief never seemed to last. Naisi eyed him warily. Ardan and Ainnle had enjoyed no shortage of bed-partners at Carnach's dun and Dunadd, but for Ardan that would not be enough. He needed a hearth that was his kin-home, with music and blazing fires, and the warm jests of family. And a wife, perhaps, and children.

The smoke of the little fire curled into the lines of Deirdre's face for a moment, before unraveling. Frowning, Naisi dug the knife into the deer, slicing along the membranes. He felt her being drawn away. He noticed how her gaze often misted over now, as if she was absorbed in some other realm. He knew he bore the fault by leaving her, but the bitter irony was that she, alone among women, also seemed to seek that isolation. She often turned from him toward the deep woods, or padded from their bed out into storms just to feel the winds. It made him afraid—and it brought relief. She gave him the space to do what he must do, to take the shattered pieces of himself and bind them back together into something she could love. And it was so close now. He jerked the knife, freeing the deer's glistening liver.

"You should not be from home so much." Ardan's voice was keener than the dagger. He tipped glowing rocks into the hole, wafting up steam from the lining of reeds. "I am surprised you leave Deirdre alone like that."

For a moment, Naisi could not reply. He never missed Ardan's glances at Deirdre, either. It was not something he wanted to admit, let alone confront. *It's not his fault. She is beautiful and he is young.* It was lust and that was fleeting, Naisi had always found. He cleared his pained throat. "The passes are protected by Carnach's men, and she knows we have to win Cinet's favor." He suddenly realized his heart was racing, poised as if in defense. He breathed through it. Ardan's desire would pass in fighting. Everything would.

Ardan nudged the pile of dug earth with his toe. "I hope she feels the same way."

Did Ardan see more of what absorbed Deirdre than he did? "That is between her and me," Naisi murmured. A gulf hovered between them, dark and cold.

A shout went up from the other fire, and Ardan strode toward it, then came back hauling Ainnle. Their younger brother boasted a black eye and an inane grin. Ardan shoved Ainnle down by their fire. "I bet four of them they couldn't get me flat out on the ground," Ainnle crowed, his breath reeking of ale, "and they lost!" He flung down three hide pouches sloshing with liquid.

Naisi peered at the drip of blood from Ainnle's nose. "You should save your ire for the Venicones."

Ainnle unsteadily batted him away. "Come on, they want us back and it's going to be a long night. We'll leave the meat cooking."

Ainnle's fever for battle was at boiling point. As he waved his arm, Naisi's eye was caught by the cut his youngest brother had taken in a skirmish with a band of Venicones scouts. The makeshift bandage was filthy, the ends shredded.

Naisi stared at it with tight eyes. It was his lead Ainnle followed so eagerly to battle, Ainnle's need to prove himself to Naisi that quickened that hot blood.

Boots pad through dappled woods, each sole tracing the same laddered pattern as the feathers marked on his arrows, forcing his soul into the barbs to give them greater power. Trancelike, he reads the throb of earth through his feet, sensing the ripple of deer-heart that threads through the pulse of Mother Forest. The bow is held as taut as his muscles. He crouches low... makes his cape brush the wind-blown leaves like the hide of his quarry. He paints the shape of the deer against the cave wall of his mind... holds it still. Mother, let him creep so close the stag feels his blood as its blood, his warmth as its own.

Deirdre's palms molded to the stone beneath her, this place so imprinted by the ancient echoes of human reverence. *This* was how she glimpsed a oneness with animals—by reaching to him, this breath of hunter caught in the wind.

Now she understood that unlike his clear, crystal soul, surrendered into Oneness, her mind was like broken rock, the stone veins tangled by fear and self-doubt. It made her struggle to cross the boundaries to the fleet, silver spirits of the beasts and birds by will alone. No matter how she longed for that immersion, she was afraid to lose herself completely, to spread roots into soil and grow a skin of silvery bark, for then Naisi would walk by and never see her again...

She woke with a start on the stone, dew caught on her eyelashes from the night mists. Around her, the *sídhe* raced across the face of the moon, whirlpools of radiance pouring over the meadow. Reaching up with unsteady hands, she brushed against their savage glee, for they were drawn by the vivid emotions that filled her when she walked with the ancient hunter.

Belonging. Clan. Motherland. Womb-place. That is what the hunter felt—and every time she woke from that trance, she was choked by the terrible grief of being sundered from it. For she remembered being a spirit-walker, and now she was just Deirdre, and men wanted to mold her into something else, when she needed to find the shape she already *was*.

Drawing in the night air, she drifted back through the woods, her raised lips drinking in the moonlight. She stopped when she saw a flickering glow.

Deirdre paused to clear her sight, anchoring herself in the here-and-now. It was a bloom of flames through the dark trees. She crept closer, the hunter's senses still clinging to her so that she reached a vantage point behind an oak tree in silence.

It was Naisi, his weapons and amulets spread out beneath the moon. He held each up one by one, his fingers reverently tracing its shape, bathing it in sacred light. He kissed the cold blades of sword and dagger, then the curves of the antler necklet and his father's torc. At last he took up his Red Branch arm-ring, murmuring to it as if imparting secrets, or praying. His expression as he gazed at it was wrought from the most unguarded pain, his brows shadowing hollow eyes.

Deirdre pressed her breast against the oak to quell a swift ache. When he left the valley, he never looked at her with such loss. In her distress, she forgot herself, and her foot cracked a stick. Naisi dropped the ring and in the same movement his sword was in his hand. She saw how unconsciously he caught up that blade, as if it was a part of his body.

When she moved into sight, his sword lowered. Caught by the moonlight, his face was faintly ashamed. "I thought you were asleep," he blurted.

"I thought you were with your brothers," she replied. When he did not answer, looking down at his weapons, she took another step. "I go to the rock up there when there's a moon," she said. "It is a place of power, and I draw comfort from it when—"

She cut herself off but his dark eyes flinched and she knew he gained her meaning. *When I am here in the valley alone.*

His lips drew into a thin line and he dropped his sword, running an unsteady hand through his hair, and it came to her with a spike of heat how that mouth felt brushing against her. She shivered. Perhaps the fire between them was like this one, a small, guttering flame against the encroaching dark of secrets and opposing desires. Lust had bound them, but she did not know if it could unravel—if that's what this sliver of coldness was. Such mysteries of women and men were beyond Levarcham's teachings.

"What do you do up there?" Naisi's hands seemed unsure now they were empty, and he picked up his dagger and sheathed it at his waist.

Her heart ached and she walked closer. They must weave the paths together again, share what moved them. "Many things. I practice…the bird-lore I taught Ardan and…I follow the animals, as I did the deer." He had not been afraid of that, she remembered. "And…" she thought of the ancient hunter, "and I can catch glimpses sometimes of the past—"

"The past?" An instinctive fear flared in his moonlit eyes.

A sick shock reverberated through her. He *was* afraid of her feyness, her strangeness. Why had she not seen it before? "Yes," she croaked.

He spun around, taking an agitated step across the clearing and bending for his father's torc. She came up behind him and looped her hands around his waist, burying her face in his shoulder. He stiffened at her touch, but a moment later the trembling muscles softened under her cheek, and his warm hand covered her fingers. *Fiáin*. It could have been a whisper on the breeze.

She drew a breath. "Tell me the truth, Naisi. About why you feel the need to leave, to risk your life so much…" Her voice caught.

He was still for a moment, his fingers brushing her hand. "Every time we fight for Cinet, the higher we rise in his favor and the more power we command among his men. Soon we will have warriors to recruit to our side—against Conor." Deirdre flinched and dropped her arms. Naisi turned, looking out to the shadows that crept in from the forest. She noticed he was gripping the torc tightly. "If we help Cinet to defeat the Venicones, there is no telling what rewards we will gain: land on which to raise sheep, cattle and crops, which will support a war-band, and then a dun, and then you will be protected by a ring of men and stout walls." The words rushed out in a vehement stream. Disconcerted, Deirdre stared at the outline of his rigid jaw. Walls?

He let his breath out, glancing at her. "The Epidii have taken to calling me *fladorca*," he went on more softly, "because they don't know my kin—and because of my hair." His smile was wry as he scraped a lock off his brow. "And every time we unsheath a blade, we are drawn further into that brotherhood, as we win their respect."

She looked down at her hands, clasped into a tangle now he had stepped away from her. This was his truth, then—but it wasn't hers. Fear crept up her from the damp ground. He wanted a dun again, a feast-hall, a war-band. She wanted the silence of the forest, seeking the Otherworld in the mists. This was not what she knew between them, the perfect joining, the ecstatic pleasure. This was confusing…

Then it all tumbled through her. She could not plead with him to stay, when she herself felt such an instinctive fear of being trapped that every arm-ring Naisi proudly bestowed on her— the gold from Cinet's treasury—still felt like a heavy shackle.

She could not turn him inside out, for he would demand the same of her, and how could she reveal how tempted she was by the slow dive through the Otherworld veils? It was beyond explanation, and it was still fragile, and it was hers—*hers alone*. Despite his understanding of the deer-call, he would be afraid of the vast and startling depths of this. She could not tell him how the call of the *sídhe* now bled into every waking heartbeat, offering peace, familiarity, belonging...

She started when Naisi bent for his Red Branch ring and fastened it on his arm, his touch lingering on the bronze spearhead. She watched his black hair fall over his cheekbones, and told herself fiercely that this is where she belonged.

But if he so longs to leave, then he's not happy, a cold hiss whispered inside her. *While you sink beneath the surface of the world as if you will not breathe human air again. And why should you, when he might die and leave you alone?* Was she holding herself back in anticipation of some future sundering? Her eyes stung. "If you could pretend to be a farmer, we wouldn't need an army," she murmured.

He cocked his head, looping the thong of amulets around his neck. "If I was a farmer, you wouldn't want to wrap your thighs around me half as much."

"Liar," she forced past the lump in her throat.

His smile flickered briefly, and then he lifted his face to the moonlit sky, as if he could not look for long in her eyes. "It is nearly here, Deirdre," he murmured. "The day we will be untouchable."

But it was his very need to fight that hardened him. She felt herself grow cold, and couldn't stop her heart curling up to protect itself, like a bloom closing at dusk. Unable to speak, she stumbled away from him across the clearing, toward the path. Words could not change what they felt in their hearts, the different things they wanted. She stopped in the shadows and glanced back, to see that he was already crouched by the fire, his head lowered as he tossed twigs on the tiny flames.

Naisi, she found herself pleading, *why can you not be at peace with your own heart in silence, in stillness?*

As she went, she longed to hear his footsteps behind her, to have him curl his naked body around hers in bed. They could laugh together then, shivering as they warmed each other.

He did not come back that night.

The next time the sons of Usnech returned they did not stride up the slope from the curragh singing, swords glinting over their shoulders. Ainnle stumbled along with his head drooping, arms strung around his elder brothers.

Watching from the trees, Deirdre didn't waste any words, directing them to her and Naisi's house since it was nearest and Ainnle's face had gone white with strain. The day was warm and the door-hide was tied back, and the faint wash of daylight in the dark hut picked out the clammy sheen of Ainnle's skin. He sank to the blankets with a groan, clutching his waist. His tunic was stiff with dried blood that had seeped through a crude bandage wrapped around his middle. She asked what happened as she poured water into the iron bowl and set it on the tripod over the coals, stirring them into flames and feeding them hazel twigs from the woodbasket.

"He was a careless fool, that's what," Naisi snapped.

He glared at Ardan, who was divesting himself of his weapons. The elder two looked exhausted, their hair knotted by the wind, shadows smeared under their eyes. Their tunics were also bloodied, and Deirdre thought, *They took it in turns to hold him.*

Calming herself, she knelt by the bed and tried to ease up Ainnle's tunic.

"It's all right…" Ainnle panted to Deirdre, gritting his teeth. "It's just a cut. It hurts a little…that's all."

"Just a cut!" Naisi could not stop his voice rising. He'd kept it all at bay to speed Ainnle home—his terror, his guilt—and now the relief of having his brother in Deirdre's hands, by his own hearth, was rapidly unraveling him, breaking his control. "You are both to blame! Foolhardy, mindless…"

"It was an accident," Ardan cut in, dumping his spear-carrier on the floor. "The Novantae stole those cattle off the Epidii last year. Ket and the others asked us to get them back."

"We were supposed to be guarding Cinet's carts," Naisi retorted.

Ainnle pulled himself away from Deirdre, a line of color threading his pale cheekbones. "They begged us to go."

Naisi whirled on him. "And if they begged you to leap off a cliff, you'd do that, too?" He looked between his two brothers, at their pursed mouths and the resentment in their eyes, and he could barely force air down his throat. He filled his chest and flung it back out. "How could you risk yourself like that?" he bellowed at Ainnle. He crushed the howl inside. *I am doing all this to give you back a future, and you almost throw it away?*

Ainnle gasped, his shoulders trembling. "It's up to me what I risk! You throw yourself into danger all the time, Naisi, I've seen you. *I* didn't ask to be so bound, barred from ale-feasts and women and warrior-songs—"

"No, you didn't," Naisi shot back. "But you could have gone your own way long ago." Ainnle's mouth dropped open, and Naisi's voice cracked. "Except that it's up to me to make all those decisions."

Ardan was on his feet, his eyes blazing in his pale, dirty face. "It *isn't* all up to you and it doesn't just affect you! Ainnle is frustrated, and that's why he takes such risks. We are all champing at the bit here." The movement was slight but his gaze slanted fleetingly toward Deirdre. A silence fell, threaded by their harsh, hurt breathing, and not knowing where to look, Deirdre backed against the wall.

Naisi was unable to hide the defensive bracing of his body, his hands spread over his thighs, feeling the muscles harden. Ardan swallowed, choking something down, and an instant later he flung his sword-belt alongside his spears and turned on his heel, tossing the door-hide aside.

Naisi did not follow: unable to move, unable to bind anything back together as the pieces slipped between his hands.

Ardan took his bow and snares and did not come back.

Naisi tried to help Deirdre with Ainnle, feeling his brother's forehead with a dark expression, then his shoulders and limbs, as if touching him would knit the riven flesh. He tucked him in their bed like a nestling, piling so many blankets around him that Ainnle flung them off whenever Naisi's back was turned.

At last Deirdre managed to prevail upon Naisi to go hunting for fresh meat, guessing that Ardan would not be returning immediately. In the quietness, at last, she could focus on Ainnle.

The cut was only glancing, but in the field it had begun to turn, the fringes an angry red and the center moist and yellow. It seemed to be paining him far more than he revealed, and so she dosed him with the precious vial of red-flower and bathed the wound. That night he developed a fever, and that combined with the syrup left him muttering in a restless sleep. Deirdre bathed his burning cheeks, desperately sieving her memory for the strongest healing herbs.

Leaving Ainnle the next morning, she searched the woods, lying in a shaft of dappled sun to still her mind and drawing in the scents of soil and leaf-mold. Sinking into the forest floor, she saw that trails of the Source spun brighter swirls around some plants she had not used before.

Deirdre picked those leaves and dug those roots as if in a dream, and when she drank the draft without illness, she felt reassured enough to give it to Ainnle. He gulped it like a child, his skin flushed and taut. Then she sat with him as she had with the horse, and channeled the Source through her own body into his, showing the little stars of blood how to be whole by calling them to hearken to her own flesh. After a long time, he stirred.

His eyes slitted open. "He's never...the same," he slurred. "It's never...three...anymore."

She peered at his pinprick pupils, his eyes glassy. "He loves you," she said softly, wondering if the red-flower dream meant her words might go straight into his heart, bypassing his stubborn mind. "You'd hurt him so much if you were badly harmed, so get well now."

Ainnle's cracked lips stretched into an insensible smile. "Hurt …him?" His mouth turned down. "No…he doesn't care. Not anymore…"

She clasped his clammy hand. "He needs you, Ainnle." After a time his eyelids stopped fluttering and he quieted, slipping into a deeper sleep.

When she checked him again in the night, the herbs had brought the sweat out to bead on his face, taking the fierce heat from his skin into the damp linen sheets. She sponged his torso, and though his breathing was more even, he did not open his eyes.

Two days later the fever was gone and the cut was at last crusting over. She was gathering bandages she had hung over the rafters to dry when Ainnle finally said something beyond grunted replies to her queries about his pain and discomfort. "I should not have worried him," he murmured. "I've never seen him lose his temper like that."

Deirdre glanced at him. He was plucking at the wool blanket with restless fingers, a little furrow between his brows. Now he let out a sigh and rested his hand under his head, turning his face to the heather roof.

"It's just love, Ainnle." She went to the oak shelf pegged in the wall and picked out an earthen pot of goldenrod salve, and taking the yarrow broth sat on a stool, peeling away the pad of sponge-moss from his wound. He winced, his hand jerking. "The only time Fintan, my foster-father, ever raised his voice to me was when I nearly got myself killed," she said.

Ainnle stared at her. "You…nearly did what?"

She smiled, gently dabbing the cut with the yarrow. "I was only five, and a fox had made its den in a little cave in a hill. I was wriggling up, trying to see the cubs, and was about to slide over a cliff when Fintan appeared and pulled me back." She shrugged, amused at Ainnle's amazement.

"So he caught you."

She nodded. "He yelled so loudly that all the game vanished for a week. And then when we got home, it occurred to him I was about to crawl *into* a fox den and if the cliff had not killed me the vixen would have, so he yelled even louder."

Ainnle snorted with reluctant admiration, and Deirdre grinned. "I actually got a birching for that, a whack across one hand, and he had tears in his eyes as he did it."

Ainnle gaped. "That's all? We'd get a whole sapling across our rumps."

"I assume you got up to worse escapades than me, so no doubt the punishments fitted the crimes."

He chuckled. "No doubt."

They were silent for a moment, embarrassed. She smeared the salve on the wound, packed it with more moss and made Ainnle hold the pad while he sat up. Then she eased him to the side of the bed and began winding the bandage around him.

She tried not to touch any part of his body, conscious that the only young man to whom she'd ever got close was Naisi, and the shape of Ainnle's torso and those dark curls at temple and neck were disturbingly familiar. Still, this opening might not come again. "You don't need to fight so hard to make him see you," she said softly. "You don't need to struggle for what you already have, or push others away to gain it."

From the side, she thought he looked a little shamefaced, and pressed her advantage. She could not rid her mind of the anguish in Naisi's eyes when he looked at Ainnle's wound, though at least now he would see what they risked, and there would be no more expeditions. "You and Ardan are his breath and blood; he would not be whole without you." She wound the bandage again. "Don't you remember how your mother suffered when your father died?"

Ainnle was quiet, his chin turned away. "Yes."

"There you go." She tied off the strip of linen and sat back. "Anyway," she added dryly, "I don't have all of him, either, so we are alike there."

His head swung around and he looked at her in surprise, his

eyes for once unguarded. She rinsed her hands in a basin while he eased down his tunic and lay back on the covers. She saw how his rawboned, rangy body was thickening, his shoulders developing the same bulk as Naisi's. He had that same stubborn tilt to his mouth, too, she thought. Then another came out of nowhere. *And he will fight by Naisi's side until his last breath is wrenched from him.* She rubbed a tight spot between her collarbones.

"Naisi has always been a mysterious bast—" Ainnle checked himself. "He's always kept his thoughts close, as if I was too young to understand." His nostrils widened like those of an irritated colt.

"Then we have something else in common, because he isn't telling me much right now, either."

His eyes were wryly amused as he cleared his throat. "I haven't said thank you yet, for tending me." He shrugged his good shoulder. "I suppose it's not a bad thing to have a healer in the house."

"So I have a purpose now?" she observed, throwing the bloodiest bandages on the fire.

He snorted. "I'd probably drive Naisi mad if it wasn't for you keeping him sane."

Naisi had been hovering over Ainnle for days, feeding him a stew from the hind he'd caught and telling him strained stories about when he was small. Bathed in that attention, Ainnle recovered with startling speed. The wound itched as it healed, the salves doing their work even better now that the skin had knitted.

Ardan came back down the mountain trail on the fifth day with a brace of hares across his shoulders, and he was not alone.

Behind him walked an Epidii scout leading a stocky pony laden with food and sleeping hides. "I met him on the trail from Carnach's dun," Ardan told Naisi, throwing the game down beside Deirdre where she changed Ainnle's dressings at the fire. Ardan's cheeks were wind-scoured and his eyes were clearer, as if he had burned off his wrath. "He said he's got a message of great importance for Finn—so important he would not deliver it to me." He cocked a brow at the scout.

The Epidii messenger nodded at Naisi. "I cannot stay; I am on my way across the glen to the southern valleys. Every warrior who can wield a spear is being summoned."

"Why?" The word shot out of Naisi like an arrow from a bow.

Deirdre fixed her gaze on the rug beneath her knees, the thick wool woven in bright colors—another gift from Cinet. She wrapped a loop of linen bandage tight around one finger.

"The Venicones have sent a war-banner to Dunadd." The man's eyes were bright, and he spoke to Naisi as if he delivered an honor. "There will be a battle, the greatest for years, and the king is calling in all warrior oaths to fight at his side. Men are gathering at Dunadd from across the Epidii lands, getting ready to march in a seven-night in full force."

Silence fell in the little firelit hut, and with every moment that passed Deirdre's pulse beat harder, until the tide pushed her to her feet. She did not see the other faces, only Naisi's, and the way his gaze went straight to her. "You can't be serious," she whispered.

Naisi drew himself up, containing himself as he always did. "My brother will give you any supplies you need," he said formally to the scout. "Count your errand fulfilled."

Without another word Naisi walked stiffly out the door, and Deirdre flung the bandages on the bed and followed him. He strode along the path that climbed the hill until they were within the shade of the dappled birch leaves. As soon as they were out of earshot, he turned. "One last fight, *fiáin*." He gritted his teeth, though above them his eyes sought for understanding. "The one I knew was coming—I told you in the woods that night. A chance for a great triumph, not this scuttling about in wind and rain."

"No." Her voice shook. "The last time, Ainnle was wounded. How can you even *think* of fighting again?"

To her horror, part of her was feeling strangely light, already fleeing up the trail to the wild places where there was only the whisper of the *sídhe*, and she could float there, removed from pain. It would be so easy to escape into that Otherworld haze, for so much of her wanted it, had always longed for it. This was how far she had gone from him. The recognition of that staked her to the spot.

Naisi's eyes were smoldering in his tense face, and that long-honed control forced all the suppressed emotion between them back on her. Her voice cracked. "What do you run from so badly that you would leave me? You ride away without a backward glance, *craving* something so much that you will tempt death over and over, senselessly!"

A fine trembling passed beneath his skin. "Nothing I ever do is senseless," he said quietly.

But she was past all hearing. "How can you risk such a sundering of us when I give you all of me?"

The blood rushed to his skin, his nostrils widening. "Do you give me all of you, Deirdre? I don't think so. You take off to commune with who knows what—gods, even when I am here you leave one foot on the floor, to fly from our bed!"

Her eyes stung. "I knew you were afraid of me, what is inside me."

Naisi shook his head. "No, I am not, but when you called the deer, we were together in that, and I felt it, too." His pupils glittered. "And now you say you are mine, but I see in your face when this *thing* takes you over. You long to disappear into the wild, to the *calleach*, to find what you are—and what if you don't come back? If I build no other life than this, what will I be left with?"

They were blindly flinging hurt at each other, making no sense. "I am glad the land calls to me, for I have nothing else to fill my heart when you are away," she cried. "And anyway, I'm sure you're happy I don't trap you like those other girls at Emain Macha." He recoiled as if she had hit some mark and, not knowing what it was, her heart faltered. "Is that what this really is, Naisi? You are tired of me, and this is your way of loosening the bonds between us?"

"As you disappear into the mists on a whim, then run back to me whenever you want?" He stepped forward. "You seek something outside of us, too, Deirdre, and I don't demand that you share every pulse of your heart. It seems that there has been something hidden in your eyes ever since we first came here!"

Her throat burned. "So that is why you leave. Because I have my own mind, my own heart?"

"I told you why I pursue this path." He flung out a hand, and the movement made his black hair fall in his eyes. "I can ask Cinet for more now, settle properly, have a dun, a war-band—"

"I never asked for those things; they are not my future. In fact, I would rather make my own way without them, for they put me in *more* danger, not less."

"You can't survive alone!"

Her fury broke free. "Why not? I *will not* depend on you, I don't need you!"

"And I don't need you!" he roared. "I have oaths to fulfill—kin bonds and family ties. And I can't be *me* hidden away in the wilderness like this!" He was panting, and there were white lines of strain around his mouth.

They stared at each other, appalled that they had stumbled over some boundary that was not meant to be crossed. Naisi tried to retreat, spreading his hands. "Never have I felt for anyone what I do for you. When we are in the bed-furs—"

"We consume each other," she finished in a strangled voice. "And that craving was easy to feel, wasn't it? It eased our pain, Naisi, and blotted out everything else. But what if it burns out?" The fear was terrible but she had to speak it, for it was like a blade against her throat, slowly parting the skin.

Naisi's eyes held a pained warning. "Deirdre…"

"Because now you are clearly consumed by something else." Her hand reached out in some strange impulse, to touch him so she could sink inside and drift among the sparks that made him. "You told me you were proud, but if you do this from blind pride, I can't forgive it. You have to accept what has been—Leary's death, leaving Erin, everything. For no matter how you run, Naisi, you still take it with you."

His jaw lifted like that of a rearing horse, his eyes narrowed. "And if you struggle against a rope, the knots tighten around you,

Deirdre. You are so afraid of being trapped by Conor, by any man, that you never let yourself bind fully to *me*."

Her hands dropped to her belly, crossing there protectively, fingers pressed into the curve of the muscle. "And you're so desperate to be some famous warrior you will chase that at the cost of all else—of the lives of your brothers."

A choked sound was all that leaked from him, as if she had punched him in the chest. He took a faltering step back. "Is that what you think of me?"

The pain in his eyes… "No." She gulped back tears. "That's not what I mean…"

He didn't hear her, a wild, vulnerable hurt flooding his face and wiping away the remnants of his sense. "Gods, you do not trust me. You do not think me worthy of trust." An old, haunted agony looked out at her from his wide eyes, and she desperately tried to cram her thoughts back together into some kind of answer.

But she could not force a single word past the thundering of her heart—because what if he was right? Perhaps she kept a part of herself hidden because she did not trust it with him, didn't understand what drove him.

Naisi saw the truth in her unguarded eyes and he threw his head back, gulping a great breath and then spinning around, staggering away down the path. Deirdre turned slowly, her limbs aching as with a fever, and her hands came out before her blind eyes, pushing the birch branches apart.

She let the twigs scrape on her cheeks and tear at her hair until she could hear nothing but the birds above her, the scent of damp soil dragged into her nostrils by her pained breaths.

CHAPTER 34

In his empty house, Naisi tied his cloak with fumbling fingers. He must get away, for her eyes were so fierce and painfully clear, so piercing, that at any moment she would see all the way into him. And he wasn't ready.

One more battle, and then she could know it all, and she would still love him. For the only thing that was straight was his sword in his hand, and if he threw all he could at this fight, then he would tell Cinet they must build a stronghold now, somewhere near Carnach, in a place that could be defended. And he'd throw *that* in Conor's face, and have the power at last to protect all of them—his brothers, and Deirdre—and make the world *whole*. The word snagged on his heart with a physical pain.

What if it burns out? Her cry was an echo inside his bones. He paused, summoning her to him, her gleaming body in the firelight... no, not that. That was easy. How she was just then on the path, with her face all twisted and tearstained, ugly with pain. He heard her words again, felt the full lash of them this time. *Has it burned out?* Gods, no. She filled him with agony and frustrated rage, and that could only *be* there if the flame still burned. *Deirdre ...Deirdre...* He pressed his thumbs into his forehead, grinding pain away and forcing thoughts back together.

"I heard all that." Ardan had come from seeing off the scout. "It was too loud to miss." He watched Naisi warily.

"It's none of your business," Naisi muttered breathlessly, strapping his sword around his waist.

Ardan took a step toward him. "You blame Deirdre for your pain when it is your own guilt that drives you. You think you set us on this path…" Naisi's body tensed—did Ardan *know*? "But it was Conor who killed Dallan," Ardan went on. "And Conor who killed Leary. You take on too great a burden. You don't share it, so what choice do we have but to fill that gulf our own way?"

Naisi spun around to hold Ardan's gaze. "And what secrets do you keep, brother? What takes you away from me?"

The glint of dark guilt in Ardan's beloved eyes thrust Naisi back. He groped for his cloak so he did not have to see any more. His pack was still there by the door; he had not even had a chance to empty it. "I will make my own way to Dunadd to ready for this battle."

"You can't go alone!"

"You must follow your own hearts; I cannot make decisions that risk you, you are right. And if Ainnle wants to fight, then he needs more time to heal. But I will go, because I gave my promise to Cinet." He paused at the door, staring up at the sun-splashed hill, and all he could think to say was, "Tell her this: I said I will know the day, and it is not this day, this battle. There is no need for that farewell." *Though she might wish it upon me right now.*

"The day of what?"

"She'll know."

"You should damn well tell her yourself!" Ardan called, as Naisi dropped the door-hide behind him.

Conor drove himself into the slave girl and, buried there, reached for his cup and guzzled ale. It spilled down his chin and over the maid's face, onto the pillow, and he drained it and threw it on the floor. He wanted to curl up, drink himself into oblivion, but he had to narrow his mind to the slack breasts jiggling before him so the men in his hall below would catch the faint sounds and know he was still powerful. *Staring at her wet lips so he did not have to remember the dried blood coating Cúchulainn's face.*

The slut turned her cheek to the side, her fist in her mouth, but his responses were dulled and it seemed to go on for an endless time.

The bedcovers were abruptly torn away. "Out!" A staff poked the slave-girl in the leg and she squealed as Conor twisted over. "Out!" Nessa cried, prodding any skin that came within reach. Conor tried to fend off the blows, but the girl kept squawling until she eventually fell off the bed. Nessa hooked her discarded dress and flung it at her, and the whimpering maid fled down the stairs.

Conor sat up, dragging the covers across himself. The room lurched horribly. "What is the meaning of this?" he hissed.

Nessa snorted. "I should be asking you the same thing. I hear that Connacht warriors took a dash over the border for cattle and the guards at the Gates repelled them. And here *you* huddle, sucking on ale and shoving yourself into some stupid slut!" She jabbed the staff toward his groin. "You should ride there yourself, exhort the men to greatness and go on the attack. Burn Connacht's steadings around their ears, and they'll know we are back in our power!"

Conor feebly knocked the staff aside, belching ale fumes. "You've been listening to too many tales," he slurred, his mind slowly spinning.

The staff struck the bed-post so the frame shivered. "For the sake of the gods who made you, forget the girl and that foolish boy. He's skewered her a hundred times already by now, so why do you still want her?"

Conor's nausea stirred.

"Draw your sword and *fight*! *Then* the men might follow you."

Not when they now look on me with such contempt. His drunken thoughts grated, like broken bones rubbing on each other. "They will not follow my lead into battle." His words tumbled out hoarsely. "There are others that stir their hearts." To his horror, he felt an unfamiliar sourness in the back of his throat, his control dissolved by ale.

"That is your own crop you reap, not mine." Nessa's bitter gray eyes swept over him. "Gods, is this what I bred from my body? How can you forge such strength, such control for thirty years, only to lose it all now?"

The ale roiled in Conor's belly and sloshed in his head. Suddenly his legs were under him and he was advancing on his mother, naked. "This is all your doing—"

"I won you your kingdom!"

"You *bought* it by clamping your thighs around mac Roy!" She gaped as he staggered forward, his temples caught in a vice of pain. "And they all know it. You sucked the life from Fergus through his cock, and you sucked the life from me."

She slapped him, sharp and stinging, and his legs collapsed. He fell on all fours. The whirl of his head swept all sense away and surges of pure, mad feeling began surfacing, like rotting things bobbing up from the fetid pool of ale. How could he lose thirty years of control? Because at last he had allowed himself one fleeting moment of pleasure, a release from that vice of discipline, a sliver of an opening to smell one gust of fresh air… *Deirdre*…And through that chink she and Naisi had stabbed him, and the wound would not close and it wept his strength from him.

No. His mind weakly tried to deny it. Not him.

But his body did not listen, throbbing with an older memory of sharp hurt, buried deep. Deirdre's youth and beauty had called to the remnant of his own child-self, the boy that longed for perfection when everything of him was so *flawed*. His slight body, his clumsiness with a sword, his mother shaming him before the warriors. The moment he lost Deirdre, all these old agonies had engulfed him. And now he could not drag himself from their thrall.

The men hate me, his darkest secrets chanted. Worse dregs were lurking at the bottom of that pit, however, and instead of words his belly convulsed and a stream of sour ale splashed over his hands. *For I didn't earn my throne in blood, in bravery.* The pain of years forced more vomit from him. His mother thought she'd given him the greatest prize, but it was a hollow triumph. A woman gave his power to him and trickery kept it, and he was sick of it all. He wanted something pure and unsullied for once, like

Cúchulainn's battle-fire. Like Fergus's rousing songs with his warriors.

Like Deirdre, her glow spreading through him like sunlight, washing this darkness from him forever.

The shrine to the Father God, the Dagda, smelled musty from the sheaves of barley that had decorated its altar. The air was hazy with chaff and Conor had to suppress a cough and rub his throat, his knees aching on the rushes.

In the harvest rite, the king was hailed in ritual words to praise his fertility and his safeguarding of wealth and fruitfulness for all. His people had gazed up at him hollow-eyed that morning, though, for he was merely a husk that spoke with no life. And there was no queen beside him, swelling with child.

Afterward, he stumbled to the Dagda's shrine. He could not face the great temple and the goddess Macha's faceless, accusing presence. He needed the king of the gods.

This smaller hut was dark and comforting, the daub walls curved close, the roof-posts a grove of silent trees. It was lit by tallow candles on a stone plinth that held the silver rowan branch, the gold bowl of blessed water and the spoons filled with salt. Behind it another oak pillar was set in the ground, invoking the Tree that held up the universe of Thisworld and Otherworld, its roots in the depths of earth, its branches in the heavens.

Conor had been praying on his knees all afternoon, muttering so many pleas he had sent himself into trance. The acid of the ale burned his breast and his tongue was gritty, his head pounding. Manannán, Lugh and the Dagda—he was utterly beaten. Only the gods could give him a way out now. For a breath, he was filled with panic at the thought that in the Otherworld they might actually scorn him, and he would not eat at their table. *Help me.*

Something white glimmered behind the altar and Conor's head jerked up. The lamp-flame hissed as something was thrown on it and a stream of thick smoke obscured the room. Through the smoke he made out a hazy figure that glowed with a much larger outline than a person, and his pulse began to race again.

"You have come here for salvation. Ask what you will." A woman's voice, was his first thought. But no. As it spoke it lowered, and became more sonorous, neither male nor female but imbued with a resonance beyond human capacity, vibrating as if from the air itself. It was the gods speaking through one of the druids…or the Dagda himself, revealed to Conor because he was a good king, a just king.

Conor felt that divine essence wrapping about him in the smoke, prising open his soul. "I have lost my way," he stammered. And even as the uttering of defeat at last left his tongue, the poison began to seep away from his blistered flesh.

The voice floated from the shadows. "The gods see all." The white figure drifted in and out of focus through the smoke, a light emanating from the altar and its pale robes so he could see nothing clearly. Was it Cathbad, come to hear his confession? An arm lifted, and a finger pointed at him like a spear piercing his breast to expose his beating heart. "For your relief, they need the truth from you."

The truth? Conor passed a hand over his dry lips, thirsting for that promised ease of pain, and it all rushed out of him. "I craved her sweet flesh in my bed, to touch and taste, to bury my body in hers. Aye, I did! I wanted to fill her, possess her, and for the men to bow to me for commanding such a woman."

Cold air touched his neck—was it a god's hand? "There is more," the wraith intoned. "There is a man, cloaked in the darkness of your hate."

Closing his eyes, Conor made himself picture Naisi, and when the blackness surged up he forced himself to look it in the face. "I am withered by age, and…I was jealous of the women's love of his smooth skin, his black hair."

There was a soft hiss of admonition. "That is not all." The spear-tip dug into Conor again. *The gods could see inside him, pierce him with their light.* "Let thy burden go," the whisper came again.

Panting, Conor scrutinized Naisi's face. Those long, narrow

eyes glowed with intensity, and that refined nose lifted high, like a fine-blooded horse, with challenge. With strength. "The warriors loved him." He thought he might die from strangling fury, and his thoughts splintered. *All the young ones looked to Naisi...even Fiacra.* There was power in Naisi's eyes, and a hunger to inspire. Conor's truth crushed him, bowing him over his pained knees. He'd been a weak child, his mind his only weapon, and he had disdained what he could not have, what he hungered for—to win kingship with a sword, so the men's eyes glowed, too, when they looked at him.

"Yes," the voice breathed. "Feel it all."

Conor's belly cramped and in the wake of hate came shame, a tidal surge of it, hot and bitter. Self-disgust was a stink in his own nostrils: for being controlled by these desires, for fearing the young. He was a king; he should have been stronger. There was a rustle of robes and a hand came down on his brow in blessing. It felt thinner and lighter than he had anticipated, given the throbbing weight of that godly presence. "That is truth," he heard the gods speak. "At last."

The touch on his head, the forgiveness, undid him, and he did not know how much time passed in that paroxysm of shame. His eyes clenched as if they wanted to squeeze out tears, though none came, and a silent sob was caught in his gullet. At long last, the pain began to ebb, the burden lifting enough for him to breathe. The hand retreated, as did the footsteps.

Conor leaned on wrists and knees, gasping, and at last crawled painfully upright. His thoughts grew clearer. He remembered Lughnasa and the disappointment on people's faces. He saw his mother, bony hands poking at him, contempt in her eyes. Dizzily it all came together, and it was like the sun rising, and his sight was filled with the wavering candle-flame, the temple receding into shadow.

His kingship was corrupted by a woman from its very birth. His warrior blood was sullied before he ever felt it running through him, bled out by her ambition and greed, by duty and his own hopelessness.

Now the balance must be redressed, yes, by a sacred union with the Goddess, in the person of a divine maiden untainted by Nessa's worldly lusts. He *must* find Deirdre, because only then could he free himself from his mother's original corruption, cleanse his kingdom with the blessing of Macha. As the counterpoint to the dark mother to whom he'd been born he would turn to light, and *Deirdre* would give him the power to hold the warriors with sheer force of personality, making him unassailable.

"If my kingship is faltering," he said hoarsely, "if I have been led astray by lust and envy, then I have to return to what a king truly is." The air glimmered with possibility.

"Oh, my son." That voice came from behind him and he opened his eyes and twisted about. He blinked, the glamor clearing to show Cathbad hobbling up the aisle as if he had only just come inside the shrine. Conor turned toward the narrow eastern doorway but there was no one there now...no robed god cloaked in smoke and fire.

He turned to Cathbad, wiping his face. The chief druid also spoke for the gods...all the priests did. Did it matter who had been taken by the divine spirit to offer him comfort? Cathbad was wheezing, slowly limping. The old man had been getting weaker with the many chest fevers that gripped him, and now his eyes were cloudy and the strength was melting from his wasted face.

"What did you teach me about the inauguration of kings?" Conor bowed his head to Cathbad.

The chief druid grasped his staff in two hands to brace himself, coughing. "The mound of Macha is the breast of the Goddess, and in the rites a king must be wedded to the Goddess of the land in divine blessing." His voice rattled with phlegm.

Conor smiled with relief, his cheeks aching from that unfamiliar expression. "You also said a man becomes king by vowing to ward the three realms: those of spirit, war and fruitfulness of the land." His mind galloped on, leaving the shadow of shame behind. "Lost in lust and folly, I did not ward the realms and so disaster creeps upon the Ulaid. I did not listen to you, my teachers of spirit. I do not lead the warriors, for they do not trust me. And people are afraid to pasture their stock and till their fields for fear of Connacht. Worst of all, I broke my vow to the goddess and do not have a divine bride at my side to shower the land with fertility."

As a shadow of confusion crossed Cathbad's face, Conor stepped forward. "*This* is what you felt in Deirdre, Father. *She* is the Goddess incarnate!" He stared hungrily into the darkness to see if he could conjure a shimmering image of her. "I have been chasing her for my loins, but the gods have shown me my folly. She was meant to be the goddess for us all—and when she stands in the temple of Macha with me, my joining with the Source will be complete. She will be treasured and loved, and the land will be reborn." Though he was exhausted by his fervor, the shining pattern unwound in him, filling him. She must come back in honor and state, not beneath a cloud of shame. Once she saw that the Ulaid's safety hinged on her taking up her divine fate, she would bend her head for the crown of flowers, he was sure. Once she knew this was not about an old man's lusts but about the gods, then she would understand.

"It…is possible." Cathbad passed a trembling hand over his eyes. "But you presume too much, my son. And what of Naisi?"

Conor looked to the world tree for strength. "The gods showed me. He is a true warrior, loved by my men for fighting and hunting. He must return with his honor restored to stand beside Deirdre and me on this mound and link us, king and queen, to the battle-throng."

Cathbad's breathing was labored. He groped behind him for a bench and sank on it, resting his head on the mud wall, his cheeks flushed. "You must…set them free because it is the right thing to do, my son. You cannot control them…not their hearts, nor their flesh. The natural order must be restored. Don't bring them back. There is foreboding in me…" His voice cracked and he coughed again.

Conor sat next to him and gripped Cathbad's hand, the bones beneath his fingers brittle, the joints swollen. "You don't understand. In view of everyone, I will kiss Naisi and give him a position of high honor in the Red Branch, and he can lead his own dun, as his father wanted. Those boys are Red Branch and they will sicken without it, and the Red Branch without them. Cúchulainn even said so; he said to bring them back. This *is* the natural order. And when Deirdre sees how she can mend what was riven, I know she will want to fulfill her destiny!"

Cathbad tried to speak again, forcing air from his clogged chest. "We do not know what they will feel. You must force them to do nothing—"

"You never saw her as a woman. You have not seen what I have …the dance, the Goddess shining from her. If you had, you would know you were right all along—and that she is here not to bring ruin, but grace." He leaned in to kiss Cathbad reverently on both cheeks and leaped up, full of renewed vigor. "The efforts to find them will be doubled, tripled, I don't care how much it costs me in gold!"

He hastened to the door, and Cathbad's voice struggled up weakly from behind. "If you bring them back, you must let them be their true selves, and follow their own hearts."

Conor barely heard, breaking outside and drinking in fresh air. *Lift this blight of jealousy from me*, he prayed. He saw himself standing with Deirdre and Naisi, holding their hands up as one. And in his warriors' eyes he would see the shine of pride, at last.

Levarcham was already back at her fireside, unsteadily feeding the flames with scented resins to shake off that profound healing trance that had overcome her in the shrine. She had followed Conor as she often did, like a crow watching him from the trees, but when she saw him at last break…heard his prayers…she was filled with the first hope that had come to her since Deirdre fled.

The energy that surged through her…the godly voice that deepened her own…it felt like truth, Conor's truth. If no one here had been able to reach him, then perhaps at last the gods had done so.

She had felt his shame and self-disgust inside her own body, sensed the tide of his spirit changing as he knelt before the Dagda's altar. Now he had seen the degradation of his madness, and surely would release the fugitives and they could come back with their honor restored.

Deirdre, Deirdre.

The song filled her now and she allowed tears to pool in her eyes, though they dried in the heat of the fire before they could fall.

CHAPTER 35

The challenge rang out from war-horns cast in stallion-heads of bronze, the leering snouts flashing the blazing sun over the battle hordes as they blared a cacophony of fury and defiance.

The Epidii had drawn up their forces below mountain slopes splashed with bright swathes of heather. At its base, the hill flattened into an immense, boggy plain covered in pale sedges and red marsh grass, the ground pockmarked and sodden. On the other side of a brown stream, the Venicones army were massing in kind, their trumpets wolf-headed and howling.

The air was hazed by clouds of insects that whirled up from marshy pools, and a breeze wafted over snatches of sound from the Venicones lines, a murmuring hum of taunts that sounded like bees swarming. The darkness of their cloaks, hide armor and hair was shot through with the glitter of spear-tips and swords. A gleam of gilded helmets and fur pennants marked out the nobles in their chariots behind the foot warriors, their banners wrought with wolves in outline, green and black.

Naisi and his brothers were gathered on a knoll making their last preparations before joining the ranks, divesting themselves of tunics and sword-belts, leaving them clad only in leather breastplates, war-caps and trews tightly bound up the thigh with buckhide thongs. Kneeling to his boots, Naisi was calculating the number of enemy when Ardan moved up beside him, removing a piece of grass from his mouth to remark, "Five hundred, by my reckoning."

Their minds had always run as one. Naisi rested his chin on his knee, breathing out, before standing next to his brother and gazing out, hands on hips. Ardan had convinced Ainnle to wait for his wound to knit at home for a few more days, during which Naisi had spent his time at Dunadd training Carnach's men. His brothers had arrived the day the army left for the battlefield, and Naisi and Ardan had only exchanged curt words since.

Now they were standing before this immense wall of men, that unspoken rift had turned into a bodily ache. Ainnle darted looks between the other two, his brows lowered. On the march, Naisi had questioned his ability to fight, only to be forcefully told that the wound was strapped and it wasn't Ainnle's sword-side, and that was that. Naisi gave in, satisfying himself that Ainnle wasn't wincing in his line of sight.

As the Venicones trumpets blared again in a discordant screech, Ainnle turned on his brothers. "If we fight, it has to be together." He stared hard at them both. "You are driving me insane."

Naisi snorted and looked down at his feet, kicking his heel into a clod of dirt. His blood had already begun to pump faster, making his temples thud. He could sense his muscles coiling up, his hands tingling for the heft of the sword. They had to join as Red Branch or it was dangerous, and he had weakened them enough. He cocked his head at Ainnle, squinting into the sun. "That makes a welcome change from you," he said wryly.

Ainnle pretended to scowl as he did when a boy, and Naisi went to cuff him behind the ear. When Ainnle ducked with a grin, Naisi caught him instead and held him close. Ainnle squirmed and thumped his back. "Gods, don't break my arms, I need them!"

Naisi let him go, and without looking in his face he turned for Ardan, and Ardan moved at the same time so they met forcefully in an embrace of men. Naisi closed his eyes. *Forgive me.* It was more fervent inside him than he could ever say.

Another face hovered there over Ardan's shoulder, close enough to touch. The plea for forgiveness had to wing its way to her, too, before he risked his life. The ghostly sigh of death that blew over the ranks before battle brought feelings into sharp relief, and he was sick with regret that he had allowed his hurt to drive him from her like that. *Fiáin. My wild one. Mine.* He would make her see that after this, when he drew her back to him with the force of his heart.

Ardan's eyes were bright when they broke away, and he held Naisi's arms for a moment. "It's yourself you must forgive, or you will not be strong."

The enemy began to roar, and Naisi looked to the gleaming ranks of swords they held to the sky, the light rippling along the blade-tips like the sun on ocean waves. "I do not know how." It slipped out, naked and despairing.

"There are some things we just have to accept," Ardan murmured.

"Yes," Naisi said, meeting his eyes, and after a moment it was Ardan's turn to look away. They faced the battlefield, leaving a hand on each other's shoulders before dropping them.

"What we need," Ainnle said fervently, twirling his unsheathed sword, "is to be back in civilization, so Ardan and I can have two women apiece—at least."

Ardan smiled and laced his own boots, while Naisi stretched his arms out, one by one. "Then may the greatest fight yet bring the greatest rewards," he said, and at last caught up his sword. *Manannán fill you,* he murmured to the cold blade. *Lugh fire you. The Dagda strengthen you.*

When Cinet met with his commanders at Dunadd, Carnach had named Naisi the second-in-command of his men—a choice

Cinet endorsed with a strange smile, promptly honoring Carnach and his men with a position at the center of battle. After all, Carnach told Naisi, his warriors had not stopped talking of the brothers, and everyone was clamoring to have them join their war-band. As soon as they were ready, the brothers therefore made their way through the noisy ranks of the Epidii to the first lines. Carnach turned to them and grinned, his polished iron helmet boasting a crest of black horse-hair that fell to his waist.

Naisi could feel the eyes of the Epidii warriors fixed on his back. He and his brothers were winning a name, even if it wasn't their own. Soon they would be strong enough to say the truth aloud once more. *The blood of Usnech would be restored to them.*

He turned and scanned the Epidii forces with narrowed eyes. Their banners depicted a white mare on a blue background, and they were covered in the marks of the horse: tail tufts that hung from braids and spear-tips, manes stuck to helmets, stallion hides padding out shoulders and splashing torsos with mottled hues of brown and black. Studded breast-plates were decorated with horse-teeth and ochered bones clattered around necks. All the men's tattoos had been freshly drawn with iron dyes during four nights of ritual singing on the plain of Dunadd, and the scything arcs and spirals shaped their faces into fierce masks.

On the hill behind, Cinet stood on a war-chariot that had been laboriously dragged over the mountains. The wicker sides had been painted orange and the hubs were gilded. His weapons and those of his guards were also polished in bronze and gold so the sun itself appeared to have come to rest there, a defiant sign of favor from the gods.

The noise of the battle rousing was swelling now, the Epidii screaming and spitting curses at the Venicones, smashing their spear-butts into the ground to drive themselves into a frenzy. The clash of swords on shields punctuated the throb of war-drums, the trumpets all ululating like banshees. Druids walked up and down the ranks, arms raised, and the warriors joined in with their chants to the gods.

Naisi was pleased to see that amid the chaos, Carnach's men were staring stonily at the Venicones army, mustering their energy, their bodies humming with it. There had been no possibility of forging a Red Branch bond in so short a time, but Naisi had urged them to focus their power, concentrating it and then expanding it outward to encompass their sword-mates. As he spoke to them, he had been filled with the memory of what it felt like in a great mass of warriors, and his long-dammed passion had fired his words.

And so the Epidii felt a glimpse of it, at last.

Cinet's heavy legs were aching. The sun baked his head inside his helmet, tightening his scalp with a sharp headache. His ringmail was so tight he'd had to loosen the bindings, and with the bands squeezing his arms he felt stiff as a beetle in a shell.

The vibration of the war-drums thrummed in his ears and down below his warriors shouted insults, puffing themselves up so their necks swelled. Men were thrown up on one another's shoulders and borne aloft before sinking back into the heaving crowd. On the flanks, riders held fractious horses at bay.

Cinet's heart strained to burst free, but he would not be pounding down the slope into the fray. It had been a few years since he had been able to fight for hours: too many luxuries had come his way, too much feasting to placate nobles and envoys. He could not claim the glory of this day, something in him muttered. But that would soon change. He would invigorate himself with *her*.

"If we leave it much longer, the heat will sap our blood," Bridei observed from his horse.

Cinet reined his thoughts back with an angry grunt. These men were fighting for *his* name. "Sound the advance," he growled, gripping the sides of the chariot and standing tall so his men could see their king. His nephew yanked his horse about and set it down the slope.

The massed trumpets skirled as one and the drummers beat

out the rhythm of marching feet. The warriors grew more enraged until they were screaming in fury, their spears waving in
glittering lines, the banners sweeping across the sky.

Now the Venicones were on the move, all of them breaking into
a trot, and with bellows and screeches Cinet's army joined the
rush, the horse-riders curling around the ranks of foot-fighters.
From the king's vantage point, it seemed as if the entire hillside
was collapsing into the valley beneath his feet.

His front ranks splashed across the stream and through the
shallow pools, the sun scattered by the frothing water. Cinet
stopped breathing as the armies rolled toward each other, and instead pushed all his will into his army to give them strength.

Naisi plunged toward the Venicones lines, his feet pounding in
time with those of his brothers. Their three swords reached out
like the fangs of one great beast, and they paused at the same
point to fling their spears. The ash lances soared into the sky,
raining down on the Venicones army along with Epidii spears
and a glittering hail of arrows.

Red Branch! Red Branch! the three brothers shouted, though it
was lost amid the bellows of the Epidii warriors around them. As
Carnach's men raced across the plain Naisi sensed a faint flicker
of the same connection he'd had with his old comrades. He
watched the Venicones coming at him in a whirl of flashing
blades, picked a target—a yowling, black-haired fighter—and relaxed into white light. The sunburst was so bright that all the
background shapes and colors and even sounds receded, leaving
only his brothers.

He was conscious of Ainnle on his left more as a shift in the
air, a presence that pushed against Naisi's awareness, and when
Ainnle swung his arm Naisi felt his own muscles clench. On the
other side, he knew when Ardan's body tensed to strike, for
Naisi's own lungs sucked in a deep breath. Sparks traveled along
his limbs and into his brothers' bodies, joining their flesh. They

were one again…and for a moment he floated in the ecstasy that encompassed them all.

Then his focus narrowed to the spiral tattoo on his opponent's snarling face as it raced toward him, and the blue circle began to spin in Naisi's mind as if his own body was an arrow soaring toward a target. Just before the front ranks of the armies collided, the sunburst around the enemy warrior shimmered, signaling to Naisi that the man's shield arm would drop, not rise, to halt Naisi's feint. As the Venicones shoved his shield down to block the lunge, Naisi switched and unexpectedly sprang high, his sword shaving down from the spiral target to bury itself in the man's throat. Before the echo of the collision of armies had faded from the peaks, Naisi's first enemy was down.

Naisi killed Ardan's second attacker while Ardan turned to his third. Ainnle, meanwhile, surprised his own opponent with a backward swipe, knocking his shield aside and sliding in beneath. It seemed madness, but everyone else was fighting high, so while Ainnle's enemy desperately cast about for him in the chaos, Ainnle thrust his sword up between his legs, cutting off his bellow.

Ainnle jumped up, screeching, and stuck Naisi's next attacker in the back, and he fell in the tangle of bodies. All three brothers glanced at one another, panting, the Source glinting in their eyes like stars.

The stink of blood and loosed bowels, urine and sweat assaulted Naisi's nostrils, and he coughed and lifted his face to the sky to gulp a sweet breath. All around him, the crowds were a mass of writhing limbs, and at his feet severed pieces of flesh and squirming bodies were lost in a sea of churned mud and blood. White faces were splashed with gore, mouths opened in hoarse screams. Swords came from all directions, the sheen of iron already nocked and pitted, and streaked with scarlet. Broken spear-ends were thrust at him and arrows whizzed over his head.

Despite the chaos, Naisi could see that Carnach's band were keeping to his orders with determination. They fought back to back, and there were flickers of light around them now—licks of

molten fire that flowed together for moments and then broke
apart. Glimpses of the Red Branch. Whereas the rest of the lines
had splintered, Carnach's band still held together as a knot, fighting outward.

Deirdre had been lying so close to the fire that her lips had dried
and cracked. She brushed them dazedly with a finger and felt the
ridges of broken skin. For days, the flames had played out her
emotions, writhing in flares and gouts of vivid red and orange,
the veins of wood splitting, the resins spitting and popping. The
fire roared up with every draft from the door-hide, then hissed
out her buried fears in tiny jets of flame.

At last it burned down to coals, which radiated a steady glow
on her face. *Naisi.* She heard his voice as a breath in the shadows
and her head snapped around.

You never let yourself bind fully to me.

Even when I am here you leave one foot on the floor to fly from our bed.

You long to disappear into the wild.

A gasp leaked from her, the first sound she had made for days.
She dragged her feet under her and she was standing, her legs
shaking. All anger had gone; the fire had taken it. Now she saw
him again, his dark hair framing his cheekbones, his gaze unwavering. And it wasn't desire for that skin and body that flooded
her, but the terrible knowing that the light in those eyes *was* him.
He did reveal himself to her, for it was there in the lambent
depth of his glances, the crooked smiles. It was in the gentleness
in his hands when he tucked the furs around her. She had become so enamored of the unfolding world inside her, the light
falling through the veils, that she *had* turned some part of herself
from him.

She felt a tear on her cheek and touched it, tasting it on
her tongue to understand the truth. *Gods, Naisi, let me hold your
face again, and I will not let you go from my heart, no matter how far you
wander.*

She crept outside, the light hurting her eyes, and moved to the lip of the hill on unsteady legs. It was a strange, ghostly day that only Alba's extremes of cold and damp could conjure. Although the sky was clear directly above her, a dense bank of mist had settled over the loch. The upper reaches of the hills and the far mountains were glowing in sunshine, mottled with heather, but the water and shore were obscured by an impenetrable veil of vapor.

She stared at it, and turned her head to where the high meadow was lifted to the sun by the peaks. Everything would be drawn in sharp relief there by the clear light, she knew: the leaves and grass sparkling with dew; the glitter of the veins that ran through the standing stone; the *sídhe* dancing like sunlit insects over the stream. Familiar ... warm and enveloping.

She did not have to consciously decide; her steps simply took her the other way, down the steep path to the shore and the thick curtains of mist.

As she got closer, the cold from that bank of fog breathed over her cheeks, and the vapor swirled, halting her. She and Naisi were not only light and fire, the bright patterns easily read by a body saturated with desire. What also joined them was subtle and baffling, difficult and fearful ... yes, fearful. And her courage had failed and she'd turned from those mists where the truth of her heart was hidden.

She could not seek him at the stone, in the sun. She had to seek him here.

Deirdre paused with her hand out, swirling the droplets as if to form his face. But that was not courage. She still lingered on the fringes, the boundaries of the veils between child and woman. She knew the borders well, but now she had to allow herself to lose her way.

Deirdre threw herself into the clammy fog and stumbled along, knowing only that she traced the shoreline by the ghostly lapping of the water. She could see nothing and kept one hand out to grope through the drifting mist. The path was littered with rocks and puddles—in the daylight she skipped from one to another, fleet and sure of herself. Now she could see only what was right under her and so she tripped and fell, barking shins and grazing palms on the stones.

The mist clogged her throat, creeping into her lungs to strangle her with an instinctive panic. She fought it, seizing that primitive desire to flounder her way back to the light and brutally crushing it. *Naisi.* Her feet hit a low wall and she fell on it, scraping her knuckles, and hauled herself back on her knees in the grass. Weathered oak trunks shadowed the mist all around her; she'd wandered into a copse of them. She heard a faint trickling beneath a pile of wind-blown branches. A spring.

She became aware of a thickening in the atmosphere, a stirring of power like a whirlpool that anchored her at its heart. The burbling grew louder, seeping right through her, the ripples running from feet to head. She pulled away the fallen branches and dense sludge of leaves, wiping mist from her eyes. The stones had been placed there by human hands to form a tiny pool.

Deirdre peered at a worn carving in one of the stones. Her hand was drawn to it, as if its heart pulled her flesh toward it. At last she cupped the spiral and heat pulsed through her palm, and with it came a snatch of vision: a woman leaning over to scatter a blessing of flowers in the spring, weaving magic with a breathy song. The woman's necklace fell from her gown as she bowed…a crescent of pearl shell…a moon-crescent. A Goddess sign. The woman cradled the necklace before plunging her hands into the water—and the image guttered out. A wisewoman, a druid.

Desperately, Deirdre leaned over to cradle the spiral with both hands and, as if the sun was burning off the mist, the droplets of vapor ignited into an iridescent cloud. Dazzled, Deirdre gazed around her as the world turned silver and the oak trees were clad in their glimmer, and the spring was sheened as if by moonlight.

A star came flying out of the oak leaves, hovering so close to her eyes that she was blinded. Instinctively, her hand went up to shield her face. The *sídhe*'s light pulsed before her—twinkling, capricious—and as it flew off, it threw a mantle of light around her, pulling the pinprick of her consciousness from her body and sweeping her with it.

The *sídhe* soared between the substance of existence in graceful spirals. It streaked ahead of Deirdre, growing smaller and more incandescent as the motes of Source around them became larger.

Pulled in its rippling wake, Deirdre sank through the glittering rafts of air and then they were stars, and she flew through a night sky. Then she saw that each spark was a moment, an instance of time caught in light. The streams of moments stretched not in a single path but in nets spreading out in every direction. She focused harder, and saw how the webs curved and folded, bending back on themselves in endless whirlpools and starlit peaks.

She once saw through water to Naisi fighting in another place ... but now she flew close to the star-dust with the *sídhe* and saw herself and Naisi in other times. There were fleeting glimpses of glances passed between them, and touches. Walking through dappled woods, hands linked. A gleam of firelight on their faces, moisture on their lips. These were memories she already held in her heart, and here they drifted among the sparks of Source, caught like moths in amber.

The life-force of the *sídhe* felt not tiny and flickering now but immense, amused, and it lifted her toward knowing with its light, as once Levarcham did with words. There was no straight line of *before* or *after;* somehow all points of time spiraled around one another in the same instant, past and future. All the many possibilities of every moment existed in the droplets circling around the eternal moment of One. With Thisworld senses, people could only perceive one of every time-droplet. But now, if she sought it, she was sure she could look into what she knew as before and after. Immediately, she thought of going *back*...to where many of these priestess women sang over the spring and carved the rock spiral. Back...so she could use their magic to send protection to Naisi.

Instead, she felt a tug and she was flung in an entirely different direction.

The specks of Source streaked past her like falling stars, their swirling patterns dizzying, until at last she collided with a flaming ball of light that shattered all around her. And she was enveloped by a *moment*, the fragments of streaming silver forming up into shapes that her mind could understand.

It was night.

There was a vague blur of a black sky and below it the lurid glow of flames against wooden buildings. She was floating above it, and now she looked down. Naisi was there, on his knees. His black hair curled around his pale neck as he bent his head. Deirdre's mouth opened to scream a warning before she even felt the terrible *wrongness* of the moment, and then the sense of it crushed her and her scream was silent.

Naisi's shoulders were already bowing, and his arms clutched at his belly. Dark figures clamored around him, howling and baying like wolves. She wanted to drag them all away to get to him, but then they fell back and she did see it all...

The firelight glanced off polished iron and glistened on smears of wet blood as the long sword was drawn out of Naisi's body, to the sound of a great cheer.

Cinet was trying to make sense of the chaos with his older captains when Bridei came thundering back on his pony, red hair flying from under his helmet.

"Do we have the field?" Cinet bellowed, peering through the mass of ragged pennants.

"Not yet," Bridei crowed, "but see what Carnach and Finn are doing!"

The armies swarmed about like ants, and at first it was hard to discern anything. Ruddy Epidii heads were mixed in with dark Venicones; the banner of the wolf lay shredded and tangled with the Mare. Then Cinet saw that Carnach and his men had not splintered like all the others, and he recognized what could only be seen from the slopes above: Carnach's warriors had made a fist of men that punched through the ranks of the Venicones, driving to the left of battle.

Bridei rose in the saddle. "They are outflanking them, and the Venicones bastards don't realize they are there!"

The conversation of the guards around Cinet became an excited rumble. Carnach's warriors were curving around the rear of a large group of the enemy, driving them into the paths of the Epidii riders, who herded them back on themselves to be crushed between both pincers of men. The Venicones warriors soon realized their retreat was being cut off and they panicked, fighting desperately but also tangling weapons and feet, tripping over one another as they were squeezed ever tighter between Carnach's fighters and the Epidii horsemen.

Bridei let out a hoarse war-cry. "We must do the same at the other side!" he yelled, and before Cinet could speak he was racing down to the right to exhort the Epidii commanders there to launch the same tactics. The Venicones army was soon outflanked on both sides, their men pushed into a slippery mire of blood and sprawled bodies.

At last their battle-horns blared out a desperate retreat.

Avidly, Cinet watched his army decimate that of his enemies and the saliva ran over his tongue. He clutched his scabbard as the sun caught the sides of hundreds of Epidii swords held aloft, the great flash filling him with fire. *He* would go down and touch the blood to his brow now, and claim the victory!

At that moment, one chant arose to Cinet's ears from the roar of battle-cries and screams of pain. The Epidii king paused on the slope and found he was swaying, the sound driving through his chest.

Fla dor ca! Fla dor ca!

Deirdre came back to herself by the spring, her hands clawing at her own neck to release her strangled breath, her jaw strained by her silent cry. She tore the rest of the broken twigs and leaves out of the water and plunged her face in, gulping at it to free her throat.

What she'd seen was already receding into the dark recesses of her mind, fleeing her sight. All she knew was what her heart continued to hammer out: danger stalking Naisi, a treachery he did not see coming. Not battle and screeching enemies after all but... betrayal.

Cinet...the Epidii.

She wiped the water fiercely from her cheeks, gasping. It hadn't happened yet; she had only glimpsed into future moments that might be. Her broken mind clutched at that; they were only possibilities. Her fingers grasped the rocks placed there by other hands so long ago. A faint vibration of chanting seeped into her from the stones, chinks of memory caught in the fabric of this valley, embedded in oak and mist. *Sister...* Was that a whisper, or a breath of longing from her own heart for a belonging she once had?

She rested her cheek on the cold rock. She had not understood she was bound to Naisi through time and the many worlds, through soul-life. *No.* It was guttural, that moan—a denial with all the power she possessed. Her eyes opened.

The gleaming stars of Source were drifting all around her now, and they were not flames but spheres. She could see them with her own body's eyes. They floated like raindrops, turning slowly on their axes. And in the glowing droplets she saw the moments of the past that were anchored *here:* women circling this pool with offerings in their hands.

One by one they hovered over the spring and scattered in flowers, milk and grain. They also dropped in gold, rings that kings gave to the forest and the *sídhe* of the pool. In return for those gifts, Deirdre saw the women—*priestesses*—standing on tomb mounds of the ancestors, taking the light of the Source into themselves from the earth and focusing it into a stream of blessing that they radiated out to the people.

Deirdre pushed herself up on her arms, the water dripping from her hair. The flame the wisewomen gathered for the people was...warding, protection, love. She saw them dancing, bending lithe bodies like trees in the wind and leaping and spinning as animals, invoking the powers of the goddess earth to bless their clan. Deirdre was on her feet now, absorbed into the flow of that ancient dance.

And at last, she felt the true power she had forgotten.

The Venicones horns were still blasting a retreat, and more and more of the enemy were breaking away to flee. The Epidii army let out hoarse screams and streamed after them, cutting them down from behind.

Naisi had little heart for massacres during retreats and he pulled back, his brothers slowing with him until they all halted together to catch their breath. The field spread out in an ocean of bloodied turf scattered with broken bodies. Warriors lay in piles of tangled limbs, arms hacked, scarlet whorls pooling across exposed chests.

"Water," Ainnle puffed, extracting his feet from the bodies piled around his ankles. Naisi's hilt was so slick with gore he could barely hold it. He dragged his hands down his trews one by one, and wiped his sweat from his brow on his shoulder. The three of them staggered toward a trickling stream that crossed the plain, picking their way between Epidii warriors who were tending the wounded and swarming over the dead, stripping off weapons and armor.

The water ran red but they found a place upstream and pulling off their caps plunged in knee-deep, bending to splash their burning faces and bare arms, lapping at it with dry tongues. The icy water cleared the last vestiges of the battle frenzy and Naisi scrubbed dried blood from his cheeks and blinked his sore eyes. He heard the roaring of many men and lifted his dripping head.

Fla dor ca! Fla dor ca!

Someone grabbed his arms from behind.

Mired in the gore of the battlefield, Cinet snapped his head around. Epidii warriors had plucked Finn out of the stream and hoisted him on their shoulders, while all the men about him cheered madly.

Carnach was now clambering over the raised arms, crowing with laughter as he clapped an iron helm on Finn's dripping bare head. The helmet was heavy and ornately worked in iron banded with bronze and copper. Its crest was a leaping wolf with paws out and bared teeth—the mark of Venicones royalty.

At first Finn struggled to get down, embarrassed, while his brothers screeched and shouted encouragement. The faces of all the young men around them were alight with bloodlust and triumph, their eyes glowing.

The heat in Cinet's blood was extinguished, the lingering images of the girl instantly wiped from his mind. How could he not have foreseen this danger stalking him from behind? A wolf, yes, and there he was—a black one with snapping jaws. It should be the king of Dunadd and Lord of the Isles who was so honored; it should be Bridei, his heir, hoisted on those shoulders.

Finn had been squirming to get down, but then a change came over him. He gave up struggling and sat straight, flinging dripping hair from his flushed cheeks. Over the heaving crowd, Cinet saw the savage flash of hunger in his eyes.

For this. For more.

Deirdre stood knee-deep in the loch, her hands falling open by her sides. Something glimmered through the last shreds of the breaking mist, pure and white, softly gliding.

The pair of swans carved an arrow over the glassy surface, paddling close together as they had all sunseason. Their gray cygnets lingered farther back, dipping their long necks to the bottom of the shallows. Deirdre watched the mated pair sail past her, and the ripples of their wake touched her finger-tips with a jolt of cold wakefulness. She looked down and saw the drifting feather and, picking it up, held it before her. It was white like the glow of the moon's face, the white goddess. As she brushed the silky tip against her cheek, the dance of the women again wove through her mind: the most sacred dance of all. Priestess and king.

Her legs sparked into life and she was clambering ashore, staggering at first then leaping over the rocks that with the lifting of the fog were bathed in sun. Urp and Arda looked up at her from their fireside when she appeared, startled at her wild-eyed appearance.

Urp set aside his awl and the leather shoe he was working on. "Lass?"

"Where is Dunadd?" Deirdre said between breaths.

Arda rose from the fire, wiping dough from her hands on her skirt. "Child, it's three or four days away."

"Just tell me where," Deirdre replied, trembling all over. "Finn is in great danger and I have to go to him there."

Urp's white brows drew together, and he glanced at Arda. "It's time for the leaf-fall fair—many will be going there for the horse-trading, the feasts and games, lass. I can come with yeh—" Arda's soft cry cut him off; she knew he would be in danger.

"No." Deirdre looked deeply into him. Her limbs felt numb, her mind faintly humming, as if she had detached from her body, her spirit already flying over the hills. "The mists are my own realm—only I can pierce them for him." Arda and Urp never questioned her odd appearances and strange pronouncements, and they did not do so now. Deirdre realized then that they genuinely believed her to be a *calleach* after all. The *sídhe* wife of a mortal. Distant tears clouded her throat. "You must stay here," she said huskily to Urp, "and guard what you love. He would want that above all other things."

Arda braced herself, as if overcoming a deep superstition, and dared to touch Deirdre's cheek. "We'd not keep yeh from his side. Go to the village and upriver to the loch of the waters, then follow its southern shores and the ancestor valley south to Dunadd. No one will notice yeh at the fair, for the gates are open to all."

Deirdre laid a hand on Arda's wrinkled fingers and summoned a smile. At the door she turned, lingering below the lintel. "If we do not return, then everything we have is yours, for your care of us and your open hearts." Their eyes shone with fear and sorrow, and she had to go before their gentleness made her waver.

At her own house, she flung back the door-hide and stood poised by the hearth on the balls of her feet. She looked past the gleam of the furs on the bracken bed, and the pots of healing salves on the shelf. Past the hearth-stone on which she baked bannocks, still dusted with flour, to the baskets stacked up against the walls.

Naisi had given her freedom, and sacrificed his honor for her. He risked his life for her. There was no time to lose.

She walked toward that beckoning glimmer of pure-white, glowing there in the dark.

CHAPTER 36

Levarcham, Ferdia and Cúchulainn stared at one another by the light of a single lamp in the druid's tiny lodge. Levarcham looked like a crow, her body had wasted so, the loss of flesh from her neck sharpening her jaw, her cheeks pared back, making her nose a narrow beak. But her smile was triumphant. "I have starved myself to bring on the mind-swoon, and taken the herbs that are not named." She flung her chin up to Cúchulainn. "They are in Alba, in the Epidii lands. My heart led me over the sea, like a gull. At last."

She groped for a bench, and Cúchulainn paused only to press a cup of water into her cold fingers before turning to Ferdia.

"Conor and the Epidii king are great enemies," Ferdia mused.

"Surely they cannot have been hiding there? That would be incredibly foolhardy."

Cúchulainn laughed, swept with relief and a thrumming desperation to get his friends back. "That would be incredibly brave."

His eyes must have betrayed his excitement, for Ferdia frowned. "*You* are not going. You are known all over Alba. Imagine if the Epidii found they had Erin's greatest champion in their midst! I am dark and look like the Caereni, the island people."

Cúchulainn eyed him. "The Caereni are short," he growled.

"Cú, be reasonable. You must stay and keep the pressure on our king, hold the Red Branch together." His smile was tight. "I am expendable."

Cúchulainn was watching Levarcham, who was now swaying in her seat, utterly spent. He glanced sharply at Ferdia. "Not to me."

Ferdia shrugged. "Nevertheless, I will take a curragh and be gone—though the Epidii allow no Ulaid boats into their harbor, and so I cannot risk someone knowing me there. I will land elsewhere, and go overland to Dunadd."

Cúchulainn held him by both shoulders. "Be as careful of yourself as you would be of me." That had always been their farewell.

The victory feast was held at Dunadd three days after battle.

By moon-rise, it had dissolved into a fog of drunkenness wreathed with thick smoke that wafted up from the spits turning over the crackling hall-fires. Cinet's belly gradually distended with greasy chunks of meat sliced from the glistening pig carcasses, while the massive body of the wild boar was taken down and laid out on a platter to be carved in the warrior toasts.

With a fixed smile, he licked his fingers and roared jests at the nobles who crowded his benches, gulped ale and groped his sluts, and all the while his mind rolled his dark thoughts endlessly around, like dice in agitated fingers.

The sacred horse-fair was the perfect time for such a victory. Even those chieftains who had not fought with him had streamed in from their duns to join the others in renewing their yearly oaths of allegiance, stocking his storehouses with gifts for the long dark. Bathing them in generous rivers of ale and showering them with food bound them to him ever more tightly, and allowed him to boast of his success. This triumph against the Venicones would show all his warriors and nobles that he was still in his prime.

And yet…

He watched the eager young warriors clustering about Finn and his brothers, while in a rousing voice Carnach extolled every minute detail of their fighting skills and bravery. Cinet listened, and the ale stream turned bitter inside him. Grating voices replayed each sword-stroke of the battle, each near-miss. Strong, young arms slapped the backs of all those whose glorious actions were branded across the minds of the warriors like an afterglow of fire. He remembered what it was like, and it was just a memory.

It was time to bestow the honors. Staggering to his feet, Cinet gifted Bridei with a gold arm-ring and, vacillating, called up the commanders who had taken the right of battle. As the chatter grew more animated, he came to Carnach. Just as Cinet looped a necklace of jet around the young man's neck, Carnach turned, his face flushed with ale. "I say give Finn, Bran and Conn the boar-haunch!" he cried.

"Aye!" another of his men shouted. "The champion's portion to divide between them!"

This suggestion was met with bellows of approval and Cinet blinked the stinging smoke from his eyes, pushing his slack face into a smile. It was the greatest of honors; one he could not refuse if his men demanded it. Carnach flung up his arms, exhorting his men to chant the names of the brothers.

The chants spread until the hall rang, the vibration entering

Cinet's belly and stirring up the ale and greasy clods of meat. Swaying, he reluctantly beckoned the brothers forward and summoned some banal words of praise that stuck in his gullet. Even the women were gazing at these foreigners with speculative eyes.

The youngest brother grinned, shouting amusing retorts to Carnach's men. The middle one was quiet, his face impassive. The eldest was trying to hide his pride, but even so Cinet saw that hint of hunger again, the thirst for this acclaim.

To openly harm a warrior who had killed bravely for him... no king would risk that, not in this pit of smoke and ale, heated blood and war-songs. As the crackling skin of the boar was speared by a lance, Cinet sank back on his chair. Steam wreathed his face, shielding him from curious eyes, and he breathed in the damp, salted cloud.

The tantalizing picture came again, of *her* reclining beside his throne on the gleaming furs of seal and beaver. He would clad her in more soft, white hides, her hair combed by slaves into a shimmering curtain, and adorn her with a golden bow. He imagined her fierce, passionate features crowned by the ancient antlers on the wall, so all knew she was his own wild goddess of the woods. Something utterly different, unimaginably exciting. He put a hand to his belly.

Everything around him in this moment shouted his power, his wealth. He only boasted the rarest luxuries and she would be the jewel to outshine all others—something only the greatest of kings could possess. As always when he thought of her, the power flooded back into him, wiping away his doubts.

The blood flowed first to his loins and from there spread to the rest of him. This game had to be brought to an end now.

The feast had descended into chaos. The hall was so packed that Naisi was jostled by warriors as they shouted and slung arms about one another, singing blearily. Drunken revelers danced to the ragged music of pipe and drum that could barely be heard above the din. Some had cleared spaces in which to wrestle and spar, catching up any wooden object that came to hand, since iron blades were banned under the king's peace. Others clustered about *fidchell* boards on the floor or threw dice to loud roars, while bets feverishly changed hands.

Naisi tried to brace his feet as the crowds surged about him, his tunic stuck to his chest and back with sweat. He had allowed himself to get drunk because, after this, he knew they had won the power they needed. He felt like his heart would burst. Ardan was watching the wrestling to one side, gulping ale with determination while a girl whispered in his ear and wound a black curl of his hair about her finger. See, his brothers needed such distractions, to be back where they belonged.

He closed his eyes as he felt Deirdre's fingers on his neck, remembering how in the shelter of her he shed all the fierce armor he had to don for the world. Now he could let it all go, and whisper into every gleaming pore of her body that he would not be sundered from her again. The fingers moved to his lips and his eyes sprang open, his head spinning. A bejeweled woman was pressed up against him with an inviting glint in her eye, bronze rings at her ears. The nudge of her hip in his groin was pleasant indeed, but he gently returned her hand to her with a smile.

He had a rift to heal with one woman only, and she would see all the way into him and there would be no secrets. For the first time in his life he wanted that, *needed* that. Turning his shoulder, he squeezed through the crowd. He reached a clearing where Ainnle knelt, throwing dice against four others, screeching every time he won. Bets of brooches and daggers, buckles and rings were being passed back and forth over their heads.

"See?" someone hissed in his ear and, thrown, Naisi took a faltering step before balancing himself. It was the king, his bulk pushed up against Naisi in the crush. "By the end of the games, your arms will all be heavy with rings, and your bellies with the sacred haunch of boar. All you need now is the soft flesh of one of my dancing girls, and the triumph will be complete."

An odd undertone threaded his words. Cinet's eyes were fixed on the dicers and so Naisi watched them, too, his dulled mind scrambling to wake itself up. He cleared his throat of smoke. "Speaking of triumphs, my lord, I do have something to ask of you."

"Ah! Here it comes. I thought you had no need for any reward."

Though the king slurred, the edge to his voice kindled a little spark in Naisi's mind and he turned to face him. Cinet's heavy cheeks were veined, his eyes glazed and his mouth pursed in a small, hard smile as he watched the betting. Naisi's thoughts struggled back up from the warm depths of the ale.

"But then again," Cinet said, "you have done me a great service and I am the most generous of kings. Now we have taken the mine from the Venicones, my supply of gold is assured, which gives me the means to take all the trade routes across to the east coast for my own."

Naisi closed his eyes and opened them, shaking his head to clear it. "*Took* the mine?"

Cinet's eyes slanted toward him. "Of course. My war-band attacked the Venicones dun that guarded it, and other, swifter warriors chased the remnants of their defenders and secured the ore before it was lost." His brows went up. "Oh, but you had a hand in that victory, did you not?"

The lurid blur of bright clothes and glinting jewelry and bellows of laughter all whirled around Naisi. He had lifted his sword for this king to defend what was right. He had poured himself into every fray to empty that black well that glinted inside him; to fill it with the light of pride again.

Cinet's teeth were a yellow smear in his red face. "Surely you heard my men speak of it, Finn. After all, you should always stab your enemy before he stabs you."

Though men had not spoken openly of it, Naisi had heard snatches of things that made no sense, because he didn't want to know. He longed to fight for the weak, not kill for a king's greed. Not again. His hand came out to steady himself, but there was nothing to grasp. Sweat trickled down his face.

Cinet chuckled at his expression, stroking his beard. "So you want a fort, then, a hall and men to rally to you, and women to bear your brats?" He waved an indolent hand toward the musicians. "Take one of my dancing girls, then, as your prize."

Naisi desperately scanned the room for Ardan. He had to get away from here. They must leave.

"Oh, but then you said you have a wife." The words came to Naisi from far away, drowned out by his racing heart that was belatedly sounding an alarm. His attention swung back. The king's mouth was working as if he was savoring something, his gaze greedy. "You are a man who seeks the best in life, Finn. So I imagine this wife of yours is untamed, her walk as lithe as the wildcats that roam the mountains. I imagine her limbs clad in deerskins, her woodland eyes disappearing into the leaves themselves. A pretty picture, indeed."

Naisi was plunged into a coldness that wiped away the ale stupor. The king's huntsman. He stared blindly into Cinet's face as that avaricious smile fell away like a discarded mask, revealing pure loathing in the king's unshielded eyes. *All the gods above.*

Naisi had thrown himself so desperately into battle, sword thrust out before him, all his fire and fury poured toward that one shining prize just ahead—redemption. And so he'd left his rear completely undefended. He'd exposed his back to the blade, his heart to oblivion because she was there in it and he hadn't held her close enough...*Deirdre*...

People were jostling closer, bellowing in disappointment or screeching their success, so no one could see Cinet step closer. "She is mine." The king's spittle landed on Naisi's icy cheek. "And you will stand there and watch me with my hand tangled in that hair and my fingers on her milky skin..." Naisi was quivering now, every nerve tingling alive, "...and under her deerskin her breasts will be panting from fear of me, my proud prince—or will it be desire?"

Deirdre's face looked at Naisi from that vision, her lips parted with terror, her eyes glittering with pain...and in that moment he understood he had failed her. For the first time in his life, all his control slipped away. He did not feel the muscle in his arm stretch and contract, reaching down his leg, his fingers grasping the hilt of the hunt dagger in his boot. He did not realize he had whipped it out to grip it before him in some futile defense against that image Cinet summoned. He didn't even know what he'd do with that blade, because there was no mindfulness, only a blind rage to which his body reacted, the need to protect her overwhelming. He saw the king's gaze snap straight to the dagger and fire with triumph.

Naisi wildly backed up, pushing people aside to get to the door. But there was no chance of escape. The king's bodyguards appeared as if they had been lurking behind him, taking hold of his shoulders. *Ainnle...Ardan...* Shouts had broken out all around him. He heard the king bellowing—*Treason! Betrayal!*—and a clamor of voices exclaiming in disbelief and confusion.

Naisi was slammed against one of the oak pillars that held the thatch roof, and when his brothers tried to push their way through the crowd to him, Cinet spat, "Let them through. They are dishonored together as they were so honored!" And still all Naisi could see was the king's face twisted with a hidden smile.

At last a shocked silence fell, the music trailing off with a drunken slide of pipes.

"He has broken the law and threatened the king!" Cinet bellowed again, prowling before Finn. A *knife*, he exulted silently. He did not expect that; better than Finn sending a fist at him, indeed!

"It's a mistake," that obstinate pup Carnach growled. "We are all the worse for drink, my lord."

Cinet turned on him. "He still holds the blade in his hand!" To his pleasure he noticed that the bulk of the warriors who had fawned so readily over these strangers were now thoroughly shocked and dismayed, glancing at the brothers and back to their king. Whispers and mutters went around the throng like a wind through barley.

Finn spoke past the sword-blade pressed against his throat. "He said he would...take my woman unlawfully, dishonor me..." The weight of the guard's sword cut off his words.

Cinet spun toward him. "Woman? I have never seen your woman; none of us have." He smiled coldly at his warriors. "She is a ghost-maid, we all think: a product of your fevered imaginings, my friend." He pointed at Finn, holding the eyes of his nobles one by one. "And this must indeed be madness, to break the peace of my hall at this sacred time."

Bridei appeared at Cinet's side, frowning. "It must be a mistake, uncle. Finn would never—"

"And what do you know what he would do? What do any of us know? You call him dark prince because nothing is known about him. We have let foreigners squirm their way into our favor." He whirled again, striding back and forth before the fires. The warriors and their women crowded back, necks craning, glazed eyes bulging. "He must have been sent to kill me by one of our enemies, who will then attack when we are weakened. Look at him; he's not Alban! These traitors are from the British westlands, or sea-wolves from Erin, or Gauls in league with Rome!"

More cries of disbelief ensued, while Carnach began shouting to the men that the brothers had fought bravely and proven themselves to be true.

Under cover of that bleating, Cinet turned his head and leaned in to Bridei, speaking under his breath. "Are you blind, you fool? The men love them in a matter of moons more readily than they did you in your whole life. These pups will have your throne off you the moment you turn your back! Do you honor them enough for that?" As it sank in, Bridei gradually blanched until freckles stood out on his cheeks, and he gulped down any further rebellious words.

Cinet cut Carnach's rant off with a raised hand. "It does not matter how bravely they've fought. This could all be some ploy to get close enough to murder me. Why else did he have a dagger concealed, and why draw it on me if not?"

"I never ... would have done ... such a thing ..." Finn gasped. His brothers launched themselves at the guards to drag their arms from their brother, until more men piled on them and they were also seized.

Cinet watched the fearful looks darting among the fighting men. Warrior blood ran so swift and hot it could be turned from adoration to suspicion in a moment, simply by invoking danger to the heartlands of the Epidii. They swore to protect *that* above all other oaths. Kin and tribe won out at such times—and Finn had done it all himself.

"I will be merciful," Cinet declared. "They will be kept under guard until the warrior-games in two days. There they will be put to trial."

"But they haven't done anything!" Carnach protested.

"He has drawn a blade under the king's peace," Cinet snapped. "And for that alone he will have to prove his loyalty in a way that cannot be misconstrued. The druids will decide on single combat to the death, or warrior ordeal, as they see fit." He glared around at them all. "And no one will be allowed to see them or break my peace again lest they suffer the same punishment."

Bridei reluctantly spoke up. "Take them away," he said to the guards, "and let them sleep off their ale."

The three brothers were shoved toward the doors amid a subdued silence. Cinet shook his head as if saddened, then clapped his hands to call for more ale and mead. He whipped up the musicians with a raised hand, summoned his dancing girls and scattered them among the nobles, for once sharing their pleasures. He didn't need them now.

He sat back on his chair and sent one of his messengers to seek out the hunter Fidech among the campfires on the river meadow. He was calming himself with a cup of cool, foaming ale when Fidech slunk through the crowd to his feet like a grizzled hound.

"Bring in our little bird," Cinet murmured. "The snare has sprung."

In Nessa's house at Emain Macha, Conor's gaze bored into the firelit walls while a man knelt before him, his hands clasped around a sword.

The man had flaxen hair and the rawboned, lantern-jawed look of the people over the northern sea in the colder lands, his traveler's hides bleached by salt and wear. His pale, blue eyes were shrewd in the nest of creases carved by sun over bright water.

Dark prince, he said. *Three brothers*. Rumors that drifted from the docks and onto the deck of his ship in the banter of sailors and fishermen.

Conor hefted the leather bag tied to his belt, and flipped a few silver and bronze coins to where the man's knee rested on Nessa's rug, much to her evident distaste. "The rest is for when there is proof. You will take my own men back with you, and they will see for themselves."

The man touched his fist to his head and got up, taking the reek of fish with him.

Unavoidably, Conor's gaze slid from the walls to meet that of his mother. Her eyes were as hard and gleaming as the stone pendant she rubbed between her fingers. "Dunadd," she breathed.

CHAPTER 37

Cúchulainn thrust the doors of Conor's hall open with a bang. The king was sitting in his carved chair, the firelight playing over his glassy eyes while the warriors drank and muttered to themselves on the wall benches. As Cúchulainn strode toward the hearth he sat up, and while necks craned and all the chatter fell silent, Dubthach, who had been primed by Cúchulainn, cried, "Hail to the champion!"

Cúchulainn reached the pool of torchlight and halted.

He wore his red cloak gathered on the shoulders by sun-disk brooches. An immense, twisted gold torc sat on his collarbones above a breastplate of burnished hide, over a tunic and trews of dyed check, embroidered in gold thread. Emer had limed his hair in a crest and he braced his body with his ceremonial shield, the Red Branch emblem polished to gleam. His dagger-hilt was set with a single piece of crystal that glittered like a star at his waist.

"My king." Cúchulainn drew his breath down to his belly and pushed it out like a flung spear. "I hear the great news that the sons of Usnech have been discovered in refuge among the Epidii in Alba."

The warriors all roared with surprise and excitement. Conor sat still through their cheers and demands for explanations, before slowly placing his mead-cup on a table beside him. His veined eyes locked with Cúchulainn's, his withered cheeks shadowed by the hair that escaped his circlet in lank tendrils, now completely gray and bleached of its last gold. "I just myself received these glad tidings, Hound, and was waiting for you to arrive to share them."

Cúchulainn swung about to hold everyone's attention with the light flashing off his adornments. Ferdia surely would be reaching the sons of Usnech any day now, so there was no chance for the king to cover up what he knew. Cúchulainn must drive the spear home. "We have suffered, riven by suspicions that lodge deeply in the heart of the Red Branch." He prowled around the circle of men, drawing them in with his eyes, his rousing voice. He had summoned the battle-light with care, letting it fill him slowly so it would shine from his face and resonate in his throat. He met the gaze of every man who had spoken against Naisi. "Now the blackness can be lifted. Now the light will return and we will be restored!"

The warriors were already imperceptibly relaxing, relief flowing like the mead through their tense bodies. Illan, Fiacra, Cormac and Dubthach's glad faces lifted Cúchulainn's heart. Conall still seemed wary, then his shoulders lowered and he looked to his cup, as if he too breathed out.

"Let love and trust flow between us again," the Hound cried, "for we know how it feels to fight side by side as the Source pounds in our blood, do we not?"

"*Yes!*" the bellow went up.

He scrutinized the king, and his heightened senses saw the light around Conor writhing with darkness, threaded by a bloody red. It was resistance even now…a struggle with himself, Conor's need for peace fighting with his old fears. *No,* Cúchulainn thought fiercely. *If you want your kingdom, you will bow to the Red Branch now.* "We will be able to stand in strength once more, shoulder to shoulder with all those we love—and as One we can beat Connacht's raiders back to Cruachan and trample their blood with our boots!" A cheer erupted from the drunken throng and Cúchulainn put his head back, eyes closed, arms out. "Sing your pride to the gods!"

The cheers turned to a hot-blooded chant that rose and fell in waves, reverberating through every muscle and bone in his body. *Red Branch! Red Branch! Red Branch!*

Only when the hoarse din disintegrated did Cúchulainn seek Conor's gaze through the smoke of the hearth-fires. "And so your warriors ask you, great king, when will you bring Naisi, Ardan and Ainnle home?"

Conor pushed himself unsteadily to his feet, and in that moment, as he and Cúchulainn stared at each other, something passed between them—an understanding. In publicly bestowing his trust, the champion was forcing the king to be trustworthy.

Conor waited until the last voice faded. "For moons now I have given all I can to summon the sons of Usnech back and make amends…" His words faltered and to everyone's shock he bowed his head, spreading a hand over his breast where a gold necklet covered a ladder of bones. "…make amends for how I wandered in such blindness." He lifted his face and there was a wetness on his lined cheeks. Cúchulainn gazed in amazement at the shifting hues around the king, recognizing true despair there. The surprised warriors all murmured approval, for the strength required to display humility and emotion before the Red Branch was as compelling as Cúchulainn's booming voice.

Conor drew a shuddering breath and his hands fell slack by his sides, looking utterly broken. It was real, Cúchulainn thought exultantly; he had repented. "The light has at last pierced my darkness," the king croaked, "and from you I beg forgiveness."

Cúchulainn's inner fire flared with hope, while the warriors rustled and muttered, not knowing how to react. The king's surrender had affected them all.

Now Conor lifted his chin and spoke more strongly. "On Naisi's return, I will stand with him and Deirdre on the mound of Macha and do both of them great honor, I swear on my own blood. The strength and skill of the sons of Usnech will further the glory of the Ulaid once more, and do honor to the Red Branch, our brothers!"

His voice rose at the end and the younger warriors went wild, expressing the same wave of relief in Cúchulainn's heart. Amid all the cheering, only Conor and Cúchulainn remained unmoving.

The Hound nodded at his king, his kin, and Conor sketched a grave bow with his head while men's feet stamped the floor around them.

Thud.

Thud.

Thud.

The drumbeats rang through Deirdre's slight body where she waited in the porch of Cinet's great hall at Dunadd. She crushed herself against the wattle screens, making herself as small as possible in the shadows. The rhythmic thumping only increased the trance into which she'd fallen, where all the memories of the last few days were adrift like pale gulls on the ocean inside her.

She remembered a jostling of crowds on Dunadd's meadow; the whinnies of ponies in their pens and mingled reek of dung, smoke and churned mud. Dusk light picking out the helmets and spears of guards pacing the high timber walls. Her own cracked voice summoning words, asking for news of three

brothers. The shudder when she heard they were alive but imprisoned. And the punishment? she had whispered. Trial by the
sword, she was told. *A sword of iron, washed with Naisi's blood.*

From the day by the spring, she had not truly known what the
snatches of vision meant, or what drove the impulses of her
hands—she had let herself be taken by the current, the winds.
However, when she discovered that many nobles had brought
gifts to the king to mark their allegiance at this sacred time, then
she understood.

A gift.

The king's hall reared from the crest of the crag, its banners
blown by the sea-winds, and below it on a rocky shoulder of the
hill there were painted houses whose doors were decorated with
fur pennants on spears. After passing beneath a carved gate in the
stone ramparts of the crag, Deirdre had squeezed between the
fine houses to a place where the hill fell away in low cliffs, looking out to a marsh reddened by the gathering dusk. Crouching
there, she studied her fingers and saw they were trembling.
Immediately, she wrapped her arms around her pack and its precious contents, drawing herself deeper into self-containment.
Fear was an indulgence she could not afford.

She had gradually breathed it out into the shimmering cloud
around her, until she felt her own skin glittering from within.
She could wield no sword to break Naisi from prison, summon
no physical force to stand up to warriors.

She had only herself. They only had her.

Thud.

Thud.

Thud.

Cinet belched and sat back as his steward strained to make himself heard over the din. His head was splitting from the ale-
guzzling and his belly fit to burst, but he had never felt more
flushed with vigor, now his last problem was dealt with. Gifts of
fur, cloth, antler and bronze were piling up behind his chair now.

His nobles saw him gilded with triumph, and with bent knees and bowed heads they hastened to acclaim him their lord once more.

So what was this now? One of the chieftains had sent him a most unusual gift—a dance. Cinet snorted. It would be diverting, at least. He nodded to his steward, and the man pushed through to the hearth-fire and clapped his hands, dragging the attention of the warriors from their drink and the groping of their women. The pipes and drums broke off and the screeches of laughter gradually trailed away. The lines of dancing revelers came to a halt and threw themselves down on the rushes and cushions, panting, their faces sheened with sweat.

When the steward announced there was a special entertainment, people murmured with excitement, their heads straining toward the doors.

Cinet lolled back in his chair, letting his flesh spread out. The brothers would be done away with by entirely legal means, and if there was any danger of them escaping that, he had druids who appreciated subtleties of power that his warriors did not. He tilted his head to breathe the clearer air above the sweating crowds. And *she* would be here in only a few more days when Fidech returned.

His own gaze was on the doors, and so he was the first to see the glimmer of white in the shadows. The stillness of that pale figure gradually spread around the room. Warriors nudged their women and moved back. Servants paused with platters of meat and cheese, craning their necks. Cinet gestured a server forward and took a leg of duck, tearing at the meat with his teeth as he settled in to watch.

The girl took a step forward, and another, her chin tilted down. She did not move with the sensual swaying of hips Cinet expected, and there was no clink of bells on ankles. She glided as if she was not touching the ground, but floating. The effect was eerie, and he stopped chewing.

Just then, the dancing girl emerged into the full glare of the torches, and the crowd gasped, and the meat caught in Cinet's gullet. She was sheathed from head to foot in a hooded cape that was completely covered in white feathers, and over her face she wore a primitive mask with an orange beak and slanted eyes. There was no hint of anything human besides her hands, holding the cloak closed.

She lifted her averted head to look up at Cinet and he thought her pupils dilated for a moment before she blinked. Then the gleam of her eyes steadied and became penetrating. She bowed to him.

Cinet lowered the gnawed duckbone to his lap, an odd cramp of superstition running across his shoulders like a trailing hand. "Dance, then," he slurred, "and we will see if I am pleased."

The musicians lifted their pipes to their lips but the girl shook her head at them, the feathers at her neck and crown fluttering. "You do not know this tune." She stood back, spread her arms into wings and stood poised with one bare foot extended. After a faltering start she began to sing her own accompaniment.

It was apparent at once that this maid was no trained singer. Her voice was husky and low and the melody was simple, almost childlike. Yet the cracked tone and the haunting mask with its slanted eyes created a surreal air that stilled all the fidgeting and jesting. The poignancy of that plaintive, wavering voice in the vastness of the cavernous hall made Cinet catch his breath.

And then at last she began to move.

She bent and swept out her arms then twirled and spun, the cape flying out in a cloud of white. Her voice grew stronger until it rebounded off the soaring thatch roof and the carved oak pillars, the pale mask and orange beak transformed by the leaping firelight into disturbing shapes. For a moment, Cinet was transported to some ancient world of the *sídhe*, in the dark forests before time began.

And then he forgot to think at all, for the spell that fell over him.

Cinet. Galan.

Deirdre let that realization fuel the spiral of white flame inside her, and it became a towering column, unfurling bright. And it wasn't rage or despair because they wouldn't leave her strong enough for Naisi. She had to be more powerful than this king—stronger in this moment than any warrior and his sword.

It was the ferocity of love.

She let it consume her, watching the flame lick along her up-held arms and blind her so she saw no faces in the crowd. The hall, the shadows, the hearth-fire, the rustling of feet and whis-pers—they all fell away and she was the swan maiden, gliding over a black pool with her wings folded.

She saw him, the hunter—Naisi—bending to drink at the pool, his bow in his hand. The expression of her heart became mute in a swan's throat, the yearning to show him she was human, that she needed him. That the gulf between them could be crossed. *You are bound to me, wound through me, and I did not know it.*

She spread her wings, and her feathers were lifted by love.

The savage urge to defend it was nothing she had felt before, and the blinding cloud around her broke up until she was danc-ing through whirlwinds of the *sídhe* with tears running beneath the mask. She was open, her heart unimpeded, and so the stars fell through her in a rain of light and at last she knew what drew the *sídhe* to her, what bonded her to them.

It was purity of emotion unclouded by thought—the flame of a soul's absolute truth. The harmonic dance of the natural order, unfurling life, creation. The *sídhe* were thrilled by joy, rage, grief, love and unbridled courage, and she had always burned with those. She would not let any man's need to destroy, his fear and greed, usurp the flow of life or obliterate any flame in her.

This time, she did not cast her soul out to a bird. Instead, she summoned a memory of a swan into her own body. One mo-ment, somewhere, that captured an echo of its spirit. She called it to her with a blessing under her breath, a pulse of her own Source, and allowed it to inhabit her utterly.

Cinet was watching the girl slack-jawed now, everything else forgotten.

Her underclothes of fine, bleached kidskin were bound so close to her that when she extended her limbs from the cloak, he could see every graceful curve. Her arms became sweeping wings, then were folded back as she mimed landing on an imaginary pool. The pale feathers glowed against the backdrop of ruddy flames.

Cinet sat up, his mouth going dry. As she turned he swore he saw a swan itself, an ethereal tracing of arched neck and spread wings that blurred the outlines of her body, like mist. He had never seen such illusion, such sorcery. Goose-flesh dappled his skin, and he found this fear even more arousing.

He was conscious of his sister, Eithne, the royal priestess, rising from her seat with her gray head alert and her penetrating eyes fixed on the dancer. Perhaps he was not the only one to recognize this maid's magic. She must be a priestess or witch from some far eastern temple of Egypt or Greece—an expensive gift, indeed. He had heard that they possessed sexual skills of a divine nature that were unknown on these shores.

As if she read his mind, the girl leaped lightly up on the platform that held his chair and began sweeping in great arcs through the space left around him. She glanced at him over her shoulder as she passed, eyes slanted and glinting, then paused to stretch seductively just so he could feast his eyes on the curve of her breasts when the cape fell back. His head spun to follow her, making him dizzy, and the reeling sensation increased the flood of heat into his loins.

When she at last swept back down to the hearthside he caught a salty, wild smell of feathers and a musky waft from her own body as she went by.

As the hunter trained his arrow upon the swan maiden, Deirdre silently cried her love to the sky so the world would know the moment of ecstasy that powered her flight. She thrust upward to feel the last moment of soaring, for the hunter could not know her in this form, and for him to love her she must surrender. She must die for this love.

A piercing pain...and she was falling, transforming back into the shape of a fair maiden so the young hunter would hold her and know her before she died. There was a collective gasp as Deirdre flung herself to the rug before the fire, and her cloak shimmered into stillness around her and she lay with arms in the posture of death, eyes closed. The breathless silence in the hall stretched out, Deirdre's fluttering ribs pushed into her by the weight of her own body.

Naisi, Naisi, her heart sang, as mute and lonely a cry in this den of enemies as that suffered by the swan in the tale.

At last the hush was broken by a great clap from the direction of the king's chair. Another clap came, and another, and the people joined him, smacking their palms together and murmuring in the relief of tension. The applause quickened until a few cheers broke out, which only swelled when Deirdre drew herself upright. She swept the swan cloak out to bow to the king.

Cinet was standing now, sweat running from his plump cheeks into his beard. He raised his arms for quiet, and as soon as he could speak over the excited chatter, he yelled, "By the gods who made me, any gift is yours after that!" He beckoned Deirdre closer. "A bronze ring for your ankle, then? A band for your hair?"

The dancer dipped her head and looked up at him. "Did the king feel the power of the Goddess in this dance?" Her voice was low and breathless.

Confusion muddied Cinet's mind. It must be some kind of ritual question; perhaps it was part of her seduction. He laughed. "How could I not? I have never seen its like." His nobles were all awestruck, their mouths half-open, their mutters excited.

His sister climbed up beside his chair, resting her hand on the twisted roots of oak that formed the back; his druids were also hovering. The girl's gaze did not waver from his face, however, and she spread her wings again, her voice more forceful. "So a priestess brought the Goddess to the king this night."

Priestess? He was right, then. His thoughts were eclipsed by an image of that eerie mask leering over him in the half dark of his bed, his fear sharpening his desire. *Gods.* "What questions are these?" he growled good-naturedly, smiling around at his warriors.

The girl tilted her head, making him think of a bird cocking its beak before stabbing it down. "There is an ancient rite, a sacred pact of priestess and king. She gifts the power of the Goddess to him with her dance, the fertility of the earth itself, the power of the land—and if she has moved him, he grants her a boon."

Relief flooded Cinet. It was a riddle, a game. This was more diverting than anything since he saw the wild maid of Finn's. His sister suddenly turned to whisper in his ear. "My brother, what she says is true."

"Eh?" Cinet scowled at her.

Eithne was his opposite, stately and gray-haired, her gravity a product of her sacred position as Ban Cré, mother of the land. People listened to her. "It is older than the kingship rite in which you took part," she added. At Cinet's inauguration, Eithne, as the Goddess incarnate, had lifted a ritual cup of mead to his lips and in so doing gifted the blessing of the Mother to his rule. "Much older," she murmured, watching the girl. "It was danced in the lands of the sunrise, our ancestor lands. The Sisters on the Sacred Isle use a variation to inaugurate the Caereni kings." Now there was a little frown between her brows. "I have never seen anything of this power, brother. Beware."

"Beware?" Cinet muttered. "Of course I will beware. Do you think I'll let some wily old chieftain outsmart me?"

She gave him an odd look. "I meant beware you do not offend the Goddess."

This was all nonsense. "In this *ancient* rite, sister, does the priestess bestow these blessings with her body, by any chance?"

Eithne pursed her thin lips. "At times, but—"

"Well, then!" He raised his hand to the girl. "And is this favor some sly attempt to gain riches for the lord who pays you? Rings, ships, furs, a reduction in his tithes?" He chuckled, drunk and flushed with lust and the triumphs of this night. There was a smattering of answering laughter among the nobles.

The intensity in those slanted pupils was arresting, for he could see no whites in the holes of the mask. "This sacred plea is for me alone."

"Ah! As long as this favor is the same as comes to *my* mind, sweetheart!" The laughter was louder and Cinet clapped his hands in delight. "Whoever honored me with this gift will sit by my hand and drink from my own mead-cup!" he roared.

Two of his druids moved to his other side and began whispering in his ear. *This could be a trap, it is dangerous, rash. You give your word and it is binding.* His sister weighed in again. *Binding, yes, and she invokes something that is not of this world.*

Cinet snorted like an impatient stallion, flicking them away. This maid would keep his flesh invigorated until Fidech came back with his other prize.

The *sídhe* were still glittering on the boundaries of Deirdre's sight, and she felt their song in her blood. *Truth.* Behind the mask, she closed her eyes.

At this moment, her truth was a love that was a flaming star in the dark. Powered by the chorus of the *sídhe* and their hunger for all truth, she thrust her own light toward Cinet. The flare entered the king's soul like a torch through the hidden caverns of his spirit.

The paths inside him were as tangled as briars. The charges of ethereal lightning that were his life-force anchored knotted cords in heart, mind and belly, and as those patterns of emotion grazed her own spirit she understood them, felt them.

The fear of being supplanted was a terrible force that drove all the others. Then there was greed and lust...*I want this no matter what it costs.* Pride...*I am invincible...I have triumphed...all will bow to me*. A disdain for women. A jealousy that others had their youth and vigor, and he must clutch what he could of it and twist it to serve *him*, for this dancer was another enchantress who would dazzle the lords who fawned at his feet.

Flooded by the *sídhe*-light and Deirdre's own flame, all the patterns of his myriad fears glowed more vividly, lit up like a branching silver tree. And what had already taken root there over long years of resentful nursing was only given greater power by that sunburst. Pride was intensified into hubris, and anger into contempt for weak females, and the exquisite throb of it made him laugh. *What maiden could be a danger to me? Not Cinet the Bear, Lord of the Isles, possessor of all my desires!*

His white-robed druids tried to speak again, but Cinet's unsteady hand struck them away. "Your wish is granted!" he shouted. "You have my royal word. Now take your mask off, that I may see who has so ensnared me."

With one tug, Deirdre pulled it from her face, dragging her hood back and shaking out her braids. The mask floated down to her side, held loosely in her fingers.

Cinet appeared to turn to stone.

"I am Finn's wife," she said in a ringing voice, "and my boon is this: release my lord and his brothers from their trial, and banish us from your kingdom forever."

There was a stunned silence. Cinet's hands groped behind him for the arms of his chair and he sank on it, his knuckles strained. A moment later loud exclamations and a tide of consternation broke out among the warriors, pierced by the shrill excitement of their women. Cinet collapsed down in his chair, his sweaty face gray. "They are ... They must be punished for their transgressions."

Deirdre swayed as the fury rose from him like an acrid reek. "Exile is surely punishment enough, my lord."

The rumble of mutters was growing. The tall woman with the crescent of shell at her neck inclined her head to Cinet once more, and as she did she looked at Deirdre, and there might have been sympathy in those steady blue eyes. "You gave your word to the Goddess, brother." This time she did not drop her voice. "It was a binding oath, made before your nobles. At this moment of your greatest success, do not call the wrath of the gods down upon us, lest what you have gained is snatched away by storm and famine, or a blight of the earth." Cinet was still blinking glazed eyes, his lips clamped hard together.

Some of his warriors began to argue now. A young fair-headed man called out, his angry gray eyes and scowl saying more than his words. "Exile *is* enough, my lord, especially when the crime is unproven! Show the generosity of your great heart, and inflict no more than banishment upon our honored sword-brothers for the bravery they have shown in your service."

There was a general murmur of approval, before someone else yelled, "They deserve their lives for how they fought for us!" The murmur rose to a clamor of agreement.

Deirdre was slowly coming back to an awareness of her body, her blood slowing, the memory of feathers sinking back into radiance. Her sense of the Otherworld veils also faded, until she knew only the flickering torchlight, the sour air, the walls glinting with shields.

A red-haired man who bore a resemblance to Cinet had now joined the king. "It is the right thing, uncle," he said, looking around at the frowning warriors on their benches with a tension about his shoulders. He glanced at Cinet. "Keep your word, let them go and leave our honor unsullied. The unlawful act Finn committed can be set against the blood they shed for us, and the bravery and beauty of this dance that has astonished us all." His brief smile to Deirdre was strained.

Cinet's small eyes were coals in his pallid face, his gaze roving slowly around the hall, alighting on warriors, who stared defiantly back. His throat bobbed and he moistened his lips, until at last he gestured at two spear-men standing behind his chair and they swiftly disappeared outside.

Deirdre let his eyes bore into her and was untouched. So much of what she thought she was had been seared away in that dance, leaving only the core—and that he could not oppress. A touch came on her arm. The gray-eyed young warrior was pressing a cup into her hands. "Take this for your thirst, lass," he said. "Your man will be here at any moment." He looked relieved, but also profoundly sad.

Just then the doors opened, and though Deirdre's back was to them she felt the change in the air. She turned. Naisi halted in his tracks, and in the leap of glances between them her soul took flight again, for she saw the light of her dance flood his face, the moment when the hunter at last sees what he holds in his arms.

She returned that searching, hungry gaze. There were bruises on his cheek and another cut along his jaw, the scab a darker slash through his black stubble. His tunic was filthy and his braids untangled into sweaty knots. He looked exhausted, the grime and shadowed anxiety in his face stripping everything back so his eyes blazed out with all the defiance he held at bay in his body.

Before anyone else could speak, the king's sister stepped forward. "She has bartered for your lives with her courage and her surrender to the Goddess—and in so doing has bestowed Her blessings on this hall."

Ardan and Ainnle merely stared at the woman, confounded. They were just as grubby, their hair scattered with straw, and Ainnle had a trickle of dried blood under his nose. Cinet obviously realized he had to say something and dragged himself upright. "I see your woman holds as many secrets as you do, Finn." His eyes shut briefly, and opened.

Naisi had still not broken his and Deirdre's gaze. She felt it as a caress on her eyelids, her mouth...as if his palms cupped her cheeks. Now he dragged himself away and turned to Cinet. "As you said, you've never seen her, my lord." His smile was cold. "I am sure you can now appreciate why I needed to be at her side—and why my temper got the better of me in drink."

Cinet glowered. "In my infinite mercy," he hissed, "I have transmuted your punishment to exile."

As the other brothers shared glances of apprehension, the young Epidii warrior who had given Deirdre the cup went to

Naisi and held his shoulders. "You are to be banished. The sword is lifted from your breast." He embraced Naisi, and Naisi's hands gripped him and they murmured together before they released each other.

Naisi bowed to Cinet, his face hard, and Deirdre suddenly knew how he looked going into battle. "We thank you for your mercy and forgiveness, and the generosity of your heart in over-looking my transgression."

Cinet grimaced with every word. "Collect your belongings from your steading," he ground out, "and be gone from my lands before I change my mind."

There were more mutterings at that ill grace, and Naisi's gray-eyed friend lifted his chin, raising his voice. "After that, come to my dun, Finn, and I will supply you with food for your travels. You saved my hall and gave my men a victory in battle they will remember for years to come."

Other men crowded around the brothers now, somber and subdued, touching their shoulders in salute. "Return their swords and their packs to them!" the red-haired nephew of Cinet's called to the guards. "They shall not go unprotected when they leave our lands—and I think we can accept their word not to use them in revenge."

He looked meaningfully at Naisi, who bowed. "You have my word on it," Naisi said quietly, straightening to address Cinet. "After all, my lord, you did once say I was an utterably honorable man."

Cinet waved them away, and though he turned his head to take a gulp of ale, Deirdre felt his eyes lingering on her back as they strode from the hall.

As soon as they were clear of the pool of torchlight outside, Naisi grabbed Deirdre's wrist and dragged her off the path that led left toward the upper gate. The brothers hastened right instead, along a narrow trail that crossed the hill, past a temple of oak pillars open to the sky. They scrambled over a stone outcrop that formed a natural rampart around the peak and slid down the ramp of rock until they were all standing beside the houses on the shoulders of the hill, along the cliff edge.

"That was a fine saving of Cinet's face," Naisi muttered, still gripping Deirdre's hand, "but his guards will be searching for us already—and this time armed with a silent blade in the dark."

"Does he seriously think we will go home?" Ainnle said.

"Of course not." Naisi's voice was brisk, all warrior. "They'll expect us to lose ourselves in the crowds, then use the northern roads to get back to our boat."

"There's a trade path that goes west to the harbor," Ardan put in.

"West and south is the direction they will least expect," Naisi agreed. "But not the road." He turned to look out at the sea of darkness that spread away from the crag, devoid of the twinkling campfires that covered the river meadow. "We'll go over the marsh. I went fowling with Carnach; there are not many pools or mudholes. It's just hard going." Naisi looked at Deirdre in the starlight. "It will be the hardest race we ever run, *fiáin*. Can you keep up?"

An explosive snort came from Ainnle's direction. "After whatever she's just done to bring this about, I doubt anything will beat her, brother. She will keep up with us. She always has." The warmth in his voice brought an unseen heat to Deirdre's face.

As the rush of the dance faded, the lack of sleep and the strain of travel were beginning to swamp her, and she could easily have sunk to the ground. Instead, she kissed Naisi's knuckles, made a fist and held both their hands to her chest. "I will not falter."

The dim light shone in his eyes. "There's an old gate in the wall here." His voice sounded husky now. "It's unguarded because the slopes outside are too steep for enemies to attack—though they never thought about people escaping down them. They throw their waste out there, too, so will not expect us to choose that foul path."

"How do you *know* all this?" Ainnle demanded.

Naisi merely dropped Deirdre's hand and turned, cocking his

head. Someone was scrambling down the rocks behind them, and as Ainnle and Ardan went to spring forward Naisi held them back. "Carnach," he murmured.

The dark figure slid down and gripped Naisi's wrist. "Cinet's guards are looking already," Carnach said breathlessly. "I saw them racing through the gates to the meadow."

"Then thank the gods you told me of this other way."

Carnach grunted. "I won't waste time telling you of the fury in my heart. Just let me know how I can throw them off your scent."

A thought came to Deirdre. "Here." She dragged off the swan cloak and pressed it and the mask into Carnach's hands. She felt the wood slip from her touch, the carving Levarcham had smoothed with her fingers.

"You could throw it in the river upstream, and they will think we ran southeast," Ainnle said eagerly.

"Perfect." Naisi clapped a hand on Ainnle's shoulder.

"I left my pack close by," Deirdre added. "It has my old tunic and trews, and my cloak…"

"Yes, the kidskin is too pale to hide," Naisi agreed. "But hurry."

Ardan crept along the alley with her and waited while she threw her old clothes over her close-fitting hides. There he drew her close, pressing his long dagger into her hand. "Put it through your belt," he said. She could not see his face in the shadows. "I would not want to be on the receiving end if it's your will to send it home." He tentatively touched her cheek with the back of his hand. "Even on difficult ground there is a way to run like Red Branch, letting the light bear you up. I saw the glimmer in you in Erin. Now I am sure you know it." He paused, his hand falling away. "That is how warriors run."

Deirdre nodded, wanting to weep as the memories of their little house, the gleaming loch and the brooding hills flooded her, then receded. As Ardan led her back, she smoothed the amber hilt of the dagger and it was warm in her fingers.

"Tell Urp and Arda what happened," Naisi was saying to Carnach. The Epidii warrior nodded, embracing the brothers one by one then turning to go before Naisi stopped him, seeking his eyes. "Tell Urp that Naisi mac Usnech, of the Red Branch of the Ulaid in Erin, thanks him for his friendship, as do his brothers, Ardan and Ainnle."

Carnach paused, one hand holding Naisi's shoulder. "Naisi." He tasted the name, then nodded. "I will not break that sacred trust, or forget you as I live. Ardan. Ainnle." He gripped their hands again as he named them, before disappearing, the glimmer of Deirdre's swan cloak at last swallowed by the dark.

Ardan and Ainnle dragged open the timber gate and lowered themselves down the rocks, and for a moment Naisi and Deirdre were alone. Amid the reek of the dung spilling down the hill, his arms crushed her to him and his lips sought her brow. Her hand went to his jaw and she felt the wet blood. His new cut had opened, smearing her skin. He had marked her again. She put her copper-tainted fingers to her nose and drank in his life-scent, the stink around them fading away.

"It was because of you."

She pulled away a little. "We have to run, Naisi. It doesn't matter anymore."

"It's all that matters." The sheen on his eyes showed what he was suppressing to be strong. "A spear can still stake our backs in the next heartbeat, *fiáin*, and then I can say nothing to you again." His teeth were bared, the smile dazed. "At one word he might harm you, I threw away everything I had fought for. I couldn't think of anything but you, after thinking too damned much about too many useless things. How the gods must be laughing!"

She saw the wild despair in him, and gripped his arms. "I thought I might die in the darkness around this king, but I could see only you, too." She brushed the hair from his brows, that raven-black plumage. "My love."

His gasp was a release. "I wish I had time to kiss you properly," he muttered, sounding more himself.

She leaned her forehead on his chin. "It's fortunate, then, that I know what it feels like—and won't forget again."

His arms went about her and he let out a great breath.

CHAPTER 38

The crossing of the marsh in the darkness was like a terrible dream. Deirdre felt she stumbled over that sucking mud and pockmarked bog for nights on end, with only the sheen of the river and the bulk of the southern headland against the stars to guide them.

A faint murmur of sound carried from Dunadd, the shouts and screams of revelers, but the damp air tricked them and made it seem as if the voices were close behind, in pursuit. They plunged through pools of sour brine, and as soon as they reached the narrow river mouth over the mudflats they all plunged in, washing off the stink of dung and urine that had coated them in their descent from Dunadd's cliffs. When they emerged on the other side and began to climb the hills there was nothing left of them but the clothes they wore and their swords. They were stripped once more of any allegiance and belonging.

Dawn was breaking when they reached the shore, far down a peninsula that speared south into the sea. There was no path of safety now but to take to the ocean again. They stole another curragh from a cluster of fisherhuts and this time had nothing to exchange for it, wearied beyond endurance.

They rowed for five days among the offshore islands far into the sea, seeking a place with no smoke or glimpses of thatched huts. Finally they found a small islet that was too rocky and steep to support a steading and crops, and exposed to the force of the storms and lashing waves. There was a spring and a few tiny beaches cupped by the jagged rocks, and some wind-blasted oak, hazel and birch trees huddling behind the outcrop that formed the island's spine.

They pulled the boat into the trees, lit a fire in a rock shelter to hide the smoke, and huddled beneath the dank stone roof in their wet clothes, too drained to speak.

Only sleep offered the comfort of oblivion.

Deirdre fell sick with a cough and fever, her body too stressed by the flight from home and the power she had mustered at Dunadd. Those first days passed for her in a painful daze, her throat so sore she could barely speak but to whisper to Ardan and Ainnle the healing plants to gather for her. They spent their time scouring the shores and taking the boat to nearby islands to search for thyme and coltsfoot, then boiling them in a hide pouch of water over the little cave-fire.

Naisi piled up the sleeping hides close to the flames and held her while she shivered and burned, smoothing the sweat from her face.

In the moments she could open her eyes a crack, she thought she was still lost in strange dreams. The waves and wind threw fine clouds of spray and streamers of sea-fog over the island, and the earth quivered with the constant, faint roar of the ocean. Her mind feebly wondered if they had found a place that hovered between the worlds, where they would be hidden at last.

After a few days, she got over the worst of the illness, though Naisi insisted she stay in bed. The constant slipping in and out of sleep made the dreams become fractured and anxious. One night as she drifted off, she thought she heard gull cries, high and wheeling. But only the waves sang at night. It was another bird's cry, fey and piercing.

And suddenly she was on a beach at dusk, her legs pushing through the sand. She looked out across the crested waves and there on the horizon the meeting of sky and sea was a sheet of flaming sunset, with the underbellies of the clouds soft as feathers and hemmed with gold.

A movement caught her eye, and she shaded her brow and watched as three black shapes approached across the fiery sky. Birds.

They swept over her in a rush, the wind of their wings brushing her temples, and she craned her chin to follow them. The rosy light glimmered on something dripping from their beaks, and the droplets fell onto her upturned face. She touched a droplet to her lips—it was honey. As they spun away to the east, she realized it had changed on her tongue. The taste was wrong...sour...

Deirdre struggled awake, recoiling from something painful.

She was alone in the cave, the roof washed by gray daylight. Naisi had carefully tucked her cloak into a ruff about her neck, leaving a cup of water beside her. The soreness in her joints and throat was gone and her mind was clear again, the remnants of the dream stirring her body with restlessness.

Moving stiffly, she drank water and wound her tangled hair off her face, then gingerly got up. Outside, her eyes slitted, unaccustomed to the glare of the cloudy day. The rowan trees on the ridge above were bent in the sea-wind, and it flapped her cloak as she picked her way along a sandy path. The curragh was gone. Ardan and Ainnle must be away fishing, but Naisi would not leave her alone.

At last she found him sitting on a rock on the western beach, his scabbard propped between his legs. The waves crashed on the rocky headland and drifted spray over him.

He only moved when he heard her, startling at the sound of her step. "*Fiáin!* You shouldn't be out here."

She linked her arms about his waist from behind, resting her chin on his shoulder. "I am better, and I need some fresh air before I go mad."

It was the first time she had been able to focus on anything other than her illness, and her smile faded as she straightened and gazed into his upturned face. Though his skin was reddened by wind and sun, it had a sallow cast to it, and there were bruises under his eyes and a furrow between his dark brows. His hair hung in tendrils from the sea-spray and it also coated his cheeks, as if he was melting into the mists and the ocean. He drew away from her scrutiny, averting his face to kiss her hand.

He had been gazing west. The dread of her dream still clung to her, forcing out fearful words. "Do not call them with the cry of your heart."

He placed her hand across his breast and she leaned her belly against his back. "There is no point looking to Erin." Sorrow roughened his voice, and the weight of it rushed out of him. "There is no point seeking anywhere. There are no other shores to flee to now, *fiáin*. Nowhere for us to find home." He turned his hilt so the dull daylight played over the bronze. "I wanted to fight for honor, and instead it was for Cinet's greed. So now I know—every time I grasp for light, I bring ruin instead."

His skin began to tingle under her touch, the sparks of knowing coming alive. To her, being here brought a lightness, freedom. They had escaped; no one ruled them anymore. But now she saw despair in him, and heard bitterness in his voice. "Some things have not come to ruin. Me, and your bond to your brothers."

His shoulders tensed, and he turned his head against her breast. "I did nearly lose you, though."

"And I you," she murmured. "The bond stretched, but will not break. It cannot."

After a silence he looked up at her and forced a wry smile that did not reach his eyes. "Perhaps I will need to become that farmer you long for," he said. He nudged the bag of mussels with his toe. "Or a fisherman. For we cannot hunt deer here. Not even that."

She knelt on the sand. "In the druid stories, to reach the light you must first descend along a dark road, a shadowed valley. And the more beautiful the dawn that beckons over the hills, the more difficult the trail to get there. I don't know why." She smoothed the pain from his jaw. "We have all walked through the worst darkness now, which means the light is nearly ours. Once you reach the shadowy depths, you can only climb up—or so the druids say."

Naisi spent the days wandering the rocks and gathering shellfish, and sometimes stayed overnight on the sands when the stars were out. Deirdre let him be, hoping the salty wind could scour this terrible darkness from him.

Ardan and Ainnle were just as morose, taking the curragh out in turns alone on the sea. It was an island of dreams, Deirdre thought, sitting beneath the rowan on the ridge. It floated in the mists and so the brothers were suspended also, and had not begun living again. She drank her life from such wild places, but their paths had closed behind them and they had not yet dreamed of what lay in front.

One night, a storm bore down on them, and when Naisi came back the next dusk he said a fisherman's curragh had been blown up on the rocks, the man taking a knock on the head. Naisi had lashed the cracked timbers back together and gave the fisherman water to send him on his way. Ardan and Ainnle stared at him across the campfire. "You showed yourself?" Ardan said.

Naisi broke up driftwood and tossed it on the flames. "He would have searched ashore for water, anyway."

"You should have left him alone." Ainnle frowned.

"He was bleeding. He could have been badly hurt."

"But—"

"I will not stand by and leave someone else in pain!" Naisi snapped.

As his brothers gazed at him, baffled, Naisi jumped up and went outside into the dark. Deirdre followed him, catching him on the sandy path. With a gentle hand she lifted his chin to the sky, blazing with stars. "There is no end to the world, Naisi. There is a sea we can sail upon together, and travel far."

He lowered his head and his hands went to the small of her back, drawing her to him. "Can we?" he whispered. "Help me, *fiáin*, to find what I can be now, because *I don't know*."

In answer, she kissed him fiercely. "We will find a path to-gether."

Even as that left her lips, the plunging dread of her dream

returned in force, and she did not know if it flowed from his flesh into hers, or crept inside her from the sea-mists themselves.

Naisi.

   Naisi.

The call entered his dreams.

Naisi's eyes flickered open. Sun played over the roof of the cave, picking out the veins of stone above him. It was past dawn. Deirdre stirred in his arms, curling up and nestling her head into his belly, and then he remembered why he was still in bed.

He had found another little fissure of a cave along the ridge for them to sleep in—a place to be alone for the first time since Deirdre's illness. Now he slid the deerskin from her bare shoulder to see it gleaming, remembering how he had lapped it in the dark, nipping her neck. His tongue summoned the taste of the skin between her thighs, and he savored his hardening again and the throb of desire—the first thing that had felt pure for days. He smiled as she burrowed into his warmth, then kissed her shoulder and covered it up once more.

Naisi. He paused, as if a voice had echoed in his hollow belly. A gull cried far away...or was it voices? He must be going insane. A thin thread of sound came, as of a distant shout, but this place was washed by the endless murmuring of the sea and he could not be sure it was a different noise at all. And yet his head turned to it, his heart racing.

Despite the heat of Deirdre's flesh beside him, Naisi was drawn from his bed.

Deirdre climbed down from the cave to find Ardan and Ainnle in the little hollow below the ridge, rubbing their bleary faces.

"I heard something," Ainnle was saying to Ardan, buckling on his sword. "I'm sure I did."

Deirdre stopped, her eyes darting between them. "Naisi is gone. I thought he was with you."

They heard another noise, a low bellow. Stags? There were no deer here. Ardan and Ainnle looked at each other and, as one, swung for the trail that led to the eastern shore. Deirdre hurried after them, her senses eclipsed by such a bound of fear that she could gain nothing from the air around her, or the pulse of the earth.

They came to a halt at the fringes of the beach, and as Deirdre choked back a cry, Ardan pulled her roughly behind a scatter of rocks. A ship was anchored offshore, with a timber hull and sails. They couldn't see the banner it flew, for the west wind was streaming it out behind the mast. Three men had lowered a tiny curragh from the larger ship, and beached it on the sand. They had just come ashore, their dark figures obscured by the white foam that had pushed them in.

And there on the beach stood Naisi, like a pillar of rock on the sand.

It had all happened so suddenly that Deirdre seemed to have lifted out of herself, the vivid colors of the blue sea and the white sail, the green standard and the dark rocks all sharp-edged, like a tapestry. It was just a moment of imagination. Of nightmare. Surely it was.

Ainnle would have flung himself after Naisi, but Ardan gripped his tunic, anchoring him. "Wait!" he hissed.

One of the men had stuck a pennant in the sand, and with another gust of wind the cloth streamed out. Deirdre could not make out the design in black and green, but Ardan answered her unspoken question, his voice sounding queer and breathless. "Fergus."

"And Illan and Buinne," Ainnle finished. He glanced at his brother with wild eyes, his mouth drawn into a rictus somewhere between snarl and disbelieving smile. "We have to reach Naisi!" Squirming from Ardan's grasp, he streaked off over the sand.

Ardan whirled to Deirdre, scraping his hair back as he tried to force his thoughts into order. "You should stay here."

Deirdre shook her head. "We are as one now—for good or ill."

An unguarded glimpse of immense strain and pain flitted across his face. "Very well, but only because the banner means this is no attack. And Fergus has been our friend since we were in breech-clouts, and Illan as close as a brother. Come."

An enormous silver-haired man was standing beneath the banner. Beside him was a slim, young warrior with flaxen locks, and another ruddier youth whose features were stamped with the massive jaw and proud nose of the older man.

Deirdre saw the glint of Naisi's sword in his hands, and the slight sway of his body. *It's too much for him*, she thought desperately.

The silver-haired giant was reaching for his own blade, murmuring something to Naisi she couldn't hear. Ainnle and Ardan made it to Naisi's side, kicking up a flurry of sand and whipping their weapons from their sheaths. But the big man was only unbuckling his scabbard and now he flung it from him with great force, leaving himself unprotected. "Father!" his elder son shouted.

Fergus spread his huge paws, and his teeth were white beneath his drooping moustache. "Lads," he said in a rumbling voice, "I have never been so glad to see such pretty faces in all my life."

Deirdre kept her hood tight around her cheeks in some futile defense, and Fergus and his sons barely glanced at her hovering behind Naisi.

"Tell me," Naisi said in a strained voice. He had not lowered his sword, and it wavered in his hand, the tip trembling. "*Speak.*"

The red-haired man scowled, while the fair one darted a wary look at his father. Fergus only dropped his hands, and the warmth in his eyes faded a little, though more with sadness than wrath.

"Disarm and we will speak," the elder son broke in again, until his sire gestured him sharply to silence.

Fergus cocked his silver head, studying Naisi. Deirdre could only see the side of Naisi's jaw and how the muscle along it formed a hard ridge. "The king has seen his folly at last." Fergus's voice boomed from his barrel chest, giving it a great force of authority. "He's had men searching for you ever since you left, as has Cúchulainn. Ferdia is missing, and though I will not ask the Hound, I suspect mac Daman has come to Alba looking for you, too. We all heard the rumors that you were with the Epidii, but even as warriors set out for Dunadd, worse news came—that the Epidii had turned on you and their king sought to kill you."

A tremor went up Naisi's back. "We know. We have lived this fine tale that provides such entertainment for Conor's hall."

Fergus shook his grizzled mane. "It isn't like that, my friend. The loss of you has splintered the Red Branch, and though it has taken time, Conor saw it at last. He doubled his efforts to find you. And when the men discovered he would have you back in peace … You have never heard such cheers, lads." He met Ainnle and Ardan's eyes in turn, smiling broadly, his heavy cheeks crinkling his eyes in a nest of wrinkles.

"He's right," the flaxen-haired young warrior broke in eagerly. He took a step forward and Naisi's sword nudged toward him. Bravely, the youth stayed there with the tip only a breath from his breastbone. "When Conor sent the order to retrieve you from Dunadd, it's the first time since you left that we felt whole, Naisi. Everyone was smiling. The Red Branch spoke of you with love and honor. We slaughtered a boar for you and marked ourselves with the blood!"

Naisi's shoulders lowered fractionally, and Ainnle let out a sharp sigh. "They feasted?" Ainnle said, his tone rising into wonder.

Fergus grinned. "A terrible cloud has been hanging over us all since you fled, but with the news you were found, it lightened. And when we knew that these foreigners were stalking you— well." He snorted and shook his head. "The Red Branch bayed at Conor—howled like a pack of wolves!—that he must find you now at all costs before the Albans did. He's practically emptied his coffers. Thousands of fishermen, sailors, traders, passing travelers—everyone has been scouring these seas."

There was a pause. "A fisherman." Naisi's voice was faint. "Someone came ashore … I was too used to hearing Ainnle and

Ardan's voices, and those of the Epidii, all blended together. I did not notice he was of Erin."

Fergus gazed on him with pity, scanning his face. "There's no mistaking you, lad," he said, with more gentleness than Deirdre would have thought possible from that massive frame and rough-hewn face. "One description was enough, and a day later Conor was humbling himself at my own gates, and there he begged me and my sons to act as his envoys." He paused, eyes glinting beneath bushy brows. "Because he hoped you would trust me above all others—all others but one." And with one hand spread in peace, he reached to his belt and withdrew a dagger carefully by the tip, and handed it toward Naisi, hilt first.

Naisi stared blankly at it for a moment, before the youngest warrior took it from his father and, reaching past Naisi's sword, pressed it into his hand. Naisi took it silently, turning the hilt in his fingers, and Deirdre saw the light shine through it. It was a polished ball of crystal, clear as green glass. Naisi's head bent over it for a moment.

Ardan at last spoke up, harshly. "Cúchulainn's dagger is one thing, the Red Branch another, and even your own appearance, Fergus, for we esteem you well. But what of Conor himself?"

Fergus turned to Ardan. "He has seen sense, I swear it. In the Temple of Macha, he heard the words of the gods themselves—that he must honor you. Cathbad was there, and he vouches for what Conor said. And I am convinced he means it. I looked in his eyes as he asked me to go to you." He placed a hand on the enormous bronze ring around his thick arm, the braided design familiar to Deirdre. "He gave me his oath, and now I give you mine. You are pardoned by the king of the Ulaid, and I am here to escort you back to Emain Macha with the undying protection of my own house upon you."

There was a silence, while the wind cracked the pennant on its spear. Deirdre was rooted to the spot. Why did she not feel any shock at this? It was almost as if she knew it was coming; she knew her path would lead her here. The foreboding sprang from the primitive, instinctive core of her belly, at the base of her spine, and spread up her body, setting the world alight.

Danger.

And yet Fergus himself was clothed in luminescence, fingers of it winding from his heart toward Naisi and his brothers. Even in Fergus's sons she could see no evil intentions. The elder was guarded, though none of his thoughts were bent on his blade, but the younger was a pure flame that eagerly reached for the sons of Usnech to surround them with fierce protection.

In that cloud of spinning radiance, only one thing had drawn a thread of the surrounding darkness into the heart of the moment, like a black spear thrust into the pool of light. And that was Naisi.

"What if we do not agree to come?" Naisi was saying.

His words snapped Deirdre back from the mist, confusing her. How could he even consider going with them?

At that Fergus stepped to Naisi, and with one hand pushed the sword blade aside, and Naisi let him. Fergus took hold of his shoulders and Naisi for once looked vulnerable within that massive grip. "Then I will leave," Fergus murmured hoarsely, "and say you have gone from our shores, to the east, and no one will seek you again."

Naisi bent his head back to look up at him. "*Now* you would defy the king?"

Fergus's smile was crooked as his fingers squeezed Naisi's shoulders. "Gods' breath, lad, I would have done so long ago, but you never gave me the chance. By the time I knew of this, you had already fled." He stared at Naisi. "Perhaps you should have trusted us. This did not have to be you three alone."

Naisi took a shuddering breath, and his sword at last slipped from his fingers. After an awkward pause, Illan bounded to Ainnle and threw his arms around him. "It's good to see you," Illan muttered, and the stiffness went from Ainnle's stance. A moment later, they were thumping each other's backs. With a wry smile, Buinne extended his hand to Ardan and they gripped wrists. Then Fergus was giving them each a bear hug in turn, crushing them so hard he almost lifted them off the ground.

"Fergus." Naisi broke away and turned to Deirdre, though when she looked in his face he hardly seemed to see her, his eyes glittering and dazed. "This is Deirdre." He beckoned her forward, and she had no choice but to warily approach the former king she had heard so much about.

As she pushed back her hood, the elder, red-haired son of Fergus turned, and his eyes bored into her. The younger one was staring over Ardan's shoulder with open curiosity. Fergus, meanwhile, gruffly bowed his head. "So this is the lass all the trouble's about." His eyes swept her up and down, not with cruelty but with the swift appraisal of a man who appreciates woman-flesh for pleasure only.

Her cheeks and jaw felt heavy and cold, her expression hardening. "That is Conor's trouble, I think you'll find," she said throatily.

Fergus's brows rose with surprise and amusement. Illan glanced at Ardan, who merely shrugged, while Ainnle scratched his sprouting beard, hiding a smile.

Naisi's hand reached for her own even though his eyes were not aware; his body simply craved her touch as she did his. "You can see," Naisi said softly, "why we are now mated. And she is right. None of this was her fault. That is something we must all know from the outset." Still his words hovered in the realm of *possibility*, and Deirdre realized her pulse was racing erratically, as her own fate slipped from her control once more. "We must think on this," Naisi said, stepping back.

"Share one cup of mead with us, lad, at least," Fergus urged. "When I knew we were coming to see you, it was the first thing we packed!"

Naisi reluctantly agreed and a horn edged in bronze was passed around, and after an initial stiffness Fergus began firing questions at the brothers about where they had been and what they had done, and telling them how, when rumors came of dazzling new warriors among the Epidii, all the Red Branch knew it must be them. His beaming smile drew the brothers from their wariness, and their words began to flow about the battles they had fought in Alba.

Fergus's sons exclaimed and threw questions at them only a warrior would ask, and all the while Deirdre stood silently, as unmoving as the rocks. At last Naisi remembered her, and with a swift look at her face said they four must speak alone. "Give us until sunset," he said hoarsely to Fergus. "And do not leave the beach." He paused. "This is the only realm we hold, and it is ours alone to walk."

He turned, and Deirdre pulled her grasp from his and stayed at the rear as Naisi led his brothers back to camp. She could hardly lift her feet from the sand, stunned that he had not refused this pardon.

It could not be true.

CHAPTER 39

Ainnle erupted as soon as they reached the hollow outside their cave. "So it comes at last—the pardon we have been waiting for!" The heaviness that had hovered over his brow for so long had suddenly cleared, like the sun breaking over his face.

Ardan was standing with his chin lowered, rubbing his temples. Deirdre wondered if he was overcome by the same storm of confusion that was charging through her. Naisi, meanwhile, had collapsed onto an oak stump, his head falling into his spread hands, fingers buried in his hair.

"What is this? Why are you not rejoicing?" Ainnle's voice rose, shrill and disbelieving. When Naisi did not stir, Ainnle stormed past him and spun about. "After all these moons of running, hiding, barred from everything we love and know…Can you even be considering for one moment *not* going back, when our heart's desires are once more in our grasp?"

Ardan abruptly straightened at that, his face going pale.

Deirdre was staring at Naisi's bent head as he neither moved nor spoke. Why was Naisi not denouncing this insanity? She could never trust Conor…none of them could. She crouched before Naisi. "We are free here, and we have love, Naisi. We need nothing else."

"You might not," Ainnle snapped, his eyes sparking. "You have your love and belonging, but what do we have?" He jabbed a finger toward Ardan, making his middle brother fall back a step. "We have to forge our own path, and being stuck on some windswept island grubbing for food in the mud is not what we were born for!"

A shudder went over Naisi at that, his black hair stirring between his fingers. Far back in Deirdre's mind, she remembered the sensation of the raven's flight; the world-wheel arresting, the hub straining. Again, the flow of fate had paused around them.

She touched Naisi's forearm below his clenched hands, and the muscle was so hard it startled her. She got up slowly. "You never told me," she whispered, "what drove this hunger to prove yourself to Cinet. I always felt there was more, but when I saw you at Dunadd I thought…I thought it had gone forever."

There was a silence. "And it would have," Naisi whispered. He pressed a fist into his belly, his other hand forming a shield across his face. "It would have if Fergus had not come."

He was the spear of darkness. "A terrible shame," she said wonderingly, her gaze roving over his bowed shoulders and the despairing tilt of his head. "And it is tearing you apart even now."

"Tearing?" Ainnle frowned. "How can you be *torn* about this?" He strode forward and gripped one of Naisi's shoulders. "You will not keep me from my heart's longing with secrets. Tell me!"

Naisi jerked away from that touch and his hand dropped to reveal his face, and it was terrible. Deirdre had seen it transfigured with light at Dunadd, when he laid eyes upon her again; seen the truth of love revealed there. Now came the dark—his pupils, pits of despair, hollow and frightening; his mouth clamped and twisted on itself.

"If this is still guilt over Leary's death and the Red Branch," Ainnle said harshly, "then you have to damn well accept it. Conor pardons us. We can mend those rifts and honor Leary, and the rest will be as it once was."

A hiss escaped Naisi's lips and he staggered up, putting the stump between himself and his brothers. Then he looked right at Deirdre, as if straining to imprint her features on his mind. As if he thought he would not see them anymore.

A wild fear pierced her. *You will always have my face before you.* She was about to cross that gap when a convulsive movement of his shoulders halted her.

"It's not that." His voice was strangled, before he gulped and it rushed out of him in a sour torrent. "It has always driven me. I kept trying to quench it, but then I saw I was cursed, that the thoughts in me were black, and always would be."

Ainnle shook his head. "What are you talking about?"

Naisi spread his arms, and bowed his head as if he was opening himself to a blade. "I did not merely hate Conor." The words were surrendered. "I wanted to utterly overthrow him."

Ainnle's hands fell to his sides like a sail that has lost the wind. Ardan froze for a long moment, then forced himself to speak. "But...you are the greatest Red Branch fighter since Cúchulainn. You have served the Ulaid with your blood and breath!"

Naisi's bruised eyes flicked up, staring through his falling hair. "I wanted to feel that Red Branch fire, that glory—but when the darkness moved in me, I wanted these things only so I could be powerful enough to take the king's hall and lead the people." He grimaced as if the words pained him, then whirled to Ainnle, flinging his head up. "See, brother, what you love so well—a fool with an infernal pride who, in summoning such thoughts, betrayed my king, my Red Branch brothers, and you, Ainnle. Betrayed you."

Shock had wiped all the anger from Ainnle's face. "I cannot believe that of you," he stammered. "Not you."

Deirdre understood nothing of this warrior talk. "All this time you tortured yourself for this? You never killed anyone but in battle; never ravaged a woman—"

"You don't know." Naisi's voice was dark; he lifted a hand to his brothers in a despairing gesture. "They know the sacred oaths we take, the loyalty we swear—to think only of the people, to shine in battle only to further the Red Branch and the Ulaid, and the sworn king placed there by his nobles. We are not the kin from which the kings are chosen. If you are, and the gods smile and the chieftains acclaim you, and you have earned kingship with the bravery of years...then that is something pure. The men have put you on your throne, and it is sacred. But to lust after it in a black corner of your heart, while so young, foolish, undeserving—to usurp a king annointed by the nobles for some hatred you don't even understand—that is another thing entirely. An evil thing."

Ardan shook his head. "I will not listen to you say that of yourself..."

"But there is worse!" Naisi strode toward him with agitated steps, as if he would strike him. "Go on, hear it all!" His eyes were wild as they held Ardan's. "I should have been content in being our clan's chieftain, leading our dun, guiding our people—father's people. They trusted me, but I turned my back on them to chase glory. I abandoned them, and so broke that trust!"

In that cry, Deirdre remembered their argument before the battle, and the hurt in Naisi's eyes. *You do not think me worthy of trust.*

"We all wanted Red Branch glory," Ardan said in an unsteady voice.

"It wasn't your place to protect our people; it was mine."

Ainnle looked sickly, and his words whistled from between his teeth. "Father was Red Branch."

"Father came back from Emain Macha."

Anger was dawning over Ardan's face as the shock disintegrated. "I thought you defied Conor just to release your own frustration."

"Nothing was an idle game for me. To shine in the Red Branch meant one day leading the kingdom." Naisi spun toward Deirdre, and the agony was naked in his face. "And when you asked me to take you away, my *fiáin*, I thought that could be the start. I could expose what Conor was—a jealous, miserly, unjust king—and rally men to me. I never knew his retaliation would be so traitorous, so swift and complete. I never understood, as I do now, what drove him to keep you by his side at all costs. What would make him attack men by stealth, set Red Branch oaths at odds and kill children, just to possess you once more." His lip curled, inviting her to hate him. "So you see, when I rescued you, I thought only to use you."

All she could think about was getting beyond that terrible pain and holding him. "I used you, too," she murmured, crossing her hands over her breasts. Despite the warm day she shivered as the shadows crept over them from the hazel trees. "There is no sin against me unless I sinned against you."

"I told you I forgave you that long ago," he snapped. "And this is why."

Ainnle blinked, still taking in what Naisi had just said. "*This* was what you planned when you took Deirdre? To stir up the chiefs and overthrow Conor?"

Naisi's eyes glittered with the coldness he had cast over them, the lids narrowed. "Something like that."

Ainnle looked between his brothers and his face crumpled. "You risked our lives for this, for something you kept secret from your own brothers?"

"I did not know it would escalate so swiftly. And then when it did, I could not tell you because it was my folly that had broken our lives apart." Naisi sucked in a breath, his chin down, shaking his head. "And so I fought desperately to make a place for us again here, a life of honor, so I could look you in the face and lay something at your feet that was good, and fine." He laughed bitterly. "And yet all I wrought was more ruin."

Ainnle's jaw jutted out. "And now, brother?"

"Can I go back? Is that way open? I don't know, Ainnle."

Deirdre had been concentrating so hard on his pain that his words crashed in upon her heart. *Go back.*

Ainnle stared at his brother for a long moment, then he turned and, plowing through the bushes, struck out toward the northern cliffs, disappearing among the thorn-scrub.

Ardan was flexing his fingers at his sides with convulsive movements, trying to expunge his feelings. "Speak to me," Naisi demanded. "If anyone wields the blade to rend my heart, it is you. You always gave me your trust when I did not deserve it."

Ardan's hands settled into fists. "Why didn't you tell me?"

"Because you would look at me as you are doing right now."

Ardan fell back one faltering step, his eyes wounded. "You didn't trust me."

"I wanted to spare you."

"You treated me like a child!"

"None of this was planned."

"No, it was just dark dreams, you say. But we always shared our dreams!"

Naisi sighed, his shoulders lowering. "Once we did."

Ardan was backing away. "I do not need to say anything to punish you, my brother. You do that for yourself." Then he, too, stumbled from the hollow into the shadows under the ridge, disappearing among the rocks.

Deidre and Naisi were left alone. "Why didn't you tell me?" The hurt of how they had nearly lost each other was still so raw, and now she went to him, reached for him. She circled his waist, and though his back stiffened, he touched his thumb to her cheekbone with a pained smile.

"Because, my *fiáin*, I wanted you to be proud of me, to believe in my good before you knew my darkness." He snorted without mirth, and the self-contempt in that hurt her more.

She closed her eyes. "I don't care about warrior oaths and pride—"

"But I do." He removed her hands and held them in the cold space between them, making her look up. "You are not listening if you forgive me so easily, Deirdre. When I took you away, I was not thinking of you. Only of…that." He could not name it again.

"And I made you rescue me by playing on your pride, and I hated myself for it!" she exclaimed. "But I was desperate…" As she heard her own words, her voice trailed away.

He let the moment unravel, before saying quietly, "And my desperation will follow me wherever I go, and I cannot conquer it so easily."

"My own pain faded at your touch," she stammered, cradling his hand to the hollow of her throat. "Let yourself sink into me, and that will be healing."

He was silent for a moment, his lashes closing along his cheeks. "No, Deirdre. You found your peace in the mountains of Alba. And I found love, yes, but nothing of me. I have burned sick with this for years…" He struck himself in the chest, making her flinch. "I have been hounded by this shame from Erin to Alba, and because of that sickness everything I turn my hand to is cursed. Can't you see that? And now I am cornered, with no way out!"

His words sunk in. "Goddess…would you really return to Erin, to that traitorous king? Would you risk all we have because of *pride*?" A taint came to her tongue and she tensed, her eyes glazing. The dream…glistening drops shed by three birds, words of honey that turned to blood. She tasted its coppery bitterness again and knew it now for what it was. "I dreamed that these men would come, and that their words brought great danger to us. *Death*."

The orbits of his eyes were sunken, his lips cracked where he had gnawed them. All at once she saw him clearly, as if a veil had dropped from her eyes: it was he who had wasted while she lay abed in her fever. "I do not need a dream to tell me that," he croaked. "I am a warrior, and blood is washed all over my fate." He crushed her hand to him. "Try to feel into me, *fiáin*. I need you to understand."

She sought to make the daylight blur around them, to see the fragments of emotions inside him as she had seen into Cinet, but the fear was strangling. She glimpsed a storm-darkness blowing around them, and at the eye was her hand over his heart and there she felt the surrendering of his truth, all the depths she had tasted and longed to know, his love for her a bright fire.

"I am dead without my honor," Naisi murmured, "and wherever we run, whatever seas we sail, this darkness will poison me."

Her throat cramped, and she blinked tears away. "And if we return, you might be taken from me."

"I am not *me*," he countered raggedly. "I am not whole. I dishonored the Red Branch, and though I bear no love for Conor, I honor the office of king and must find the humility to renew my oaths—and rule our dun the way Father would want me to."

"And I will be left to pace those walls year after year, not knowing if you will return to me on your feet or on a bier," she cried. "Unless Conor kills you as soon as we set foot on that shore."

"I trust Fergus, and Conor has made oaths—"

"This is not about oaths. It is about men who kill one another out of greed, and lust, and jealousy. There is no sacred honor among such men!"

He tilted his head and looked down at her, and she felt his heart thudding under her fingers. "And yet I will live the rest of my life in that truth, even if all about me fling theirs away."

Truth. That word rang through her, dragging her to see the heart of this, but she could not. "You would choose the Red Branch over me." It was an old ache, and it came back to her with breathtaking clarity.

He was struck by that, rocking on his heels. All at once he dragged up his trews, pointing at a faint scar on his shin. "I dropped my sword the first day I bore it, and sliced my bone... there... and I could barely walk for weeks. The Red Branch jest of it with me to this day. And that scar you asked about: when I first bedded a girl, her father chased me and I tripped and fell on a thorn-bush, and he caught and beat me." His hoarse laugh was almost a sob. "Fergus bound those wounds with his own hands; he said I'd been touched by enough women for one day." He straightened, his blue eyes fierce with memory. "In battle, death stalks so close you feel it panting on your neck. You love me, *fiáin*, but when I wield my blade you are not beside me. There is only Red Branch, and their kinship might be the last thing I feel."

"We can find other lords, other war-bands, if that's what you need. There is no end to the far lands we can seek."

"And though I travel with my face turned desperately outward, this will rot the heart of me, and everything I try to bury will come back tenfold because it is not being healed. It is how the gods work; you know that."

"The gods want us to choose life, and love!"

"They want us to be truly ourselves. And if you have found that light, then no one can take it from you—not Conor, and not me. So give me that, as you have found it!"

The plea made her gasp, and with a curse he cupped her face, leaning their foreheads together. "I will be able to return to my own dun, and my own hearth, and put aside my weapons with my soul clean, and love you with the last traces of that fire in my blood, and you will have all of me."

Crushed against him, the defeat swept over her, bleak and cold. *No matter how happy I make him, I cannot free him with love. I cannot free him.*

The inevitability of that choked her and she dragged herself free of his touch. She did not hear him call her back, as the storm rose and roared through her, borne of an old agony. *Why can I never be free?*

She left him and stumbled blindly. She did not know where she went, only that her legs carried her up the rocks, toward the clouds, until the sky swallowed her and she was barely tethered to the earth.

CHAPTER 40

Deirdre climbed the ridge with fingers spread, stirring the air with her touch so that as she let go into pain it ignited around her.

Conor. Erin. Red Branch.

She trailed a mantle of stars, gathered to her from the earth and the clouds by the clarity of a heart torn open, and the oaks in the shelter of the hill flamed into torches at her passing. The folds of air were whipped into a quickening radiance as she walked, breaking into a thousand glittering jewels that became a whirlwind, and she felt the agitation of the *sídhe* as they flew around her.

At the top of the ridge, the west wind hit her, buffeting her body, flooding her nostrils with the scent of salt air, and sea-plants and the mineral taint of the rocks. The streaming motes of Source rushed about, drawn by her hurt. *Where is peace?* Where was home?

Her feet slid down the other side of the hill as she made her way along the trail, desperate to reach the beach and the crashing waves. The spring from which they drank tumbled down both faces of the ridge, and on the west side it emptied into a waterfall that had carved a tiny ravine. She heard the pounding of the water and realized her throat was parched, and plunged through the browning ferns under the stunted birch trees toward it.

She stumbled into Ardan, hidden in the undergrowth of bracken.

His back was pressed against one of the birch trunks, his head tangled among the leaves as he stared down into the boiling white foam of the pool. The thundering falls had blotted out all sound of her approach.

He recoiled at her sudden appearance, knocking his brow on the branch above him. Clapping his hand to it, he stared at her hollow-eyed, while she teetered there on the balls of her feet, about to turn and flee. Then he took an unsteady step in front of her, and the helplessness of the movement stopped her.

"Why are you here?" she croaked. "I thought you'd be with your Red Branch friends, plotting your glorious return."

"I thought so, too," he replied, his eyes never leaving her face. "But then I found myself here." He chewed his lips as if to halt his words, but they leaked out anyway, hoarse and broken. "Deirdre, Naisi *will* return to Erin." Her senses snapped to attention, for by his wild-eyed, hungry look—so different from his familiar placid expression—she saw he was also strained beyond reason.

She felt behind her for the birch trunk. "He's confused."

"He's eaten up by guilt—why didn't I see it before? And he is too pure of heart to run from this anymore." His face contorted and he dropped his hand.

Deirdre stared at the seam of blood that had opened along his brow.

"And I know I should go home, too, but..." His eyes flared with anguish. "As I stand here, I have not been thinking of Erin at all, but of *you*." Her gaze leaped to his mouth as she struggled to take that in. "I know you will not return, Deirdre. I have seen this brightness in you, this light of Alba that you cannot hide..." Stunned, she could not stop him rushing on, "and though I love my brother with all my soul, there is something I need even more than him." He gulped a ragged breath. "It is you...it has always been you."

"No."

Ardan's eyes pleaded for understanding. "He will leave because he needs the Red Branch, and you will stay because you need the wilds of Alba. And if you do, then I will stay—with you." The words hammered the air between them, but it was Ardan who was felled by them, and his legs crumpled as his strength gave out and he sank on his knees. He raised a hand, warding something away. "My brother," he muttered breathlessly.

"You cannot leave Ainnle and Naisi," she stammered. "You cannot survive."

He lifted his head and his eyes glistened. "It is this sickness I cannot survive, this emptiness in me." His voice was thick with self-loathing. "I am nothing but weak, and lost, and alone, and every part of my body and soul spends its time longing for what I cannot have. How can I be Red Branch filled with this yearning? My brothers are renowned for their bravery, but where is my courage if I am so unmanned? All love is cursed, I know that now, and I can take no such curse back to Erin when Naisi is so crushed by his own."

She closed her eyes, appalled. Her and Naisi's love could not spawn this; it wasn't possible.

Her eyes opened again to see a storm of spinning sparks, as if all the motes of Source that had streamed to her from the air and soil were now centered here. They were not whirling around her, though, but drawn to *him* . . . brushing his black hair, his gray eyes, cloaking his whole body with a sparkling aura. *They wanted him.* Couldn't he *feel* it?

Alone. Longing. Yearning. His words could be about her own self as it once was.

The charge of the *sídhe* rushed through her, buffeting her like a glowing wind. *See him, heal him.* The radiance did not penetrate Ardan, for his pain was a twisting column of black in his heart.

Yet she had beckoned the life-force of the stallion back to memory of life. Now Ardan had to remember what wholeness called him, too. She was only barely aware that her fingers had reached for the dagger at her belt, and as Ardan stared at her, she spread out her palm. He had to absorb it, and he would not open.

She sliced her hand, the pain a burst of joyous fire, and pressed her bleeding palm to his cut brow. "If I can know it, then my blood will show it to you," she muttered, and with all her will forced her own light to stream through the vibrating particles of blood and life-force in him.

Suddenly, she was in the glowing river inside him, that dance of flesh and charge of life. She knew the song of her own soul now, and so she immediately recognized the harmony of Ardan's light all around her, and how it chimed with her own. The same yearnings of their hearts. The same seeking for the *sídhe*. Her desperate hope to heal called to the disrupted sparks among the dark rents of his pain, and because they resonated already so closely with her own, all the luminous stars in him became attuned to that pure note. *Come. Take this blessing.*

Ardan gasped and swayed on his knees, gazing about him as if he could at last see the veils of light among the trees, and wonder wiped away his pain.

"It is not me for whom you sicken," she whispered, soaring through the truths of his heart, the star-patterns making her body throb with his emotions. "It is the Goddess you yearn for—communion with the Mother, with the *sídhe*. Belonging. You saw Her light through me, that is all, and it confused you."

My brother, she breathed into him. *The brother of my heart.*

And there, in the droplets of light that surrounded Ardan, she saw glimpses of a future. Ardan in a hooded mantle wandering the oak groves on an Erin hill. He reached the dark opening to a stone tomb of the ancestors and, entering, he lay there in vision, the spirals on the walls spinning with a light only he could see. She saw him walking with his face tilted to the sky, dew coating his smiling lips.

Look beyond to what your heart truly seeks, below the surface of it all. The meaning lit up the strands of his being, and there was no need for words.

Ardan broke away from her, his eyes widening as the pool and tumbling stream shimmered into light. This flame was not for her, though. He turned on his knees and plunged his hands into the water, touching the surface, breaking the drops and letting them drip from his hands, and his heart flowered inside him, as if it had seen its desire.

The intimacy of that was so raw that Deirdre could watch no longer. She left him with a touch on his head, her steps taking her down the path toward the beach. The flood of Ardan's light had cleansed her, letting her breathe.

Ahead, the sinking sun turned the sands gold, and sent a ridge of flame along the crashing waves.

A single rowan tree grew close to the shore, a last bastion against the wild sea. Its roots were anchored in the rocks and the wind had pressed it almost flat, the trunk worn by rain and storms into a long, undulating shape.

She lay on it, molding herself to it, for it was her spirit formed in wood. The strength of the branches bore up her limbs and the wind tangled her hair in the twigs and yellowed leaves. She could not face the west and Erin, so she lay with the roar of the waves at her back, her chin stretched up the trunk toward the heart of the island, and Alba.

Alba, where the wiry heather had to crouch close to the ground, huddling from the wind, yet still flamed with the brightest of blooms. A land where she had found silence within the cry of wild storms, and burned with the Source among the frosts. The pain in her throat was held at bay by the trunk beneath her ribs, and blood from her hand smeared the wood. She looked up at the ridge of the island, the birch crowns yellowing with the approach of leaf-fall, the oaks turning brown.

And she saw herself like Ardan's druid, wandering the shores in a deerskin cloak, mottled with brown so she merged into the woods, rowan-berries wound in her hair. She would sit by the spring and drink of the Source and her skin would glow as she dissolved into it, forming a cloak of shimmering fire. People would hear of the wisewoman, the *calleach* on the island, and leave offerings for her. And as a seer she would stir up the Source in the water and see their fates. Years would pass, and she would bleach the same hue as the rowan, and hide in the trees and watch people landing, and forget what human voices were. She would at last become *sídhe*. A cramp of pure longing bent her body.

Her thoughts called the *sídhe* and they drifted about her in clouds. She lifted a shaking hand—she could feel an agitation among them, a gathering of force that drummed in her blood. Did they call her deeper into their clan, beckoning her to slip her human bonds? Did they warn her not to let go?

She gasped as she saw the webbings between her fingers, the light traveling through her veins and out into the world. *To Naisi.* She touched her lips, remembering the honey of his kiss and how she had fought for him. She had felt the loss of love in the vision of him stabbed by a sword. She had known the ecstasy as his hand touched hers beneath the stars on Dunadd. A breath of denial escaped her lips into the clefts in the bark. She couldn't give him up and watch him sail away.

You could make him stay. That was her own dark whisper.

Yes. She could weave her new power about him, anchoring him to her with stroking touches, enslaving him with tongue and lips. She could tantalize his body until he was buried in her, then make him swear they would not return. She could bind him with love, desire, heat, beauty.

Like seaweed strangling him until he drowned. She would be a selkie, twisting him with enchantments until he was no longer a man. She would have most of him—and pretend to have all. But when she was asleep, his dreams would break from hers and turn to nightmares of Erin. And at the heart of him there would be an emptiness she would circle, and rend herself knowing it was there and be powerless to heal it.

In making him choose to sacrifice what made him Naisi, she would unman him as surely as if she wielded a blade.

The wind had been rising and with raw eyes she staggered up and over the rocks that led into the foaming waves. There at the borders of sea and land she spread her arms, her hair streaming behind her, her tears numbing her face.

You are so afraid of being trapped you will not bind to me. Naisi's words. And so she had nearly lost him.

The *sídhe* were gathered before her in waves of crashing luminescence that echoed the seas beneath them. Their murmuring was the sound of oceans thundering on far shores, and she wavered, imagining plunging into the water and at last shedding her human self, kicking down through depths lit by phospor and moonlight.

Then there would be no pain, no human cares, no tangled webs of longing and love to break through, anymore.

Naisi was still sitting on the oak stump, his hands slack on his knees as if he was emptied of all he had carried. A last shaft of sun spilled from the clouds, bathing him in that warmth.

He looked up at Deirdre's soft step, and his eyes blazed in his white face.

Slowly, Deirdre turned. The *sídhe* had drifted inland with her, in sea-mist veils that draped themselves around her with every step she took back from the beach. She watched them with trembling lips as they hovered, shimmering in luminescent waves. Waiting.

A tremor went through her and she extended a hand and turned it like a petal unfolding, bestowing a loving touch. And before they could stream around her with their wild beauty, she dropped her hands and turned away from them. The light was extinguished from her eyes and heart. "If you must go back," she said huskily to Naisi, "then I will not be parted from your side." To bind to him, she must be a mortal woman, and no more.

He was on his feet in a bound, his face flooding with relief, but as he hastened toward her she held up her bloody palm, uttering the next words as an oath. "I fled a life at Emain Macha, for I knew how my spirit would wither. But I tell you now: you are never to doubt my constancy or question my love, no matter what lies are told to you. For no man, god or beast could make me walk back into the jaws of the wolf I fled, except you."

He came and pressed his cheeks to hers, their foreheads touching; cradled her hips with gentle hands and stroked her tangled hair. He kissed her eyelids with disbelief and then turned her hand up, staring at the blood before folding her fingers gently over that wound. Finally, he withdrew his sword from its scabbard and sank on his knee before her, raising his face. "Then I make my own oath to you, my *fiáin*, before any others. No one will ever know that my love is given not to the beauty of your face but to the spirit of fire in you, and that will keep me for all the long years on this earth. I will never adorn you with a single ring of gold, for there is no jewel to compare with the heart of Deirdre, and I would dishonor you if I laid at your feet all the riches of Erin. You will go unadorned, so that we alone know we are one in soul, and have no need for the wealth of this world. And after, the druids say there is nothing in the Otherworld but that flame, and yours will shine the brightest to me."

She knelt so they were on their knees together then, and held his face and kissed him, and his heart beat against hers. She tasted joy on his lips and knew it would hold her through a mortal life. She had chosen a fate with him.

They built an enormous fire in the clearing, and dragged their sleeping skins from the cave and were sitting by it as dusk fell, when Ainnle and Ardan came back together.

Ainnle strode up and with chin high set his scabbard tip on the ground, both hands folded over the hilt. "I have chosen to return to Erin," he declared. He looked at Naisi, and Deirdre recognized a more mature cast to his face, as if something had been stripped away, the agitated sharpness gone. A redness around his eyes said he had wept, but his irises were clear and his gaze was not restless or defiant anymore. "No decisions will burden you any further, brother, for now my choices are mine alone—and this is my first."

Naisi scrambled up from Deirdre's side and grasped Ainnle wrist to wrist, like warriors. "Do you forgive me, then?" he asked somberly.

Ainnle's smile was lopsided. "That, I have not decided." But he drew Naisi into an embrace.

Ardan, meanwhile, sat down on the hides cross-legged. "I am going back to Erin, too," he said. "Something calls me that I can only find there—a new fate, perhaps." Without shyness, he reached out and placed his hand on Deirdre's, his smile rueful, and though he looked unutterably weary there was no anguish there, only a peaceful light in his eyes. *I can go on*, his glance said. She squeezed his hand. The force that came from his flesh now was strong, pulsing with her own heartbeat.

Naisi looked between his brothers. "Then we are not to be parted—for Deirdre and I will also return to Erin."

Ainnle broke into a slow, relieved grin at odds with his defiant stance. "Ha! Then I will go and tell Fergus and Illan, and break open another mead-cask with them, and find out something of Erin other than Conor and his ills."

"Come back at full dark, then," Naisi said. "We should share our last night together by this fire."

Ainnle nodded, kissing Naisi and Ardan on the cheeks and flicking a strand of Deirdre's hair in what passed for a caress, and with a spring in his step headed for the eastern beach.

Ardan looked at the reddening sky. "I need to go back to the sea." He brushed Deirdre's hand and got up, hovering before Naisi. "You must know," he said softly, "that you might inflict guilt upon yourself for your failings, but nothing would change my heart toward you, except for you shutting me out. Don't do it again."

Naisi ducked his head and nodded, and they embraced, both dark heads together, and Ardan swiftly let go and turned as if he did not want to be anchored by human touch yet.

Naisi and Deirdre sat by the fire and did not speak. His look sank into her like something settling after a long fall, cloaking her with warmth. He brushed her cheek and she turned his hand and kissed it, and that melting of skin to skin was enough.

Under the stars that night, the sons of Usnech honored Alba with their voices, and the resonance that came through Naisi's hand into hers made Deirdre's body ring with their song.

CHAPTER 41

Down at the water, the little curragh wallowed, the waves nudging it back onto the sand as if it was reluctant to leave. Deirdre stood wrapped in her fleece cloak against the brisk morning wind while the three brothers and Fergus and his sons clambered around the boat, packing in bundled weapons and barrels filled with water.

Deirdre's awareness hovered between the clouds and Alba beneath her. She would not let herself melt into that hazy glow of the *sídhe* that merged sea with sky, the beckoning glints on the waves. She had chosen Naisi and a mortal life, binding her fate to his.

She would not stray down the path toward the glints, the whispers, again. That meant being torn in two, an inexorable drift away from him, and that she could not bear.

She looked at Naisi. His decision had brought a sureness to his movements, and he stood more solidly, taking deeper breaths—for even though the path to Erin might reveal darkness, he was striding down it now and not away. He must be her anchor.

"Fiáin." He turned before her, arms out. "Let me carry you to the boat." She blinked to focus. His black hair was ruffled by the wind and he was squinting in the rising sun, but she could see the determination that now framed his features, smoothing out the pain and firming flesh and bone into those of a man, not a youth. Indeed, if the Epidii thought him a prince then he had never looked more so: his far-seeking eyes reflecting a glimpse of seas and wide skies, his jaw lifted to the west like the defiant prow of a ship cleaving the waves. A glimpse of the life such a

man would lead, and she by his side, flashed through her and she clamped down on it with a ragged swallow.

That new resolution in his voice was more sure than any foreboding of hers.

She reached out a finger to his palm. "No," she said slowly. "I want my feet to get wet."

Understanding shone in his eyes. He felt the pulse of her heart now, knew her grief. That gaze said, *I should have known you'd walk every last step,* and hers returned, *Yes, by now you should have.*

Rolling up her trews and bundling her cloak over her arm, she plunged into the freezing shallows. The water was liquid crystal over pale sand, the grains shifting between her toes. The cold went into her bones but she did not brace herself. She wanted to have that ache follow her over the sea, and Alba's salt still drying on her skin when she set foot in Erin.

Ardan was in the boat, reaching out a hand, his eyes holding the clear, pure light of the sea. She gave him her boots and then clasped the rail.

Her heart contracted the moment her feet lifted from Alba's waves, and she drew a fold of her cloak around her head as the men jumped in and rowed out to the timber ship at anchor. There, she was hauled up again into a wide, open hull crossed with oar benches. The sailors gawped at her, but she sat in the stern and curled her knees under her cloak, and looked out so she saw only water.

After lashing the curragh aboard, the sail was raised, and it billowed out with a fresh wind as they turned to the west and the open sea. Deirdre gazed back. The island bays swept around in thumbnail curves, cupping iridescent water. She tried to absorb that beauty, to push aside the picture of their little hut, the roof falling in over a bracken bed hollowed by the weight of Naisi's body wrapped with hers.

As the water darkened and the island faded into the blur of Alba's mountains something began to stir in the pit of her belly. The heaviness rose up her throat, its taste metallic, like blood, and a song formed itself from her breath.

The melody was raw and wandering, the whispered words coming from an unconscious place inside her.

> Dear is the land in the east,
> Alba with its wonders,
> Never would I leave it
> But to go with Naisi

She paused, her breath taken by pain, and from the corner of her eye she saw Naisi's dark head by the steering oar turn toward her. "Honor that which we will miss," he said softly.

Deirdre swallowed, and nodded, for a moment allowing herself that sweet pain.

> The river of hazels
> We would sleep by its gentle murmur.
> Fish and venison, and the fat of meat boiled,
> Such would be our food by the hazel river.
> The bower of deer
> Tall its wild garlic, fair its oak branches
> We would wade through its grasses
> As we crossed the craggy peaks of the Shepherd mount.
> The roaring glen, in which we raised our house,
> Delightful were its groves on rising
> When the sun struck on the silver loch.
> The hill of the birches
> Sweet is the voice of the cuckoo
> on the bending branch on the hill
> Dear to us is the isle of seals,
> Dear its waters over the clean sand
> I would never have come from it, but that I came with
>   my beloved.

She named the little valleys and peaks she had climbed at Naisi's side, the riverbanks they had lain upon, the high corries from which she had watched the sun fade from the sky. Her voice cracked, the words almost lost in the slap of water on the hull and the banter of the sailors, which grew hushed as the oar strokes slowed. Ainnle paused in his rowing, his head turned toward her, and Ardan's eyes were fixed on the shore as Naisi watched the hills.

Deirdre's eyes blurred the water-glitter into a tide of receding light, and as the memories rushed away, she became aware of Naisi's finger-tips around her own. He tethered her, enlivening her flesh with warmth.

All the moments from leaving Alba's shores, the landing in Erin, the trek inland—these unfolded around Deirdre like a vision she was merely watching, a cloth unfurling that had already been woven by other hands.

She held herself fiercely detached from all about her—the smell of Erin's trees, the sand beneath her feet, the men's harsh laughter—for she wanted to know nothing of the pattern of that cloth. Still she did not allow herself to seek the murmur of the *sídhe*, for the glimpses of that stream now seemed dark and cold.

My oath was to honor my warrior husband. I will be a warrior's wife.

Instead, she kept herself contained to a tiny flame that was kindled only by *his* touch, allowing herself to feel only the moment of vivid life that was wrapped close about him. This was the only path: to stay strong as the currents of other men's fates swept them up again.

This became her world, then: Naisi's back moving under her hand when she walked up behind him on Erin's shore, burying her face in his shoulder. The sun-browned curve of his neck, gilded with fine hairs. The sense of his heart beating against her breastbone. Naisi's shoulders softly rising as he took a sustaining breath of Erin, while she only smelled the salt on his skin.

When she let him go, she kept a finger trailing in his, and saw then the strain gradually creep over his face again as he gazed inland, his body yearning toward the western horizon and Emain Macha. She was alive to him and so she knew the touch of Erin's soil had awoken it, the shame settling over him once more. In the lift of his set jaw, the gathered light in his eyes, she also saw a determination to bear that shackle until he could strike it from his body forever.

They walked along the cart-track that led west, and her touch never left Naisi, cradling his hands, his arms, moving to the small of his back if he turned to speak to his brothers. The rough calluses on his palms were more real to her than the outlines of hill and rock, the wind in the trees and the scudding clouds. *Erin*. She moved through it like a dream.

At high sun, a horseman hailed Fergus from a ridge-top, galloping down to tell him he had been waiting for the former king, and begging him to turn aside from the path. These words swirled strangely around Deirdre like a memory...something she expected.

Fergus was needed to resolve a cattle dispute in his own lands that was about to break into outright fighting; they had need of his counsel right away. Tempers had been escalating for days, the man said, and Fergus's own warriors were involved. Buinne offered to go in his father's stead, but Fergus dismissed that, leaving Buinne glowering.

At last, Fergus shook his head. "I must turn aside and deal with this; it will be a day's delay at most. It is too important to forfeit this cattle portion now, or weaken my own dun." He clapped Naisi on the shoulder. "I'll bash these chieftains' heads together with my own hands as soon as we get there, lad."

Naisi's face was grave, though through his fingers Deirdre felt the rising of desperation, like a parched man thirsting for sweet relief. For resolution. "You stay if you must, Fergus, but we will push on to be at Emain Macha by tomorrow night."

Fergus frowned, pulling on his moustache. "I gave my word I would escort you home. Come! Have one warm night on the way, fill your bellies with Erin mead and lay your head on a proper pillow at last. I could put my arm through the rings around your eyes."

Naisi held Fergus's gaze very steadily. "We have waited nearly two years for Conor's pardon. I will wait no longer. I can neither feast nor rest my mind and heart until I look in his eyes and hear it from his own lips. Only then will I lay down my sword and sleep freely."

His quietly impassioned tone silenced Fergus and he looked Naisi up and down. The older man's eyes were surprisingly tender, and he rubbed a fleshy hand across his nose before gruffly nodding. Illan broke in. "We are our father's blood, and his word is our word. Buinne and I will escort you in his name." He looked at his brother, and Buinne shrugged and nodded broodingly.

Fergus turned to Naisi, his hand on his sword. "If you will accept them in my stead, mac Usnech." Naisi started at the formal address, and some color came back into his face.

The party split and the other men went ahead on the road, and Naisi paused and held Deirdre to him, their bodies touching all the way from thigh to cheek. He took a breath, hoarding pained thoughts, and she heard them as if they were placed in her own heart. *If I'm to know any pride, I must go to Conor as if the whole world is arrayed against me and still I do not hesitate.* Her fingers felt for his soft lips, because the memory of their taste was more real to her than the cold wind and brooding hills through which they walked.

Night fell, and they made camp in a forest. Deirdre went to gather firewood, for she was struggling with the pressure prowling around the edges of her awareness. She hovered on the boundary of the black woods, wondering if she should reach a hand to that sibilance beneath the trees. But if the fear of Conor undid her, she would fail Naisi.

Something stirred behind her, and Ardan was there. He asked her why she was so silent, why her eyes were glazed. He spoke so simply now, his voice unguarded, his face softer as it turned to Erin's skies. She was glad he had that.

"I made a vow to be Naisi's, and face his fate alongside him," she said. "I am just trying to be strong."

"Do not fear," Ardan replied, his hands on her shoulders. "I saw myself at peace here."

A dark dream woke her, though she could not recall it. She drank from the stream beyond the camp, then Naisi came for her, his hair as dark as the inky sky, his eyes sheened by starlight. All sensation and emotion condensed in that moment to one vivid spark of *him*, and her nerve-endings tingled awake, becoming exquisitely raw.

She and Naisi were enveloped by the shadows of the whispering trees, as if the veils hid them, calling them to slip into their own world between the shimmering layers of Source. One stolen moment alone.

Naisi's hands wove a sacred dance, caresses that drew her cloak and tunic from her as softly as their mingling breath. His lips annointed each expanse of gleaming skin as he exposed it to the air, from shoulder to arm and down the cleft between her breasts. He reverently trailed his lips over thighs and calves and up the tender dip of her spine to the nape of her neck, raising a shudder under her skin.

Then he drew her down to kneel with him on their clothes, their bare limbs silver in the light, their thighs pressed together. Their exhalations stirred the mist, which was lit by the rising moon, as Naisi brushed each side of her face. "They cannot take from us." He framed her cheekbones, his fingers spread like feathers over her brows. "We both must vow to it. I will never leave your side, and you must not leave mine."

She softly kissed his full mouth, his eyelids, the slanted slopes of his cheekbones. Drawing his thick hair between her fingers she brought it to her nose, then tasted the skin beneath his jaw, where it dipped beneath the bone. Naisi moved between her thighs in the dance then, linking his hands in the small of her back and lifting her waist. He kissed the pulsing hollow below her ribs and she arched up to meet him, her arms draped back like wings. His mouth drank of her glistening flesh, as if it was a mead-blessing for the gods.

She flowed up and into him, so absorbed in every touch of his lips that when he at last slid inside her, the realization of their joining emerged only gradually. The stroking was a song her body slowly woke to, until it was rising with his in the long resonance of sea and winds. In the midst of that undulation, he buried himself in her and paused, locking them together. His fingers brushed the hair from her brow and her hands cradled the great expanse of his shoulder-blades. Neither of them stirred, desperate to hold that moment still, to capture it and leave them here like this, inviolable.

For a heartbeat, the illusion engulfed them. Then some night creature stirred the leaf-litter and the wind shook dew upon them from the branches, and the moments of time rolled on.

Naisi plunged into her now with a gasp of defiance, for that was the only response left to them, and Deirdre clung to him as they sought to melt together in a way that brooked no sundering. The sunburst was so intense they did not cry out, and only as they fell together from the peak were hushed cries wrenched from them at last. They were cries of fury, flung out as a fierce challenge to all the forces arrayed against them, as if with passion alone they could thrust back the encroaching darkness.

As if they could beat back the coming day.

CHAPTER 42

It was as he moved through the sunburst of battle-light that Cúchulainn felt the sons of Usnech.

Conor had at last ordered the Red Branch to the southwest border in response to rumors of a Connacht war-band massing. The anticipation of the return of the brothers had poured fiery light over those dark rents he had once seen, healing them. The

Red Branch were One again, freed of the dark weight of the king's malaise, joining their hearts in a flame that was incandescent with relief. *Brother warriors again.* And so with Ferdia by his side once more, Cúchulainn and the other Red Branch had decimated the Connacht raiders, beating them back over the hills.

It was then that it happened.

The Connacht-men were in retreat, Ferdia and the others pursuing the stragglers…

…and on the battlefield of churned mud and blood, Cúchulainn's head was thrown back, his awareness spreading like a light-storm in the ecstasy after battle. His consciousness soared up to the sky in an explosion of Source, and in one lightning flash of expelled breath he saw the whole island in blinding silver. There were the traceries of vivid life and fire and—

—*there, four flames that had come to rest on the eastern shore like falling stars, brighter to his eyes than all the others, for the force of heart he had bent toward them for so long.*

By the time Ferdia turned back from the battlefield, Cúchulainn was already in the saddle of the Gray of Macha, the swiftest horse in Erin.

Cúchulainn was barely aware of Ferdia standing by his bridle as the Gray reared and pawed, absorbing his energy, unable to stand still. The hairs on the back of the Hound's neck stood up, and his legs were already melting into the horse's back, to make them One, to force his own urgent power into the stallion's ride. "They are back," he croaked, his voice hoarse from war-cries. "I feel them."

He dragged himself from the light that still rimed everything, bringing his gaze to Ferdia to see joy and pain struggling in his friend's eyes. Ferdia had not found the brothers in time, had searched the shores of Alba fruitlessly for days before returning to the news that Conor's spies had succeeded where he had failed.

"It doesn't matter," Cúchulainn said to him, touching Ferdia's fingers on the bridle. "We are all drawn back to Emain Macha now, and will be reforged as one blade. It doesn't matter." He moved his hand to the Gray's neck, holding him for a breath, the coiled muscles bunching under his fingers. "I must go. These hooves will bear me back before the dead of night." There was a long, pale road he could follow that cut across the plains, and the cauldron of the moon goddess was full and would spill silver light across his path, making it as bright as day. "Ensure the borders are guarded and lead the others home as soon as you can."

"I will." Ferdia nodded swiftly, relief flooding his face. "Bear my love to our sword-brothers, and tell them I will be with them soon." After gripping Cúchulainn's wrist, he let go of the bridle.

The Gray was off like an arrow from a bow.

At the fall of dusk, Emain Macha was a citadel of light on a dark, rolling plain.

Like a cluster of stars that had come to rest on the earth, the low mound was lined along its ramparts by torch-light, and flaming braziers cast a red tide over the sweeping roofs of its halls. Off to the east there was another mound, and the flames there burned more steadily—a great bonfire that spilled a ruddy light out into the gathering darkness.

Pausing on the track that led down from a low ridge onto the plain, Deirdre held Naisi's hand as the wind brought the musty scent of woodsmoke and the whiff of sour waste and feet-turned earth. Dog barks echoed off the hollows, along with the wails of children. She glimpsed the red flowers of hearth-fires flickering as people lifted door-hides and let them fall. A human place. A place of men.

"The temple," Naisi whispered, pointing at the mound of the bonfire. Her heart shuddered unexpectedly, wondering if Levarcham was there, if she even knew they were coming. Naisi had not allowed Illan or Buinne to send a message of their arrival, and when the foot and cart traffic on the track increased the closer they got to the fort he made them take the more deserted paths. Now, as night fell, people were inside in the warmth and they were alone on the deserted road.

Naisi moved forward a step and stood like a quivering hound at alert, his brothers flanking him, their bodies tilted toward those high timber ramparts. Deirdre's palms spread over his back, absorbing the tremors in his flesh. The muscles in his shoulders coiled, and she saw him swallow. "Remember that the dark valley only leads to light," she murmured. His answering smile was crooked as he grasped behind him for her hand.

Naisi then turned to Buinne and Illan. "We will not announce ourselves." He blew out his breath in a steadying rush, his shoulders lowering. "I don't want everyone knowing we are back until we reach the upper fort."

Illan stared at him with a frown. "My father would have an honor guard out for you, and the horns singing of your return."

Naisi glanced at his two brothers. "I need to walk into Emain Macha like any other warrior." He cleared his throat and raised his face to the torches. "I want to tread its paths in freedom again, remember when the thrill of being Red Branch at Emain Macha was pure."

Buinne was scowling. "I do not understand."

Ardan placed a hand on Naisi's shoulder, his soft eyes on his brother's face. "No one can. This is between us and Conor. We do not want to have to *be* anything to anyone until we have that pardon from him."

Ainnle regarded Naisi with frustration—he would want the glorious return—but then his face softened and he grinned. "There will be time enough for all of that."

They were challenged by the guards on the tall gatetowers and Buinne and Illan had to give their names. Deirdre unconsciously drew her cloak around her face, as if she could thus contain herself in her own world. "They are not Red Branch," Ainnle whispered to Ardan. The brothers had also hooded themselves. "These guards have not heard of Fergus's mission, plainly."

"Conor must have kept the news among our sword-brothers," Ardan remarked. Buinne and Illan's rank was enough to gain them all entrance, and the little party was waved under the great, dark arch of the gate, flanked by the wooden towers that reared against the dusky sky.

No one recognized them as they climbed the paths, though that would not hold long, Buinne growled. "Time enough," Naisi said in a low voice, and drawing Deirdre into the warmth of his body, he murmured in her ear as he walked up the mud paths. "There is the king's stables, and the practice green." There was a little catch in his voice. "And the houses of the nobles, and the granaries. And up there, against the sky, the highest hall is the king's, but the one with all the banners is the Red Branch hall." He paused, his hand tightening in hers. "Our hall. Yes." He spoke to himself, under his breath. "Ours."

The night wind was blowing along the narrow laneways between the rows of squat roundhouses, and whistling in the fringe of the low thatch roofs, streaming out pennants on roof-posts and stakes. Fire glowed from doorways, accompanied by the noise of people laughing and children chattering.

With a sense below hearing, Deirdre felt the ponderous scrape of the gates across the stony path behind them. Emain Macha had closed its arms about her.

Levarcham was standing by Conor's great chair in the hall when Fergus mac Roy's son proudly threaded his way through the servants around the fire-pits. As the light of the flames fell on his lean, eager face, it took a moment for his features to register, for her focus these past days had been solely on the king, as if by hovering close enough she could read the currents of his mind.

Cathbad's fevers had finally brought him to bed, and in the hollow place inside her, Levarcham did not think he would rise again. The druids were all embroiled in that crisis, praying over him, burning herbs in the temple, calling the spirit-trance for guidance in choosing a new chief druid. Levarcham, though, had worldly cares; she would stay by Conor.

Illan's flaxen hair was distinctive, but the servants paid him little attention, and there were no warriors or nobles in the hall this night, as there had not been for moons. Fergus had not sent word, so no one was expecting the search party's return—or knew if they had found their quarry.

Crushing the wild leap of her heart, Levarcham glanced at the king and saw the shock take hold of him.

Illan sank on one knee before Conor. "I have accompanied the sons of Usnech back from Erin, and the girl, too," he announced. Levarcham closed her eyes, sending a pure dart of gratitude to the Goddess on Her temple mound.

Conor said nothing for a moment, one hand feeling unsteadily for the gold torc at his neck, fingering the bull terminals and their eyes of amber. "So soon?" It came out faint and he had to clear his throat. "How is it that I had no advance word?"

Illan looked uncomfortable. "My father was unavoidably detained, but we all decided to press on, to get here as soon as possible. Naisi is in a great rush to be reconciled with you."

Conor sat back in his chair. Levarcham hobbled forward, grasping her staff. The king seemed paralyzed. "And how do they fare?" she squeezed out, trying to rein in her breathing.

Illan stood and smiled at the king. "They are overjoyed at being home, my lord, and grateful for your wisdom and generosity. Shall I go and get them?"

"No." The word slipped out swiftly, before Conor collected himself, waving his hand. "They must be exhausted, cold and underfed, and we have had no warning to prepare for them. Take them to the Red Branch hall and there they can rest until we are ready."

Levarcham opened her mouth to argue, then shut it. The fact Conor agreed to allow them back at all had been a great breakthrough. Her contempt for him had been moderated by his change of heart, and after all this time avoiding his hall, immersing herself in ritual and prayer—the sacred rhythms the only thing keeping her sane—she had reinstated herself at his side. She had not forgotten the look on his face in the shrine of the Dagda, the truth of his regret. She must be here when Deirdre got back.

She and the king had continued to dance about with stilted words, but he needed her, too; the people were reassured of his good intent when Deirdre's tutor stood by him. And that had brought relief. People were moving about more briskly now, their fear lifting. There was a bustling air of life being resumed, as women dug up roots from the gardens and men wove thatch on their roofs against the coming storm season.

Now Levarcham narrowed her eyes. She knew Conor, and he had been caught unawares. His gray hair was unbound, his clothes musty, and Illan's appearance had brought an ashen cast to his face. He would feel more secure if he had time to summon the trappings of his royal rank—a lavish feast and crowds of warriors, fine clothes and gold. And if Conor was secure, they all were safer.

Illan was clearly taken aback and had been hesitating, unsure. "They can wait, if you will it," he said at last.

Conor stood, and Levarcham did not miss how his hands trembled. "I must receive Naisi before our nobles, so my regard can be publicly acknowledged. And I am sure he would rather meet me and his comrades bathed and dressed in his finery."

Illan frowned. "Certainly." He gazed around. "But where are the Red Branch? Why do they not attend you?"

Conor stared down at him. "We had rumors of Connacht mustering a war-band, and Cúchulainn and Ferdia have led most of the Red Branch to the borders. Conall is at his dun supervising the southern defenses, and Cormac and Dubthach are riding between those forts nearby to ensure their fighting men are on alert." He smiled thinly. "You see that our strength is already waxing, and Naisi's return makes it complete. I will send messengers this moment to those Red Branch near enough to come and feast with us."

"And Fiacra?"

"He has been lingering at Emain Macha for your return, but this day took my horses downriver to ready them in case I must ride out with the army."

When Illan's face fell, Conor gestured again, glancing once at

Levarcham. "This may make up for the absence of the Red Branch. Tell Naisi that when he comes before me to renew his oaths, he may bear his naked blade into my hall. I will take his vow on his own sword again, as I did at his initiation."

This was a great honor. Custom demanded that all men disarm as they entered the king's hall. Illan's brow cleared and he nodded more vigorously. "I will, my lord. That will gladden him greatly." He swept out.

Conor watched him go, his eyes hooded, and Levarcham's voice became brisk. "It is as grim as a grave in here. You must welcome the brothers back with honor and gladness, to show the warriors that this rift is mended. We need to stoke the fires, lay out gilded cups and platters, summon bards and musicians."

He stirred and rubbed his palms over his face. "You are right." He lifted a hand and his steward came rushing over from his place by the door. Conor's bowed shoulders straightened. "Fill both fire-pits and make them blaze," Conor growled. "And bring out my best furs to soften these benches—and the bronze cups from Greece set by my side for Naisi and his brothers! And is there a boar hanging in the coolhouse?" The steward swiftly nodded. "Then get it on the spit, man! The champion's portion will be for the sons of Usnech."

The steward wrung his hands, bobbing his head. "Certainly, my king. I also have word that the chieftain Eogan has arrived from his dun to treat with you. He asks leave for his men to camp on the meadow by the river."

Conor nodded broodingly, and at Levarcham's scrutiny, he waved a hand. "The man has come to make peace with me over some minor dispute. Tell him he has leave," he said to the steward, "and take Eogan to a guestlodge and offer him every comfort there."

When the steward had bustled away, Conor cocked a dry brow at Levarcham. "Will that spread of food and gold cups satisfy you?"

She held his gaze. They had both aged these past moons. "It is not for me you must do this, but for you."

"Do you not think this has all been for me?" Conor replied testily, his tension leaping out of him. "Do you think me grown so soft that I suddenly love that foolish, black-haired pup, that I will revel in his triumph?"

This outburst, oddly enough, allayed Levarcham's misgivings. "No," she said. "I know that only cold self-interest would ever change your mind. I am glad you have woken to it at last." The sense of Deirdre's presence was pulling Levarcham now like a subterranean river, taking over her body. "I must...go to her." Unavoidably, her throat tightened and her voice grew rough.

"Yes." Conor clung to the chair, the veins standing out across his hands. "If I just knew what she looked like...So much time in the wilds, living rough...She must be changed by that. Changed beyond all recognition."

Levarcham's stomach turned. *Changed from what she was—what he craved.*

And then perhaps he would not want her any more. She cursed that sick hope with the same breath that she prayed for it.

After Levarcham's exit, Conor was still staring at the doors when he realized he was alone in a pool of silence. The only people rushing about him were servants.

Women hurried past with baskets of blackberries, hazelnuts and bread, setting them out on the low tables before the fire. Men heaved the skinned boar up onto a spit and threw more wood on the flames, building them high. There was no one who sought his presence unless ordered. All year, the chiefs had avoided his hall, preferring their own duns, and without the hearty voices of crowds of warriors the cavernous building now seemed bereft, the walls mired in shadow, the metalwork glinting coldly at him.

His legs ached as he climbed the stairs to his bedchamber. Normally there would be servants to comb his hair and wash his beard, and fold about him the heavy, embroidered robes of a king. This night he could bear no fawning hands or the obsequious murmurs of those who were only afraid of him.

He sat on his bed and massaged the folds of his belly, digging in his fingers in a vain attempt to rid himself of the knot that tightened every time he caught a glimpse of anyone's dark hair.

Was it not enough they were back? Did he have to pretend a joy he did not feel? He desperately strained to summon the requisite relief that he also craved, but every time he tried to force those thoughts, something rose to block them. He had resorted to drowning that bitter gag at the back of his throat with ale, until its comforting haze descended over him again.

Closing his eyes, he grasped for the glowing picture of him in regal splendor leading Naisi and Deirdre to the Temple of Macha. Standing between them, Conor would hold up their arms, their hands in his, and show the people that all wounds were healed.

Deirdre was the key to this sacred bond, and he tried to imagine a chaste goddess with flowers about her feet. Instead, he saw again the blush of her skin through the fine linen that hugged her thigh, swan feathers fluttering from her wrists.

Stumbling up, he groped for the jug.

The Red Branch lodge was a vast structure, rearing from the slopes below the crest of the hill and the king's hall, its stone walls thick and strong. Its majestic thatch roof bore carved beams at the eaves, and a gilded apex at its peak that lifted red banners to the sky. Before the great doors, a line of flaming pitch torches in the ground gleamed on rows of shields nailed to stakes.

Two boys in leather armor flanked the entrance with short spears tilted to ceremonially bar entry. They peered at the brothers with surprised recognition before they remembered their duties, demanding to see Red Branch arm-rings. The sons of Usnech now wore them proudly again, and with nods and awed glances, the boy-guards stood back.

Inside, the hall was empty—Illan had already told them the Red Branch were not at Emain Macha. This was not unusual, Ardan murmured to Deirdre, for the high-ranking warriors had their own duns, and only filled the hall when they were all together for feasts or before battle.

Yet Naisi prowled around the hearth like a caged wolf, frowning at the shadows that lurked in the vast, echoing room, at the lack of glad greetings to warm the air.

Deirdre dragged her eyes from him, overwhelmed by this glittering cave around her. Most of the hall was one arched space, though a partition near the back denoted rooms beyond. In the main chamber, a roaring hearth-fire and glowing lamps sent light bouncing off shields that lined the walls like scales. Flocks of spears hung from the ceiling, caught as if in battle-flight, barbed tips glittering. Unsheathed swords were pegged up the walls in chevron patterns, polished to a bright sheen.

The colors were lurid and rousing, the array of cushions and wall-hangings dyed in bright yellow, green and orange, and embroidered in gold and silver thread. Furs strewn over chairs and benches gleamed in wolf-stripes and the rich browns of beaver and fox. Low tables bore jugs of bronze and horn cups rimmed in gold. It was a dazzling spectacle after the softer greens and grays of the woods and ocean.

And yet for all its vaunted glory, Deirdre found it oppressive, the decorations an assault on the senses. It was among the unroofed pillars of the forest, on the bare earth, that she could breathe freely.

"The king should have had you to his own hearth immediately," Illan remarked uneasily, his eyes following Naisi's agitated steps.

Deirdre was jolted from her reverie, some old lore of Levarcham's running through her head. *Once you have supped at a man's hearth he cannot harm you.*

Buinne snorted, sitting and kicking off his boots. "You take the bard tales too much to heart, little brother. The king grants Naisi an unprecedented honor if he intends to let him come before the throne with his sword. What do such courtly rituals matter if a man gains that? He has something great in mind for you, my friend, making such a statement." His eyes glinted at Naisi from under ruddy brows, and Deirdre was faintly aware that her back stiffened at that look.

Ardan threw his cloak on a bench and rotated his shoulders. Despite his words to Deirdre, he, too, darted glances around as if affected by the strange hush. "Perhaps it's a good idea to gather our strength before we see him."

Ainnle had his hands on his hips, looking around at the shields on the walls and the swords with obvious excitement. "Such doubts! The gods are merely testing our courage," he declared boldly. "And to be installed here shows to all that we are still esteemed warriors. Why, it must be a good sign that the first thing we see is our own father's shield before us!" He pointed at the wall, his brows lifting encouragingly at his eldest brother.

Naisi nodded slowly, rubbing his stubble with his finger-tips. At that moment, a boy came in lugging two large earthen jugs by their handles, leaving them on one of the tables with a little bow. He lit a clutch of pine tapers in the fire and disappeared toward a corridor at the back of the hall. Behind him, two older serving women carried in baskets of bread, and a willow platter holding cheeses and cups of honey, and a bronze plate piled with slices of pig-meat, edged with brown crackling.

"Ha!" Buinne exclaimed, and reached for a bannock, shoving it into his mouth. Ainnle leaped on the nearest jug, peeling back the wax lid, and Buinne accepted a cup that Ainnle poured and took a gulp, before chewing some more. He leaned back in the chair, his bare feet propped on the cushions. "At last we get to quench some thirst and hunger, eh?" Those dark eyes slanted once toward Deirdre, then back at his bannock. "I am famished."

When Deirdre tensed again, Naisi glanced at the men divesting themselves of their cloaks and swords, accompanied by the clink of cups, and taking the tips of her fingers drew her toward the back of the hall. "There are some bed-chambers here. You might want to rest away from this noise, *fiáin*. And I can try and get you some hot water in which to bathe."

She wanted to say, *I cannot be away from you*, but then he cast a glance over his shoulder, his face taut, his eyes searching. "Perhaps we can draw from Illan and Buinne something more of Conor's state of mind that they would not reveal before their father." The strain carved into his face stopped her. This is what he needed—to sit at the Red Branch fire with Red Branch warriors.

Daub walls formed a corridor and two chambers at the rear set into the curve of the walls, each with scatters of beds piled with hides. In one, the boy was lighting lamps with the tapers. At their appearance, he bowed again and hastened out.

Deirdre pulled Naisi close, resting her forehead on his chin. Her hands ran from the curves of his shoulders down his arms, remaking the outlines of his body, fervently weaving a silent protection over him with her touch.

He kissed her behind the ear and left her there, as if he could not bear to be still.

Deirdre sat on the bed. These were the most lavish rooms in which she had ever set foot, boasting soft feather mattresses and silky furs, the wooden chests and sideboards ornately carved and painted. The boy had lit a brazier, an iron bowl of charcoal on a tripod that already gave out warmth and a red glow. Lamps wrought of polished horn hung from chains in the roof, throwing off the pungent scents of seal-oil, and a few tallow candles flamed in soapstone bowls.

Everything here was meant to encourage comfort and ease, the setting aside of weary cares. Instead she began to feel stifled, the stone walls pressing in upon her. Conor's walls were about her again.

She leaped up, striding to the rear wall and frantically pulling back the wool hangings until she discovered a small window high up, whose wood shutters had been boarded a long time ago, for they were rotten and cracked. After dragging a small table over and climbing up, she managed to rip away a few shards of splintered wood.

Night air rushed in through the gap, and Deirdre pressed her face to it and closed her eyes, burning with unshed tears.

At the Red Branch hall, Levarcham stood rigid, eyes desperately sweeping the group of men by the fire. The conversation gradually died as the five warriors became aware of her, hovering near the door.

Head erect, the owl feathers brushing her neck, she forced herself to glide toward them as though her twisted gait was graceful. One of the men uncurled from the hearth-bench and stepped toward her. She had glimpsed Naisi only amid the mass of warriors around Conor. To her surprise, he held her gaze steadily. "You must be Levarcham. She has described you to me many times."

The intimate *she*, the hint of possession, told Levarcham the true state of affairs between this young man and her Deirdre. She took him in with one trained glance: black hair framing a vivid, sharply drawn face that had a watchful hunger about it; limbs boasting a lithe grace, though right now they were coiled like bow-strings. He had fierce eyes of a light color that blazed—not in a boastful way, but with a gathering and containment of strength, as in the lauded Cúchulainn. This Naisi held more inside than he ever said, and wanted more than he would ever admit. Yes, she could see the depths that would intrigue her Deirdre.

Before she could even speak, he pointed down the corridor. "She is there," he said softly, watching her, and the back of Levarcham's neck prickled at the knowledge that such a buck could read her desperation. But then, he had been hunted, this young man, and living in the wild brought its own keen senses.

Moving in a daze, Levarcham's footsteps were silent, and she was standing at the door to the chamber by the time Deirdre swung around.

Teacher and pupil stood frozen for a moment.

Levarcham was conscious of a roaring in her ears and both

hands reached for the door-posts, bracing herself. Conor wanted Deirdre changed, and something *had* been worn down by her wandering, but it was only the iron crust beaten away to free a blade.

Muscle had replaced childish plumpness, leaving her waist smaller and her breasts and hips more pronounced. Lean limbs were poised and balanced on the earth, and her stance was that of a wild creature now. The agitation that had always run through Deirdre's body as a girl, as if she was constantly on the edge of flight, had been replaced by self-containment. Levarcham had seen that in druids after their nights with the gods, and in warriors after initiations—the mark of one who had been tested and had passed through trials. It was a fire burning alone in the dark, a spirit that had come to know itself.

But it was her face ... *her face* ... "My child," she said huskily, and as she moved forward, so did Deirdre. Levarcham went to cup her chin and was halted by a throb of shame, of unworthiness, and her hand dropped away.

Deirdre stared at her without recognition, her gaze blurred by veils as if there was a film of water between them. Levarcham watched her struggle back to the surface of that other realm and blink, her eyes clearing. She took a shuddering breath, and confused, Levarcham searched her face, desperate to know her again.

A flush crept over Deirdre's cheeks as awareness returned, and in that instant her expression revealed itself with such clarity that Levarcham saw it all: the fear and weariness, the defiance and marshaling of great strength. Pain was carved in thinner cheeks, resignation framed by starker bones. And that mouth was no longer child-sweet, for it had savored a man's lips now, and tasted tears. Love and sorrow were written in the tiny creases around her eyes. If her child's beauty was that of a statue, then the idol had come alive, and this knowing strength was more beautiful than innocence could ever be. What was once a frustrated spark in those eyes was now luminous—and Conor would know it. He was too clever not to see what she had become.

Levarcham's hand curled across her own chest and she felt her way to the bed and breathlessly sat on it. "I do not have long, for the king waits to hear from me."

She thought Deirdre would press her with questions, as of old. But she merely sat beside her and took Levarcham's fingers, and looked at her from the hidden realm behind her eyes. "I understand. I endangered you when I fled, and I would never do that again."

Levarcham's laugh was a bitter croak. "I care nothing for that. It is I who have failed you." All that she had carried for nearly two years was crushing her, and it bled from her heart, the tumble of words surprising her druid composure. "I should have done more long ago. You should have been able to tell me..."

Deirdre touched the feathers in Levarcham's hair to stop her, and the druid was so undone by this reversal that her voice failed. "It doesn't matter now," Deirdre murmured. "You were my friend, my family. I seem to remember you telling me once that guilt was a waste of precious time between those who love."

Levarcham arched a brow, grasping for the familiar rhythm between them. "I doubt I ever said anything so poetic, fledgling."

Deirdre blinked again and looked around her as if waking to where she was—the walls, the roof—and a wariness came over her and her body drew in on itself once more, her hands crossing in her lap. "You only did what you had to as servant of the king— as I did what I had to. And you worried you betrayed me, and I have sorrowed that I betrayed you. That makes us even, doesn't it?" Levarcham barely registered the hint of mischief that struggled to animate Deirdre's mouth.

"Why the gods did you risk coming back?" the druid demanded hoarsely, digging her fingers in between her knees. "At least I knew that you were out of his reach, and I hoped happy."

Deirdre raised her face to a slight gust of air entering through the window above, scenting the night. "I was happy, but Naisi was not whole." She turned, her gaze intense. "He could not find his true self in Alba; he could not be complete. Something would not let him go—it called him back—and I would not leave him."

Levarcham stared, as the roaring grew louder. Something about her words. A calling. *A circle made complete.* And the old, hidden darkness at the bottom of the well rose up and overflowed, desperately needing to be released. Amid all this grief, she had put aside the lie that lay at the heart of Deirdre's life—the secret she had kept to protect a child. But this was a child no longer.

"Fledgling." Now it was Levarcham's eyes that glazed over, holding to the flickering lamp-flame because she could not bear to see Deirdre's face change. The girl must gain the truth from the one who had most truly betrayed her, before she heard the harsher whispers. Levarcham's numb lips moved. *A prophecy... Cathbad's hand on her mother's swollen belly, saying this girl would be fair beyond all reason—and bring strife to the Ulaid fighting men, and ruin to Conor's kingship.* That was why, Levarcham forced out, Conor had wanted Deirdre. That was why he had hidden her away.

Levarcham sensed the warm body beside her slowly withdraw. Deirdre did not make a noise, staring at the wall as the silence drew out. Eventually, she whispered, "So that is why I was always alone. Because a druid foresaw a dark fate for Conor and his men."

Levarcham swallowed and turned to her. "Yes."

Deirdre swept upright in one movement, a ripple from within bringing her to her feet. She stopped before one of the embroidered hangings, and her breath stirred her unbound hair into a halo of light before the lamp-flame. "And this king's fate is why my Naisi was pierced by an arrow, why he was hunted—why he is left to struggle with fear, here in this place that was his home."

"Fate, yes, " Levarcham said, rising beside her. "But listen to me—"

Deirdre spun around with eyes ablaze. "I reject fate!" she cried. "I reject this prophecy, these words from the gods that drive Conor so. I will not bow to them, to him, to anyone!" The force of her voice rushed through Levarcham's body, sweeping her back a step. Uttered with such power, they were an oath. "Fates are woven not by gods, but by the choices of humans—their greed and jealousies, their loves and courage. If men look upon me and kill, this has nothing to do with my *destiny*, but with the weaknesses of their own hearts. I have seen the droplets of time held in stardust, the possibilities that every moment holds." Deirdre's eyes flared with understanding. "Fate is but one moment the gods extend to us, a test for us. But it is the choices we make that take us to that fate, or away. And so I will forge my own life!"

Stunned, Levarcham's utterance was trapped by her tongue. This could not be…druid lore of the most arcane and hidden kind. How could Deirdre know this when she had never been taught? *The gods create destiny as a challenge, not a fate; the paths to it are our own to forge.* Did the gods place those prophetic words of Deirdre's birth in Cathbad's heart to *test* Conor, not to set down the Ulaid's future in stone?

"And what of this fated beauty?" Deirdre stormed. "Conor expected something else, did he not? A soft, demure maiden, a vacant doll painted with all his desires." She laughed bitterly. "And he got *this*…" she flicked a hand down herself. "Dirty boy's clothes and knotted hair, and too much to say and too many thoughts. How disappointed he must have been! So I was not this perfection after all. I was only me."

Levarcham's eyes blurred. *You became more than he could ever have imagined.* "Listen to me." She uncurled Deirdre's hands and held them. "You are right, my dear one. And Conor himself has made the choice to change his fate. I have seen the transformation in him, as has Cathbad and Cúchulainn. His follies ruled him for too long, but he overcame them with a great struggle. He has changed the path, and the prophecy is broken. The moments that might have been are now extinguished in favor of this one, where he won against his darker heart and welcomed you back."

Both of them were silent as their breathing quieted, and the color flooded Deirdre's white face once more. "If the gods," she said shakily, "pronounced something over my birth that brought Naisi such pain, then they can bring him comfort now, in exchange. Something burdens him, and it may be he can lay it down at their altar before he faces Conor. Will you take us to the temple?"

"I…of course." Though Deirdre was a wild thing now, untamed after so long in the forest, she was once her child, and so Levarcham drew her resisting body into an embrace. At last Deirdre softened, trembling and unsteady as she stretched her head on Levarcham's shoulder. She did not weep, but she let her weight rest upon her teacher for a moment, and Levarcham bore it and never wanted to let go.

CHAPTER 43

Levarcham stood at the entrance to the Temple of Macha as Deirdre and Naisi paused before the oak statue of the Goddess. Deirdre was still, but Naisi was not. He wavered on his feet, his body shaking with subtle tremors that she recognized as the blows of his pulse.

Deirdre turned to him and raised her hand, and he copied her. They touched palm to palm. Levarcham's mouth went dry as their fingers entwined, curling up to nurture and hoard that moment.

Their silent absorption made her back up and turn away, for this was too sacred to be witnessed. She slipped into the night and gulped the cold air, and her hands fell at her sides as she gazed at the torch-light of Emain Macha.

Then something caught her attention behind her and she turned. A full moon was sailing into view over the eastern hills, streamers of mist wrapped about its bronze face that would soon flame to silver.

The moon goddess, watching them all.

Confronted by the silent Goddess statue, Naisi's pain grew until it scalded him. The enigmatic wooden features were more daunting than any frown of anger could ever be. Her intense, expectant expression could summon secrets from dark souls, and She stared out with the endless gaze of the unknown that made strong hearts thunder. That echoing silence bent men's deeds back upon them, until they crushed them to their knees.

Naisi sank.

He bent his head and Deirdre's hands came upon his crown, cradling the curves of bone. She muttered fervently under her breath, her palms pressing his skull as if she tried to reach for something. "For *him*," she murmured fiercely. "Give me something not for myself, but for him alone. Use this vessel if you must. *Help him*." Her voice cracked with all the grief Naisi was struggling to control. "*Release him!*" she cried raggedly. "*With mercy*."

Naisi bit hard on his lip because the pressure in his chest was unbearable and he could not weep, only face the judgment of the gods as a man. That might be the only scrap of honor he had left.

A moment later, Deirdre gasped and her body went rigid, her fingers digging into his scalp. Alarmed, he went to catch her arm but she had already whirled away from him to face the Goddess, and he saw her sight had turned inward, her eyes filmed with a glistening light. Startled, he stayed where he was, his hands clenched on his thighs.

She whispered something in a sibilant stream, her palms spread to the oak stump. "So many voices in song and blessing, hands in offering and prayer, feet dancing the sacred spiral…all of them calling the Source, anchoring it here. The light of people, of thousands. I have never…" She broke off and her breath caught, then flooded from her and she took a faltering step, and another.

Berries and nuts from the gathering time were piled at the statue's feet over the crumbling sheaves of harvest grain, but it was not to these offerings Deirdre walked. The talismans of the kings were placed around the temple walls: shields and spears, scabbards and helmets; and sacred things that were not weapons, such as faded cloaks of many colors, and cups of horn, bone and gold.

Deirdre paused and reached for a shield, tracing the studded rivets with a finger, the iron burnished and oiled by the tending druids. For a moment, a noise moved in Naisi's throat, the instinctive taboo against handling the sacred talismans, but he forced it away. There was a nimbus of light around Deirdre's hands that was not the lamp-flame, and the look in her face… She held only blessings in her touch.

She began to move in a slow, dreamy dance, bending to touch the talismans as she passed, turning in lithe sweeps to cradle them with reverence. She held crested war-helms to her mouth and blessed them with her breath. She drew the thick folds of royal mantles through her fingers, and held the mead-cups of transparent horn to the light so they glowed.

And all the while she whispered, and at length Naisi rose and followed her, desperate to hear what she said.

Her voice was a low murmur and it was not hers alone, but deepened by a more resonant note that made it a song, a chant. Entranced by the graceful spirals she wrought with her hands, Naisi moved close enough to breathe the scent of her hair, drawn to her voice and the spell of her dance like a starving man to sustenance. And soon the shadows and the smoky air of the temple began to lighten with a strange luminescence, and as it grew so Naisi's pain crested, as if drawn inexorably upward by it.

He gasped and Deirdre immediately spun around, her hands clasped under her chin. Her face glowed with rapture, eyes closed and chin lifted, and her eyelids quivered at something unseen. He was sure she was not aware of him or her own voice. The radiance in her face was so great he could barely see her features, and he bowed his head to the Goddess.

Deirdre whirled once more and continued her blessing of the hallowed relics, circling the temple, and Naisi kept pace, hovering behind. She wove snatches of vision with her chant and they were of the ancient kings, as if the things they had borne had been imprinted with something that Deirdre could now sense with fingers and heart.

Men in gilded helmets leading armies…throwing themselves between a blade and a sword-brother's heart.

Meadows lit by bonfires…kings twined in sacred joinings with women on the earth to make it fruitful.

A war-lord singing a battle-song of bravery and love to bind his men to-gether as they weave their shields before the charge.

A chieftain emptying grains of barley with his own hands into pits be-hind a rampart, as hollow-cheeked people bend their heads for his blessing.

Priestess and king, the gods murmured through Deirdre. *The blessing of the Goddess in return for his protection, healing, warding. His body, breath and blood given for the people.*

Dazed, his heart already awakening with some faint pulse of hope, Naisi followed Deirdre as she came to the altar. There she stood gazing up at the Goddess face, swaying, and at last reached out and placed both palms on the wood. Her head fell to her breast with a little cry, and she shuddered, but Naisi did not break the trance.

Tell me what you will. That fervent cry spilled from his heart, and with that surrender of his vulnerability and pain, She heard him at last and bestowed Her blessing.

The roots of an oak anchor the ground, Deirdre whispered into the aged wood. *The trunk stands against the storm. The branches shelter those below. So a god…so a king. The god shields the Goddess so she can birth cre-ation. But a king shields the people.*

Now she reached behind her and gripped his hand with a ter-rible force, dragging him so that as Deirdre pressed her belly against the tree, Naisi curved around her back. She took his palms and spread them on the stained bark. *Feel it.*

The surge took him, a deep resonance throbbing through the wood and Deirdre's body, then pouring into him in a wave of song.

"The memory of kings is channeled by my flesh, and the chant of the gods echoes through this tree," Deirdre cried, "but you can only feel them because the same song runs through you."

Her words shattered the hurt into shards that were sharp in his throat, and Naisi fell back a step. Deirdre faced him, and the strange shimmering outlines of the light across her features made them an echo of the enigmatic wooden Goddess behind her. Though Naisi stood alone now, the vibration still thrummed through him, and he held his hands up in wonder as the desperate hope billowed out into full life. His flesh rung like the clean bell of a pure-wrought sword struck on an anvil.

Deirdre opened her eyes, and they were bright with an intense flame that shot a bolt of joy through him even before he heard her words. "All you felt was the god-energy rising in you, because it is the song of your soul. It is your calling to inspire, lead and protect—a calling beyond men and their oaths, so hear now that you did no wrong. There was no lust to usurp, or greed for power. You heard the summons of the gods, the cry to make all stronger, and you simply hearkened to it as others need to breathe." She paused, her voice a powerful sea. "There is nothing to forgive."

The words seared Naisi's soul and he sank to his knees again and this time made no sound. The years of hoarded pain were released by his muscles in one long cramp of agony that bent him over, silent and fierce, his arms crossed over himself. And beneath him the ground sang, lifting him, bearing him aloft.

As the pain drained out of him into that sacred earth, so bright thoughts came leaping like fleet deer from the heights. *I only ever saw how we could be more. Red Branch. Ulaid. Greater. All of us together, not me alone.*

Deirdre's hands came down upon his head again and this time her touch was gentle, a caress of a mother through his hair. "You did not see the beauty of the pattern, and so twisted it into shame."

A vivid rush came then of him walking the walls of his dun, the chieftain's torc at his neck, the fields of barley gleaming around it in the sun. He felt it all unfurling in him—the need to be the father of his people, to hold them with the fire he had always known inside. But this time, he could let it burn freely.

His arms came about Deirdre's waist and he clung to her, his face pressed into her belly, and there he let the tears flow at last, cleansing him.

Levarcham came back to Conor and for once the inscrutable druid mask was stripped away.

"Well?" he snapped, descending the stairs from the upper gallery. The heavily-embroidered robes rustled stiffly against his legs, armoring him, and there was a circlet of gold on his brow. That, and the arm-rings and neck torc, the brooches and braided hair, helped numb his flesh beneath.

There were more servants scuttling around now, and Levarcham glanced at the boar that had been hoisted on the spit and was being rubbed with butter and thyme. Other maids were piling up layers of cushions and furs around the warrior benches by Conor's great chair, and setting out cups.

He paused a few stairs up so he was above Levarcham, and she lifted her face to him. Lines pulled her mouth down, but there was also a wondering look in her eyes and a flush to her cheek that raised his hackles. "Yes, she has changed."

An unsteady thump shook his chest. He covered it by lifting a brow. "Indeed?"

Her expression sharpened, as if she awoke from dazed thoughts, and the sorrow that came in their wake was a light falling away down a dim tunnel. "You will see soon enough."

He was conscious of an odd sense, an aversion to laying his own eyes upon Deirdre. "I want you to tell me."

Levarcham's pupils shrank again. "The time in the wild has taken the girl she was. She is a woman now."

"That tells me nothing! Is she worn and broken, rough-skinned and faded? Has she grown coarse?"

She tilted her head to capture him with the full force of her druid gaze. "They are more bonded than you can ever know. Listen to what Cathbad said. You cannot order their flesh, their hearts. You want to honor her, but you cannot rule her. If you want her glory to light your hall...the goddess in her to bless us...then *let her be his*, and put aside all thought of her as a queen. It is over."

Her words brought relief for a moment, and he drove away the other feelings that flapped up like black crows, circling his heart. "I am giving them the greatest of honors," he murmured. "All will be witness to my forgiveness. Will you question that sacred vow I made before the gods?"

Her eyes flickered and she pursed her lips, swallowing further argument. "She is bathing, and I am finding some fine clothes for her. I thought that would be to your liking."

It could not be over yet. He just needed one more moment to lay it to rest. "Wait." His voice was colder. "You will supervise the feast preparations for me. You know I want it to surpass any other, and the serving maids and cooks are terrified of you." From the side, he saw her features settle into hardness. "You, more than anyone, know what this means, to receive Naisi and...and the girl. You appreciate the finer points of ceremony. If you care for her, you will help me to show everyone how lavishly I honor them both."

He felt their wills clash and struggle, though neither moved. "As you wish." She changed direction, toward the door to the cookhouse at the back of the hall.

The king waited a few moments, then gestured one of the servants to help him into the generous, obscuring folds of his riding cloak. The oiled leather weighed him down, hiding his gold and taking his remaining feeling with it.

Without a glance at anyone, he swept out of his hall and into the night.

Conor paced in the shadows along the rampart and paused beneath the stairs that ran up to the walkway. He rested his aching forehead on a dank oak post, his nostrils stung by the fumes from a nearby dungheap. So long he had pursued her and, now that she was here, he could not bring himself to *see*, but must prowl around like a skulking wolf.

This way, circling fate, avoiding the clarity of his own eyes, he could pretend to slow time. But that was impossible.

His legs were moving, he vaguely realized, the dun passing by in a haze of damp and darkness, pierced by ghostly flickers of torch-light.

From the shadows at the rear of the Red Branch hall, he looked up at the looming stone walls, not knowing what he would do, why he was here. *She was bathing.* It took some time for his eyes to resolve that dull glow high up into a window. Lamp-light. The bed-chambers. There were piles of logs stacked against the wall, and ale barrels. A ladder the thatchers had left leaned against the house behind him.

Many times, Conor had partaken of druid herbs for kingly rites and experienced this same dizzy detachment of body from mind. He knew the sense of numbed limbs animated by druid suggestion and desire, so a king would lie with a maid in a circle of fires. Deirdre had enchanted him like that, it must be true, for this was not *him* stealing through shadows to spy. Not the king of the Ulaid.

He bent his chin back. Smoke wafted the comforting scent of roasting meat over him, and somewhere nearby a dog barked. Behind door-hides, before glowing fires, children shrieked and voices were lifted in argument and laughter. *Alive.*

Something punched up from his chest, and a compulsion set his hands on the ladder and propped it on the barrels. Heedless of royal dignity he hauled himself frantically up, the embroidery on his robes catching on the splintered wood. If she was naked, then at last he would see their lust, their shameful betrayal, and it would be over. He could make himself feel only disgust.

He put his face to the opening in the boards over the window. There was only one lamp lit, and a brazier, and at first he saw only the moving shadows. He shifted, until at last *she* was caught in the dim glow—and then he forgot to breathe at all.

Deirdre was standing in a wooden basin, dipping a cloth in the steaming water and running it over her arms and legs. Tongues of firelight played over her skin, sheening her curves and casting mysterious shadows in her collarbone and down the sloping line of her belly to the hair at her groin. She raised an arm and her breast hung in the golden light like an apple on a tree, and when she leaned over to wet the cloth again, Conor's palms prickled with sweat and itched to stroke her flesh. Her unbound hair gleamed when she turned, the firelight gilding each strand.

A symmetry of feature and limb were one thing, but Conor had seen them before. This was something else. The ease in her muscles, the absorbed, wondering way she drew the cloth over herself…It was the dance all over again, as if she utterly inhabited her body. Envy took him by surprise, a longing for that ease to seep into him from her wet skin as he kissed her. He ground his chest into the icy wall, so that it pushed his ribs back into him, the physical pain distracting.

Then she began singing under her breath, unconsciously calling some blessing into her skin, and where her hands trailed he swore he saw an afterglow of light. Conor sensed the throb of power in the room, a thickening of the air he had only felt around the druids. Forgetting about her nakedness, his gaze went to her eyes, light and fierce in the firelight. She did know magic. She *was* magic. His heart plummeted.

Footsteps sounded in the corridor and she turned and stepped out of the basin. Conor sagged, his foot slipping on the rung before he dragged himself back again.

Naisi.

The pup crossed the rushes toward Deirdre with a confident gait, catching up a linen towel from the bed and looping it around her neck. "I do choose the best time to interrupt you." He used the towel to pull her against him, one hand sluicing the trickles of water from her smooth buttocks, cradling them as if he owned them. Conor's nails gripped the rough wall. Lust, he told himself. He'd been prepared for this.

"Are you rested?" Naisi asked more quietly. "I see the temple has tired you."

Deirdre shook her head, blowing a tendril of damp hair from her mouth, and Naisi leaned back. His tunic was wet from her body, and Conor could not tear his eyes from that dark imprint of her on Naisi's front. Naisi gently tucked a strand of hair over her ear. "*Fiáin*, you have no idea what you have given me this night."

Deirdre captured his hand and kissed it, burying her nose in his skin. "I do not know, since I cannot remember, but…" She smiled with a gradual radiance. "I can see it in you." She paused and her look became somber, deep and tender. "I can see all of you." A shudder went up Conor's body at the note of husky warmth in her voice, at that *look*.

Those words seemed to make sense to Naisi, for he nodded, brushing her hair back with long caresses now, then trailing his hand over each cheekbone with a soft wonderment that chilled Conor.

Then Naisi kissed Deirdre's eyes and tangled her hair through his fingers before at last claiming her mouth, and Conor leaned in with a strangled grunt. If Naisi coupled with her like a dog now, then the spell would be broken; she would be like any other woman.

But Naisi only drew her bottom lip between his lips and sucked on it gently, before sprinkling the corners of her mouth with kisses. Then he nestled Deirdre into him, nuzzling her hair. They stood there merely breathing… not rutting, not exposing themselves as animals that Conor could disdain.

Instead, Deirdre laid her head on Naisi's shoulder and her eyelids lifted, and Conor saw what no one was meant to see. With subtle movements—a flicker of her lashes, a graceful melting of muscles—she sank into Naisi, curling about him like a flower folding up to hide its heart. Eternally joining them as one living thing.

It was a gentle, secret movement, and yet its force reached to Conor, took his heavy heart and savaged it.

His feet were not his own, and he was only distantly aware of them slipping down the rungs one by one. What was vivid was the dread of night spreading below him to the bottom of the world. All he knew was the plunge, and the endless whistling of wind through an empty place.

CHAPTER 44

The sky darkened to night and the wind skirled about the thatch, and still no summons came. The brothers scraped the mud from their boots and oiled their swords with seal-grease. They drank the ale and ate the bread, though it lodged in Deirdre's belly in a hard knot.

Some of the rush lamps burned down and guttered out, and still there was no word. Ainnle found a *fidchell* board and played with Illan halfheartedly, though both heads snapped around at every noise, and soon the game was forgotten. The three brothers went to wash their faces, and when Naisi came back, Illan merely shrugged.

Naisi began to prowl the room again then, circling beneath the lines of shields, tracing the tips of swords, a cup of ale clasped in his fist. Deirdre could not take her eyes from him. She did not remember what had happened to her in the temple, though her body still quivered slightly with its aftermath. She did not want or need to know. She cared only that the Goddess had come for him, and that he had been released.

The change she saw in him now was not some measure of tranquillity, though. His eyes were clear of shadow, but it only made them blaze more purely, their light compelling. In his coiled, powerful body and restless hands, she felt the echo of something her flesh still remembered from the temple. The god. His bearing was unbowed, his chest open, his face expectant. When she touched him in the bed-chamber, she had felt the fire rising in him, and it was not fear that drove him now, but an urgent desire to unleash the strength and certainty coursing through him, to stand before others and have them see it. In his strides around the room, she saw the longing that drove him: to take the oath to the king in a ringing voice; to reclaim the leadership of his dun before all.

He swept past her again where she sat by the fire. The brothers still wore the clothes in which they had fled, and Naisi's red tunic was stained and frayed, his trews crusted in mud. His green cloak was now an indeterminate shade of brown, and the only jewelry he had left was his father's torc and his Red Branch arm-ring. All this dirt made his own coloring more vivid to her, though: the gleaming black hair and clear skin and flushed lips she had first seen in the snow. There was no excess of gold, curled hair or lurid embroidery to distract from the fierceness of his naked gaze.

"I would have liked fresh clothes," Ainnle said, flicking dried mud from his trews.

Naisi stopped. "We bear the travails of our journey in these marks of scars and dirt. We made mistakes, we showed courage, we suffered and triumphed and our comrades and the king should know that when we are brought before them."

Levarcham for her part had sent Deirdre a dress—a long, sleeveless column of green wool that fell in folds about her feet, accompanied by brooches of bronze for her shoulders, jeweled pins for her hair and golden ear-bobs and finger-rings. She donned the dress, but left off the finery, instead combing her hair with her fingers before the flames to dry it. After a time, she glanced up and caught Buinne's gaze fixed with fascination on her, and she dropped her arms and met his look steadily until his eyes slid away. He groped for the jug and sloshed another measure of ale in his cup.

Ainnle pushed open the doors of the hall, leaning against the force of the wind. "The guards are gone," he said over his shoulder. "Hopefully they are bringing more food and ale."

Naisi ran a hand over the shield on the wall beside him. "I pray they bring a message from Conor that we are summoned." He looked up at the flock of spears near the roof, filling his chest. "By all the gods, he *must* receive us now!"

Illan got up, hovering close to Naisi as if to reassure him. "Perhaps the fact he wants to make some great statement is testament to how important this is to the king," he offered. "After all, we were not expected."

Naisi cast a rueful glance at him. "And you are too polite to blame me for that, brother." Illan flushed a little, shrugging.

Naisi rocked on his heels, arms crossed, his fingers resting on the Red Branch ring. "If *I* had been Conor," he declared in a resounding voice, "I'd have brought us to the king's hall the moment of arrival, to seal the oaths with mead. Conor always thinks too much."

"You can talk about thinking too much." Though Ainnle smiled at his brother, his forehead was shadowed by a frown. "Though if you *were* Conor, none of this would have happened in the first place."

Naisi held Ainnle's eyes with a slight smile.

At that moment, Ardan returned from the bed-chamber, the neck of his tunic wet. "Let's not talk about our grievances anymore, lest they gain new life." He sought to calm Naisi with that tranquil glow that now lit his face. "We will all be clean and fed soon enough."

Illan's head turned to the door, listening to the wind. "I still don't like it. I will go and see what is going on."

His hand had only reached the crossbar when an enormous blow was struck on the wood, accompanied by a metallic ring. Deirdre's mind was not attuned to anything beyond, holding to the fierce thread of Naisi's gaze. So it was only when Illan leaped back from that sound, his body braced in a warrior pose, that she was jolted from her warm cocoon. *A sword.* Her mind reluctantly filtered that knowing down to where her soul floated, holding her world still.

A booming voice came through the crack. "I bear a message from Conor, the king of the Ulaid, for Naisi, eldest son of Usnech. He must show himself."

Every shred of Naisi—mind, body, heart—had already sprung into movement without pausing to absorb the startling stab of adrenaline that hit him, the warning.

Illan blocked that lunge with his own body. "No!"

A moment later Deirdre's hand was also on his arm, anchoring him to her.

Illan's frown spread, darkening his fair face. "Let me see. Stay here."

Deirdre's hand pulled on him, and Naisi looked down at the pale flower of her fingers on the bronze arm-ring. Her eyes were dark in the firelight and there was a tender warning there, a plea.

Buinne shouldered in next to his brother. "We vowed to protect you," he muttered. "Until we know the meaning of this strange summons, you must hold back. Or would you have Father know you did not trust him?"

Naisi released a grunt of frustration and let himself be drawn back to Deirdre's side. "Open it and see what the devil this means," he commanded Illan in a hard voice. "I will stay behind if you see for me."

Illan pulled back the bar once more and creaked one door open to a small sliver of night that he blocked with his body. Over his shoulder, Naisi glimpsed the guttering light of torches in the yard against a backdrop of stars. "Are you Naisi mac Usnech?" the voice demanded.

Illan paused, the air blowing back his pale hair. "Why do you not know that? And who are you? You are not of Emain Macha!"

"I am a herald for the king. I bring a full pardon for this son of Usnech."

The pardon, at last. Yet the word fell into a hole inside Naisi, for this was not how it was meant to be. His body was reacting its own way, feeling something in the gust of night air that his mind would not admit. Every fiber of muscle, nerve and tendon drew up, his soles feeling for the floor, his weight balancing between heel and ball of foot, his fists flexing and grasping the hilt of sword and dagger.

"Naisi deserves this pardon from the king himself," Illan replied angrily. "Let him come and clasp his hand, and they can meet before this hall as brothers."

The voice outside held a disturbing contempt. "I have been ordered to offer Naisi his pardon for the wrong he did the king of the Ulaid. He will be absolved of all guilt in this matter and his family name restored to full honor."

His family's honor was not Conor's to give or take. It was for Naisi to claim for himself, and he had done so in the temple, when the light of the gods filled him and Deirdre's words drifted upon his shamed heart like rain on parched land. A growl escaped Naisi's throat, deflecting those dark words. "Why does he not tell me this himself?" he demanded.

There was another pause, while Illan's breath bounced off the wooden door, harsh and swift.

"Because first he requires the payment."

The knowing settled over Naisi, and where it met the tension in his body he felt armor forming over skin and limbs. Behind him, there was a soft exhalation from Deirdre, and he longed to take even that breath of pain from her. "And what is the price?" he asked heavily, knowing the answer.

"You will gain your pardon if you give up the maiden Deirdre to the king."

Naisi's curse parted the hair at Illan's neck and both his brothers exploded with exclamations at the same time. Illan reacted instinctively, barging back to close the doors and yanking across the bars, before turning with his back against them, panting.

Ainnle was incandescent with rage. "That prick-sucking *bastard!*" he shouted, dragging his wet hair from his scalp as he stormed back and forth, his eyes wild. "I knew we made a mistake trusting that pap-stuck son of a whoring *bitch*!"

He paused for breath and Naisi looked past Buinne's slack-mouthed shock and Ardan's dismay and fixed his gaze on the only other still person there. *Fiáin.* At the eye of that tempest whipped up by Ainnle, he and Deirdre merely stared at each other. Her hand crept to nestle at her breast in a tiny movement of protection, and her pupils were enormous in the shadowed green of her irises. She knew this was coming; he saw it in those dark wells. But he also saw a light force its way back up, reaching for him, and he felt what joined them now: their awareness of each other's most subtle thoughts and senses, the deep sharing of their hidden hearts. This is what they had already won.

"No," Naisi said softly, cutting off Ainnle's renewed tirade. "It wasn't a mistake to return. It was the right thing." *For I know myself now as a strong oak that can stand against the storm.* He held Deirdre's eyes and smiled, and though her throat moved while she struggled to breathe, at last she nodded.

Ainnle blinked and turned to Buinne. "And did your father know Conor intended this?" he bellowed.

Buinne glowered and pushed out his chest. "Of course he did not! You slur our family honor—"

"Stop it!" Ardan pushed between them, nudging Buinne back with his elbow.

Illan rounded on Naisi, his face stricken. "We knew nothing of this, I swear! Conor was resolved."

Ainnle shook off Ardan's hands and, spinning around, smacked a palm on the doors with a guttural grunt of fury. They were all silent then, until Buinne dropped his chin and turned to Naisi. "I rail, too, but perhaps it was inevitable it would come to this." He spread his fleshy hands with their livid sword-scars, sucking his lip between his teeth before delivering the blow. "Perhaps you should give up the girl, before this escalates any more."

"No." Illan thrust himself futilely between them to stop those words, of all words.

Buinne doggedly ignored him, bracing his thick, bull neck. "I know why you want her, Naisi, but none can have such a one except the king."

Naisi was aware of Deirdre's gaze boring into the back of Buinne's ruddy head, and realized that the glacial contempt in her eyes must be mirrored in his own. For at Naisi's glance, Buinne went still as fallen men do the breath before a sword descends. And when Naisi said nothing, merely continuing to stare at him, Buinne stepped away.

With smoldering eyes, he turned to his brother, Illan, instead. "I will go and see the king myself," he said stiffly. "And remind him of his oaths to our father." Illan nodded unhappily and Naisi did not argue. Buinne levered the door open, holding his arms away from his sword as he went out.

Naisi stepped to Deirdre's side and linked their fingers, looking at her hands. So it had come to this; some part of him had known it would. The crushing weight kept passing over him in waves now, spiked into peaks by anger, then sinking again. He pushed it all out of him, striving for that clarity he gained in battle. The peace of the temple.

Buinne squinted across the dark expanse of yard and stopped. A silent ring of strangers surrounded the building, each holding a flickering torch. The only thing that moved were the torch-flames guttering in the wind, making the wash of ruddy light over the grass writhe as if alive. The messenger who had banged on the door gestured him over the green toward a rise of ground near one of the storehouses. Buinne approached a cluster of the flames, the light glinting on the swords and spears of a group of heavily-armed warriors surrounding the king.

"Let him through," someone croaked, and suddenly Buinne was in front of Conor. He did not know what to say; his thoughts were mired in confusion. All these men were strangers, dark-haired and bearded. They were clad in sleeveless leather jerkins despite the cold, their bare arms oiled.

"If he has not come out or sent her in his stead, then I assume he has said no to my offer."

Buinne had to peer at Conor to see if that cracked, torn voice had really just issued from the king. In his voluminous cloak, he looked oddly shrunken, his hood a dark cave. Torch-light caught the ridge of his nose with a pale gleam, and outlined one eye that was fixed open and disturbingly glazed.

A big, black-bearded man standing next to Conor wore a wolf-fur cloak, his narrow eyes hungry. No one else was around, neither the Emain warriors who guarded the ramparts nor any of the people, though it was dark now and in this cold wind everyone would be by their own hearth-fires farther down the mound. With no Red Branch present, the upper circle of the fort contained only servants and the king's household, and as yet these strangers had made no sound beyond that one demand to Naisi. Had they entered by stealth?

"He..." Buinne's breath rushed out. "I do not think he will accept your terms, my lord." He still felt the visceral thrust of Naisi's gaze through his bowels. He was older than Naisi, more experienced. It should be Buinne by Cúchulainn's side, Buinne at the heart of the Red Branch.

Conor swayed for a moment as if that was a blow, his head dropping to his breast, his shoulders sinking. Then he sucked in a wheezing breath. "So, Naisi defies me yet again." His head jerked unsteadily toward the wolf-fur man. "What would you do to one of your warriors, Eogan, if he defied you like that?"

The warrior's smile was a snarl. "He would not draw another breath to fling such contempt in my face."

Conor nodded, his hand wound in the folds of the cloak, pushing it into the hollow of his throat. "No king could call himself powerful and let a mere boy undermine him." That wraith-like figure swung toward Buinne. "And you, son of the great Fergus mac Roy." His voice rose to an unnerving pitch. "Will you, too, defy your king and lend your sword-strength to the traitor of the Ulaid?"

Surely that curse was reserved for the worst crimes of all? But then, Conor had always said Naisi's actions were treason. Buinne wrestled with these conflicting ideas, trying to beat them into some sense.

At Buinne's hesitation, Conor began to laugh hoarsely, until the laugh was cut off by a spluttering fit of coughing that made his bowed shoulders quake. The king at last gained his breath and, wheezing, he stepped closer to Buinne's shoulder. "For your loyalty," he hissed, "you will be well rewarded. A man like you must chafe under the rule of your father. He uses up all the air in a room, like a great bonfire, does he not?"

Hot shame and an even older anger were kindled in Buinne now, wiping away any memory of Naisi. *Yes.*

Now he could see both the king's eyes, the glassy surfaces licked by a reflection of the flames. "It may be time," Conor murmured, "for a dun of your own."

Buinne's mind cracked under the weight of confusion and went blank. His father's face was there before him, and the oath he had given was still branded on his tongue. "And a woman..." he heard himself stammer. "A beautiful woman."

Conor's smile twisted. "Almost as fair as my own."

"It has been too long." Ainnle paced before the closed doors. "Buinne is not coming back."

He glared at Illan, who was standing with his head down, his hand on his sword-hilt. Illan was almost never still—he and Fiacra both embodied the quicksilver hue of their hair—and Naisi was chilled by that frozen stance. Illan had always been with his friend, or following his idolized father. Now he was alone, and he didn't know what to do. Illan cleared his throat. "Perhaps my brother is treating with the king."

"There is nothing to be said," Ardan replied. Naisi glanced at him. Ardan was on the floor by the fire, legs crossed, hands resting on his knees. It was not a surrendering pose, though, for Naisi knew him like his own self. Ardan was drawing strength and power into the core of him. His hands were open for the hilt, his

limbs loose and alert. "You are Buinne's brother." Ardan looked at
Illan with a quiet intensity. "You must know him as we know one
another. Do you think it is in him to abandon us now?"

Illan struggled to answer, then his fair skin darkened and he
felt behind him for the bench against the wall and sank heavily
onto it. He nodded just once and lowered his head in his hands.

Naisi stepped over to him, and when Illan looked up, he
smiled at him with great pity. "Go, Illan," he said softly. "Too many
sorry deeds have already been done this night, and there are
more to come. I would never be the one to part brother from
brother, or son from father. Save yourself, and we will not think
ill of you."

To Naisi's surprise, Illan's eyes glistened, even as his face grew
harder and more determined. He got up and held Naisi's shoulder, staring deep into his eyes. "I would rather die with you than
live with the brother of my blood. It is left to me to carry our
name back to honor, so my father can think well of me when he
hears."

Outside, the wind was rising.

A dozen Red Branch warriors led by Lugaid and Brecc had heard
the news of Fergus's landing by chance near the coast, and so
were the first to thunder in on their horses beneath the full
moon. They streamed up the path from the stables, their blood
fired by a tide of jests and eager chatter as they savored the anticipation of good ale by the Red Branch fires, and a rousing feast.

They spilled out into the grassy yard before the Red Branch
lodge and were confronted by an unimaginable scene—strange
warriors surrounding their hall with torches, a greater mass of
them crowded at the side of the green, and no Emain guards in
sight. *An invasion.* One of them saw the hooded man on the rise
surrounded by a thick wedge of the dark strangers, and hissed to
the others that the king was taken, the king was trapped.

They had come upon the rear of the crowd and the wind
had covered their voices; no one had seen them yet. Fired into

recklessness by their night ride, they did not hesitate. The flame of the Red Branch leaped up in an instant roar, and they swept swords from scabbards and, hoisting down the shields strung across their backs, barreled into the unsuspecting enemy from behind.

The invaders spun about with screams and war-cries, springing to life. The first ring of iron blades split the air, followed by a din of shouts and bays that broke out in all directions. The confusion of darkness and the guttering, wind-blown torch-light bred chaos, with men desperately hacking out and ducking fire-lit swords, and slipping in the mud.

Torches were flung to the ground, lighting the scattered straw.

Illan's ear was pressed to the doors. "I hear fighting! Perhaps the gate guards have come." He looked at Naisi. "I will bar one of these shut and hold the other while you get out another way."

"No." Naisi shook his head. "This is our fight."

"Conor only wants you and the girl; he's found some unknown filth to do his dirty work for him. Let me hold them while you escape. Once they know you are gone, they will leave me unharmed, for I am Fergus's son and Conor's kin. I can give you that chance."

Naisi was holding Deirdre to his chest, his arms muffling everything but his enveloping heartbeat. She tried to become conscious of her voice again. "I found a window," she said. "It's not wide, but we might be able to squeeze through."

Ainnle had calmed enough to stop shouting, though his face was still mottled with the aftermath of rage. He dropped his shoulders, lowering his tone. "If we get out the back we could surprise them—fight our way to the lanes and use them to access the main gate." He had not even countered the idea of giving Deirdre up to save them.

"It will be easier to protect Deirdre out there than being trapped in here, with no retreat," Ardan agreed quietly.

Naisi frowned at Illan. "If it goes bad, promise you'll surrender and save your life." Illan answered with a sharp nod and the four men dragged heavy kegs of ale to wedge one door closed. Naisi embraced Illan. "We will be back at your side soon. Hold fast."

Turning, Deirdre and the brothers crossed the hearth and ran down the corridor to the bed-chamber.

In the stables by the rampart, Fiacra thought he heard shouts and raised his head from between his father's chariot horses. He'd spent the evening bathing the animals at a river some way distant and was still wearing a sleeveless hide tunic and trews, dark with river water, his wet hair bundled under a leather cap. His skin and clothes were smeared with mud and horse-dirt, and he was longing for a bath.

There it was again. He caught one of the guards from the western gate, who was running past the stable door. "What has happened?"

"I don't know," the man babbled, shaking his head. "The sons of Usnech…"

They were back? Fiacra heard an unmistakable bellow of anger now, and did not hesitate, racing up the path and pulling out his sword. As he got closer, the shouts resolved themselves into screams of pain and savage growls, and his heart crowded his throat.

He was sprinting so fast that he propelled himself from the stable track into the yard before the Red Branch hall and collided with a group of men engaged in furious fighting in front of the double doors. Fiacra's vision was confused by the lunging black shapes and bloody shine of swords, the waving torches and burning straw. His Red Branch brothers were desperately struggling against strangers with black beards and hair, and at the doors of the sacred hall itself.

Naisi has come with Alban men and attacked! No, no; his sense intervened. Never Naisi. And yet it had been so long, and the sons of Usnech had been so angry with his father…and with the Red Branch after Leary…All these thoughts lurched through Fiacra's mind as a cloud of smoke billowed from the pile of flaming shields at his feet, choking him—the Red Branch trophies knocked to the ground.

Someone came at him with a dagger, slicing his brow, and he gasped in pain. An instant, mind-blinding rage took him. *Invaders, here at the heart of Emain Macha.*

Fiacra braced his sword and launched himself into the fray, stabbing and lunging, and the black-haired strangers backed away from his whirling blade. He was jostled by the crowd until the tide forced him up against the doors. The blood was running down his face, blinding one eye and tainting his mouth with a copper sourness that mixed with ash, the smoke stinging the other eye so he could hardly see in the chaos of lurid flame and leaping shadows. A man with a glinting sword had just felled someone right across the doorway of the hall, his back turned.

Fiacra growled under his breath and lunged at the man, and the other warrior turned as if he sensed him and with a scream blocked his descending slash. They twisted in the writhing smoke, struggling to get under each other's guard, Fiacra desperately trying to clear his eyes of the blood from his cut. Then their swords grated until the blades locked at the hilt, their faces so close the other man's spittle hit his cheek.

A discarded torch burst into flame on a stack of barrels by the door, the mead-soaked wood sending up a gout of flame as bright as day. In that bloody light, Fiacra stared into Illan's soot-smeared face.

Illan's eyes went wide, and Fiacra's mind jammed. Then Illan's features unfroze, drawing themselves into a snarl. "And so you, too, would betray me for that foul beast who calls himself king?" he cried, shoving Fiacra backward with a two-handed push. "You are no more than traitor's spawn, after all. Your blood is as black as his!"

His words stabbed Fiacra. Naisi and Illan had attacked the hall with Alban warriors in some twisted act of revenge—or an attempt to overthrow his father. His heart could not admit the evidence of his own eyes, but Illan was Fergus's son, after all...Was

Fergus plotting to take back the king's hall? Then this treachery must have been lurking there in Illan all along. *Not Illan!* his anguished soul howled.

"Not you," Illan wailed, and before Fiacra could speak, all sense slipped from Illan's black face and he lunged at Fiacra with a scream of pure despair.

Conall shouldered aside all the terrified people who were crowding the lanes, mouths agape, and sized up the situation with a glance.

Enemy warriors struggling against Red Branch fighters and Emain guards...then his eyes were unerringly drawn to two men slashing at each other before the very doors of the sacred hall. One turned to the light...Fiacra, his face twisted with effort and pain. The king's son, defending the door of the hall alone...Had Conor been attacked?

Everything was red from flame and blood, the two fighters covered in soot and dirt so it was hard to tell them apart through the cloud of smoke. Only Fiacra's anguished eyes swam in and out of Conall's sight.

Roaring, Conall flew at the two struggling figures as Fiacra's foot slid in the churned earth while he desperately tried to defend himself. The stranger's arm rose above Fiacra's head—Fiacra stabbed up with his own blade, twisting his wrist to block that falling sword. And at that moment, Conall swept in.

He grabbed Fiacra's attacker by the shoulder, setting his sword-tip between the blades of bone and wrenching back the man's arm joint to brace him. Then with a great bellow, Conall drove his blade into the man's back, pushing it home.

The enemy let out a terrible scream and Fiacra's anguished bellow followed, threading through that death-cry until both of them faded as one. Fiacra shoved Conall aside and grabbed for the body slipping off his blade. "No," Fiacra sobbed. "I would have disarmed him when his rage was spent! *No!*"

Baffled and panting, Conall looked down at the soot-smeared

features held up to the light of the torches, the man's cheeks flecked with blood from his foaming mouth. *Illan*. Stunned, Conall felt his legs give out until he was kneeling in a spreading pool of blood on the flagstones.

Illan clutched at his sleeve, twisting the cloth so that Conall's head was dragged toward that fair, young face that had so often turned to him with awe and an eagerness to share sword-talk with him, the great hero. A hero who had killed Fergus's beloved son. Conall's throat spasmed and he cradled Illan's head with bloody hands.

"Conall," was all Illan got out, his fingers slipping nerveless to the ground.

CHAPTER 45

Naisi dropped down from the window and his face filled Deirdre's vision, for an alert stillness had settled over it. "There are men prowling with torches around the hall," he said, and his voice was steady. "They will spear us before we can reach the ground."

The three brothers stared at one another, but before anyone could move, there was another kind of roar outside, an eerie hiss and deep growl of wood catching alight, and an ominous crackling from the direction of the front doors.

"They mean to burn us alive!" Ainnle exclaimed.

The scent of smoke was already creeping down from the thatch roof. "We will not die trapped in flames," Ardan said, almost dreamily, as if he floated in some other state.

"No," Naisi replied, his shoulders spreading and his chest opening as the anger fell from him. "I will not be driven before

the storm of other men's greed and hatred again." He was staring
at the hanging on the wall, an image of the god Lugh with the sun
as his shield. "I will wrest control of my own steps from them,
charge ahead in the fire of my own heart, with no retreating anymore." His fierce gaze went to his brothers, and there Deirdre
saw the hoarded flame rising. "We will break from the great
doors, and so pass beneath the shield of our father as we go." And
he smiled and reached his hands around Ardan and Ainnle's
necks, drawing all three of them into a circle.

Ardan held his wrist with a tight grip; Ainnle's arms went
about his brothers' waists and he bent his chin so he was almost
nestled into Naisi's shoulder. A moment, a breath of them as
boys.

Then they straightened and their hands fell to their sword-
hilts, and they drew the power from this hallowed warrior
ground up their backs again, bracing their heads. "Go, brothers,"
Naisi said "and soak our cloaks in water to cover ourselves
against the flames."

As Cormac and Dubthach arrived from the gates, one of the
posts of the Red Branch hall collapsed, skewing the roof and
bringing down a war banner in gouts of orange. The banner
broke free as it fell, whipped into writhing flame by a gust of
wind that blew it toward them. Cormac and Dubthach had to
leap aside, along with a crowd of screaming people who surged
away from its heat.

Cormac flinched as the sparks seared his cheek. *The sons of
Usnech were back*, his father's messenger had reported when he
found them downriver. Cormac stared wildly around at the
chaos of hacking men, the fire and blood.

"Connacht!" Dubthach gasped, echoing Cormac's plunge of
horror.

Connacht had darted in at their rear, through the rents their
own folly had torn.

Cormac did not pause, barreling into the enemy warriors and

fighting blindly in the smoke. He couldn't see the gold of his father anywhere. *The hall. He was with Naisi in the hall.* Cormac tossed someone from his blade and, leaping over the body, dashed through a gap in the wall of struggling warriors, a bank of white eyes in soot-blackened faces. Fixed on the goal of the burning hall doors, he quickly lost Dubthach behind him.

Red-haired Conall was fighting desperately against two men on the grass, his tunic and arms drenched in blood. Cormac was momentarily blinded by a cloud of sparks that rained down on him from the flaming roof, but as he shook them off and strained through the smoke, the catch of his breath made him cough up acrid ash.

A man was propped against the hall doors, dark blood splashed over his chest and the wood behind him. His head hung forward, his bright-silver hair spilling down his breast. *Illan.* And the man who had killed him was leaning over him in victory, pulling on his tunic with one hand while the other clutched his sword so feverishly that his tendons strained under his skin, the blade hovering over Illan's brow. He wore the sleeveless hides of these dark strangers, the dirty helmet and scum of mud on his limbs making him look like a wraith trying to suck the life out of Illan. Surely he was about to sever Illan's neck and take his head!

Cormac didn't pause, emitting a screech of fury as he raced in and pushed off from his toes into the wild, whirling spin of the Red Branch. Mid-leap, he hacked his blade with all his power across the back of the attacker's neck.

The leather cap flew off with the force of the killing blow and as Cormac thudded to earth all he saw was a familiar flaxen mane tumbling free, its fair glints soaked through with blood.

Levarcham was in the underground storehouses behind the king's hall sorting barrels and sacks when she heard the gabbling of the servants. She flew back up the steps and then ran past the hall down the path, toward the fire. There she pushed her way to the front of the crowd of terrified people that had streamed from their houses, their massed bodies a black outline against the lurid glow.

Deirdre...Conor...She could not see anything for smoke and fire. The Red Branch hall was burning.

She ground her fingers into her temples to halt the panic, so she could think. Desperately scanning the crowd, her eyes caught upon a man standing on a rise of ground on the other side of the yard. Conor. He was hooded, but she knew his stance. He turned, and she saw how he watched this terrible slaughter with glazed eyes and a mouth stretched into an avid leer, the light of all those flames playing eerily over his face.

He made this happen. It must be for Naisi, for Deirdre.

The press of hacking, capering warriors was too thick this close to the hall to break through. Instead, her steps drove her toward Conor. Deirdre.

There were so many onlookers now that Conor's guards did not see her until the people fell back from the wrath in her face. She flung down her hood to reveal the druid owl feathers, her sudden appearance and crooked limp making the warrior-guard hesitate. In that moment she lunged to spit at Conor, and one of the scarred warriors caught her in his arms. "Traitor!" she screamed. "I curse you with the breath of the gods, Nessa's spawn, for betraying your oaths and doing ill to those who trusted you!"

She struggled in her captor's grip. A curse was the only power she had—something that could unnerve even hardened warriors. "A king who so vilely dishonors the gods will hereby be brought to ruin, and your blood will never be honored among us again!"

Conor's eyes gleamed with a kind of madness. "I am cursed enough!" His laugh was the harsh caw of a crow. "It is ended now!"

Levarcham squirmed around to fling herself into the skirmish, desperate to force her way through to Deirdre by any means now...and if she was dead, to join her on that pyre. She heard an unfamiliar, deep growl behind her—"Bind and gag her, you fools, before I run you through with my own sword!"—and hard fingers forced her to her knees. Encouraged that they were not struck down by the gods, others piled in on her as well and she was gagged with a strip of bloody cloth, her arms roughly tied with a leather belt. "Deirdre!" she screamed behind the gag, her voice forced back down her aching throat.

On the other side of the clearing, a line of flame ran up the ridgeline of the hall, toward the great standard of the red-and-gold branched tree.

In the bed-chamber, the cries and ring of blades were a distant storm.

Naisi framed Deirdre's face with his hands and they seemed to glow with a force deeper than heat that slowly spread through her, bearing up her faltering heart.

His eyes were ablaze with it, the flecks of silver around the pupil summoning the defiant light of a steel blade held to the sun. "I told you I would know the day I died." She stirred to escape those words, but he held her. "This day, *a stór*."

A shudder went through her. Her awareness had bloomed along with the fire, for to savor this moment of being exquisitely alive with him, she needed to experience his senses as he did. So now she let the faint roar of the flames and the shouts and screams pass through her and did not shut them out, for fear she would lose a precious drop of time with him. The world that had been a blur leaped into vivid life around her, and she felt the force sweep through her body, as if tumbling them through rapids and then over the great falls. "Naisi...I love—"

"No." He cut her off fiercely. "We never loved by mortal rule so words will not be the last thing we share." He pulled her to the window, both of them clambering up on the table, and with a growl under his breath tore the remaining shreds of wood away. He held her there, his belly against her back. "See," he whispered.

His voice now was a lover's murmur that should be shared by firelight and the touch of furs on bare skin. The acrid smell of burning was blown away by a gust of freezing air, and Deirdre could see a veil of darkness lit by stars and moonlight. Through the window came the scents of wet soil and a whiff of rotting wood and moss from the marshy forest below the dun. The tendrils of the wild had overcome the smoke, twining about them. "For love of you, I turned my back on men and only the forest held us." He hesitated, his breath a sigh in her ear. "I should have stayed there with you. I am sorry."

She shook her head, touching his hand braced on the wall. "I know about the prophecy, and why you never told me." A waft of smoke from the roof above them made her cough. "I know what fate you risked when you let yourself love me."

"Not once did that ever matter to me." Over her shoulder, the blaze in his eyes swept her up and she felt it could drive her into the sky like his lifted blade, freeing her with a cry of defiance, of release. "I think we make our own fates, my *fiáin*."

He lifted her down to the floor and she dragged him to her and kissed him, catching every spark of sensation to hoard it in her heart. Her fingers traced the angle of his jaw, the strong bone and give of flesh, the tips absorbing the scrape of stubble. They moved to the tenderness of lips that softly parted, heated by his breath, and leaning in she drank in the sweet scent that rose from the warm hollow at his neck.

She cupped the part of him that had given her pleasure, worshipping it with her touch, tracing the grooves up each side of his groin to his hip-bones, as he echoed that caress over her thighs and breasts with his own fingers. Her hands grew desperate then, shaping the wings of his shoulder-blades, remembering how they moved when he was inside her. He possessed her mouth again, nestling her head in the crook of his elbow to hold her still, until at last he broke from her and rested his chin on her brow. "How strange," he whispered, "that even now I would bury myself in you and let this burn down around me. Even now, I would make you mine in defiance of him."

Her laugh was hoarse from smoke, but a pure chord was ringing through her flesh now. "Imagine them breaking in to find us, naked and oblivious." Her fingers moved endlessly, molding his cheekbones, the dip above his mouth, brushing the pulse at his temple. *Naisi. Naisi.* "They would say we are beasts after all." Their heads curved on each other's shoulders like swans caressing. *Naisi. Naisi.*

It was a song she could not stop singing.

There was a distinct crackling above their heads now and the clashes of fighting and screams had grown louder. Ardan appeared at the door to the chamber. "Here." He flung Naisi's soaking cloak at him, and then Deidre's. "Illan is gone and the door is shut. He must have left to fight."

"Then we must join him," Naisi said, and Ardan nodded and hurried down the corridor.

With no sense of urgency, Naisi tenderly wrapped the wet wool around her, smoothing it down as if it were not clinging in freezing folds to her skin but a fur to keep her warm. Tilting up her face he kissed one eyelid and then another, annointing her. "Come," he murmured, inviting and soft. "Come, my love."

In their absence, Ainnle and Ardan had wedged the doors closed with a heavy sideboard until they were ready to leave. Now they dragged it aside, leaving only one barrel holding the crossbar over. Smoke was gathering more thickly here, seeping down through the thatch. Blows rained onto the oak doors and the wood shivered with each strike, as hoarse yells and shrieks came through the cracks.

The brothers restrapped their swords over their backs, and then Deirdre's eyes met Ardan's and she walked into his embrace. He held her arms. "It wasn't this future we saw after all," he said, with a slight smile. If his eyes had ever looked far-seeing before, now they held the washed light of wide skies, and his hands quivered not with fear but with the tension that comes as wings spread to lift a bird from the earth. "Yet this was how I had to return to Her, I see now."

My brother. The blessing and the gratitude left her heart and as he sensed it, he kissed her brow.

A few stalks of flaming thatch were beginning to drop upon them, smoldering in the rushes. Deirdre hesitantly folded her fingers over Ainnle's where he held his sword strap, and after a moment he turned them to grip hers, his swift grin belied by the rueful glint in his eyes.

Naisi embraced his brothers and moved before the door, unfurling to his full height like a wave the moment before it falls. Ainnle was to one side, Ardan the other, and Deirdre between them. "No man can sunder the sons of Usnech if we hold together," Naisi said. "Summon the Red Branch fire as never before!" His jaw turned and his head tilted toward Deirdre with a small, intimate movement. "We can pass through fire. Don't forget, *a chuisle mo chroí*." Pulse of my heart.

She nodded and could not stop coughing, tears streaming from her eyes into the flakes of ash on her cheeks, her lungs reaching for breath...for life. She had a last moment to tangle her fingers in the tendrils of dark hair falling down Naisi's back. A warmth came through her palm and she imagined the light there at his core, burning forever. He took a breath that moved her fingers, and even as she clutched that sensation to her he shoved the barrel away and drew the crossbar back.

Letting out an ear-splitting cry—*Red Branch!*—Naisi kicked the door open.

The sons of Usnech with Deirdre in their midst flung themselves through a rain of cinders and clumps of burning thatch ripped away by the wind. They burst out into a confusion of cold air and starlit sky, and black figures struggling before sheets of flame, and behind them the porch collapsed in a great whoosh of sparks.

The momentum of their charge carried them over fallen bodies and through the first lines of screaming men. Deirdre glimpsed contorted faces and twisted arms through the smoke; the glint of bloody light catching the flat of swords. The din of shrieks, battle-cries and the crackle of flames beat on her ears, and the reek of burnt flesh and charred wood assaulted her nostrils and made her gag.

Then all she could see were disembodied, firelit eyes charging at them through the gray veils, and they halted as a wall of dark men took shape through the smoke.

Deirdre's hand was still on Naisi's back and so the first clash of blades shuddered up her arm. His muscles bunched under her fingers as he blocked blow after blow, twisting and lunging. And then there were too many blows to distinguish. They melted into one storm of clangs and sparks on steel, and grunts of effort as the brothers hacked and scythed.

They faced outward in a triple-knot, covering one another's flanks, Deirdre at their heart. The howling attackers surrounded them on all sides and the movements of the sons of Usnech became one endless, deadly flow of iron and flesh. As they lunged and braced themselves, they jostled her, and she struggled to keep her feet.

A cracked voice floated over the confusion. "Harm the girl and I'll have your heads on stakes!"

Something warm dripped down Deirdre's cheek. She thought it was tears, but when she wiped it away, her hand came back bloodied. Its stink filled her nostrils as more gore sprayed from slashed flesh and pooled in the mud at her feet.

"Enough!" came Conor's roar. "Enough!"

Behind Naisi, the Red Branch hall was disappearing in a conflagration, the proud walls and roof falling down amid gouts of flame. The banners of the golden tree were no more than shredded, flaming ruins.

As the fighting paused, so an eerie hush descended, and the press of dark strangers lightened around them. Though he stared ahead to the rise where Conor stood, Naisi's eyes did not see. His awareness had burst free of his confining body in one brilliant rush. He felt as if it flowed from every pore, sheathing him in silver, and flamed from the crown of his head. His soul roared with it, strong and free, a gust of flame reaching for the sky. *Cúchulainn's ecstasy.*

Naisi had been joined to his brothers and comrades in the Source many times, but that sharpened the senses of flesh and battle-field only, and was confined to that time and place, those breaths that danced between the veils of death. This was an explosion, an eruption, as his awareness spiraled up from the earth and flooded the land for an endless moment, joining him to something *beyond this*, behind the sky.

Below him, in one flash, he saw Red Branch dead splayed on the ground, the rest of their sword-mates bent over them. Dubthach was slumped against a wall with a badly wounded Conall across his lap. Cormac, the king's son, was also insensible, not with blood loss but with grief, keening in a broken voice over Fiacra and Illan's bodies that he cradled together on his knees.

Where once Naisi would have fallen into shame at this loss, the great flame that lifted him would bear only one pure rush of piercing grief that flowed through him unimpeded and then away. The flame blazed out even brighter, pouring from his body and the aura of spirit that hovered around his flesh, spilling a luminescence across the yard like a lamp burning against the night. *He knew himself; he was himself.*

The horrors of this night were not of his making. He had been filled only with the fire of creation: to lead his people, strengthen the Red Branch, protect with his blade. He grew conscious of the senses of his body once more. The warmth of Deirdre's hand radiating into his back; that was of his making, that love. The weaving of his brothers' breath and blood with his own—that was forged by them. And that was all that mattered.

He watched Conor take pained steps toward them. The enemy warriors parted and let the king through, until he stopped, a cloaked figure as bent as a gnarled yew. All Naisi could see was the white line of his hawk nose inside his hood.

Almost in supplication, Conor put out his hand. "Even now, I offer you life." The bony fingers quavered, and that strained voice held desperation. "If you give her to me, it can all be laid to rest, as I promised. Even now."

He was no more than an insubstantial wraith on the fringes of

Naisi's sight. Instead, Naisi's eyes were raised to the sky above the dark valley around him; to the rising dawn that beckoned over the peak ahead, just as she'd said. His heart pounded in great blows on his chest, to race for that hill and see the far views she had longed for, to expend this fire in a great shout of ecstasy. He took a breath and laughed. "She was never mine to give."

A hush fell again, and suddenly Deirdre laid her head against Naisi's back and turned her cheek to rest along his shoulder-blade. And in that one, subtle movement she gave of herself, re-jecting the king and his warriors and the charred walls that enclosed her. Instead, her hand reached around Naisi's waist and settled with great tenderness in a star across his heart.

Conor's gaze was riveted on her fingers, his glassy eyes trans-fixed.

A harsh growl tore the silence in two. "What is this?" The bearded man in the wolf cloak pushed through the crowd. "I heard the Red Branch were the bravest warriors in Erin, loyal to their king unto death." He spat on the ground, looking around at his pack, their eyes glowing greedily in the light of the flames. "Perhaps this path to honor is open to other warriors now!" And he stabbed his sword into the air with a bellow.

The flood of howling warriors engulfed Conor as if he was no more than a shard of broken wood in a stream, rushing past him to pile in upon the brothers once more.

Naisi swept his sword before him, a flame piercing the dark. "Follow me!" he cried to his brothers. *Follow the path up to dawn.*

Cúchulainn thundered up the track from the main gate on the Gray of Macha, the bodies of horse and man still joined, as peo-ple leaped out of the way of the flying hooves. He had been drawn by the angry glow of flames against the sky and by the leap of foreboding that had split his chest on sight of the dun.

Red Branch! Red Branch!

Time slowed, the Gray a flowing wave beneath him, and he saw the black mass of howling men surrounding the burning hall—comrades dead and wounded. And there…a blinding flash of lightning that was a silver shield thrown up against the bloody flames, the rain of cinders, the cries of grief and rage. *Naisi*.

He saw it all: the sons of Usnech were the last defenders of the hall and Emain Macha against a tide of screaming invaders. Enemies.

In the hush of the Source, Cúchulainn leaned down to tear off his boots and then he let go of the Gray's reins, pushing himself up to crouch on the galloping horse's shoulders. The Gray snorted, knowing the shift of weight…*the horse-feat of Skatha's Isle, practiced with Ferdia on the Plain of Muirthenne in the long dusks of sun-season.*

Cúchulainn tangled the mane in his fingers as the Gray collided with the crowd of warriors, and they screamed and fell back from his slashing hooves. *Cúchulainn!* they cried.

Rolling with the flow and lunge of the Gray's back, Cúchulainn stood, the soles of his bare feet curved to balance on the stallion's shoulders. The throng of warriors had parted beneath the onslaught of their charge, ebbing back to leave a clear space around the brothers. As the horse streaked along the alley of grass, Cúchulainn waited until the Gray was level with the brothers. Then, bracing thighs and calves, he propelled himself off its back with a great shout, in a soaring reverse somersault.

He landed with a thud, his hand already reaching over his back to whip his sword from its scabbard. Taken unawares, Ainnle and Ardan flung their blades up to defend, but Naisi did not. He had followed the Hound's entire flight with eyes ablaze.

The knot of brothers opened and Cúchulainn leaped in among them. The Gray carried on to the edge of the crowd, the shock of his appearance and his pawing legs keeping the enemy warriors at bay for another breath. The men all milled about, trying to rally to their commander's shouts.

It left enough time for Cúchulainn to cling to Ardan and Ainnle, their disbelieving laughs like a breath of pure air among the reek of smoke. Enough time to grip Naisi's shoulder and see the Source spilling from his face in a silver glow.

"Well met, brother," Naisi panted.

Behind him, the fabled beauty of Deirdre was obscured by soot and splashes of blood, but her eyes were just as fierce as Naisi's. And in this breath of peace, Naisi moved back and she held him around the waist as if he was all that existed for her. Of all the shades of the Source Cúchulainn had ever faced, he found he could not look at her fire, for it was too raw, too intimate and bleak. It was for Naisi alone.

"Sorry I was late," was all Cúchulainn got out, for a breath later they had to turn, bracing themselves as the sea of men crashed over them once more.

The fighting renewed more fiercely, and Cúchulainn and the sons of Usnech swept through the enemy ranks like a flaming brand thrust into a field of dry tinder. The fight was a dance, a dream, and Cúchulainn did not know how much time passed, only that each breath inward seemed to fall through a calm place of silence, shared by them all. And each breath out sent a brighter flare up their blades.

But though he held the moments tight in his fist, there was no end to the waves of baying attackers—scores of them—and even the Hound of the Ulaid in his battle frenzy and the sons of Usnech in the flame of their youth could never prevail.

Rents opened in the shield of the Source through sheer force of numbers: a strike on Ainnle's sword knocked him sideways a step, and Ardan stumbled when a blade caught his arm, spinning him. Naisi slammed his back against Cúchulainn's so they could speak without lowering their swords, Deirdre crushed between Naisi and Ardan on his other side.

Naisi's whisper went through Cúchulainn like a sweeter breeze blowing far above this mire, the Source-light flowing between them, joining their hearts. "Save her," Naisi breathed. "I cannot bear it after all."

Cúchulainn would have argued, but the whites of Naisi's eyes flashed toward him even as he desperately blocked a swinging sword. "Give me this honor as a man, and argue not."

The black sea in which Deirdre was tossed was scented with blood, but the great glow around Naisi suddenly expanded now, growing into a towering spire of brightness that obscured his body and Cúchulainn's beside him. The radiance flamed brighter, a shield between her and her terrible fear of Naisi's pulse guttering out.

It is death, she thought, dazed by the bloody dream. She and he were passing into the Otherworld together—death was the light that cradled their pain, taking her in its glittering mantle to bear her into peace with Naisi's eyes upon her.

And then strong, sinewy arms wrapped about her, and the shrieking din of the night broke upon her once more. It was not death—it was Cúchulainn. The great warrior bound her flailing body with his own and lifted her from the brightness into dark. The blow as he flung her body on the ground woke her. She was lying against a wall, and before her was a horse, a bulky shape between her and the men and the flames. It stamped and snorted, facing outward, and the warriors stayed well clear of it. She was in the space it guarded.

Deirdre's fingers dug into wet grass, her hair tangled in her mouth... and time began again. "Give me my death with him!" she cried. But Cúchulainn had already leaped back to join the fray, though he was now confined to the back of the crowd as a mass of fighters all piled in on him at once.

Winded and sick, Deirdre tried to straighten, but at that moment an invisible blade stabbed right through her breast. She gasped and bent double, holding her chest as if the flesh had indeed been torn open, though no weapon had touched her.

The seething throng of warriors erupted in a great roar of bloodlust, and as Deirdre knelt there, clawing at the wall, a vision of Ainnle burst upon her mind—his hair wet from the loch, his eyes bright with mischief. *Ainnle.* His cry of fury echoed all through her and she threw back her head and howled with it, the pain cresting before his voice faded into nothing, like the gust of a storm whirling away.

She barely had time to gulp a breath before a second blow came, and she fell on all fours with a moan. A violent blow seemed to strike her neck then, as if entering her spine, and she clutched her belly with one mud-stained hand. *Ardan,* she whispered. Saliva mixed with blood and flooded her mouth, running down her chin.

A second hoarse cheer lifted to the sky, and Deirdre's back hunched. She vomited over her hands. The bitter stink caught in her hair, making her retch again, over and over. *Ardan.*

Then her body arched in a long spasm of anguish, and the third and last death-blow fell. This skewered low in her belly, twisting on itself like a spear thrust through her vitals. The darkness roared over her, wiping out air and firelight, noise and touch.

The last thing she knew she was falling facedown in the blood-soaked mud, as the loudest cheer of all enveloped her. It rebounded off the walls of the houses and up to the clouds and back until it surrounded her, obliterated her.

But the wild hills beyond and the scattered stars were silent.

CHAPTER 46

The lilting song wove through Deirdre and she floated on the notes in a dreamy haze. She was ten again, and sick in bed. She could feel cool sheets against her sweat-soaked body and smell the taint of herbs. She was ten, and Levarcham was tending her with gentle hands.

The singing was husky and the melody wandered up and

down, and Deirdre's child self listened in wonder. A song of the Ulaid heroes! How she loved to hear such tales when she was ill, and Levarcham lifted a cup of honeyed water to her lips and smoothed her aching forehead. She was cosseted and warm. She was safe.

The song faltered and then took up its rhythm again.

> *Behold, the proud-striding sons of Usnech*
> *Naisi, washed by me in firelight*
> *Ardan with the stag slung lightly*
> *Ainnle with a load of wood high-lifted*
> *Though you praise the rich mead*
> *Conor mac Nessa drinks*
> *I have known a sweeter drink*
> *By the forest pool*
> *Out of the fire-pits Naisi dug*
> *In the flat-swept forested plains*
> *Meat issued more melting than honey*
> *Under the three sons' hands*
> *Naisi!*
> *The black flower of his head*
> *On stem-white shapely body;*
> *No need of welcome now for the dead*
> *Never-coming sons of Usnech*

Levarcham's grip on her hand grew tighter and her breathing was hoarse in Deirdre's ear. The druid was not singing after all. So whose was that plaintive, broken voice?

> *Forest daybreak when he stirred*
> *With open gaze I dressed in sunlight*
> *His blue eyes a rapture to women*
> *A fierce terror to foes*
> *I loved our coupled step in tree-dusk*
> *A chant threading through dark woods*
> *Now I do not sleep*

Nor tint my fingernails
There is no need to be welcoming
He will not come
The first son of Usnech

The voice trailed away to a cracked whisper.

"Shut her up!" The man's anguished growl rang through Deirdre's hollow head. "Bind her tongue, I command you!"

Levarcham's voice was more terrible than Deirdre had ever heard it. "She wanders in fever; I can no more command her thoughts than extinguish the sun." Deirdre plucked feebly at the blanket trapping her legs, for the two voices were like sharp points cutting her flesh.

"Don't you *ever* let her say his name again," the man hissed.

A pause. "You cannot take a name from a man or the fact he lived. You can no more take that, son of Nessa, than order the gods to remake the world."

That word *Nessa* hinted at another, darker name, a different memory, and Deirdre felt herself taking wing and thrusting her feathers down to flee from it. At the last moment, Levarcham's voice halted her, winding a tether around one talon. She was tugged back, desperately beating her wings. All she could see below was a bank of roiling cloud, a storm that cloaked the land she had left, while, above her, sunlight spread across the world. "Deirdre!" Levarcham's hoarse mutter. "I will have you back. I will."

Deirdre was torn between the sun spilling across the mountains and the voice of her teacher. She must be dreaming, that was it; Levarcham was calling her. She was ten, and if she woke the druid would be smiling down and Aiveen would have bannocks baking and Fintan would be setting his nets over his shoulder.

"Come." Levarcham's call was breathless and insistent. "Come back to me."

Deirdre was struggling, blinded by the urgent light above and buffeted by the clouds below. Then Levarcham's arms were about her and she was caught by the familiar, mingled scent of thyme, myrtle and linseed. Something bitter was thrust under her nose, yanking her back. Her spirit spiraled down, and a heaviness crept into her limbs. Now she vaguely recognized the pressure of blankets and sour smells. Her eyes were fast shut, their lids crusted over, and when the spinning at last slowed she had to strain to drag her eyes open.

She was in a strange chamber, lavishly decorated with cushions and rugs in lurid colors that pained her eyes. Levarcham was not smiling at all but hunched over, her hair a gray tangle, her cheeks sunken and smeared with soot. Those twilight eyes were cold and dead.

Deirdre stared up at this broken woman, then down at the pale hands spread on her own chest. She turned them over. They were not soft and young after all, but roughened, with broken nails and callused palms. A scar scored one finger. *A burning ember that escaped the fire … she had tried to brush it back in and he had laughed when she cursed in pain. And he had sucked on the burn to soothe it, smiling around her finger …*

The storm consumed her.

Levarcham saw it break over her, and her face crumpled. "I am sorry … I am sorry I brought you back." Then she began to weep.

Conor sent gifts: amber and crystal rings, nets of spun gold for her hair, carved boxes inlaid with pearls. There were silks, and bronze drops for her ears, and blackbirds tethered to perches so they could sing for her.

Deirdre neither saw, nor spoke.

Conor curled his beard and hair with perfumed fat and sat by her bed. Her hand remained limp in his, and when she stared at the wall her eyes darted back and forth as if she was absorbed in her own unfolding world, somewhere he could not reach. He had swans slaughtered on the lakes and their feathers sewn into a blanket that lay across her unmoving body like a soft drift of snow. Only the flutter of her breast showed she lived, and a ladder of bones ran down her chest.

Guilt was a place Conor would not go; coldness was his only strength.

Outside, the black ribs of the Red Branch hall rose up in a charred skeleton. The dun was hushed and people crept about on silent feet. There were no warrior voices lifted in jest or song. The Red Branch warriors who returned with Ferdia were shamed and still in shock. There was no one to lead them, or to challenge Conor. Fergus had ridden back to his dun with Illan's body. Some hand of the gods had come upon Cúchulainn after the brothers died, and though he had killed more of Eogan's men, the battle frenzy left him and he staggered to his horse and rode it away. Conall was badly wounded. Cormac would not see him. And Fiacra, Conor's fair-silver son, was gone.

In these few days, Conor had called to him his most loyal chieftains from all over the Ulaid—those who wanted no part of Red Branch squabbling—and they had come with their guards and so there were armed men ranged about the gates and the walls once more. Eogan's men still roamed the dun and he had been too afraid to send them home yet. He would give Eogan enough gold to satisfy him, and not look upon him again.

All he could focus on was that he had to make this mean something. He had to have the triumph of Deirdre to set against the ruin.

"What happened?"

Dozing on her stool, Levarcham sat upright. She clutched at Deirdre's hand. "My love…"

"What happened…after?" Deirdre's voice was strained from the screaming.

Levarcham cradled those cold fingers to her face. Deirdre's bone-white cheeks were sunken, the hollows of her eyes purple. The druid had combed that tangled hair, but the girl's lips were cracked, her brows furrowed with pain. Levarcham told her of Illan killed by Conall, and Fiacra by his own brother; of Fergus riding in that night to find one son a traitor and the other dead, and how he wept over Illan.

"And where are…they?" That was a whisper, the only vibration of feeling so far.

Levarcham squeezed her fingers. "They lie as close as they did in their mother's arms, in a place where wild roses bloom in sunseason."

Deirdre absorbed that, sinking into the pillow as if she was wasting into a wraith. "The king has lost everything," she murmured.

The cold from her hand spread up into Levarcham's heart, deadening it. "Yes."

Deirdre's numbed mouth moved for the first time into an icy smile.

Cathbad had been getting weaker, and one of the novices came to Levarcham where she brewed a healing draft by Deirdre's bed. Cathbad was dying, he said.

Levarcham went to him as the light faded, the dusk throwing banners of mist around Emain Macha and its smoking buildings. The footstep behind her was as insubstantial as the fog, and when she turned she glimpsed a slight, cloaked figure. Deirdre had at last risen.

Levarcham swiftly hurried on, those ghostly steps trailing her to Cathbad's hut. No one was about, for people kept to their lodges, too afraid of what the coming days would bring. A sickly scent crept along the narrow alleys from the pyres on the plain, the burning of flesh seeping into the mist of ruin that hung over the dun.

Druids were singing dirges at Cathbad's fire and sprinkling the herbs on the flames; others were scattering the bones of divination. Levarcham approached Cathbad's cot behind a screen of rowan-wood, its berries wound about his bed. He was wrapped in a pure-white bull-hide, the fine skin dotted by drops of sacred water and specks of salt to mark the journey he would make over Manannán's Ocean to the Blessed Isles. Lamps at each corner of the bed spat and flickered.

Cathbad's spark of awareness had been coming and going. When he saw Levarcham, though, he feebly waved his attendants away. She sensed the ghost-maiden hovering behind her, but the singing druids did not mind Deirdre, as if she had already faded into a shadow world. "The veils are parting, daughter," Cathbad wheezed, his breath stirring the wisps of white hair clinging to his scalp. His eyelids quivered, following something unseen. "It is ...nothing I expected. I feel myself...slipping from one world to the next. It is becoming...blurred. And there is light! Where the mists become vivid again, on the other side of the sea." At times of death, druids were preoccupied with the great journey, and Levarcham focused her will on that and joy for him, and not their loss. Yet he left at such a time, with the Ulaid at their weakest.

She heard a faint sigh in the shadows behind her, and took up Cathbad's frail hand, every bone showing through the leaf-thin skin. His mind had already wandered so far that though the druids had told him what happened, he had no counsel for them; they must find it themselves. The dying often remembered long-ago events, though, and this is what filled her heart. "As you saw for her before she was born," she murmured, "have you no comfort for Deirdre now?" She squeezed Cathbad's hand. "*Please*, Father."

His irises were cloudy. "Deirdre of the Sorrows." He spoke her name like a chant, and Deirdre stirred behind Levarcham. "Most beloved of the *sídhe*." His eyes closed, flickering rapidly under his transparent lids. "Yes...yes..." His breath came faster as he clutched the side of the bed, speaking with the unseen. "No, I... no." Levarcham could not make out that muttering, the words slurring into a hoarse song, his eyelids showing glimpses of the whites. His throat began to rattle and the druids looked over without pausing in their singing.

"Father!" Levarcham cried in alarm. She glanced to the table where potions stood by to ease Cathbad's breathing, but before she could reach out he tensed, his hand clutching his chest. She held him by the shoulders, vainly trying to transfer some of her own strength into his frail body.

"No…no…" His head fretted from side to side. "So blind… how can it be?" His eyes sprang open, and he looked over Levarcham's shoulder as if she was not there, his gaze fixed on Deirdre. Levarcham heard a faltering step as Deirdre came close behind her, though the druid dared not release Cathbad, her ear close to his spittled lips. "When I saw your beauty to be…" Cathbad croaked to Deirdre, "I did not perceive the fullness of the pattern that arcs over me now…"

Deirdre moved to the bed and Levarcham dared a glance at her. The girl's hood had fallen back, her fists were clenched and, in the middle of her icy face, her eyes blazed at Cathbad with every scrap of animation left in her. "What pattern? What did you curse me with?"

"Ah…" Cathbad moaned, his eyes full of wonder. "No curse… for look at what she holds in her, how bright it is, stripping away illusion, yes, burning it away in fire. It is not your beauty that brings death, child…" His face filled with anguish, and tears leaked from his clouded eyes.

Suddenly, Deirdre swooped past Levarcham and grabbed Cathbad's hand, and the old man spasmed with the shock of that touch. Their palms made a fist, his fingers clawed, hers small and sturdy, covered in healing scratches. "Then tell me the truth!"

"A man…*looks into you*…as a mirror…" Cathbad whispered, locked into Deirdre's gaze, "and sees his darkness…what he covets, fears…hates." Amazed, Levarcham let go of Cathbad and stood back. "To feel worthy…" Cathbad's breath escaped in a hiss. "Possession, greed…the terror of encroaching years."

"Conor." Deirdre was barely audible. "And Cinet."

"A banshee…come to take his brother from him, bring the loss he so feared."

"Ainnle," Deirdre breathed. "And Ardan saw the Goddess he longed for."

Cathbad gripped her hand with fading strength. "They saw what was missing in them…But not him. You know what he saw." Deirdre bit her bloodless lips as Cathbad drew a rattling breath. "All their longings…and it reflects back…even my own." He dragged his other hand from beneath the covers. "Though in the end, you are no mirror but a flame, and by you the darkest depths are laid open to the light." He gasped, his hand shielding his wet eyes. "Was my pride so great I thought mere dreams to be the word of the gods?"

Levarcham struggled to force her thoughts into order. *It was not Deirdre's fault.* She went to move, but was arrested by the stillness that had now fallen over Deirdre as she stared down at the dying man. Whatever her eyes held made Cathbad shake, utterly undone. "Forgive me…" he cried behind his trembling hand, "forgive me…"

Deirdre hesitated and then lowered their fists, and at last this kinless girl placed a gentle hand of blessing on the chief druid's head. "You did hear true at last," she whispered. Cathbad searched her face, and a shudder went over Deirdre and her chin dropped. "I forgive. I would send no one to death bearing the pain I now bear." After a moment Cathbad's body sank into the mattress beneath her touch, his breath sighing out.

Moving stiffly, Deirdre turned with sightless eyes, her hands groping for the screen at the end of the bed. She grasped for the wall and steadied herself along it before stumbling around the hearth, making for the door.

Levarcham would have run after her but Cathbad was turning his face up, his hand feeling for her own. "I hear singing…is that your voice, daughter?" he wheezed. "Draw them all closer…I want to be wreathed in song."

The fields around Emain Macha were silent and the wind blew in spatters of rain as if the sky was weeping, washing the paths in rivulets of soot. Cathbad was on his deathbed, and druids walked the paths in ghostly robes, the still air full of their chants.

Conor needed Deirdre on his arm as a balm for this wound. Emain Macha must be envied again by men for its luxury and grace, and she would decorate his hall so all men knew that Conor of the Ulaid was still powerful. That he had won.

He went to his mother. "Break her," Nessa croaked, as shriveled as a dried husk, too afraid to leave her house. When he hesitated, she got past his guard, jabbing at his prick with her claw. "Use this like a man, by the gods!"

He struck her hand away and, stepping forward, slapped her across the face with his palm, sending her sprawling to the floor.

"Who cares about her spirit?" she hissed, her eyes hollow with accusation. "Break her, *claim* her, if that's what you need, or there will be nothing left for us. That crow of a druid is at Cathbad's bedside; she's been there all night. Do it now!"

Conor gazed down in horror. Cathbad. He moistened his lips. "I should be giving him due honor—"

"He is beyond you now." Nessa pulled herself into a huddle on the floor. "We must think of the living, of holding control of the men in any way we can. Sweet Brid, you can't let her humiliate you anymore!"

Conor stumbled from Nessa's house and to his horror felt himself grow hard with frustration. All the curdled shame and fury poured into his loins, for it had nowhere else to go.

"Leave us!" he barked at the serving women tending Deirdre in the guestlodge. When they just stared with frightened eyes he roared, "Leave us!" They fled, and he dragged a stool in front of the door.

Throwing aside his cloak, he approached Deirdre, who was curled on the bed. He would not look at her face. She was *his*, and he had never even seen her body. He wrenched back the sheets. The mattress was barely hollowed beneath her, and her bones stuck out beneath her linen shift at neck and wrist. *Now* she looked worn, when it did not matter anymore.

Her pale face was a blur on which he would not focus. Panting, he dragged up her shift so he could finally see what he had yearned for, exposing an expanse of smooth white thigh and a curve of buttock. With a catch in his throat he sank on his knees and touched his nose to Deirdre's knee to scent her. *His prize.*

Beside him, her nails imperceptibly pressed into the mattress, the pink paling into the white. He smiled. *So she did feel.* His breath quickening, he moved along on his knees and, extending a quaking hand, cupped one breast through the fine linen. She was trying to be still, but could not hide the tremor of her heart under his fingers.

Unsteadily, he grasped her other breast, the globes firm and warm in his palms. At last. He should have claimed her long ago. She was a wild thing that needed breaking, not gentleness. He staggered up with a grunt, and tore Deirdre's shift from neck to knee.

She lay awkwardly splayed, making no effort to cover herself. Her skin was as pure and translucent as he'd imagined, the bright gilding of her hair echoed by the darker smear between her legs. He ignored her protruding hip-bones and ribs and feasted his gaze on her nipples and the dent in her belly, savoring his painful engorgement. He was not an old, broken king but a potent lord, and everyone in Erin would quail before him when she renewed him all over again, her presence summoning this fire of lust and vigor. "You can lie like that now, my love," he whispered, brushing her thigh, "but you cannot ignore me forever." He fumbled with his belt, clumsily unlacing his trews and kicking them off. His prick sprang free, eager and proud. "See?" he hissed, his pulse galloping erratically. With a growl he clambered on the bed and, grabbing her knees, wrenched them apart.

His mouth went dry and he stared at the prize for which he had waited so long, that tender pink flesh and mysterious cleft. He would plow this furrow and seed it; make it his. *Naisi did not get a child on her.* When she stood in the temple with a swelling belly, that would be the completion. He strained toward her, desperate to sheathe himself in that pliant body, knowing she did not fight because she had accepted this inevitability, too. His focus narrowed on the shadow between her legs and…

She moved, her muscles spasming.

He startled and forgot himself, involuntarily looking in her eyes. A cry was torn from him. In the center of that stark, bony mask, they were coals of hatred, the rest of her fading into the pillow as the hungry flame grew. It reached for him, sucking his life away. She lifted a thin, white hand and, before he could twist away, she hissed loudly and touched a finger-tip to his shaft.

He sprang back, his fist lifting to strike her. Then he halted, for her touch burned all the way up his body and suddenly he saw...

A black-haired man moving over Deirdre, those white thighs wrapped around him, her face raised in rapture. The young man slipped from her, both of them sweat-soaked and replete, and from Deirdre's body his seed ran, milky white. Naisi's seed.

Conor moaned and his prick shriveled, curling up beneath his flaccid belly. He tried to stiffen it, then threw himself over her to force it in. But it shrank away from him until it was no more than a slug lying in his fingers. He could only twist his head up, his sight filled now not by her eyes, but by the barest hint of a cold smile on her lips.

Conor's senses deserted him and he leaped off her, dragging his trews up to hide himself from that smile. The door banged with an enormous thud, catching on the stool. Conor struggled into his tunic as fists pounded, and then something was hurled at the door. He spun as a third blow pushed the door back, slamming the stool out of the way.

Levarcham advanced on him at a swift limp, forcing her way before Deirdre and turning at bay, her teeth bared. "I will not let you touch her!" she cried. "This time you will slay me to get to her!"

Deirdre rose to her knees, the sheet thrown around her. Both of them looked at him as if he was something deformed. He dragged up his aching body, the touch of Deirdre's finger still burning, and fought the simultaneous urge to retch and let go into blackness, rending them both into pieces. "I have given you every honor and desire, everything tender in me," he hissed to Deirdre. "But if you will not be a queen, then you will be a slave.

Eogan's blade broke Naisi's back and that will crush you more than I ever can—to lie beneath him and be split by him—and then you will come back to me broken. If you will not give yourself to me as a woman, I will have you as the shell of one!"

The fear that crossed Deirdre's face was a sweet, satisfying pain, but while he was still savoring it Levarcham darted in and, drawing a great breath, slapped him across the face. "You will kill me before I let your brutes near her!"

He let the sting invade him, smiling at her. "Cathbad is dead—I see it in your face—so who will protect you now? I should have done away with you long ago."

Levarcham held the staff sideways, bracing the oak with her pitifully thin arms, so weak compared to his, which could strangle the life out of her even now. She lifted her chin. "No, you will not, O cursed one. You may have called to you the chieftains you bought with gold, and told them this destruction is wrought by Red Branch pride. But there are other nobles, and Red Branch warriors, and all the common people of dun, field and byre—and though you will excuse *these* deaths as battle slaughter, *you cannot kill a druid and hold your hall.* Not after this, when you must wrest control back from the ruin of your darkness!"

He glowered at her, panting, and his fingers itched to fasten around her neck.

"I will go." Deirdre got up and turned to Levarcham, the folds of the sheet draping the floor. "Nothing anyone does can harm me again. I will not have you hurt for me." She looked at Conor. "It will take me away from *him*, and that is all I desire in this world."

A coldness blew over Conor as if a wind had climbed the hill, sweeping through him and taking every shred of feeling with it. "Tomorrow, so that everyone knows your shame, Eogan and I will drive you from the very gates of Emain Macha to his own dun, and he will feast me. And in return, I will bestow the gift of you upon him for six moons, to use as he sees fit." He paused by the broken stool and, grasping one leg, hurled it against the wall, where it splintered, the shards grazing one cheek as he passed into the night.

Deirdre squatted by the fire and fed it feverishly while Levarcham stood with helpless hands.

The lodge was silent but for the crackling of the wood as it caught. Levarcham forced herself to move, putting her palms on Deirdre's head. "My child, I failed you utterly, and my life is worth nothing." A dry sob hovered in her throat that could not be released.

Deirdre's arms were wrapped about her sheet-clad knees, her spine pushing through her bare skin. "No…" she breathed, and when Deirdre looked up, Levarcham could see nothing but a penetrating light—no features, no pain, nothing. "For you, too, have learned about love, and that is all you needed."

She strips away illusion. And as Levarcham tasted the full draft of her failure in that revealing flame—the pride in Conor's honor that blinded her, her lack of courage—she realized that the teaching had not been from druid to pupil after all.

All at once, Deirdre reached up a hand and pulled her down beside her. Through the broken door came the faint chanting of the druids, warding Cathbad's bier for three days before they burned him.

"I sought, and I found things," Deirdre whispered, and when Levarcham sank on her knees she saw the icy hue of the girl's skin was warmed by the firelight, her glassy eyes reflecting the flames. "You taught me the lore and, from the opening you gave me, I learned more. But though I turned my back on them, and the shining ones must shun me now, perhaps you can reach them for yourself." Levarcham stared at the trembling curve of her cheek, baffled.

Deirdre hesitated, her hands tracing shapes in the air. "Below the surface of what we see, there are…stars…" She paused. "And… they sing, and the resonance they make is the light of Source…

and…" She broke off, biting her lip. "There are no words, I must show you."

Deirdre turned toward Levarcham, her pale fingers urgently gripping her arm as if trying to force some knowing into her. And all unnoticed by the girl, the druid could swear that a plume of fire-sparks swirled toward her, ever so slightly.

CHAPTER 47

It was dawn, and Levarcham's palm bore a stark imprint of the comb she had drawn through Deirdre's hair. She uncramped her hand, rubbing the marks away.

Despite Conor's words, she would not send the girl out before men like a slave. The servants had dressed Deirdre and were now coiling her hair and holding it with gold pins. All through these attentions, Deirdre had gazed into the fire, her back straight and head down, while layers of fine linen and wool were tugged over her and twisted around, then knotted with brooches.

At last, a horn blared from the gates below. Deirdre tilted her face to Levarcham like a flower on a stem. "Leave me some time alone," she said. She no longer spoke to Levarcham like a child to a teacher.

Levarcham could hardly push the words past her numb tongue. "I will stay outside the door—"

"No." Deirdre held her eyes. "I cannot bear one more person being punished by aligning with me. Stand by the gates with the people."

"Don't be ridiculous," Levarcham retorted, struggling to summon breath to argue.

Deirdre gripped her hand with surprising force. "I need to know you are safe or I cannot be strong."

Levarcham started at the subtle vibration in Deirdre's fingers, just as she had the night before when, in halting words, Deirdre had tried to impart some glimpse of what she had found in Alba. Now as then, Levarcham could not grasp this stream of wonder with her grief so thick around her, and even this day her mind only skated over it, fragmenting whenever it came near to the senses of which Deirdre had spoken. She could concentrate only on her child.

Nevertheless, she bowed before Deirdre's fierce gaze and called the servants away. Outside, the light was as gray and cold as beaten iron, and guards fell into step around her, their spears a fence of blades. Levarcham walked in silence, but inside she was furiously thinking. Now that she and Deirdre were together, there would be a way to escape once more, just the two of them. At Eogan's dun, she could make the men think she was broken, and then run... There must be a haven for them somewhere.

Before the gates, Levarcham raised her head and finally became aware of the crowd that had been drawn from their hearths into the cold morning. People hung over the timbers of the ramparts, peering down, clustered the stairs to the gatetowers and lined the paths, straining to see. The entire throng was hushed, though, their hoods and shawls thrown around their heads, their breath mingling with the mist that had descended over the dun, blurring the edges of the world.

Levarcham's gaze was drawn to the gate, and her body jolted with dismay.

Framed by the towers, two groups of warriors faced each other. On one side, the king stood by a wicker chariot lined with shields, the brute Eogan at his flank surrounded by scores of his own men. On the other was Fergus mac Roy, returned from his dun, and Cormac, his neck and arm bandaged. Dubthach and other Red Branch warriors were behind them.

Fergus was no longer puffed and proud. His bulk had sagged

with grief, threatening to slide from his enormous frame like a hillside collapsing, and his eyes were reddened and glassy as he stared at the king. Off to one side, Cúchulainn was by his chariot, standing between his stallions with one hand on the black's neck and one on the gray's.

Uncaring for once of her limp, Levarcham continued with chin high, until, when she got close to Eogan's chariot, the king stirred and her flanking guards crossed their spears to stop her from going farther.

Deirdre plucked the pins from her hair as she slowly circled the hearth, burying her fingers at her scalp and loosening the braids until her hair tumbled untamed around her shoulders.

All the details of the world—the lamplit outlines of furniture, the cold coming through the door—were broken edges grinding against her, prodding her from numbness. She circled faster, her hands spread across her belly and pushing inward as if digging into mere flesh and muscle could distract her from the agony of that which she could not reach: soul-heart and life-flame. At least bodies could be beaten until they were cold and unfeeling.

She turned her hands over and knuckled her belly, trapping the endless howl inside her. If she refused to go and became limp and lifeless again, they would only carry her to Eogan, and someone else would animate her limbs for her. *This flesh that was once alive to his touch.*

She could not say his name. Never.

She had to find some shred of strength, and not let him down. It made her think of Levarcham's whisper in the night, of a life they would lead together as wandering druids, where no one would know their names. They would be wisewomen, bestowing blessings on the land. And she would have the freedom she had always longed for—the freedom *he* had died for.

She stopped, her hands falling numb at her sides, and let those words sink through her for the first time.

⚛

Deirdre walked away from the lodge with a cloak wound about her, grasping it closed at the neck and pressing the folds to her side. She was vaguely aware of a blur of faces lining the path down through the fort. The mud sucked at her bare feet, and the sky was a bank of pale mist.

She forced herself to focus on nothing but Conor under the gate, the iron strips on his helmet framing pale, frozen features that made his face a death-mask. To summon her strength, she had been forced to wake again, and as she met his gaze and saw the glint of hunger there—even now—her hatred was a blinding spark that set her alight. She walked toward him and something began to rise in her, filling muscle and hollow bone, spilling over into the mantle of energy that clad her body. Deirdre trapped Conor's gaze as he had trapped her, and poured everything she had always felt for him into her eyes.

He was rooted by it; bound by it.

Holding that fiery thread, Deirdre relaxed her grip on the cloak and let it slide from her shoulders to the ground, her chin held proudly. People gasped, for she was naked. Stripped back to nothing but herself, she savored the ground through her soles, and her limbs swung free, moving in ripples she knew well as the flow of the wildwood.

He had thought to shame her, but he could only do so if she allowed herself to be shamed.

The stillness of the people became complete, the shuffling of feet, the coughs, the whines of children fading into silence. Perhaps because of the carriage of her neck, her straight back, she became aware that they were not staring at her nakedness but bowing their heads as she passed. She saw Fergus, his mouth agape, and the other warriors whose gaze fell to her body but then swiftly lifted to her face, from which they then did not look away.

By the time she stopped before Conor, rage had become her cloak, and she felt it expanding her stature like great, dark wings unfurling around her. She wondered if she had summoned Badb or the Morrigan, the crow goddesses of war, with the force of her silent scream.

Her gaze moved to the older nobles with their glittering rings—the men who had raised no finger to halt the injustice done to her. She looked at the Red Branch, which held to a code that took from her the most honorable of men; which had the power to shape a world and used it to destroy. Would they walk alone, naked and bare-handed, into a nest of their enemies? Would they risk shame to conquer it?

She could not see Cúchulainn, but could feel his presence as she could sense no one else here but Levarcham. In contrast to the blaze she had seen in battle, his spirit felt dark and cold now, turned and crushed back on itself so that no light escaped. And yet it seethed there beneath that black surface. Though she hated that he had torn her from *his* side, she drew a strange comfort from the Hound's pain.

The murderer Eogan, all bare, brawny arms and oiled black beard, shuffled his feet uneasily and glanced from Conor to his warriors. Levarcham was endeavoring to push through the arms holding her, until Deirdre told her with her eyes to stay still.

She returned her gaze to Conor, laying it like a brand upon him, and his bloodless lips twitched as a pulse jumped in his neck.

"This flesh I gave to him, and it will always be his, because he did not take." The howl of her soul fragmented into human words, her voice cracked and torn. "And in the Temple of the Goddess, I felt in him the God, the mantle of what a king must be."

There was a subtle movement of Eogan and his men, hands drifting to swords to stop her words. And yet as that ripple passed among them, so there was an answering stirring from Fergus and the Red Branch to warn them back—a fine tightening that only warriors would sense. Then Cúchulainn was there beside the king, and though Eogan scowled at him, Conor did not order the Hound back. The king merely stared at Deirdre, trapped by the blade of her words, and for a fleeting moment she wondered if he longed for her to twist it on its hilt and lay him open.

"A king serves the people and not himself, sets aside the furthering of greed that feeds the destruction of conquest. He summons power not to revel in it, but to shape it into a flaming sword to protect the people, and bless the land so that their souls may be nourished, and forge the cup of plenty so that they may grow in fruitfulness. This is a king."

She saw the altar of Macha again, and beside it a fair, strong-jawed face framed by black hair, his expression transfigured by light. Her voice grew like a wind into a rising storm, the shriek of the banshee. "And he was more a king in spirit, Nessa's son, than you will ever be as flesh and bone—for rather than ward the Source, you bring ruin, and though love is all, you slaughter it, and in so doing utterly destroy the very glory of the gods." Tears washed down her face and dripped from her cheek to her bare breasts. "I will not even name you a man. You are nothing but a carrion-eater, a slavering wolf, a coward. *Usurper!*"

Every person there was riveted by her cry, and still the king raised no hand against her. His eyes had opened wide and his mouth slackened, and he stared through her to someplace beyond, struck with horror. She extended her finger to point at his groin, and Eogan spat and would have struck her, but Fergus's growl stopped him.

The storm howled and Deirdre felt her winged self tower over Conor, her shadow cast across his face, her tears dripping like dark blood. "Your loins will wither and there will be no more seed, and no heirs of yours will hold Emain Macha again. When you at last seek the Isles of the Blessed, the shores will shun you, and you will be lost in the dark sea, never to drown. You will hear the songs of the gods floating across the water, smell the meat from their table, but never sing beside them and never taste their grace." Deirdre's curse was a roar that issued from her throat with the same fire cloaking her naked body. "There will be only salt and bitterness in your mouth; and in your heart, the wasteland!"

The curse swept over the throng, fanned by invisible, dark wings. Levarcham broke from the men holding her and they let her go, gawping at Deirdre. The druid sagged to her knees and raised her arms as if to the altar of Macha. The women in the crowd bowed their heads and sank to the ground, murmuring of the Goddess, their faces anguished and tearful.

Before the king could utter a word, the horrified silence was broken by Fergus.

"By the Dagda!" With an eruption of breath he faced Conor. "The ash of my son's pyre taints my very flesh, but to be shamed by a maiden... You are beneath my contempt. You broke my word, you broke my life, but it is *she* who finally lays your foulness before us. Because of you, there has been too much betrayal to resurrect the Red Branch again!" He wrenched out his sword and swung it over his head, and before Eogan's men could leap before Conor, Fergus buried its tip in the earth at the king's feet. It swayed there, the blade splashed with mud. "There!" the old warrior breathed, his hands raised to the sky. "My blade was blessed by this king of the Ulaid, and I fling it away from me lest I be poisoned by its touch!"

Conor's mouth creaked open but no sound came from it, and then another young warrior stumbled forward, his arm bound to his shoulder with bloody linen, his face haggard, his eyes dead. "Father, I am shamed beyond bearing for the deed you forced upon me, and am cursed as Cormac the kin-slayer forever!" He stared at Deirdre, his pain raw. "Will a maid prove stronger than your own son? Stronger than these warriors who have walked in uncertainty for days?" Holding his hilt in his good hand, he thrust it in the earth beside Fergus's. "I can find no pride by your side," he spat at Conor, "and though I am doomed to wander, I take this punishment gladly, and rejoice to never see your cursed face again!"

Conor did not wipe the spittle off his cheek; his hand only twitched a little toward his son as the younger man turned and limped away.

As if ignited by that cry, scores of warriors by Fergus's side let out the same hoarse yell and slammed sword after sword into the soil at the king's feet, until he was ringed by a circle of iron. Fergus's smile was a grim streak. "I will bear their rule in exile— and wherever we go, your enemies we will be. To me!" he bellowed, turning his shoulder away, and the men streamed after him.

Deirdre's fury still beat around her, but through that haze she saw that as the men left one remained unmoving: a lean, dark-haired man in shining plates of horn armor. Cúchulainn blanched when he saw that grim face, whose very hardness spoke of suppressed pain, and when the man strode forward, dragging his sword from its scabbard, Cúchulainn sprang between him and the king with a muttered curse.

They squared off, the Hound of the Ulaid and this dark man, and Deirdre was close enough to hear the whistle of anguish in Cúchulainn's voice. "I cannot believe you would leave."

The other man's eyes were narrowed, hoarding their emotion. "I cannot believe you would stay."

"I told you why, Ferdia." They murmured as if they were alone, and Cúchulainn sounded breathless and strained. "My oath is to the Ulaid, and now they need me more than ever. Do you think I do not wish to skewer the rest of these carrion on my blade?" His glance at Eogan's men was a stab of fire, and they all jostled back, muttering among themselves.

Ferdia had recoiled at Cúchulainn's words. "Then why didn't you, with the blood of the sons of Usnech on the grass at your feet?"

"You were not there," Cúchulainn hissed. "You did not see the ruin. I would have let go into the frenzy and heaped destruction upon slaughter, and now we would have blood feuds within the Ulaid drawing all men into that fire. And the people would be left with no protection when our true enemy swoops down upon them—*Connacht*. How can you think I would blind my eyes for even a moment to the greater threat?" He paused, and whispered, "How can you not know how it burns?"

Ferdia flinched. "I would have you be my brother and not the

Hound. Let other men bear this burden of protection, and follow your own heart."

"I have no heart if I abandon the people, and you should look to yours if you go!"

Ferdia's lips were knitted by a white line. "But my name is not as hallowed as yours, Cú." There was a bitter turn to his smile. "I am no champion of the land. I look to my own honor alone—as you should do, for once. Ferdia and Cúchulainn should never serve a man who taints the very air we breathe with treachery!" His gray eyes skimmed over Conor, but the king did not hear him, slowly stirring from a dream, his head straightening with effort as if too heavy for his thin neck.

"Ferdia!" Fergus growled, down the slope toward the river. "Come."

Ferdia hefted the sword and stuck it into the ground with the others, his dark face haunted and bloodless. "As much as I love you, I can call you no friend of mine, or claim you as a brother again. I sever all connection to one who serves a king of such evil."

Cúchulainn stood there empty-handed as Ferdia left. More warriors hurried behind Fergus and their women joined them, people running after them with shouts and tears.

Conor said nothing for a long moment, his back slowly bowing. He turned away from the ramparts, hiding his face, and dragged himself onto the platform of the chariot.

When Eogan gestured at his guards to seize Deirdre, Cúchulainn spun on his heel and in the same movement his own sword crossed Eogan's path. Eogan's dark eyes flashed, but Cúchulainn kept his sword across his chest. "You will treat her with respect," the Hound said in a low, strained voice, "or death will come when you least expect it, so no kin of yours will be able to claim any blood feud with mine."

Eogan grimaced and snorted like a bull, but eventually he motioned his men back. He whirled with a toss of his black head and clambered up beside Conor in the chariot.

"Why do you not betray me, too, then, Hound?" Conor was gazing out from the chariot to the woods.

Cúchulainn lowered his sword and, dragging off his cloak, went to wrap it about Deirdre's nakedness. The quivering tension in him was like heat rising from his skin. "Because," he said over his shoulder, "I will not skewer this murderous wolf before Emain's gates, and so rend the Ulaid from within—like you. I will stay strong to fight Connacht. Our land has need of me when so many others desert it." He dropped his voice to a whisper for Deirdre. "There may come a way." She understood he meant to free her somehow, though the shame in his eyes was like an endless drop into a void. "In the meantime, I will not let you ride this dark road alone."

At that moment, Deirdre caught the scents emanating from the folds of his cloak: wool-fat, leather and birch-tar; sweat and horse musk. *Warrior smells*. She drew back. Such fighting men took *him* from her.

"It is my mantle she will have." The confused guards made no move to stop Levarcham as she shrugged off her own cloak. She nestled the wool about Deirdre's shoulders and crushed the folds to her cheeks, her gray eyes luminous with pain.

Deirdre leaned her forehead on Levarcham's chin, grasping for that last scrap of warmth. "Mother," she said.

Levarcham tried to speak again but Conor hissed an order, and hard arms reached for her. Deirdre was tossed into the back of the chariot, between an unmoving Conor and Eogan, who turned with the reins and looked her up and down with sly lust. His horses were as black and shiny as his beard and eyes, their harness pulling on his arms.

He flicked the reins and the stallions sprang into motion, and behind them, Cúchulainn took to his own chariot alone. The line of men on horses and the chariots rumbled over the muddy ruts of the road that led east from Emain Macha. There were no cheers or blaring trumpets, only a subdued murmur of the crowd that was soon muffled by the thick mist.

Behind Deirdre, Levarcham's blurred face and the dark timbers of the fort gradually disappeared into the swirling vapor.

CHAPTER 48

Deirdre existed only as distant sensation…
The chariot lurching beneath her feet, her silent body parting the mist like a cold blade…

The gray blur of rocks, somber hills and ghostly trees floating past unfocused eyes…

The sharp spears of men's voices surrounding her, piercing her…

Conor's presence was a void beside her—a man who had ruined a kingdom for this body, and now recoiled from it as the chariot jarred over ruts in the mud.

The towering rage had shrunk and hardened into blackened stone inside her. Her lungs that had expelled a laugh in the sunshine with…*she could not name him*…now struggled to draw each breath; she did not want them to ever move again. She felt staked through the throat, for the trapped scream there burned and would not be released nor swallowed, nor ground to oblivion by the force of clenched teeth.

She would acknowledge no other senses, send out no tendrils of seeking through the filmy layers of existence. For there were no other realms—no life when she could not feel him. There was only *nothingness*, where once she had turned to him like a flower to sun before she even took a breath of the morning.

There were no gods, only cruel jests. There were no *sídhe*, only tricksters. They had beckoned her to surrender to love, and taken it from her. Only hatred sustained her and kept her frozen in this moment, as the chariots rumbled over the stony path and men shouted harsh jokes…the same men whose blades had drained his blood.

Levarcham's words came to her in half-remembered snatches. They would both wander as druids, blessing the land in secret rites, far from the gaze of kings. But Deirdre knew her voice would only be a bitter hiss through cracks in the stone, for withered souls can bless nothing. The mist mingled with the ash on her cheeks…or was it tears? She did not own them, merely smeared them over her cheeks with nerveless fingers.

Near dusk they reached the east coast, and the sea-wind began to fray the mist and blow it away, the sun shafting over iridescent green turf. The track turned south and fell away into low cliffs and broken ravines against which the white water rolled, the faint pounding of the sea shuddering through Deirdre's body. The wind dragged on her unbound hair, streaming it out like a banner. Only, she could not be swept away to freedom, because of the stake through her throat and the blade piercing her heart—just as she was hemmed between Conor's dark spirit and the bitter smell of Eogan's sweat.

While Conor avoided looking at her, Eogan stood proudly at the reins, reveling in his moment of triumph. He turned to grin lasciviously at her, but to Deirdre he hardly existed.

Suddenly, the narrow path opened out into a wide expanse of pasture running along the edge of a low sea-cliff. The drumming in Deirdre's body became louder and she realized it was hooves thundering over the soft earth, and the rumbling of wheels. Eogan turned from looking at her and cursed as Cúchulainn's chariot streaked past, and once ahead scythed around in sweeping arcs over the pasture, releasing sheer frustration with a burst of speed over the now-open ground.

Cúchulainn was a spire of fury, snarling at his mounts and slapping their reins to race faster, his chariot carving great spirals and loops in the turf. The whirl of gleaming horse-flesh and spinning wheels, the Hound's bared teeth and the flying clods of mud, made Deirdre's head snap up, and the sun-flashes on horse trappings and bronze hubs dragged her awake.

"What is the dog doing?" Eogan spat. "Has he lost his mind?"

Cúchulainn turned and flew past much closer and Deirdre perceived a towering black cloud enveloping him—a thunderhead of emotion—and recognized in it her own cloak of darkness, her own rage. The desperation in his face to somehow release himself with this charge, expend himself, instead of rending the world into oblivion, radiated palpable waves of energy through her.

Eogan's horses shied at the rush of wind and hooves and he desperately tried to get them under control, with little room to maneuver near the cliff-edge. Ahead, Cúchulainn wheeled the chariot again, expertly bracing his legs to ride its bucking back as if it was a living thing. As he did, he threw back his head and screamed in incandescent shame and fury, forcing it out like a great spear flung to the sky.

It pierced the stifling cloud surrounding him, the anguished bellow sounding as if it dragged Cúchulainn's very bowels with it, emptying him. The roiling darkness about him shattered and was blown apart into shreds that faded like ash. Heedless of the chaotic gallop of his horses, Cúchulainn flung the reins aside and put back his head as far as it would go, his arms out.

In the wake of that cry, Deirdre saw a wild surge of life flood his face, transforming it with pure joy. He had surrendered his rage. For a moment, it was as if she shared his senses: the wind pouring through him, the savage scent of the crashing sea, the sun streaming through the last mist over the water. The joy was a starburst around him.

Deirdre's inviolable spirit was spun of such wildfire, even though she had forced herself to forget. But now that crackle of lightning leaped from Cúchulainn to her, like to like, and where the charge met her own it set off a brilliant flash that burned through every mote of her being.

The droplets of time froze; the world-wheel stopped.

That blinding brightness swept all darkness away, and reverberated through her flesh and soul. She was *Deirdre*, her heart alive to every moment, every taste and scent and touch of Thisworld. How could she allow this? To be crushed by despair, suffocated by rage so that her spirit sat in her like stone?

There, in that infinite instant, she let go. She took a great draft of air, imbued with the tang of the sea, and she felt bonds slipping from her skin, shackles she had allowed to become locked about her own limbs. Despair was the only prison that could ever hold her. Men could only trap bodies, not the limitless reaches of thought and will.

Grief had made her forget the glimpses of her greater self that glinted through the veils.

The tide of her soul broke free and poured through her, searing all the sorrow and hate and consuming them utterly. It rushed up her body then and spilled out, and the wheel resumed its turning and the worlds shimmered into vivid life for her once more.

There on the chariot, heedless of Conor and Eogan, she *saw*. A web of glistening light spread in all directions, the filaments pulsing with the streams of star-motes. Tree and hill, rock and water were formed of denser pools of brightness, and life coursed along the glowing strands as well, the song of existence beating out the heart music of the beasts and the harmonies of wind-blown leaves.

The silver motes stirred now, and one by one the flock of *sídhe*-ravens took shape from the scatterings of stars, drawing on a mantle of bird-matter from light. Wings unfurled and, emerging from the sparkling web, the birds spun on their wing-feathers and soared over her head.

Cúchulainn's chariot now streaked ahead of them along the cliff, and Eogan shouted and whipped up his own mounts, cursing the Hound. Deirdre was thrown against the railing as one of the ravens flew alongside, tilting so its wing brushed her cheek, its black feathers outlined in flickering silver. Its eye held her, gently mocking. *What was your first love?*

Her answer was a swift dive of thought. *Birds.* Creatures that travel between land and sea, air and rock. Her knowing arose from the ether as the raven's wings had condensed from light. If Source is One, then all realms were hers to roam. She did not have to choose one path, mortal or *sídhe.*

The rush made her smile, and she remembered the sense of a vaster self, greater than Thisworld could hold. How could she have felt separate from that song? Or bury the knowing that, though Thisworld seemed so vivid to her, its threads were but a dim echo of the luminous strands of all the otherworlds of spirit, the filmy layers that were inextricably wound through it like cloth?

Her eyes were glimmer-bright. The Otherworld was not *there* but here. And souls could flow from one to another, as easily as a bird taking to the air.

Oblivious to the lurching chariot, Deirdre traced the outlines of a face that had only triggered the darkness already dormant in men's hearts. She touched her breasts, hips, waist and thighs with reverent fingers, honoring them. Yet this body was merely a mantle she had taken as the ravens had their wings. Her shimmering essence was already being drawn elsewhere, the destiny still calling to glimpse the light of the One, to create from the star-dust of otherworlds. An ancient longing rose in her, and with it, a longing for him.

Her raven squawked with something that might have been laughter, and as one they spiraled up and flowed off toward the hills. In their place, a bugling cry sounded far out at sea, resonant with power and yearning and the slow pulse of vast wings, beating in time with her heart. The cry came again, piercing her. *Come.*

The lowering sun sent shafts of gold over the turf that illuminated the mist, and there, glowing white, three swans arrowed in over the waves.

The cry again. *Come.*

And as if he stood over her shoulder, she felt Naisi breathe it in her ear, smelled his scent, tasted the essence of his soul. The brothers had remembered the days in Alba, their bodies stretched on the warm rock, spirits adrift on mountain winds.

There was no sundering.
There was no death.
There was always choice.
She chose.

Cúchulainn's stallions were thundering for the cliffs, maddened by the flame of the Source that for that brief moment had burned through their master, lifted him from despair to release.

He began drawing them around in a circle, reasserting control. Behind him, his charge had left Eogan's mounted guards in disarray as they tried to avoid colliding with him. And farther back, Eogan's chariot was still bouncing along the cliff-track, the chieftain's teeth bared in a sneer. As the stallions settled back in their traces, taking up their familiar twinned rhythm, Cúchulainn's eye was caught by three pale streaks over the sea, swift and bright like falling stars.

Conor and Eogan were distracted by the terrified whinnies of their own horses and their tossing heads, and Deirdre was forgotten for a moment. So only Cúchulainn saw her glide to the rear of the chariot, as if she was not bound by a dense body or shaken by lurching wheels.

His heart rose in his throat, pushing out a shout, but before he could let it free he was arrested by a look of intense rapture on her face as she lifted it to the sky. The stark hollowness of her cheeks and cracked mouth were softened by an ecstatic smile, a lover's greeting.

And there, gracefully poised, Deirdre raised her arms.

She spread her wings and was lifted, feather-light. All sense of earthly bonds released and she soared unfettered, drawn by the updrafts. Her joy met the sky in a great cry, an exquisite surrender, a name she would sing forever.

Naisi.

CHAPTER 49

Cúchulainn's shout echoed out even as she leaped. *The graceful dive from the chariot, the sea-mist swallowing her.*

Conor's scream was unearthly as he reached desperately to catch her, his chest slamming into the rail of the chariot while Eogan bellowed in impotent fury. Cúchulainn hauled his horses back and the fight went out of them. He leaped to the ground, the stallions trembling in their traces.

The Hound outdistanced the others and scrambled down the cliffside where the ground gave way to a ravine, clods of earth and sticks showering down around him. He tore along the rocky shore to a headland and came to a halt.

The sea had been gentle, washing her into a hollow of the rocks where the waves would not break her on their sharp edges. Cúchulainn stood over her as she was lapped against the land, his head forced down by unbearable sadness.

She was curled on one side, so the violence of the fall was hidden in the water. The force had torn the cloak from her and she was naked once more, her golden hair trailing all around her and her skin so white she was already one with the sea—a water-goddess of seaweed and foam. Her lips formed a soft, wondering smile, the slow lift that comes when someone is taken by gladness.

With a crushed sob, Cúchulainn reverently lifted her out of the sea's embrace, winding her hair about her body so no man would look upon it again. His guilt would not let him breathe, but he cradled her to his chest above the jagged rocks as he struggled back to the sand. She would lie in Naisi's arms, and no king would sunder them again.

His eye was caught by a flash of movement and his chin swung up. Four swans soared in from the sea in a graceful arc above him, and his head circled in wonder as his shattered heart took flight after them. The men clambering down the path did not notice them—not the dark chief burning with wrath, nor the king with his terrible, lost face. No one else watched that flight, as the swans glided so close their wings of mist and light overlapped, merging together.

The trail of their glimmering feathers was a shaft of brightness across the dark slopes of the mountains, until they grew faint as stars at dawn and he lost them in the clouds.

NOTE ON MYTHOLOGY
AND HISTORY

This is a novel based around the old Irish tale of Deirdre and Naisi, not a straight retelling. I highly recommend reading the original myth, as the translations from the Irish are beautiful.

The story of Deirdre and Naisi is part of the group of old Irish tales called "The Ulster Cycle," the most famous of which is the *Táin Bó Cúailnge*, translated in English as *The Cattle Raid of Cooley*. The Ulster Cycle revolves around the exploits of King Conchobor (anglicized as Conor) and his Red Branch warriors, including the famous Irish hero Cúchulainn. The *Táin* describes a war between Queen Maeve of Connacht and Conchobor over a famous bull. Central to the story of the *Táin* is the defection of a large number of Red Branch warriors, led by Fergus mac Roy, from the Ulster side to the Connacht side. The tale of Deirdre appears to be a foretale that explains this defection. Maeve's part in the *Táin* will be told in the next novel in this series, *The Raven Queen*.

The historical background to these tales is confusing. The early peoples of Ireland were not literate, and before Christianity the tales were passed on orally by bards. Nothing would have been written down until after the coming of Christianity in the fifth century, but the earliest surviving manuscripts were made in medieval monasteries much later than that.

I based the basic plot of *The Swan Maiden* on Thomas Kinsella's *The Sons of Usnech* (Dolmen Press, 1954). The same version is included in the more widely available *The Táin* by Thomas Kinsella (Oxford University Press, 1969). Kinsella takes his Deirdre translation from the twelfth-century text the *Book of Leinster*, although the language of the prose sections is actually eighth- or ninth-century, and the verse sections a century or two older. Further than this, we are stretching back into the mists of time and orally transmitted tales.

That is why there was an early belief that the Ulster Cycle described the Irish Iron Age in the centuries before Christ, known by many as the time of the ancient Celts. Modern scholars don't like this idea and, instead of the tales giving us a "window" on Irish prehistory, think they merely reflect the later period in which they were written down. Since they were transcribed by Christian monks, no one really knows how faithfully these tales of so-called Celtic pagans have been copied, and whether the bias of the writers and the society in which they lived—medieval Ireland—meant that events have been changed, or even left out. We will never know.

However, many of the aspects of these tales—the feasting, cattle raiding, boastfulness and courage of the warriors, single combat of champions, taking of enemy heads, riding in chariots—fit in with what Roman writers observed firsthand about the Celts in the years B.C., as well as the archaeology of the Iron Age in Gaul and Britain. We don't know how much of this applied to Ireland, but for the purposes of this novel, I have set the tale of Deirdre and Naisi in the Irish Iron Age in the few centuries before Christ.

There were no actual historical events for this story to follow, but I have tried to ground the story in the archaeology of Ireland, Britain and Gaul and the writing of the Romans about the British and the Gaulish Celts, with regard to weapons, dress, food and houses. This has been liberally mixed in with the mythical world outlined in the original tale. For example, the Iron Age swords found in Ireland are not very big, yet those in the myths are described as large hacking swords—the sort more in use when the stories were transcribed in medieval times. Chariots are also described in the tales. They have never been found in Ireland, but are known from Iron Age graves in England, France and Switzerland, and there are wooden trackways in Ireland made for wheeled vehicles. In such cases, for fictional purposes, I've stuck to what was described in the myths.

I have mainly followed Kinsella's sparse early version of the Deirdre story, which includes Deirdre's prophecy, how she escapes with Naisi, settles in Scotland and is wooed by the Scottish king before having to flee again. However, from the time that Conor's envoys are sent to retrieve the fugitives, I switched to the later fifteenth-century version of the story. This was found in the Glen Massan manuscript, discovered in Scotland, for Scotland also lays claim to the Deirdre story. This later version was used by Lady Gregory in her famous retelling of the *Táin, Cúchulainn of Muirthenne* (reprinted, Gerrards Cross, 1970), which embroiders the story with much more detail.

Kinsella's version, based on the earlier sources, has Fergus, Cormac and Dubthach bringing the fugitives back; Lady Gregory's version, based on the later sources, has Fergus accompanied by his sons Illan and Buinne. The dream of the birds with drops of honey in their beaks comes from this later version, as does Deirdre's lament as she leaves Alba. The events that overtake them at Emain Macha, the time in the Red Branch hall and the fight outside are also drawn from Lady Gregory's tale. I then change back to Kinsella for the last chapter, because the earlier version of Deirdre's fate I found much more moving, and it fitted my story better.

The text of Lady Gregory's book can be seen at http://www.sacred-texts.com/neu/celt/cuch/lgc10.htm. See the chapter on "The Fate of the Sons of Usnach." A good version of the *Book of Leinster* used by Kinsella is at http://www.maryjones.us/ctexts/usnech.html. If the page has changed, go to Mary Jones's site at http://www.maryjones.us/ and look under Celtic Lit; Irish texts; the *Book of Leinster;* and the section "The Exile of the Sons of Usnech."

The Glen Massan manuscript has the fugitives living on Loch Etive in Argyll in Scotland, and I have followed this. There are still many sites around Loch and Glen Etive named after Deirdre and the Sons of Usnech. One rendering of the name Loch Etive is "the roaring loch," probably because of the Falls of Lora at its mouth, a spectacular tidal waterfall of white rapids that is indeed a sight to behold at full spate.

Folklore says that the sons of Usnech and Deirdre flew back to Loch Etive in the form of four white swans, and to this day you can see them gliding over the dark waters in Glen Etive, in the home they so loved.

SOURCE
ACKNOWLEDGMENTS

Deirdre's first recital to Conor about the sons of Usnech and the beautiful and famous lament of hers near the end are both adapted from *The Sons of Usnech*, translated by Thomas Kinsella (Dolmen Press, 1954). The song Deirdre sings on leaving Alba for Erin is written down in many forms; I have very loosely adapted the version found in *Cúchulainn of Muirthenne*, by Lady Gregory (Colin Smythe, 1970).

ABOUT THE AUTHOR

JULES WATSON was born in Western Australia to English parents. After gaining degrees in archaeology and public relations, she worked as a freelance writer in both Australia and England. Jules and her Scottish husband divided their time between the UK and Australia before finally settling in the wild highlands of Scotland. She is the author of the Dalriada trilogy—*The White Mare, The Dawn Stag* and *The Song of the North* (U.S. title)—a series of historical epics set in ancient Scotland about the wars between the Celts and the invading Romans. *Kirkus Reviews* named *The White Mare* in the top ten Science Fiction/Fantasy releases of 2005, and *The Song of the North* was featured as a "Hot Read" in the April 2008 *Kirkus* special Science Fiction/Fantasy edition.

If you enjoyed *The Swan Maiden,*
be sure not to miss

The
Raven Queen

BY

JULES WATSON

The second of these two interlinked stories tells the tale of another of ancient Ireland's best-known women: King Conor's former wife, the fiery Maeve—the woman who aspired to be king.

Much as *The Swan Maiden* breathed new life into one of
Ireland's greatest tragedies, so too this narrative brings vividly
to life one of its most infamous and complex women—a free-
spirited warrior who wanted to be no man's plaything, but simply the ruler of her own destiny. In the midst of war and chaos,
however, comes an unexpected redemption, resurrecting a part
of her she thought dead long ago ...

Coming in 2010 from Bantam